fall out

Loved and trusted... hated & abused...

By
Martin Winter

All rights reserved
Copyright © Martin Winter, 2015

The right of Martin Winter to be identified as the author of this work has been asserted by him in accordance with section 78 of the Copyright, Designs and Patents Act 1978

The book cover is copyright to Martin Winter

This book is published by
Lapwing Publishing
The Old Summerhouse, 19 Lancaster Avenue, Kirk Sandall, Doncaster, DN31NW
www.lapwingpublishing@hotmail.com

This book is sold subject to the conditions that it shall not, by way of trade or otherwise, be lent, resold, hired out or otherwise circulated without the author's or publisher's prior consent in any form of binding or cover other than that in which it is published and without similar condition including this condition being imposed on the subsequent purchaser.

A CIP record of this book
Is available from the British Library

ISBN 978-0-9932490-0-6 [Hardback]
ISBN 978-0-9932490-1-3 [Softback]

	Overview [I'd never show 'im a bird's nest]	
1	Let he who has never sinned…	1
2	The gospel according to John [and Gary]	9

Loved and trusted…

3	May you never have everything you wished for	28
4	Do you want a receipt for £5?	75
5	The deal at Pizza Hut	84
6	An Austin Ambassador Y Reg?	93
7	Well I could couldn't you?	98
8	2.4 Million SAGA readers	106
9	Golden Child or last one standing?	125
10	Puppet Meister or Apparatchik?	145
11	You can have it any way you want it, John	178
12	A germ of an idea – building an ideology	207
13	After the mayor making	280
14	One million people – a view from a hotel room	314
15	Favourite car journeys of the world	332
16	Loyalty's a two way street	339
17	Why did he just call me Jim?	430
18	A long Good Friday	473

hated & abused…

19	Between the wars	542
20	A very English coup d'etat	596
21	In search of FLO [the calm before the storm]	658
22	Exit stage right – pursued by…	716
	Afterword	785

I'd Never Show 'im A Bird's Nest

> *"If you really want to hear about it, the first thing you'll probably want to know is where I was born and what my lousy childhood was like, and how my parents were occupied and all before they had me and all that David Copperfield kind of crap..."*
>
> JD Salinger

I was born on April 9th 1962 in the village of Kirk Sandall, a rural spot, 4 miles north-east of Doncaster – a passionate mining community right in the heart of what became known as The People's Republic of South Yorkshire.

My father was John "Bryan" Winter; JB to his friends – but BJ to me. He was a painter, decorator & sign writer for Pilkington Bros, a professional Rugby League player and a part-time artist. The youngest of three children, he was from a relatively affluent family; the son of Stan, a time-served blacksmith who had worked as a wheelwright, ironsmith and farrier in the Somme trenches of the First World War; and Blanche [my grandmother] who had worked for many years as a pâtissier for Hagenbachs bakery in Leeds.

My mother is Marie Winter, nee Rowland, who was a wages clerk at Peters Wholesale Fruit & Vegetables. The youngest of four children, two boys and two girls, her upbringing contrasted greatly with Bryan's. Originally from Alfreton in Derbyshire, her mining father William followed the work down to Kent, where he and his wife Gertrude's first child was born; and then back up to Armthorpe in Doncaster in 1929. William died from a stroke at 42, when my mother was just 5 years old, leaving Gertrude to raise the family on a paltry widow's pension. But tragedy dogged the family and the following year Gertrude was struck down with chronic rheumatoid arthritis. By the age of 8, Marie was the principal carer for her bed-bound mother and would spend the next ten years looking after her and running the busy household.

Gertrude's death, when Marie was just 18, left her living with her elder sister, June, and it was then that she met my father at a local dance.

At ten years her senior, some might say she married him to escape the predicament she found herself in. But she and BJ were married for more than 45 years and never once doubted their love for each other.

Over the years they developed their loving, married relationship into an even stronger business arrangement, running the local newsagents and buying and selling property. All in all they made a wonderful team.

Home births were the norm in those days, almost "*de rigueur*", and mine was apparently a relatively easy birth.

It was to herald an easy and phenomenally happy childhood.

I spent the majority of it roaming the fields in and around Kirk Sandall, particularly the small hamlet of Sandall Parva – the ancient name for the original village of Kirk Sandall but the place everyone knew as the 'the old village'.

The old village is derelict now but back then it was a beautiful spot and the centre-piece of my growing up. First mentioned in the Doomsday Book, it was a traditional feudal community with a farm, schoolhouse, gardener's cottages, a chauffeur's house and housekeeper and servants' quarters. Central to the village, of course, was the big house – "Grove House" – and St Oswald's Church.

During the 1920s the entire Sandall Parva estate had been bought by the Pilkington Glass Company as the place where it would build its new glass factory. In its heyday, "Pilks" employed more than 3,000 workers from the immediate and wider community constructing the new village of Kirk Sandall to house its workforce. Within this new 'model village' of more than 500 houses, each road, street and square was named after a counterpart in Lancashire – Lancaster Avenue, St Helens Square, Eccleston Road etc. – to recognise the Pilkington family's proud Lancastrian heritage.

The industrial revolution and the arrival of the railway had also attracted other businesses like The Malt Kilns and Kirk Sandall and its surrounding villages were an attractive place to live for the newly- established working class.

Pilkington's – and my father – maintained the model village to the highest possible standards.

The company provided quality leisure and recreational facilities for a treasured workforce, including "the Glassmaker" public house, a sports ground, cricket, bowling and pensioners' pavilions, separate "boys club" and assembly halls.

Its benevolence was legend with "Pilkington's Pensioners" receiving free electricity, household repairs, gardening, hampers at Christmas and summer outings each year.

BJ was a true loyalist to his employers and to their philanthropy but he also introduced me to a wider, shared sense of a community's social responsibility.

He explained how in 1830, alongside other villages in Yorkshire, the people of Sandall Parva had petitioned parliament for the total abolition of the slave trade. The petition from Kirk Sandall asked that slaves be restored the *"Rights and Priveledges* [they had been] *long and unjustly deprived of"* [sic.].

He also introduced me to the concept of the nobility, the bourgeoisie, the proletariat and the class struggle. But he didn't do it as some kind of a political zealot; it was more to give me a moral compass, if you like; something to guide me through my life.

So there I was, enjoying a wonderful childhood, roaming the fields and lanes with my dad.

I can picture it now, St Oswald's' Church bells chiming in the distance.

It's another sunny summer's day and we're laid on the grass at the back of the cricket pavilion. The skylarks are climbing high in the sky, singing to their hearts content; the grasshoppers are chirruping and my dad and I are watching a lapwing walking to and from its nest.

BJ is explaining the paradox of the bird. The closer you get to the nest, the less interested the lapwing pretends to be – displaying complete nonchalance the nearer you get.

The further away from its nest you are, the more it attempts to distract you, plunging earthwards with a drunken spinning and turning fall, as if mortally wounded, in order to draw you away.

BJ tells me how lapwings are incredibly loyal to each other – seldom being seen alone and only rearing one brood a year – but that they will lay up to four or five replacement clutches if the eggs are lost.

He says Victorian farmers used to exploit this loyalty, "harvesting" lapwing eggs, as a crop and explains how the government tried to protect the birds through the introduction of the "Lapwing Act" in 1928 – banning the collection of eggs after a certain date and giving the robbed birds time to lay a new clutch and rear their young.

As I grew up, my life revolved around the countryside; I was always bringing home one animal or another.

Shamefully, I was an ardent egg collector – a "nester" – selling the lapwing's eggs I collected each spring for "two bob a dozen". With a loyal and demanding customer base to satisfy, particularly the elderly residents of the old village who had a taste for them, I had different morals then.

However, the egg collecting didn't just stop with Lapwings. I loved the challenge of finding other birds' nests as well – researching their habitats, observing their courtship displays, establishing their territories and looking for nest sites. To this day, I think there is nothing more captivating than a beautifully-made nest with a pristine clutch of eggs in it.

Victorian egg collectors used to take the full clutches and the nest as well. At least I had a greater sense of moral decency, never taking more than one egg, so the bird could still raise a brood.

There's something quite anal about boys and collecting; whether it be train numbers, coins, stamps or cigarette cards. They are all indices of a less complicated past. I collected them all, save the train numbers, but it was the eggs that kept drawing me back. Everyone knew I was a good "egger". People used to love to show you an egg they'd got; they would tell you where the nest was and how they'd found it and the end result was that the bird's nest would be robbed of its remaining eggs.

I never told anyone where "my" nests were.

There is something immensely disloyal about an individual who would rob a bird's nest, having been shown it by someone else; to have been taken in to that person's confidence, and to then repay that trust by destroying it, seems to me the ultimate act of betrayal.

Having said that, isn't betrayal the defining trait of humanity? It certainly defined my tenure as Mayor. It provided the aegis by which I judged an individual's worth and it's why I have written this book.

It reminds me of how Margaret Thatcher would carefully assess somebody's level of trustworthiness before admitting them into her circle.

"Is he one of us?" she'd ask.

My own comparable euphemism became: *"Would you show him a bird's nest?"* In other words *'Can we trust him?'*

"Well I wouldn't show him a bird's nest...."

"Enough said."

In some ways my early life feels like it's from a bygone age. I was always out with the terriers and lurchers, ferreting and enjoying everything the countryside provided. To this day I love collecting fungi and I reckon nothing beats the taste of giant puffballs fried with a sliver of fresh rabbit on a misty late summer, or early autumn, morning.

In those days our house was a veritable menagerie with owls, foxes, jays, jackdaws and hedgehogs all residing there at one time or another.

During dad's latter years he began to reconnect with that time. After seeing a partridge nest in the garden he was mortified when a fox, or some other predator, killed the mother bird.

He bought a 'broody bantam' hen, hatching and hand-rearing a full clutch of eggs before releasing them into the countryside around our house.

I'll never forget my mother's face when, after buying the broody bantam, the farmer yelled after them that they had forgotten the cockerel that came with it.

After waking the whole house at 3.00 am the next morning, the cockerel was promptly despatched to my uncle's smallholding.

I'll also never forget the bizarre sight of my, by then disabled, father 'calling in' his squadron of partridges one summer's evening. After a few enthusiastic shouts and a good rattle of their feed tin, a dozen or so birds would darken the sky and then land on the lawn at his feet.

It was a spectacle to behold and it undoubtedly helped keep dad's spirits up in his old age.

So this is the backdrop to my early life. My father taught me how to draw and paint the wildlife we discovered together. He taught me how to play rugby and he was the reason I entered politics. He developed in me a greater strength of purpose, a real sense of what is right and wrong and a desire for a fair and egalitarian approach to life.

Together, my parents showed me the value of organisation; of doing a job properly; getting it right first time and every time. It is to them that I dedicate this book.

Let he who has never sinned...

"It is much safer to be feared than loved because... love is preserved by the link of obligation which, owing to the baseness of men, is broken at every opportunity ..."

Nicolo Machiavelli

Sunday December 12th 1980...

I suffer a flake fracture of my right thumb playing rugby and I have an operation at Doncaster Royal Infirmary to pin it.

This is a setback to my studies because I'm in the final year of sixth form at Armthorpe Comprehensive School, taking 'A' Levels in Art & Design, Geography and General Studies. It's a direct blow for my Art 'A Level' because I have a cast all the way to my elbow, restricting my ability to draw and paint; however, several of my school friends have offered to let me use their course notes to revise for my other subjects.

ooo

Monday June 2nd 1980

I attend Doncaster Royal Infirmary to have the cast removed. It's the day before my Art & Design 'A' Level and the week before my other 'A' Levels begin.

ooo

August 1980

Not surprisingly I flunk all my 'A' Levels and I'm less than pleased that the school failed to apply for special dispensation because of my injury.

ooo

September 1980

As an eighteen year old, I begin a one year Art & Design 'Foundation Course' at Doncaster College of Art.

I meet several new friends, including "Jamie" [James Robinson], a ceramicist who had been at Pocklington Grammar School, and his vivacious girlfriend Carolyne.

At the same time, my parents are preparing for a [successful] court case against a former employee at their newsagent's – a woman who was caught with her fingers in the till in the late 1970s.

This is one of my first recollections of thinking intuitively; as a 'naïve' 15 year old I'd told my parents she must be guilty – on the basis she immediately jumped to defend herself when my mother joked that the shop's reduced takings meant *someone* was fiddling.

The woman was caught 'red-handed' by the police with marked money in her purse, and subsequently admitted stealing over several years. But she only confesses to taking £4,500 even though my parent's accountant and the police estimate it is more like £12,500.

The police and prosecutors argue that it will be difficult to prove she's taken more – yet Customs & Excise request the VAT on the full £12,500 and are demanding immediate payment of £1,875 from my parents.

Meanwhile the court has ordered the thief to repay the £4,500 at the rate of £10 a week so it will take more than eight years for her to reimburse them!!

This, my father argues, is madness: the law's an ass [which it is] and everybody he speaks to about it agrees with him.

Except me. As an innocent and inexperienced eighteen year old, I argue it differently... my second recollection of thinking intuitively:

"*Look dad – you can shit with the Inland Revenue as much as you like – and they won't [can't] really do anything. But Customs & Excise is a different animal – if you shit with them, they'll come and get you!*"

But 'BJ' knows better and says he won't be paying it.

"*I won't pay it... I won't pay it...*" he roars. "*I wouldn't have paid it if it was 8% but its bloody 15% now... fifteen bloody per cent!*" referring to Geoffrey Howe's VAT increase the previous year.

"*The robbing bastards...*" he continues... and then [prophetically] "*I'd rather go to jail!*"

I can see the picture as vividly now as if it were yesterday. It's several weeks later and early on a beautiful sunlit summer morning; my mum and dad have returned from their 4.00 am stint at the shop and are having their breakfast.

I'm sorting out my equipment box, ready to leave for college – and, as I look through the dining room window, I see a large black Mercedes pull up outside. Three suited men get out, two walk up the house and the driver waits, standing beside the car.

There's a knock at the front door and my mother shouts my father, telling him these people have come from HM Customs & Excise.

I can hear an argument and as I walk into the hallway, I can see that they've arrested my father, handcuffed him and are taking him away.

For a big, belligerent man, he seems extremely compliant – which I think scares my mother more than if he were fighting with them – *"Martin... Martin..."* she's calling *"... they're arresting your dad"*.

She's crying and as I join her on the drive, we watch them sit him in the rear of the car and drive him away.

"Where do you think they've taken him? What am I going to do?" she asks. *"What am I going to do?"* she repeats again *"They're taking him away"*

To be quite honest, I had been expecting it, and I think my dad has as well.

"Well don't tell me this is a surprise?" I say. *"So you can start by writing out a cheque to them."*

Despite my mother issuing a cheque through her solicitor straight away, they don't "release" him until 6.30 that night. But I think a lesson is learnt.

ooo

October 1982...

By the time I'm twenty, my rugby career is going from strength to strength. Having been selected at eighteen for the British Amateur Rugby League Association [BARLA] Yorkshire 'Open Age' team, I am being acknowledged as a very strong young prospect.

I am now in my second year at Sunderland Polytechnic, studying Fine Art [Sculpture] and French Philosophy.

Although I have refused to sign professional terms, not wanting rugby to get in the way of my studies, I am still managing to play an awful lot of the game and captain the British Polytechnics Rugby League team; indeed, my tutors would argue I am playing too much rugby!

I train regularly while I'm at college and travel home on a weekend to play professionally with Doncaster Rugby League Football Club, although still retaining my status as an amateur.

ooo

Sunday January 2nd 1983...

This being the start of a new calendar year, the Rugby Football League has introduced the sin-bin. Only penalties involving violent play, dangerous play, professional fouls or repetition of a specific offence result in a *sin binning*, where the offending player must spend 10 minutes off the field.

It was introduced yesterday, for the weekend's live televised game; however, the referee didn't need to use it, which scotched expectations that it could be a passport to violence for the thugs in the game, or a cop-out for lazy players.

"*Players will be willing to risk at least one determined act of aggression at an opponent if they think they are only risking ten minutes in the sin bin,*" says Doncaster General Manager Tom Morton.

"*There will also be the opportunity for a tired player to 'earn' himself a ten-minute rest,*" he continued… "*when a tired player may well take a whack at somebody to get a rest and return refreshed.*"

The referee will raise both hands and spread his digits to indicate "10 minutes" off the field of play; and in a marvellous example of South Yorkshire scepticism and distrust at 'change', Mr Morton continues: "*It may be clear to see in the sun of Australia or New Zealand where the scheme has already operated, but it is a different matter on a misty January day at Tattersfield*"

ooo

2.00 pm – Doncaster versus Keighley, Doncaster RLFC Tattersfield Ground.

Today's game is against Keighley and we're playing in front of a crowd of about 1,000.

Although we're having a bad season, we're expected [and expecting] to win. I could certainly do with a win, not because I'm ultra-competitive and can't bear losing at anything, but because, although I'm classed as an amateur, I still get paid – and when you're a poor student living on a grant, that comes in very handy.

I'm really on top of my game at the moment and have been selected to play for a BARLA XIII against 'Tweedhead Seagulls' – a highly-rated Australian side touring England in two weeks' time.

As we approach the kick-off at 2.15, I'm feeling supremely confident, I'm as strong as an ox – frequently shifting stone blocks at college – and getting plenty of exercise.

The first half is a very close game between two well-matched teams. It's not particularly rough but it is hard and, after 25 minutes, we have a player substituted with a broken ankle.

With ten minutes to go before half-time, I'm pleased with my performance. It's a very tight game with the score 4:3 to Keighley; they having scored two penalties to our one penalty and a drop goal.

As play continues near the half-way line, I receive the ball at first man. As I take it up to Keighley's defensive line, I look first to my inside, where I have a support player running and then to my outside, where I have another. I'm waving the ball as if I'm going to pass to my outside, while two Keighley players get ready to tackle me; turning slightly, I look to my inside and feign a pass to the inside runner and one of the Keighley players moves across to tackle him. As he does so, I keep the ball and break through the gap he has created.

Accelerating away, I'm making good ground and turn again to my outside, where I now have the two Doncaster centres running wide for me – but the Keighley centre, Malcolm Dudley, is coming straight towards me and the full back is also racing across for a tackle.

I consider a long looping pass over the centre's head but it's only the second tackle and we're now in the 'Green Zone' – the Keighley defensive '25 metres'.

So I decide to take the tackle from the Keighley centre and get up to play the ball quickly before Keighley's defenders have time to get back behind the play-the-ball line. As I do that, I can see we're going to have an over-lap and I start to run in support; but as I do, I feel the Keighley player trip me up and I fall to the floor.

As I get up, I'm feeling pretty disconsolate, I'm having quite a good game and this bastard has just tripped me up – so I turn to give him a mouthful and the clever bastard is smirking at me.

Now I work on the basis that if I take it from him now, I'll be taking it every minute of the game – I've had this drilled in to me by my dad and many coaches over the years.

This bastard will think he's got one over one me – he's top-dogged me and asserted his superiority – so I've got to give him one back and let him know I'm not some kind of a pushover.

As I walk over to remonstrate with him, he comes for me so I hit him straight away. I hit him with the most perfect straight arm punch I think I've ever thrown and he goes straight down.

But it's not a perfect punch at all and as I look at him with a sense of justice, I can also clearly see that I've broken my right 3rd metacarpal – the third bone in the back of my hand.

A boxer punches with knuckles one and two and I'm that bloody good I hit him with knuckle three! It's sticking up. It's not particularly painful but it's firmly sticking up and it's uncomfortable.

While I'm considering this, the Keighley centre gets up and starts to pummel me. He's not hurting me much as I wrap my arms around him and wrestle him to the ground, but he's giving me better than I can give him!

The scuffle develops into a melee as several players join in – but they're not coming to my aid, just using the brawl as an excuse for a wider "dust up".

After a short while everyone calms down and the referee calls me and the Keighley centre to his side. *"It's an unusual day,"* the ref says as we approach him *"Normally I'd send you straight off…"*

"That bastard tripped me," I exclaim, cutting across him and sounding like a small child.

"Shh… shh… shh… I'm talking" replies the ref, holding his finger to his lips *"And all I saw was you lunge at him,"* he nods towards the Keighley centre.

"Ask the touch-judge," I appeal pathetically

"Shh… will you? I am talking" he repeats. *"And if the touch-judge saw anything he'd tell me…"* he raises his voice towards the linesman

"Nothing sir – the Doncaster player was the main assailant" replies the touch-judge

"As I was saying – before you interrupted me" he nods at me *"It's an unusual day"* and he looks to the stand and signals to the timekeeper that he is sending us to the 'sin-bin' – there's a triumphant cheer from the crowd.

The ref awards a penalty to Keighley. I've lost us possession on the second tackle and I leave the field. As I trot off towards the dug-out, the coach Alan Rhodes is waving me towards the changing room and comes to get me.

"Tha's got t' leave t' field Martin" he says and he takes my elbow to lead me towards the changing rooms.

"Tha's got t' go in t' changin' room – and wait fo' thee ten minutes…

"Th' dirty bastard,… 'e fucking tripped thee – and th' bastard's gotten away w'it" he tells me as we are met by the kit-man with the keys to unlock the newly fashioned 'sin-bin'.

"Has he not sent 'im off?" I ask, unaware that the ref only 'sin-binned' me.

"Nah – did 'e bollocks… Mind you" he laughs as he hands me over to the kit-man *"It wer' a cracking punch tha threw."*

"Yeah… but look at me hand." I show him the raised bone.

"Ahh bollocks," he says – and walks back to the dug-out.

ooo

3.00 pm – Half time

I've been in the sin-bin for about five minutes now, and the half-time hooter has just sounded, with the score still 4:3 to Keighley.

As the players troop in one or two of them are laughing and ruffling my hair, calling me a sinner.

I join my teammates for the half time talk from Alan Rhodes.

As the hooter sounds for the start of the second half, I reflect on what Alan has told us.

He's broadly happy with our performance and wants us to get the ball out wider to Ray Wilson, the former Featherstone player, who's been making a lot of progress in his position as one of our two centres.

After only two minutes our stand-off, John Buckton, races in for a try which David Noble converts to make the score 8:4 – we're leading.

As the crowd goes wild Ray Wilson receives the ball almost straight from the re-start but just as he is making good ground, he takes a very heavy tackle from the second rower who is covering across.

Ray is clearly badly injured and, after a long time on the ground, the team 'Physio', Don Brookes and two others escort him from the field and towards the changing rooms. He has a badly broken ankle and a collapsed cheekbone.

But Don seems more concerned with me and starts to strap up my broken hand.

"We've used all of our replacements up now Ray's had to come off..." he tells me *"... so you'll have to play the whole of the second half Martin."*

After a nightmare, bad tempered second half, I'm massively relieved to hear the final hooter sound.

I've struggled to make any progress with the ball and had even less success making tackles – as I desperately try to protect my broken hand.

My teammate, Ken Ellis, was also sin-binned for a high-tackle.

The history books will record how, after leading 8 to 4, ten minutes into the second half we collapsed and lost by 42 points to 8!

ooo

6.00 pm – Doncaster Royal Infirmary, Armthorpe Road, Doncaster

I attend DRI with my broken hand and see that Ray is also there. I like Ray and I've got a lot time for him – he's an ex-school teacher with a good sense of humour.

As we laugh and joke, Ray mimics the touch-judge at the game *"... the Doncaster player was the main assailant,"* he says – and we are both laughing.

"The main assailant... main assailant..." exclaims Ray *"It might be full of 'em – but they don't know what assailants are in Doncaster!"*

ooo

Monday January 10th 1983...

10.00 am – Sunderland College of Art & Design, Backhouse Park, Sunderland

My tutors are not happy with me. Not only am I missing an increasingly large amount of studio time, through travelling to rugby matches, I am now struggling with my workload because of the injuries I sustain playing.

I reflect on the injury I got in last week's game, which also means I've also lost the opportunity to play against the touring Australian side "Tweedhead Seagulls".

However, the main issue is that I lost the team their winning bonus – we were all set for a victory until I lost the plot; I decided my game was more important than the team's and I need to learn from that – sometimes the team agenda is more important than the player's.

ooo

Footnote

Ray Wilson took a well-paid job in Saudi-Arabia in the mid-eighties and, following a tragic accident in a swimming pool, was confined to a wheelchair.

He died on the 19th January 2012

ooo

As far as can be ascertained, I have the dubious "honour" of being the first player ever to be sin-binned in English Rugby League.

The Gospel according to John [and Gary]

In the beginning...

'John and Gary' are two former senior offices at Doncaster Council, having both worked for the authority for 30 years.

They each took early retirement in 2003; a decision brought about, they say, by the unremitting pressure from the new corporate management team, ever-reducing resources and a feeling of constant dissatisfaction with their work.

I was disappointed that they should seek to leave the organisation so early into my tenure as Mayor but remained in contact with them. Since they had known and worked with me for several years, I asked them for feedback on early drafts of this book. Both commented that it did not reflect how bad the situation was before I became Leader in 2001...

As a result, we agreed that they should draft this Chapter.

Here goes...

ooo

The Gospel According to John...

Around 1991 I took over the management of the car parks, including 25 staff, fabric maintenance, on-street parking & enforcement and a raft of other services. My Chairman was Councillor Ray Stockhill and Vice Chairman was Councillor Tom Roebuck.

ooo

Tommy Roebuck and the demise of an officer...

Tommy Roebuck was a big man. Correction – Tommy Roebuck was a huge man – and, standing at more than six feet, he must have weighed in at a good twenty five stones.

Always sporting a huge cigar, Tommy Roebuck was 'Mr Mexborough' and he saw DMBC staff as his, to do with as he saw fit. He had famously done time in the seventies as part of the John Poulson scandal – jailed for conspiracy and corruption whilst in office as a Mexborough councillor.

At this time, I was the Principle Officer [Services] within the Environmental Services Directorate.

I was in the Old Guildhall Yard offices, our main office, when I heard Tom giving his horse racing bets to one of my car park staff to be taken to the bookmakers:

"... 'ere thy is Graham – tek these t' bookies and bring t' slips back 'ere, arl be in t' office wit chairman, just come in when tha gets back."

When I later saw the attendant coming out of the chairman's office I asked him what he was doing...

"Gerrin 'im 'is bets, we do it every day and tek 'em t' bookies"

Being his manager and knowing this was completely contrary to any council policies, I said *"not today you're not."*

"Well Tom says he wants 'is bets purrin' on and we always do 'em."

"Put it this way – if I catch you in the bookies you'll be on a disciplinary and likely to lose your job, so take his bets back to him and tell him I've said you can't do it anymore."

"I'm not telling him – we've always done it."

"Wait here," I instructed. *"I'll tell him."*

So I went to see Councillor Roebuck who was sat with Chairman Councillor Stockhill in his palatial office.

"Tom," I addressed him, trying to be friendly *"... unfortunately I can't allow my staff to take your bets to the bookies."*

"Why the fuck not?" Stockhill intervened.

"Because it's a disciplinary offence and he could lose his job if he's seen in the bookies, Chairman" I explained, trying to appease him.

"Well Tom can't walk far so they always done it"

"I'm sorry Chairman, I can't allow it," I began, worrying how career-limiting such a stance might be... and a full-on row ensued with me on the rack. Needless to say, that was the beginning of the end of any aspirations I had while Stockhill had the chairmanship.

I could hear my career start to slide, but I stopped the trips to the bookies.

Other staff members were less brave – or stupid [!] and to say my Assistant Director wasn't happy was an understatement; these 'politicians' were rabid in their pursuit of power and whatever Stockhill wanted, Stockhill got... no matter who or what got in the way.

ooo

Autumn 1995 – Roebuck and the Parking equipment...

As officers we were looking at making the parking experience more customer-friendly for visitors to the town and considering a "pay on exit" system as the way forward. We had been signposted to a system Leeds City Council was operating and decided to go and have a look at it.

Off we trot to Leeds – me, an engineer and my, then new, Assistant Director along with Tommy – who was still Vice Chairman of Environmental Services.

We duly arrive at 9.00 am, to be greeted by the company representative who asks us where we would like to start. I suggest we start at the 'entry equipment', so off we go with Councillor Roebuck in tow. We get to the entry barrier and the representative is just explaining the equipment when a Japanese gentleman pulls up in his car and tries to get his entry ticket. Tommy Roebuck sees his opportunity to embarrass everyone!

He bends into the window of the Japanese man's car and says…

"Nah then owd love, this is a greeting from South Yoksha – wid like to welcome thee to Leeds and 'ope y'ave a nice day"

The man drives off totally confused… especially as he is in West Yorkshire.

The officer continues with his explanation of the system – five minutes later, Councillor Roebuck interrupts him again: *'as tha gorra cuppa tea organised and few biscuits for thy Uncle Tom?"*

"No sir…" replies the rep', clearly embarrassed by Roebuck's behaviour *"… but we can go to the Queens hotel and get one,"* he ventures sheepishly

"Ah that'll do son – tha's learnin'…"

So, following several more interruptions as the officer attempts to present the workings of the machine, we adjourn to the Queen's Hotel.

As we sit down to morning coffee – all struggling to hide our embarrassment at being with Roebuck, he says to the rep'… *"as tha got one o' them theer mobile phones?"*

"Yes I have, would you like to use it?"

But Roebuck ignores the question and simply orders him: *"Rate – put this number in."*

There are no niceties, no please or thank you — but he puts the number in and hands the phone to Roebuck.

"Nah then…" says Tom, to the voice on the other end of the line *"… can tha put me two two-bob* [10p] *doubles and a two-bob crossed…"*

It's Roebuck's bookies. The officers present just want to melt away, but the day is still young!

Eventually we go back to the car park to look at the 'back office equipment'.

It's about 11.00 am when Tom interrupts again.

"Nah then owd lad, as thar gor any dinner organised."

"As a matter of fact we do" says the rep' triumphantly. *"I'd like to take you all back to our factory where we have a rather nice buffet laid on for you."*

"A buffet? A buffet?" replies Roebuck *"Nay nay lad, ah dun't ate buffets – gerron that phone o' thine and tell thy gaffa that tha's tekking us to a nice restaurant cos ard like a nice steak and some chips…"*

"Arm a councillor tha knows," he continues, *"An ah dun't want a buffet"*

"But we have the buffet ordered," protests the representative

"Tha can gee it t'staff – gerron that phone an tell em," he says again.

Which the rep' duly does and off we go to a nice restaurant in Leeds.

Tom being the sartorial, foul mouthed gent that he is, sits there swearing and throwing back as many beers as possible – with his tank top inside out and dried food down the front of it.

After a difficult lunch during which he succeeds in offending several other customers, we head back to the factory to have another look at the 'back office equipment' for the proposed parking system.

While we officers look semi-intelligent and ask pertinent questions. Tom sits in the corner totally disinterested in the system, reading the racing pages and showing complete disregard for the officers' discussion and activities; suddenly he pipes up:

"Sithee, arve got to get back to Donny soon, ah need to be gerrin off."

I say we need to see this equipment, because it's a lot of money to commit the council to without fully understanding what it can do.

"ah dunt care", says Tom, *"ah need to be in Donny, av important stuff to do, t'engineer can stay and do yon stuff."*

So my boss, the Assistant Director, negotiates with the engineer [who agrees to stay] and off we go back to "Donny".

When we arrive, Tom says: *"tha can drop us 'ere… this'll do"*… just outside his bookies!

Nice one Tom – you can always rely on him for the most appalling behaviour.

Suffice to say there's a very humble telephone call made to the supplier the following day apologising for the Councillor's behaviour – but never put in writing!

ooo

1995 – The Funeral…

Within most organisations it's custom and practice for staff and officers to attend the funeral of a former colleague, to show support and respect for the deceased and for the benefit of the family.

One of my supervisors, Bill, wants to take early retirement but circumstances are such that I'm unable to let him go – despite what people might think it's not that simple and there are lots of factors to consider and hoops to go through.

One of our staff members has passed away and we are out in force at the cemetery for a burial. Bill, the supervisor who wants to leave, is there and, surprisingly, the Chairman, Ray Stockhill, is also there, swanning around in his own inimitable "aren't I nearly a god" manner allowing the lowly staff to talk to him and call him Ray – just as any man of the people would!

Eventually he comes to Bill: *"Aven't you retired yet?"*

"No..." Bill replies, surprised the Chairman should be taking such an interest in him *"No... they won't let me go".*

At which point Stockhill looks at me and says in a very loud voice.

"Who won't let you go, that bastard there?" he nods towards me *"I'll fucking get you out, don't you worry."*

Even at a funeral he can't help bullying me – and all because I stopped Roebuck's betting and took control of managing the car park staff for the first time ever.

ooo

Autumn 1996 – The Town Centre CCTV and what they thought was the end of a career!

One of the things I have always wanted to do, at whatever level I have worked, is to leave a legacy whereby I could look over my shoulder and say *"I did that – and it's made things better..."*

So when I am given parking as a responsibility I want to make sure all our car parks are safe for the user – and, to achieve this, I want the 'Safe Parking Award'!

I arrange for all Local Authority car parks to be painted so they are bright and colour coded but that isn't enough; I want them safer and I identify Closed-Circuit Television [CCTV] as the answer!

The police know all the criminals, or so I reason, and if I can put together a package which offers good quality images of the miscreants, stealing or vandalising a car – then it's bingo – and off to jail they go!

As I begin to research the market, I inform my Director, Richard Sprenger [a man I continue to have huge admiration for] and to say he's supportive is an understatement. After a few days Richard returns from a meeting with the police and informs me they are looking into the same thing for the town centre – and we agree that I should meet with them to discuss a joint project. I'm absolutely buzzing with excitement at the prospect, so we meet and get a common consensus that we should work together to achieve these mutual objectives.

My Assistant Director, however, takes another view – making it clear he is completely against the project and wants nothing to do with it. His rationale being that the Chairman, Ray Stockhill, despises the Director because he's refused to fund Stockhill's drinking at conference [!]; consequently, anything Stockhill dislikes my sycophantic Assistant Director dislikes. And anything my Director wants, my Assistant Director doesn't want…

In the middle of all this symbiotic behaviour, I am introduced to a company trading as 'Executive Security' – a Doncaster firm specialising, they say, in security and CCTV installations and trading out of Mexborough.

We appear to be doubly blessed – a Doncaster firm installing a town centre CCTV system, in Doncaster, for Doncaster people – what could be better, and it creates employment! We agree to meet them and I get approval for them to install a trial camera in one of my multi storey car parks and I'm happy… for a few days!

Then I receive a call from my Car Parks Manager, a really dedicated guy, who very sheepishly tells me that I'd better come and have a look.

As I arrive at the car park I can see the camera has been ripped off its roof mounting and smashed.

Undeterred, I have a look at the recorded images and – bingo – we've got 'em. The film shows a group of guys in the middle of what appears to be a 'drug deal' when suddenly they see the camera and set about pulling it down.

I've got the most crystal clear, perfect images of it all. So I make a call to my [new] police colleagues thinking they'll know who it is instantly; second disappointment… of course they don't know, why would they? They could have come from anywhere. However on the upside it has proved a point, CCTV works!

I ask for the camera to be repaired by Executive Security and they invite me and my police colleagues to their offices to see their set-up. By this time they know we are looking into a possible town centre wide CCTV system, which they say they can install and then monitor from their Mexborough base – again, I'm buzzing with excitement.

They say things come in threes, well disappointment number three comes when we realise they are just establishing their business; console desks are set-up but there are hardly any consoles and there's a really amateurish look to the whole thing.

Not to be put off we move on with the meeting and the Executive Security officers begin their presentation, outlining what they can do. Suddenly, out of the blue, one of the police officers tells me he doesn't trust them and he think's something is wrong. He just can't quite put his finger on it.

At the next meeting, with me and one of the police officers present we are advised that one of the Executive Security Directors owns a 'car hire & sales' company and surprise, surprise, he can get us both a car "at the right price…"

Needless to say we don't take up the offer – but make our excuses and leave as soon as possible.

But as this potential scheme gathers momentum, we begin engaging with some of the 'big players' in the newly emerging CCTV and security market – companies such as Mercury, Telecom, BT, Philips, Serco, <u>et al</u> with a view to getting a scheme design and indicative costs.

We estimate the cost to be in the order of £2.2 million and want to work with companies capable of putting together a team with a track record on delivery, quality of product, aftercare service and financial stability.

We looked at due diligence issues and do background checks into every company and for completeness, we also have Executive Security checked out. It transpires that they neither have the capability to build the scheme nor the finances to fund it, with slightly over £12,000 in the company bank account.

So the steering group puts together a tender list from the major companies and I prepare a report to seek political approval to progress the project.

Together with our police colleagues we then deliver a joint presentation for the Cabinet. The room is packed and every councillor in the room supports the idea; we get approval to move the project forward, with the caveat that we have to raise external funding to pay for it.

Somewhere along the line, and I'm not sure where, a meeting must have taken place between the senior councillors and Executive Security because shortly after the presentation, I receive a phone call from the Leader, Councillor Gallimore.

Councillor Gallimore was a very powerful politician in those days and, to be fair, not unintelligent; however, it's a stressful call because back then the leader was next to God and far too important to ever speak to the likes of me.

"*John…*" he begins, and I'm flattered that he knows my name, "*I want you to put Executive Security on the tender list for the CCTV.*"

"*I can't leader – they don't have the technical capability or the financial standing, we've done background checks to support that.*"

"*I know all that John but just put them on the list. We know they won't get the work,*" he continues "*… but just put them on. We know Mercury will get the work.*"

You will note the insinuation here. Ray Stockhill has seen police officers and me at the races with employees from Mercury. We paid our own entry and bets, but with Mercury providing the food and alcohol the councillor clearly believes we were on the take.

I explain to Gallimore that it's highly unlikely Mercury will get the work and it is most likely to be Philips because they have the greater technical knowhow. He seems happy with this and simply says: "*Well, see what you can do, but I would like you to add them on the tender list.*"

In other words – do it!

Now we are in a partnership with the Police on this project, so I ring Superintendent Brian Mordue, the force commander, and tell him.

He responds sarcastically *"That's fine John... put them on the list,"* he tells me, and I'm momentarily relieved, *"And I'll start making the arrests in the morning."*

I'm in a really invidious position here. *"Oh come on Brian,"* I plead *"I've been told by the leader..."*

"I don't care John, put them on the list and I'll make the arrests tomorrow." End of conversation!

So where do I go from here?

I have a chat with my Director, Richard Sprenger, who advises that since the Leader of the Council is involved I speak to Doug Hale, the Chief Executive. Again, staff at my level don't normally speak to the Chief Executive, so I'm anxious, but to be fair he is receptive and understands my dilemma. I'm told to carry on and that he will sort this out with Gallimore.

The following day I'm called into my Assistant Director's room for a meeting with him and Ray Stockhill, as Chair of Environmental Services. The room is set out with the AD's desk and meeting table in a "T" shape; Councillor Stockhill is behind the table and the Assistant Director is behind his desk.

Councillor Stockill isn't over-burdened with brains but well-blessed with bad manners and abrasiveness; he kicks off straight away:

"We want you to put Exec Security on t' tender list for this CCTV system," he tells me aggressively

I explain that I can't put them on the list and why; but Stockhill is persistent because he saw me at the races with the Mercury team.

"I'm tellin ya, we want 'em on the fucking list"

I try to dig in, reiterating why I can't and advising him that the police will not support this decision, I daren't tell him what Supt. Mordue has said.

Then Stockhill comes out with an absolute beauty. *"Listen... I'm tellin ya they're goin' on the list and we all know Mercury have got you in their pocket!"*

I'm immediately on the defence. *"What do you mean they have me in their pocket? I've never taken anything that I'm not entitled to."*

He repeats: *"We all know yurrin their pocket."*

I continue: *"You can check my balance anytime you want"*

"Aye – and ya can check mine n'all," he responds.

Ray Stockhill is probably the most corrupt person I have had the misfortune to know. Later it would all come out about Stockhill but I knew he was corrupt, he couldn't possibly afford all the holidays he was taking otherwise.

I look at my Assistant Director for support and he quickly leans back in his chair, puts his arms up as if surrendering and says: *"I fuckin' told ya. You're on yer own!"*

"What do you mean I'm on my own?" I say

"What I say – Ah fuckin' told ya – yer on yer own!"

So that's what it feels like to be hung out to dry!

"I told ya not to do this fuckin' project," he continues *"But you would side with that fuckin' idiot Sprenger. Fuckin' waste of time.*

"Fuck what the fuckin' police say – put 'em on the fuckin' tender list."

End of meeting!

A couple of days later one of the police officers I'm working with comes to see me. He tells me Chief Executive Doug Hale, has had a meeting at the highest level with the police. He tells me he's seen some minutes he shouldn't have, recording that Hale and the Chief Constable have been discussing the CCTV system as an example of the level of corruption throughout the council. I'm surprised the minutes show it is being discussed at such a high level.

After the police officer leaves me, he goes back to the main police station where Superintendent Mordue confronts him, challenging him over the minutes and wanting to know whether anyone else has seen them. As a result, they are taken from him, never to be seen again; to this day, we don't know how he got them or how Mordue knew he had them!

I have to go to the Mansion House and Peter Welsh, later to become Leader of the Council, sidles up to me with a magazine in his hand:

"This is who's gonna build that CCTV system," he says, tapping a page of a magazine and showing me a photograph of the central control at Executive Security's base in Mexborough!

For Christ sake, when is this shit gonna go away – back to the explanations again…!

A day or two later, an officer from Executive Security invites me and a police colleague to have a 'pie and pint' with him. Given the political pressures we accept and meet up in 'The Corner Pin', a traditional old pub on the edge of the town centre, close to the train station.

The conversation very quickly turns to the CCTV system and when I start to talk about the tender for the work, and the officer says *"what fucking tender?"*

I tell him we are preparing a tender and it will have to go through the European tendering process because the value of the work exceeds EU limits. At this point, he goes bright red and tells me it's not going out to tender. I tell him it is and he stands up, almost purple now.

"It is not goin' out to fuckin' tender," he shouts. *"I'm fuckin' tellin you, you're gonna fuckin' put it out in £20,000 tranches and we're fuckin' doin' it."*

I'm glad the copper is with me. I tell him that what he is saying is impossible and it will never get past the District Auditor – and we both make a timely exit.

It's about this time that the District Auditor sends his letter to the Council about the corruption inherent within the Council, particularly elected members. We finally get control of the process over the CCTV system and the contract is awarded to Philips.

ooo

The backstory to all this is that the AD who so ably supported Stockhill, is promoted thanks to his political allegiances. The council advertises his job – and I decide to apply.

There are three internal candidates, myself and two colleagues. Three weeks before the interviews I find myself chatting to Richard Sprenger, who seems really depressed and tells me I'm wasting my time; that one of my colleagues is going to get the job because Stockhill wants 'his boy' in post.

When I tell the colleague, he won't believe it – and seems to think it's gamesmanship on my side.

A week or so later Head of HR, Geoff Bray stops me on the staircase: *"I think you want to talk to me about your Assistant Director application,"* he tells me; his code for 'I'm going to tell you some stuff to help with the interviews'.

Geoff wants to know what my Achilles Heel is. I tell him it's the CCTV system, which at the time is in its initial development stages, but that everyone is content with it. Geoff says: *"I'll tell you what to say John. Tell them that despite what councillors might think you have always acted in the best interests of the council."*

"I'm not saying that, they will think I've done something wrong," I tell him.

By the day of the interview it has become clear that two of us are just making up the numbers. I enter the interview room to see Tony Sellars as Chair and several other councillors sitting around the table, along with Geoff Bray as the HR/Personnel Advisor.

Sellars opens with: *"We're running late – you've 25 minutes – so keep your answers short."*

Great start, I think, and then they go on the attack. John Quinn is a powerful politician and a miner with a very thick Scottish accent:

"You've been in charge of gypsies, John – tell us how you're going to keep them out of Doncaster."

Trying to ignore the inherent racism in his question, I reply: *"Chairman, I can't keep them out of Doncaster, they have a legal right to move anywhere they want, just the same as anyone else."*

Quinn comes back at me: *"Well we don't want 'em in Doncaster, we're sick of it, so tell me how you're going to stop 'em coming in."* ; and so the interview, or barrage of attacks, goes on until it's time for Peter Walsh to ask his question

"Tell me John, if a councillor or your Director asked you to do something that you felt wasn't in the best interests of the Council what would you do?"

I look at Geoff with a face that says "you bastard"; he just smiles and shrugs his shoulders. I knew I was screwed before the interviews but not by my so-called colleagues.

Needless to say I don't get the AD post and Richard Sprenger's information turns out to be 100% accurate. I eventually bump into Geoff in a corridor and let him know I'm not happy. He simply shrugs the whole episode off. *"Ah well, politics is a dirty game,"* he says – and walks away.

To be fair Richard Sprenger creates a better career path for me and I finish up as a Head of Service.

ooo

Autumn 1998 – My Trip to London with Councillors Roebuck and Collins…

JC Decaux is a highly reputable firm; the number one outdoor advertising company in the world and internationally renowned for the installation of street advertising media and automatic public conveniences.

Given that we are always looking to generate additional income for the Council we genuinely believe that selling advertising space can realise a considerable sum for the benefit of the council tax payer. As such, I begin a dialogue with the people at JC Decaux who are delighted to put a package together for us. It's a bread and butter job for them.

As part of the package they invite us to London where they have a variety of automatic loos installed which net substantial advertising revenues. I get approval to go but am told I have to take 'uncle Tom' [Councillor Tommy Roebuck] with me, because public toilets are part of his portfolio… yeah right I think … another excuse for a councillor jolly!

So with a slight grimace on my part, we plan the day and I eventually catch the train to London. Coincidently Councillor Roebuck has to stay in London overnight on other 'official business'; and, also coincidently, Councillor Mick Collins is on the train on the same business as Roebuck – what are the chances of that…

Collins is supposed to be one of the brighter and more respected councillors at the time, so I feel I should make an effort, be respectful and give him some credit.

We meet the rep' from JC Decaux in London and he takes us to see this loo. All very interesting, Collins controls Tom and we get a fair understanding of how the loo works and how the advertising would fund such a facility. It's going great and then the rep' utters the fatal words:

"*Would you like some lunch? I know a really nice French restaurant in Covent Garden?*" I want to die, Noooooo! Don't take Roebuck there... here we go again...

We arrive at the restaurant, to be greeted by a classic and classy French waitress:

In a delightful French accent *"Bonjour gentlemen may I get you a table."*

"Ah, that'll be rate," says Roebuck

"Can I get you a drink Monsieur?"

"Ah, arl av' a pint o' bitter."

And so it goes on – no class or finesse – but at least Councillor Collins is trying and has a glass of wine.

"Gentlemen, can I take your order"

Tom says *"Ah... arl av' steak and chips."*

The French waitress is somewhat embarrassed: *"I'm sorry Monsieur, we don't have simply steak on the menu, the closest we have to that is Chateaubriand."*

"What's tha' then?" asks Tom and she explains it's a cut of beef roasted and served with fresh seasonal vegetables but that it's for two persons.

Fully expecting him to tackle it on his own, and ever the diligent officer [!], I quickly interject: *"I'll have that with you... if you want Tom?"*

"Ah... rate, w'ill av that then, burrah want chips wi' it."

After a while the Chateaubriand is served, beautifully carved and very pink. Tom takes one look at it and says, totally aghast: *"What's that?"*

"It's the chateaubriand monsieur!"

"Well tha can tek it back. Ah aint 'ating that – ah like my mate <u>cooked</u> not raw"

"But it is perfectly cooked Monsieur."

"Arm telling thee I aint 'ating that, ah want it <u>well cooked</u>, tek it back"

I don't know what to do with myself – I'm absolutely humiliated and want the whole world to swallow me up.

Eventually Tom's food returns; it's nearly burnt to a crisp and comes with a huge portion of chips. We all begin eating, chatting nicely over the meal. After about half an hour Tom leans over to me:

"Ah can't ate any moor o' this mate," he tells me, gathering his plate in one hand and his knife and fork in the other *"Eeyah tha can av it,* " and he proceeds to scrape the remains of his meal onto my plate.

I'm trying not to gip... anybody who knows Tom will tell you he isn't the cleanest of men... his false teeth are too big for him, so god knows what is trapped in them.

"I'm sorry Tom I can't eat any more, I was full anyway," I say, wanting to be sick and crawl away.

Afterwards we thank the rep' profusely for a very informative day and a very nice meal. I'm looking at my timetable to see when I'll get back to Doncaster when Collins asks me: *"You're stopping down aren't you?"*

I explain that I can't, I don't have approval for an overnight and my wife is expecting me home.

"Gerron that phone and tell Sprenger that tha's staying down 'ere," says Collins unexpectedly. *"And tell 'im ah said so!".*

So I duly ring the Director and get approval. Despite not having much money and no fresh clothes, we get a cab to the Plaza on Hyde Park. As we arrive Collins says: *"Tha can get this John."*

"Oh I get it" I reply *"The officer pays the man at the front a brown drinking token [a £10 note]"*

"You've got it," replies Collins *"Now you're learning son."*

At the hotel the two councillors get a typical room. I, on the other hand, am dispatched to what I can only describe as 'a cupboard' somewhere at the top and back of the building.

We agree to meet downstairs at the bar in an hour and, knowing I am in for a rough night, I find the nearest cash dispenser and get some money out, before joining Collins; it's early and he's on gin and tonic, which is good because it means I can just drink the tonics and they won't know.

It's a pleasant enough atmosphere, a decadent piano lounge with a pianist playing easy listening tunes and Collins and I are idly chatting away until Roebuck joins us.

To be fair, and up to a point, Roebuck is reasonable company and tells me some of the story behind him going to jail over the Poulson affair; essentially arguing that he took the fall for a lot of other councillors... his reward being a relatively comfortable prison sentence.

However the acceptable behaviour doesn't last... and Roebuck and Collins are soon knocking them back as if there is no tomorrow; with it always seeming to be my turn at the bar!

Seeing a group of ladies pass our table in all their finery – pearls & twin sets and classic blue rinse hairdos – Roebuck, grossly overweight and scruffy though he is, can't resist trying to 'pull'.

As the pianist performs a Burt Bacharach classic, he opens his arms towards the ladies, pint in one hand, huge cigar in the other:

"*Na then love, does tha wanna sit with thee uncle Tom,*" he calls to one as she attempts to pass.

She glances anxiously at her friends, who have found an alternative route past us.

"*Na dun't ignore me luv...*" he addresses her again, as she retreats to follow her companions

"*Come and av a drink with thee uncle Tom,*" he pleads as she escapes and scurries off with her friends.

"*Well that's her fucking loss,*" he proclaims, as she disappears into the distance "*Your round Michael,*" he hollers... and, despite it always being my turn, Collins decides to get a round in!

"*Gerrus a cigar will tha Mick?*" Roebuck says

The bar itself is about three or four tables away from where we are sitting, with the pianist seated a couple of tables to our left; Collins duly takes the order to the bar – two G&Ts, a pint and a cigar. I have to have a gin this time otherwise I'm undone!

As Collins leaves us, Roebuck finishes yet another pint with a loud sigh, smacking his lips; "*Does tha no' drink pints John?*" he asks me, but he's not really concentrating on my response... and before I can answer, he literally shouts across the pianist to Mick Collins at the bar in the Plaza on Hyde Park:

"*MICK, THA WAINT FORGET MI CIGAR WILL THA?*"

The entire lounge falls silent, even the pianist is knocked from his playing.

"*Memory like a sieve – 'im,*" Roebuck informs the entire room.

Tommy is totally oblivious to the scene he's caused – but then 'gods' don't worry about what mere mortals might think.

ooo

John's Summary

We don't have a book long enough to report them all but there are many other, equally outlandish, yet true, stories that describe the elected members' greed, bullying, arrogance, vindictiveness, jealousy and stupidity... including:
- The time the chairman wanted to see an electrically powered bus – so insisted on going to Sweden to view it even though they would have delivered it for inspection at the Mansion House.
- When another chairman wanted a trip to Germany – any trip [because Ray Stockhill had been!] so he was taken to see a paving scheme... in Germany, when there were acres of the same paving schemes in the UK.
- When nearly a dozen councillors went to Dandong, our twinned city in China, and flew back 'First Class'; ordering as much booze as they could

- drink on the flight, and stuffing their pockets so full of miniature bottles, they could be heard clinking as they walked through the airport.
- The occasion a colleague was disciplined – because he hadn't introduced a new [female] member of staff to Stockhill.
- The councillor who was checking other councillors expenses – so he could claim the same amount, even though he hadn't been on the trip they were claiming for!
- The story of the hotelier who made rooms permanently available for senior councillors to use, as they saw fit, including for drunken orgies with prostitutes...
- The chairman who used corrupt money to pay for holidays with his regular prostitute – who he pretended was his niece…
- The time they made a mistake on a plaque for an opening ceremony, crediting Robert Grainger with an MBE as opposed to the British Empire Medal he had actually been awarded. He quietly and magnanimously let it go, but it's still there to this day.

Perhaps these stories will be told on another day.

ooo

The Gospel According to Gary…

It would be wrong to assume that Doncaster Council's problems started with the damming District Audit [DA] Report published in January 1997 – the demise started long before that. But Gordon Sutton's report did at last start to bring things out into the open – with a little help from 'The Independent' newspaper.

I attend the "informal meeting" on the 20th January, 1997 where Labour Group Officers listen to the DA report on "sensitive management processes" like foreign visits, receipt of hospitality and gifts by officers and members; working lunches where 'given the amount of alcohol consumed' the DA is surprised anyone could get back to the office afterwards let alone get any work done'.

It is the most critical report by an auditor I have ever seen – in fact I am amazed I have been invited to the meeting. Sutton pulls no punches and, in varying degrees, every councillor from the Doncaster District Labour Party 'miners group' sat around that table is involved in the abuse being highlighted, and they know it.

When the DA intimates that his investigation has come as a result of a tip off, John Quinn is naïve or stupid enough to ask where it has come from.

Leader Peter Welsh who is in the Chair [with Chief Exec Doug Hale at the side of him] is involved and his response is classic.

"We'll sort it art won't we Doug? Tha can leave it to us, Gordon, we'll sort it art."

To my utter amazement Sutton seems to accept the response, I can't believe it. I'm convinced they are going to sweep this under the carpet and it looks like the DA is going to let them. That will be an absolute disgrace and I can't leave it there. That evening I go to see a former Councillor and friend Ron Rose, who in years gone by has had the Labour whip withdrawn for trying to expose the abuse of the ruling 'miners group' and I tell him what has happened.

Ron Rose says he will ensure it won't get buried and the following Sunday I receive a telephone call from Christian Wolmar, the Westminster correspondent of The Independent newspaper. He runs some quotes past me with regards to the DA's comments in the meeting, all of which I have given to Ron and I confirm they are accurate. I also tell Christian that if my name is associated with this, my career is over. His response is that if it becomes public, so is his!

Two days later the front page of The Independent runs a headline "Blair Hit By Old Labour Junketing". I take one look and think 'they can't bury it now'. All this leads to the Operation Danum Police Inquiry – described by Eric Pickles as "the biggest and most extensive investigation into wrongdoing in local government for a generation". For once he is right. In addition to a plethora of expenses frauds, a multi-million pound manipulation and abuse of the planning system is exposed whereby Deputy Leader Ray Stockhill, and Planning Chairman Peter Birks, are both found guilty of accepting inducements running into thousands of pounds from property developer Alan Hughes. Tory Group Leader John Dainty is cleared of corruption in that case but later jailed for 15 months for inducing a £5,000 bribe from a local landowner for smoothing a planning application.

Truth be told, some councillors have used the system to their advantage for as long as I can remember. But 'the system' at least tried to exercise a degree of control over the whole process. For example free tickets for the races, access to the Portland Suite, a free bar – all dispersed by the Leadership – were regarded as legitimate perks of a councillor's job. Some perks were less generic than race tickets, more relative to the seniority of the councillor or granted at the grace and favour of the leader.

For the Chairman and Vice Chairman of the Housing Committee there was the annual Institute of Housing Conference at Harrogate. It was my job as Head of Housing to accompany [perhaps chaperone would be a better description] my two elected members. We had full delegate tickets which were not cheap at nearly £300 but gave access to numerous presentations in the main exhibition centre. This usually culminated with an address by the Housing Minister, customarily on the last day. My 'job' however was not to ensure our politicians were present at key Conference sessions. I had one role… to ensure they were well wined and dined every lunch and evening, at no cost to themselves, courtesy of a corporate attendee.

Despite their political position and full delegate status, it was quite common for our politicians not to attend a single conference session. The best that could be expected was a trip around the exhibition to collect some freebies. When Bev Marshall was Chair, his food and drink consumption was legendary. The Institute of Housing Conference was no different to the other professional conferences like Planning, Environmental Health and so on, which councillors saw as an opportunity to eat, and in particular drink, as much as they could – courtesy of a contractor or an officer's council credit card.

This may sound like an abuse of the system but, believe me it was nothing in comparison to what was to come. When Gordon Gallimore was Leader he was happy to accept a gift of £1000 worth of travel vouchers from the Board of a large developer to celebrate his retirement but he did exercise a degree of control over the largesse. The catalyst to the escalation of the abuse was without doubt the appointment of Peter Welsh as the new leader in 1994.

Welsh was often referred to in the local press as 'a bit of a lad'. Not a bad description. In those days I regularly took my father to Tattersfield on a Sunday afternoon to watch the Doncaster Rugby League Football Club play – we paid, I hasten to add. On one occasion at half-time, I saw Peter coming out of a box at the rear of the stand, obviously for a cigarette. He spotted me and made a beeline for us. He was extremely well-oiled and after "Aye-up son" every sentence was interspersed with 'fucking this' or 'fucking that'. After his cigarette he shot back to his box, at which point my father [obviously disgusted with who I was mixing with] asked *"who on earth was that?"*

"Oh, only the Leader of the Council, dad!".

Peter's most classic laddish act was however saved for an event at the Doncaster Dome while he and several other Elected Members were enjoying a very liquid evening watching a concert. Pistol Pete [his other affectionate name] decided it was too much trouble to go all the way to the toilets at the end of the corridor; particularly when there was a convenient window nearby! With many of the audience below understandably distressed by the Leader's "behaviour", the Chief Solicitor earned more than his salary ensuring this was all kept out of the press.

Many Members saw authorised travel as an opportunity to make a few bob on the side. Quite simply, they would travel standard class, claim 'First Class' and pocket the difference. They did not regard this as fraud – but a 'perk'. It might not sound a lot but, as the DA pointed out, the Council spent almost £24,000 on 'First Class' rail travel in the year in question.

This is how it worked.

When Terry Sellers was Vice Chairman of Housing he accompanied me to an event at Westminster where, prior to their election victory in 1997, the Labour Party set out its manifesto for Local Government. Terry and I were delegates and he travelled with me in 'Standard Class' – when we arrived in London he turned to me and said:

"If anyone asks I ant bin sat w' thee" and he proceeded to get the next train back to Doncaster.

One of our biggest "problems" was the fact that Terry wanted to enjoy the same largesse as his brother Tony, the Chair of Environmental Health. Tony was known as the Council's wine-taster for his penchant for fine wines consumed at the tax-payers' expense. Terry would quite regularly go in to the Housing Offices at Conisbrough and insist that one of the officers take him for lunch, his rationale being: *"Our Tony only has to go and inspect some garages and they tek 'im for lunch and all I get is a sarnie"*.

He would also come in to my office and say *"I want thee to find a reason for us to gu t' Dublin, our Tony's bin an I want to gu"*.

"But Terry I need to have a reason for us to go, and there isn't one". Fortunately Terry didn't have the acumen or the bullying nature to take the argument further…

Perhaps my fondest memory of Terry though was a phone call I once received from him.

"Morning Terry, what can I do for you?"

"I want thee to ger our Darren a job".

"It's not that easy Terry, we are losing staff, not taking them on [as you well know]".

"Look! 'e's a good lad, and 'e meks 'is own bed ev'ry day".

"Ok Terry, in that case, I'll see what I can do".

Of course nothing further ever came of that phone call; and, in some respects, I was lucky that these were conversations with Terry and not some of the other senior councillors who would not have let such requests drop so easily.

ooo

fall out   May you never have everything you wish for

Loved and trusted...

May you never have everything you wish for

> *"Even a slight remark... Makes no sense and turns to shark*
> *Have I done something wrong?*
> *What's wrong is wrong, it's always wrong."*
>
> Billy Mackenzie and Alan Rankine

1989...

Most of 1989 is a recuperation period.

The second half of 1988 has been spent physically recovering from, and dealing with the trading aftermath of the car crash which has ended my career – both as a rugby league player and a professional sculptor.

I was driving home from work with my business partner Mike, whom I had met at college, when we were hit head-on by a car travelling on the wrong side of the road. I suffered a serious head injury, brain trauma and significant orthopaedic injuries including a compound fracture of my left tibia and fibula. Mike suffered facial lacerations and a fractured femur, which left him in traction for more than six months.

On crutches for over three months and suffering from traumatic brain injury symptoms, I spend much of the time sitting on the settee at my parents' house with a plaster cast up to my groin, phoning anyone I can think of to speak to.

One day I get around to ringing Carolyne, Jamie's ex-girlfriend. She has moved on and is living in Huddersfield and soon we start seeing each other seriously. In years gone by, Carolyne and I used to enjoy working together on her classic MG. She's an attractive woman, petite with blond hair, an hour-glass figure, a killer sense of humour – which has always attracted me to her – and a great sense of style.

ooo

At around this time, Leigh Environmental applies to build a waste incinerator right in the heart of Kirk Sandall. The Toxic Waste Out [TWO] campaign is launched with its headquarters at the Assembly Halls, a facility bestowed on the community by the Pilkington Glass Company. The Assembly Halls are directly opposite my house and since I am by now at least mobile, I become heavily involved.

The campaign and Assembly Halls become the focal point of the community's activities. Almost every house, every car and every business has a yellow TWO sticker on it. We have differing committees meeting every night of the week and we march on Doncaster's Mansion House – the historic home of the council – to make our feelings known. Democracy prevails and the plans are turned down. Leigh Environmental appeals against the decision and, as we prepare for the forthcoming public inquiry, our petition is signed by more than 100,000 people.

When we bench-mark our community's response against others, we notice Greenpeace and Friends of the Earth are central to their campaigns. We begin asking questions as to why we are receiving no advice and support.

Greenpeace tell us: *"You are actually very well organised and don't need any help...you're doing a very good job on your own"*.

Their energies are better spent helping less capable communities, they say. We don't necessarily feel so confident.

But as an introduction to community politics, the campaign is fantastic – bringing people together with great passion for a shared NIMBY vision. It gives me a real opportunity to display some of my attributes; commitment; expertise; enthusiasm; loyalty; energy; team-working and humour; I'm having a ball!

As a result, local councillor Pat Mullany and community activist Liz Jeffress ask me if I will consider standing as a Labour Party candidate for the parish council. I agree, taking my place on the Labour slate, which now reads Jeffress, Mullany, Skinns, Stoppard…and Winter.

ooo

January 1990…

By now and Carolyne and I are a definite item, sharing our love of socialist politics and being Northern together. Since we are expecting our first baby in May, I need to find a job.

I begin work at Doncaster Metropolitan Borough Council as a Training Officer. It's my first real experience of Local Authority operations and, to be frank, I'm appalled; both by the inefficiencies and the waste and by the nepotism, rife within the system.

For a while I work alongside an officer called Alan Jones… or 'Jonesy'.

ooo

Thursday May 3rd 1990…

I am elected as a parish councillor for the Barnby Dun with Kirk Sandall Parish Council, polling only thirty votes less than Liz Jeffress and 107 more than the DMBC councillor, Pat Mullany.

Pat Mullany is a stern looking, upright individual who is always seen in a black gent's Crombie coat, wearing his black leather driving gloves and carrying his triple thickness DMBC briefcase.

Whilst he congratulates me on my success and is publicly friendly, in private Councillor Mullany warns me against thinking I could ever challenge him for his seat– welcome to local politics!

ooo

Thursday May 17th 1990...

Carolyne gives birth to our new baby girl – Bethany.

ooo

Sunday March 17th 1991...

My dad is rushed to hospital suffering from a stroke. As a result, I open my parents' newsagents [at 4.30 am] four days each week.

ooo

Friday May 10th 1991...

After just fifteen months working for Doncaster Council, I decide to leave. I just cannot relate to the workings of the Local Authority – it appears completely disconnected from reality.

I have been a good team player and my colleagues are reluctant for me to go, highlighting some exciting projects in the pipeline; not least the "Museum of the Earth" [sic.], a concept outlined in a paper that the elected members are presently considering – later delivered as the Earth Centre.

As a leaving gift, I'm presented with some red socks – partly because I never wear socks and partly as a comment on my "political leanings". Alan Jones, who has by now become a good friend, organises a collection for me – but then delights in telling me he drank it at the local pub!

ooo

Monday May 13th 1991...

I begin work as national training manager at the Royal Society for Nature

Conservation [RSNC] in Lincoln.

ooo

Monday November 11th 1991…

Success! After three-years, Leigh Environmental's appeal for the incinerator to be sited within our community is thrown out. Over the following weeks, and after several celebrations, the successful TWO campaign is wound up.

At one of the final meetings, I challenge those involved to consider what we could achieve, if we use our energy, enthusiasm and phenomenal spirit for something more tangible; to bring something positive to the community.

My comments go down like a damp squib. People want to celebrate the last campaign's success not plan the next one. Unperturbed, I suggest we campaign for Pilkington's fifty acre cullet dump – a waste glass landfill site on the edge of the "Old Village" – to be closed down and opened up for the community as a recreational resource.

I take the resounding silence to be acquiescence and begin to map out my campaign for the "Pilkington Country Park".

ooo

1992…

I am doing well at RSNC and have a sideline as an external moderator in environmental conservation and a variety of land-based programmes for EDEXCEL BTEC, City & Guilds and the National Proficiency Testing Council.

My work on the "Pilkington Country Park" concept continues apace, and I develop the project further seeking support, advice and assistance from a wide network of contacts within RSNC.

ooo

Thursday April 9th 1992…

General Election Day

ooo

Friday April 10th 1992...

3.00 am – Our House, Kirk Sandall
Having campaigned energetically for the Labour Party in the 1992 General Election, Carolyne and I are devastated by the unexpected defeat.

We are both sat up in bed crying over the election result – because of it we seriously consider emigrating to New Zealand with our young family, but eventually decide to stay and fight on.

ooo

Sunday June 14th 1992...

7.30 pm – Doncaster North Constituency Labour Party, Spring Gardens, Doncaster

I have been invited by Pat Mullany to my first Doncaster North CLP meeting – and to be frank I find it pretty tedious.

One of the last items on the agenda, however, is Kevin Hughes with his MP's report, describing how lucky he has been since getting elected [on my birthday] and that he won the raffle last week!

Mundane, he admits – until you realise it's the raffle to see who gets first crack at Prime Minister's Questions next Tuesday!

What an opportunity! I think to myself.

As the meeting wraps up I make a beeline for him. *"Congratulations Kevin – I have an idea for your PMQ, if you want to hear it?"*

He takes a drag on his cigarette. *"Go on then,"* he humours me. *"What are y' thinking of?"* And I go on to explain that John Major has just attended the United Nations' Earth Summit in Rio De Janeiro and signed up to a variety of conventions and commitments with regard to 'saving the planet'...

He takes another drag on his cigarette.

"Well you need to pin him down on 'thinking globally – acting locally'..." I tell him. *"And get him to commit to saving Thorne & Hatfield Moors."*

I stare at him attentively; convinced I'm a fucking genius!

Kevin looks back at me, his lips open, his cigarette grasped between his teeth; then he takes the cigarette from his mouth and says: *"D'you know Martin... that's exactly what I was thinking of doing".*

ooo

Monday June 15th 1992…

10.00 am – RSNC The Wildlife Trusts, Waterside South, Lincoln

I meet with Caroline Steel and Charles Couzens to talk about drafting a PMQ for Kevin.

ooo

Tuesday June 16th 1992…

2.22 pm – The House of Commons

> **Kevin Hughes:** *"Given the commitment that the Prime Minister gave to the Biodiversity Treaty in Rio over the weekend and in the House yesterday, while he advises other countries on how to solve their problems, will he try to solve some of the problems that we have in this country? Thorne and Hatfield Moors in my constituency have been totally devastated by the peat extraction carried out by the Fisons company. Will the Prime Minister introduce legislation to stop the devastation of sites of special scientific interest, not just at Thorne and Hatfield Moors, but throughout the country?"*
>
> *Hansard – June 16th 1992 - Vol 209 cc771-6*

ooo

Monday July 13th 1992…

Carolyne and I are heartbroken when our second child, a baby boy, dies when Carolyne is 26 weeks pregnant.

ooo

Sunday August 14th 1992…

5.30 pm – Our House, Kirk Sandall

I arrive home, having spent the previous week in Edinburgh at the RSNC Education Conference and the Edinburgh Fringe Festival. As I open the door, there

is a note from Carolyne waiting for me…
> *Martypants – taken dog and Beth down Moor Lane with Susie and Jonathan [from Greenpeace!] – Cazza*

I get my bike out from under the carport, jump on it and cycle down the lane; it's my grandfather's old "sit-up-and-beg" style gent's cycle, made by Upperdine of Balby in Doncaster in the 1950s. Who the fuck are Jonathan and Susie [from Greenpeace]? I think to myself…

I ride past the cullet dump and towards the "Old Village" – and find them near St Oswald's Church and the farm. I get off my bike to cuddle Beth, Carolyne [and the dog!].

Carolyne introduces me to Susie and Jonathan and their son Gabriel, who is the same age as Beth. She tells me how she has been explaining the concept behind the "Pilkington Country Park" to them – access to the countryside, sports pitches and recreational areas, planting new community orchards, re-connecting the public with food production and creating a business unit on the derelict farm.

What transpires, as we walk around, is that when Jonathan came up to Doncaster, I was recommended to him as a good contact for "their" project – the Earth Centre – the rebranded "Museum of the Earth" officers had mentioned when I left my job at Doncaster Council..

It turns out Jonathan is the former Managing Director of Greenpeace and Susie is his partner and a sculptor – what a result! There is tremendous synergy between our two projects and I am excited at the possibilities for future collaboration.

We spend an immensely enjoyable few hours together and Susie explains they are completely new to the area and don't particularly know anybody – she says they see Carolyne and me as kindred spirits.

As Jonathan and Susie are leaving, we ask them what support we can give them.

It's an embarrassing moment. Jonathan looks at Susie and she looks back at him. Together they look at Carolyne and me and then ask, in unison…

"Will you be our friends please?"

We all laugh.

ooo

Tuesday October 13th 1992…

It's almost six months since the general election victory and the smug Tory government is continuing Thatcher's assault on our mining communities.

Trade & Industry Secretary, Michael Heseltine, has announced the second phase of its pit closure programme – the shutdown of 31 of the 50 deep coal mines that remained in the UK after Thatcher's closures following the 1984-85 strike.

Liz Jeffress was heavily involved in the "Women Against Pit Closures" programme with the likes of Anne Scargill, Brenda Nixon *et al* during the 1984-85 Miners' strike. Liz is a good organiser and, since I was elected as a Labour parish councillor, we have become good friends.

Together with Carolyne and our young daughter Bethany, we attend a rally in Chesterfield against the pit closures.

With Tony Benn, Dennis Skinner, Arthur Scargill and Rodney Bickerstaffe all speaking at the event, I'm all fired up. However, I'm flying out to the Czech Republic tomorrow for a British Council [Know How Fund] project in the Carpathian Mountains; the revolution will have to wait!

ooo

Tuesday October 27th 1992...

After establishing the Central & Eastern European Working Group for Enhancing Biodiversity [CEEWEB] during an excellent conference, I fly back into Heathrow. I hire a car and drive to Framlingham in Suffolk for a Wildlife Trusts' Conservation Conference.

Having been out of the country for more than two weeks, I am expecting widespread disenchantment with the Tory government; nay an emerging culture of civil disobedience following Heseltine's Pit Closure programme.

Nothing... the miners are broken.

ooo

January 1993...

We establish the Kirk Sandall Community Wildlife Group – an urban wildlife group with the specific aim of progressing the Pilkington Country Park project.

ooo

Saturday June 5th 1993...

Carolyne gives birth to our new baby boy – Joss.

ooo

Monday October 3rd 1994...

My work at RSNC is going from strength to strength. I'm developing a good national profile and receiving a number of offers to take on private consultancy work. I'm also becoming more and more obsessed with delivering what I'm now calling the Glass Park Project.

    I make the decision to leave RSNC and establish the Martin Winter Consultancy [MWC] specialising in organisational analysis; occupational standards; NVQs; organisational standard setting; quality assurance and environmental management standards. The focus is on the voluntary and not-for-profit sectors.

    RSNC reluctantly agree to my departure and I negotiate a 100-day retainer across my first eighteen months of self-employment.

ooo

Sunday October 9th 1994...

Having received a final settlement last year, from the 1988 car crash, we move from our three bedroom end terrace on Dentons Green Lane, to a much larger four bedroom semi-detached house in Lancaster Avenue; some two hundred yards around the corner.

    We have the property substantially extended with a downstairs bathroom, playroom and double garage as well as a teleworking cottage constructed from "The Old Summerhouse", to act as the office for my increasing private consultancy.

ooo

Wednesday January 25th 1995...

Carolyne gives birth to our new baby girl – Marcey.

ooo

Wednesday July 17th 1996...

Pilkington Country Park is re-branded as the "Glass Park" and continues with a new-found energy.

ooo

October 1996…

The Barnby Dun with Kirk Sandall Parish Council agrees to work in partnership with the Kirk Sandall Community Wildlife Group to deliver the "Glass Park" as a suitable project to celebrate the millennium.

ooo

Tuesday December 22nd 1996…

6pm – Cumberland Hotel, Wheatley, Doncaster

As a manager at Doncaster Council, Alan Jones is on a relatively good salary, as is his wife, who works in a managerial post; so they aren't a family who struggle financially.
    Nonetheless, whenever we're out, Alan always claims he has no change on him, borrowing a quid here or 'ten-bob' there. He's forever borrowing tools and never giving them back. Not deliberately, I hasten to add, but through a selective amnesia – knowing it annoys me.
    Alan has suggested we go out for a Christmas drink together and we meet up at the Cumberland Hotel at Wheatley. The landlord is a man called "Gadge" as I know him from when we played rugby together.
    Alan brings two colleagues with him, introducing me to Ian Spowart, a bus driver who is looking to stand for election as a Doncaster Councillor, and John Curry who works for the Regional Labour Party in Wakefield. Because we are all members of the Party, the conversation about the forthcoming General Election flows as easily as the beer.
    The pub is getting very busy and we are laughing, joking and insulting each other; by 9.00 pm we are very merry.
    "D'you wanna buy a raffle ticket Martin?" asks "Gadge".
    "Ayeup Gadge… No thanks mate," I reply slurring.
    "Go on you tight bastard," says Gadge *"You can afford it… you're fucking loaded"*
    "Well… you've certainly got your customer care sorted Gadge," I respond but Jonesy jumps in.
    "See… somebody else who knows you. Go on… buy a fucking raffle ticket… you tight bastard."
    "Has he always been a tight bastard Gadge?" Jonesy asks of his new friend the landlord.
    "There's a £1,000 accumulator on" says Gadge laughing at Jonesy's insults.
    "Nah… I never fucking win anyway," I say.

"Here you are mate" says Alan demonstrably "I'll have one please" and he puts a £5 note on the table "Not like this tight bastard," he sneers, nodding at me. "Just one mate," he concludes, leaving his change next to his beer mat.

"Yeah here you are mate," says Ian, putting a pound on the table.

"There you go mate" says John, passing his pound to Gadge.

"You are such a tight fucking bastard," says Jonesy, slurring at me once again.

"No I'm not..." I protest. "I never fucking win anyway. Besides I'm always fucking subbing you."

But then I had an idea.

"Actually... yeah... Gadge," I shout after him "Here you are..."

And Gadge comes back to the table.

"I will have one," I say, as Gadge tears me a ticket out. "And he's paying" I shout, passing him one of Alan's four pound coins.

Both Ian and John laugh like hyenas.

"That'll fucking teach you... you clever twat" I tell him, and Alan just laughs into his beer glass.

By 10.00 pm the entire pub is heaving. Jonesy is in the middle of a story about his 1950s Morris Minor, which is costing him a fortune to keep on the road. We're taking it in turns to mock him, insult him and shout him down.

"It's Green 674... on yer ticket," says the tannoy.

As a classic car enthusiast, I have restored many cars over the years, including recently a Porsche 356 which Jonesy had towed back for me when I bought it five years earlier.

"It's Green 674... on yer 'Play Your Cards Right' raffle"...says the tannoy again. But we're having too much fun mocking Alan. And we're getting louder and louder.

"It's Green 674... on yer 'Play Your Cards Right' raffle. Over near the conservatory."

"Oh just fucking missed it..." says Ian, looking at his ticket "... it must be you John?"

"Nah not me – oh fucking 'ell it's you Martin," says John.

It is. I've won the pub's "Play Your Cards Right" raffle!

With the entire pub screaming "higher, higher, lower, lower" I somehow manage to lose the "Play Your Cards Right" £1,000 accumulator prize; nonetheless, the audience goes wild and I still win £500 cash.

As I bring my winnings back to the table, Jonesy is even more abusive.

"Oh no... not me... I never fucking win..." he mocks.

"Oh shut up" I tell him, as Ian and John laugh on. "I wouldn't have bought a ticket if it wasn't for you..." I say

"With your money!" jumps in Ian.

"So I'll split the winnings with you," and I give him £250.

ooo

Saturday January 11th 1997…

Our House, Kirk Sandall

Alan Jones and I often "swap days" with each other. We have both relatively recently moved into new homes and, as usual, there are hundreds of jobs that need doing.

Alan comes up with the concept to make the work more enjoyable and easier; helping each other out, lending tools and equipment etc.

For this particular "swap day" I decide to build a large family table in our back garden, so our family and friends can eat out during the coming summer months.

To be honest these days are flawed from the outset. Whenever Jonesy is due to be helping at our house, we plan and ready ourselves religiously so that the moment he arrives we can put him to work with the correct tools and equipment and what we want him to do.

When I [or we] are helping at Jonesy's, he never knows what he wants doing, how it's going to be accomplished or what tools and equipment are needed. As a result, more often than not, the days are wasted, planning, arguing and re-planning. I contend this is not a good use of our time but it does provide an appropriate metaphor for Jonesy's approach to life.

I plan this particular day meticulously and as a result, we are able to construct the table and spring-clean our back garden while our children playfully tidy up all the leaves and other garden detritus into my new compost units.

ooo

Thursday January 16th 1997…

Martin Redmond, the MP for Don Valley dies unexpectedly aged 59. With a General Election set to be held in 16 weeks, no by-election is called.

A bloody selection process commences with Doncaster MBC Councillors Pat Mullany, Tony Sellars and Peter Welsh [Leader] all vying to be chosen as the next Labour Candidate for the Don Valley Constituency.

ooo

Monday January 20th 1997...

District Auditor, Gordon Sutton, sends a damming District Audit 'Management Letter'; and a routine part of his responsibilities, to the Chief Executive of Doncaster Council. In the 'Management Letter' he paints a picture of widespread abuse by officers and members including foreign visits; receipt of gifts &hospitality; expenses and others issues.

At a meeting with the Senior Executive members of the Council, he outlines that a further, more detailed, report will be made available and public within two months.

ooo

Wednesday January 22nd 1997...

Carolyne's music hero Billy Mackenzie has died from a drug overdose. He was found in a shed at his father Jim's home in Dundee – he was 39.

Singer Billy, famed for his operatic voice, formed The Associates with guitarist Alan Rankine in Dundee in 1979. They had a top 10 hit in 1982 with Party Fears Two and the band were said to have influenced acts including The Smiths and The Cure.

Carolyne is a huge fan of eighties new wave music and says he had the voice of an angel. She also says that what first attracted her to me was that I looked like his twin!

ooo

Following Martin Redmond's death there is a relatively short campaigning period, which is becoming increasingly marred by allegations of fraud and corruption among council candidates. As a result, the Labour Party's National Executive Committee [NEC] has taken over the process of selecting the candidate.

Following CLP's meeting, a "long-list" of eight potential candidates is drawn up to be considered by the NEC; interestingly, Doncaster Council Leader, Pete Welsh, is not on it.

ooo

Saturday February 15th 1997…

Labour Party's National Executive Committee Shortlisting Meeting

The Labour Party's National Executive Committee produces a shortlist of four to seek selection for the Don Valley CLP seat at the forthcoming General Election:
    Cath Ashton – A convener for the AEEU union in Yorkshire.
    Caroline Flint – A Senior Researcher for the GMB Union in London.
    Mark Walker – A National Political Officer for the RMT Transport Union.
    Mike Watson – The MP for Glasgow Central [loses seat – boundary change]

ooo

Tuesday February 18th 1997…

"MP Snub for Councillors" cries the Doncaster Star, before going on to report how "The NEC verdict leaves Don Valley activists with no local candidate" in the final part of the selection process.

ooo

Saturday February 22nd 1997…

Don Valley Constituency Labour Party [CLP], Parliamentary Selection Meeting

After a selection meeting that many members have boycotted, Caroline Flint is selected to contest the Don Valley CLP seat at the forthcoming General Election in May.

ooo

March 1997…

During the fallout from the Don Valley parliamentary seat selection process – and the publication of the District Auditor's Report – Doncaster Council is wracked with allegations of high-level fraud and corruption.
    The thrust of these is that the council is controlled by a small cognoscente – the "ruling mining group" – and that this is operating as a cabal, or faction, making all the decisions about council resources for the benefit of select communities and individuals.

In response, South Yorkshire Police has launched *'Operation Danum'* – an investigation into claims of widespread wrongdoing by members and officers of the council – a scandal that becomes known as "Donnygate".

As a result of this, and also because of its general 'dysfunctionality', Doncaster District Labour Party is suspended by the National Labour Party.

ooo

Wednesday March 5th 1997...

The leader of Doncaster Council, Pete Welsh, and his deputy Ray Stockhill, resign in the wake of the second, more detailed, damming District Audit Report. However, they only resign from their positions as leader and deputy leader and remain as councillors on the Local Authority; thereby retaining their 'Members Allowance'.

ooo

Wednesday March 12th 1997...

Malcolm Glover is appointed as new leader of Doncaster Council.

ooo

April 1997...

Work on the Glass Park continues and, having secured a successful bid for Millennium Green status and funding, the demands on my time are now significant.

I'm getting more and more obsessed with delivering the project and, as a result, my time management and prioritisation is going awry. I'm spending too much time working for free, doing the work I love, and not enough time earning the money that allows me to work for free.

Carolyne and I agree to re-mortgage the house, enabling me to concentrate on developing the project further.

ooo

Thursday May 1st 1997...

The Day of the Labour Party's Historic General Election Victory

Carolyne and I have campaigned energetically for a Labour Victory. In a manner different to the triumphalism of 1992, we know victory awaits us. Everybody does; it is our destiny as a Party.

ooo

Friday May 2nd 1997...

10.00 am – Our House, Kirk Sandall

A fantastic sunny day, both literally and metaphorically; the whole country seems to have a new sense of optimism. I ring Jonesy to ask him if he wants to come round to our house with his wife and children, and mark the Labour election victory with a proper socialist celebration – fish & chips and pink champagne.

In the meantime, we agree that to make the celebration go with a bang, we should nip to the Chinese Firework Company in Leeds, just off the A64 Ring Road. Jonesy picks me up.

ooo

2.30 pm – The Chinese Firework Company, Leeds

As we enter the shop, Alan rushes up to the counter and declares: *"I'd like to buy a rocket to celebrate the Labour Election victory please – and it's with his money,"* pointing at me.

"So can [he] buy the biggest "fuck-off" rocket that I can legally purchase, please!"

The staff laugh and seem to know straight away which one to get; somebody disappears into the back and returns with one that matches Alan's description exactly – it's huge and it costs £60.

ooo

5.00 pm – In the garden at our house, Kirk Sandall

We have a lovely evening with the children running and playing, and at about 7.35pm – *"Just as they're sitting down to watch Coronation Street"* says Jonesy – we decide to light the celebration rocket.

Alan and I have fashioned a launch tube from a piece of old cast-iron drainpipe and used several breeze blocks as support – it needs it because it's such a big, heavy device.

We get everybody ready and standing on the patio – Carolyne, Beth, Joss and Marcey; Alan's wife Sue, and their children Libby and Oscar.

I get the rocket from the house, introducing it to the children…

"This is something to remember the 1997 Labour election victory by… it carries with it our hopes and aspirations…" to which Jonesy adds *"… and let's hope that the Government lasts longer".*

The rocket shoots into the air, ever higher and higher. It seems to be going higher than I've ever seen a rocket go before; flying, with northern bias, towards the Pilkington's Bowling Green appropriately enough.

Then, just as I expect it to disappear over the horizon, it explodes! And it explodes with such a bang and with such a force, that we feel the shockwave hit us in the stomach where we are standing. Not only that, but practically every car alarm in Kirk Sandall and Barnby Dun seems to be going off and every dog is barking frantically.

Now I love fireworks, and I have seen many displays over the years, but I have never heard a bang as loud as that, before or since.

In the corner of the square next to ours, in a direct line with the rocket's trajectory, an upstairs window opens – and out pops the head of my friend and Labour Party member Martin Hilton:

"Oh… You're here then?" he shouts at the top of his voice…*"I might've known it was you!"*

The whole village knows we're here thanks to that explosion.

And we all sit down to more pink champagne.

ooo

Monday July 7th 1997…

Councillor Pat Mullany is Chair of Doncaster Council's Education & Culture Committee. As a time-honoured councillor, he is obsessed with being the longest standing chair of education in the country.

He is also chair of the Association of Metropolitan Authorities [AMA] Education Committee and, without a doubt one of the better-known and respected local government politicians of this time.

Pat can see how well my company is doing; now employing two associates on a part-time basis. I occasionally ask questions of Pat and Liz Jeffress, as qualified teachers, about issues related to contracts I'm working on. One is a quite lengthy piece of work for the RSNC/RSPB and St John Ambulance Brigade. The work has been commissioned on the protection of children and young people as a response to the Home Office's "Safe From Harm standards and guidelines", themselves a response to the Lyme Bay canoe disaster – which left four teenagers dead in 1993 – and other recent tragedies.

Ever keen to bench mark my work, I ask Patrick, as I like to call him, if he can get me a copy of the Council's Child Safety Policy and Guidelines – which he duly does.

ooo

Monday July 14th 1997...

There are some mornings when you just work away, oblivious to how the day may turn out– not knowing what's just around the corner – and this is one of them.

Pat Mullany has rung to ask if he might drop in to see me – nothing unusual in that – and we agree he'll pop round late morning.

He joins me for a coffee and I show him the new triple-bay compost station I've constructed. As a result, we are in my garden talking, stood near to my compost bins, when he suddenly says:

"I've been thinking about what you asked me with regard to child safety, Martin..."

"Oh yes Patrick,"...oblivious as to what he is to say next.

"... and it started me thinking... how I could help you with the work that your company is doing..." he pauses to see how I am receiving him.

"... and I was thinking if... as one of my constituents... you were to ask me a detailed question... and I emphasise the detailed, Martin," he explains "... I could get the officer core [of the Council] to research this for me, providing me with a detailed written response... which I could then provide for you, as the researched answer to your detailed question"

"Go on Patrick..." I say, wondering where this might lead.

"... and if I gave you such a detailed answer... well that would be valuable to you wouldn't it?" he pauses: "It would have a value to it wouldn't it? ... and if you were pleased with the answers... and I could get you them on anything... <u>absolutely anything</u>... you could make a donation for them, couldn't you?"

[Pregnant pause]

"I suppose I could," I say, somewhat taken aback by his gall.

To be honest I'm embarrassed– annoyed at how he is compromising me. So to give myself some distance from what he is proposing, I adopt the royal "we"...

"We pay for research all the time – in fact we budget R&D into most projects," I lie. "But we would need to be buying it from a recognised and legitimate company. We couldn't just pay you for it Patrick – particularly with Donnygate happening."

But he is ahead of me:

"I've already got one!" he exclaims, apparently sensing a business opportunity "We have a company already set up... of which I'm a director....because I need it for other work that I do."

Oh bollocks, I think, I was just about to wriggle off the hook. Then I wonder. What's the "other work that I do"? Who's the "we"...?

"Well it's certainly something we can think about Patrick"

And I see freedom again "... *the only thing I'm a little unsure about is that we specialise in working with the voluntary, not-for-profit sector and it can be very different to the public sector."*

"Well it's there anyway... isn't it?" he replies, sensing I'm pulling away. "*If there are any opportunities... I'm sure you will let me know won't you?"*

It's at this fateful meeting that I realise Patrick is as bad as the rest of the bent councillors. Constantly on the make, they are always looking for a way to make a quick buck from their [elected] positions and, frighteningly, they see it as legitimate!

The situation clarifies one point for me though. Patrick has to be embroiled in "Donnygate" in which case I need to distance myself and the Glass Park from him.

ooo

Christmas 1997...

The deputy leader of Doncaster Council, Ray Stockhill, finally stands down as a councillor – after nearly a year claiming his 'Members Allowance' and only turning up at council twice. By failing to attend in one six month period he has forfeited his seat. Amid widespread claims of fraud and corruption a by-election is called.

ooo

Saturday January 31st 1998...

The Doncaster Star runs with the front page story "Blair backs the new regime" with the sub-heading "Prime Minister praises Doncaster Council" and reports:

Prime Minister Tony Blair has backed Doncaster Council's new leadership and praised its handling of the Donnygate crisis.

The Prime Minister spoke out during an exclusive interview with the Doncaster Star yesterday. Mr Blair was in town for a few minutes as he caught a train to London... but he promised he would return to Doncaster soon.

Giving his seal of approval to the authority's new leadership, the Prime Minister said: *"I fully support the changes that have been put through. We take very seriously any problems that arise and took action very quickly. I am very* happy with changes that have taken place."

"All the things that have been criticised have been dealt with and people can see how deep these changes are."

"I am very happy with the new leadership who have taken over..."

Council Leader Malcolm Glover and his deputy, Councillor Colin Wedd were away on business in Brussels. The Council did not even know Mr Blair was going to be in town, a spokesman confided [!]

ooo

Friday February 13th 1998...

The by-election for the Stainforth Ward took place yesterday. Despite Blair's shocking attempt at voter manipulation, by coming to Doncaster and announcing he is "… very happy with the new leadership…"just two weeks before the election, the Lib-Dems have still capitalised on the public furore over "Donnygate" and Doug Porter, an ex Postman, has won the seat.

MASSIVE SWING TO LIB-DEMS IN DONCASTER BY-ELECTION

A swing from Labour to the Liberal Democrats of 37% saw Paddy Ashdown's party capture one of Labour's safest seats on Doncaster MBC yesterday. In May 1996 the Lib-Dems got only 10.7% of the vote in Stainforth.

The result makes the Liberal Democrats the official opposition on Doncaster Council, and if repeated in May's local elections will see an unprecedented 15 further seats fall to the Lib-Dems.

Doug Porter said: 'As of tonight, Labour are on a three month notice to quit. If Labour councillors won't resign over the Donnygate scandal, then the people of Doncaster will kick them out in May's elections. This is an enormous swing in one of Labour's safest seats.

The Liberal Democrat opposition will not rest until we have the full truth about Donnygate; until we have the names of those involved; and until we have kicked out those sleazy councillors.

'Let tonight's result send one clear message to the town hall bosses.Labour may refuse to say sorry for the Donnygate scandal, but the Liberal Democrats and the people of Doncaster are going to make them sorry'.

Local Government Chronicle

Sunday February 15th 1998...

Our House, Kirk Sandall

Pat Mullany has come to see me. He is up for election in May and, having seen Ray Stockhill's seat go to the Lib-Dems, he's convinced he's going to lose.

I tell him that, like most politicians, he always thinks he's going to lose when he stands for re-election; however, Pat's paranoia seems more acute than usual and he is showing considerable signs of stress. Having been "approached" by him with a bent deal, I begin to wonder how deeply involved in "Donnygate" he is.

He tells me he wants me to be his agent for the forthcoming election in May – and I detect he is desperate to lend an air of respectability to his campaign by attaching my name to his.

I am very reluctant and put forward a faux argument based on the huge workload I have – but he is relentless and won't take no for an answer. I finally agree to think about it over the next few days.

ooo

Tuesday February 17th 1998...

The Old Summerhouse, Our House, Kirk Sandall

I'm under a horrendous workload – and running behind at the moment. But it's feast or famine when you work for yourself; you can't afford to turn anything down and as soon as there is a lull in the work, you worry it might have dried up.

I'm also struggling to get a grip on a particularly difficult piece I'm working on for a new client – the Ross & Cromarty Footpath Trust.

Patrick rings to ask if I have decided about acting as his agent for the May election. Knowing I'm being dragged into something I don't want to be, I make my excuses again – citing my heavy workload, long hours etc. But he's having none of it and asks me to reconsider – showering me with compliments about my capabilities. Yet again I bat it into the long grass.

Thank god for that, I think as I put the phone down and get back to work. He knows, and I know, he's going to be annihilated. But I'm premature...

Half an hour later the phone rings again. It's Patrick – supposedly calling about a Glass Park issue and then asking me questions pertaining to his election campaign. I fob him off yet again.

The scene repeats itself another three or four times over the next three hours – finally I snap and plead down the phone: *"Patrick... you've got to let me get on with my work – you're costing me fucking money"*

But he's not listening... *"Patrick... what've I got to do to stop you ringing me?"*

"Just agree to be my agent" he stipulates – adding rapid fire *"You don't have to do anything – just agree to be my agent on paper"*.

So I do – just to get him off my back I agree to be his paper agent. I tell him I will only be able to undertake the bare minimum of canvassing and will struggle to prepare leaflets for him. But Patrick is both desperate and relieved – and agrees he will do all of the work.

ooo

Wednesday May 6th 1998...

Assessor Training – Caravan Industry Training Organisation – Aldershot

Because I am frequently working across the UK, often in difficult to access areas, I often hire cars. They're fully tax deductible and as everybody knows, you can drive a hire car harder than you might your own!

I've been working down south for a few days and, having just finished work in Aldershot, I'm driving back up to Doncaster. Beside the northbound carriageway of the A1, just north of Stamford, is a pub called the Ram Jam Inn. As I approach it I notice the white flag of a deer's backside at the edge of the road.

I pull the car into the pub car park and walk back to the deer – a newly killed muntjac, only slightly damaged and still warm. Ever a fan of road-kill, this is venison I think to myself, and I drag it back and throw it in the boot of the hire car [another benefit of hiring!].

When I get home, I show it to the children before hanging it in the garage.

ooo

Thursday May 7th 1998...

Election Day!

I've taken today and tomorrow off because it's the DMBC elections. Current practice is to meet for breakfast at the "Election Rooms", a rather grandiose title for the candidate's house!

But I'm in no rush to get there this morning – I've grown increasingly disappointed with Patrick and have been trying to distance myself from him. There's a sense that there is going to be a backlash against sitting councillors and the Lib-Dems have fought a particularly dirty campaign against him. I think he knows himself that he's going to get a kicking today.

So as much as I enjoy election day, taking my place alongside a politician who's on his way out is not at the top of my wish list – and I decide I'm better employed butchering the deer I picked up yesterday and preparing the venison. I have a new full sized professional butcher's block – one of the best pieces of fly-tipped waste I have ever "rescued" and I'm looking forward to using it for the first time.

I have to say, as a self-taught butcher I am pretty good and very quickly have the animal skinned and gutted. Its large intestine has burst where it was struck by the traffic and I clean it thoroughly before preparing two cuts of haunch, a saddle, two shoulders and the neck.

I thoroughly wash down my butcher's block and notice that I've nicked myself on my left forefinger – it's not bleeding too badly, so I wash the cut in warm water and disinfectant and then dress it with an Elastoplast.

It's 11.30 am, so I go for a breakfast at the local greasy spoon café and then join them at the Election Rooms.

ooo

Friday May 8th 1998…

2.00 am – Election Count – The Doncaster Dome

Pat Mullany loses his seat to Karen Page in a further humiliating defeat to the Lib-Dems, although the turnout is only 30.3%. Mrs Page polls 52.5% of the vote – 22.5% more than Mullany.

Karen Page	[Lib Dem]	1881 [52.5%]
Patrick Mullany	[Lab]	1074 [30%]
James Nelson	[Con]	396 [11%]
Kathleen Boulting	[Ind]	230 [6.5%]

A total of 7 Labour seats fall to the opposition on the night.

Armthorpe Ward – Jean Elwick [1359] lost to Margaret Pinkney [Ind][2086]
Mexborough Ward – Robert Gilbert [717] lost to Peter Firth [Lib Dem][1472]
Thorne Ward – David Oldroyd [1049] lost to Martyn Williams [Community][1202]
Rossington Ward – Annette Harking [717] lost to Terry Wilde [MDIL][1174]
Hatfield Ward – Rossetta Cousins [828] 3rd place lost to John Brown [Con][1067]
Bessacarr Ward – Roni Chapman [1086] lost to Montague Cuthbert [Lib Dem][2020]

ooo

Monday May 18th 1998...

In a shocking display of political expediency, nay manipulation, the new council leader, Malcolm Glover, convinces the ruling Labour Group they need to appoint a civic mayor from the opposition.

This, he argues, will calm down the furore over Donnygate. As a result, Councillor Yvonne Woodcock is elected as the first Tory civic mayor. The Local Government Chronicle reports "New Tory Mayor to get Doncaster going again".

ooo

Tuesday June 9th 1998...

7.30 pm – The Glass Park Trustees Meeting – Barnby Dun Parish Hall

The Glass Park project is making fantastic progress and, as a requirement of Millennium Green funding and support, we have to establish an all-singing, all-dancing charitable trust.

Before he lost his seat in May, Pat Mullany had inveigled himself into chairing the "Shadow Trust Board".

Despite my reservations and the fact that I am now certain he [was] a bent councillor, I'm thankful for his support. It's a job not many want or are capable of doing; and, to be fair to him, Patrick is doing admirable work steering the charity towards establishment, in line with the requirements of the Charity Commission.

I take the view that it's easier to avoid the issue – even the police seem to be having difficulty investigating it and Patrick is still a very powerful individual. If I cross him it could be bad for the project – and me!

As usual, I had been to Patrick's to brief him on the meeting and matters of importance, a couple of days before.

Unusually for Patrick, as I arrive at the meeting, he is already sitting down talking with several of the shadow trustees. As the meeting begins, he asks me if I mind leaving the room whilst they have a discussion. On my return, he tells me the Board has just made a decision.

"The Board would like you to know, and for it to be fully minuted, that we are uncomfortable with the amount of time you are contributing to the project without remuneration Martin..." he begins

"... and, to this effect, the Board has agreed to a £1,000 honorarium with respect to your work"

I don't know what to say. I look at the board members; I'm incredibly embarrassed and looking for a way out.

"Well... I don't know what to say really... thank you very much for this kind

offer" I say. *"I'm certainly not undertaking this work, to be paid..."* and I spot my out. *"So can I suggest that I check out the impact on our finances [for you] and then report to you at a future meeting?"*

I already know I won't take the money. The trustees agree and the meeting continues. Afterwards as I load up my car in the Parish Hall car park, Patrick collars me *"Did that surprise you Martin?"*

"What's that Patrick?"

"Did my moving of that honorarium surprise you?"

"It certainly did Patrick – you know money is not the motivation for me doing this work."

Patrick either doesn't listen or ignores me. *"You could argue that you wouldn't have got that money, if it wasn't for me moving the resolution,"* he goes on.

"I suppose so Patrick"

"So you could argue that half of that £1,000 is mine."

Once again, Patrick stuns me with his greed and desperation. Once again, he appears to be trying to drag me into his web of deceit. But this time his corrupt actions have not only compromised me but potentially damaged the trustees and the trust.

I am left with only one option. I request a meeting with Chief Inspector Colin Lomas, one of the trustees, with regard to the honorarium. I explain that I am in an incredibly difficult predicament – and cannot and will not accept it.

I tell him in confidence what Patrick has said…

The Glass Park Millennium Trust – Minutes of the Trustees Meeting – 9th June 1998

6.7 Honorarium for Glass Park Millennium Trust Project Director
The Chair led a discussion on this matter.

<u>Action</u>   MJW to be awarded an honorarium of £1000.00 *as a token of appreciation for the previous work he has put into the overall Glass Park project.*

<u>The Project Director was asked to return to the meeting</u> *and informed of the Trustee's decision. MJW thanked the Trustees for the award.*

ooo

Monday June 15th 1998…

External Verification – Kirkley Hall College, Northumberland

I have never been a particular fan of football but, like most people, every time the World Cup comes around I believe we can win it once again – and this World Cup in France is no exception.

With England's opening game against Tunisia being played this afternoon, I set off at 6.00 am, so I am ready for an 8.30 am start and can listen to the game as I'm driving back to Doncaster.

After an enjoyable day's work, I manage to get away in time and settle down to a steady drive home. By half time, England have taken a 1:0 lead but I'm distracted by an abscess behind the nail on my left forefinger which seems to be getting increasingly painful as the match goes on.

By the time I'm approaching Scotch Corner the second half is just kicking off and I'm constantly looking at my fingernail, pushing it down as I drive. Then I suddenly experience the most intense pain as the abscess bursts into my face.

With my finger now extremely painful and bleeding, I pull into Scotch Corner Services and get some paper serviettes to wrap around it. I purchase some Elastoplast and continue the remainder of my journey home.

ooo

5.30 pm

I arrive home and have tea with my children before reading them a story and putting them to bed. I'm reading 'The Wizard of Oz'; they love it because I substitute each of their names for the Tin Man, the Lion and the Scarecrow. I use Carolyne's name for Dorothy and our dog [Breeze] for Toto.

Later I set off for Southampton where I have booked a hotel for the night before work the following day.

ooo

Tuesday June 16th 1998…

10am – Caravan Industry Training Organisation
Sandy Balls Holiday Centre, Fordingbridge, Hampshire

I have been asked to attend a meeting of the British Holiday &Home Parks Association as a representative of CITO. This is to respond to and advise members regarding training and support issues specific to the new "Park Operations" NVQs.

After a very constructive meeting, I set off home after lunch.

ooo

It's a lovely sunny day and I am making good time as I drive up the A34, continuing north past Oxford. Approximately five miles south of the M40 motorway, this dual carriageway has no hard shoulder, and I notice a ten ton truck that has broken down and pulled over as far as the driver can manoeuvre it.

I pull into the outside lane but a white van, a hundred metres in front of me has remained in the inside lane and hasn't realised the lorry has stopped. I watch in horror as it crashes into the vehicle's offside rear edge.

The van flips and starts to roll across both lanes of the carriageway, disintegrating, with all manner of car parts, tools, boxes and debris scattering across the road. As I hurtle towards the disaster unfolding before me, I am horrified to see the driver flung out and rolling across the road. I brake hard and swerve to miss him but realise that the full wrap-around bumper has now disconnected from the van and I brace myself for the impact as I have to literally drive over it.

I pull over in a state of shock and, gasping for breath, look in the rear mirror at the scene behind me. The driver lies motionless at the edge of the road with vehicles coming to a stand still further behind him and I think the worst. I wait for a few seconds to gather my thoughts before getting out of the car to see if I can help; but I am certain the motorist will be dead.

As I walk back to the scene, I am stunned to see him roll over and try to stand up. I rush to his aid and help him to the side of the road, where he sits wiping his face and his hands on his shirt. He is shocked and dishevelled, with a bloody grazed face and hands but appears to have only superficial injuries.

After some 15 minutes consoling the driver, whilst police and ambulance teams arrive and others clear the carriageway, I swap my contact details with him and continue on my way.

ooo

10 minutes later

As I drive onto the M40, I am suddenly gripped by the most intense pain emanating from my left ear and down my neck. It is so strong I have to pull over to the side of the motorway. After some 5 minutes I begin to drive home again, intense pains still shooting down my neck and ear.

ooo

One hour later

Having had to pull over twice more, I am now struggling along the A43 towards Silverstone. As I approach Towcester and the M1 northbound, I park up in a filling station; the pain is so unbearable that I can no longer drive. I call Carolyne to come and get me but she can't find anybody to look after our children.

ooo

3 hours later

The journey from Oxford, which would normally have taken around two hours, has now taken more than four! But I'm home and Carolyne immediately takes me to Doncaster Royal Infirmary's A&E Department.

I explain my symptoms, the car accident and the evasive action I had to take and they treat me for whiplash injuries from the crash.

ooo

Wednesday June 17th 1998…

External Verification – Halton College, Widnes, Cheshire

Having had a restless and uncomfortable night, the neck pains have subsided and I attend Halton College as normal; however, I am struggling for most of the morning, with headaches and nausea. I feel absolutely terrible and call Carolyne to make me a doctor's appointment for when I get home.

I finish earlier than usual, make my apologies and leave at about 2.00 pm – as I begin my journey back I have to pull over at the side of the road to be ill. Again, I stagger homewards in huge discomfort.

ooo

4 hours later

At my Doctor's Surgery

By the time I get home I'm suffering from fatigue, headaches and vomiting and have a severe rash on my forehead. The doctor ventures that the rash is sunburn and that I have heatstroke.

"Look at the colour of my skin" I tell him, pointing to my black hair and olive complexion. *"I've never been sunburnt in my life"*. Nevertheless, he prescribes medication for sunstroke.

ooo

Thursday June 18th 1998...

09.00 am – External Verification – Knowsley Community College, Merseyside

I have had a shocking night's sleep; the rash is much worse and I am now shaking with fever and have a severe headache. Carolyne calls to postpone my visit to Knowsley Community College.

She also calls the doctor for another appointment. None is available until this evening – if Carolyne is worried, they suggest I see a locum.

ooo

09.30 am – Locum Doctor, Armthorpe Road, Doncaster

The locum doctor seems at a complete loss over my condition and symptoms but declares it is not sunstroke. He tells me not to take the "sunstroke" medication and prescribes a further course of drugs – but admits he is not sure what for!

ooo

4.30 pm – At my Doctor's Surgery

The doctor has called in one of his associates for her opinion on my affliction. I have the rash across my forehead and scalp, my forehead is now swelling-up, I have pains in my neck and ears, I'm feverish, shaking with the chills and have sickness and vomiting. I'm tired and I'm worried that nobody seems to be able to give me a reliable diagnosis.

I look at the doctor. *"Look doctor... I work as a consultant... I work across the country and diagnose organisational behaviours and advise on interventions... and I see as many different ways to con me as there are – in short, I can spot a bullshitter – and you're bullshitting me! Aren't you?"*

My doctor looks embarrassed *"Well I wouldn't call it that,"* he replies. *"But I have to say I'm a little perplexed by your symptoms."*

"That's fine – but all you're doing is making educated guesses," adds Carolyne, nodding towards me *"... and he's getting worse – not better."*

We conclude that the doctor will monitor my condition and symptoms on a daily basis. He prescribes a new course of antibiotics and books me in for a further appointment tomorrow morning.

ooo

Friday June 19th 1998...

10.00 am

The symptoms seem to have calmed down somewhat but my doctor says he still needs to monitor my condition and I should come for a further appointment after the weekend.

Carolyne makes contact with colleges I have been visiting recently and the lecturers at Hopwood Hall tell her they are particularly concerned because I was sampling candidate portfolios in a Micro-lab there the previous week.

ooo

3.15 pm

I am in my dressing gown, under a duvet, on the settee in the living room at home. Carolyne is worried that I now seem to be delirious.

She leaves me to go and pick the children up from school.

ooo

4.15 pm

Like me, Carolyne is known for her sense of humour. I awake in a cloudy haze to see her, Liz Jeffress and several other friends and neighbours stood in the entrance to the room.

"Is that it?" I ask them *"Have I died?"*

"Not at all sweetheart," says Carolyne. *"I just wanted people to see your unfeasibly large head!"*

"Oh... that's alright then..."

ooo

Saturday June 20th 1998...

10.00 am – Our House, Kirk Sandall

Last night was terrible, the rash on my forehead has now become more bloody and scab-like, my head has swollen to the point that it has enveloped my not insubstantial ears and I'm in real pain.

Carolyne makes me an appointment with the locum for 12.30 pm.

12.30 pm – Locum Doctor, Armthorpe Road, Doncaster…

It's a different doctor from last time and, as I walk into his consulting room, he welcomes me by asking what appears to be the problem.

"*What's the problem?*" barks Carolyne *"Just look at him,"* she laughs, and starts to imitate the Elephant Man… *"My name… is… John Merrick."*

"*And he's delirious, so you won't get any sense from him!*" she adds.

But Carolyne's humour belies her worry and, as the doctor examines me, she regales him with the story. He seems much clearer about what's wrong and he's perturbed that I've been treated for a whiplash injury and sunstroke.

He asks us to wait outside while he makes one or two phone calls.

The doctor then calls us back in and expresses significant concern at both a lack of action and misdiagnosis – he tells me he is having me admitted to hospital immediately and directs Carolyne to take me straight to the ward.

ooo

1.30 pm – Doncaster Royal Infirmary, Armthorpe Road, Doncaster…

The hospital is literally 50 metres away from the surgery. As Carolyne and I walk down the corridor towards the ward, she says: *"Your head is MASSIVE Martin – it's really swollen… stick your tongue out"*

"Why… is my tongue all swollen as well?" I garble, struggling to obey her request.

"No… not at all" – and she starts doing a salsa in the corridor *"It's like I'm in Rio!"* she giggles hysterically *"At the Carnival!!!"*

ooo

2.30 pm – Doncaster Royal Infirmary, Armthorpe Road, Doncaster

I am admitted to a single room with limited access and put on an immediate course of intravenous antibiotics. I will be in hospital for several days.

ooo

Tuesday June 30th 1998…

2.15 pm – Doncaster Royal Infirmary, Outpatients

A doctor looks at my scalp, checks my pulse and asks me a few questions about my symptoms.

"So what do you do with pigs?" she says.

"That's a rather personal question... And it was never proven!" I've clearly got my sense of humour back.

She smiles. "You must do... You're recovering from erysipelas – it's a streptococcal infection of the skin – it's also called Pigman's Disease or Diamond Skin Disease"

"Nothing – I visit agricultural colleges and farms – but nothing specific to pigs," I respond.

"Well, I'm telling you, you've had a fairly severe case of it and it's pretty likely that you've got it from pigs – Pig men get it from cuts that are infected with the streptococcus bacteria which they get from the pig's faeces," she informs me.

"It's also known as 'holy fire' and 'St. Anthony's Fire'," she continues consulting a book "It's an acute infection of the upper dermis and superficial lymphatics, usually caused by streptococcus bacteria."

"It can be very serious. Pope Gregory XVI died from it in 1846, as did Queen Anne in 1714"

She's on a roll.

"And George Herbert, the 5th Earl of Carnarvon, who was the man who bankrolled Lord Carter when he found Tutankhamen's tomb – he died from it in 1923 – which led to the story of the 'Curse of Tutankhamen' – the Mummy's curse," she closed.

"So I dodged a bullet?"

"Well I wouldn't go that far – but it can be pretty nasty."

And then it comes to me – pigs have cloven hooves and so do deer. I explain to the doctor about the road kill in May, cutting my finger and the abscess under my nail. She agrees that this is the most likely cause.

"There's no such thing as a free lunch," she tells me as I take my leave.

ooo

Saturday September 12th 1998...

The Glass Park [Millennium Green] Trust is formally accepted by the Charity Commission. Meanwhile MWC is successful in its tender to prepare a feasibility study and business plan for the "Friends of Fishlake Old School".

ooo

Monday September 14th 1998...

Pat Mullany is arrested as Part of the Operation Danum police inquiry. He immediately offers his resignation to the next Glass Park Shadow Trust meeting.

ooo

Tuesday September 15th 1998...

Glass Park Trust Meeting – 7.30 pm Barnby Dun Parish Hall

The Shadow Trustees accept Pat Mullany's resignation as chair of the Shadow Trust.

> *Emergency Agenda Item* – *MJW reported in more depth on the present situation re. Pat Mullany's position as both Chair and as a General Trustee, after his arrest following investigations into Local Authority expenses irregularities. The Project Director reported that he had discussed the matter to some depth with Pat and the potential implications to the Trust; during which Mr Mullany had offered his resignation to the Trust. MJW reported on the various scenarios that were, of course, dependant on any future legal procedures.*
>
> *The position was discussed in some depth and it was decided, with regret, to accept Pat's offer to stand down from the Trust's Board.*
>
> *Action* – *MJW to write to Pat Mullany and to accept his offer of resignation and to stress that this is solely on the basis of protecting the public perception of the Trust; and, as such, completely without prejudice to any legal position. MJW to express the Board's gratitude for the work he has put in to the Glass Park project and the excellent lead he gave in establishing the Charitable Trust itself.*

ooo

Wednesday September 16th 1998...

MWC is successful in its tender to prepare a feasibility study and business plan for the "DuPont Sports & Social Club's Lottery Submission".

ooo

Sunday October 18th 1998...

Andy Lanaghan, who has been ill for some time, announces to the ward Labour Party that he will be standing down as a councillor at the election in May 1999.

    I let it be known that I see the seat as mine.

Thursday November 5th 1998...

The Glass Park holds its first Annual Community Bonfire on the site. Some 3,000 plus tickets are sold and, despite the day being a wet one, on top of the previous week's rain, the evening itself is dry and the event is a huge success.
Two consequent years' bonfires are also significantly affected by heavy rains and the trust agrees not to hold any more.

ooo

Monday November 16th 1998...

MWC is really going from strength to strength and has now secured one of its largest contracts ever. After some eight or nine years offering varying degrees of support to Jonathon Smales as he develops the concept from scratch, I am appointed Consultant Director [Staff Recruitment, Training &Development] at the Earth Centre – a £60million millennium project funded by the Millennium Commission.

My role is to specify the staffing requirements with regards to job skills, knowledge and training & development needs. I will also develop a recruitment scheme and market the opportunity to potential staff from within the local communities, recruiting them and providing a tailored training and learning package to get them job-ready in time for the opening in five months.

To achieve this I put forward a development programme for The Earth Centre Training Academy. I propose to provide the syllabus, overall programme direction, specialist input and pastoral support needs for delegates; I will also co-ordinate specialist input from the likes of the Findhorn Foundation – a spiritual community, Scottish eco-village and international centre for holistic education – and the environmentally aware cosmetics business, Body Shop.

This means I have an intensive six-week period in which to put the entire programme together, specifying individual and team learning outcomes, identifying and recruiting the partner trainers and agreeing their individual contributions; all ready to begin the marketing and recruitment fairs in the early new-year.

ooo

Wednesday November 18th 1998...

7.00 am

My first meeting has been called for 6.30am on a cold morning. The agenda is a contractors and staff progress meeting followed by a walk around the construction site of the £60 million visitor attraction – now less than four months away from opening.

I attend, bright and breezy, to a pitch-black building site. The weather is awful – stormy and raining.

Jonathan introduces me to the team and I listen to the progress meeting for approximately thirty minutes. As he is about to move outside, he realises its pitch black and the site is a serious health and safety risk.

"I didn't realise it would be so dark – has anybody brought a torch?" he asks, naïvely.

Unbelievably, none of the contractors have them.

I am stunned that such a massive operation can be responsible for such a fiasco; they appear to have no common-sense.

It looks as if the site inspection is to be cancelled...except that I have twelve flashlights in the boot of my car!

The Glass Park's volunteer stewards had used them at the Community Bonfire event eleven days ago and I put them in my car last night, knowing it was going to be pitch black this morning.

As I get them from my boot, I notice that two or three people have sourced torches from their own cars. I distribute the flashlights, telling the collective:

"These flashlights belong to the Glass Park project, which is a voluntary community project in Kirk Sandall – can you make sure you return them after the site visit please..."

After the visit, and despite appealing to those present several times, only nine flashlights were returned!

I'm reminded of the irony of the Earth Centre strapline...

earth centre

You'll never see the world in the same way again.

Thursday November 26th 1998

The Leader of Doncaster Council, Councillor Malcolm Glover, is arrested as part of the Operation Danum enquiry.

ooo

Friday November 27th 1998

Colin Wedd is appointed as new Leader of Doncaster Council.

ooo

Thursday December 24th 1998

My workload is becoming unbearable; it turns out that the new Managing Director, who started at the same early morning meeting as I did five weeks ago, is leaving for a month in Australia today!

As a result, I now have more than one hundred Job Profiles and Person Specifications to prepare alongside all the supporting administrative paperwork for the marketing fares in January. It's a huge additional workload but one that I am being paid additionally, and handsomely for, which is symptomatic of this Millennium Commission funded project as we approach the opening day deadline.

To deliver on this additional workload, Carolyne and I agree that I am going to have to work over Christmas!

ooo

As well as the above, I'm still delivering on the Glass Park Project, have substantive contractual work for the Environmental Training Organisation [ETO], the Land-based Training Organisation [LANTRA – formerly ATB Landbase] and significant contracts for the Caravan Industry Training Organisation [CITO] and the Ross & Cromarty Footpath Trust. I am also externally moderating at more than thirty university and college courses around the country.

In addition I have contracts for Business Plans at Fishlake and the DuPont Sports & Social Club's Synthetic Running Track Lottery Consultation and Submission.

ooo

MWC is doing very well, and because Carolyne now has to travel between home and the Earth Centre on a daily basis, and it's also tax efficient, we buy a new VW Polo.

Alan Jones's Morris Minor has broken down [again!] so I give him Carolyne's old Fiat Uno, with six months tax and test on it.

ooo

Tuesday January 19th 1999…

10.15 am – The Old Summerhouse, Our House, Kirk Sandall

It's a dismal, foggy, cold day and there is no let-up in my workload; with the start date for the Earth Centre Training Academy only four weeks away, I'm under phenomenal pressure. I now have two consultants working with me full time, including Charles Couzens a colleague from my days at RSNC, but the demands on my time are still substantial.

Carolyne calls me from the house *"Martin – I know that you're really under the cosh at the moment but Jamie's here…"*

[Pregnant pause]

Jamie is my former best friend and Carolyne's ex-boyfriend. I'd first met Jamie during our "Foundation Course" at Doncaster Art College in 1979, when I nearly killed him undertaking a full plaster cast of his head. Friends forevermore we had set up an aerial photography company together some three years earlier – but I had moved on, unhappy with the sustainability of such photographs and the unnecessary air flights.

"Is that your answer?" she asks of my silence.

"No – well probably yes…" I correct myself *"It's just that I'm snowed under – you know I am. He was only here a fortnight ago… What's he here for?"* I ask irritably.

"He's just popped in for a coffee – he should be flying from Gamston [Retford Airport] *but he's been fogbound"*.

"Look – I just can't spare the time." I defend my rudeness desperately. *"Tell him to look at me in the office"* I plead. *"It's just that I just can't spare the time"* – and I wave at him from my office window. *"He'll understand – he knows I'm not being an ignorant bastard."*

ooo

Thursday January 21st 1999…

Having been fog bound for two days Jamie finally gets the plane off the runway.

He is killed one hour later, along with three others, when a Tornado jet collides with his Cessna aircraft above Mattersey in Nottinghamshire…

ooo

Monday January 25th 1999…

The Earth Centre workload is becoming completely unwarranted. I have now found out there is no real budget allocated for the recruitment, training and development of the visitor attraction's staff.

Jonathan appears completely relaxed by this omission and introduces me to David Copeland as his "funding guru".

David is extremely impressive and, as a result of our meeting, not least on the "to-do" list [now] is that David and I have to prepare a £250,000 European Social Fund [ESF] submission for the funding of the recruitment programme, Training Academy and a wage subsidy for the staff.

I have some experience of preparing ESF and ERDF [European Regional Development Fund] submissions and it's usually a very long-winded affair. I'm not convinced we'll get the funds in time – if at all!

ooo

Jonathan Smales has introduced local councillor Tony Sellars to me as the "fundamental link" to the local community. I don't really understand what this means or what Tony does.

While I have been planning the Academy, Tony has acted as a kind of minder to me. He accompanies me around community facilities as we try to identify a geographical base for the Academy. Tony knows every venue and every landlord, steward or manager in Conisbrough & Denaby. Wherever we go, there is always a pint waiting for him.

Tony also introduces me to Aidan Rave, a young man who works for CDDT, the Conisbrough & Denaby Development Trust. He says Aidan will be the next DMBC councillor, replacing him when he stands down at the election in four months. Knowing that I'm standing for election at the same time, he says I should watch out for him 'because he's extremely bright'.

Personally, I think he's a real surly individual who doesn't say anything and seems frightened of his own shadow.

We visit a number of potential venues; the Catholic Club, CDDT's building 'The Terrace', 'The Ivanhoe Centre', Northcliffe School, the Earth Centre itself and many others. At each one Tony gives me his assessment of the level of support for the Earth Centre from staff and punters and of his success in turning the community's views around.

It's at this point I realise what Tony does. He's a professional drinker! Jonathon Smales said the locals always ask him *"What does the Earth Centre make?"*. Well Tony's job was to convince Jonathan that [Tony] was the "fundamental link" to that local community and that he needed to schmooze them on their terms – what an operator!

We eventually agree to base the Earth Centre Training Academy at the Denaby Miners' Welfare.

Work continues to establish the Academy. The opening day for the Earth Centre itself is Good Friday, so its first weekend falls at Easter.

On a count-back basis, we have identified the optimum date for the Training Academy to begin as Monday February 22nd. This will allow us five full weeks.

With a trial Community Open Day on Saturday March 27th, that gives us a final week to fine-tune any teething problems, ready for the opening.

ooo

Wednesday January 27th 1999...

I am having difficulties with the Earth Centre's management; several key senior staff have failed to grasp the implications of sustainable development and the reasons why this former mining community was chosen for the visitor attraction.

I explain to the new Managing Director how we have developed the ESF submission and how the European Union has prioritised the project through the EU's Objective 2 status. I explain that we have requested funding on several levels including a wage subsidy, which tails off over the first 12 months of the site's operation.

It's a tense meeting, during which I have to increasingly assert my position. I try to get him to understand that we need to recruit the majority of the staff from the deprived Doncaster communities – and how I propose to prioritise applications from such areas.

The MD looks ashen-faced as the reality hits home.

"Look" I tell him. *"You have to understand that this area is suffering from significant levels of unemployment... it has poor educational attainment... the residents frequently have poor health and housing... and there are high levels of crime as a result."*

"It is classed as deprived... This is why it qualifies for European Structural Programmes and funding"

"Oh my god" he exclaims *"How can I be expected to run a world class visitor attraction with the unemployed!"*

Friday January 29th 1999...

Jamie's mother, Mary, his sister Susie and his brother Andrew have asked if they can spend the night before the funeral at our house, having a Chinese take-away with Carolyne and me – just like we used to with Jamie in days gone by.

Despite my horrendous workload, it's important that we support them at this sad time and we look forward to seeing them.

ooo

Sunday January 31st 1999...

I have made sure throughout that we keep MP Kevin Hughes involved in the Glass Park project. He has been a keen supporter and a frequent visitor to the site. The Countryside Commission Millennium Greens people have also said they want a large public launch. Because of the project's quality and integrity, Kevin has suggested we might get Deputy Prime Minister, John Prescott.

Duly charged, Kevin liaises with us over the date and time, giving us about two to three weeks-notice – and comes back with 8.40 am on Monday February 22nd, twenty minutes before the first day of the Training Academy starts!

I'm desperate to have the DPM there, so I agree.

I explain my dilemma to Jonathan Smales along with my plan for addressing the problem. He is fine with my strategy and confesses they struggle to get any political acknowledgement of the Earth Centre; despite this £60 million enterprise being the largest Millennium Commission funded project in the country, they cannot get Prescott to visit.

ooo

Monday February 1st 1999...

6.00 pm

The night before Jamie's funeral. Mary is grief stricken and before the food arrives we all sit in the living room reminiscing over the photo-albums she has brought.

She sits next to me on the settee and shows me a picture in the album – it's Billy Mackenzie from the Associates.

"Do you remember this one Martin?" she asks. I don't really know what to say, I look at Susie, Carolyne and then back at Mary. I *really* don't know what to say... why would she have a photograph of Billy in a family photo-album?

After what seems like a lifetime and with tears streaming down my face I say:

"Ah... Billy – bless him... he's dead as well – isn't he".
   This time it's Mary's turn to look nonplussed. *"What?"* she asks.
   "Billy Mackenzie – bless him – he's dead as well. He died a couple of years ago – didn't he?"
   I look at Carolyne for support but she has tears streaming down her face and is unable to speak. I look to Susie but she doesn't seem to know what to say.
   "What do you mean? Billy Mackenzie?" asks Mary.
   "What I say – it's Billy Mackenzie" I insist *"Bless him – he committed suicide a couple of years ago – didn't he?"* I plead, looking at Carolyne.
   This time she responds *"Yes"* she agrees *"I took it* [the photograph] *from the cover of an album when Jamie and I were getting used to his new camera a few years ago."*
   And Mary starts smirking *"Oh god"* she laughs, the tears still falling *"We thought it was you Martin,"* she exclaims *"It's been in this album for about fifteen years!"*

ooo

Tuesday February 2nd 1999...

3.00 pm – Rose Hill Crematorium, Cantley, Doncaster.

On a very sad day, we attend Jamie's funeral and the wake afterwards.

ooo

Wednesday February 10th 1999

Government Office informs us that the £250,000 ESF bid for the Earth Centre Training Academy has been successful – just over two weeks since we submitted it!

ooo

Tuesday February 16th 1999

I have a contract with the DuPont Sports & Social Club in Doncaster to deliver on a Business Plan and Feasibility Study. The contract has been novated into a submission to the Sport England Lottery Fund to deliver a synthetic running track.
   Work on this has been delayed because we have been requested to take the lead in the 'transfer of ownership' negotiations; as part of this we launch a "55

Days to Save the Club" campaign.

ooo

Monday February 22nd 1999...

7.30 am – The Deputy Prime Minister's visit to launch the Glass Park Millennium Green Project – Glass Park, Old Kirk Sandall

Carolyne has been organising the PR for the Deputy Prime Minister's visit, liaising with the Countryside Commission's Millennium Greens people who are delighted with the high profile event and are using the Glass Park as one of their key sites, a national exemplar of community involvement and organisation.

The DPM's security and police have visited us the previous Friday to familiarise themselves with the site.

His office has confirmed he will arrive at 8.20am and leave at 9.00; we have him for a 40 minute visit and we're thrilled. I work out if I can have all my subsequent interviews finished for 9.30, traffic permitting, I can get to the Earth Centre for 10.30 and our [revised] 11.00o'clock start time.

Knowing JP is always good for a laugh, and looking for something a little different as a photo opportunity, we agree a shot where he is at the controls of a crane, which is positioning a footbridge ["Prescott Bridge"] connecting a public right of way onto the site.

One of the committee members I met through my work with the DuPont Sports & Social Club has a local metal fabrication business 500 metres from the site and agrees to construct the bridge for free in support of the project. Liaising with the DPM's Office proves both problematic and a real eye-opener:

- We have to provide a pair of size seven wellingtons for him; but these cannot be green, says the aide, because of a competition in the media to publish a mocking photograph of him wearing 'Green Wellies'.
- We have to provide six umbrellas for if it rains, and these must be in non-primary colours, because they signify political parties.
- We also have to notify them that we will be providing a marquee for the launch speeches and to confirm there will be a lectern available and a glass of water on a table beside it.

As JP's arrival gets closer the site becomes absolutely packed. Several TV companies including the BBC and ITV have turned up, along with local and national journalists; the Countryside Agency has made sure it has several key individuals and partners in attendance, as have our own trustees; and many local people have also turned out for the visit. The fifty-person marquee isn't going to be big enough!

ooo

8.00 am

The DPM's security team arrive to make sure the site is secure. They tell us he will be there at 8.40 – not 8.20. That's okay. I reckon I can still make the start of the Academy for 11.00 – just about!

ooo

8.40 am

The DPM arrives at the site with Kevin Hughes. After welcoming him in the marquee, and giving him chance to put on his [black] wellingtons, we take him on a guided tour round the site. JP is on great form.

It's a bitterly cold day with snow on the ground and the positioning of the bridge goes well. Della Georgiason, JP's Office manager, takes Carolyne on one side and says:

"John's really pleased with the visit Carolyne – this is a fantastic project – and he's going to get a later train [to London] *so he'd like to stay for a further half hour."*

What can we do – say no?!

As we move into the marquee, everyone makes a beeline for the hot tea, coffee and Bovril we're serving; it's heaving and soon starts to warm up. The speeches go down famously and my children present the DPM with a glass apple paperweight, as a commemoration of his visit.

Inspector Colin Lomas, in full uniform, representing the Trust and trustees, thanks the DPM for his time and we wave him off at 9.45.

At 10.15 we complete the post-event interviews and I leave for the Earth Centre Training Academy.

ooo

11.05 am – The Earth Centre Training Academy Inaugural Day

I arrive at Denaby Miners Welfare almost on time. The delegates started at 9.00 am and after a 10 minute introduction of the morning's activity, Tony Sellars and the personnel manager have spent 90 minutes enrolling them onto the programme and the Earth Centre's staff data-base.

They have then had a 20 minute tea break ready for an 11.00 o'clock induction session. Phew… I've managed it!

ooo

Friday April 9th 1999

12.30 pm – DuPont Sports & Social Club

The "55 Days to Save the Club Campaign" has been a huge success and the club is now in a much stronger position to move forward into the new millennium.

Today is a fundraising event for the Campaign organised by Malinda Lygo and Terry Barker. They are massive supporters of the club – not least, through their ballroom dancing events. Today's event is a lunch-time meal and celebration tea-dance with the Doncaster Civic Mayor, Councillor Yvonne Woodcock in attendance, alongside the Managing Director of DuPont and other dignitaries.

Carolyne and I are invited because we have been leading on the transfer of ownership negotiations for the club. Sat alongside us at the "top-table" is Michael Parker, the Human Resources Manager for DuPont [and his wife], because he has been leading on the logistics of the factory's closure and is also a member of the club's management committee.

After lunch, Mike confesses to the Civic Mayor and the guests that he cannot dance and is petrified at the thought of it; his wife however says she loves to dance, but never gets the chance to. Carolyne allays Mike's fears by telling him that we don't dance and that he can choose to simply watch from the side.

As we enter the ballroom, with its beautifully polished, sprung dance floor, the dancers and guests are already seated awaiting the Civic Mayor and dignitaries' entrance. There is also a Master of Ceremonies with a microphone. While we parade past and start to sit down, the MC leaves his seat and walks across to the bar. I notice a look of mischief on Carolyne's face as she quickly walks over to the MC's mic.

"*Madam Mayor, ladies and gentlemen… Can I thank you for attending today's tea dance at the DuPont Sports & Social Club…*"

She pauses to let the audience compute that somebody has begun speaking – and what she is saying.

"*Will you all now put your hands together as your Manager Michael Parker and his lovely wife, lead you all off in a foxtrot.*"

"*I thank you!*" she concludes, and then starts the applause, with her hands high in the air, nodding towards a red faced and furious Michael.

At this point Michael's wife grabs hold of him and marches him onto the dance floor. The band, though somewhat startled, begin to play…

We are all howling with laughter, and as they swirl around, Michael is taking every opportunity to attract Carolyne's attention and pull faces at her. His wife, meanwhile, is grinning widely and chuckling to herself. She is loving it.

As the foxtrot finishes, Michael marches straight over to us and I expect the worst. But thankfully he can see the funny side!

ooo

Wednesday April 21st 1999…

Amid all the other activity, I have also been campaigning energetically for the local elections next week.

After losing the last two seats to the Lib-Dems, the media is expecting the Labour Party to get a drubbing – but I know, and expect, different. As both a former Doncaster RLFC player and the main driver of the Glass Park project, I know that I have a fantastic local profile.

I'm campaigning on the anti-sleaze, anti-corruption stance that I am a complete break from the Labour Party of the past – with the strap-line "It's time for a change".

The campaign has been going well and Liz Jeffress tells me she had a phone call from the Labour Party saying "The Times" wants to come up for a feature on the "new blood" standing for Labour, as part of its "Project 1999" campaign. Although I've never heard of "Project 1999", I'm delighted the Party seems to be aware of my capabilities and has put my name forward.

ooo

Friday April 23rd 1999…

6.00 pm – Canvassing, Kirk Sandall

The Times journalist and photographer join us and follow me while I'm canvassing. We've got a good turn out again – we are being received well on the doorstep and I'm having fun!

As I joke with one prospective constituent, she gives me a friendly slap across the face. The photographer's camera goes into overdrive.

ooo

Thursday May 6th 1999...

Election Day!

Breakfast at the "Election Rooms" is a more relaxed affair today – it's at our house. Our canvassing has identified the Labour vote – now all we need do is make sure that we get the vote out.

ooo

Friday May 7th 1999...

3.15 am – The Count, Doncaster Dome...

Success – I win the seat left vacant by Andy Lanaghan and in doing so give the Lib-Dems a massive slap in the face. Karen Page, who defeated Pat Mullany the previous year, had been absolutely cock-a-hoop that the Lib-Dems would secure their third victory on the trot and consequently put forward her husband for the seat.

Martin Jon Winter [Lab]	1,858 [53.1%]
David Page [Lib-Dem]	1,137 [32.5%]
James Prestwick Nelson [Con]	504 [14.4%]

My victory represents a 21.5% swing back to the Labour Party.

ooo

July 1999...

Alan Jones rings me to complain that the Fiat Uno I gave him six months earlier has failed its MOT and he has had to pay £150 to get it through the test.

I tell him to go fuck himself.

ooo

Footnote

In terms of failing to attract political bigwigs to the Earth Centre site, I believe political naïvety was largely to blame.

Certainly getting the Lib-Dem Environment spokesperson, Simon Hughes MP to chair a round table meeting there didn't help when it came to attracting big names from other parties. We were able to get John Prescott to launch the Glass Park mainly because of Kevin Hughes's loyalty and his belief in and support for me.

ooo

I consider the Earth Centre Training Academy and staff development programmesome of the best work I undertook as a consultant; and it became the recipient of several high-profile awards including the Yorkshire Tourism Best 'Customer Care Offer' for 1999.

Do you want a receipt for £5?

> *"Lies don't fit snugly into disguises. Eventually the cloak falls off...*
> *... and you're left staring at the naked truth which is always an uncomfortable situation"*
>
> Richelle E Goodrich

Tony Sellars and his brother Terry have been Labour ward councillors on Doncaster Council for many years, both representing the Conisbrough & Denaby Ward. They are part of the "ruling mining group", and right at the heart of "Donnygate".

I'd first met Tony in 1992 at a District Labour Party meeting at Spring Gardens in Doncaster. A community activist who fancies himself as a real political operator, he is both streetwise and smooth; though I remember thinking it strange that a man approaching his sixties should always wear a Wrangler jacket and jeans. In later years, my Deputy Mayor Aidan confides that he aspires to "be Tony Sellars" on the basis of Tony's ability to know several key facts about everything. Aidan sees him as a *bon viveur*, philosopher, wit, and master raconteur – I see him as a bull shitter.

As a councillor embroiled in "Donnygate", Tony is responsible for the council decision to curtail foreign trips. As one of the main beneficiaries, he moves the motion in an attempt to appease the Labour Party's National Executive Committee, as it decides on the shortlist for the local Don Valley seat.

Councillor Sellars tries to paint the [Donnygate] controversy as "*... nothing but a plot by the Tory-owned media, and a continuation of the damage Rupert Murdoch inflicted on our community during the miner's strike*".

But his tactic doesn't work and he fails to secure the Labour Party's Prospective Parliamentary Candidate position for Don Valley – despite getting the backing of seven out of the eight Ward Nominations.

If truth be told, Tony would never have been victorious, regardless of local support – the NEC simply couldn't afford the damage the coronation of any of the leading Doncaster councillors would cause the Party.

Tony will later get a 3 month suspended jail sentence for expenses fraud.

But ever the survivor, he sees the writing on the wall and, despite being in line to be mayor the following year, makes the decision to stand down at the May 1999 election. He makes sure, however, that he has both "groomed" and "managed" his anointed successor, Aidan Rave.

There are many theories as to who is responsible for bringing the Donnygate scandal to public attention. Some say it's the writer and ex Doncaster councillor,

Ron Rose, who blows the gaffe.

Others credit Tony for spilling the beans on the expenses scandal – purely for political gain.

Tony is one of those long-listed for the Don Valley seat, alongside councillors Pat Mullany and Peter Welsh [then Leader of the Council]. The story goes that, ever the Machiavellian politician, Tony decides he has to remove and/or damage his competition by leaking evidence of their fraudulent activity – d'oh!

The truth is, it's probably more to do with an extremely critical district auditor's report which points to councillors taking business-class flights to China, America, Hong Kong and Japan, and tucking into drunken "working lunches" at £100 a head.

ooo

Monday November 16th 1998...

6.30 pm – Labour Party Panel of Candidates interviews – Doncaster Trade & Labour Club

I am being interviewed to have my name placed on the Panel of Candidates list, for potential selection as a Labour Party candidate for the May 1999 DMBC elections.

I'm looking to be accepted onto the Panel, in the hope I'll be chosen by the Stainforth Ward, as their Labour candidate for the election next May. The Ward has lost out to the Lib-Dems in the previous two elections – Ray Stockhill's seat in the by-election in February, Pat Mullany in May.

The interview panel consists of Nan Sloane [Labour Party Regional Director], Bev Marshall [Chair DMBC Corporate Services Panel and Vice Chair of South Yorkshire Police Authority] and Russ Williams [Doncaster North Constituency CLP Member], the husband of DMBC councillor Di Williams.

Nan is a thick set woman, not unattractive, with a strong head of deep red hair, and beautiful full lips, which are always adorned by bold, dark lipstick. She is known as 'Stalin's Daughter' by the party faithful, a name I think she quite enjoys. I find her authoritative to the extent that she can be intimidating, but fair, and always willing to listen to a cogent argument.

The interview is going relatively well; although Nan has scoffed at my ideas of 'market stall' type street surgeries and consultation events held outside TESCOs and other places where people go in their masses.

"We need a strong candidate in Stainforth" she says.

Presumptuous cow, I think. *"Well that's for the Party in Stainforth to decide"* I reply.

"What do you mean?"

"Exactly what I said. I'm here to be interviewed for the Panel of Candidates and not for the Stainforth candidature" I remonstrate. *"I might not want to seek the Stainforth Ward's support, I may want to try for another Ward – or I might have too much work on and choose not to seek any Ward... whichever, it will be the people of Stainforth who decide who stands for election in May, not this Panel"* I declare.

I look at Russ, whom I know well and admire, and he's making eyes at me as if to say "shut the fuck up!"

I finish my interview and go home.

ooo

10.30 pm

Russ Williams rings me."Fucking 'ell you're hard work you are Martin"
"What d'you mean?"
"You sackless bastard – couldn't you see me telling you to shut up?"
"Yeah but she was fucking wrong – she was telling me what the people of Stainforth want and it's now't to do with her"
"Y'see you're doing it now" he says... *"Anyway you stupid bastard, she didn't like what you said to her and they've turned you down. Bev just agreed with her and they two-oned me"*
"Oh fucking hell – the stupid bastards" I respond *"Don't they fucking realise what they've got [with me]."*
"I think that's just it Martin. They could see exactly what they'd got with you – and it pissed them off"
"Ah bollocks to 'em then." I say.
"Anyway, I just thought you should know" he finished. *"But I thought you'd make a fucking brilliant councillor"*

ooo

Wednesday November 18th 1998...

10.30 am

Chris Taylor rings me. Chris is a time-served Labour Party activist, who lives and breathes the Labour Party. He's well known around local government in Yorkshire and has worked for everybody from Ken Livingstone, in the old Greater London Council days to John Pearman the Leader at Wakefield District Council and Kevin Hughes, the MP for Doncaster North. Incredibly well known and well-connected in the unions, Chris was frugal to the extreme and, to this day, he carries a NALGO plastic bag that he has had for over twenty years!

A self-confessed 'anorak', Chris is extremely well read and obsessive about cricket, socialism and jazz. He hails from the Black Country and has a delightful Wolverhampton brogue, which belies his intelligence.

No telephone conversation with Chris is ever quick but he tells me he's heard I've failed to get on the Panel and thinks I should appeal.

Furthermore, he says he'll advise me on the appeal and accompany me to the re-interview. I'm really humbled that he should consider me so worthy of his time and accept his kind offer.

ooo

Monday November 23rd 1998…

7.15 pm– Labour Party Appeals Panel – Rotherham Town Hall

The interview panel consists of three regional members with Nan sitting in as an observer. Chris briefs me beforehand to agree with everything they say.

"Remember" he whispers as we go into the interview room *"Yes sir… no sir… three bags full sir…"*

The interview goes well and all three interviewers appear to be just going through the motions.

"Why do you think you were turned down last week?" asks one.

"Because I was asked a question that I considered outside of the panel's terms of reference" I say, glancing over at Nan and readying myself for the same argument.

I feel Chris treading on my foot and ankle under the table.

"What do you mean?"

"Well let's just say I mis-interpreted a question that was posed" I say diplomatically.

"But I've realised I made a mistake and was wrong. So I'm looking forward to seeking selection as the Stainforth Ward Candidate before Christmas"

I can sense Chris physically relax.

The chair concludes the interview and, as we leave, Nan asks us if we can wait outside for ten minutes.

ooo

8.00 pm

"Fucking 'ell Martin..." says Chris *"You nearly blew it again; but you did a good job pulling it back"*

    "Well... they piss me off. They can't accept that they were asking the wrong questions..."

    He cuts me off: *"No... no... no... no... no...!"* he says in extremis

    "What you can't accept... is that they can ask whatever questions they want".

    "Fair comment" I concede.

ooo

8.15 pm

Nan comes out of the interview room. *"Well... congratulations Martin... you're on the Panel of Candidates..."* she says smugly.

    "And you will be standing in Stainforth after all this... and you will, of course, be towing the line... and Chris will be making sure of that... won't he Chris?"

    Chris smiles.

    "Thanks very much Nan" I say. *"I won't let you down"*

    "I know you won't. And that's the last I want to hear of your stupid market stalls... Is that understood?"

    "Yes Nan"

    "Good... Then say thank you and good night Nan"

    "Thank you and good night Nan"

ooo

December 1998...

My work at the Earth Centre through MWC continues. But while there are some fantastic individuals involved with the scheme, they are also the most disorganised set of tossers I've ever worked with.

    As I say to Carolyne when I'm first offered the work, it gives me a real dilemma on three levels:

    Firstly, we can't afford, from a credibility point of view, to be associated with such a project. My analysis is that it will more than likely fail, due to poor planning and a distinct lack of understanding around sustainable regeneration issues, outside of the environmental impact.

    Secondly, we can't afford, from a credibility point of view, NOT to be associated with it. If it works, it will be the biggest most successful community-based 'environmental' project in the country. What would that say about MWC, as a company, if it weren't involved in such a project in its own back yard!

And lastly, that we can't afford, *financially,* not to be part of such a project. Top-dollar is being offered to get the best people.

ooo

Friday February 26th 1999...

The Denaby Miners Welfare Club, an old red brick building in the heart of the community, is perfect as the base for the Earth Centre Training Academy.

It has a relatively plush function room downstairs alongside a more basic, slightly threadbare "taproom". But much more importantly, there is a very large concert room upstairs which will easily cater for 150 plus delegates – the number of new-entry staff we are planning for with the Training Academy.

Tony Sellars, soon to be an ex councillor, remains involved with The Earth Centre and I'm spending more time with him.

Having helped me identify the Miners Welfare as our base, it's there, at the end of the first week of the Training Academy, that he tries to entice me into his web of corruption.

We have just returned from the first of our Friday Bus Trips – a weekly series of visits to visitor attractions around the region in order to recognise best practice and competition and to relax and wind down after a heavy week's work. Tony, Carolyne and I are each in charge of a bus, co-ordinating the day and delegates' pastoral needs... which are many.

We have just waved the delegates off and the three of us are having a de-brief on how the first week has gone. After about an hour we begin to wrap up, and Carolyne leaves early to pick up Beth, Joss and Marcey from our child-minder. I am tidying the training venue so it's in a neat and tidy state for the following Monday, and should the steward, Neil, wish to use it for a function over the weekend.

Tony sits, watching me work, while he drinks a pint of bitter. We laugh and joke about events of the first week.

"You've budgeted for how many each day Martin?" he says.

"For what Tony?"

"For the snap Martin"

"£5 a head – she's done a good job hasn't she?" I reply, praising the work of the steward's wife. Tony doesn't respond – just pauses for a sip of his beer.

"Aye but you're okay for money each day are you?"

"Yes... I'm fine thanks Tony, they're not bad payers at the Earth Centre...

and we've turned it round a lot cheaper than we originally budgeted... and we [MWC] have got a good cash-flow at the moment. But it's good of you to offer, thanks" I say, mistaking his interest for support.

"Oh that's okay Martin – I just wanted to make sure you were alright" and he pauses again.

"How many have you budgeted for each day Martin?"

"Oh, I've budgeted for 150 staff each day Tony, at £5 a head so £750 a day."

"£750 a day eh? Every day Martin?"

"Well it's for 4 days each week, with the fifth being the provision of a packed lunch for the bus trips"

"So how much is that each week then Martin?"

"Well its 5 X 750 Tony, so that's... fifteen hundred... three... its £3,750 each week Tony"

"And how many are we *actually* catering for?" he asks, stressing the actually.

"Well there are 90 enrolled on the Academy, plus four or five trainers each day and a fluctuating number of Earth Centre staff... who usually come up for lunch [to the annoyance of the Academy members!]... so the actual number fluctuates... but I've asked Neil's wife to cater for 100 each day [which is plenty enough] and we let her give the leftovers to the punters downstairs... which has led to a greater number coming in for an early afternoon beer!"

"And how much is she charging you?" he asks.

"£3.50 a head..." and I realise where he's going.

"So what does that work out at?"

"Well its £100 each day at £3.50 a head so £350 a day Tony"

"So how much is that each week?"

"Well its 5 X 350 Tony, so that's £1,750 each week..." But Tony is well ahead of me – and itching to get his hands on the £2,000 we are saving against the budget I've put together.

It's at this point he says something that simply highlights how corrupt he and presumably other councillors within Doncaster have become.

"Well do you want a receipt for £5 a head Martin?"

Even though I know this is what he's been angling for, his brazenness still surprises me.

"I can't believe you Tony..." *I say* "... am I such an easy lay? Am I so easy that you don't even try to charm me knickers off?" Tony says nothing. His eyes are fixed on the wall in front of him, as he takes another sip of his pint.

"In fact... I can't believe you're even saying it to me... here we are in the middle of Donnygate... and you're trying to stitch up a dodgy deal with me..."

"You know the crack Martin. It's public money – they won't miss it. It'll only go back to central government..." he says. "And if I get you a receipt for £5 –

that'll make it £500 each day – which means we can make £150 a day and we're still saving the Earth Centre £250 a day. We can split the £150 each day, which makes £75 quid for each of us, each day, which makes £375 quid a week [each] Martin – it's nothing to be sneezed at"

Tony has certainly been doing his sums.

"You know where I'm coming from Tony. The Earth Centre is my bag – it's my value base and I'd prefer to leave it for the Earth Centre"

"You can have £100 and I'll have £50 then" he said immediately, almost in desperation.

"Nah I'm fine Tony." I say, getting irritated.

At this point Tony changes tack. "There's a lot of people been complaining about the packed lunches... and there's not a lot of choice each day, Martin" he proffers.

I lose patience with him "Do you think I'm fucking stupid Tony. Do I fucking look stupid?"

"I'm just telling you that there's a lot of people been complaining about the lunches..." he counters.

"Aye – and you're gonna wind 'em all up aren't you? – telling 'em the food's shite... and I bet your mate'll do a better deal for a fiver... won't he Tony?"

"Don't treat me like a fucking moron" I begin to rant.

"Don't try to... don't even think... that you can manipulate me... like one of your other fucking cronies! It might work in the fucking council chamber... but it won't fucking work with me... you... you..." I am so exasperated I'm stuck for words.

"You and your fucking jumped up... fucking Mickey Mouse... fucking operations!"

"Enough said" Tony raises his hand and quickly finishes his beer. "I'm going – I'll see you on Monday". He leaves the building and the subject is never mentioned again.

ooo

Footnote

Having reflected on my conversation with Tony for several years now, I'm so glad that, not only did I refuse the approach, but that I frequently discussed the scenario with anyone who would listen. I did that to protect my integrity but also to make sure I had a fairly strong audit trail of individuals who would remember the incident and provide testimony should I need it.

It probably wasn't the brightest thing in the world to do, to have a blazing row with one of Doncaster's political cognoscenti; but I've always worn my heart on my sleeve and, as the saying goes, *"The kings is dead... long live the king"*.

My star was in the ascendancy and I didn't think I needed Tony Sellars' approval for where I was, or thought I was, going. Tony's star was fading and I needed to let him know I now "owned" him. I'd got him and he wasn't going to fuck with me again.

It seems to me the "ruling mining group", as it was known at that time, worked very much like the Mafia, or *Cosa Nostra*; if he had persuaded me into the "brotherhood", Tony would have "owned me" and I would have been forever subservient to his manipulations.

Having refused the deal; having stood firm, I had "top-dogged" him. I would not be beholden to him – and he knew it.

He on the other hand would be beholden to me – as someone who knew of his dishonesty. I would also never trust him again.

The truth is I was paid handsomely, and on time, for all the work my company did at the Earth Centre.

Having said that, several years later I was involved, as Mayor, in negotiations with the Centre's CEO and Dick Caborn, then Sports Minister and Chair of the Millennium Commission. Sadly, we were negotiating the project's closure and administration/liquidation. The Earth Centre CEO became quite obsessive about the fact that their records allegedly still highlighted me listed as one of their creditors, to the tune of a significant financial amount.

Although I denied this on several occasions, it concerned me on three levels:
1) If true, it would have ruled me out of making Earth Centre decisions, by virtue of a pecuniary interest in the outcome;
2) The claim could have been, in itself, an attempted bribe [although I suspected not];
3) It might suggest a much wider malaise – that finances paid to me, were accounted for elsewhere and I was identified as an "unpaid creditor" simply to balance the books.

The deal at Pizza Hut

"Clowns to left of me... Jokers to the right... Here I am, stuck in the middle with you... "

Josh Homme and Jesse Hughes"

Monday May 17th 1999...

My first full council meeting, Doncaster Mansion House

It's the annual council meeting and all the newly-elected Labour councillors are sat together on the back benches of the council chamber. The Labour Group's chief whip has chosen to sit me by the aisle, with Aidan Rave on my left and Margaret Ward on Aidan's left.

Margaret is a lovely, friendly, gregarious woman; a self-confessed 'biker girl' with strong family ties and a solid commitment to helping the community.

I have met Aidan before, at the Earth Centre, when he worked for the Conisbrough & Denaby Development Trust. He's a geeky young man of 26 and an ex-head boy at the local catholic school. He's slightly balding [especially for his age] and incredibly conscious of what he considers his two main attributes; his high intellect *"I have a brain the size of a planet."* he tells people; and his unfeasibly large penis which he conspires to "reveal" to me at the earliest opportunity! Call me a philistine, but I'm more impressed with his penis than I am with his brain.

The Agenda for the meeting is as follows:

Doncaster Metropolitan Borough Council Annual Meeting – 10.00 am 17th May 1999

Part 1
1. *Prayers*
2. *Election of Mayor*
3. *Election of Deputy Mayor*
4. *Presentation of Badges to the Retiring Mayor and Consort*
5. *Mayor's Inaugural Speech*
6. *Vote of thanks to the Retiring Mayor and Her consort*

Part 2
7. *Borough Election Result 1999*
8. *A New Democratic Framework for Doncaster – Creation of a Standards Committee*
9. *Acceptance of Urgent Items of Business*

10.	*A New Democratic Framework for Doncaster – New Political Decision Making Structure*
11.	*Board Memberships*
12.	*Membership of Panels and Sub-Groups*
13.	*Appointment of Chairs and Vice-Chairs to Boards and Panels*
14.	*Appointment of Representatives on Outside Bodies 1999/2000*

Diary of Meetings 1999/2000

To be quite frank, we're in a world of our own. We don't have a clue what's going on. We've had no induction, no briefing from the [Labour] Group leader, chief whip or anyone else – we are just expected to understand what's happening. Remembering what Pat Mullany has always told me, I look at Aidan and Margaret and say in a sage-like manner *"This is sitting on your hands stuff – we should only speak if we're invited to... watch what's going on... and take the lead from the other, more senior, Labour politicians..."*.

They both nod in agreement and Aidan says: *"Yes – Better to remain silent and be thought a fool than to speak out and remove all doubt... D'you know who said that? – Abe Lincoln – that's who said that"* he continues without pausing for the answer.

I look at Margaret and she rolls her eyes at me, exclaiming *"Ooh... he knows his stuff"*.

So there we sit, in glorious ignorance, just happy to be part of 'New Labour'. Two years into a new Labour Government, we are going to change the World, the Country and Doncaster... and, as far as I'm concerned, all on my 'It's time for a change' 'anti-corruption' ticket.

I'm standing on that because the council, and more specifically Doncaster Labour Party, is still reeling from Operation Danum.

So far, five Labour councillors have been arrested and found guilty as a result of "Donnygate":

Jack Riley:	*July 1998. Jailed for 28 days for falsely claiming £214*
David Jobes;	*August 1998. Jailed for six months for falsifying expense claims totalling £3,700.*
Derek Hughes:	*September 1998. Fined £500 after pleading guilty to one charge of falsifying an expenses claim.*
Mick Collins:	*September 1998. Jailed for eight months for expenses fraud involving Doncaster Council totalling £2,000. He denied stealing nearly £2,000 from his local Labour Party branch. The judge ruled these charges were not to be proceeded with, but ordered compensation to be paid to the party branch.*
Len Dyson:	*February 1999. Jailed for four months after admitting falsely claiming £325 in expenses.*

The whole meeting is an incredibly turgid affair, beautifully choreographed by officers who are well-versed in the pomp and ceremony of civic occasions. But I'm stunned by how disingenuous they are.

The way they greet us, as newly elected councillors, their overt humility and general insincerity is Uriah Heep like.

Outside of a game of Scrabble, sycophancy has never been a favourite virtue of mine. But the Labour Group's *de facto* chief whip, Danny Buckley, positively exudes it. A good-looking, fit, young man who has worked for many years down "Broddy Pit" [Brodsworth Colliery], Danny has a strong sense of sartorial elegance. He's also fond of horses, though better known for having an eye for the ladies. *"There's a nice looking little filly..."* he'll frequently be heard to say.

I'm spellbound by Danny's behaviour. Here's a man with no senior role within the Labour Group [or Party] for all I know, yet by creating one through complete bluff he is making himself totally indispensable. He flutters around the meeting, like a painted lady butterfly, whispering in people's ears, laughing and congratulating them, shaking hands and patting them on their shoulders; Danny Buckley is "the man" – and he knows it.

Danny is making sure everybody knows where they are going and what they are doing. He flatters us by making sure we know who he is and we are honoured – particularly Aidan because Danny exchanges pleasantries with him. I'm more disdainful of the Armani clad spiv.

Agenda items 11 [Board Memberships] and 12 [Membership of Panels & Sub-Groups] come and go. Despite Danny's choreography, there's a great deal of confusion every time a vote is called; not least because although they have been told what to do, each time the opposition changes the script, or failed to act true to type, the Labour Group falls into disarray.

I'm stunned. The majority of Labour Group members can't think for themselves! The vote is not going as planned and, failing to grasp the more subtle political nuances at play, Labour councillors are frequently confused as to what the next steps are, or should be. It's difficult to credit what we are seeing; the Group is being wrong-footed by its own stupidity! And with a chief whip who is unable to get round them quickly enough, and without the wherewithal to call an adjournment, it's like herding cats.

I, nay we, have assumed, somewhat naïvely it appears, that the longer standing Labour councillors will be excellent political operators; that they'll guide us, showing us how to behave; like a Greek scholar and his pupil. How wrong we are.

I've often marvelled at the herding instincts of politicians, blindly following the lead member, happy that they know what they're doing. But that requires clear guidance from those in charge, so everybody knows their part in the performance and when they are required to act. We are witnessing a level of controlled anarchy here.

There's a simple need for one chief and several assistant chiefs who are able to read the political situation, as it plays out.

Danny hasn't been made the "chief" but he certainly knows what's needed and like Derek Hatton in Liverpool in the mid-eighties, he hasn't needed to be elected as leader to be "in charge".

Agenda item 13 comes up – The Appointment of Chairs and Vice-Chairs to Boards and Panels. This is the most important meeting of the year for councillors – because it's the meeting where the money is dished out.

Each and every councillor receives a basic allowance of £8,146, just for being elected. However, in addition to their "basic pay", the majority are desperate for a "Special Responsibility Allowance [SRA]" for being appointed Chair or Vice-Chair to one of a myriad Boards and Panels. Arguably, this is where the power lies because it's where the additional, internal money is. And further SRA money is available for appointments to "outside bodies" – Agenda Item 14.

Consequently, this is where the 'Leader' parades his loyalties – practising his patronage and "buying off" the malcontents for the next however-long. There's no room for error here and Danny has made sure nothing is left to chance. We're talking money – and every base has been covered! Danny is magnificent. With all the deals having been done previously, the Labour Group, with its two thirds [41 out of 63] majority, gets exactly what it wants.

Nobody seems very clear what direction we're going in, but apparently that doesn't matter; the political cognoscenti know where they are going and each is elected to a position of power and remuneration.

Name and Position within Labour Group	Board/Panel Appointment	Special Responsibility Allowance
Colin Wedd Leader	Chair Policy & Strategy Board	15,600
Michael Farrington Deputy Leader	Vice Chair Policy & Strategy Board	7,900
Danny Buckley *De facto* Chief whip/leader	Chair of Community Development	3,940
Chaz Harrison Secretary	Chair Education & Culture	3,940
Martin Hepworth Chair Labour Group	Chair Environment Health & Housing	3,940
Bev Marshall	Chair Policy & Strategy Panel, Corporate Services Panel	3,940

Each Chair has a [Labour] Vice-Chair working alongside – a post which also comes with money. The cognoscenti then agree further appointments to a whole series of remunerated "outside bodies", external to the Council, including South Yorkshire Passenger Transport Authority, South Yorkshire Police Authority, South Yorkshire Fire & Civil Defence Authority and South Yorkshire Pensions Authority.

Given that most also have other, more regular, paid jobs, functioning as a councillor in Doncaster can be extremely lucrative; particularly if it's a job with a public sector employer, who will allow you time off for civic duties.

For example, ▇▇▇▇▇▇▇▇▇ is a fully paid union convenor and receives the following "allowances" in addition to his union salary:

Name & position within Labour Group	Employment	DMBC Allowance	Internal Appointment	SRA	External Appointment	SRA
▇▇▇▇▇ No position	Union Convener [+/- £30,000]	Basic [£8,146]	A Board/Panel	Chair [£3,940]	A Joint Authority	Vice-chair £14,000

In effect, as an elected councillor he's able to double his not insignificant union salary to around £56,000... And this in 1999, when average take home pay is less than £16,000.

ooo

1.00 pm

As the meeting finishes, Aidan asks me if I want to go for lunch with him. Surprisingly mature, I think... until he suggests Pizza Hut across the road from the Mansion House.

Aidan isn't paying of course; he seldom does in all the time I know him. It's a trait that draws frequent observations from other councillors, most notably Barbara Hoyle, the delightful Leader of the Conservative Group.

But these are early days, MWC is very successful and now employing six staff on a very strong profit margin, so I tell Aidan I'll treat him to an "all you can eat" buffet special.

As he begins tucking in following the first of his many forays to the buffet, Aidan and I have our first real discussion about all things political. Aidan can't wait to start dazzling me with his knowledge of political history and, with this as a starting point we discuss World, European and UK politics as well as, of course, Doncaster's local government scene.

Aidan explains his relationship with Tony Sellars. He tells me Tony has been impressed with the size of his brain and that, when *"Tony decided to stand down to make way for a younger tomorrow..."* he had done so *"... from a position of respect for Aidan's abilities, support for him and the wish to nurture his* [undoubted] *talents."* Aidan declares the feelings are reciprocal.

"So the fact that he'll get lifted soon for his involvement with Donnygate has got nothing to do with it?" I say.

Aidan nearly chokes on his 10 inch Meat Feast *"No, I don't think so. There* have always been the rumours... but I've always found him an incredibly hardworking and sincere man..." he defends him.

"*Careful Aidan...*" I say "*... if you carry on like this, you'll be denying the Holocaust soon*".

"*What do you mean?*" He says, playing dumb.

"*I mean that this denial of the truth is what's holding the Labour Party in Doncaster back*" and I explain how Pat Mullany has been my de facto political mentor; but not from a position of respect, support or the wish to nurture my talents but more from a position of holding me down – keeping an eye on me as the 'young Turk'.

I tell him of my disillusionment with Labour politics in Doncaster – our obsession with control from within, but with no apparent purpose. Frequently, we manoeuvre to control an organisation, group or individual – not in order to do some good, but to stop anyone else, other than the Labour Party, "controlling" it – ever fearful that someone else might actually do some good.

This obsession is clearest through the manner in which we are encouraged to "control" school governing bodies, I say. Frequently, the schools themselves are careering downhill, failing our children and our communities; but we don't care, from a [local] Party perspective, as long as the Labour Group is in control.

We can send down as many dictats from on high as we want but the reality is that no matter how well intentioned and transformational, Labour Party policies are, they will always be received or interpreted as transactional instructions. For me, this is the eternal dilemma; how we identify the policies that will truly transform communities without the need to transform the political community first.

I say I saw this paradox written large in the simplicity of Lincoln's statement, from this morning; "put your brain into gear before engaging your mouth" [in the vernacular] – which really means "don't say anything, or do anything until we tell you". The result is that Labour Party activists become merely "voting fodder" protecting the *status quo* rather than being the architects of a progressive agenda.

The mantra is to get the Labour machine rolling, get into a position of power and sit tight in that position of power – but don't rock the boat, don't draw too much attention to yourself, otherwise you might get shot.

I've never been able to understand why some local authority Labour leaders are given such reverence and paraded up and down the country, when their 'leadership' hasn't actually delivered anything for their communities.

Often the only things they have accomplished are the stability of the local Labour Group and keeping their own powerbase and job. Their only doctrine is self-preservation.

Aidan says I'm being disparaging and he thinks Colin Wedd is an excellent Leader. I say I don't even consider him a Leader, simply another Labour Party journeyman, serving his time.

I concede that Colin and Danny are incredibly adept at balancing the multiple demands, tensions, jealousies and stupidities of the Group's membership; no mean achievement, when you consider how dysfunctional some members are – and that this is a picture being played out across the country.

"*But I believe leaders should lead*" I say "*...and deliver a progressive change agenda, not just protect the status quo – and themselves*".

During a long lunch I tell Aidan about my father's influence; the Glass Park Project and its multiple objectives; and that real sustainable development must be about balancing social, environmental and economic objectives rather than about political rhetoric. I say this is what we are trying to achieve with the Glass Park, creating access to quality leisure facilities, employment, education and skills opportunities by encouraging communities to re-connect with food production and their local environment.

Aidan talks about his and my involvement with the Earth Centre; his work with the CDDT, and the direct links to Prime Minister Tony Blair's "fairness agenda". He discusses delivering social justice, employment, education and skills under a New Labour government.

We congratulate ourselves on our elections and our masterful campaigns and tactics. Truly there are no greater young politicians than the two sat in Pizza Hut that May afternoon; basking in the mutual masturbation of our egos. As Aidan begins his first visit to the dessert trolley, the pie is far from humble [Toffee Apple Meltdown, if I remember].

Nonetheless, we agree that we have a much deeper understanding than the others, that we are possibly the only two councillors, this morning, who grasp the bigger picture. We are destined for great things...

It's at that point I make prophetic declaration: *"The reality is Aidan, that if we're not in charge of this bag of shite within two years, then we need shooting".*

"How will we achieve that?" Aidan asks, with childlike simplicity.

"Oh I haven't got a fucking clue!" I say. *"All I know is that this lot are a bunch of fucking idiots... they don't know what they're doing... and they're constantly in denial about what's going on. You only have to see how they refuse to discuss the "D word"* [Donnygate] *– as if it doesn't exist – it's the arrogance of power. We just drift from one arrest to another. There's no real defining ideology or vision".*

"So what are we going to do?" asks Aidan, still concentrating on his dessert.

"I just think we'll have to wait – but be ready for it happening at any time... because it will happen. And when it happens we've got to do what's necessary".

"That's dangerous talk... from someone so young and bold" Aidan replies, impersonating Obe-Wan Kenobi from Star Wars.

"Well what would you have us do?"

"It's just dangerous talk... plotting at your first meeting of the High

Council..." Aidan laughs continuing the impersonation.

[Pregnant pause]

"And you don't know if you can trust me yet" he goads, breaking away from his food.

"I can trust you... as much as I can trust anyone" I add... but Aidan remains silent. *"Because I know you'll let me down – just like everyone else does"*. Aidan goes back to his pudding in silence... considering what I've said. *"Anyway, we're not plotting,"* I add. *"We're just planning to respond to future [and foreseen] events appropriately"*.

Aidan throws his spoon on the table in mock anger. *"What d'ya mean you can't trust me and I'll let you down?"* he says, dropping into a broader vernacular, because of his agitation.

"I can trust you..." I emphasised *"... as much as I can trust anyone else. That's why I don't have close friends... because they always let you down"*.

"Not me – I won't let you down – I'm incredibly loyal" he protests.

"Of course you are" I patronise *"So am I... In fact nobody's more loyal than I am... but I know you'll let me down at some point in the future – People always do."*

"I don't think you realise how insulting you're being" he says. *"I am incredibly loyal and it's really important you understand that"*.

"It's not really important I understand it..." I say *"... but it is really important that I experience it"*.

"But it's really important to me that you understand my motivations" he goes on.

Me, after a pause: *"Have you ever read David Copperfield?"*

"What?"

"Have you ever read David Copperfield? It's incredibly pertinent, given what we've witnessed this morning".

No answer...

"Well if you'd ever read or seen a production of David Copperfield... you'd clearly understand that a truly 'umble person, doesn't need to constantly tell you about 'ow 'umble he is".

"What? I haven't read Dickens – what about Shakespeare? "Methinks you doth protest too much – mate"

"Ah... Hamlet... and you got it the wrong way round..."

It's clear Aidan is desperate for me to accept his loyalty, and his friendship, so at the famous Pizza Hut across the road from the Mansion House, we agree to look out for each other.

It's an echo of Blair and Gordon Brown's so-called Granita pact – when in the summer of 94 the pair are said to have met in London's now-defunct Granita restaurant following the death of Labour Party leader John Smith and in return for certain promises, Brown agrees to stand aside to allow Blair to become leader of the party, and, as it turns out, future prime minister.

But we're oblivious to that as we agree our own deal: that as newly elected councillors we will always protect each other.

Me: *"Well let's do that then... if you want to".*

Aidan: *"Yes – let's agree that we'll watch each other's back"*

"Whilst ever we have a reason to trust each other" I add.

"I'll never let you down Martin. I'm extremely loyal and you need to know that. I'm often so loyal that I'll damage myself in sacrifice of our relationship".

"I'll trust you 'til you let me down... Aidan. And let's hope I'm not proven correct on this one..."

Little do I know then, the manner in which my prophecy will come true....

ooo

Footnote

Of the sixty three Councillors represented at that particular council meeting, sixteen were subsequently found guilty of financial irregularities in one form or another.

The outgoing Mayor at that meeting was the Conservative councillor, Yvonne Woodcock. When I asked why we had had a "Tory Mayor", given there were only five Conservatives elected to the council, I was told it was to 'get the newspapers off the Labour Group's back'.

She was appointed as a sacrificial lamb – to 'prove' the council was not being run by a Labour cabal.

An Austin Ambassador Y Reg

"Don't keep asking me why, Reg
It just happens to be that year"

John Shuttleworth

Saturday June 26th 1999…

10.00 am – St Oswald's Church, Kirk Sandall

… And I'm in old Sandall Parva, once again. The church bells are chiming and it's another beautiful day. Today is my first official 'civic duty' as a fresh, newly elected, baby-faced and proud "New Labour" Doncaster councillor.

I was elected 51 days ago on an "anti-corruption" ticket with the mantra "it's time for a change" – reversing a three election-losing streak to the Lib-Dems – and I'm here as the special guest to open the St Oswald's Church Art Fair.

But I'm a father first, so time management is all important and I'm squeezing this in between several family commitments during the day. I'm with Carolyne, Beth, 9, and Marcey, 4, and we've already dropped off our 6 year old son, Joss, at football training.

The Art Fair is a lovely event and, to thank me for attending, I'm offered *"a picture of my choice from the exhibition"*. Naturally, I decline the gift.

After an hour we leave for my mum and dad's house – to herd up and catch a mallard duck and her eleven ducklings. Having discovered the nest in his garden, next to the pond, BJ and my mother have been watching her sitting on her eggs for several weeks.

Each evening, the mother duck troops them out of the garden single file, down the road to a small stream approximately 100 yards away. Like clockwork, an hour later she walks them back, settling them down for the evening in a bramble patch. But BJ is concerned for the ducklings' safety and asks me if I'll catch them and take him to 'release them' on Tickhill Mill Pond, approximately 3 miles away.

As we drive towards my parents' home, we filter left onto Tickhill Road in Balby. Tickhill Road is a fast road –a single carriageway road that transforms quickly from a busy urban arterial with a 40-mph speed limit to a fast winding rural 60-mph link road with many blind bends.

It's where I was wiped out in a car crash in 1988. I know it well and I drive it carefully.

Next to St Catherine's Hospital we stop at a crossroads and traffic lights and as the light turns to green the car behind us, an old Austin Ambassador, immediately pips his horn. Now, if there's one thing I can't abide it's anti-social drivers and as we pull away, I say something about his behaviour and my children strain to see who it is being so aggressive.

A hundred yards further on a bus has pulled in to the bus stop on the left, stopping on the herringbone lines, and opposite, cars are parked outside a car showroom – so the space between them is small. The road is fairly busy and I'm struggling to find a gap in the on-coming traffic. The car behind us pips again! In response, I put my arm out of the window and raise it to the heavens; the universal language for "what can I do?".

The driver pips his horn two or three times now – and when I take advantage of a brief lull in the stream of cars he starts to pip rapidly in short busts – almost mock applause. As I look back, I see him put his arm out of his window and raise his clenched fist, cartoon like.

We continue up the road, leaving the town and approaching open country. Suddenly, the Austin Ambassador is hurtling up behind us again, flashing his lights and pipping his horn. This time he's attempting to pass us. Annoyed that he should be driving so dangerously, I gesticulate "tosser" out of the window; and tell Carolyne that I'll drive exactly as the traffic and the road dictates, slowing down to 40 mph.

This seems to incense him and, as we drive through the winding countryside, he constantly tries to pass us in dangerous situations, forcing the on-coming traffic to take evasive action. I remark to Carolyne that the man is driving like a lunatic and tell her that as soon as we arrive at my parents' she should take the children inside and be prepared to phone for the police.

Despite my speed, the driver constantly struggles to overtake us. As we approach the ninety-degree turn into my parents' village, I indicate to turn left. In one final mad desperate act, he attempts to overtake us yet again but then swerves immediately hard left in front of us. The turn is too severe though and he starts to lose control of his car on the rural road, spinning it on the gravel.

My parents' house is 50 yards further on in a small cul-de-sac, and as we pull into the drive, Carolyne quickly ushers the children into the house. I adopt a more leisurely pace, locking the car and pretending to inspect the garden.

Within seconds, the old car screeches up on the road outside and out steps a man of about 50. He's around 5 feet 10 tall and weighs about 12 stones. He looks scruffy in a threadbare blue/black turtle neck jumper with matching trousers and Doc Marten shoes. Anticipating his arrival, I've already turned as if I'm walking towards the house.

"Can I have a word with you?"
I ignore him.
"Can I have a word with you?"

I ignore him again, idly examining a prized buddleia bush. But I notice out of the corner of my eye that he's walking up the drive towards me.

"*Can I have a word with you?*"

"*No*" I say. "*I have no wish to speak to you*"

"*But I want to talk to you*" he says.

"*Well I have no wish to talk with you... and can you leave these premises.*"

He's standing on the drive, in front of my car and about fifteen metres from the road.

"*But I want to talk to you...*" he says once again "*... about your driving*".

By this time I'm getting pretty annoyed and I begin to walk down the drive towards him.

"*I want to talk to you... about your driving*". He says again.

"*And I've told you... three times now... that I have no wish to speak to you.*" Then, slightly pre-empting my inheritance: "*Will you please remove yourself from my land.*"

At this point, he moves a few paces towards me, and puts his hand in his trouser pocket and I think he's about to pull a gun or a knife...I'm going to have to flatten you here mate, because you're going to have a go at me, I think. How wrong I am.

"*But I'm a policeman*" he says, pulling his warrant card from his pocket.

Now I've never been a huge fan of the boys in blue. Like all trades, some are good and some bad; but the naivety of this man, to attempt to excuse his behaviour in this way, just infuriates me.

"*D'ya think that makes any difference whatsoever...*" I say raising my voice. "*Now remove yourself from my land – this is my final time of asking you*".

"*But I want to talk to you about your driving...*" he says, trying to assert some kind of authority.

It's then I realise Carolyne has come out of the house to join the emergent mêlée.

Now Carolyne's a feisty character and, one of my greatest regrets is that she never saw me playing rugby when I was at the top of my game. Bolstered by her presence, I decide I'm going to take him out – so I begin to enunciate at him... "*Get – off – my – fucking – land – before – I – fucking – throw – you – off*"

But this stupid, stupid man just stands there looking slightly puzzled.

Now at 5 feet 10 and 15 stone plus, I outsize him considerably; we Winters are well known for our broad shoulders and barrel chests. We're also known for having fairly loud voices and in all my time as mayor, I never struggle to project my voice.

By now, I am so incensed with this man's behaviour, that I rush the remainder of the distance between us and push my face right up to his – so close that our noses are less than an inch apart.

"*Get – off – my – fucking – land – before – I – rip – your – fucking – head – off,*" I scream at him.

It begins to have the required effect. The man turns and scurries away – only to stand in the drive's gateway, adjacent to the footpath.

I run towards him now and push my face into his again *"Get off my fucking land... or I'm gonna fucking eat you"*. I scream again.

Carolyne decides she's having some of it too, *"Piss of you little man"* she cries. *"I bet you've got a really small dick – haven't you?"*

He runs round to the driver's door of his car, now open, and places one foot in the foot well.

"You haven't heard the last of this," he says. *"You don't know who I am"*.

"Ah ha... you have" Carolyne taunts *"... you have got a really small dick – haven't you?"* as she raises her little finger and waves it at him.

Full of the glory of victory – having driven him from "our land", I raise my voice in mock rhetoric once again *"D'ya think that I give a flying fuck who you fucking are?"*

And with that, he gets into his car, drives to the end of the cul-de-sac and turns round. As he drives back towards us, Carolyne can't resist raising her little finger and waving it at him.

As he nears us, he slows and winds down his passenger window... *"I'll get you for this"* he shouts in a Dick Dastardly cartoon kind of way.

"Who...you and your little dick?" calls Carolyne.

As he drives off out of the close, I keep repeating his car registration number... "_ _ _ _ _ _Y... _ _ _ _ _ _Y"...

Entering my parent's house, I confirm it with Carolyne, writing the number on my mother's wall reminder... "_ _ _ _ _ _Y

"Did you see that – I demand of my father?"

"What?" he asks.

"We've just nearly had a fight in the garden" I exclaim.

"I've been playing with these two" he nods at Beth and Marcey; and we proceed to tell him the story.

After we recover our composure, I say: *"I really thought he was going to pull a gun... or a knife... or something"*.

Now my father has never been a lover of the police either; ever since he witnessed an innocent man being arrested for public disorder – but that's another story.

"Well... y'know what those bastards are like" he says. *"Just look what they did over Hillsborough – he'll be claiming you did it to him"*.

"You're right" I say, thinking of the 96 fans that were killed in 1989.

"*He said he was going to get us... I'm going to put a formal complaint in to the police about him road-raging us*". And I ring Doncaster Police Station to make a formal complaint about his behaviour. After I put the phone down, Carolyne says: "*Did you see what he was driving?*"

"*Of course I did...an old Austin Ambassador*".

"*Not any old Austin Ambassador*," she says – and she begins to sing...

"*An Austin Ambassador Y reg... [Why Reg]...[Why Reg?]...*"

"*... an Austin Ambassador Y reg... [Why Reg]...[Why Reg?]*

... and we both sang in unison: "*It's a car that I revere!*"

My father looks at us, as if we've gone mad.

ooo

AUSTIN AMBASSADOR Y-REG

My Austin Ambassador Y reg, Y reg, Y reg
My Austin Ambassador Y reg is a car that I revere
My Austin Ambassador Y reg, Y reg, Y reg
Don't keep asking me why, Reg
It just happens to be that year

Now you may covet a Clio
Or a Mondeo
Marvel at the Montego
Fine but not me, no

Now you may be utterly sold on
Your Peugeot, your Proton
Your Mitsubishi Shogun
But I'll always dote on

My Austin Ambassador Y reg, Y reg, Y reg etc.

I'd even say no ter
A Rolls with a chauffeur
A brand new Toyota
A Skoda? Give over!

I've got an Austin Ambassador Y reg, Y reg, Y reg
Don't keep asking me why, Reg
It just happens to be that year

Lyrics courtesy of: http://johnshuttleworth.tripod.com/lyrics.html

Well I could... couldn't you?

*"Under certain circumstances,
profanity provides a relief denied even to prayer."*

Mark Twain

Saturday June 26th 1999...

"They never bleedin' answer when you want them to... do they?"

"Have you tried going through Thorne?" asks my mother; now back from shopping and appraised of the morning's events.

"Why on earth should I want to go through Thorne?"

"Because I always have to go through Thorne... or Sheffield," she says.

"Y'know isn't that fucking typical... we've got a mad copper..."

"Or police impersonator" Carolyne interjects.

"What?"

"He might be an impersonator".

"Ooh... that's a bit Rutger Hauer" I say. "So we've got a mad knifeman impersonating a copper... and road-rage attacking innocent residents... and I've got to go through fucking Sheffield".

"And stop swearing... " says my mother.

"Okay... so we've got a mad knifeman impersonating a copper... road rage attacking innocent residents... and I've got to go through...".

"Oh I'm sorry... I didn't realise you'd picked up" I say in best Received Pronunciation. "Yes... I'd like to put in an official complaint please – preferably to the Independent Police Complaints Commission please – about one of your police officers please..."

"Sorry... okay, can I make a formal complaint about one of your police officers then please. Look its really quite simple... one of your police officers has just road rage attacked me and my family... in front of witnesses..."

"And he's harassed us and intimidated us whilst trespassing on private land..." Carolyne interrupts.

"Yes... yes... he has... he has harassed us and intimidated us whilst trespassing on private land..." I repeat.

"And I wish to make a complaint".

"Sorry... yes it was an Austin Ambassador... registration number "_ _ _   _ _ _Y"...

Carolyne's singing quietly *"An Austin Ambassador Y reg... [Why Reg]...*

[Why Reg?]"

"Shh..." I sign.

"Okay... yes... thank you – my number is Doncaster ▓▓▓▓▓... Have you any idea when you'll ring us back... okay... thank you"

After about twenty minutes the phone rings and my mother answers it before handing it to me...

There then follows the most bizarre telephone conversation which, following a preamble, goes something like this...

"The registered owner of the vehicle is not a police officer with South Yorkshire Police sir"

"That's a strange way to answer me – what's that supposed to mean?"

"It means he not a registered officer with this police force sir"

"Well... are you saying that it's a man impersonating a police officer or are you saying that his car's registered at a bogus address?"

"Neither... I'm simply saying that he's not an officer with this police force sir".

"Well which police force is he an officer with?"

"The Metropolitan Police force, in London sir"

"What's that supposed to mean? Are you saying that this man lives in London?"

"No... the car is registered in Doncaster sir... but it would appear that he works for the Metropolitan Police force in London sir"

"Why are you giving me all this information?"

"I'm just trying to be helpful sir... you're wishing to put a formal complaint in and I'm just trying to furnish you with some of the information you require sir"

"Well it all seems very strange to me... so what do we do now? ... Okay... yes... thank you... We'll be there at some point next week then... okay... thank you".

As I put the receiver down, I turn and look at my audience *"Did you hear that?"*

"Hear what?" asks Carolyne.

"That bastard works for the Met, in London, but lives in Doncaster..." I'm wondering why no-one has jumped to the same conclusion I have.

"What does that mean?" asks my mum.

"Well which coppers commute to London each day?"

"Top ones do..." volunteers Carolyne.

"Yes... and..." I patronise.

"Undercover ones!" she jumps in.

"Bang on! "Surveillance... Special Responsibilities Units...." my mind is racing, "... the Secret Service even! I bet this bastard's licensed to carry guns – he's with some special responsibility team that means he commutes from

Doncaster... or can't live near to where he works"
  "Don't you think you're getting a bit carried away?" says my mother.
  "No I bleeding don't. You didn't see him. The man's a fucking lunatic. He could've killed us. He's an arrogant little fuck pig... and I'm gonna 'ave 'im".

ooo

The following week...

So there we are, at Doncaster Police Station, Carolyne and I, waiting to be interviewed about our complaint.

It's a typical police station reception – cold lino floor tiles in blacks and greys; a laminate hardwood reception desk with the edges worn off revealing the chipboard underneath; safety glass on all the doors, the type with the wire mesh contained within it [and only produced by Pilkington Glass Ltd!]; black vinyl seats with holes picked in the seating to reveal the polyurethane foam with a patchwork of black electrical-tape repairs.

Now I'd like to describe this anecdote in the style of Quentin Tarantino; that is, from several differing perspectives. I'd like to describe it as the two police officers interviewing us saw it; I'd like to describe it as Tony Sellars saw it; as his lawyer saw it; and as the police officers behind the complaints' desk saw it; but I'll stick to one perspective – mine.

As I've already said, I'm not a fan of the police and Carolyne and I have always lived by the motto "life's too short as it is, so whatever's happening, make sure you have fun".

I like playing linguistic games with my colleagues, friends and family; a favourite being whether we can get key words or phrases into speeches and interviews. Indeed, to this day, my children love to play the "malaprop game" collecting malapropisms they hear people using; current favourites are "*... this one gave me pacific concern*" and "*... are you incinerating that I am wrong*".

To this effect, Carolyne and I enter into these interviews with two objectives: firstly we are concerned that this "off-duty" police officer has endangered our and our children's lives; and secondly, we are determined to have some fun at the police's expense.

In order to understand this game, you need to be familiar with the South Yorkshire vernacular and our tendency to speak in a lazy manner; we frequently replace the "*t*" before a vowel with an "*r*" so that "getting better" becomes "gerrin' berrer", "get off" becomes "gerroff", "put it down" becomes "purrit down" etc. There's also a tendency to drop letters completely, so "going to" becomes gonna; and "should not" which becomes "shouldn't" as you move up the country, turns to "shunt" as you reach the people's republic of South Yorkshire.

To wit, as far as Carolyne is concerned, the game is on – and she hates to lose.

After about ten minutes, a police officer comes into the waiting area and asks for Carolyne; he is extremely polite and explains they are "under-staffed" today. He asks if he can interview Carolyne first and if I wouldn't mind waiting a while, to which I graciously agree; exit Carolyne stage left.

In a typical police station reception, there's a limit to the number of times you can read the same poster, and only so many walls you can look at, or types of human behaviour you can subtly observe.

But after some twenty minutes of waiting, a smartly dressed man carrying a briefcase comes into the room and sits down on the bench seat next to me. He places his opened briefcase on the bench and begins tidying papers. At this point, I notice the title of the document paper clipped to the back of his briefcase.

"Affidavit of Anthony Sellars"

That's interesting, I think to myself. Here we are at Doncaster Police station, in the middle of the "Donnygate" saga and I'm sat next to Tony Sellars' "brief".

My mind's racing again. I haven't seen Tony to speak to since the opening of the Earth Centre, some three months ago, and certainly not since I've been elected.

I know what I know about Tony Sellars and that Tony is the ex–chairman of the Labour Group on Doncaster Council, so it must be over Donnygate – I wonder what his brief's here for?

The more I strain to read his affidavit, the more obvious it becomes that I'm doing so; and, frankly, the more annoyed I'm becoming about the complete lack of discretion displayed by his lawyer.

After a further 15 minutes, he closes his briefcase and goes up to the desk. He speaks to the desk officer who opens the door and the brief disappears into the back.

Another five minutes passes and suddenly there, outside on the pavement, is Tony Sellars, Wrangler jacket and all, coming up the steps. I make sure he can see me as he approaches. He smiles brightly, and then the smile gradually fades as he begins to wonder why I too am at the police station.

"*Hiyah Tony*" I say, feigning a worried look as he comes through the doors.

"*What are you doing here?*" he asks "*Oh, by the way, congratulations on your election*". Tony is always saying "*Oh, by the way...*" I guess he somehow thinks it hides his Machiavellian asides.

"*Oh yeah... thanks...*"

Then: "*Haven't they told you?*" I say "*... it's something to do with the Earth Centre... apparently they've identified some kind of a fraud and they're concerned about the receipts I submitted.*"

"They've asked me to give a statement about when we worked together at the Earth Centre... something about the receipts I submitted for the Training Academy not being consistent with yours..."

Well you could have knocked him down with a feather – his face is ashen. *"They've said what?"*.

Now Tony was an extremely quick thinker. Why on earth would I have been called at exactly the same time as him? Surely they would have kept us apart? They wouldn't have told me what they were interviewing me about?

All of these thoughts are written all over his face – so I give him a break. *"Nah... I'm talking bollocks Tony..."* I laugh *"... for a change..."*

"Aye... for a change" he echoes back at me. Tony has a huge relieved smile on his face and he's laughing quietly... but I know he's thinking "bastard"...

"What happened?"

"Carolyne and I are making a statement... she's in already... about some lunatic copper attacking us in a road rage attack..." and I give Tony a substantially abridged version of the story.

Tony has a lovely way of communicating with you, he shows complete attentiveness and listens to everything you say to him frequently calling you by name, constantly mirroring your behaviours and checking back with you.

One of his failings, arguably, is that he loves to interject and finish the story for you; parading his political nous and intuitive powers.

True to form, he stops me in mid flow.

"Stop there" he says *"He works for the Met? Well what was he doing up here then?"*

"Oh he lives here... in Doncaster..." I say. *"I fancy he's with some special responsibility team which means he has to commute from Doncaster each day... to protect him"* I'm in full flow now.

"He's licensed to carry guns y'know?"

"How old is he? What colour hair has he got? What kind of a car was he driving?" Tony continues rapid fire.

"An Austin Ambassador Y reg..." I say.

Tony immediately looks up at me.

"I know him" he says, his face pensive.

I'm taken aback: *"How do you know him?"*

"I know him" he repeats to himself again. *"It's a guy called ▮▮▮▮▮▮"*.

"How do you know him?" I ask again. *"Is he a twat? Is he a member of the Met's armed response unit? Is he licensed to carry a gun?"* I imitate Tony's rapid fire questioning. *"I bet he's a fucking Mason"*.

Tony looks at me – the colour has drained from his face. *"Oh fucking 'ell – he is a fucking Mason... Are you a Mason? No... no... bollocks... of course you're not... you're a left footer aren't you... you Catholics have your own version of the*

Masons, don't you?"

"Yes... and no – I'm not a Mason". Then, repeating himself for a third time, "Yes... it's a guy called ▮▮▮▮▮▮▮▮."

Tony is smiling. He knows something I don't.

"How the fuck do you know him?" I plead.

"Well I can tell you, but it's very confidential... And it can't ever get out – how I know" he clarifies.

"Everything's confidential Tony – that's why I haven't seen you here today".

"Anyway... y'know I won't say anything ..." I touch my nose.

"Okay. But it had better not ever get out".

"For fuck's sake Tony... you know how loyal and trustworthy I am".

"Okay" he says "He's my son-in-law's father... and you're right... he's a right fucking wanker"

ooo

Just then, with almost comic timing, a door opens and Carolyne comes out into reception with a police officer. Giddy as a spring lamb, I smile at her: *"Hi,"* I say, *"Are you okay?"*

"Mr Winter is it?" says the officer.

"Yes".

"Are you alright for time?" he asks "Only we're very under-staffed today – and I haven't had anything to eat yet... is it alright if I see you after lunch?"

"Yes – that's fine" I say.

"So shall we meet back here at half past two?"

"Yes – well go and get some lunch ourselves" – and the officer turns and goes back through the door.

Still giddy, I smile at Carolyne again *"Are you okay?" "Yes"* she said *"I've got something really funny to tell you"*

"You know Tony... from the Earth Centre" I interrupt.

"Yes – Hiyah Tony" she said "I'm sorry Martin but I've got something really funny to tell you" she's almost bursting with laughter.

"They told me his name" she declares.

"We know his name" I say, nodding at Tony – and dampening her enthusiasm.

"How did you get that?" she asks.

Just then we are interrupted, as Tony's brief comes out again and they greet each other.

"I'll see you later Martin" says Tony as he walks away with his lawyer and disappears behind the door; but not before he's made eyes at me. "I told you so" they seem to say.

"How did you find out his name?" I question Carolyne.
"Because of these" Carolyne looks down at her [wonderful] breasts.
"Ah... no contest" I respond.
"Nah..." she laughs "... he had to put it into the statement".
"Anyway... you should've seen the windup I got Tony with..." I told her.
But it's too late, Carolyne isn't interested. She has already "won" the game and wants to regale me with her victory speech.

ooo

12.16 pm – South Yorkshire Police, Doncaster Central Station, College Road

Interview Room 7

[Acting] Inspector ▓▓▓ is reading Carolyne's statement back to her. *"And Mr ▓▓▓ was in the car behind you Carolyne"* says [Acting] Inspector ▓, reading from Carolyne's statement...
"No"
"Excuse me Carolyne?"
"The man – I now know to be Mr ▓▓▓ was in the car behind us"
"Okay... Sorry... the man – you now know to be Mr ▓▓▓ – was in the car behind us"
"Yes... I want you to change it then... I'm not signing it unless you change it" she insists pedantically. *"I'm not letting him come back to me at a later date – saying that it was a vendetta and the proof of the pudding is in my statement, where it suggests I already knew him"* ...
"Okay... that's fine..." says [Acting] Inspector ▓▓▓ *"... and then what happened?"*
"He pipped us when we did not set off immediately the lights turned green... but Martin never sets off straight away, especially on that road because it's near where he had his car crash. Then..." she continues *"... a bus was stopped at the bus stop, just near St Catherine's Hospital, and because we couldn't see the road ahead, we stopped – and he started pipping us again"*
"How far could you see Carolyne?" [Acting] Inspector ▓▓▓ asks.
"Oh I couldn't say"
"Well was it a short distance. Say less than ten metres. Or a longer distance?" asks [Acting] Inspector ▓▓▓ helpfully.
"Oh I couldn't say – I'm not very good a judging distances" says Carolyne, teeing him up. *"I couldn't even tell you how long this room is..."*
"Surely you can" says the officer.
"No I can't... could you?"

"*Yes, I could...*" says the officer.
"*You c'unt...*"
[Pregnant pause]…
"*Could you?... well that's very clever of you Superintendent. I could never do that*" she covers her tracks by playing the 'dumb blonde' – a role she's incredibly adroit at.

Knowing full well what she has done, the officer gives her a sideward questioning glance. Carolyne just smiles sweetly, gently squeezing her ample bosom together, before continuing with her statement.

fall out

2.4 million SAGA readers

> *"It may be judged indecent in me to come forward on this occasion;*
> *but when I see a fellow-creature about to perish through the cowardice of her pretended friends...*
> *I wish to be allowed to speak, that I may say what I know of her character"*
>
> Mary Shelley

Friday September 3rd 1999...

Surprise surprise, I receive a letter from South Yorkshire Police informing me that the police are not taking matters further with regard to any motoring offences against the officer I have made a formal complaint about.

ooo

Tuesday October 5th 1999...

South Yorkshire Police are really dragging out the investigation into my complaint against a police officer for my alleged "road rage" complaint. Consequently, I write to the Chief Constable, Mike Hedges stipulating that in addition to the original complaint I now wish to make a further complaint about the shoddy, unprofessional and discourteous manner that our original complaint has been dealt with. I copy this letter to Bev Marshall as the Vice-chair of the Police Authority.

ooo

Tuesday October 12th 1999...

I receive a suitably embarrassed letter from South Yorkshire Police, countering their shoddy behaviour, missed customer-care timescales and response times etc. and protecting their "Charter Mark".

ooo

February 2000...

Michael Farrington is arrested as part of the Donnygate investigations. He immediately resigns his position as Deputy Leader of the Labour Group [and

Council]. As a result, an election takes place for the Deputy Leadership.

ooo

Monday February 14th 2000...

Gerry McLister, a youth worker for Derbyshire County Council, was first elected four years ago- when he was the ward colleague of Tony and Terry Sellars – and is now the ward colleague of Terry Sellars and Aidan Rave. He is, and always has been, very wary of the Sellars brothers, but as a passionate Ulsterman, Gerry is wary of most people.

He is also possibly the hardest working Doncaster councillor; a dogmatic man, committed to leading an ethical, honest, socialist agenda.

Gerry decides to challenge for the Deputy Leadership and, in a two horse race, he is in competition with Councillor Bev Marshall; a battle portrayed as the 'New Broom' against the 'Old Guard'.

I don't dislike Bev Marshall but I've decided I'm voting for Gerry McLister, because we've got to draw a line and move forward. When I tell Aidan this, he seems evasive and slightly uncomfortable, however, I've counted him in [because he's Gerry's Ward colleague] and we appear to have got the numbers.

ooo

Monday February 21st 2000...

After a relatively brief campaigning period, the election is upon us. When the votes have been counted Gerry has lost 16:15!

The Group is split straight down the middle and, although I'm not happy with the result, I don't think Bev will be a bad Deputy Leader – he certainly can't be worse than those who have gone before!

ooo

Tuesday March 14th 2000...

I receive a letter from the Metropolitan Police informing me that the matter has now been referred to Police Complaints Authority for their consideration.

ooo

May 2000...

Twelve months into my role as councillor and I'm constantly struggling to balance the demands of council work with those of running my company, MWC. Significant conflicts are also emerging between my contract, to project-lead the embryonic Glass Park Development Company [GPDC], and the desire of our many partners to associate themselves with its success.

To gain more from a community perspective, we have established the GPDC as a community-owned model, operating as a not-for-profit company. I have diverted the majority of the MWC work I'm securing to the GPDC in order to train others and develop the company's capacity – which by this time has grown to employ 9 people. Nonetheless, I'm torn by the need to liaise with the council whilst simultaneously keeping them at arm's length – a position I have always advocated to the Glass Park trustees. This is particularly troublesome when council officers insist on writing to me as "Councillor Winter", in what I perceive as mock subservience and despite my protestations.

> *Glass Park Development Company – Modus Operandi*
>
> The company is a Private Company Limited by Guarantee. The Memorandum & Articles have been adapted from standard Memorandum & Articles of the Industrial & Common Ownership Movement [ICOM].
>
> This structure is also known as a "not-for-profit" company. As such, we can apply for EU, Lottery and landfill tax funding, amongst others. However, we are not able to pay dividends or issue shares, as the company has no shares. Profits are intended to be used to further the aims & objectives of the company; with additional and residual profits being covenanted to the Glass Park Millennium Green Trust.
>
> Any individual can join as members of the company, for a fee of £10.00 Members can also be elected as Directors.
>
> The structure is democratic, with a pattern of meetings to lead and review the work of the company. The work of the company is led and reviewed by the members through:
> - Management Group – six directors meeting on a monthly basis
> - Quarterly and ad hoc steering group meetings
> - Annual General Meeting of members

In addition to my increasingly complex business life, I am becoming ever more dissatisfied with the way the Labour Group is running its affairs and the style of leadership of Colin Wedd. This position has been compounded by what appears to be the Leader's unimaginative patronage when bestowing chair and vice-chair positions.

I have performed particularly well in my first year, or so I think. Colin must be able to see our capabilities, Aidan and I reassure each other in the run up to the

Annual Council Meeting and the 'Appointments to Panels and Outside Bodies'.

"*I'm expecting to be given Chair of Community Development*" Aidan tells me, as we massage each other's egos – which is ironic because it's the minimum I'm expecting as well!

ooo

Wednesday May 3rd 2000...

9.30 am – The Labour Group Office, Mansion House

Our second Annual Council is approaching and Danny Buckley has asked to see me. I arrive expectantly and on the dot. Danny asks me in. As usual he is wearing a sharp suit.

"*Let's dispense with the pleasantries...*" he instructs. "*I've got a shit load to do because I'm preparing the committee report for next week's Annual Council...Suffice to say, the Leader wants you to take Vice-Chair of Employee Relations*"

He looks at me with spaniel eyes... I swear I see him tilt his head sideways.

"*Fuck me Danny – is that it?*"

"*What do you mean? Why do you say that?*" He sounds confused and slightly pathetic; he's suddenly lost his air of authority.

"*Well I'm good at this*" I say. "*I thought you'd have at least offered me Chair of Community Development*".

"*Well this is a good position... it's an important position*" he's spluttering, like a car misfiring. "*To be offered this so soon is recognition of your capabilities. It takes years to become the Chair of Community Development... and it's another fifteen hundred quid for you!*".

"*It's not about the money Danny... who am I Vice-chair to?*" I ask with a sigh.

"*Malcy Wood*"

Malcy is a time-served Labour Party member representing the Sprotborough ward. He's one of the "old guard" a loyal foot soldier who is well aware of his value to the Labour leadership and how to get what he wants in return.

Malcy is also the spitting image of Charlie Drake, both in his looks and his mannerisms. He is a gregarious little man with an obsession for horse-racing – hence his nickname "Jockey".

"*Fuck me Danny it gets worse – Apprentice to "Jockey" Wood eh. It'll be like Ray Allen and Lord Charles*".

I look out of the window, blowing out my cheeks, petulantly.

"*Well what did you expect me to say?*" I ask, thinking I might have gone too far.

Having composed himself, Danny slips into gear: *"You see Martin... politics isn't a meritocracy... And you'll forever struggle... if you expect to progress based on your capabilities".*

"Well what should I have said?" I sense I'm being taught a new trick by an 'old dog'.

"Well I would have said I'll be glad to serve the Leader in any way I can... and I'll do any job he asks me to do". He's motoring like a purring Jaguar now.

"Well it's not as simple as that – is it?" I tell him. *"What's Aidan got?".*

"Vice-Chair of Corporate Services..."

Ah... That's his payback for supporting Bev for Deputy Leader... I think.

"... and Aidan was delighted with it" he adds.

"Can you thank the Leader for his foresight... and tell him I'll be glad to serve him in any way I'm able to"

I sigh and leave the room.

ooo

With hindsight the reality is that the Leader doesn't have much room for manoeuvre. Despite the ramifications of Donnygate, the Labour Group is still a large group and the Leader has to balance the need to keep the time-served happy, whilst also satisfying the newer councillors who, twelve and twenty four months on, are starting to get restless.

ooo

11.20 am – Members Room, Mansion House

"What a pile of bollocks," I say to Aidan.

"What do you mean?"

"The vice-chairs appointments. What a pile of bollocks! Apprentice to Jockey Wood– me!"

"Well what's wrong with that?" he says *"... you still get your money"*

"It's not about money Aidan – anyway this'll cost me fucking money"

"How come?"

"Because I work for myself Aidan – and I don't get paid when I'm not at work. Unlike those of you who have a job to subsidise your civic responsibilities. At least you're apprentice to Bev Marshall... and you'll be able to learn something".

Aidan doesn't respond.

"All I'm saying Aidan is that I would have thought Colin would have been able to see our capabilities."

"Yeah… but think about it" says Aidan *"Danny was advising Colin… and he made sure he got Chair of Community Development…But I would've thought he would've been able to see your capabilities"* he adds – overtly patronising now.

"Maybe he did… but if he did, he fucking under-estimated me," I tell him. *"I'll give it six months."*

ooo

June 2000…

Councillor John Quinn, or "Quinny" as we know him, is a big man; a big strong Scot who came down from the Highlands to work in the pits in the 1950s. He has an incredibly strong, hard Scottish accent and an even stronger, solid union background. Tough, passionate, fiery and red-haired, he knows all about loyalty. He's a faithful family man, dedicated to his roots in Scotland and devoted to his adopted Rossington community; above all he's a lifetime member of the Labour Party and forever faithful to the cause and class struggle.

But the best, most remarkable, thing about Quinny is his nose –huge, bulbous and red, exactly like WC Fields, who, like him, poor man, suffered from rhinophyma.

Several years later it is cured following a successful operation but until then it remains bright red, raw and massively swollen. I swear blind we once had a visit from one of our twin towns in the Dandong province in China and the group all wanted a photograph taken alongside Quinny – and his extraordinary nose.

John often features in conversations about Donnygate; but while he is interviewed on more than one occasion, he is never arrested nor charged.

My first real connection with Quinny comes in my first week as a councillor. During my first Labour Group meeting, Councillor Martin Hepworth, the Chair, very indelicately asks the Group to endorse a 'decision' that Councillor Jack Meredith defer his appointment as Deputy Mayor because of the Donnygate rumours being laid at his door.

It's a decision Jack, who has already been Mayor in 1990-91, appears to take with a mixture of dignity and chagrin.

Quinny doesn't take it lightly though. He is raging and puts forward an impassioned plea to the Group to consider the pain and humiliation this will bring to Jack's family.

I can see Quinny now, ranting like Rab C Nesbitt, the alcoholic Glaswegian portrayed so brilliantly by actor Gregor Fisher.

"I'm tellin' ye… it's not right. Ye canna treat a man like this – he's done nothin' wrong. Ye canna treat a man like this I tell ye– I want it puttin' to the vote".

"Well I don't think it will do us any good," says Martin Hepworth, ever the conciliator. "I'd rather not put it to a vote... It could be very divisive".

"Wad are ye afraid o' man?" John hits back. "We's protecting Jack's human rights here?" he was really flowing.

At this point the Leader, Colin Wedd comes in with a typically pompous melancholic diatribe about the protection of human rights always having primacy but that this is about public perception.

He is quickly followed by the desperately supportive [and newly appointed] Chief Whip, Danny Buckley, keen to display his grasp of the bigger picture.

Bev Marshall, Chair of Corporate Services, then suggests "... *we might all find it useful if John reflected on the situation, over the weekend, when* [he felt sure] *he would see the sense of the decision*". Bev always suggests we should "reflect" on difficult or contentious situations. It's his standard tactic.

John, realising his defence is having little success and that he will lose any vote he manages to force, acknowledges the cause is lost. He stands up and starts putting his papers into his briefcase.

"*Ye disgust me... Ye dinna treat people like this...*".

"*Ah have bin there... haven't ah?*" he said looking to the group for acknowledgement of his own, spurious trials and tribulations – but it isn't forthcoming.

"*Ah'm not standing here watching this rubbish*" he growls; "*It's nay more than a kangaroo court... and ye's a set a vultures*" he exclaims storming out of the chamber.

It's something I become used to during his time on the council.

ooo

I always describe Donnygate as a scandal that operated on three distinct levels:

1] *The widespread abuse of expenses by councillors* – claiming for first class rail fares when they were actually travelling standard class; submitting bogus mileage claims for journeys that never took place or were exaggerated; and the abuse of overseas trips, visits to conferences, entertainment accounts etc.

It seems madness today, that simple Quality Control and Audit Systems did not pick up on such abuses earlier. The one piece of bureaucracy even the smallest, worst run organisation has is a book to manage the day-to-day use of petty cash. Yet at the height of the Donnygate scandal, members were still not expected to produce receipts for train tickets and, on several occasions, were given cash advances to purchase tickets and pay for subsistence! A situation later put sharply into context by the MP's expenses scandal.

2] *The Mismanagement of external contracts* – inappropriate political involvement in the procurement of contracts, where councillors would make sure "favoured" businesses were awarded contracts in return for alleged paybacks.

Within this area were fraudulent claims from contractors – where companies would submit bogus claims for work done on houses. For example claims for fitting nine windows, two new external doors and a bathroom to a property – when only five windows, two doors and a new toilet had actually been fitted.

3] *Allegations of fraud within the planning process* – various allegations were made and I accept they dog planning committees across the country. But these were specifically focused on the inappropriate designation of land for housing, within the Unitary Development Plan [UDP] process.

Manor Farm was one of four or five sites allegedly included in the UDP right at the last minute – without going through the usual robust consultation process. The allegation was that the sites had been included for corrupt reasons; an easy accusation to make, but a difficult one to prove.

The Manor Farm application was for a large residential development of approximately 1000 plus houses on hundreds of acres of predominantly agricultural land and ancient woodland. The site lay south of a large housing estate called Bessacarr and east of Potteric Carr SSSI [Site of Special Scientific Interest] Nature Reserve; being sandwiched between these and the M18 motorway. Access was difficult and any improvements were set to add to an already impossible rush-hour traffic problem known as the Cantley Crawl.

If the application was successful, this agricultural land, worth less than £2,000 per acre would rocket in value to £200,000 per acre. This was serious stuff.

Jonesy had become fixated with Manor Farm, alongside other sites like Poppyfields at Branton, and was determined to expose the 'fraud' that he claimed had taken place.

He made sure he cranked me up with plenty of information on the application and on my need to stake my claim as "the new broom" – a reformer who was going to sort out this bunch of corrupt bastards once and for all.

And it worked. Jonesy's manipulation played to my arrogance. To be honest, I'd already decided this was going to be a defining moment for me as a councillor. I just didn't realise quite how significant it would prove to be.

ooo

Monday June 12th 2000...

I receive a letter from the Police Complaints Authority fudging the whole issue and, basically, saying that it is my word against his. The letter states that after nearly twelve months of investigations:

> "... there is such a conflict of evidence between the different accounts of what happened that I cannot be satisfied that the officer's behaviour fell below the standard set out in the police code of conduct and therefore disciplinary action cannot be justified."

Of course we all know that police never lie.

ooo

Tuesday June 13th 2000...

The morning of the Planning Committee dawns but I don't mention the stance that I'm going to take, in case anyone tries to 'water me down'. I never discuss it with Carolyne either. Despite how closely we work together over the years, I always tried to leave work 'at work' and not to bring it home with me. Carolyne, on the other hand, always wants to talk through everything and my reluctance to debate every ephemeral issue is a constant bone of contention between us.

I look over at the Press Box. The Doncaster Star, Doncaster Free Press and Yorkshire Post reporters are all in attendance. A good turn-out. They must know the importance of this application...

The Schedule 1 agenda item comes up and the Chair introduces it.

"Sit on your hands", I think to myself "... you need to bide your time and listen to what the others have to say".

Councillor John Hoare [Lab] speaks first on the application, a fairly anodyne approach that overall isn't particularly supportive, although his opposition is well hidden. He is swiftly followed by Councillor Malcolm Jeavons [Lib-Dem] who, buoyed by Councillor Hoare's approach, gives a slightly more self-assured presentation that suggests he isn't happy either.

The whole meeting has an air of inevitability about it and a real sense of lethargy.

This isn't particularly dynamic, I think. They clearly don't want it but they're reluctant to say why they don't want it – I'd better liven it up a little.

I indicate that I wish to make an intervention and wait for the Chair to introduce me...

"I'm a relatively new councillor... and this is my first substantive opportunity to let people know where I'm coming from" I say, warming myself up.

"We all know that this land wasn't originally designated for housing; it was designated as Countryside Policy Area... and it was only designated for housing right at the last moment, along with several other sites, at a meeting to accept the new Unitary Development Plan wasn't it? People have always argued that it was a dodgy decision... and one that put this site right at the heart of what has become known as Donnygate".

The sudden interest of the gallery is palpable; I look up and the journalists are scribbling furiously.

"If it was a questionable decision then... and I stress *if it was*... then we need to look at whether it could be a questionable decision now".

I'm cheerfully disregarding the "material reasons" planning committee members have to consider by law.

"My colleagues earlier made reference to the fact that the only access to this site is by constructing a link road through a broad-leaved ancient woodland – well I'll go a little bit further and remind you that we've lost 95% of this type of indigenous habitat in the last 40 years...so I suppose we could argue, what difference will another 5 acres of priority habitat make?"

"But it does matter. Of course it matters. Because we'll be obliterating pristine habitat for treecreepers, nuthatch, woodcock, badgers and roe deer – never mind all the ancient woodland indicator species such as bluebell, ramsons [wood garlic] and arum lily – all beautiful flowers found in this habitat".

"So it does matter! It matters because I want my children to be able to see this type of habitat in Doncaster and not have to make them trek to Clumber Park".

"And let's not buy the developer's argument that we can recreate such a habitat off site... because we can't... and they won't".

"This site is an ancient woodland, because it's exactly that – an "ancient" woodland – not because it's an "instant" woodland. You can't get it out of a packet... or a spray can".

The cheap seats love it.

"When I stood for election as a Labour councillor, I did so because I thought it was time to draw a line under Donnygate. And for us to start moving Doncaster forward again"

"Enough is enough, I said to myself. And to the electorate I said 'it's time for a change' – vote for me and say 'it's time for a change' "

"And you can all say this too... today. You can say 'it's time for a change'... by voting against this planning application today... you can show the people of Doncaster that we can change".

I can see Quinny is getting uncomfortable with what I'm saying.
I start to come to a close.

"Each and every one of you on this planning committee today... can show the people of Doncaster that you can change – and you can do so by voting against *this planning application"*

And I start to speak, and point, to each of the key members; one-by-one I say to them:

"You... can draw a line with the past – today..."

"You... can draw a line with the past – today..."

Each time I re-emphasise the *"you"*– occasionally using their names; *"Bill... Councillor Burrows [Louise]... Councillor Simpson... Councillor Dainty"* [which is particularly apposite given that this Tory Leader will be found guilty of planning fraud three years later].

I begin to build to a crescendo *"You can say to the people of Doncaster... 'it's time for a change' now – because it was a corrupt decision then and it's a corrupt decision now..."*

By this time Councillor Quinn is getting really agitated– huffing and puffing and noisily gathering his papers together. He wants people to know he's uncomfortable with what I'm saying.

He stands up and with great aplomb puts his papers into his briefcase before slamming it shut.

"Ah'm not lissening to this, Chair" he growls.

"Ye canna let him get away wi' this, Chair. We took the advice of officers" he remonstrates, both acknowledging his involvement with the committee's previous decision while denying any culpability. Then he storms out of the council chamber, again.

"Sometimes... the truth can be very uncomfortable..." I say in closing; and I sit down to applause from the cheap seats.

"Go geddum tiger – you're on fucking fire" says Bill Mordue, another of my newly-elected colleagues. *"Mind you – you're probably dead as well..."*

Now I sit and watch as the later speakers follow suit; it's as if my tirade has liberated them – allowing them the freedom to similarly speak out against the application.

Finally the Chair moves to the vote and the application is turned down by a handsome majority.

ooo

After the meeting finishes, Councillor Yvonne Woodcock speeds across to me – *"Well done Martin – somebody has to stand up to them"* she says, giving me a big kiss. I notice she glances over at the Press Box as she does so.

"Thanks Yvonne – but I see the Lib-Dems aren't too enthralled".

"That's because you've stolen their thunder" she tells me. *"I've been against this from day one..."* she's speaking so that the journalists can hear *"But we've always been in danger of being out-voted by the Labour numbers".*

"The Lib-Dems have been trying to stop it and claim a victory for their campaign but you were fantastic!" she exclaimed. "Did you see John Quinn's face as he stormed out – I thought his nose was going to explode."

"Do you think he'll be giving an interview to the newspapers?" I ponder naïvely.

Bill Mordue, a colleague of Quinny's on the Coalfields Communities campaign, comes in again. "I bet he stormed straight down to see Colin".

"Why... d'you think I was a bit over the top?" I already know the answer.

Bill: "Let's say it was a bold move in your first term".

"Ah bollocks to em... " I cut him off. "If they want a row... then they've fucking got one"

ooo

Friday June 16th 2000...

I receive a letter from the Chief Whip...

> Dear Councillor Winter
>
> An allegation has been made against you, that your conduct has been unbecoming of a DMBC Councillor and that it has brought the Labour Party into disrepute.
>
> Would you please ring me to arrange a meeting where we can discuss the allegations?
>
> Danny Buckley
> Chief Whip

I rip it up and put it in the recycling bin. For the remainder of the week, the word is out that I am making a stand. I assess the Council as being divided into four camps:
- Those who think I am plain stupid – and are going to get me for what I said.
- Those who think I am plain stupid – and shouldn't have said what I said.
- Those who don't care – and just carry on as normal.
- Those who are as naïve as I am – and think my stance might mean something.

The reality is I'm living in a dream world. Nobody really gives a shit about what I've said or done – except the newspapers, of course. As is often the case with situations like these, we tend to be in a goldfish bowl and think that the whole world is teetering upon our every word; not at all, the world carries on regardless.

Having said that, there is a fifth camp. Three or four officers [and growing], some from within the planning department, are letting it be known they are supportive of the stand I'm taking. Most notable of these is Ken Burley, the Chief

Planning Officer, who unbeknown to me had previously been questioning members' 'unhealthy' involvement in planning issues.

ooo

The media reports of my outburst are quite interesting with the Doncaster Star and Free Press giving me reasonably good press coverage. The local newspapers now have a champion; somebody who will say what they want to say – though their use of my notoriety is relatively short lived.

The Yorkshire Post on the other hand barely mentions the matter. My analysis is that they don't want Donnygate to go away; the Yorkshire Post is generally considered to be on the right of the political spectrum, supporting the Conservative Party – in fact its owners used to be known as Yorkshire Conservative Newspapers Limited until the 1960s. An anti-Labour Party story helps this Tory rag sell so they don't want to report on an anti-corruption stand by a Labour councillor.

ooo

I speak to Aidan about my tirade. My analysis is that Aidan is firmly in "Camp 2"; he's trying to ingratiate himself with Colin and I can tell he thinks I'm foolish and unnecessarily rocking the boat. I suspect the views are not his own.

"They can fuck off. They can't whip me in for a planning issue – there's no whip on planning issues" I say, practising my defence.

"I just think you should think a little more strategically" Aidan says – code for "they're gonna screw you mate".

I don't give a shit.

ooo

Friday June 30th 2000...

I receive another letter from the Chief Whip.

> Dear Councillor Winter
>
> We haven't received a response from you concerning the allegation about your conduct. Would you please ring me as soon as possible to discuss this situation?
>
> Danny Buckley
> Chief Whip

I make a plane out of it this time and fly it at the dog asleep in front of the fire – he just lifts his head and looks at me through tired disdainful eyes, as if to say "twat".

ooo

Friday July 7th 2000...

9.30 am – Council Chamber, Mansion House

We're attending a Members' Seminar "The Members' Role in Waste Management" appropriately enough. As I arrive I notice Danny coming up the corridor from the Group Office.

"Martin, can I have a word with you please?"

"Sure Danny – what is it?"

"We need to have a word about your conduct at planning the other week, Martin. The Leader's concerned that you aren't aware of the full facts".

"I don't need to be aware of any facts" I say, moronically "But I think you should be aware that I'm not going to be whipped in for a planning issue".

"No that's not what it's about at all, Martin".

"Isn't It? Well perhaps you'd like to let me know exactly what the allegation is then. If you let me know in writing, then I'll consider attending. But until then, I won't be attending... And in the meantime, Colin needs to be aware that he's on dodgy ground here... in fact... this is very thin ice you're all skating on" I mix my metaphors. "Now I've got a seminar I'm meant to be attending – see you later!" and I walk off up the stairs.

ooo

As usual, refreshments are being served in the Salon before the Members' Seminar and everyone is congregating. I chat to some of the members and, out of the corner of my eye I see Quinny. I also notice Danny having a quick word with him before the meeting starts.

The Seminar is what is fast becoming the usual self-serving pile of crap. Only there to benefit those compiling statistics on member involvement, these seminars are held simply to justify government regulatory auditors. After about an hour we break for "refreshments" again; it seems officers don't expect to be able to hold members' attention for longer than 60 minutes without a fag break.

There's an immediate exodus to the Members' room – the only room in the Mansion House where smoking is permitted. I stay in the Salon for a cuppa and talk to Bill Mordue; Quinny makes a beeline for me.

"D'ya feel better after yez attack on woz all Councillor?"

"Sorry John?"
"D'ya feel better after that attack on woz all Martin?"
"I'm sorry John, I didn't quite catch that?"
"Dinna act clever... Martin – I said d'ya feel better after that attack on woz all last week"
"Which one would that be John?" I patronise.

Bill seems uncomfortable, constantly shifting his weight from one foot to another and looking at his watch. He gestures at the portrait on the wall *"That picture of Alderman Tuby... is that Roger Tuby's grandfather?"* He gets no response.

"Some of us wez on that planning committee when the Manor Farm decision was made..."
"I know you were John"
"Well... are yez saying woz all corrupt?".
"No, I'm not saying any of you are corrupt..."
"I think I'll get another cup of tea..." says Bill.

John won't let it drop: *"Yerseez we woz all corrupt"*
"No I never said you were corrupt John. But I am saying... that the <u>decision</u> was corrupt... ... there's a big difference".
"Nah... dinna try and be clever mon – yerseez we woz all corrupt".
"No I said the decision was a corrupt decision...I was using the word "corrupt" as a verb to describe the state of the decision and you were hearing it as an adjective", to describe the planning committee".
"Dinna be s' fuckin' clever – I knows wot yer deeing" John is pointing at me now.
"I'm not trying to be so... fucking... clever...as you put it" I protest. *"I was simply using the word corrupt as a verb to describe the condition of the decision – it was a corrupt decision, as in a distorted decision... But you heard corrupt as an adjective to describe you and your colleagues".*
"Yer clever bastard" John reiterated.
"I'm not trying to be clever..." I protest again.

The truth is I'm as confused as he is over the linguistics, he just doesn't know enough to put me right. There are several people watching now and, almost on cue, Quinny decides he's had enough.

He begins ranting, *à la* Rab C Nesbitt.
"Let me tell yez this sonny... " he starts prodding me in the chest with his finger.
"Th' woz nothing wrong wi' that decision wen it woz made... an yeez shud back off... de yeez understand?".

Now I've had enough and, ever conscious of the developing audience, I hit back:

"*No... let me tell you this Councillor Quinn*" I say very calmly and I grab his finger tightly with my fist and start bending it right back towards his chest.

"*Don't you ever... fucking... touch me again!*" I warn him, bending his finger further. "*Or I'll snap your fucking finger off and shove it up your arse – do you... fucking understand?*"

I let go of his finger, turn and walk out of the Salon.

John and I don't speak again for more than three years.

ooo

Fishlake and Sykehouse are both part of the Stainforth electoral ward, the ward I am elected to in May 1999. Fishlake Endowed School is a beautiful little country school in the heart of this pastoral oasis, nine miles north east of Doncaster.

Councillor Pat Mullany, the Chair of Doncaster Council's Education & Culture Committee, makes the decision to close the school in 1994 to get rid of surplus places – yet another victim of the Tory's swinging cuts within UK local government.

Pat makes no secret of the fact that if he has to close schools, he'll do so in affluent Tory areas like this and not in Labour's heartlands; relying on families and friends to drive the children three miles to the next nearest school in Stainforth.

Ironically the school made news for its 'monkey children' in Edwardian times, when parents removed their children from the school because the head teacher, a Miss Winifred Gould, was teaching Darwinism. Back then parents preferred them to walk to Stainforth; a theme later echoed in Spencer Tracey's 1960 Oscar-nominated film "Inherit the Wind".

After the school's closure the "Friends of Fishlake Endowed School" campaign for an alternative community use for the school's buildings; ably led by Stephen Cooke, a Labour Party member and activist, who is the son of a previous head teacher at the school.

My company undertakes a feasibility study and business plan for the "Friends" in 1997/98 and, consequently, I am intimately involved with the Fishlake community for some eighteen months before I stand for election.

As a result I had expected a strong showing in the "Fishlake box" at the election the previous year.

Fourteen votes, out of a box of one hundred and eighty seven polled, takes some believing.

"*The ungrateful fucking bastards*" I railed [at the time] to Stephen Cooke and Kevin Hughes.

"Fourteen fucking votes"

"Dave Page [my Lib-Dem opponent] *couldn't even spell fucking Fishlake and he got forty seven votes!"* I continued in hyperbole.

ooo

Despite my abysmal showing in the "Fishlake box", I have been elected to serve the whole community and continue to support the "Friends" in their efforts to secure the funding to "save" Fishlake Old School – ever conscious of the need to separate my councillor's duties from the work I have been paid to do beforehand.

Brian Barnes is Secretary of the Friends of Fishlake School and lives in Fosterhouses, a hamlet of 15 homes mid-way between the villages of Fishlake and Sykehouse. Brian is a genial old guy, a bright man and an ex-personnel manager at the Coal Board and at ICI Fibres – where he worked alongside my Dad's brother, my Uncle Roy.

Brian was very interested in Doncaster's politics. This was more from a position of having seen the behaviours at the Coal Board and ICI more than anything else; and because he knew that I was rabid in my disgust of the behaviours I had witnessed. Perhaps more importantly, he knew I was also quite keen to discuss behaviours I had witnessed.

As a meeting of the "Friends" is wrapping up, one of the lady members asks me about a planning application in Fishlake that will see a wonderful old orchard grubbed up [ripped out].

They know of my obsession with orchards, the large numbers of apple orchards that the Glass Park has planted in schools in the area and my scion-grafting project to save the "Sykehouse Russett" apple from extinction.

"Well, as a member of the planning committee I couldn't possibly comment..." I joke *"... and, in any case, I'm 'persona non-grata' at the moment within planning".*

"Oh, have you been making yourself unpopular again?" she asks.

"Well let's say I haven't got many friends within the Labour Group at the moment."

"Oh I wouldn't worry about that" she says, disdainfully.

"Oh I don't know... SAGA were impressed with you Martin" Brian interjects.

"Sorry Brian?"

"SAGA were impressed with you – they had an article about the young man that's standing up to the corruption in Doncaster after you stood up to them about Manor Farm. I assume that's what you're referring to".

"Yes. Did they really?" I'm stunned *"It's marvellous isn't it – I can't get the Yorkshire Post to cover the story but I can get featured in SAGA's magazine! Why should England tremble – eh?"*

"It's all very well you taking the Michael, Martin, but you shouldn't underestimate SAGA's readership"
"Shouldn't I?"
"Oh no... it's nearly two and a half million you know"
"I'm not underestimating them at all Brian..." I say "... but how many of 'em vote in Doncaster?"

ooo

Footnote

Looking back, even before the planning committee meeting John Quinn wasn't particularly disposed to me; despite my long-standing family connections with the village of Rossington and the fact that for many years I captained the village rugby team.

He first started to mellow after Carolyne sat next to him at the "Chair of Council's Inaugural Banquet and Ball" where they both charmed each other. Quinny had let it be known he was standing down in 2004 and the Group nominated him as the Chair of Council for his penultimate year. Carolyne obviously knew of our 'disagreement' – most people did – and she was looking forward to the challenge of winning him over.

Carolyne's father, Roland Hunter, was injured in the D-Day landings and there's nothing she likes better than reminiscing over the War and her father's involvement in it. As a result of his injury, Roland required plastic surgery and became a member of Sir Archibald McIndoe's famous Guinea Pig Club; McIndoe achieved international recognition during the war for his pioneering work with plastic surgery on Battle of Britain fighter pilots [also see Sir Patrick Duffy - Chapter 17]. As her father became ever more frail and blind, she took him to the 60th and 65th Anniversary commemorations in Normandy.

Turns out that, not only was Roland stationed at the Royal Naval Dockyard in Rosyth, but he and Quinny's father, a sheet metal worker, were there at the same time.

In the event Carolyne, Quinny and Quinny's wife Ella, all had a whale of a time and ended up singing old time songs together, like 'Edelweiss' and 'Don't Sit Under The Apple Tree...'

Notwithstanding that, I think John was getting disillusioned with the way the council was moving. He understood loyalty and discipline; he'd done his political apprenticeship and some, and he knew that internal Labour Group rows should be just that – internal. As the Father of the Council and serving the Rossington ward and community for some 24 years, I think he was also growing disillusioned that politics wasn't what it had been; that the Labour Group had no socialist backbone or ideology and that the executive [mayoral] model of local government was disenfranchising him and his colleagues.

I also think, and I never spoke to him about this, that he was beginning to realise there was an internal Labour Group campaign to discredit me and the mayoralty and that many of the problems we were experiencing were not necessarily created by the 'despotic' Mayor.

Certainly as the onslaught against me grew stronger, Quinny seemed to become ever more supportive; indeed, the Rossington Branch Labour Party was one of my stronger allies when I was attempting to deal with the bullying and victimisation.

I think John was becoming disgruntled by how I was continually attacked, and frequently by our own side. He was a passionate defender of an individual's right to be presumed innocent until found guilty – something that was lost at the height of the Operation Danum investigations.

Golden child or last one standing?

"I did not become someone different... That I did not want to be...
But I'm new here... Will you show me around
No matter how far wrong you've gone... You can always turn around"

Gill Scott Heron

November 2000...

Six months on and the disenchantment is growing. The Labour Group continues to lurch from crisis to crisis with arrests now commonplace under Operation Danum and averaging one a month. Sixteen Labour councillors have now been found guilty and, as a result, fourteen have either stood down or lost their seats at elections.

The Labour Party's stranglehold is loosening but Labour is still king in Doncaster. Despite all the arrests there are still forty one Labour members of the majority ruling group – leaving room for just five Conservatives, nine Lib-Dems and eight Independent councillors.

Of the eight Independents, Steve Judge and Michael McAteer are both ex-Labour councillors who, despite having been convicted, are not disqualified from holding public office because their sentences were relatively minor. Indeed, one of my lasting memories of this time is the number of councillors awaiting trial or questioning who are suspended from the Labour Party as a result. During my first 12 months as a councillor, I note that Gillies, Glover, Martin and Terry Sellars only attend council meetings once in each six-month period, to avoid being struck off.

Of the remaining six, four – Pinkney, Wilde and the two Williams's, Martin and Carol – are all said to be former members of the Labour Party, with multi-millionaire Martin Williams having funded Kevin Hughes and Rosie Winterton's election campaigns previously.

The forty-one remaining members of the majority ruling group are divided into three camps:

1] Councillors implicated in "Donnygate" – those who know they have done something wrong and are waiting, in abeyance, on the call from the Police [12 of the 41 Labour councillors at this time].

2] Councillors who think they may be implicated by association – those who are not sure whether they have done something wrong or not but are not prepared to discuss it just in case [11 of the 41 Labour councillors at this time].

3] Councillors who know they have nothing to worry about – [18 of the 41 Labour councillors at this time]; who, in turn, divide themselves into two sub-categories:

    3a] the newly elected councillors [11]
    3b] the longer-standing, time served councillors who had
           been rigorous in upholding the standards of their office [7]

By now the newspapers are having a ball regularly reporting on the police making "yet another arrest", yet the Group never mentions it.

<u>11 Labour Councillors found guilty between May 1997 and December 2000</u>

Pat Mullany:	Sentenced to 200 hours community service in July 1999 after admitting expenses fraud totalling £1,290. He had already repaid it to the council and was ordered to pay £500 costs.
Steve Judge:	Sentenced to 120 hours community service in August 1999 after falsifying his expenses. He was ordered to repay £289 and £500 prosecution costs.
Terry Sellars:	Sentenced to three months suspended for two years in September 1999 and ordered to re-pay £490.
Tony Sellars:	Sentenced to three months suspended for two years in December 1999 for falsifying his expenses and ordered pay £664 in compensation.
Roland Cox:	Sentenced to two six-week jail terms to run concurrently [suspended for a year] in April 2000 for making a false claim for £137.60 hotel accommodation and for claiming a £120 rail fare when he had paid less.
Michael McAteer:	Fined £250 in May 2000 for falsely claiming £139.60 for two nights at a hotel.
Paul Farley:	Ordered to carry out 120 hours' community service in May 2000 after pleading guilty to making a false claim for accommodation and train fares totalling £243. He was ordered to pay £118 costs.
Malcolm Glover:	Sentenced to three months suspended for a year in July 2000 on each of three charges, to run concurrently and ordered to pay £1,000 costs. False accounting, claiming first class rail fare when he had travelled standard and making a mileage claim for a 450-mile round trip when he'd travelled in a company representative's car.
Gordon Jones:	Fined £250 with £118 costs in July 2000 for falsely claiming for a £140 rail ticket when his ticket had cost him £66.
Norman Fisher:	Sentenced to nine months in September 2000 for falsely claiming £639.20 for hotel accommodation.
Brian Day:	Fined £300 with £250 costs in October 2000 after pleading guilty to making a £69.70 false claim for overnight hotel accommodation.

It's my most obvious bone of contention with the Labour Group at this time – their complete refusal to acknowledge that we somehow have a problem and that the

Group is in paralysis as a result.

There is a quite remarkable paradox here in terms of the lack of accountability and sheer arrogance displayed by the Labour Group then, compared with the Mayoral model now; specifically the manner in which the mayoral system opens up the decision-making process for the public to see exactly who is making the decisions.

Indeed, such is the arrogance of the leadership; I liken it, rather laconically, to the "disappeared" in the Argentinean Dirty War. There is frequently an empty seat at the end of a table but no discussion of the previous occupant, no mention of the "missing" member.

I discuss my on-going frustrations with my family and my good friend and confidante Liz Jeffress; and, after much soul-searching, I make the decision to stand down.

I request a meeting with the Leader to let him know of my decision.

ooo

Colin Wedd became the Leader of the Labour group and Council in late 1998, after his predecessor Malcolm Glover was arrested for false accounting. Only four months earlier Tony Blair had famously stopped-off at Doncaster Railway Station for a photo opportunity to declare that Glover's election as Labour Group Leader finally meant "the end of Donnygate"... d'oh!

Colin was an incredibly pompous man, who looked like a slightly portly version of actor and comedian Peter Sellers. He delighted in people thinking he was a former headmaster and was truly "upper class" in a Doncaster context; a man who revelled in the misconception that he was ex-public school. He had a plum stuck firmly in his mouth and had clearly not forgiven me for the way I shunned him and Chief Whip Danny Buckley over their attempt to "discipline" me over the Manor Farm planning application.

"No thank you I'd rather not say what I wish to speak to him about. It's personal and private... but he should know that it's extremely important" I tell Alison, the Leader's secretary.

Much to my surprise, the Leader grants me an immediate audience. I'm to attend his office at the Mansion House at 8.30 am the following morning.

ooo

8.20 am – Outside the Leader's Office, Mansion House.

"Morning Martin; he's not normally too late..." said Alison, *"... his driver*

normally picks him up at 8.00 ish – but the traffic's sometimes bad on Balby Road" she fussed.

Bang on 8.30 in walks Colin, placing his hat on the hat stand and hanging his coat up on the rail.

"Morning Martin" he says in his best Received Pronunciation. *"Oh... is that your University scarf?"*

I touch the edge of my red, amber and black Sunderland Polytechnic scarf, almost identical to St John's College, reputed to be the wealthiest in Oxford.

"Yes... it's my old college scarf... you have a keen eye Colin... I really must get something a little more discreet" I mock.

"Yes... I must look out mine again" he responds, clearly deciding it would be too gauche to question further. *"Do come in."*

The Leader's Office was, by Mansion House standards, a tiny room – approximately four metres by four metres. It had an imitation Chippendale desk with a large faux-leather reclining office chair, which Colin loved to swivel on. In front was a small square table accommodating eight at a squeeze. The walls were covered in replica William Morris wall paper with Farrow & Ball painted woodwork.

On each of the two free walls he had three glorious original oils – permanently on loan from the museum – depicting the St Leger and various equestrian or rural scenes; Colin had a real penchant for works of art and loved to play up the cultured ex-Don role.

After idle chit-chat and the appearance of morning coffees, I thanked the Leader for granting me an audience. I told him of the difficulty I was having balancing the conflicting demands of running MWC, my work as a councillor and the Glass Park project and, as a result, I wished to stand down as a councillor.

Colin said he was surprised at my decision but, somewhat tellingly, accepted it straight away.

I admit I was surprised. I expected him to at least have toyed with me; to have feigned concern; been desperate not to create a bi-election. Here we were, with another eleven Labour councillors convicted in the space of two years, and the new-broom, elected on an "anti-corruption" ticket resigns.

We were looking towards eighteen months of relative calm – a fallow-year, where there were no local elections in Doncaster – so why risk a by-election now?

But nothing; nothing came back at all. There was no real response from the Leader.

'How wrong you were Martin,' I thought to myself – 'It would have been nice to feel wanted. It's quite apparent he doesn't rate you, so he can have it with both barrels.'

With this at the forefront of my mind, I told him of my concerns over the complete lack of vision or ideology shown by his leadership or within the group. I told him I felt we were simply drifting from crisis to crisis; displaying little, or no, imagination and that he – "we" – had no plan for getting out of the situation we were in.

Not surprisingly, Colin appeared taken aback and dismissed my views; but without proffering a counter argument. I can still hear his pathetic, supercilious tone now:

"Is that what you think? ... Really... Well I can assure you that this is not the case at all..."

My frustrations were raging *"You see – you don't even want to take me on"* I challenged him.

"Surely you're not going to deny the damage that these continuing arrests are doing to the Labour Party and, more to the point, to Doncaster?"

"No... I can't deny that my dear boy. But I can assure you that we've got plenty of ideas and plans for the town... Now if you'll excuse me I have another meeting to go to"...

In his delightful ex-schoolmaster's voice, he dismissed me, adding almost apologetically *"Thank you for your time Martin. I am always keen to encourage our young blood – we need to have new ideas and new viewpoints – perhaps you'll put down any that you might have before you finish?"*

Condescending bastard – I'd rather put you down, I thought to myself, as I left his office.

ooo

That evening I got a phone call from Bev Marshall. Bev had recently become the new Deputy Leader of the Labour Group and Council [with Aidan's support!] after Mike Farrington was questioned by South Yorkshire Police. They quizzed him over allegations he had used Council resources to pay for hotel accommodation for him and someone he was allegedly having an affair with.

Bev was a completely different style of operator to the others within Doncaster Council. An NUT convenor, he could wrap the Council around his little finger and was a top quality orator and bullshitter. A large man, reminiscent of Billy Bunter, he had lost out to Rosie Winterton in 1996 for the Doncaster Central Constituency MP's position. He had a joke for every single situation you could think of and, because of this, was well liked by fellow councillors; nothing short of remarkable, given their dislike of anyone with such an educational pedigree.

Bev gave me the whole nine yards. He was complimentary, respectful, funny, strategic and political.

I explained why I wasn't keen on causing a by-election and he agreed.

"I wonder if you would delay any announcement until after May" [2001] *so we may get our sister Labour Authorities to come and help with the by-election"* he suggested helpfully, creating a bogus date for me to aim for – all our sister Local Authorities had the same fallow years so why would we have to wait until after the elections in May?

Then: *"Well I've really enjoyed having this conversation with you. Perhaps you'd like to reflect on our discussion Martin... over the forthcoming Christmas break... and we can discuss your position further, and with refreshed eyes, early in the New Year?"* he flattered me.

I agreed – I'd completely folded to Bev's smooth talk and manipulation.

"Given the sensitivity of this issue, perhaps we'd be better keeping this discussion to ourselves?" he said, finishing the conversation.

"Yes I agree" I said sheepishly. *"But I've discussed it with Aidan..."*

"I don't think they'll be a problem there" he smiled. *"Aidan's a bright lad with a good future. But I'll have a word with him".*

ooo

Christmas 2000...

In my first year as a councillor, I had helped out at the Mayor's Christmas Fayre with my three children. It was a lovely event, with many councillors helping and a real sense of goodwill to all.

I've always believed my job as a parent is to create a bank of memories for my children, so "we" had decided the 'Christmas Fayre' would be our annual festive spirit bash, one that put us in the mood and got us ready for the big day.

This year was no different and I was selling gifts from a large round table in the middle of the ballroom in the Mansion House. As usual, everybody made a fuss of our children and Councillor Yvonne Woodcock [Tory], desperate to become a grandmother herself, even had a special small table set up for them to sell from.

The event went famously. The children loved being the centre of attention and made quite a few sales to boot. They were eating cakes; helping people unwrap their Tombola tickets and find their prizes; and they were happy to give the 'main man' a miss. They knew he was merely one of Santa's "helpers", having been all the way to Lapland the previous year to see the real thing – and eat reindeer burgers as well!

Suffice to say we were all feeling pleased with ourselves. As with any event like this, come 1.00 pm, it was down to the usual suspects to clear away; me; Councillors Gerry McLister, Yvonne Woodcock, Glynn Jones, his wife Diane and

Irene Raw; and the civic office staff.

Aidan had graced us with his presence earlier in the day along with his wife Maria and their two children. But they stayed for just 15 minutes, before they had to leave for 'another engagement'.

Gerry McLister had gained a lot of cross party respect for the manner in which he had conducted himself recently, voting against the Whip on a retirement homes closure issue as a matter of conscience, some six months before. He was suspended from the Labour Group for doing so.

Gerry was carrying some chairs to the side of the ballroom when he spoke to me in his strong Belfast accent: *"Are you enjoying yourself Martin?"*

"I always do at this event, Gerry – are you?"

"No... I'm fucking sick of these corrupt bastards... and not a one of them is here this morning".

I just looked at him with a face of resignation – words failed me.

"They've fucked you off as well... haven't they Martin?"

"I don't know what you mean Gerry" I told him quite genuinely.

"Aidan tells me your standing down... is that true Martin?"

"Well I'll not show him a bird's nest then," I responded.

"Who?"

"Aidan – It's supposed to be a secret" and I muttered something about the difficulties of balancing my many conflicting interests.

"It's a sad day Martin... it's a sad day Martin because I had hope... with you and me" he stopped himself mid-sentence.

"Come on – let's you and me show those bastards... let's fucking teach them a lesson... let's take the fucking thing over and remove Colin Wedd, as Leader? Come on Martin – you and me – we can do it. What do you say?"

But I was resigned to leaving. *"Nah... they've fucking done me Gerry and it's not very often I throw the towel in".*

Then, conscious Gerry wore his heart on his sleeve, I found myself advising him to beware of Aidan *"You need to be careful what you say to Aidan... Gerry. Y'know he's trying to get close to Colin".*

"I do. He'll get dragged in to it, so he will. They'll pull him in – the stupid bastard. They'll see he's weak and set him up, so they will".

"I don't know – I just think you should be careful" I warned.

"You know he's never seen in his Ward." added Gerry. *"He's known as The Tourist in Conisbrough because, when they do see him, they ask him if he's there on holiday!"*

I laughed; partly because it was funny and partly because I was glad that soon I wouldn't have to deal with such bitchiness.

I made my excuses and left to have lunch with my children.

Monday January 22nd 2001...

Former councillor Jean Elwick is found guilty of falsely claiming expenses. She lost her seat, in the May 1998 elections to Margaret Pinkney, former Labour Party member and anti-Donnygate campaigner.

ooo

Monday February 5th 2001...

Ex-Deputy Leader Michael Farrington is found guilty. He is given a two-month sentence, suspended for a year for claiming two extra nights' hotel accommodation valued at £137.60.

Farrington is not disqualified from holding public office because of the length of sentence and takes his seat as an Independent, bringing their total to nine.

ooo

March 2001...

Chief Whip Danny Buckley is found guilty and given a two month sentence, suspended for a year.
    Although having been found guilty, Danny is not disqualified from holding public office because of the length of his sentence. Danny takes his seat as an Independent, bringing their total to ten.
    He and Councillors Judge, Farrington and McAteer operate as a *de facto* Labour Group.

ooo

Wednesday April 18th 2001...

2.25 pm – The Labour Group Office, Mansion House

Nineteen Labour, or former Labour, councillors have now been found guilty.
    Gerry McLister decides enough is enough and is nominated as a candidate for the leadership of the Labour Group at its AGM on May 1st. He is proposed by Councillor Ted Kitchen and seconded by Councillor David Hughes.

> **NOMINATIONS FOR OFFICERS OF THE LABOUR GROUP**
>
> **LEADER** Gerard McLister PROPOSED BY :- E Kitchen
> SECONDED BY :- D Hughes
>
> **DEPUTY LEADER** PROPOSED BY :-
> SECONDED BY :-
>
> **CHAIR** PROPOSED BY :-
> SECONDED BY :-
>
> **VICE CHAIR** PROPOSED BY :-
> SECONDED BY :-
>
> **SECRETARY** PROPOSED BY :-
> SECONDED BY :-
>
> **CHIEF WHIP** PROPOSED BY :-
> SECONDED BY :-
>
> Closing date for nominations 5 p.m. 18th April 2001.

By now the Labour Group has declined to just 36 members and Gerry is talking up a very good game. He claims he has already identified eighteen supporters and, as such, he's home and dry – Colin is history.

Interestingly Gerry never asked me if he had my support. You always know who your definitive supporters are, as opposed to the so-called 'floaters', so I wasn't overly concerned.

But I considered Gerry to be a man who dealt in certainties and I worried that he didn't appear to be covering some of the bases. Nonetheless, the media was having a ball with the story of the maverick free-thinker who was challenging the establishment.

Challenge to council's Labour leader

EXCLUSIVE
Rob Waugh

THE leader of scandal-hit Doncaster Council is to face a leadership challenge which could result in a radical power shift away from Labour's "old guard."

Gerard McLister threw down the gauntlet to current leader Colin Wedd last night and said both the Labour Party and Doncaster needed a fresh start after years of suffering from a reputation tarnished by the "Donnygate" saga.

In a statement, Coun McLister said: "I've been approached by a number of Labour councillors to stand as a candidate in a forthcoming leadership race.

"It's time for a fresh start, a new beginning. The past four years have been painful, embarrassing and not as productive as they should have been. It's now time to move on.

"I appeal to all sections of the Labour Party to support me – in particular I appeal to those new Labour councillors elected after 1980. We have to take the reins of leadership and move our party forward."

The move follows recent disquiet in Labour ranks over Coun Wedd's leadership. Concern over his handling of revelations surrounding the council's links with the controversial Yorkshire Compensation Recovery Service was followed by his decision to spend four days in Pisa, Italy, where he took in a day at the local racecourse.

About £600 of public money was put aside to pay for the trip to Pisa, but after bad publicity it was announced that Coun Wedd's Italian hosts would fund the visit, except the air fare. Coun Wedd made the trip last month, saying he was promoting Doncaster and its plans to revamp the town's racecourse.

He has yet to report back to any council committee on the results of the visit.

But Coun McLister's challenge is aimed at more than the leader's performance in office, and he clearly hopes to strike a chord with those in the party who want a clean break with the past.

Under the spotlight: Gerard McLister, far left, who is mounting a challenge to Doncaster Council leader Colin Wedd, left.

His statement added: "There are three key challenges ahead. We need to deal with our recent history and then begin the process of severing the links with this humiliating and sterile experience.

"Secondly, we need to rebuild the confidence of voters in the Labour Party by creating an administration that is more transparent and open and includes more of the talents of the new generation of councillors.

"And thirdly, we need to raise the reputation of the borough of Doncaster as a whole."

The Labour group of councillors will vote on the leadership on April 25.

Coun Wedd is on holiday, and was unavailable for comment last night.

Friday April 20th 2001...

9.30 am

It's another beautiful morning. I'm driving to Sykehouse for a planning committee visit into a housing application on the site of the former "Three Horse Shoes" public house.

I'm listening to Michael Franti on my music system, singing at the top of my voice to Water Pistol Man – a song about HIV awareness. The phone rings and I look down at the Caller ID, it's Kevin Hughes. I'm not disturbing Franti for Kev, I'll ring him back. I turn the music up. And Kev rings off.

Thirty seconds later the phone rings again. Caller ID says it's Kevin Hughes. "Fuck him" I think. The phone rings again – something must be important. I turn Franti off...

"*Hiya Kev – how are you this fine and wondrous morning?*"
"*Cut the crap Martin – have you heard the news today?*"
"*Clearly not – what news?*"
"*Colin Wedd's been arrested*".
"*Fucking hell*".
"*Fucking hell – it couldn't have happened to nicer man... not*".
"*I bet Gerry's sitting pretty – I fancied he was going to twat Colin as well.. ... what's he been lifted for?*"
"*It just says on the news that he's been "taken in for questioning" by South Yorkshire Police as part of its "Operation Danum" investigation*".
"*Bingo! Clever bastard; has he resigned?*" I uttered in quick succession.
"*Not yet – but he'll have to – all the others have*".
"*What's that? Three or four Leaders lifted now?*"
"*Three I think – Welch, Glover and now Colin – where are you?*" Kevin asked.

"*I'm just on a site visit in Sykehouse – the old Three Horse Shoes site – there's a load of your constituents attending to let us know the strength of feeling against the houses being built*".

"*Miserable bastards...*" said Kev "*... they all want it as a pub now – but they didn't drink there when it was a pub, that's why he sold it for development – he couldn't make it pay as a pub*".

"*To be quite honest Kev, I don't give a shit, they don't fucking vote for us anyway in Fishlake and Sykehouse!*" I said remembering the 14 paltry votes I got in the Fishlake box.

"*Well not for me anyway*" I clarified "*I suppose they still love you for delivering their mains drainage?*"

"Nah... they don't vote for me either – miserable bastards!" he responded.

"Fucking hell – old Colin lifted eh? Old fucking Colin... I'll meet you for coffee at yours if you want, about half eleven?"

"Can't do Martin – I've got a surgery in Thorne 'til twelve – what about yours at quarter past?"

"See you there then Kev' – who do you fancy as new Leader now then – Gerry?" I asked.

"It's a whole different ball game now. All bets are off. They'll have to re-run it – what about you?"

"Surely they'll declare a walkover to Gerry" I answered naïvely.

"Nah – this is Labour Party politics. It's not that simple. They'll have to reopen the nominations again – what about you?"

"I think I'll stay with Gerry – he and I get on"

"WHAT – ABOUT – YOU..." he enunciated "You thick bastard..."

"Oh... sorry..." he took me by surprise. I genuinely thought he was asking my opinion."

"Well I... er..." I was fumbling for an answer.

"Gerry's too much of a maverick, Martin. He won't be able to take the Group with him"

"Yes but... I think there needs to be a certain amount of loyalty here Kev – anyway I was supposed to be standing down"

"Yeah but that's bollocks now Martin – you can take over the whole fucking shooting match here"

"Yes but I think I should stay with Gerry..."

"That's why you and I need to have a chat Martin – I'll see you at yours at 12.15?"

ooo

9.55 am

"Carolyne – can I come and have a chat and a bite of lunch with you today – say 2 o'clock?"

"That's very precise – is something up?"

"Colin Wedd's been arrested... and I need to talk to you about it"

"What about?"

"Well that's why I want to come and have lunch with you"

"Well you've got to give me more than that, so I can be thinking about it"

"Well okay I'm thinking about throwing me hat in – and we need to have a chat about it"

"Why – has he resigned?"
"Not yet but it's inevitable"
"Okay – I'll see you about 2 o'clock in The Point Café"

ooo

9.58 am

Voice mail left on Aidan's phone: *"Aidan, it's Martin – fucking hell, Colin's been lifted – give us a bell when you get chance"*

ooo

10.00 am

As I arrived for the site visit, there was a fairly large deputation from the local community; approximately twenty individuals and then representatives from the applicant and a dozen or so planning officers and others.

Central to this throng was Brain Barnes. I took him to one side and told him about Colin's arrest and the fact that he will probably have to stand down.

"Are you going to stand Martin?" asked Brian.

"Well er... I don't think so".

"Well you ought to" he said. *"And don't forget you've got all those SAGA supporters."*

"Well – since you put it like that Brian..."

ooo

10.35 am

"Mum – can I come and have a chat with you and BJ later on?"

"Yes – is anything wrong?"

"No – not particularly, I could do with having a chat with you about work and stuff and I need your advice"

"Okay then. I'll see you about tea time – do you want some tea?"

"It's okay thanks. Carolyne and I are going to a concert"

ooo

11.30 am

A text from Kevin: *"It's official – he's just announced he's stepping down as Leader"*
    I reply: *"The bent bastard – he's done it then!"* [see footnote].

ooo

12.15 pm

Kevin arrives at my house, almost to the minute.
    I've been thinking long and hard about what he had to say. I've thought of practically nothing else all morning and I like the idea – I like it a lot.
    But I also think Kevin is pretty desperate. He wants the "Leader" to be back in his constituency, so he can control it again.
    Do I want Kevin telling me what to do all the time? Thinking he can control me? Ranting at me when he can't control me? Can I control Kev?
    He comes in and we go into our kitchen.
    "Do you want a coffee Kev?"
    "Aye... make it strong though will you?" "Am I alright with this here?" he asks, taking out his first cigarette and unbolting the top half of the stable door, as he speaks. He knows he is; he's done it a thousand times and he knows he doesn't need a response from me.
    Kevin smokes heavily, and has a peculiar way of holding his cigarette between his thumb and index finger when he's thinking deeply.
    He draws heavily on the cigarette, and then looks up at me as he exhales. *"We need to draw a proper line in the sand this time Martin"*
    "You're telling me... we need to draw a line" I respond, holding my hand out for a cigarette.
    "Fucking hell..." he says *"... you have that many fags off me... that I'm gonna put you on my tax return"*. I've heard it a hundred times, it's one of his standard disparaging lines – we're both good at them – and we both laugh politely.
    "We can't go through this again Kevin – they'll force an administration on us" I say.
    "Well we certainly can't risk another fucking idiot getting it again".
    By this time, Kevin was in the Whip's Office, and I thought I would have some fun negotiating with him:
    "I don't particularly want it though Kev. I've seen all the fucking idiots behaving like morons during the last two years – Do you think I want some more of that?"

"Yeah but you can't resist it Martin – you fucking love it".

"... but it's a right mess Kev"

"Yeah but you can sort it out Martin. You – can – kick – their – arses – Martin" he enunciated, to underline his point, I always thought it just made him sound stupid.

"And, what's more, the Party will be forever in your debt for doing it".

"I suppose so – but is that what the Party wants?"

[Pregnant pause]

"Because, if that's what the Party wants, then you can get TB to ring me and have a chat with me about it"

"Look Martin, he's not gonna do that is he?"

"If it's so important..."

"Yeah but it isn't... Well, it is important – he wants it sorted – but it's only that important after it's been sorted. And anyway he's fallen for that one once before... when I convinced him to get off the train at Donny for a photo call. They've got it on the wall in the Star's offices – front page it was – Donnygate's Over Hails Blair in Trip to Town... or something like that... Two weeks later Glover got lifted!"

"Fair point I suppose," I say. "Are you telling me that that's what you want me to do... because if you are, well I'll do it – I can do it!" I declared. "But I'm telling you now, there'll be blood everywhere".

"That's what it needs Martin – that's what it's needed for some time. And, if that's what is needed Martin..." he paused to take another drag of his cigarette "... then JFD it"

"What... what the fuck does that mean?"

"JFD it... Just – Fucking – Do – It" he enunciated.

"Fucking hell... I've heard 'em all now... JFD it" and I had to think fast.

"What if I... DFW... T... D... I?" I said falteringly.

"Eh?"

"Don't Fucking Want To Do It" I explained smugly.

He looked up at me, then at his cigarette and spoke in a laboured manner as he breathed out the smoke. "It needs you to sort it out Martin"

He nodded the packet towards me. I declined. You're a creature of habit you are Kev, I thought, you shouldn't play poker.

"It needs you to sort it out" he reiterated; "You're the only one strong enough to do it".

"Oh that's a bit Blade Runner – Deckard" I said, referring to the Ridley Scott film and character.

"What?"

"Oh nothing – it'll get in the way"

Kevin kept going: *"Yeah but you can sort it out Martin. You – can – kick – shit... and the Party will be forever in your debt for doing it".*

"Okay... but what's in it for me then Kev?"

"What's in it for me?" He said exasperated *"You'll be the Leader of the fucking council – you might even be mayor, if you've got the bollocks to call the referendum"*

"It's not enough Kev" I said *"I'm not massively bothered about it. Particularly given what I've been through in the last couple of years"*

"If you want something from me – I might want something from you in return"

"... and you've asked me a lot about my plans, well what about your plans?" I went on.

"What about my plans?"

"I might want your seat, Kev? How long before you retire?"

"I'm not that fucking old – you bastard"

"I'm not saying you are but none of us is getting any younger"

"When am I fucking retiring..." he drew heavily on yet another cigarette *"... I'm only a few years in front of you... cheeky bastard"* he sneered under his breath, as he smiled at me.

"I'm just saying..." I defended myself. But he interrupted me *"When am I fucking retiring... fuck me"*

Then, almost jumping to attention, he added: *"We can talk about that Martin... and I certainly don't want to be doing this all my life – not like Lady Caroline* [Flint]*"*

"I just want to get me 20 years in and then I'm happy to retire".

I was feeling brave, quickly adding it up in my head *"That doesn't quite work Kev... it's still another eleven years away"*

"Yes but its only two or three terms – and I'm telling you Mart, if you sort this bag-o-shite out, the Party will owe you big time"

Kev knew I wasn't going to pass this one up, but I'd still got him to shift quite a bit, I thought, with regards to his own seat – unless he was playing me.

"We'll piss this kid – you and me" Kev said ominously.

"Well I hope we do Kev – but you're not going to be telling me what to do all the time are you?"

"No... will I bollocks... but you and me Martin. We'll make a great team – they won't know what's fucking hit 'em"

"I want Aidan as my Deputy" I said *"I can't do it without Aidan, as my Deputy"*

"Have you spoken to him?" *"No, not yet. I left him a message but he's not come back to me yet"*

"I don't know much about him – I've never met him"
"You will..." I said "... if we're going for it – and we are going for it – aren't we?"
"Yes I think so – well I know so!" said Kevin. "But it's got to be your call"
"Well I've got a lot to do, if we're going for it – not least convincing the liddle lady"
"Have you spoken to Carolyne yet? Because you won't be able to do it without her support"
"No. I'm going to see her for lunch, now we've finished"

1.30 pm

I text Aidan: *"Aidan – we need to talk urgently – Martin"*

ooo

2.00 pm – The Point Café.

I speak to Carolyne about the opportunity before us.
"It'll mean our life will change, as we know it" I say "There'll be no more nine-week summer holidays... and months spent in France"
"The Glass Park will have to chance it on its own" I say. "And we'll have to have a more defined 'traditional' division of labour. I'll work – it'll be long hours – and you'll have to look after the house and home!"
To her credit, Carolyne never really balked at the idea.
"You know me Martin" she says "That's why we work so well as a pair... If we're going to regret anything... let's regret the things we've done – because I don't want to regret the things we haven't done."
And that was it. I'd decided. We'd decided. We were going for it.
All I had to do now was persuade Aidan!

ooo

3.30 pm

On the telephone in my garden.
"Fucking hell Aidan – Colin Wedd's been arrested"
Aidan mumbles something about not knowing who you can trust and how he feels sorry for him *"There's a lot of people who can't see him doing it, to be*

honest" he says "and he's certainly gone down in my estimation, if he did do it"
"It doesn't really matter whether he did or didn't do it – he's out of the running now. You certainly know how to back winners, you do!"
"What do you mean?" he replied.
"Well you've certainly been cuddling up to him, with your thesis this and your thesis that, haven't you... you and your hoity toity posh northern ways"
"It was just something he'd asked me if he could have a look at" he replied "Y'know I think it's the old teacher in him"
"Well... you know what I think on that one... you had a lucky escape you did"
"Oh fuck off – do you fancy Gerry as Leader then?"
"Well it's a whole different ball game now. All bets are off. They'll have to re-run it now – won't they?" I say mimicking Kevin.
"Gerry'll get it by default won't he?"
"Nah... its Labour Party politics isn't it – they'll have to re-open the nominations again" I say, very sage-like.
"You've been talking to somebody haven't you?" He deduced "You haven't worked this all through by yourself. Who've you been talking to then?"
I didn't respond. Glad to know he thinks so highly of me, I thought – or knows me so well.
"I'll be staying with Gerry though; Ward colleague and all that" he said in a fatalistic and, almost dismissive manner.
"It's a pity you didn't think like that when Gerry went for Deputy Leader" I thought – but that's not for now...
"There is another model though Aidan"
"You have been talking to somebody! Who've you been talking to then?"
"I'm just saying – that there is another model – if we want one?"
"Go on then... oh great one... dazzle me with your thoughts..."
"You've got to take the piss haven't you"
"No I haven't... I just want to hear 'Chairman Mart's' thoughts"
"Well if you can contain yourself, Grasshopper, what about us doing it?"
This time it was Aidan's turn to go quiet.
"Can you remember when we had lunch at Pizza Hut that day...?"
"Our Granitas..." Aidan said solemnly.
"... And I told you that we'd have to be ready when the time comes – well it's here now, today, Aidan"
"But what about Gerry?" he said almost childlike.
"He's too much of a maverick" I mimicked again "... and, anyway, he won't be able to take the Group with him"
"Fucking hell – have you spoken to Gerry?"

"Have I fuck! I needed to talk to you first"

After a long pause… *"I can't do it without you Aidan... you're my old Blade Runner"* I added; acknowledging our shared cultural reference point.

"Fucking hell – have you spoken to anybody?"

"Have I bollocks!"

"Fucking hell – this is real isn't it?"

"It certainly is – have you spoken to anybody Aidan?"

"Only Chris"

"What does she think?"

"She's with Gerry"

"I'm with Gerry..." I say *"... but this is a different deal now. Gerry would've pissed it, just to get rid of Colin – but it's gonna be a straight competition for a new Leader now and he'll frighten people off".*

"Fucking hell – this is real isn't it?"

"Will you stop saying that! Look... have a think about it – and we can talk tomorrow. But for fuck's sake keep your fucking powder dry and don't say anything to anybody – not even Maria... and we'll see how the land lies after the weekend".

The Star
OPINION
Shockwaves will reach Westminster

BOMBSHELLS don't drop much bigger than the latest to explode in the Donnygate scandal - with the arrest of Doncaster Council's third Labour leader, Coun Colin Wedd.

The shockwaves have ripped through the Mansion House today and will no doubt cause more than a few ripples in Westminster.

Labour will wince over the impact this could cause so close to a General Election. Opposition parties will surely make a meal of it.

Coun Wedd has not been charged in connection with Donnygate or anything else. Let's make that clear from the start.

But his arrest, with him on police bail until April 30, is damaging enough to the party and to Doncaster Council. It means he faces automatic loss of the leadership and the authority is plunged further into crisis.

And not only is he the third successive Labour leader to become a casualty of the scandal, it is the SIXTIETH arrest by Operation Danum detectives.

That's one diamond landmark which takes away the sparkle from Doncaster Council's reassurances that Donnygate is well and truly in the past.

ooo

8.00 pm

I attend a concert at The Point Building of the wonderful Spanish guitarist and composer Eduardo Niebla but I can't concentrate on the music, preoccupied instead by the battle ahead and whether or not this will mark my last night of "freedom".

ooo

Footnote

The timing of the 'arrest' of Colin Wedd has always been an area of great confusion.

Wedd was interviewed by South Yorkshire Police over allegedly travelling Second Class on a trip to London and claiming expenses for travelling First.

He chose to stand down as soon as the police announced he was being interviewed which suggested he'd done something wrong. But although newspaper reports said he was arrested, Colin always argued that he was never actually arrested but agreed to answer questions under caution – which then begs the consequent question – so why stand down with immediate effect?

> **CPS drops Doncaster case over lack of evidence**
>
> Criminal proceedings against a former Doncaster Council Leader have been halted after the Crown Prosecution Service decided there was insufficient evidence to proceed.
>
> Colin Wedd, who resigned as leader in April following his arrest on alleged expenses fraud, had the case against him formally discontinued at Doncaster magistrates' court.
>
> Councillor Wedd faced two charges relating to alleged false claims for two first-class rail fares when, it was claimed, he actually paid standard fares. The difference was £155.
>
> A CPS spokesman said: "It was felt that there was not sufficient evidence to proceed in this case and therefore the decision was taken to call a halt."
>
> With a clean bill of health, Mr Wedd is expected to be given a senior role to play within the authority. As well as being Leader, he was also chair of the powerful racecourse committee, which he stood down from following his arrest.
>
> Two previous leaders, Malcolm Glover and Peter Welsh, were given suspended sentences for expenses fraud.
>
> Independent Newspaper – Wednesday 22 August 2001

Anyone who knew Colin Wedd will tell you he would never travel "second class", period. He was known as "Little Lord Fauntleroy" and people could rather see him doing it the other way round, up-grading to first class whilst claiming standard class!

He was never charged and the timing of the "arrest" has always given cause for concern. As a revolutionary leader, Gerry McLister had challenged Colin for the Leadership of the Labour Group and, had the election taken place, Gerry would have won to become the Leader of the Council.

Somebody made the decision that Gerry McLister could not, and would not, become the Leader of Doncaster Council; nobody will ever convince me otherwise. Colin Wedd was "arrested" less than two hours after the nominations had closed.

The resultant question is who, and for what purpose?

Was the "arrest" a ruse to halt the leadership challenge that would have seen Colin defeated and Gerry McLister become the Council Leader?

That question leads to another that forever dogged Donnygate; who was actually controlling the investigation and the timing of the arrests and to what end?

Three lines of thought exist:

The first is that South Yorkshire Police were in complete control of the process and singularly intent on destroying the Labour Party in Doncaster. They wanted to achieve this, so the story goes, as "payback" for the role the Ruling Mining Group played in the 1984-85 Miners Strike.

Certainly this viewpoint has a lot to support it, not least the stance taken by former Divisional Commander DCS Mick Burdis – Head of 'Operation Danum'.

Indeed, Detective Chief Supt Burdis allegedly blamed everything on the Labour Party, and in 2001 told the council's chief executive and six new executive directors that he was intent on taking out the majority of the Doncaster Labour Party.

A Guardian piece by Martin Wainwright [March 1999] famously fuelled this rumour:

Labouring to put the town halls in order

... Martin Wainwright has been in Doncaster, where the sleaze trials are far from over, wondering whether anything much will change until one-party statelets are abolished.

... it is precisely on this boundary that party discipline is most needed. *"There are some things that are criminal, and we can deal with them..."* <u>a South Yorkshire detective in the thick of Donnygate said</u> *"But there are some things, a lot of things, that are just wrong, and that's down to the Labour Party".*

Martin Wainwright – Wednesday 24 March 1999

The second school of thought is that The Freemasons were controlling the process.

The third view is that the National Labour Party was controlling the whole process in order to purge the Party of its detritus, in a similar manner to Neil Kinnock's expulsion of Militant in the mid-1980s.

Puppet meister or apparatchik

"You learn a lot when you're barefoot.
The first thing is every step you take is different"

Michael Franti

Saturday April 21st 2001...

8.00 am

I leave a telephone message for Aidan: *"It's a good job this isn't the Cuban Missile Crisis... give me a bell when you get chance – that's if I'm not disturbing you of course."*

ooo

9.30 am

"Hiyah – it's me Aidan."
 "Thanks for coming back to me so quickly."
 "I couldn't come back to you any earlier, I've got a Surgery this morning and I've been on my way to Conisbrough."
 "Via Cudworth?"
 "I've only just got your message through – I think there's something wrong with this phone..."

Aidan is a terrible liar and the transparency of his untruths never ceases to amaze me. He is always late for meetings and, in a Reginald Perrin kind of way, always comes up with some patently serious, though completely far-fetched attempt at an excuse.

 "Anyway... never mind your fucking phone's knackered. Have you thought about it?"
 "Yep – I've got a Surgery with Chris and Gerry at 10.00 – so I'll see how they're feeling about it after that"
 "Just remember – you need to be wary of Gerry becoming blind to his weaknesses at the moment. There's a big difference between voting for one person – to get rid of a twat – and voting for a twat because you want him to be your Leader..." I say.

"Why – do you think Gerry's a twat?"

"No – course I fucking don't. But some in the Group do – he scares them... and they might've voted for him to get rid of Colin – but it's gonna be a straight competition now and I'm telling you – he'll frighten people" I continue where I left off yesterday. "See if you get chance to test that one with him or Chris and give us a bell afterwards"

ooo

12.30 pm

"Hiyah – it's me Aidan"
    "How did it go?"
"Well it was really quiet, so I got chance to have a good chat with Chris and she suggested we meet up with Gerry afterwards"

And then, almost as if he's forgotten to tell me: "We split our Surgeries and Gerry was at the Ivanhoe Centre, so we met up with him in the car-park at the Gateway supermarket afterwards."

Aidan's a chronic dissembler – so I disregard the fact he told me this morning that all three were running a surgery together.

"How is he? What's he feeling?"

"Well he's really fucking angry. He thinks he's been stitched up by the Party. But you know what Gerry's like – everything's a conspiracy – and he thinks he should just become the Leader now Colin's dropped out"

"Well it is a conspiracy isn't it?" I say "We just don't know who's conspiring and who they're conspiring against! Does he acknowledge that he can't just become the Leader? That we can't just have a coronation and that we've got to have a competition?"

"Oh yeah – but he's talking about a legal challenge"

"That's not gonna get us anywhere – anyway he can't"

"Why?"

"Because it's a private club – and it has its own membership rules – which are set by the NEC... Does he acknowledge that he's fallible though?"

"Oh yes – he seems quite delicate, for Gerry. Have you spoken to him Martin?"

"No – I don't ring him all that often and he'll smell a rat if I suddenly ring him"

"But I think these are pretty unique circumstances..." says Aidan "...I think he'd appreciate it"

"Nah that's bollocks – especially if I become Leader – it's too soon and it'll damage our relationship later and Gerry is fundamental to us taking charge smoothly... we've got to find a way for Gerry to think this is his idea."

"Yes but he isn't gonna do that – I've already told you he's really fucking angry... have you spoken to anyone else Martin?"

"Only Liz, this morning."

Like me, Liz Jeffress is from a long-standing Kirk Sandall family. A retired school teacher, she joined the Parish Council in the early 80s and was elected to DMBC in 2000. She has known my parents for years and is already both a close friend of mine and a surrogate grandma to my kids. A passionate, fiery woman, she can also swear like a trooper...

"What does she think?"

"She just says Government will think that we're all fucking bent and that having an Administration forced on us is inevitable – she'll have been talking to Mullany though."

"What do you think?" he asks.

"I think they're not far wrong. This is three consecutive Leaders that have been arrested now and we're a fucking laughing stock. Doncaster's known as the benchmark in fraud and corruption in local government and, to be quite honest, we'll get what we deserve because no bastard's got the bollocks to take them on"

Aidan: "Do we have a time scale yet?"

"No – other than the AGM's next Monday night and we don't have a District Labour Party, so I expect Region will come in; Nan [Sloane] will tell us we're all crooks and useless and this is the process. In fact I'll give her a call this afternoon. We could do with getting her take on it and talking us up as the "Dream Team" unification model... see if you can get Gerry to acknowledge that he's gonna struggle now and that we need a unification candidate" I close.

ooo

1.15 pm

John Mounsey rings me.

Sunderland-born Mounsey originally headed south to work the 'easier' coalfields of the Midlands. A huge soccer fan and hopeless romantic, he famously combined his two loves and proposed to one of his previous wives on the Doncaster Rover's football pitch at half time!

After a short interchange, John asks me if I'm going to stand.

"It's not as simple as that, John".

"It is Martin – you either are, or you aren't".

"You know me John... I'm supposed to be standing down. It'd be pretty

147

hypocritical for me to then stand to become Leader wouldn't it?"

"There's quite a bit of support for you" he says "Including from Ted – and he nominated Gerry!"

"But I'm nothing, if I'm not loyal," I say, marvelling at the speed by which Ted changed horses.

"And we've got to get it right this time...or we'll be facing an Administration".

"Well just think about it man... there's a lot wanting you to do it," John finishes.

ooo

2.00 pm

Following on from John's phone call, I start covering some bases to see who my banker votes will be. I figure out I can rely on a good fourteen already with more if I work it.

I ring Aidan to tell him.

"I'll feed it in to Gerry," he says.

ooo

2.30 pm

"Thanks for coming back to me Nan. I wanted to have a chat with you about the AGM process for next Monday now Colin's been arrested..."

"Yes... you're in a bit of pickle, over there, aren't you?"

"Certainly are... and now Gerry's talking about legal challenges if he doesn't have a coronation."

"Look, I've told Gerry... I spoke to him yesterday, and we went through all this. What Gerry needs to know..." she begins to instruct me "... is that Gerry won't be having a coronation and Gerry McLister will not be becoming the Labour group leader...

[pregnant pause]

... unless he is voted as the group leader by the majority of the Labour group... and preferably by a significant majority of the group – because we don't want a split group again, do we?" she patronises.

"Well I think the group's split regardless... but nothing's new..." I'm alluding to the tribal nature of Doncaster's on-going problems *"Do you know what the process will be?"*

"Well... we're actually having a meeting about this tomorrow, and we shall be notifying you accordingly and through the group's secretary."

"But basically, you will be opening the panel for nominations again... for an election next Monday night... and it will be a secret ballot..."

"It will be a secret ballot – as per Labour Party rules – did you hear that Martin? <u>And I will be attending!</u>" she finishes her lecture.

"When you say open the panel again... is that the full panel or just for the leadership position?"

"Well that's one of the reasons we're meeting tomorrow – but I think the full panel – because everything's changed. But we will expect, whoever is placed on that panel, to be absolutely clean as a whistle, because we are not going through this again."

"That's exactly what I've been saying to Aidan," I tell her "I wouldn't be surprised if we have an administration forced on us by Government"

"Well I don't know about that... but we were told with both Malcolm Glover, and now Colin, that it won't happen again – but there appears to be just something in the water in Doncaster... doesn't there Martin?"

ooo

5.00 pm

"Hiyah Aidan it's me – I've just had a really interesting conversation with Nan."

"Why – what did she say?"

"Well firstly, that there is going to be an election; that we're keeping to the same timescale; and thirdly, it looks as if the whole panel will be opened again."

"Well we knew all that..."

"Yes – but what she also said... [or rather didn't say]... was that Gerry won't be the Leader of the Council."

"What?"

"I think the Party had something to do with Colin's arrest"

"What! – you can't go around saying that."

"Well you give me another story then? Because I bet Colin thinks that; and you know Gerry thinks that!"

"Well I can't."

"Exactly... I'm telling you – Gerry frightens them and they're not keen on him being in charge – and I worry they had something to do with Colin being lifted. I think somebody's told 'em to have a look at what's happening in Donny because they're gonna elect a revolutionary to get rid of a fucking idiot... and they've panicked."

"*So much for fucking democracy then,*" says Aidan

"*Don't get me wrong – she didn't say it...*" I respond "*... but it was the way she didn't say it, that "said it" – if you get my drift.*"

"*Fucking dead right... Nan's been around for too long and she's gonna want to make sure we make the right choice this time.*"

"*Exactly*" I underline.

"*Did you tell her you're going for it?*"

"*No – did I fuck! But she's a cute cookie, Nan. She knows we're up to something – and I think she'd be pulling for us if she could... and that's why she came back to us so quickly*"

"*Do you think so?*"

"*Dead right I do... you know how difficult she is to get hold of on a weekend – and that's why we're the "Dream Team" – where else can she go? She... the Party... has a choice... do they go with the "old guard", in which case we'll be in the same situation in less than a year because you can't trust any of 'em.... and then the Party is well and truly fucked! Or do they go with the young guns and draw a real line in the sand? It's that black and white this one Aidan – it's young versus old! Reformers versus dinosaurs, isn't it?*"

"*Besides I told her enough for her to realise you're with me, because she likes you doesn't she?*"

Without realising it, I've opened the door for Aidan to regale me with yet another tale of his great intelligence... "*Ken Knight told me that when they interviewed me for the panel... Colin lent across to Nan and said "gold dust" to her.*"

"*Well it's yin and yang then mate – cos I failed my interview and had to appeal! Anyway... if we can get you, me and Gerry – bingo! That's why we're the dream team*"

"*Well... I think Gerry might be moving – he rang me about an hour ago,*" says Aidan.

"*In what way is he moving?*"

"*Well he's still very angry... but he acknowledged he might not get as much support now, depending on who they come up with as a candidate*"

"*Do we know who it might be yet?*"

"*Well rumour has it they can't get one. Bev's said it won't be him and Martin Hepworth won't do it either – so they're struggling*"

"*Which is why we've got to get Gerry not to blow it – we've got 'em running here but if we put the wrong candidate forward, they'll unite against him. I think I should speak to him...*"

"*Fucking hell – you ruled that out this morning!*"

"*Yeah but it's changing fast – and we need to make sure we're all singing off the same hymn sheet."*

ooo

Sunday April 22nd 2001...

10.00 am

"Hiyah Aidan it's me"
"Have you spoken to Gerry?"
"Yeah, just now – I had a coffee with him this morning – he's adamant he's standing,"
I sigh loudly.
"Well – you know Gerry..." says Aidan.
"Yeah but, if we both stand, it'll split the vote and they'll walk it – he must realise that?"
"Well, you know Gerry, Martin," he repeats. "He's incredibly principled... and sometimes he just thinks he's got to do something – regardless of the cost to him or others."
"I've spoken to Mounsey, who's been talking to Ted Kitchen... and Gerry seems to think he's lost you and Chris..." I say – but Aidan doesn't respond, which worries me – is he playing me here?
"Have you met up with Caroline?" I ask to change the subject slightly.
"Yeah – yesterday morning – we always meet up with her after her surgeries."
I feel slightly nervous, Aidan hasn't been telling me the whole story again, he's unbelievably evasive when he's lying – but sometimes it's best to just go with the flow, move with the general direction, rather than get hung up with the detail.
"What's her view?" I ask.
"She's keeping out of it."
Caroline never keeps out of anything, which makes me nervous again. "Has she said anything about Gerry?"
"You know Flinty, Martin... she can do the leader's job in her sleep, stood on her head, blindfolded; so whoever gets it will be a big disappointment to her."
"Does she know we're going for it?" I ask.
"No"
"Well let's keep it that way – for as long as we can... unless... can she deliver anything for us?"
"She's despised in her constituency, Martin." Then, delighting in his South Yorkshire mimicry:

"She can deliver us nowt."

ooo

Aidan isn't being truthful and there is too much confusion, for my liking, about what is being said and by whom. I/we need to be dealing with certainties and as difficult as it will be, I need to speak to Gerry – and preferably with Aidan and Chris present – so we are all clear where we are coming from.

I have massive respect for Gerry but the simple fact is that the thought of him becoming leader is being discouraged by many; there's a rumour now that a delegation of the 'Old Guard' went to the Labour Party Regional Office in Wakefield yesterday, threatening rebellion if Gerry becomes leader!

Nonetheless, I don't want Gerry to think I'm part of this – so I ask Aidan to get hold of Gerry and see if he, Aidan, Chris and I can all meet up.

ooo

1.30 pm

"Hiyah Aidan it's me"
   "Have you spoken to Gerry?"
   "Yeah – it's taken me ages but I've tracked him down – we're meeting him at 4.00 in 'The Cecil' car park"
   "Excellent – is Chris coming?"
   "Yes."
   "Brilliant – I'll meet you there at 3.30 then, so we can go through the choreography"

ooo

3.30 pm – 'The Cecil' [Public House] car park, Warmsworth

I've been waiting about fifteen minutes, when Aidan rolls up followed by Chris Mills and her husband John – Chair of the Conisbrough & Denaby Ward Labour Party.

All three sit in the back seat of my car and we discuss the emerging situation and, most importantly, how Chris and John think Gerry is responding to the speed at which events are overtaking themselves.

I leave the front seat empty for Gerry.

4.00 pm – 'The Cecil' [Public House] car park, Warmsworth

When Gerry arrives I open my door, shake hands with him and thank him for joining us.

As he sits in the car, the atmosphere is strained.

I explain the situation to him as I and others are beginning to see it; that Gerry is single handedly responsible for the insurgency campaign and that it has succeeded. But that we are in danger of snatching defeat from the jaws of victory.

I explain how we can't risk losing the leadership and that I am standing for leader – but want to do it with Gerry's support, not opposition.

"And I'm going for deputy as well," pipes in Aidan, which is a little previous, I think!

He looks directly at me – staring deep into my eyes – he doesn't appear angry but you never can tell with Gerry.

I explain again my thought process and that I see the three of us being the "Dream Team", the unification model that can't, nay won't be stopped... and Gerry may struggle now but we need a unification candidate, rather than a rebel leader.

Gerry doesn't seem to be buying it– and why should he? To all intents and purposes I've just pissed all over his bonfire and I have to respect that.

I draw the discussion to a close, telling Gerry I think it's really important that we all know where we're coming from because we all want the same thing – to get rid of the corruption of the past.

Gerry says he'll think about the "offer" and we agree I will call him to discuss it further in an hour's time.

ooo

4.20 pm

After he leaves we agree it was a difficult meeting but that Gerry has handled it, and himself, impeccably.

ooo

5.30 pm

"Hiyah Gerry it's me Martin – how are you feeling?"

"Well not happy, Martin." His Belfast accent is now much softer, more thoughtful... *"You see, Colin's horse fell after the race had started – and in any*

other arena, that would make me the winner"

"True Gerry – but we're not playing by the Marquess of Queensberry rules are we?" I mix our metaphors.

"What do you mean Martin?"

"Well we're members of a private club aren't we? And it's called "The Labour Party club" isn't it?" I patronise him *"And they can have whatever rules they like – and it's not for us to say whether we can abide them or not"*

"Well maybe we can't, Martin"

"Straws break camels' backs Gerry... but I sense this isn't the straw that'll break you..."

"It's a fucking big straw Martin..."

"You're a principled man Gerry... but I don't think that even you, in your heart Gerry, thought for one moment they were gonna simply gift it to you..."

"That's not the point Martin... Wedd may have been removed... to stop me."

"I think your right Gerry... but that begs the question of who's actually running this investigation or this council, for that matter... but we need to look for that answer in the future because we won't get it answered now." I'm on a roll...

"We've got to concentrate on doing what we need to do now... to make sure we complete the takeover Gerry... otherwise we'll blow it."

"You're right Martin... but the simple fact is that Colin Wedd was removed by somebody to stop me."

"You're right Gerry... so what else would they do?" I insinuate that "they" will sink to any depth.

"I'd like to see them try... because they'll bite off more than they can chew, if they try to set me up," Gerry's tone is menacing.

But I can also hear the realisation in his voice; that as much as he detests him, Colin might have been 'set up' to block Gerry. After all, it's much easier to smear the man who is "in charge" at a time when practically everyone is being arrested for fraud, rather than a man who by most people's yard stick is morally, and ethically bullet-proof.

Gerry changes tack.

"So you're standing Martin?"

"I am Gerry – but it shouldn't be as simple as that"

"Well it is Martin – and you are," he sighs with an air of resignation tinged with anger.

"You know me Gerry... I wanted to support you... and I would've done... but there's something else at play here... and we don't know who or what it is."

"I'm also worried that those who would support you to rebel against Colin... might not support you to become the leader when they have a less stark choice – and it'll mean we lose the takeover [we both want]"

"There's quite a bit of support for you," Gerry says suddenly, turning the tables on me.

"But I'm nothing, if I'm not loyal Gerry," I restate what I've told Mounsey... but this time I'm thinking of Aidan protesting his loyalty at Pizza Hut.... "And we've got to get it right this time... or we'll be facing an administration."

"Well we might be having that anyway..." says Gerry.

"And I suspect Flint has been interfering as well [which will probably make it worse]" I add.

"... and that's because you're a threat to her." I'm massaging his ego... but it's true:

Everybody was a threat to "Lady Caroline", as Kevin referred to her, not least Gerry.

"But your still standing against me," he reminds me, in his straight-talking Belfast way.

"It's not that black and white Gerry... I wish I wasn't – I really do. I want to support you Gerry – but I'm worried we could lose, because you frighten people. Not me... but you do frighten some people... and then we both lose"

"If I stand... and you stand... we split the "Reformer's" vote – and we both lose."

"If you stand down – and I stand... I'll win because I'll corner the "Reformer's" vote – but you and I will both lose Gerry, because we're principled"

"I won't lose..." said Gerry "... because I will have only acted honourably," he's taunting me...

"... and I am standing..." he says defiantly, his Belfast accent becoming harsh again...

"But what you do is up to you, Martin."

I decide to leave it there for a while and we agree to keep talking to each other.

ooo

Monday April 23rd 2001...

8.30 am

"Martin, its Aidan – they've announced the Panel is open again"

"How do you know?"

"I've just seen Bev Marshall this morning and he told me."

"That means they think you're quite key," I say.

"Nah I just got in early for Corporate Services; they'd all been in early and *were fussing about and looking important"*

"But you're NEVER in early Aidan."

"I am when I have a reason to... and I wanted to know what was happening"

"You're not going to double-deal me are you Aidan?" I demand *"Because I'm solid with you and have been throughout; this is a partnership Aidan."*

"Do you fucking realise how insulting you're being," he shouts *"I fucking told you before. I am incredibly loyal and it's really important you understand that."*

"Of course you are. But remember our discussion at Pizza Hut? I know you'll let me down at some point in the future – I just hope this isn't that time."

"Stop being so fucking paranoid Martin; I don't think you'll ever understand my motivations," he continues. "Anyway, Region has instructed them to open the 'Full Panel' again for new nominations."

"The Full Panel eh? That will allow us to put forward a full slate." I completely ignore that this is against Labour Party rules.

"The Panel is open starting at 9.00 this morning and closing at 4.00 on Friday, for an election next Monday night."

"What else did he say?"

"Nothing really, you know Bev he's a real operator. He just warmed me up a little in terms of the importance of the vote."

"Is he standing?"

"He didn't say. But I get the general idea that he's not"...

ooo

11.30 am

"Martin, its Aidan – they've announced John Wain is standing."

"How do you know?"

"Martin Hepworth's just told me. And before you ask, I saw him at the end of the Corporate Services meeting."

"Well why didn't Bev tell you this morning?"

"I bet they didn't know; but there was a lot of coming and going during Corporate Services."

"What do you think?"

"Well he's really old-school – but a clever candidate because he was a councillor until 1999 but then lost his seat to Paul Coddington [Lib-Dem] and got re-elected again last year."

"So he won't be tainted then," I interrupt.

"Exactly – he's worked with them all before, so it really is young 'uns versus old 'uns – but he's a real fucking dinosaur."

"He fucking hates me," I say.

"Nah – he fucking hates everybody," Aidan replies. "He's like a bulldog chewing a wasp." "Actually – that could play to our advantage. It'll polarise opinions."

"Dead right. It's ideal – particularly if we can get Gerry to stand down."

"Did you let him know how many "definites" we've got?" I ask.

"No – he was having a downer about how he'd been shafted by everybody and I thought it would be rubbing salt in."

"Is he standing?"

"I haven't spoken to him today... but you know Gerry"

ooo

2.30 pm

"Martin, its John Hardy."

John claims to have once been a session drummer, playing with, among others, Australian band Python Lee Jackson on Rod Stewart's 1972 top ten hit "In a Broken Dream". He isn't in good health having suffered with polio as a child and scoliosis as an adult; but he's a genial man and, as it turns out, fiercely loyal to me. He also fancies himself as a smart political operator – which he isn't.

"Hiyah John – how's things?"

"Oh er... good, thanks mate," he stumbles. "Martin... can I ask you a question?"

"Fire away John"

"Martin, are you planning to stand for the group leader's position?"

"I'm not planning to John – there's a few who'd like me to but at the moment I'm thinking no," I lie.

"Have you seen they've put John Wain forward?"

"Yes – it's certainly gonna split the Group – it'll be like playing cops and robbers when we were kids."

"Well I've had a meeting today with my ward colleagues, Martin, and we think you're infinitely qualified to do the job and we think we're best backing you and that you'll do the best for Doncaster and Askern – if you'll stand that is."

"Well thanks for the vote of confidence John, I'll certainly think about it – but do you think there are any others who would support me?"

"Oh I know there are Martin – everyone I speak to thinks it's a good idea. Let me do some ringing around."

"Be careful though John – I don't want to piss Gerry off and we don't want

them to get wind of what we're doing"
"*Do I fucking look stupid?*"
"*Only saying*"
"*Thanks a fucking lot mate!*"

ooo

Tuesday April 24th 2001…

5.30 pm

"*Martin, its John Hardy*"
"*Hiyah John – how's it going?*"
"*Well there's an awful lot of support for you out there Martin, the only problem is Gerry McLister. With Gerry having thrown his hat in originally, there's quite a bit of sympathy for him and nobody knows what he's doing now. Having said that, he frightens one or two and they would prefer to support you of course.*"
"*Well that's good to know…*" And John cut across me.
"*So I make it you've got fifteen, at the moment, Martin mate … and you need eighteen.*"
"*Excellent John, as I was saying, that's good to know… but this Gerry thing is going to become a problem though.*"
"*It is Martin. I'll tell you what one or two of them are suggesting*"
"*What's that John?*"
"*Well they want to see the support you've got and they're suggesting we get together to have a meeting to discuss tactics…*"
"*They want us to hold a caucus John?*"
"*Well I wouldn't go as far as that.*"
"*Well I would John, and I'm sure the Labour Party would as well, which is all that matters.*"
"*No… No… they just want to see the support you've got and to discuss tactics…*"
"*That's a caucus John; they're not only illegal in terms of the Labour Party's rules but you're suggesting we have an illegal political meeting, at which we show our hand, as near as damn it, and discuss our tactics as well.*"
"*It sounds to me as if we're being set up here,*" I go on. "*And we're fucked if they put in any infiltrators!*"
"*No… I don't think we're being set up at all Martin. It's simply that people are worried about what'll happen to the Party and they want to make sure they get it right?*"

"Ah well... if you're talking about holding a crisis meeting, to discuss what we do because of the emergency that we're in – well that's a different situation John... we just need to be careful what's said."

"Like I said..." says John "... we need to hold a crisis meeting, to discuss the situation we're in... ... I'll get Gerry to come as well," he enthuses.

"You can't do that... it's a bit insensitive"

"Is it bollocks insensitive; we need to know what's going on and Gerry's got to be there. It'd be more insensitive to not invite him."

So John takes it upon himself to organise an emergency meeting to discuss the leadership crisis.

ooo

Wednesday April 25th 2001...

7.30 pm

A text from Kevin:	"How's it going bro'?"
I respond:	"It's going – can I call you?"
Kevin:	"We're in the division at the moment and Lady Caroline just asked me what's going on. I'll ring you later – about half ten."

ooo

9.30 pm

A text from John Hardy:	"Emergency meeting to discuss the leadership crisis 7.30 pm tomorrow night – Thursday 26th April, Alexandra House, Askern.
I respond:	"I hope you're going to be able to keep this quiet!"
JH	"Of course they'll keep it quiet – we're all on a mission"
MW	"How do you know you haven't got a mole?"
JH	"We haven't – just trust me, this is really black and white."

And I find myself agreeing with John. The group really is split into two definite and polarised camps: those fed up with lurching from crisis to crisis, predominantly the newly elected councillors; and those protecting the old way.

Provided we can deal with the Gerry thing, we are odds-on to succeed. So why would someone try to stitch us up? Nearly everyone's camps are well known;

everyone on our side knows they want change, so why would someone switch from the winning side, to the losing side?

John is right, we are working to a short timescale, and we are all on a mission, but, we should never assume we won't have a mole working against us. And just to be on the safe side, we need [I need] someone on our side – someone nobody would even consider – and I know just the man...

ooo

10.30 pm

Kevin rings, almost to the minute. He's checking in to make sure the bases are covered.

"*What's the position with Gerry now?*" he asks.

"*I've been working on him since Sunday Kev, but he's resolute he's standing.*"

"*Just fucking buy Gerry off Martin... you don't need him in on that vote, he could blow the whole fucking thing.*"

"*It's not that simple Kev – this is an injured animal we're talking about and he's still thrashing... but he might be doing it to con them... so they think they're home and dry and become complacent.*"

"*Listen Martin...*" and I could hear him drawing heavily on his cigarette "*... cut the crap and remove – him – from – the – fucking – process... Find out what he fucking wants and give it him,*" he orders, every inch the whip. "*You never go into a vote without having won it before you go in... that's a fucking loser's game that is*".

I'd better not mention the caucus then...

"*You don't know Gerry*" I argue. "*He's a principled man... and you can't buy him*"

"*Fucking principles... they get in the way of fucking everything. Let me tell you this...*" he growls.

"*I 'aven't met a man yet that can't be bought – you just 'ave to work out the price and the currency.*"

"*One last thing...*" he adds "*... sort yourself out a kitchen cabinet – three or four people you know you can trust. And I mean trust... with – your – life,*" he enunciates again. "*And operate through them – preferably one in each constituency – and get them to cover off their MPs... We don't want no fucking slip ups here...*"

I think it best not to point out the double negative.

"*I've just had a word with Lady Caroline...*" and the noise of him drawing on his cigarette becomes quite deafening *"... and [I think] I've convinced her to keep her nose out."*

"She can't keep her nose out of anything," I say.

"True..." he concedes *"... but her only view appears to be 'anybody other than Gerry'.*

Then: *"What's this Gerry like? I don't think I've ever met him... but he sounds alright – he can't be that bad if Lady Caroline dislikes him so much... Maybe I should be supporting him for leader?"* He thinks aloud, letting me know he's in charge – that he's the Kingmaker.

"... Anyway, I've convinced her that Gerry's out of the deal – that it's such a nest of vipers we're better off out of it – and that we shouldn't interfere with local government."

"What about Rosie [Winterton] – John Wain's one of her Councillors," I say.

"Rosie..." and he inhales *"... Rosie won't deliver the winner... she won't interfere, but she'll always back the winner. If your ship's going down, follow Rosie, Martin... because Rosie – will – always – be – in – the – fucking – lifeboat,"* he spells it out once again.

"And Jeff?" I ask, already knowing the answer.

"Well Jeff's done it, hasn't he..." referring to his Leadership of Barnsley Council, several years earlier *"... so Jeff will be very interested in what's going on... but he's only got part of Doncaster in his constituency... so Jeff will be an interested observer – he won't interfere.*

Anyway I'm going back to the flat now – I'll speak to you tomorrow."

ooo

Thursday April 26th 2001...

7.30 pm – Alexandra House, Askern

True to his word, John Hardy delivers a packed meeting, which worries me in itself. Fourteen are in attendance – Keith Coulton, Liz Jeffress, Ted Kitchen, Gerry McLister, Chris Mills, Bill Mordue, John Mounsey, John Parkinson, Aidan Rave, Tony Sockett, Ian Spowart, Margaret Ward and myself.

It's an eclectic bunch. Keith Coulton is a former council worker, quiet and confident and a good administrator; Chris Mills is a retired school teacher elected after the by-election caused by the 1999 conviction of Terry Sellars, while Bill Mordue is idiosyncratic – a strong, upright young man and a former miner and university graduate thanks to the NUM graduation programme.

Former union convenor John Parkinson is another ex-school teacher, well known for enjoying a drink or three but keen to break with the past; Tony Sockett is the retired Assistant Director for Education at Doncaster Council – a delightful, gregarious little man and a sharp dresser, he is deaf in one ear – the legacy of a teacher's slap from childhood; and Ian Spowart is the one-time bus driver who witnessed my £500 pub win back in 1996. A tall man, his fiery red hair earns him the nickname 'TinTin' after the Herge adventure book character. Spowie, as I know him, is a veteran of the Gulf War who has also worked as a security guard [at the highest level] and like most former squaddies has a ribald sense of humour.

Of those attending, all but Mounsey and Kitchen are first term councillors and of those twelve all but Gerry are in their first or second years as councillors.

John Hardy opens the meeting by setting the scene and just as he's doing so, true to form, the fifteenth – Councillor Beryl Roberts comes in late.

Beryl is an eccentric, extremely fit grandmotherly woman who plays competitive hockey well into her 70s and will go on to abseil down Doncaster Royal Infirmary at the age of 80. In political terms, however, she is more difficult to read.

"I've brought two goose eggs for you Martin..." she interrupts *"... does anybody want any eggs? Because I've got plenty in the car"*

I laugh to myself, and thank Beryl. *"I'll square up with you afterwards..."* I mouth to her.

"That's fine" she says... *"It's just £1.50 Martin,"* and then, to the meeting as a whole *"... does anybody want any eggs? Because I've got plenty in the car."*

"Beryl... Beryl... can we do that later" says John, struggling to chair the meeting.

"Well I'm only telling people John..." she mumbles as she sits down *"They complain if you don't tell 'em ..."* she continues to the person next to her.

"Beryl... Beryl... " says John, struggling to bring the meeting back to order.

He attempts to set the scene... again.

"Come on Gerry... let's all know what's happening – are you standing or not?" Ted Kitchen interrupts in his typical brusque northern manner.

Ted, a long-standing councillor who claims to be a self-made millionaire, is never seen without his elbow-patched cardigans. He has the look of a holidaying Father Christmas, although the similarity ends there...

Trying to imbue John with a greater sense of confidence, Gerry asks the Chair if he can respond.

"Yes of course you can, Gerry" says John, thankful for Gerry's assistance.

And Gerry begins speaking, almost in a Paisleyesque way.

"I believe there's a conspiracy at play here. I believe that, had Colin Wedd not been arrested, then I would be the Leader of the Labour group in Doncaster".

Everyone in the meeting is listening to him intently.

"*But I also believe that I frighten people...*"

I tap Aidan with my foot under the table – Gerry has got the messages.

"*... and I think that's because I have a value base, and ethics that are perhaps too much for sections of the Labour Party... at this point in time*".

"*I also think that... I have to acknowledge...*" and Gerry takes a long pause "*... that the important objective here... is that we remove these corrupt bastards from the leadership of Doncaster Council... and I've heard they're saying Chas Harrison is the next to be arrested.*"

"*Yeah – on Tuesday morning... so he can vote on Monday night,*" says Ted.

"Well Ted..." continues Gerry "*... that just shows you how corrupt these bastards are and why we've got to get our person in as Leader.*"

"*Will you be standing or not Gerry?*" Ted buts in.

"*I shall be standing for election... I will not be standing down,*" says Gerry "*I think that, for me to stand down would be too much for my principles. But I shall be letting everybody know that I do not want them to vote for me.*"

"*So that leaves the door open for Martin?*" asks Ted.

"*It's not that simple Ted,*" I say. "*I agree with Gerry... somebody removed Colin Wedd from the process to stop Gerry from becoming the leader... and that begs the question of who's actually running this investigation or this council.*" I articulate previously practised arguments.

"*But we need to look for that answer in the future – because we won't get it answered now and we've got to concentrate on doing what we need to do now... to make sure we complete the take-over. I think Gerry's stance is unbelievably magnanimous and shows why he is so well respected by his fellow councillors across all political divides*".

"*Hear hear,*" says John Hardy.

"*So that leaves the door open for Martin?*" Ted says again.

"*It's whether or not people want me to stand,*" I protest.

"*Of course we do Martin – that's why we're all here tonight,*" Ted's getting annoyed.

"*How do we know Gerry will only get the one vote?*" asks Keith Coulton.

"*I shall be letting everybody know that I do not want them to vote for me – and I can start by telling you all here tonight – do not vote for me*" says Gerry.

"*What if the one vote is enough for us to lose?*" asks Ted sardonically "*I don't like it – we should just have two runners*".

"*I'm getting a bit nervous with this now*" I say "*This is getting a bit too much like a caucus meeting.*"

"*Of course it's a fucking caucus meeting,*" says Ted.

"*Oh I wish you wouldn't swear like that Ted,*" protests Beryl.

"Nothing meant Beryl," Ted replies.

"He does... " Beryl mutters to the meeting room *"He's always swearing... and there's no need for it."*

Ted: *"Look... we're all clear now what Gerry's doing... that he doesn't want your votes... and we're all clear that Martin is who we'll be voting for. That's all we need to do tonight."*

I look around the room, and think we are amongst friends. Predominantly these are people I think I can trust, though there are one or two I'd think twice about showing a bird's nest to!

"Well we just need to be a little bit careful..." I say *"... it's important it doesn't get out about this meeting."*

John Hardy interrupts. *"Look Martin – this is really black and white – we've all had enough of the way the Labour group and council are being run and we are all clear what we have to do to change it. Nobody will try to stitch us up... because we all want the same thing..."*

"And that's the removal of the old guard," says Ted menacingly.

"Yes but we've only got fifteen votes here," says John Hardy *"... and I make it we need a minimum of eighteen."*

"Yeah but you'll get 'Cream Cake' as well," John Mounsey interjects. Sue Bolton, disparagingly called Cream Cake by her ward colleagues despite her loyalty to them, is a large, aggressive woman proud of her status in the community; but for the hairnet she would resemble Ena Sharples.

"Well she's not here," replies John.

"Only because she wasn't invited man," laughs Mounsey in his hard Durham accent.

"Sue will do whatever we tell her," says Ted quietly, paternally and even more menacingly.

"So that's sixteen then," says Spowie.

"A solid sixteen – so we still need a couple more."

"No... you'll only need seventeen," says John Parkinson sage-like. *"Two of them will be away on holiday Martin love..."* he fawns *"... John Hoare and Sue Knowles, so there'll be thirty four votes – and we need seventeen to win."*

"Do we know if that's true?" I ask the room.

"Only in that I've just said it." John is slightly irritated that I should question him.

"Sorry John. It's not that I don't trust you – but we have to work with absolutes."

"Well I'm absolutely certain of it," says John, sarcastically.

"I'll chase it up Martin," Aidan promises.

"So that's seventeen we need then..." says Spowie "... we only need another one then."

"Wrong" Ted comes in. "Gerry won't be voting for you in the first round Martin; so you need another two. Which is why we should just have two runners – that one vote might be the one vote that loses it."

"I will not be standing down Ted," reiterates Gerry. "And I've already said to you all that I do not want you to vote for me."

"Like I said..." said Spowie "... that's a solid fifteen, we only need another two."

"I'd rather have another three or more" I say.

"What about Margaret Robinson?" asks Chris Mills.

"Old guard" growls Ted, dismissing Chris's thought process.

"What about John Hoare?" asks Margaret Ward, oblivious to the discussion we've just had.

"Don't you fucking listen," growls Ted.

"Ted!" exclaims Beryl.

"Well she should fucking listen then"

"Ted!" exclaims Beryl even louder.

"Yes... I know what he said Ted..." exclaims Margaret "... but he likes you Martin," Margaret justifies.

"He's on holiday... and he's Central" John Parkinson sighs.

"That doesn't mean he'll support me," I comment "But you're right Mags... I think I can get John."

"He's on holiday," John Parkinson sighs once again "Does nobody listen?"

"Look I'll chase it up" Aidan closes down the discussion.

"What about David Hughes?" asks Beryl.

"He fucking hates you Martin," growls Ted.

"Aye... he's certainly not your biggest fan Martin," flatters Mounsey, laughing. "I divn't know what you've done to him... lad... but he disney like you one bit".

David Hughes is an odious little man, always looking to further himself. As a JP who loves to promote himself as an honourable and righteous man, he has never forgiven me for giving evidence against his sister when, as an employee at my parent's shop, she was caught with her fingers in the till in the late 1970s [see Chapter 1].

"I'm fine with that" I say, knowing full well why he hates me. "I can't win 'em all; but perhaps he hates John Wain more than me?"

"I doubt it man" Mounsey once again. "He disney have a good word for you!"

"I'll work on Di Williams..." says Tony Sockett. *"She's my ward colleague,"* he explains unnecessarily adding naïvely *"... and I think she'll take my advice."*

"I'll have a word with Malcolm," says Keith Coulton.

There are only two Labour councillors in Barnsley East and Mexborough, Keith Coulton and Malcolm "Jockey" Wood. As a new councillor, Keith is loyal to me and although he says he'll work on him we both know Jockey is old guard and will be difficult to get.

But we're on a roll.

"I'll have a word with Elsie" [Butler]," says Liz.

"What about John Creswell?" comes a voice from the room.

"TWAT!" barks Ted.

Beryl remains silent, either she is resigned to Ted's swearing or doesn't recognise the lower level of expletive.

"Ted disney like Cresswell," sighs Mounsey. And looking around the room he sighs again, laughing *"In fact, there's not many he does like... Ted."*

Seeing his emerging notoriety, Ted smiles at the room. *"I always say what I think,"* he professes *"But not many of you have the bollocks to do the same."*

"I don't think I know him," states Beryl.

"Enough said... he's a TWAT!" barks Ted again.

"He won the Thorne by-election..." explains Keith Coulton "... but it was a bit of a surprise. His wife's not keen on him being a councillor and no one ever sees him."

"I think he works quite a lot..." adds Tony Sockett.

"Then clearly he's a lazy TWAT as well," Ted closes smugly.

"So we've got plenty of work to do," says Aidan, ever the peacemaker.

I look around the room, and there appears to be a general consensus we can easily pick up another two or three supporters.

"What do we need to do about supporting each other?" asks Margaret Ward *"Because they're gonna come for us [aren't they?]"*

"I think that's a good point," I say. *"These people have been in charge for such a long time they aren't going to let go without a fight."*

"Ah fuck 'em" Ted gets even more menacing. *"It's about time they realised they're yesterday's men."*

"I don't disagree with you Ted..." says Margaret *"... but we need to be talking to each other and making sure they don't intimidate us, don't we?"*

"They've already been bad mouthing us all week – and they don't even know who we're putting up yet!" says Keith.

"Look why don't we all agree to keep ringing round each other, to make sure the support's still solid..." suggests John Parkinson, helpfully. *"That way, we can keep talking to each other and keep our eye on the numbers."*

And that's what we do. But we don't simply rely on everybody checking in with each other in an uncoordinated way. After the meeting has finished, I ask John Hardy [Doncaster North] and Margaret Ward [Don Valley] to take responsibility for ringing round and testing out how genuine people are sounding in their constituencies.

Doncaster North and Don Valley are our heartlands and we think we can rely on pretty much all these councillors to support us. Having said that, the division is very much as Ted has said – "old guard" versus "young Turks" – with the "young" being very much a statement of time-served rather than age.

Central Constituency is a different proposition though and poses us a real problem – it's very well-organised and partisan with a large, sometimes belligerent, membership. But the most important factor is that John Wain is a Central Constituency councillor and they are loyal to their own. They'll do everything they can to make sure he is elected.

Having said that, Ian Spowart is a Central Councillor and, within limitations, he has agreed to keep working on Central's support for me. It's here where I think I can find *my* mole.

ooo

Friday April 27th 2001...

9.00 am

Aidan rings me: *"Last night went alright, didn't it?"*

"As far as it could... I knew I wouldn't get the support of David Hughes." *"That doesn't matter... but,"* he quizzes me, leadingly, *"are we happy with who we've got?"*

"I don't know – are we? You obviously aren't..."

"Not at all..." he says *"I'm just worried that we're being double-dealt."*

"Who by?"

"I don't know – I just think it'll be coming."

"I don't see it Aidan – it's our destiny. The Group's split in two and we've got the numbers," I say. *"Why would someone try to stitch us up? We're all on a mission... everyone wants change... but why would someone switch from the winning side, to the losing side?"*

Aidan concedes I might be right.

"But wait for the power plays to come in," I add *"... when they try to shaft us"*.

I knew it would get bumpy and dirty, as people realised who was in which camp. But I wasn't expecting the play that came.

ooo

10.00 am

Ron Gillies, a former Mayor of Doncaster is charged with council expenses fraud. Ron is a former chairman of the Race Committee and has held several key posts including Chief Whip and Chairman of the Amenities and Leisure and Trading Services Committee. A former NUM Askern branch president, he has served as a JP and been a member of the South Yorkshire Police Authority.

ooo

11.45 am

Keith Coulton rings me: *"Hi Martin – you've got John Cresswell,"* he says triumphantly.
 "Excellent, thanks Keith – was he difficult to get?"
 "Not too difficult; it was more a case that he hates John Wain. He says he's got a lot of time for you Martin and he thinks you can work together."
 "Fucking brilliant Keith – we're almost home and dry now. Should I ring him?"
 "I asked him that but he says there's no need – he says he's difficult to get hold of because he works a lot and goes to the caravan in North Yorkshire, most weekends, with his wife."
 "Okay – can you keep him warm?"
 "No need to Martin. Apparently Wain shafted him over a rural partnership board project and he hates him... so it's payback time."

ooo

3.55 pm Labour Group Office – Mansion House

Aidan and I attend to submit our names for Leader and Deputy Leader for Monday's vote.

ooo

Saturday April 28th 2001

5.30 pm

I phone Spowie. *"How's it going Ian?"*
    "Not brilliant Martin. I think I've got Jane [Kidd]... but they're putting a lot of pressure on her."
    "Jane's newly elected... and she's a cute cookie... why on earth would she run with the old guard?"
    "She's Central though..." Ian replies *"... but they're pissing her off so I'm playing a gentle game."*
    "Keep talking," I tell him.

ooo

I have already explained how the political cognoscenti elect themselves to positions of power and remuneration. As most also have paid jobs, being a councillor in Doncaster can be extremely lucrative. Though by no means alone, Bev Marshall certainly makes money; and he wouldn't want to lose it.

ooo

Saturday 28th April 2001

6.30 pm

I phone Bev Marshall: *"Hello Martin, well I must say, this is a surprise..."* and, presumably because my call puzzles him. *"I trust you are looking forward to Monday night's vote."*
    "I certainly am Bev. I thought I should call you to explain my position when I win."
    "Oh... when you win eh? There's nothing like confidence is there?"
    "I wouldn't have entered if I wasn't sure we would win," I reply.
    "Ah the 'I' becomes 'we'... that's not a bit of self-doubt creeping in is it Martin?"
    "No self-doubt with me Bev. But it isn't about me; it's about us and the Labour Party's future in Doncaster. And it's about the new generation moving the old generation on,"
    "That's it is it Martin? You're putting me out to grass are you? Retiring me early, as they say"

"Not at all Bev, in fact entirely the opposite, we are a relatively inexperienced group and we'll need some political experience on Tuesday morning. I want you to know that if you come on board, I'll give you a position on the Policy & Strategy Committee" [the pre runner to the Executive Cabinet].

"Well that's very interesting Martin. And very magnanimous of you; are you looking for some kind of a response now or before tomorrow"

"No. I don't need a response Bev thanks," I say confidently *"I just wanted you to know that I respect you, and that I'll be looking for your assistance on Tuesday morning... because you know we'll win don't you?"*

"Well I wouldn't go that far Martin but I do acknowledge that it's going to be a close call."

"Close call my arse Bev. We've already got 20 identified votes and we're going to walk it. And it's best to be on the winning side"

"Well, thanks for your call Martin, I think I'd like to reflect on what you're saying if that's alright? It's interesting, isn't it, that only a month ago we were looking at organising a by-election for your seat"

"Old news Bev. You're not going to try and sully me with that one are you? Because if you are, you've left it a bit late"

"No – not at all Martin – I was just reflecting on the discussion we had before Christmas. I really ought to have seen it coming then, hadn't I?"

"Not really Bev," I reply. *"I didn't"*

ooo

Sunday April 29th 2001...

1.00 pm

John Mounsey rings me. *"It's looking good Martin."*

"As far as it could..." I say.

"Why aye it's goen fuck'n brilliant man. It's about time we taught those corrupt fuck'n bastards a lesson."

Thanks to his accent I'm struggling to make out what he's saying... *"Well we'll know tomorrow night won't we John? Is everything okay at your end?"*

"Why aye everything's fine. We can back you Martin but we cannot back Aidan as ye deputy."

[Pregnant pause]

"Well I've always said John that it's a package; I can't – no I won't – do it without Aidan at my side."

"Well dinna be too hasty man. The problem with Aidan is he was too pally

with Weddy man [Colin Wedd] *and we canna trust him."*

"Well I don't know about pally John – Weddy had asked him to do some work for him," I lie, as I try to buy some time *"But I don't know if that's a crime John. He's a bright lad."*

"Well... that's what they all say... but I'm saying that we can back you man but we canna back Aidan; we dinna trust him."

"What about the rest of the slate John? Are you going to have problems with them?"

"Nah it's Just Aidan we canna trust."

"Which begs the question – who can you trust John? I suppose you're gonna say you should be my deputy?"

"No... not necessarily – but ye'd know ye could trust me man."

"And it'd fuck the slate up John. In fact this is going to fuck everything up – do you realise that?"

"Well I'm just saying that we dinna trust Aidan; and it'll affect whether we support you or not."

"Look it'll fuck everything up John – can I come through and see you with Aidan?"

"Why aye man"

ooo

1.30 pm

I call Aidan *"Fucking hell Aidan – Mounsey's trying a power play and he's going to fuck everything up. You need to come and get me and we'll go and see him – I'll brief you in the car on the way."*

ooo

2.00 pm – en route to John Mounsey's house

Aidan and I argue in the car on the way there, as I try to explain Mounsey's position and that we need to see him to establish some kind of an understanding or "deal".

We row because I remind him that I've warned him previously about cuddling up to Colin and if he wasn't careful it would cost him, especially where a treacherous bastard like Mounsey was concerned.

As a result he's gone very quiet and seems extremely nervous. As we near John's house I give him strict instructions to let me do the talking.

2.30 pm – John Mounsey's house

"Martin... Aidan..." Mounsey nods to us as he opens the door.
"I'll put a brew on... what d'yer want?"
"Cup o' char for me John – white please"
"Aidan?"
"I'm fine thanks John, can I just have a glass of water please. And can I use your toilet please?"

John and I make idle chit chat as he boils the kettle and Aidan returns.

"Nah dinna tak this personally Aidan. It's just that there's a lot of o' people worried that you wuz too close to Weddy man."

"There's not a great deal I can say" says Aidan "I can't undo what I've done; but I don't really know what I've done..."

"The thing is Aidan, that Colin was detested." I begin "And you were seen as being too close to him" I pause. "I've told John that Colin had asked you to do some work as part of your MBA," I gamble "But some people have seen this as you being part of the cognoscenti."

Aidan fidgets and looks at his glass of water.

"I've also told John that we're a partnership and that I won't do it without you," I emphasise again "In which case we're fucked, because if they don't vote you in as my deputy, I shall stand down as leader" I look intently at John.

"Can I use your toilet again John?" asks Aidan.
"Aye lad – you know where it is."

Embarrassed by Aidan's behaviour I jump in "We're all teed up John" I apologise. "Everywhere we go we have to have a brew" I lie.

"He's a good lad," I say while Aidan is out of the room. "He's as bright as a button. And, if he's guilty of anything, then that's his crime – he unnerves people because he's so bright" [and the idiot was always parading if of course]. "Weddy's been worried by that," I lie again "... and tried to manipulate him into their way of thinking."

Aidan comes back.

"I've just been telling John that you've just finished your MBA Aidan," I patronise.

"For what good it's done me; that's why Colin asked me to do the work on strategic visioning" replies Aidan, having been briefed in the car.

"Are we a hundred per cent sure Chas Harrison's going to be at the meeting? I ask, changing the subject.

It works... "Y'see that's exactly why we've got to get rid of 'em'," Mounsey rants. "The fuck'n bent bastard's actually asked the police if he can go along for questioning on Tuesday morning, so he can vote on Monday night..."

"... *and they're fucking letting him!*" I complete the sentence for him.

"*That's what's so fuck'n wrong,*" John shouts "*We're fighting the fuck'n police as well – the fuck'n bent bastards.*"

Aidan gets up and walks towards the kitchen: "*I'll just use your toilet again John?*"

"*Has he got somethin' wrong with him man?*" asks John, as if Aidan isn't there.

And then, directly at Aidan "*Have you got something wrong with ye lad?*"

Aidan laughs nervously as he leaves the room.

I jump at the opportunity "*Can you look after him John? Can you keep your eye on him? He's a bright lad, very capable and a real little diamond, but he needs polishing. You can do that John can't you?*"

But he isn't biting.

"*You can polish him John... you can mould him...*"

"*Ah diven't know man,*" he says finally. And I know I've got him!

"*I need someone with your experience John. I need you to keep pointing him in the right direction for me.*"

"*Aye... I could certainly do that*"

"*You see... that's what we need... he's a little diamond, but he needs your polishing. You can do that John can't you?*"

"*I suppose so man.*"

Aidan's back again.

"*John's just been saying he'll mentor you Aidan... stop you getting lost when you're using the toilets, and all that...*"

Aidan laughs nervously again.

At 2.50 pm we leave John Mounsey's house.

ooo

Monday April 30th 2001

4.00 pm

Bev Marshall phones. "*Hello Martin, I just wanted to respond to our discussion yesterday and...*"

"*I said you didn't have to ring me back....*" I cut him short to put him on the back foot again.

"*Yes, I know you did Martin. But nevertheless, I wanted to give you a call to explain my position to you*"

He's bullshitting and trying to deal.

"The situation is this Martin. I think you were probably correct in your assessment of tonight's result... especially with both Sue Knowles and John Hoare being away. And I'd like to say to you 'Good Luck'... and that if you win I would be delighted to work with you and the new leadership team."

"Well that's very good of you to say Bev. But I assure you John Hoare is one of my supporters, not John Wain's," I correct him. "People want a change. But let's cut to the quick Bev, can I rely on your support or will you be voting with the rest of the Central flock?"

"Well of course I'd like to vote for..."

"Nothing's stopping you," I interject.

"Well I know that Martin, but as you rightly suggested, I do owe a certain amount to my constituency colleagues; a bond of brotherhood, we could call it... "

"Is that what you call it – bullshit and bollocks might be a more exact definition."

"... So I think that, all things being equal, I'll stay where I am, supporting my colleagues"

"Even though you're gonna get your ass kicked Bev?"

"That would appear to be my position Martin."

"Playing a captain's game eh Bev? You're gonna go down with the ship are you?"

"Sometimes our allegiances demand loyalty Martin, I think you can understand that – and if you don't, I think you'll grow to."

"Old-manning me as well! So how many votes do you think you've got Bev?"

"Truthfully Martin, I think we've got fifteen, maybe sixteen at the most, but I think the mistake we've made... is we've under-estimated how disliked John Wain is."

"Are you counting Chas in with those?"

"Well that's why I say maybe – we still don't know whether he's going to be allowed to vote or whether Region are going to veto it."

"On the basis of what Bev?"

"I'm sorry but, as much as I dislike the man Martin, he's not been charged yet; and I always thought we were innocent until proven guilty, the Magna Carta and all that Martin..."

"There's nothing more righteous than a dead man walking – eh Bev?"

"... well perhaps you'd like to reflect on what I've said and I would be delighted to work with you and the new leadership team; if you win of course!"

"Certainly Bev, thanks for the call – I'll see you later on"

"Ah... well... eh... just hold on a minute Martin, if you don't mind? There's another issue I'd like to talk to you about."

"Sure Bev, fire away"

"Well, I don't know if you know or not Martin? But the Director of Education has got us into a bit of a pickle with DfES [Dept for Education and Skills] and as a result, we have a telephone Conference with the Secretary of State, Estelle Morris, tomorrow morning... The situation is this Martin. We are facing a possible Government intervention in Education. Because of this and, if you were to be elected this evening, I wouldn't want you to be having to go into a high profile meeting, unprepared."

"And you'll prepare me will you Bev?"

"Well that's what I'm, proposing Martin"

I pause to consider the ramifications of what he's said.

Bev breaks the silence. "Perhaps you'd like to reflect on what I've said Martin. If you would like to utilise my services, I would be delighted to assist you at that meeting with the Secretary of State."

"That's assuming I win, of course, Bev."

"If you win of course!"

ooo

6.00 pm – Doncaster Council Labour Group AGM [Part 1]

We meet, as always, in the Priory Suite, Mansion House. Aidan is an absolute wreck as we go in, with an ashen-white face and cold, sweaty pallor.

Nan runs the AGM with steely determination, no introductions other than "I'm Nan Sloane, the Director of the Regional Labour Party at Wakefield" and this is how this AGM is going to be conducted.

"This will be a secret ballot... as per Labour Party Rules" she continues before asking for three volunteer tellers.

"And finally" she concludes "Before casting your vote... secretly... you need to make sure you have not been intimidated into casting your vote for a particular person. You also need to be sure the person you are voting for is completely free of allegations against them [as far as any of us can be] and as clean as a whistle, because we are not going through this again."

"Any questions" she asks. None are forthcoming. "Good then we can commence with the voting."

I'm impressed with her thoroughness and feel supremely confident. Certainly Nan's attendance adds an air of legitimacy to my campaign.

The voting goes as predicted and we beat John Wain 17 – 16 – 1. So much for Nan Sloane not wanting to see the Party split.

Gerry McLister gets his own singular vote, which he is extremely pleased with. And I am elected Labour group leader, and therefore 'Leader of the Council'.

I never find out where the extra vote comes from but, as I smile and acknowledge the room for their support, Bev Marshall leans back in his chair, folds his arms across his ample stomach and smiles at me, nodding.

Despite Gerry's vote now being with us – making 18 possible votes – Aidan only wins 17 – 16. Presumably Mounsey has reneged on the agreement and abstained.

"You've won Aidan..." cries Margaret Ward who is sitting next to him.

"Aidan... you've won... you've won..." but he just sits there, stunned, with his head drooping towards the table. He appears to have gone into a seizure or paralysis; so whilst putting her arm around him, Margaret holds him up to stop him falling from the table.

The rest of our "slate" also goes through, despite the fact that voting for a "slate" goes against Labour Party rules. The only exception is Di Williams, who is re-elected as Group Secretary.

By the fourth vote, the voting pattern has become obvious and Ronnie Chapman is getting visibly agitated, as is her manner, huffing and puffing and tutting for effect, scanning the room to make sure others have seen her parading her annoyance. *"They're all voting for a slate!"* she exclaims loudly under her breadth.

"So are you..." says Ted *"... the only difference is ours has won."*

As the meeting breaks up, Gerry McLister is practically the first to come over and congratulate me, followed by all our supporters.

More interesting is the reaction of the opposition. John Wain looks like a baby with a smacked arse, as he and his core supporters make a quick exit.

Bev Marshall comes forward with a suitably reserved but professional congratulations, whilst several others [Butler, Edgar, Jones and Woods] begrudgingly shake my hand to register their capricious support for the new Leadership.

"Martin – we need to have a chat," says Nan authoritatively.

Nan takes Aidan and me to an ante-room where she congratulates us and asks what our statement to the press will be. Aidan duly produces our pre-prepared statement.

"That's fine," says Nan, *"although it's much too long. We'll issue this part of your statement,"* And she selects a sentence from the middle three paragraphs!

"There's no need to," says Aidan *"We've already prepared 20 'Clean Broom' Press Statements to hand out as we leave the meeting".*

"Who to?" she says... *"The drunks on the corner?"*

Not for the first time, we realise we have totally overestimated the level of "interest" of the public and press in Doncaster.

"*Come on*" I say. "*I'll buy you both a drink*"

ooo

Footnote

It had become an open secret around the Mansion House that Councillor Chas Harrison was about to be arrested. What was so galling was that he let it be known he'd asked South Yorkshire Police if he could attend on the Tuesday morning – so he could vote at the Leadership election the night before!

Harrison was convicted of expenses fraud in September 2001. He had attended a three-day Institute of Maintenance Management conference in Llandudno in 1996 as a Doncaster council representative, but had gone a day earlier and spent the night with an unnamed woman. When he returned to Doncaster, he claimed for an extra night's allowance at a hotel before the start of the conference.

ooo

David Hughes resigned from the Labour Party in 2004 after failing to secure the Labour group's support as Chair of Council [Civic Mayor] for 2005. Despite blaming his departure on a complete lack of activity in his deprived Ward, he later claimed to have delivered £9 million worth of capital activity to his electorate, when he stood as an Independent Councillor in 2006.

After losing his seat in the 2010 election, he then applied to re-join the Labour Party in 2012 and was selected to stand for election as a Labour candidate in 2013.

You can have it any way you want it, John

"Why waltz with a guy for 10 rounds if you can knock him out in one?"

Rocky Marciano

Tuesday May 1st 2001...

7.00 am

Alison Miller, the "Leader's Secretary", calls me. She congratulates me on my election and asks what time I want to be picked up, informing me:

I have an 8.30 am video conference with the Secretary of State [SoS] for Education, at the video conferencing suite at Armthorpe Comprehensive School. Bev Marshall will be meeting me there at 8.00 am to brief me.

I then have a 9.30 interview and photo call with the Doncaster Star at the Mansion House and the same at 10.30 with the Doncaster Free Press. The Yorkshire Post will interview me on the phone; do I want to pick Aidan up on the way in so we can both be prepared for the interviews?

Alison Miller is a lovely, friendly, chatty and outgoing young woman. She is also incredibly efficient and the wife of Keith Miller, the Head of Programmes and European Funding. Alison is a member of the Labour Party and both she and Keith have been Secretary to the Constituency Labour Party within the previous five years.

ooo

7.30 am

Paul Lawson picks me up at home.

Initially I have two attendant drivers and I believe their observations are probably the most telling:

"You see, everybody was speculating as to who would win but nobody thought to ask us..." says Paul "... and we've seen it all before... so many times. Whether it be Weddy, Glover, Pete Welsh or Gordon Gallimore."

"We've seen 'em come and we've seen 'em all go; much as we will with you" he adds, slapping me down; something that becomes a bit of a hobby for Paul.

"But we knew you'd win all along Martin"

"How come?"

"You were the only ones not talking up your success" he replies "You had an extremely calm air of self-confidence... and you were just getting on with the job."

"Well you did" he corrects himself "Aidan was shitting himself – he looked like a frightened schoolboy"

ooo

7.45 am – Armthorpe Comprehensive School, Video Conferencing Facility

We arrive in plenty of time but Bev is already there. The school has prepared a table with coffee, tea, juices, croissants and Danish pastries.

"Good Morning Martin" says Bev as he comes to meet me. "As you can see..." he nods at the breakfast table "the school has done us proud."

"I've taken the liberty of preparing this brief for you. You'll find it concise and very candid but I think that's required in terms of you hitting the ground running this morning."

He gives me the brief, but before I have even looked at it: "Now the SoS knows me from previous meetings and also my work with the NUT... So may I suggest, therefore, that you do the initial introductions with her and introduce me as leading on this important matter, to ensure continuation and a smooth transfer to the new executive?"

"We've got nowhere to go with this one Martin; and I might similarly suggest that whatever the SoS proposes, within reason of course, we accept it, alongside eating a bit of humble pie"

"Now the Director of Education hung us out to dry with this one and both Ofsted and DfES are screaming for blood, so you need to dance carefully; but with your agreement, I'll just take the lead and bring you in, as and when. Is that okay?"

He's a fucking smooth operator, I think to myself, deciding to just follow his lead.

Estelle Morris is really impressive and has complete control. But perhaps the most surprising aspect of the video conference is that she has been briefed incredibly well on the political machinations of the last two weeks.

She seems to spend an inordinate amount of time discussing what has happened; the strengths, weaknesses, opportunities and threats inherent within an inexperienced or "novice" Executive.

Bev doesn't appear to be connecting with anything she's saying. He has very cleverly [helpfully even] pushed himself to one side so that my face and torso is predominant on the screen; no mean feat for a man of Bev's size.

Then, continuing on from a point she's made earlier, the SoS adds *"... of course that's the problem... when you have a lack of experience and direction"*

I look at Bev but he's wiping imaginary crumbs off his tie and shirt – having finished his second Danish by now. He sees me looking at him and smiles inanely, as if completely oblivious of what she had just said, which he clearly isn't.

"Can I just take you up on that one Minister" I interject. *"I'm fine with you accusing me of a lack of political experience... and I actually see that as a huge strength, in terms of where the "experience" has taken Doncaster in the last few years..."*

"... but please don't accuse me of having a lack of direction. I am very clear of the direction I need to lead the authority in"

"Oh... er... I'm sorry Martin..." she's quick to respond. *"I er... I er... I wasn't referring to your lack of direction – which I'm told is very clear"* she gambles. *"I was simply making a generic point about the inherent dangers within a lack of experience and direction"*

Good recovery, I think and let the matter go.

As the video conference finishes, I reflect on our performance. I'm fairly happy with the manner in which I have acquitted myself, for my first outing. Bev's performance concerns me though. He isn't particularly impressive and simply accepts whatever Estelle proffers which basically amounts to the following:
- we have a failing Education Directorate;
- our Director of Education has ignored an Ofsted embargo from its recent inspection report of the LEA and has "pre-reported" their findings, putting his spin on them;
- we need to acknowledge our failings and agree to a Public Partnership with a top performing LEA such as Warwickshire County Council;
- I need to agree to Estelle's "mate" [Phil Blundell] coming in as an organisational development consultant, whilst simultaneously mentoring me as a new, and relatively inexperienced political Leader.

We fall into line.

ooo

4.00 pm

The Doncaster Star front page reads... "Clear-out"

I'd told Aidan that we needed to look confident and determined at the photo-opportunity; when I see the picture, I think we look like the Krays.

"Who's the senior Labour Party insider?" he asks "Nan?"
"Nah... she wouldn't be so clear... and she's too canny to say it's the end. It sounds like Kev to me."

Clear-out
New broom sweeps through Doncaster Council

ooo

Wednesday May 2nd 2001...

9.00 am

Councillor Chaz Harrison is arrested as part of Operation Danum. He is immediately suspended from the Labour Party.

ooo

Saturday May 5th 2001...

9.00 am

Phil Blundell phones to introduce himself. During a 15 minute conversation he impresses me a lot. He explains how he was Labour Leader of Warwickshire County Council for many years and is a close colleague of Secretary of State for Education, Estelle Morris, who has asked him to head up a support package for both our "failing education directorate and our [novice] executive".

We agree he'll speak to Alison on Monday about coming up to Doncaster early next week so we can scope out such a programme.

ooo

Monday May 7th 2001...

8.30 am – Diary Briefing – Leader's Office, Mansion House.

Alison briefs me on how my week will pan out. I have a 10.00 am briefing on the Local Government Act 2000 [LGA2000]; an 11.30am briefing on Friday's South Yorkshire Leaders' meeting, and there's an email from Mark Edgell, Leader of Rotherham Council, congratulating me on becoming Leader.

Amongst many other items, I also have a 3.00 pm briefing from Chief Executive David Marlow, on a variety of issues including the failing Education Directorate, and Phil Blundell wants to have a chat with me about the partnership with Warwickshire County Council – Alison suggests tomorrow at 5.30pm. And I should not forget that I have a speech to deliver next Monday night at the Mayor's Ball at the Racecourse.

ooo

10.00 am – Local Government Act 2000 – Priory Suite, Mansion House.

Aidan and I sit in on an officer briefing on LGA 2000. Monitoring Officer Paul Evans is leading and my primary interest is on the issue of a Mayoral referendum. Kevin Hughes is very keen on us having a Mayor and it's a requirement of the Act that local authorities consult the electorate on the Mayoral model.

Paul is talking about the consultation exercise to gauge the level of support, opposition, apathy or otherwise for a directly elected Mayor or a Mayor and Council Manager running the authority.

The consultation process has already taken several weeks and despite the malcontents running a fairly public insurgency campaign, the number of responses has been low; less than 500 from an electorate of approximately 220,000.

I am ambivalent at best, but Aidan and I have both noticed former leader Colin Wedd, Danny Buckley and the Labour leadership team lobbying enthusiastically for members to write letters opposing the mayoral model. I am worried about the lengths they might have gone to get their "required response". Aidan and I privately express concerns that the "old guard" may have resorted to writing bogus letters to newspapers to bolster their campaign.

Regardless of that, LGA 2000 is upon us and the Monitoring Officer maps out a 12 month programme of learning & development, where the governance model is a shadow executive/overview & scrutiny split. He explains how we will have a "Shadow Executive [Cabinet] Meeting" [the old "Policy & Strategy Committee"] immediately followed by a "Cabinet Ratification Committee Meeting" to ratify the *de facto* Cabinet's decisions.

Paul proposes that the members of the "Shadow Executive [Cabinet]" and the "Cabinet Ratification Committee" are exactly the same individuals – only in UK local government!

Ignoring the byzantine nature of the proposed model, Aidan is quick to spot an opportunity.

"This means we'll have a whole series of new chair and vice-chair positions on the scrutiny panels to offer up as patronage," he tells me.

I remember my first Full Council and the chaos I witnessed as the then Leader bought off the group members' loyalties for the next period. But this is different, I think to myself. This time it's us doing it!

"Well let's just make sure it's more dignified than it was last year," I say.

"I'll do some work on it before Thursday's AGM Part 2". He replies.

ooo

3.00 pm – Briefing with David Marlow – Leader's Office, Mansion House.

David is a new local government Chief Executive and moved to Doncaster three months ago from an Executive Director position with Southampton City Council.

Before becoming Leader I have not actually sat down with him on a one-to-one basis so we are developing our working relationship from day one.

Having said that, I am extremely impressed. Even at this early stage I can see he is an exceptionally professional leader and strategic thinker. David's gregarious nature perfectly complements my joie de vivre and desire to see real change. Along with Aidan's intellect, we'll create a really capable team.

As we exchange views on the failing Education Directorate, however, David gets very defensive. *"I don't know whether I would describe it as failing,"* he tells me. He does, however, agree with my post Estelle Morris discussion summary:

- DfES/Ofsted are highly dissatisfied with our Education Directorate and specifically with our Director of Education;

- We must recognise our failings and agree to a Public/Public Partnership with Warwickshire County Council;
- I have to agree to her mate Phil Blundell coming in to broker the above.

I ask David how serious the issue with the Director of Education is and sense DfES want his head on platter; David becomes defensive again, backing the Director and insisting such a move would be damaging to the Directorate's staff morale.

ooo

Tuesday May 8th 2001…

5.30 pm – Meeting with Phil Blundell – Leader's Office, Mansion House.

A tall, distinguished man in his mid-fifties, Phil Blundell looks like a well-dressed, athletic Basil Fawlty from the TV comedy 'Fawlty Towers'. Our discussion continues on from our telephone conversation on Saturday morning. We agree that there is a need for support and interventions on three levels:

1]   – the executive's relationship with DfES and Ofsted
     – the LEA's relationship with DfES and Ofsted
2]   – the family of Doncaster schools' head teachers relationship with the LEA
     – the relationship between the secondary heads', the LEA and specifically the Director of Education
3]   – the new leader's relationship with Doncaster schools
     – the new and novice executive leadership
     – Political leadership and its involvement within education

Phil tells me he was very happy playing bowls and gardening – what he terms his glorious semi-retirement – but that he was also semi-decaying. As such, he is delighted that Estelle has asked him to head up the support/intervention programme.
    We agree Phil will undertake some initial work over the coming days and then get Alison to enter a series of meetings in my diary.

ooo

fall out   You can have it any way you want it, John

Wednesday May 9th 2001…

11.00 am – Priory Suite, Mansion House – Doncaster MBC Labour Group AGM [Part 2].

After a whirlwind week when everyone wants a part of our action, Aidan and I have just about settled into our new roles within the Doncaster Council structure and, arguably more importantly, within the Labour Party structure.

Today's AGM [Part 2] meeting is my first group meeting as Leader and I know I have to be at the top of my game. I also feel fairly certain "they" are going to come for me and try to put me off my stride – but I'm not prepared for the way they go about it.

The Labour Party's rules always defer to collective endeavour and collective decision making; and although I have been elected to "lead" the Labour group, I must take decisions through its structure and offices. To this end, I'm required to propose my first Policy & Strategy Committee [the pre-runner to the Executive Cabinet] to the group.

Aidan and I have discussed with all our supporters the potential make-up of this Committee and, to a large extent, it has selected itself – playing to a councillor's strengths and interests, their role in "overthrowing" the "old guard" and the need for a [politically] geographical spread, with three from Don Valley CLP; three from Doncaster North CLP and two from Central CLP.

Proposed Membership of Policy & Strategy Committee

1. Aidan Rave [DV]   Corporate Management
2. John Hardy [DN]   Social Care, Health and Wellbeing
3. Tony Sockett [DN]   Cabinet Member for Lifelong Learning
4. Gerry McLister [DV]   Neighbourhood Management
5. John Parkinson [DN]   Environment and Rural Development
6. Ian Spowart [C]   Trade, Industry and Innovation
7. Jane Kidd [C]   Crime Reduction and Community Involvement
8. Margaret Ward [DV]   Culture, Sport and Young People

As I distribute the paper proposing my executive team, I remind the group, that this is only my second week in the job and I'm still talking to members, in order to put together the strongest, and most appropriate "top team"; as such, it should not be read as complete or "final" in any way. What I mean is, it gives me a bit of latitude to bring Bev in later.

"Chair," comes a voice from the floor to Jane Kidd, who is chairing her first meeting of the group, thanks to her support for the 'insurgents'.

It's Martin Hepworth, the ex-Chair of the Labour group, who by virtue of losing his position [to Jane] has seemingly damaged himself by association and the manner in which the press has chosen to report it.

Not only is Martin well-respected as a long-standing councillor and a man of integrity, but he has recently returned after a bout of Bell's palsy, which has left him with a slight facial paralysis and also affects his speech. As a result, several members have even greater sympathy for him.

Jane nods at him to allow him to speak. *"Thank you Chair... and may I congratulate you on your election... and perhaps through you, can I similarly congratulate Martin on his election as Leader."*

He then addresses me: *"I didn't get chance to speak to you after the vote on Monday..."* he tails off *"... and I very much look forward to working with you in the future."*

You had every fucking chance, I think to myself, nodding and smiling "thank you"– now isn't the time to antagonise him.

"In congratulating you, I would be the first to argue that you have every right to put forward whom you see fit for the Policy & Strategy Committee," he begins with assurance, confidence and a statesman like presence.

"But there is one name here that worries me."

There's a nervous, almost embarrassed, silence in the room as I scan the faces.

"It worries me as a member of this Labour group," he continues. *"But perhaps more importantly, it worries me as a member of the Labour... Party."*

"... and I know it worries many other members sat around this table today."

I nudge Aidan, *"here it comes"*, I'd written on my pad.

"And that name is Gerry McLister..." he pauses for effect.

But he's struggling, He's very red and his disfigured face has begun twitching with the stress he's put himself under.

"Our Leader has, Madam Chair, through putting Councillor McLister's name forward... very probably brought this Labour group into disrepute."

What a load of fucking bollocks... But struggling or not, he has captivated the group's members; worryingly so.

"In putting Councillor McLister's name forward, Madam Chair, our Leader is putting forward the name of a man who was suspended by this very same Labour group, for voting against the whip less than a year ago"

"Not only do I find Councillor McLister's name unacceptable," he goes on. *"But I do feel that if we were to vote him in as a member of the new executive, we would very likely be voting against the Labour Party Rule Book"*

"... and I, for one, can't and won't... vote against the Labour Party Rule Book Madam Chair."

That's it. He's done it [they've done it] I think to myself; the clever bastards. They've used the member we least expect it from, to attack us – to attack me. They've used probably the most well respected member of the "old guard"; a man known as a considered politician, to suggest that one of my first acts as Leader is to propose a course of action in breach of the Labour Party Rule Book.

It's still a load of fucking bollocks, but it's a clever move. Keep your powder dry Mart; let's see what else they've got.

But that's it... and Martin Hepworth leans exhaustedly back in his seat, looking nervously around the room. I glance over at John Wain and he's grinning like a Cheshire cat – the smug bastard.

"Can I just comment on this?" says Jane Kidd, even more nervously than Martin Hepworth.

"As Chair... I'm very concerned with what Councillor Hepworth has said..." she begins *"We simply cannot vote for Gerry, if this means we inadvertently vote against the Party's Rules."*

"My point exactly, Chair" and the room agrees with Martin Hepworth.

The stupid, naïve twat, I think to myself. She's a newly elected part of the new executive – if I ever get it through – and she's fucking things up already. She thinks she's got to speak on every issue and she's talking absolute bollocks.

I lean across to Aidan *"Put a fucking mark against her name will you?"* I whisper *"She's supposed to be on our fucking side!"*

Bollocks to keeping my powder dry. We're gonna lose this if I don't grab it back.

"Can I come in here Madam Chair?" I say adopting a slightly exasperated tone. "It doesn't surprise me that Councillor Hepworth is saying this... and he's right to raise his concerns, if that's what they are. If they are <u>his concerns</u>... and not simply an attempt to undermine my leadership."

I stare straight into Martin's eyes. He looks awful; extremely red in the face, nervous and sweating terribly.

"But the simple fact is Madam Chair... that Councillor McLister voted against this group on one occasion. He is not a serial antagonist. He voted against the whip on the 'Homes Closure' issue as a matter of conscience – and was suspended from the group for doing so. He was suspended for two months [if I remember]."

"He was suspended for two months... because that was the penalty that the Chief Whip, elected by this group to perform just that function, adjudged he should serve..."

"A penalty that was commensurate with his crime, if you like, although I'm sure Gerry would argue that he is guilty of no crime".

Scanning the room, I can see several of our supporters have caught on and realise that the "old guard" are trying to stick it up us.

"Hear hear," says John Hardy and others start nodding in agreement.

"Gerry has served his punishment," I conclude "And we should not seek to punish him further through some bogus claim that it somehow limits his membership of the party in future."

I look at Gerry but he's just a passenger – completely shocked and embarrassed at the attack he is under.

Martin Hepworth comes back at me: "Well that may be how the leader sees it Madam Chair... but I am simply saying that if we were to vote for him today, members would very likely be voting against the Labour Party Rule Book...

"And consequently, the leader should reconsider the membership of his executive, because I for one cannot accept an executive with Gerry McLister as part of it."

And like a Jack-In-The-Box, Jane is up and at it again.

"This is my point... we cannot simply vote for Gerry, if..." and she pauses before compounding matters "... if in doing so, we are all guilty of acting against the Party's wishes," and she closes, having cast further doubt into people's minds.

"Fuck me," I whisper to Aidan "The silly bitch is gonna cost us the fucking vote here!"

Sensing victory, Martin Hepworth speaks again. "All I am saying Chair, is that we could be voting against the Labour Party Rule Book and, as such, we are asking you, Martin... to reconsider your proposed executive."

"Can I move that this meeting does not accept the leader's recommendations, Madam Chair, on the basis that it will force us to vote against the Labour Party Rule Book" and he smiles inanely at me.

"Yes – I'll second that, says Ronnie Chapman"

Oh bollocks, I think to myself... but before I can respond to the "old guard's" move, John Hardy jumps in.

"Can I move that we do accept the Leader's recommendations Madam Chair," says John.

There's a palpable sense of unease in the room.

"Well we need to move to a vote," says Jane.

We need seventeen votes – which we should have easily – and I am frantically trying to make eye contact around the room. Most are nodding but neither Beryl Roberts nor Bill Mordue will look at me and, interestingly, neither will John Hoare, having now returned from holiday.

"*All those in favour of not accepting the leader's recommendations,*" says Jane...

And she counts the show of hands – including John Hoare's!

"*That's fourteen votes not to accept the leader's recommendations,*" says Jane... and I immediately feel a sense of relief – we've done it!

"*Oh I forgot to count myself in!*" she laughs "*So that's fifteen votes not to accept the leader's recommendations.*"

We're still okay, I relax, we've still done it!

"*And those for the leader's recommendations...*" she announces...

"*And that's fifteen votes to accept the Leader's recommendations*" she continues. "*So presumably, two abstained*".

What? What the fuck! I think to myself – two fucking abstentions!

"*Just let me count them again...*" she announces... "*All those in favour of not accepting...*" But the numbers tally – Bill and fucking Beryl both abstained! "*So I have the casting vote*" Jane announces "*Which is a good introduction to chairing my first meeting...*" she adds nervously.

"*And I vote for not accepting the leader's recommendations,*" says Jane... "*I won't vote against the Labour Party Rule Book*" she added as mitigation.

What...? What...? What the fuck! I think to myself. But I need to be calm... "*Can I thank you Chair for your contribution in support of your constituency colleague,*" I say, staring at her as I labour the constituency colleague point.

"*I think this is all getting a little heated; perhaps we should call an adjournment for fifteen minutes whilst I reconsider my proposed executive.*"

And Jane agrees to a fifteen-minute adjournment – I look over at John Wain and he's smiling at me. You disingenuous bald, fat bastard, I think.

I leave the room and walk quickly and deliberately to my office.

ooo

11.45 am – Leaders Office, Mansion House...

I'm joined immediately by Aidan, Mags, Spowie and Gerry; and a couple of minutes later by John Hardy and Tony Sockett.

"*What do we fucking do here?*" asks Aidan.

"*Well we fucking shoot Jane Kidd for a start! What the fuck does she think she's doing?*"

And there's a knock at the door. In walks Jane...

"*What are you playing at Jane?*" I ask her "*Can you not see that you've just shafted us? [correction... ME]*"

"Well no..." she splutters *"I just think that we shouldn't be voting against the Party Rule Book..."*

But I cut across her *"Ah bollocks Jane! You've just shafted us... Can't you see what they've done? If you were that concerned about voting against the Party Rule Book... you wouldn't have taken a fucking show of hands... Nan told us that one last week!"*

And I can see it's dawned on her she's been turned over – calm down Martin, don't shoot your supporters.

"Can I just say something Martin?" says Gerry. *"Clearly my involvement is giving them [and us] a problem; I just want to say that if it makes things easier I'll stand down from the executive"*

"Bollocks to that Gerry..." I say – and it's more for Jane's sake.

"It's a bit like the opening five minutes of a game of rugby league when your opposite number puts a big hit in on you."

"What?" says Aidan.

"If we cave in the first time they hit us – we're fucked. If we take it now... we'll take it every minute of the game."

"Backing down's not an option," says Mags *"... if we back down, they've won."*

"Exactly Mags." I'm pleased she has seemingly "got it".

"Mind you – they've already won, thanks to Jane..."

"Look," Jane protests *"I just didn't want to vote against the Party Rule Book..."*

But I cut across her *"Well it's gone now – just get with the programme!"*

"I'm sorry for swearing Jane – it's just that we should've seen this one coming... You go back and get ready for the reconvened meeting," I dismiss her.

"All I'm saying is it's an option Martin, if it makes things easier," said Gerry again, as Jane leaves the room.

"Someone needs to read her her fucking future... the sackless twat," I motion after Jane has gone.

"The stupid bastards' are trying to suggest that I don't know what I'm fucking doing."

"It's an option Martin, if it makes things easier," Gerry again.

"Nah that's bollocks Gerry and they're talking bollocks – absolute fucking bollocks," I insist.

"That's a lot of bollocks," says Mags, smirking at her humour and my incessant swearing.

"It might make things easier now, but it'll make things much harder later on – they'll have had a taste of blood – my blood! And they'll want more; and they're not fucking getting it."

"But you've agreed to re-consider your executive, Martin" says Tony Sockett.

"And I will reconsider it Tony... but that doesn't mean I won't propose exactly the same executive again."

"Hee, hee, hee... I like your style" says John Hardy.

"Aidan. Get on to Nan now" I order him. *"Tell her what they're trying on. Get her view on the Rule Book claim."*

"Spowie – go and have a word with Jane Kidd and read her her fucking future."

"John, Tony – who's fucking wavering – Elsie Butler, John Hoare, Bill fucking Mordue and Beryl Roberts? Get 'em on board and remind them that we've just been elected to lead this fucking group"

That leaves Mags, Gerry and Aidan with me.

"Fuck it," says Aidan *"Nan's not available."*

"Right we've got five fucking minutes to sort this out," I say. *"Aidan get on to Tony Sellers and see what his take is. Mags, speak to Phil Cole. Gerry, get down to the group office and have a look at what the Rule Book actually says."*

And in a flash, Mags and Gerry have left us.

"What are you going to do?" asks Aidan.

"I've got a cunning plan," I say. *"Call Tony Sellers, while I try Nan again – I'm just nipping to the loo"*

Five minutes later neither Mags, Gerry nor Aidan have come back with anything; but John Hardy and Tony Sockett have done the numbers and reckon we're [now] on strong ground if I want to push it.

ooo

12.00 pm – Priory Suite, Mansion House

Doncaster Council Labour Group AGM [Part 2] reconvened.

I address the meeting. *"Thank you Chair. Can I thank members for allowing me the adjournment so that I could re-consider my proposals for the Policy & Strategy Committee. Can I also say, Madam Chair that I don't particularly want to force a vote on this issue..."* and I glance up at John Wain, who is gloating at me.

"... I think such a vote would be divisive and, at this particular time, we need to concentrate on unifying the group not further division."

"You've just had a vote... and you lost," says Martin Hepworth, the supercilious little shit is smirking at me.

These poor stupid ignorant bastards, I think to myself, they obviously don't know me.

"Well... let's not get into that Madam Chair... Whether that should be classed as a vote [or not]... But I have listened to what's been said.... and that's why, after a great deal of consideration, I have decided to propose the following for the Policy & Strategy Committee."

And I proceed to read exactly the same list as before.

When I read out Gerry's name there's an audible level of discomfort that ripples around the room; the "old guard" members are clarifying that they haven't misheard me and that I have actually proposed no change whatsoever.

"I have also taken the opportunity..." I continue "... to seek clarification from the Regional
Labour Party on the position of Gerard McLister..."

I accentuate the "Gerard" to sound authoritative, and then pause to allow them to take in what I have just said.

"And I am assured that Councillor McLister has clearly satisfied the requirements of the punishment meted out to him by the Labour group..."

"... and, therefore, he is eligible to be elected to the executive, <u>without contravening the Labour Party Rulebook.</u>"

There is a sense of relief from several members in the room – which I build on:

"I therefore, recommend to Labour group today that they accept my proposals and we move forward once again to a strong unified Labour Party, delivering for the people of Doncaster."

"Hear hear" says John Hardy and Tony Sockett joins him, and I can see that I've done the "old guard".

"I move that this group accepts my recommendations, as leader..." but Martin Hepworth buts in.

"Madam Chair. We can't have a vote – we just had one and on this issue."

Martin is looking bad – almost as if he's going to have a seizure.

Seething that they've got me again, I decide not to get into an argument which will only end in a massive, undignified row. It's what they want and it's a typical SWP [Socialist Workers Party] tactic to wreck a meeting; I decide discretion is the better part of valour...

"Well might I suggest, Madam Chair, that rather than get into an argument [now]... we postpone the meeting today, so we may seek written guidance from Region on the Gerry McLister issue..."

"Thanks very much for that Martin," says Jane Kidd, as group Chair "I think we would all find that useful" and she closes the meeting.

I wink at John Wain as I walk off to my office with the same determination as before.

12.30 pm

Leaders Office, Mansion House

I'm ranting at Aidan about the complete lack of support given to us [me] by the Labour group. Aidan defends the group's naïvety – putting it down to inexperience and insisting the public prefer it to the corruption of the 'experienced' past.

"Fucking hell, Nan left it late Martin," he adds, changing the subject.
"Pardon."
"She came back to you late."
"No. She's still not got back to me. In fact I never rang her."
"But you said you'd sought clarification on Gerry's position."
"I did. Well, correction, you did, didn't you... It's you she's coming back to..."

There's a knock at my door *"Just a minute please."*
"But you said you'd had an answer."
"Nope. I didn't say I'd had an answer. But I can understand that might be what you heard."
"You did, you said that they'd assured you he was okay."
"Nah – what I actually said was I had asked the Regional Labour Party their opinion..."

There's another knock on my door *"Can you wait just a minute please... and then I said 'And I am assured that he's okay'. I didn't say the Region assured me."*
"Fucking hell, you'll get us fucking hung," Aidan panics.

And then my door opens and in barges John Mounsey.
"Oh Pardon me," he says in his best Received Pronunciation. *"Can you wait a minute please, old boy!"* he mocks... *"Fuck'n hell man whad'ya fuck'n playen at man?*

"I told 'em," he continues *"... divent tak na fuck'n notice man – just gan in man!"*

Aidan is looking disconsolate and John picks up on it.
"Ah divent nah what's wrong wi yer... we've fuck'n won man..."
"Today was just a hiccup man," he continues *"We'll get the vote through next week... they've just played all their cards man."*
"Well I don't know, John" replies Aidan *"We might've just lost big time,"* he looks anxiously at me.
"You know what your trouble is Aidan?" I tell him. *"You worry too much – that's your problem..."*

"And do you know what the lesson is here? I'll tell you what the lesson is here..."

"Don't – try – and – bullshit – a – fucking – bullshitter!"

ooo

1.00 pm – Leader's Office, Mansion House

My office has now become a hive of activity, as everyone pops in and out to show their support- no matter how fickle it might be.

ooo

1.30 pm

Nan Sloane rings Aidan. He puts her over to me. Mags ushers people out of my office, across the hall and back into the Priory Suite.
After a short exchange with Nan I put the phone down.
"She said she'll give my number to Howard Knight who wrote the Labour Party Rule Book," I tell Aidan.

ooo

2.45 pm

Howard Knight rings me and I explain the scenario to him; that the "old guard" has almost succeeded in frightening the newer councillors into seizure and the stance I've taken.
He backs me completely but says he's worried about the apparent inexperience within our novice executive; a position highlighted by Jane Kidd's behaviour, though to be fair to her, she has come back on board now it's been pointed out to her.
He tells me he'll come up on Friday to form some kind of an action plan to develop the
councillors' capabilities.

ooo

2.50 pm

We reopen my office, which quickly becomes busy again. Mags has sent out for cream cakes which prove a focus for Labour members to pop in and have a chat.

Unsurprisingly, given the supply of cakes, Bev Marshall also pops in to wish us the best and to say he thinks I performed admirably. He wants me to know, furthermore, that I can be assured of his full support.

"That's the problem Bev..." I say "... sometimes assurances aren't all they seem."

Aidan nearly chokes on his coffee.

ooo

8.00 pm – Our House, Kirk Sandall

I tell Carolyne I think she should set up a meeting with Aidan's wife ASAP; Aidan and I need to be totally committed to each other, so it would be good if she and Maria could support each other as well.

Carolyne has already met Maria at last year's 'Mayor's Ball', when we had a very enjoyable evening. But both of us are worried about Maria, she is very indiscreet and wanted to tell us everything about Aidan, including every sordid detail of their first "date" – which would ordinarily be quite endearing but could prove a real handicap in a senior politician's wife.

Carolyne arranges to meet her.

ooo

9.15 pm

Kevin rings *"Just checking in – how's it going?"*

"Well it's going," I tell him. *"We've got a bit of a problem with Wain, who's bad-mouthing us and Martin Hepworth, bless 'im, who appears to be going into meltdown."*

And I feel a lovely reassurance as I hear him drawing heavily on his cigarette.

"Big tent then Martin."

"I don't know what you mean Kev."

"It's big tent stuff Martin... You've got to 'ave a big tent... with – as – many – people – in – it – as – possible," he enunciates.

And I understand what he's saying. *"Ah... got you".*

"Y'see... " and he draws on his cigarette again . *"You need him in the tent, pissing out on everybody else... rather than outside the tent... pissing – in – on – you."*

"Yeah... but he's a cunt," I respond *"And – a – first – class – cunt,"* I mirror at him.

He laughs, realising what I'm doing. *"I'm sure he is Martin. There are a lot of them about – especially in the Labour Party – but that's why you want a fucking big tent."*

"Get him in... Find out what he wants... Get him in to your executive," he continues rapid fire.

"What about Martin [Hepworth]?"

"Both of 'em," he orders.

ooo

Thursday May 10th 2001...

9.00 am

But Martin Hepworth beats me to it. Alison comes in to say he has requested a meeting with me and she's booked him in for 9.30 am tomorrow.

She says she "understands" he is withholding signing up to the Labour group and she presumes it's about that. What Alison means by this is that, thanks to her gregarious disposition and Labour party pedigree, members feel comfortable talking to her about political issues and he has told her.

I thank her for the tip off and ask her to arrange for John Wain to come in for a meeting with Aidan and me as soon as possible.

ooo

Friday May 11th 2001...

9.30 am – Meeting with Martin Hepworth – Leader's Office, Mansion House.

"Hi Martin – how are you?" I ask him.

"Well... I'm not very happy, as you can imagine."

"Why's that... What's worrying you?" I'm almost taunting him and his face is twitching again.

"Well, I'm not very happy with what you're saying about me," he starts accusingly.

"What's that then Martin? Because I don't think I've said anything about you."

But he isn't listening. He's got his message to deliver and he's going to deliver it, regardless.

"As far as I am aware Martin..." he begins, *"I have never been interviewed*

by South Yorkshire Police... or featured in any of their investigations... as far as I am aware," he repeats.

"Yet I'm being labelled as a crook. And I'm not happy. You're saying that you're the new broom that's sweeping all the "old guard" – and the corruption – out of the Council. And several people have told me that you're saying I'm part of that corruption."

Which I take exception to. *"Whoa... hold on a minute,"* I interject. *"Where have I said that?"*

"You've only got to pick up one of the newspapers to see what you're saying"

He looks terrible. His poor disfigured face has gone very red again and he's twitching. I can see my father in him, who had also suffered from a bout of Bell's palsy some thirty years earlier.

And suddenly I feel immensely sorry for him.

"Oh Martin," I say, thinking I sound like my father as I say it *"You should know... better than most people... that newspapers don't report what you say... they report what they want you to say."*

But he still isn't listening – just diving headlong into a row, regardless of what I say.

"Everyone is saying you're the new broom Martin; and that anyone else is bent... and therefore that I'm bent... that I'm part of the corruption."

Me: *"But I don't know what I can do for you Martin. I can't change the past. And what you can't argue against... is that you ran with the "old guard", as the Press are calling you... You are part of the past... so you are guilty... You're guilty, by association and that's not me saying that – that's how the press have chosen to report it."*

"But you need to shut the fuck up and let it go away," I tell him – *"because you're protesting too much."*

He's nearly crying.

"Everyone is saying that you had Colin removed and that everyone else is bent," he says.

"But I can't do anything about that Martin," I reiterate, raising my voice through exasperation. *"I can't do anything about that... and you're going to make yourself ill... you'll end up having a stroke – and nothing is worth that, is it?"*

But he doesn't answer, just trembles and stares into space.

"What do you want me to do for you? What do you want?"

And that seems to calm him down.

"I want you to write a letter to the papers saying I'm not corrupt... and that I'm not part of the Donnygate corruption."

And I know my answer straight away.

"But I can't do that Martin... and I won't do that," I pause to let him

compute what I've said. *"I can't say that... only you can say that [Martin]... we've made that mistake before – look at what happened with TB and Glover..."*

"Now you need to forget about this madness, sign up to the Labour group and start working with us instead of all this bollocks..."

He's petulant: *"Well I won't. Not unless you write me a letter to the papers saying that I'm not part of the Donnygate corruption."*

"Well then we've reached an impasse" I say. "Because I'm not going to do that"

And the meeting comes to an end.

ooo

10.30 am

Kevin rings *"Now then. How's the meeting with Hepworth gone?"*

I tell him Martin is refusing to sign up to the group unless I write to the newspapers.

"Nah bollocks to that one Martin, we've fallen for that one before..." and I hear the reassuring intake of smoke, as he gathers his thoughts.

"Nah... give him it," he orders, contradicting himself.

"What? You can fuck off!" I say, stunned.

"He's fucking harmless Hepworth... and you don't want an open sore. You need him in the tent."

Maybe Kevin knows more than he's letting on, I think; having been a councillor himself until 1992 and, perhaps more importantly, having worked in the Labour Party Whip's Office.

"I'll come up with something," I tell him and ring off.

ooo

11.30 am – Meeting with John Wain – Leader's Office, Mansion House.

John Wain is a large bald-headed man with the look of a bulldog. An ex-college lecturer, he's a nasty piece of work by anyone's yardstick. Most people are wary of him, having witnessed his vicious behaviour. For the past few years, many have seen him slowly frustrating the operation of Doncaster College because of a private dispute he is alleged to have had with its Principal, Terry Ashurst; with fellow councillors reluctant to intervene, frightened of crossing Wain.

For some reason, Councillor Veronica "Ronnie" Chapman, a Central Constituency colleague, accompanies him to the meeting. Ronnie is an aloof woman who, much to my annoyance as a huge fan, she reminds me of the wonderful actor Joyce Grenfell, in the guise of the harassed nursery teacher. Ronnie patronises everyone because of her superior intellect and capabilities.

"Thanks for coming to see us, John" I open, acknowledging both Aidan and Ronnie's attendance.

"The first thing I'd like to do is acknowledge your gracious behaviour, since last Monday..." I flatter him, careful not to rub his nose in his defeat. "... and I have to similarly acknowledge your huge experience," I lie.

"... which is why Aidan and I are keen to offer you a position within the [Executive] Policy & Strategy Committee."

And I lean back thinking the offer will have surprised him and he is sure to accept.

"You want me to respond?" John questions us, cynically.

"Well it might be a starting point for a conversation."

"Well... as I've said before... I am very concerned that you might be bringing the Labour party into disrepute and I'm not going to say yes, or no until I've satisfied myself that there's nothing amiss with what's going on."

"Sorry John, I'm not clear what you're talking about?"

"Exactly what I say. I'm concerned you might be bringing the Labour party into disrepute".

I realise straight away he is just going to use the meeting as an opportunity to attack us.

"I've got no idea whatsoever what you are talking about – have you Aidan?"

"No – none whatsoever [John]" he replies.

"Well, okay then, let me be more explicit," he starts to count out on his fingers.

"There's you... there's Aidan... Tony Sockett, that's three, and there's Jane Kidd. That's four of you, for a start..."

"You've all been working with communities and community groups that are funded by Government money or regeneration programmes," he leans back as if all should now be clear.

At this point I decide to fettle him, regardless of Kev's "Big Tent" theory. There's no way John Wain is going to change; he's a nasty, vindictive bully; a wounded animal waiting for the opportunity to savage me. I need to nip his antagonism in the bud, before it widens.

"Nope... I'm no clearer at all... and your point is?"

JW: "All I'm saying is that there's something fishy about it all and I intend to get to the bottom of it."

"Get to the bottom of what? There's nothing to get to the bottom of..." I'm starting to get annoyed.

"We all work or worked in one manner or another with community regeneration projects. Period. So our crime is – we're community organisers, with a profile in our communities. There's nothing illegal about that. Unless you're telling me that you can't seek election to public office if your employment falls into one of those categories! Because that's an argument I'd love to have with you."

JW: "All I'm saying is there's something not quite right where you have individuals being paid for working in communities, who then seek election within those communities."

By this time I've lost patience with him. He is patently being as obnoxious as he can and trying to rile us both; clearly with some success with me!

"Oh you're talking absolute bollocks," I blaze. "I notice you don't seem to have a problem if you're employed as a teacher or a college or university lecturer..." I say nodding to Ronnie and him in return.

"Oh yes... you're happy enough for them to sponsor somebody's civic duty aren't you?"

He just stares inanely at me.

"See... you've got no fucking answer for that have you? You clever bastard."

Ronnie tuts for effect. "There's no call for bad language" she says, chewing the cuticle on her index finger.

"Your right Ronnie," I exclaim. "I'm sorry – there is no call for bad language..." I apologise.

"... But there's no call for fucking bad behaviour either – and that's all I ever get from this twat."

"Oh... I say... This is outrageous," Ronnie exclaims.

I turn to see Aidan, who is clearly uncomfortable with my tirade.

"You – are – talking – absolute – fucking – bollocks – John," I repeat, calmly and quietly.

"The Party was happy enough for us to stand for election when we did, where we did, and with the profile that we had within our communities... so what's the problem now?"

I don't give him a chance to answer: "I'll tell you what your problem is now. The problem now is... that we've just kicked your ass in an election and you're trying to make mischief as a result..."

"Aren't you? You clever bastard... Well it won't fucking work matey... It won't fucking work with me... because I won't take your shit. Not like those other poor bastards that you usually fucking bully eh? Eh? Because it's not nice when you're being bullied... is it John?"

I don't think John Wain has ever been bullied before and he's in shock. I haven't allowed him to speak for the last five minutes.

"I don't have to listen to this," he says finally.

"No you don't have to listen to this... but you're gonna – you nasty bastard."

He interrupts me. "*I don't have to listen to this,*" he says again, and starts to get up from his chair.

"Well you're gonna listen to it!" I demand, really starting to raise my voice now. And I rush around the table so I'm stood right next to him, overshadowing him.

Ronnie has stood up now, on the opposite side of the table, and is loudly packing away her papers and pens. "*This is outrageous,*" she storms. "*I've never seen anything like this in my life.*"

But Wain has sat down again, resigned to the fact he can't get up, or out.

I point my index finger right at his nose "So listen to this... you nasty bastard."

"I've tried being reasonable with you..."

"I've tried being polite to you"

"I've tried being respectful to you..."

"... but you don't want to play ball, do you?"

"So just remember this..."

I pause, while I looked at him with pure demon in my eyes.

"You can have it any way you fucking want it, John..."

"You can have it intellectually..."

"You can have it politically..."

"Or you and me can go outside right now..." and I spit imaginary spittle into my left and right palms "*... and we can have a rumble*"

"But whichever one you go for... I'm gonna kick the fucking shit out of you. Do – you – fucking – understand?"

"*Oh... I say... This is completely unacceptable,*" Ronnie exclaims again.

"Now fuck off... and tell that to your fucking cronies," I bellow – opening the door for them.

As they leave my room, I slam the door after them.

Aidan is sitting there, stunned, two sweat marks the size of large dinner plates on the front of his shirt, so big they run together in the middle.

"*Well, that went well,*" he says.

And we both burst out laughing.

ooo

3.30 pm − Meeting with Howard Knight, Head of the Labour Party Local Government Unit

The meeting with Howard is both comforting and empowering. Just as Nan [Sloane] said, Howard has effectively written the Labour Party Rule Book, which I find incredibly liberating; Aidan less so − he views Howard as a greater "chancer" than I am.

"It's really simple Aidan," I say. "With Howard in our corner, we can't lose − he's the Labour Party umpire. They aren't going to challenge us and try to 'old dog' us again because, if they do, we'll just defer to Howard."

"That's right," says Howard. "And to be honest, whatever you say Martin [within reason] I'll agree with... because you've turned the corner in Doncaster, and it's important the Party supports you in doing away with these dinosaurs."

"They're bad news − for the Party and for democracy. But they won't challenge you Martin, because I'm your trump card and they know it."

"They know that they've tried it on − that they've tried to con you and, to be fair Martin, you played it just right. You didn't bite... in fact you were quite gracious to them; and you beat them at their own game."

I lean back on my chair, breathing out loudly: *"Don't bullshit a bullshitter,"* I exclaim... eh Aidan?" and I wink at him.

"Lesson learnt," says Aidan "But you need to be careful − it'll get you into trouble."

"You see we all live in a bullshit world," says Howard, building on my comment to Aidan "... and everyone's an expert in marketing − you have to look at what or who you have in your corner and play your cards accordingly."

"What's that got to do with marketing?" asks Aidan.

"Marketing's about bullshit," he replies. *"It's about making the claim, to the people that matter, that you're the best in the world − and justifying it [of course]."*

"You are making the claim − to the Labour Party "old guard" − that you know more about the rule book than they do. And you do. Why? Because you've got me on your side." He leans back emphatically.

"Yeah but some of these characters are really anal," counters Aidan.

"Do you think I give a fuck?" Howard is irritated by Aidan's naïve questioning. "The Party's full of barrack room lawyers like these. They won't throw anything I haven't heard before."

Howard lives in Sheffield and agrees to come to the AGM Part 2 next Monday, which seems to appease Aidan.

ooo

6.30 pm

Kevin rings *"The Big Tent worked then Martin...?"*

I don't comment – he's obviously heard about the John Wain issue. I hear him drawing heavily on his cigarette.

"He's a nasty fat bastard anyway," he adds, *"so you've probably not lost anything. But you need to watch out for him causing trouble... because he's a vindictive twat."*

"Sometimes you have to just deal with the situation as it presents itself," I reply. *"And he would, and will, always be causing us trouble – you know yourself what he's like."*

And we agree that he's probably better out of the tent than in it.

I brief Kevin on everything that is happening with particular attention to the support we are receiving from the Labour party – via Nan Sloane, Howard Knight, Phil Blundell *et al*.

Kev's view is that this is the least they can do given the significant turnaround we've achieved.

He tells me Tony is particularly pleased with what I've done. I simply don't buy it. I can't see TB being so interested in Doncaster.

ooo

Having reflected on the argument with John Wain, I'm not proud of my behaviour. I detest bullies and bullying but this was a calculated attack on a particularly nasty, vindictive bullying man.

I was new to the job and needed to show I was strong; that I wouldn't stand for idiots like John Wain messing me about. This is exactly the type of scenario that Kevin Hughes and the Labour party wanted me to deal with; and thankfully they stood firmly beside me. That doesn't excuse my behaviour, I could have avoided the battle and managed it away – but it wouldn't have gone away, it would have just allowed him the time to rebuild and grow stronger for when he came at me again.

I didn't want to have to deal with it in the manner that I did; but sometimes the only way to handle a bully, paradoxically, is to bully them!

I removed him from his role as a governor at Doncaster College at the earliest opportunity and John Wain never came at me again, he faded away and stood down as a councillor at the 2004 elections.

ooo

During the next few days, Aidan and I get on with the job of establishing a working routine; developing a relationship with the Chief Executive David Marlow and our senior Executive Officers and organising a programme of visits to the many offices and sites to meet and talk to staff.

I've already made the decision to stand down from my community development consultancy work and I encourage Aidan to do the same, citing Wain's obsessive vindictiveness as justification in itself. We also agree to focus all our attention on turning the local authority around and to do this we need to develop a "re-invention strategy"; which we will revisit in eighteen months.

The media are giving us a fairly easy, almost supportive press but we are acutely aware that we are no longer the "new broom" and have become "the Leadership".

Consequently, criticisms of the Council, which we may have agreed with previously, are now levelled at us and we have to take a less anti-politic and more corporately supportive stance.

For example, a group I call "the malcontents" are fighting a *"Name the Names"* insurgency campaign for the release of a report compiled by the District Auditor [DA]. The report names the elected members, staff and other individuals who have paid money back to the council as part of the Operation Danum police inquiry.

Practically the first thing I do on becoming Leader is to request a copy of the DA's report and a guidance note on the legal ramifications of releasing it to the public.

I'm stunned when I read it. There is very little in it, with around forty individuals named, many for petty sums of less than a hundred pounds. Nonetheless, the legal advice clearly states that releasing the report will be an infringement of human rights for those named; several of whom have actually claimed, or been paid money in error.

I want to release it, believing it will kill off the emerging allegations from the malcontents, that we are "as bad as the last lot" with regard to cover-ups. Having said that, I fully understand the reasons why we can't. Ironically, one of the non-Labour councillors working closely with the malcontents on the campaign is named for having paid back £60 he claimed in error!

I am also aware that the malcontents are campaigning vigorously for Doncaster to adopt the "Mayor and Council Manager" governance model, as part of Local Government 2000. But that's another issue. We can look at that in a couple of months.

ooo

Footnote

One of the benefits of being elected as leader of the majority group, and therefore the Council, was that you were allocated a car and attendant drivers. Having performed the role of Leader/Mayor for more than eight years, I will always defend the provision of such a "perk" – as it was portrayed to the general public.

The demands of the job could be as easy or as onerous, as the post-holder accepted. I worked like a Trojan and the more you were prepared to do, the more was demanded of you. Indeed, calls to my Blackberry regularly occurred across 18-20 hours per day. In addition to the constant demands on my time from phone calls, emails, texts etc., was the need to attend myriad meetings, read prepared briefs and prepare and deliver speeches. Being able to work whilst travelling to and from venues was absolutely invaluable and allowed the "machine" to extract even more from my position.

Within a few weeks of becoming Leader, Paul Lawson became my regular, preferred driver. After two years I appointed him as my permanent driver and he became a good friend and confidant. Not only did we have immense difficulty with drivers maintaining confidentiality and discretion, in terms of sensitive conversations and information they were party to, but he was probably the only person I could rely on for honest independent feedback. He was a man of real integrity and humour.

ooo

When I was discussing the capricious nature of political support and loyalty, several years after he left my office, Ian Spowart told me of the huge pressure he and Jane Kidd came under from the "old guard". He said the night before the Labour group's Leadership election, he was visited by Bev Marshall and Martin Hepworth and offered a deal to give John Wain his vote.

ooo

During the years I worked with Aidan, one of the defining characteristics of our relationship was his innate conservatism [with a small "c"] and my more liberal approach to issues. I always looked for other ways to achieve objectives and constantly encouraged colleagues to push boundaries.

A particular mantra I developed at that time, with respect to local government inertia when responding to government guidelines, edicts and statute, was to treat them as challenges to rise to rather than instructions to follow.

Although my approach often led to innovative solutions and a particularly creative and dynamic period, Aidan also saw my propensity for creativity as a significant weakness and pigeon-holed me as a huge "chancer".

A Germ of an Idea – building an ideology

> *"The philosophers have only interpreted the world, in various ways. The point, however, is to change it"*
>
> Karl Marx

Monday May 14th 2001…

8.00 am

Paul Lawson picks me up at home. As we travel to work, he asks me how my weekend has been. Fairly quiet I inform him, surprisingly so, apart from Aidan coming round to work on some 'big picture' issues.
  "I'd have thought you'd be getting John Wain to help you with those?" he fished.
  No… I don't think he'll be working with us [at all] now" I reply.
  "Yes… we heard – as did everybody else in the Mansion House – and half way up the High Street" he laughs.
  "Whoops! Was it that bad?"
  "Only if you knew it was you – which, apart from the two attendants who were with me, means no-one" he adds.
  "Like I said – Whoops! – but I needed to deal with him…"
  "Well you certainly did that!" he cuts me off. "Apparently, he nearly collapsed – when they got him outside."
  "Well I can assure you that wasn't my intention" I lie … "but sometimes you have to do what's necessary… or – you – have – to – be – prepared – to – do – what – is – necessary" I enunciate, looking out of the car window and thinking of the scene in Body Heat when Matty Walker's husband goads Ned Racine [William Hurt] into becoming a murderer.
  "Well you certainly dealt with him – he'll be thinking twice before taking you on again, Martin. But, I suppose, he got a taste of his own medicine – that's what people were saying yesterday at the `Mayor's At Home'.
  "Who was saying what yesterday?" I press him.
  "Oh… just the attendants and Councillor Woodcock [Tory]… But everyone agreed it was about time somebody sorted him out – and they were all glad you did it."
  We finish the journey with me deep in thought – worried about what I might

have done, searching for an answer in the distance.

ooo

9.30 am – Doncaster Council Labour Group AGM [Part 2] Second Leg and Full Council Labour Group pre-meet!

We are holding the meeting in the somewhat pompous surroundings of the Mansion House ballroom, with its splendid marbled Corinthian columns, huge sash windows and other classical motifs. This is because our less grandiose, more utilitarian, regular meeting room is now being decorated.

I notice that Martin Hepworth is not in attendance – and Councillors Butler, Edgar, Jones and Woods have now all committed their "support" to me – so we have more than the numbers we need to force a vote on anything. Also, Di Williams isn't really what I would class the "old guard". She may have been part of their slate but more because she was a time-served councillor and a good administrator who put the hours in as Labour Group Secretary.

Jane Kidd is not there, which isn't a surprise, so Vice-Chair Margaret Ward opens the meeting:

"*This is the reconvened AGM Part 2, and where the Leader introduces his proposed membership of the Policy & Strategy Committee.*"

"*I'd like to introduce you to Howard Knight, who will be sitting in on the meeting. Following the disagreement at the Part 2 meeting – over the Labour Party Rule Book – Howard has been asked to attend this meeting today...*"

"*Howard is the Head of the Labour Party Local Government Unit and Author of the Labour Party Rule Book*" she continues. "*So if you have any questions about the Rule Book or its interpretation, then Howard's your man.*"

"*Chair! Can I ask who asked Mr Knight to attend today's meeting?*" demands John Hardy, having been briefed to pose the question.

"*May I respond Chair?*" Howard chips in. "*I have been asked to attend by the Regional Director, Nan Sloane, following the behaviour she witnessed leading up to, during and after the AGM Part 1 Meeting last week.*"

He adds helpfully: "*May I also say Chair, that it's important the Labour Group gets behind the new executive and starts to concentrate on delivering for the people of Doncaster.*"

However, the "old guard" aren't biting – they've clearly been frustrated by Howard's attendance and are in no mood to make mischief.

As I spell out my proposals [again], I marvel at the speed by which things change; the Group simply accepts what I propose.

The Chair moves on to discussing the items on the Full Council AGM [to be held at 11.00 am] which will be *my opportunity* to "reward" the loyalty of those supporting me, by appointing them chairs or vice-chairs of the committees – and, subsequently, the shadow scrutiny panels.

But I speak too soon.

"Can I just ask, Margaret" says Mick Muddiman *"... before Martin introduces his nominations for the Overview & Scrutiny positions, who he's consulted with regard to these positions?"*

Who the fucking hell has primed him? I think to myself... But Mick's nudging at an issue that might prove problematic.

"Because, if we are now entering this area that is being called the 'Executive & Scrutiny' split..." he continues, *"I wouldn't want Martin to compromise himself by making a decision he can't..."*

"So can I ask, Madam Chair..." he starts to fumble... *"who he has consulted and who will be voting on these new positions?"*

Howard Knight jumps up: *"Can I come in here please, Chair? The councillor is correct – in Local Government 2000, it is extremely important to make explicit the dividing line between the 'Executive' and the 'Scrutiny' functions..."*

"In a similar manner to the way Select Committees hold government to account – this is one of the reasons Labour Group AGM's are now held as Part 1 and 2 meetings – in order to allow you to consider how you might best structure the membership of your scrutiny function <u>after</u> the executive has put forward its membership."

"Oh bollocks" I think. *"The cat's out of the bag now. Aidan's done all the work on who will chair and vice-chair the committees and scrutiny panels, and we're going to have to give the control back to the "old guard" again."*

But they are either asleep, don't understand or don't care. Probably all three [!]; and Aidan has played a blinder by priming Keith Coulton to introduce the nominations.

"Ah I think this is my bit, Madam Chair..." interrupts Keith. *"Obviously Martin has been putting together his executive. Me and my colleagues have been asked to put forward the membership of the scrutiny panels, in discussion with Aidan as the deputy leader"* he bluffs; and then introduces them according to Aidan's script.

"Before we move on to voting on these positions, Chair?" Howard says. *"May I ask if there is anybody, other than the present members of the Policy & Strategy Committee [as the shadow executive], who should not be voting..."* He knows full well that I intend to bring Bev Marshall on-board.

There's a definite silence as everyone looks around the room.

"Yes, thank you Howard" I interject nervously. *"You will remember that I have only put together a Policy & Strategy Committee, as the new executive, with*

nine members" I look questioningly towards Bev Marshall... and I can see him desperately urging me to move on, not to say anything.

Well bollocks to that. I'm not going to fall for some kind of double-bluff, leaving me forever beholden to him if I keep schtum. Plus – what would Howard think? I'd be as bad as the old guard.

"And we are weak in experience in this crucial area..." I can see sheer terror in Bev's eyes. He knows what's coming. *"So I have asked Bev Marshall to take up the remaining position within the executive..."*

You could hear a pin drop.

"... and I'd like to thank Bev personally for all the support and assistance he's given me recently." I sit back to enjoy the seeds of doubt I have planted in the minds of the old guard.

There is no response. The entire room is silent. With everyone looking at him, Bev simply acknowledges my statement, nods and smiles at them – though slightly sheepishly as he adjusts his position on his chair.

Whoops! That's Bev dead, I think to myself, seeing the quiet rage in the eyes of John Wain, Ronnie Chapman *et al*. Still, what did he expect?

ooo

The remainder of the meeting is fairly pedestrian with all the positions filled as planned. As we finish, I look around the room and several members still appear shell-shocked over the Bev Marshall appointment.

ooo

10.15 am – Leader's Office, Mansion House

We've returned to my office. Aidan and Margaret Ward are discussing how the meeting went with Howard Knight, whilst I'm quickly going through a diary update with Alison.

"I think that was a good meeting Martin" says Howard *"They just accepted what you said – they've got no appetite for a fight now"*

Howard says his goodbyes and re-states his offer of support for me [and the group] – inviting me to call him day or night! As we walk together, Bev stops me and asks if he can drop in to have "a quick word".

I see John Wain at the end of the corridor – and wave to him – but he turns and scuttles off. *"Clever bastard!"* I exclaim *"I don't think he wants to speak to me... but he might want you Bev."*

Bev doesn't say anything immediately.

"*Oh I'm sure it's you Martin*" he responds finally – but there's no punchy follow up, as normal.

He's not the Bev we all know and love dearly – and I note he is looking nervous and slightly more reserved than usual.

As we enter my Office he spots Aidan and Mags and reverts to his normal affable self, telling us he would rather have left it until a little later to play his "new executive" hand.

I apologise and we agree I was bounced into an early announcement. But what was he holding back for anyway? He's a shrewd operator, Bev – I think to myself – he wants to run with the hare and hounds and shit on his former colleagues whilst still retaining his dignity. But I suppose that's how politics works. You have to be prepared to betray somebody whilst expecting no comeback whatsoever.

After Bev has left and Aidan, Mags and I are reflecting on the situation, my door opens...

"*You stony faced bastard*" exclaims John Hardy, having entered the room without knocking.

"*Nobody saw that one coming... did they.*"

"*Ah, come in John*" I smile at Aidan and Mags "*Nobody saw you coming either John, did they?*" but my humour's lost on him.

"*Fucking hell, I'm never going to play poker with you... you stony faced bastard*" he says again.

"*Did you see their faces? Wain had a face like a baby's smacked arse – and Ronnie Chapman couldn't even manage a tut!*"

"*They'll think twice about fucking with you three*" he fawns. "*Was Bev your mole Martin?*" he harks back to the discussion at the caucus meeting in Askern.

"*I've got to be quick as I'm on double yellow lines. I just wanted to say congratulations again Martin – another first class performance from you. Fucking hell eh? I'm, glad I'm on your side...*" and he edges towards the door – "*Fucking Bev Marshall eh...*"

And like a 'will o' the wisp' he's gone. I look at Aidan and Mags and we all start laughing. "*Good old John eh?*" I say. "*He always sees conspiracies that aren't there...*"

"*Fucking hell*" Aidan exclaims. "*I didn't realise we were so Machiavellian!*"

All three of us look at each other again. "*Y'see that's the thing with John...*" I begin all sage-like "*... he's playing all the right notes...*"

"*... but not necessarily in the right order!*" Mags choruses with me, as we all laugh in homage to Morecambe & Wise.

"*Did you set Bev up with Howard?*" Mags looks stern suddenly.

"*Look...*" I say falteringly "*... this is hard enough as it is... but how can we plan for every single eventuality?... and if they want to create an aura that we know exactly what we're doing – that we're top political operators, that we're much better than we actually are – then I'll take it all day".

"On the other hand I do know exactly what I'm doing – and I am a top political operator" declares Aidan.

"Eeh"... says Mags disparagingly, "*he's only just out of his nappies*"

ooo

11.00 am – Full Council, Doncaster Council Chamber

ooo

2.00 pm

Jeff Ennis calls me. Jeff is a really friendly person; a tall, well-built man, who looks like a thin Oliver Hardy. An ex-teacher, he has a great sense of humour and was Labour Leader of Barnsley Council from 1995 to 1997, standing down when he was elected to Parliament as MP for Barnsley East and Mexborough.

With such a constituency, he has only a toe-hold into Doncaster but this doesn't detract from his commitment to the Borough or to me. As an ex- Local Authority leader, he has a better than average understanding of the world of local government and the ramifications of government policy on local authorities.

A keen race goer, Jeff says he is just ringing as a courtesy because he is aware the Part B AGM has taken place with Howard Knight in attendance this morning.

"*Did Colin get Chair of the Racecourse Committee?*" he asks.

"**Yes he did – and there's an argument to come.**" I know the opposition will make mischief out of the fact I put the "disgraced" ex-leader back in a very senior position.

"*That's good politics, Martin*" he says. "*I know it was a difficult decision for you to make but you'll get the benefit of it. It's important you have someone who knows racing politics in charge there – or they'll turn you over.*"

"**Well I hope the bastard doesn't try and bite me**" I say, hoping Jeff will pass the warning on to Colin. Jeff knows Colin from previous years when they sat together as councillors on South Yorkshire County Council.

Keith Coulton has kept Jeff in the loop and Jeff is gauging my views on the Mayoral referenda taking place across the country – but I keep my powder dry on the specifics in Doncaster. He moves on and gives me his opinion on the various old-guard politicians who are causing me trouble.

"That's fine Jeff..." I interject *"but they're not politicians; they're just greedy self-promoting, deluded twats."*

"Hee... hee..." he laughs *"Kev told me you don't take prisoners."*

"... but Malcy Woods is on-board now and very supportive of you – isn't he?" he fishes.

"Oh he is now – they all want to be on the winning side now... after the event" I tell him.

"Well of course – that's politics – isn't it? But now he's with you, you'll still be inviting him to the races won't you?"

"Fucking hell, that's politics is it?" I ask rhetorically "He can try and shit on me... But as long as he gets you to do his dirty work it's all okay is it?"

"Well it's not a question of doing his dirty work Martin – but you need a big tent, don't you?"

This all sounds familiar.

"And Malcy has a pretty good understanding of racing form and some useful contacts in the racing world... that's why we call him 'Jockey'..."

"Well that and the fact that he's only four foot ten!"

"You know there's nothing more useful than having an individual who can pick [and give out] the winners to guests you're entertaining at the races, Martin"

Reluctantly I agree and thank Jeff for the call.

"And you can tell 'Jockey' Wood that I'll be inviting him to attend the St Leger with me, Jeff"

"Bollocks to the St Leger – that's months away!" he closes. "I'm talking about next weekend!"

ooo

10.15 pm – Mayor's Ball, Doncaster Racecourse

Aidan has drafted my speech for the Mayor's Ball – a fairly innocuous homily that presents us at the dawn of a new age, looking forward to Doncaster achieving its destiny over the next period.

The Ball is a successful event with more than a sense of optimism in the air – certainly everybody wants a piece of our action. I make a beeline for Stephen King, the Acting Divisional Commander of South Yorkshire Police.

The discussion inevitably nudges at Operation Danum and corrupt councillors.

"Well you don't have to worry about me – I'm as clean as a whistle" I tell him.

"Oh I know you're as clean as a whistle" he replies. *"Don't you think we've looked in to you? And do you think I'd be having such a public discussion with you if we had any worries on that account."*

"Well that's nice of you to say... It means a lot to me – and us."

"As far as I'm concerned Martin, you've done your bit and it can't have been easy – and now we'll do whatever we can to help you. That's the least we can do"

ooo

Tuesday May 15th 2001...

2.30 pm – Meeting with Phil Blundell – Leader's Office, Mansion House.

Phil and I have been having regular meetings, phone conversations and briefings. He is coming to the end of his initial scoping exercise and proposes a formalised support package including:

1] Interviewing several secondary heads, individually and in groups, to discuss their relationship with the LEA and specifically the Director of Education.
2] Making a series of visits to the heads, senior staff and key players within Doncaster's schools to discuss and develop the relationship between the heads, the New political leadership and the LEA.
3] Organising a weekend public/public partnership conference with the executive of Warwickshire County Council to develop the partnership model further and agree a concordat and operational model.
4] Providing an on-going coaching and support role for the new leader; the political new executive leadership and the Labour group.
5] Providing on-going liaison with the SoS for Education, DfES and Ofsted.

I ask him to liaise with David Marlow on this and prepare a fully-costed proposal to this effect.

ooo

Friday May 18th 2001...

10.30 pm – Meeting with Martin Hepworth – Leader's Office, Mansion House.

Martin is still refusing to sign up to the Labour Group until something is done about his [perceived] public image, thanks to the media's reporting of the "new broom" leadership. He tells me everybody is looking at him and making comments, and as a result he has stopped socialising and has had several rows at work.

To be quite honest I'm getting a little fed up with how high-maintenance Martin has become; but as per Kevin's instructions, I'm trying to cuddle up to him as much as possible. I draw the line at putting anything in writing however – a position backed by both Phil Blundell and Howard Knight.

ooo

3.00 pm

The Doncaster Star runs with the story – "Public Vote Call on Mayor Issue – Petition bid for referendum to have elected Mayor".

In it the paper reveals: "Sources say that councillors want to approve a leader and self-appointed cabinet system on Monday, despite a campaign opposing them... Official rules state that a 1,000 signature petition for a mayor elected by the people can be thrown out."

As usual, the newspaper doesn't let the truth get in the way of a good story; its reporter has confused the new democratic structures, miscalculated the size of the electorate by a shortfall of 100,000, and failed to mention that the new Local Government Act 2000 allows the electorate to force a referendum on an elected mayor – if more than 5% sign a petition requesting one.

Despite the poor showing from the public consultation exercise, the mayoral question seems to have captured the imagination of the media and the paper reports that nearly 70% of the citizens' panel favoured an elected mayor model while less than a third wanted a leader and cabinet system.

ooo

5.00 pm – Briefing with David Marlow – Leader's Office, Mansion House.

David has been undertaking work for some time as the author of a "big picture" vision for Doncaster. He has now put together what he calls the "Achieving Our Full Potential" action plan and transformational goals.

These are areas of activity that, when delivered, will "transform" Doncaster and include:
- Tackling deprivation within the borough
- Raising educational attainment

- Access to information and communications technology
- Achieving an urban renaissance
- Community participation in democracy
- Sustainable and rural communities
- Increasing employment opportunities

We agree these are highly laudable objectives and, to a certain extent, self-selecting. Nonetheless, nobody has attempted to put together such a comprehensive action plan before and David displays a real ability to articulate aspirations and turn them in to deliverable programmes.

I am a little concerned that this is "David's vision" and would prefer a more community-owned agenda, however, it's early days and I concur with his thought process – we need an agreed goal, objective, mission, vision, or "dream" even; one that we can all subscribe to and work together to achieve.

Consequently, I decide it is phenomenally important that I support and push this vision; particularly given that I have been vocal in my concerns over the complete lack of vision or ideology shown by the previous leadership or Labour group.

This is "it" – this is the plan for getting us out of the situation we are in, provided we can get the public and our partners to "buy in" to this bigger picture and leave the past behind us.

ooo

Monday May 21st 2001...

10.00 am

This is our first real Full Council Meeting and as the new leadership Aidan and I are fully aware of the implications of a poor performance. As if this isn't enough pressure, the meeting has the hugely important "Local Government Act 2000 and the New Democratic Structures" on the agenda.

David Marlow, Paul Evans and several other officers have been briefing us regularly on the matter but we have both kept our powder dry, declaring views both in support and opposition to different aspects of the report.

Amongst other issues, today's meeting has to decide whether to undertake further consultation; call a referendum; or choose one of three governance models within the act:

    i]   Leader and Cabinet Executive
    ii]   Mayor and Cabinet Executive

iii] Mayor and Council Manager

The malcontents are out in force and have taken a very strong line on the Council adopting the "Mayor and Council Manager Executive" arrangement. This would effectively relieve the councillors of their duties as politicians with the council manager physically making the decisions, in consultation with the mayor. The council manager would have to merely inform Full Council – on a regular basis. Doncaster's 63 elected councillors will, in effect, become redundant.

When you look at the mess the elected politicians have made of Doncaster Council, it is easy to see why the malcontents are campaigning for a mayor. They have played their part bringing the Donnygate scandal to the public's attention – mainly through a coordinated letter writing and whispering campaign. Now, having tasted blood, they want more; all political power handed to the council manager – which will be quite a coup if they can pull it off.

The headlines read: "A Mayor for Doncaster – say campaigners". But the campaign masks the real objective – removing power from Doncaster Labour Party.

As usual, the _de-facto_ king of the malcontents, Ray Nortrop, has done the ground work. A former disc jockey and music impresario, Ray boasts about his friendships with the likes of Jonathan King and Jimmy Savile with Savile having 'fixed it' for Ray, then aged 20, to become the resident DJ for Doncaster's 2,000 capacity Top Rank Suite on Silver Street when it opened in 1964.

The irony of such claims has never been lost on those who know the inner secrets of this self-styled promoter; some call him Svengali and there have been questions raised over his friendships with, and influence over, widowed and lonely women shortly before becoming a beneficiary in their wills.

This time though Ray has excelled himself. He's got a Scottish bagpiper to attend dressed in full army regalia, and play the likes of 'Caber Feidh', 'Black Bear' and 'Blue Bonnets over the Border' on his behalf. These traditional blood and thunder battle cry marches are extremely emotive when played live on the pipes and really send a shiver down my spine.

As I enter the chamber, I think how motivating it must have been to go into battle knowing your piper was playing – the hairs on the back of my neck are stood on end. But it's important not to be intimidated by the pipers or by the malcontents haranguing you. Many councillors prefer to use the rear stairs, entering the chamber discreetly, away from the troublemakers.

Remembering my rugby days, I choose to confront the threat, to face them out and walk in the front way with the public – deliberately approaching them to say hello.

I recognise at least a dozen regular letter writers to the local papers. True to form, the journalists are fawning over them; feigning interest to get good copy. They look startled to see me.

"Morning Mr Nortrop" I address him. "It's a beautiful day for Doncaster today – don't you agree?"

But he doesn't reply; he never does.

I smile and fuss over those I recognise – smiling at the supportive compliments from well-wishers. "Call a referendum on a mayor, Martin" says Ted Moffat, a long standing campaigner.

"Yes" enthuses his wife Joan, a little pathetically.

"That's one of my options Ted" I tell him.

Like most of the malcontents, Ted Moffat is retired. A seemingly genial man, Ted often bullies others to get his way. He is a long-standing member of the Labour Party, despite his protestations. He stays on, he has been heard to say: "So I can keep me eye on these corrupt buggers!"

"Aye – but tha's freetened o' the public in't tha" he bellows, in a deliberately broad South
Yorkshire accent – but so everyone can hear.

"Clearly Mr Moffat – but then you're not a member of the public are you? No... *you're a member of the Labour Party*... aren't you Ted?" I emphasise loudly.

"It's a good job we're all on the same side – isn't it?" Then I walk off to take my seat.

ooo

10.35 am

As the Chair of Council introduced the agenda item, I gather my notes together.

"Thank you Madam Chair" I begin.

"Thank you for allowing me to introduce this extremely important agenda item and lay out my position as the new Leader of Doncaster Council – on `Local Government Act 2000' and the new democratic structures proposed by the act."

As the newly appointed leader, I need to make a strong statement to the electorate that I'm going to be different; that I won't take their support for granted. It's important to state that the public should decide the governance model best suited for Doncaster – not another DMBC Leader and Labour group who have let the electorate down so badly in the past.

Now this is, and remains, the background to why I have called the referendum on the Mayoral model. However, the truth of the matter is that I am petrified the previous leadership may have "cooked the books" somehow; making sure the DMBC consultation is against any new form of governance and, as such, leaving a bomb waiting to go off.

If they have, then they have failed because the consultation has proved inconclusive with just over 300 responses from an electorate of more than 220,000 – less than a 0.1% response rate.

But while the poor response rate is a fairly big worry, I am more concerned about the depths the disgruntled "old-guard" might sink to in their efforts to undermine me – that they might try and blame a "sham consultative process" on the new leadership.

I have to tread carefully. In in my preamble, I cite a number of ways in which a mayoral model will be wrong for Doncaster, but welcome other aspects of the act, such as increased accountability, the introduction of a standards board for England and the new overview & scrutiny function.

I take the meeting right up to the fence – where they can see the 'Promised Land'. As I look around the room and towards the press box, there is no eagerness, no excitement, no sense of a big decision pending – more a feeling of lethargy. Full Council, the malcontents, the media and the Labour group all wait for me to do exactly what they expect me to do – carry on where the previous leadership left off, keeping the *status quo*.

But I don't. I move the calling of a referendum on adopting a "Mayor and Cabinet Executive" model.

The guidance from Westminster advises that "where public consultations have proved inconclusive, a referendum should be called". If I don't call one there is a chance central government will ask me why not.

There's also a chance the malcontents will organise a formal petition to force a referendum on us – and we will forever be on the back foot.

I cite my new leadership as a point in time, a chance to break with the past; I ask for the public's support, promising to adopt a much more conciliatory, consultative leadership style – saying this is a sign of things to come.

I want to let the people of Doncaster choose the model of governance they want – in essence, to draw a line under the so-called "Donnygate" saga.

Full Council is shocked; the public and press are shocked; the Labour group are shocked – even though I'd given a similar speech to them, before asking them to follow my lead. Only Aidan knew what I was going to do.

Now call me naïve, but I half-expect the malcontents to applaud my stance. They have been banging the drum for a mayor for six months or more. But they hardly take a breath before their letter writing and whispering campaign turns on its head:

What do we want?
A Mayor!

When do we want it?
Now!

What do we want?
A Mayor!
When do we want it?
Now!

"Which is why I am proposing we call referendum on the Mayor and Executive Model and let the people decide..."
[Slight pause]

It's a waste of public money!

ooo

Tuesday May 22nd 2001...

10.00 am – Briefing with David Marlow – Leader's Office, Mansion House.

David has asked for the meeting because he is keen to understand my thought process with regard to the mayoral referendum and whether I see myself standing for mayor, should the decision be yes.

ooo

3.00 pm

"People Will Decide On Mayor Issue" reads the front page of the Doncaster Star; and goes on to report how Council Leader Martin Winter proposed the shock plans for a vote..."

However, the newspaper has confused the issue again by misreporting that the vote will be "... on how the town's affairs should be run from October".

Ever one for a scholarly or thespian jibe, the public school-educated multi-millionaire [Independent] councillor, Martin Williams says: *"It's a bold move to call for a referendum; it's unexpected but very welcome. I must say that most of us were expecting a summer of discontent and now are in store for a winter of surprises".*

ooo

5.30 pm – Leader's Office, Mansion House

I have asked for a diarised meeting with Aidan after it transpires he's agreed to lecture on a strategic leadership programme with Doncaster College.

I point out that I have already made the decision to stand down from my community development consultancy work [MWC] and encourage Aidan to do the same, citing Wain's obsessive vindictiveness as justification in itself.

I remind him of our earlier discussion when we agreed to focus all our attention on turning the local authority around and our "re-invention strategy".

"Come on Aidan – we agreed to remain focused on this for the first eighteen months!" I exclaim.

"Stop fucking worrying about it, you wuss" he hits back. "It's only a once a week lecture on their MBA programme"

"I don't give a fuck when it is and what it is!" I begin to rant "We agreed we would put all our energies into the leadership for the first eighteen months... and you've only just managed eighteen fucking days!"

"Ah shut up fucking worrying y' moaning twat. I've told you – it won't get in the way." But not for the first time Aidan has planted a seed of doubt in my mind. I'd asked him for his full commitment and he has failed me. Maybe "failed me" was bordering on hyperbole but it certainly worried me; I'd been one hundred per cent clear that we needed to support each other totally if our leadership was going to work.

ooo

I'd previously asked Carolyne for her views on Aidan and she said she wouldn't trust him as far as she could throw him! This was a pretty devastating assessment of my "right-hand man" so early on in our relationship, but I'd already become concerned about his level of commitment to "the programme", as we termed it.

When I ask her to elucidate, she said he seemed to be one of those people who always looked at how a situation could be manipulated for his own benefit; a typical social climber!

ooo

Tuesday June 19th 2001...

7.30 pm – The Glass Park Millennium Green Trust Meeting
Pilkington Glass Offices, Kirk Sandall

For more than ten years, the Glass Park has been my passion and driver. Having conceived the project as a successor to the "Toxic Waste Out" campaign of the late 1980s, I have since written many reports and lobbied many individuals and companies to realise the community's dream.

I established the Development Company as a community-owned, not-for-profit company, which means the trading arm covenants its profits to the charity. The project has a very strong local brand and regional profile and is going from strength to strength.

During the last eighteen months, I have diverted most of the MWC work I was securing to the Development Company; as a result, it now employs 9 people. We have just entered the first year of a five year action plan that will deliver significant economic and social benefits to the community.

But as our partners battle to associate themselves with the Glass Park's success, I face constant problems directing the project. I decided to resign, so as not to create a conflict with my new position as Leader of the Council.

This evening's Trustees' Meeting is to be my last and is arguably the most difficult I have ever had to attend. I ask to speak to the trustees and thank them for their support and commitment over the years, saying I believe I'm leaving the project in a very strong position, both financially and from a capacity perspective.

But I also leave them with a warning; they should be under no illusion as to the pressure they will come under during the forthcoming months and years. I tell them I worry about the project's future – particularly as I have had to abandon it so quickly, with no real succession planning. I say I believe it will become a political football, as individuals and groups attempt to destroy my credibility as the senior Local Government representative in Doncaster.

Little do I know what a prophecy this will prove to be.

ooo

Tuesday July 3rd 2001...

4.40 pm

Aidan and I are attending our first Local Government Association [LGA] conference in Harrogate. Paul was due to pick us both up at noon to take us to our hotel – The Imperial on Prospect Place.

After booking into the conference and collecting my delegate pack, I sit on the hotel balcony and reflect on what a strange day it's been... Aidan began by giving me really spurious excuses for not being ready as arranged, and whilst I call him regularly during the day, he constantly tells me he's already set off and will be with me soon, claiming he's stuck in traffic, until he finally arrives some four hours late!

ooo

7.30 pm

Aidan and I take the opportunity to have dinner with a former school friend of mine, who now lives in Harrogate and works for the local authority. The dinner is quite illuminating, not least because Aidan reveals his obsession with visiting the council's Cold War bunkers.

ooo

Wednesday July 4th 2001...

5.30 pm

David Marlow joins us and, after an exhausting day at a wide variety of workshops, seminars and keynote speeches, I am impressed by the way he constantly wants to report back to me and Aidan and explore a Doncaster-centric take on the issues.

I have to return to Doncaster this evening for a private meeting and also to put my children to bed. I give my apologies and Paul drives me home.

ooo

Thursday July 5th 2001...

6.30 am

I awake refreshed, feeling like a more "complete", less "irresponsible" parent. However, my motivations are not solely altruistic – I have the opportunity, nay excuse, to head back to Harrogate in my 1956 Porsche 356A Cabriolet, which I seldom get the chance to drive these days.

8.30 am

Before today's conference gets underway, I breakfast with Aidan, Bev and David, who brief me on what I missed yesterday evening.

Throughout the morning Aidan regularly takes calls from Maria Graziano, his former manager at Conisbrough & Denaby Development Trust [CDDT]. When I complain that she's constantly interrupting us, he blusters that "she's reluctant to let me go"; and is always asking for advice and guidance.

ooo

7.30 pm

All four of us attend a dinner given by Fujitsu, at which Aidan, David and I are stunned by Bev Marshall's consumption levels – both of food and alcohol. Having said that, Bev's a fantastically popular individual and seems to be at the centre of a huge amount of discussion and fun.

ooo

Friday July 6th 2001...

This morning, we have a meeting set up with a colleague at the Local Government Management Board [LGMB] whom I know from my previous work with LANTRA/QCA and the
Awarding Bodies.

Although I breakfasted with him some thirty minutes ago, Aidan simply fails to turn up! After the meeting, I ring him to find out why – but his phone is switched off. I notice he's left me a text saying he has been called back to CDDT to deal with an emergency.

ooo

As the afternoon wraps up, I drive David Marlow home in my Porsche. It's a beautiful sunny afternoon and we discuss some of the ramifications of the conference on our challenges in Doncaster.

ooo

6.00 pm

After dropping David off, I pull over to phone Aidan and confront him over his unprofessional behaviour at the conference. During the conversation it becomes obvious that, despite my instructions and Aidan's protestations otherwise, he is still working for CDDT.

I am not happy; deceit is seldom a beneficial virtue and frequently destroys trust and effective teams.

ooo

Wednesday July 11th 2001...

All week we have had an information and consultation exhibition in the Frenchgate Centre, promoting the "Achieving Our Full Potential" action plan and transformational goals.

There appears to be fairly widespread "buy-in" to the idea, with both our public and private sector partners eager to support it.

Rob Hollingworth, the Star's editor, seems particularly supportive of our new leadership and the direction we are pushing the authority in, and has prepared a two-page feature entitled: "The Only Way Is Up – launch of blueprint for town's future".

ooo

Wednesday July 18th 2001...

10.00 am – Shadow Cabinet Ratification Committee, Mansion House.

Since taking over in May, one of the areas I have been enthusiastically promoting is inward investment and I have significant concerns about one of our flagship projects – the Lakeside Development.

The Lakeside Development is a huge mixed-use regeneration project on approximately 4 square miles of agricultural land, former aerodrome and landfill site to the immediate south of Doncaster. With a sixty acre lake and quality quayside as the aesthetic drive for attracting inward investment – and the Doncaster Dome, one of the UK's Top 5 most visited leisure attractions, as its anchor tenant – the area has undergone a certain amount of private sector-led regeneration in the eleven years since its inauguration in 1990.

The decade or so of development is key here, because although the project started positively and made good progress, it has now stalled and is beginning to look unfinished and unkempt. As a result, I have instructed our officers to bring forward proposals to re-energise the development to attract further investment, whilst dealing with the particularly problematic hillside area to the west of the lake.

Chairing Cabinet Ratification Committee today, I invite Bev Marshall, as the [shadow] Cabinet Member with responsibility for Trade, Industry and Innovation, to introduce the report and the decision for £1,000,000 of funding to overhaul this entire area in a soft-end landscaping and tree-planting scheme.

"May I say Chair, that I am delighted to introduce this report for a decision today" he begins.

"... and in making my introduction may I ask you to envision, if you will, Doncaster in two years' time, as passengers make the first flights from, and to, our new international airport at Finningley"

My [shadow] cabinet colleagues are captivated by Bev's presentation.

"As the aircraft is approaching our runway... the longest runway in the UK..." he adds with a wry smile *"... and they look down at the now-completed Lakeside development, they will be able to admire the tree planting scheme you agree to this morning..."*

"Whilst enjoying the cherry tree blossom, wafting in the spring sun, they will marvel at the design aesthetic that represents the steam and smoke billowing from the engines of some of the world's greatest steam trains..."

"Trains such as the Flying Scotsman, Mallard and Sir Nigel Gresley – trains that were all built here in Doncaster..."

Bev is on a roll: *"And these first passengers will wonder, will they not, which people – nay which politicians – had the foresight to make the decision this morning to "complete" the lakeside development with this scheme."*

Bev goes on to describe the specifics of the scheme including the more detailed costings, safety and environmental considerations, and legal aspects.

I am delighted with Bev. He is his usual masterful self, highlighting how an experienced politician takes the information before them and links it to other policies and practices to deliver an excellent, informative presentation; one that assures his audience he has a strong grasp of his portfolio area.

But perhaps more importantly, Bev has nudged at an issue I am keen to explore further; he's reminded me that the skilled workforce of Doncaster used to lead the world in the heavy industry of the railways. Not just the railways though, alongside many of our fellow northern towns and cities, we also led the mineral extraction industry.

A world-class skills agenda for Doncaster.

Friday July 20th 2001...

2.00 pm

Rosie rings to question me on how we might "welcome" Martin Hepworth back into the Labour group "fold", given that he is one of her constituency members.

Rosie's Constituency Labour Party [CLP] is Central Doncaster. It is a very well-organised partisan constituency with a large, sometimes belligerent, membership and she is always keen to keep them on her side. She's pushing me to write a formal letter of apology to Martin – and is clearly annoyed when I flatly refuse.

She senses, correctly, that I won't budge and moves on to the issue of the mayor. As usual, it's difficult to gauge Rosie's opinion; she tends to toe the party line in a non-committal manner. The subject of the mayor is proving very divisive within the party however, with a great deal of misinformation being peddled. Rosie is keen to keep her own counsel but eager to know the Labour group's stance. I tell her there's generally a sense of ambivalence to the whole of Local Government Act 2000.

ooo

2.30 pm

Kevin rings for two reasons. Firstly, he is being dragged into the Martin Hepworth row and has now decided to have it in public. He tells me the Doncaster Star will be covering the argument in tomorrow evening's edition. I realise this must be why Rosie's getting annoyed as she feels Kevin is meddling.

Secondly, he wants to make sure I have a position on the mayor. He is very relaxed about the whole issue and, quite surprisingly, is in favour of us having one in Doncaster.

He spends quite a lot of time explaining how overview & scrutiny functions in a similar manner to government select committees – and he invites me down to Westminster to see them in operation.

I tell him Rosie's "view".

"You see that's it with Rosie" he says, drawing heavily on his cigarette *"She's very good at avoiding having to take a stance."*

"Not like Lady Caroline who always – has – a – view – on – every – fucking – thing" he enunciates.

"But that's not a bad thing..." I say *"... at least Caroline's not frightened to take a stance on an issue"*

"Aye..." and I can hear him smoking again *"... but when the ship goes down, don't follow Caroline, Martin. You follow Rosie every time – because she'll always make sure she's in the life boat."*

ooo

Thursday July 26th 2001...

3.00 pm

The Doncaster Star features a page 5 story "Leadership Row – MP Hits Back". The newspaper reports that Councillor Hepworth resigned from the Council's Labour group on Monday after Mr Hughes pressurised colleagues into supporting current leader, Martin Winter, following Colin Wedd's departure from the post in April.

Generally the story belittles Martin Hepworth, and Kevin attacks him for complaining about being on the losing side.

"Not being on the winning side all the time is something you have to live with in politics" Kevin is quoted as saying. *"That's politics, let's get on with it."*

But the article incenses me. *"Listen to this"* I rage at Aidan and Gerry McLister.

"He believed he had been frozen out of the council cabinet unfairly... the stupid bastard."

"He believed!" I reiterate in exasperation *"He says the leadership tarred his reputation by demoting him from Chairman of the Environment Committee."*

"The Environment Committee – and the whole committee system – disappeared with the introduction of Local Government 2000" I begin to rail at a non-existent audience *"... the thick bastard... and if he really thinks I should've given him a Cabinet position, after he tried to turn me over..."*

"He doesn't know you Martin" completed Gerry.

I smile at him, acknowledging his interruption: *"Know me? Know me?"*

"Listen to this – and he's claiming he resigned from the Council's Labour group on Monday, which is news to me, but that he remains a member of Doncaster Central's Labour Party..."

"And..." I command the almost empty room to listen. *"Are you ready for this?"*

"...Which is supporting his bid for a public apology from the Council Leadership – fucking Rosie, she's fucking interfering again."

"Well she's got to support her councillors" says Aidan.

"Oh yes – she has – but she needs to give him a reality check. Kev's right. He needs to fucking grow up – he's bleating like a spoilt fucking schoolboy."

"Which is supporting his bid for a public apology! Why the fuck should I apologise to him?" I ask the room.

"Oh... sorry Martin, you've run with the hare and the hounds and been caught out – and now no-one wants to run with you – have a cabinet position..."

"Except Rosie" says Gerry.

"What d'you mean?"

"Except Rosie. She's looking after her councillors – and she'll run with him. Which might be dangerous for you Martin" Gerry closes.

"Know me? Know me? I'll fucking show him how little he knows me" I threaten.

"Whoops... well if he will tickle the tail of the tiger." says Aidan knowingly.

"Fucking dead right! Aidan – find out what the Labour Party rules say for someone who is refusing to sign up?"

ooo

Tuesday August 7th 2001...

3.00 pm

The Star's headline reads: "Stand and Deliver say Frustrated Fans – frustrated Doncaster Rovers fans are calling for answers over the lack of movement over a proposed new town stadium".

"Fuck me – what do they expect? We've only been in charge for 12 fucking weeks... Did they ask me for a quote? Did they ask anybody for a quote? Did they bollocks!"

I ask Alison to set up a meeting with Chaz Walker, the Rovers' Supporters Club Chairman; Ray Green the Chief Executive of the Dragons, who I used to play rugby with; and a senior representative from the Doncaster Belles.

"Y'know it's fucking typical of the Rovers fans – and the Doncaster mentality. We hate the fucking Council... in fact we don't even vote! But we aren't gonna do it ourselves" I rail at a non-existent inquisitor.

"Ask not what the Council can do for you – but what you can do for the Council" Aidan paraphrases.

"It was Kennedy's call for the electorate to participate in public service" he adds helpfully.

"Theodore Sorensen wrote it for him... in 1961".

I ignore Aidan's attempts to annoy me. But the issue has given me an idea. As a community we just lie there and expect things to be done for us. As a local authority we are unbelievably passive – simply waiting for things to be done for us, acknowledging "our lot" is not a very good one but always expecting government to step in and help.

Thatcher has to take a large dose of blame for this mindset. Maggie's 1980s economic policies – like her Pit Closure Programme after the 84-85 miners' strike – destroyed our communities, yet she continued to drive them through regardless of the social and environmental damage they were wreaking, leaving community resilience at an all-time low.

But that was nearly 20 years ago and we need to move on. We need to get on the front foot, actively encouraging investment to come to us, rather than just waiting for it to happen.

Admittedly, government should step in – but when and at what level? Local, national or European? In terms of large scale economic restructuring, we are part of the European Union's Objective 1 funding programme, and we frequently benefit from UK Central government programmes and strategies.

I have seen massive success, albeit on a very local level, with the Glass Park project where we have been proactive in attracting public, private and voluntary sector funding and support for a mixed use regeneration project with economic, environmental and social benefits. That success, however, relied very much on my energies, my enthusiasm, my networks and my relationships.

Since I became leader, we have benefitted from projects like Finningley Airport, the plans to upgrade Doncaster Racecourse, the Frenchgate Interchange and others; but these have taken years to come to fruition and are still several years away from delivery.

How then do we encourage the same "can do" approach and mentality? Bizarrely, the answer comes to me while I'm watching an interview with Robert Mugabe. He is explaining how Zimbabwe's future cannot lie with their present economy; that they had to be able and allowed, to compete with the rest of the world and that this is *his* priority.

We need a similar single point of contact for investors; whether that be the "Leader" or the "Mayor" – that person needs to be able to make all the decisions the investors need.

Doncaster's success relies not on being recipients of Third World aid but on our ability to compete globally and being seen as an attractive destination. To achieve that, we need to empower the citizens of Doncaster. If Doncaster is to achieve its full potential, then we must encourage each and every person here to achieve theirs.

ooo

Thursday August 9th 2001

6.00 am

Carolyne and I have always been huge Francophiles and we are leaving for our annual family vacation in France.

With the Mayoral referendum coming up, I am beginning to take more than a passing interest in their attitude to government and their simpler approach to life, less influenced by any [English] thirst for or race towards Americanisation.

Ever since our children were born, Carolyne and I have sought to spend as much of the summer holidays with them as possible. Indeed, as they have grown, we prioritise spending at least three or four weeks in France with them each summer as well as at other religious and cultural festivals during the year.

Obviously some family commitments have had to be sacrificed as I took charge in Doncaster, but I still insist on a three week break with them each summer; and with August being the silly season, we are heading off to enjoy the French sunshine again.

ooo

11.30 am

Aidan calls me. I complain I haven't even got out of the country yet and he's disturbing me, but he says he needs my okay for an emergency purchase of 100,000 paper clips!

He says he's been thinking and, as a result, is having a meeting with Martin Hepworth to try and resolve the impasse. It seems strange he hasn't mentioned this in the past couple of weeks, despite me asking for him to find out what the Labour Party Rule Book says about someone who is refusing to sign up.

I assume Rosie has been lobbying him. The Hepworth issue is becoming a bit of a running sore and needs resolving.

"Let me know how it goes" I tell him. *"But on no account commit me to an apology because I've done, and we've done, nothing wrong."*

ooo

Friday August 10th 2001...

11.30 am

Aidan meets with Martin Hepworth.

ooo

Tuesday 14th August 2001...

11.30 am – Saint-Maxine, Cote d'Azur, France

By now Carolyne has become used to my phone being permanently switched on, so when Aidan calls again, it's nothing unusual.

"Thirty five degrees yesterday so very much enjoying living an al fresco lifestyle; some interesting ideas for us in terms of encouraging a café culture" I respond to his opening gambit.

"What are you wanting Aidan?"

"We've had a request to submit a bid for city-status. It's for the Queen's Golden Jubilee next year – and we've got to submit an expression of interest by the end of the week."

"Nah – we haven't got a fucking chance" I dismiss *"We got kicked back the last time we put in for it – you know we won't win it.*

"... and they'll be deciding it early in the new year" I continue *"Right in the middle of the first of the Donnygate trials in Nottingham – nah bollocks to it – we don't stand a fucking chance."*

"Don't be so quick to judge" he calms me *"What if we go for it... knowing we won't win?"*

He repeats himself: *"What if we go for it... knowing we won't win... purely and simply to get people to 'buy in', to start backing Doncaster and the new agenda? "We can really push the town... get Rob Hollingworth* [Doncaster Star editor] *to Chair the Bid."* He's on a roll.

"Who've you been talking to?" I ask *"Because this isn't your idea – is it?"*

"No-one!" he defends. *"You cheeky bastard"*

"Well you've just rung me up... without priming me – whilst I'm on holiday – what do you expect me to say?... I think it's a ludicrous idea – it's one borne of pure madness" and I adopt the voice of an evil dictator *"But it's so mad it might even work."*

"So are we going for it?" he asks.

"Of course we are" I laugh. "If that's what you're advising me. Let's just hope it doesn't become a "Dough Boy"

"What's that mean?"

"Let's just hope it doesn't become a "Dough Boy – Doughboy was a scene in Oliver Hardy's last ever film role – with Bing Crosby in the 1950s – called Riding High"

But the analogy means nothing to him so I explain it's a film about a horse trainer who has fallen on hard times and looks to his horse, Broadway Bill, to win the big race and get him out of hock. They need some betting money and set out to con a punter, an easy sucker – Hardy.

They give Hardy the name of the 'dead cert' – for £25 dollars – and tell him to keep it strictly to himself. But he tells everybody and it spreads like wildfire.

Put all your money on Doughboy, the word goes round the course! Give me a hundred and fifty bucks on Doughboy – all the money my wife's got in the world, says Hardy.

The trickster ends up getting swept away in his own hysteria – and bets the money they conned on the old nag – which finishes last.

The scene ends with a semi-comatose Hardy being carried away on a stretcher, muttering "Doughboy" over and over again; and the trickster uttering the immortal line: *"I've been milked by my own chicanery"*.

"I'm just saying – we need to be careful about raising expectations that can't be realised. We might create a problem we don't want."

"You boring fucking bastard!" he says *"I'll submit the expression of interest then."*

ooo

Wednesday August 15th 2001…

The Doncaster Star runs with the story "Labour In Search For Truce – talks to see if councillor will come back into fold" and gives a fairly detailed account of Martin Hepworth's meeting with Aidan.

ooo

Wednesday August 22nd 2001…

10.00 am

Aidan rings me to say the Crown Prosecution Service has announced that no charges are to follow Colin Wedd's arrest.
    This just adds to the air of invincibility that surrounds us at the moment – the sense that I/we have simply had Colin Wedd removed. But it makes me nervous. I know I didn't have him removed – so who *is* controlling the process?

> <u>Guardian Newspaper – Wednesday 22nd August 2001</u>
>
> The CPS drops Doncaster case over lack of evidence.
>   *Criminal proceedings against a former Doncaster Council Leader have been halted after the Crown Prosecution Service decided there was insufficient evidence to proceed.*
>   *Colin Wedd, who resigned as leader in April following his arrest on alleged expenses fraud, had the case against him formally discontinued at Doncaster Magistrates' Court.*
>   *Councillor Wedd faced two charges relating to alleged false claims for two first-class rail fares when, it was claimed, he actually paid standard fares. The difference was £155.*
>   *A CPS spokesman said: "It was felt that there was not sufficient evidence to proceed in this case and therefore the decision was taken to call a halt."*
>   *With a clean bill of health, Mr Wedd is expected to be given a senior role to play within the authority. As well as being Leader, he was also Chair of the powerful Racecourse Committee, which he stood down from following his arrest.*
>   *Two previous leaders, Malcolm Glover and Peter Welsh, were given suspended sentences for expenses fraud.*

ooo

Friday August 31st 2001…

Rosie calls to discuss the Martin Hepworth scenario. Mags and Gerry are with me so I raise my finger to say "shh" and write on the whiteboard that it's Rosie.
    Clearly Aidan's recent meeting with Martin has left Rosie thinking some form of apology is in the pipeline; it appears to be Martin's one and only negotiating point. I explain I won't be apologising – particularly given the Labour Party Rulebook's position *vis a vis* members not signing up to the Labour group – and that she and he both need to move on. She appears a little riled.
    I quite like Rosie, and we haven't had a disagreement so far, but she needs to know I won't budge on this one.
    "You need to tell him to get out of the corner he's backed himself into, Rosie. This has gone on for three months now and, to be quite honest, I'm fucking fed up of it."

"Firstly, the Party's own rules say he's now 'left' the Party – and the only thing stopping him from being thrown out is that I or we haven't formally let the National Executive know yet. Fuck knows what Nan's thinking about all this – because she's got to be aware."

"Well..." she stumbled *"She is... and she's not very happy but I've asked her for a bit more time in view of Martin's ill health and long standing membership of the party."*

Rosie, very expertly, has gone into listening mode. She's not going to get in to a row over this one with me – so I can put on a show for Mags and Gerry.

"Bollocks to his ill health – he's deliberately making himself ill! He's trying to dictate to the leadership and it's not gonna fucking work..."

"He needs to be aware he's got nowhere to go on this one. If they throw him out, it'll be five years before they'll consider him for membership again. Can you afford to wait for him for five years Rosie? Because, to be quite honest, he's not that fucking good."

And I remember my second point: *"And secondly – who the fuck does he think he is? Briefing the papers directly about our own internal arguments..."*

"If he's such a stickler for acting in the party's best interests and not breaching the Rule Book, then I've got him bang to rights for not following communication procedures and bringing the party into disrepute."

"Well there does appear to be quite a distance between the two of you, doesn't there" she says with a fake laugh and moves on to discuss the upcoming Mayoral referendum.

ooo

Monday September 3rd 2001...

2.30 pm

I meet with Martin Hepworth and ask him why he chose to say I "tarred his reputation" and had been "heavy handed" in the leadership selection process.

Predictably, he denies saying it. *"I didn't say that..."* he starts – but stops himself in full cry...

"Oh... I thought you did – because that's what they fucking reported!"

"You've been around for long enough Martin" I tell him *"... you know newspapers don't report what you've said – they report what they want you to have said."* I repeat the comments I made to Rosie – leaving him in no doubt he's out on his own and needs to come back to the party, before it's too late. He leaves to consider his options.

I draft a letter to Martin Hepworth and ask Alison to make sure it catches tonight's post.

Dear Martin

I write with reference to your position and continued membership of Doncaster MBC's ruling Labour group.

I'm saddened to have to write this letter to you because, as I have said to you before, I feel that the ruling Labour group has an important job to do for the town and people of Doncaster. The challenges presented as we move towards the new democratic structures and as we implement the "Achieving Our Full Potential" Action Plan and its transformational goals require a strong and committed leadership team.

I cannot make a public statement about things I know little about; in particular, any activity within Doncaster's ruling group in the years previous to my election as a Councillor. However, through this letter, I would like to make a private statement to you as a colleague and friend.

I have always been uneasy at the way the media has apparently tarred those outside of the "new leadership" with the same brush and, as a result, that you personally have been criticised by some of your constituents. I have always had respect for your sense of right and wrong and considered you a person of integrity. Consequently, I can assure you that I, my deputy Aidan Rave and others within the group's leadership have never commented adversely or otherwise to the press with regards to you or other members of Doncaster's ruling Labour Group. It is unfortunate that you feel the media's coverage has been injurious to your character, however, I feel this is a factor outside of my influence as Leader and a sad reflection of the world we live in today.

I trust this letter has gone some way to assuaging your concerns; and that you can now reflect on the matter in a more objective manner.

Yours etc.

ooo

Friday September 7th 2001...

11.15 am

Jeff Ennis calls *"How do you feel about the Mayoral referendum?"*
"I'm fairly relaxed about it Jeff. I'm not sure which way they'll vote though – the electorate are quite fickle in Doncaster and often buck the trend"
"So do you think they're going to go for it? Because these elected mayors are one of Tony's babies – he's quite obsessed with them."
"If I'm dispassionate about it, I think they'll go for the status quo – we're not that radical in Doncaster. But there's always the chance they might turn around

and bite us because of the way politicians have let them down in the past."

ooo

3.00 pm

The Doncaster Star runs with the story "Labour Man Back In The Fold Again – Councillor rejoins group after exile of 2 months".

ooo

Monday September 10th 2001...

Mark Eales is appointed [Acting] Director of Schools. Mark has joined us from Coventry City Council's Education Service where he has held a number of posts, including General, Senior Principal Adviser. In addition, he has led and managed primary, secondary and special schools in times of crisis, and deputised for the Strategic Director on a regular basis.

An acquaintance of Phil Blundell, Mark is also highly regarded by Eric Wood, the County Education Officer for Warwickshire.

ooo

Mathew Simpson, the Executive Director of Education, goes on long-term sick leave.

ooo

Tuesday September 11th 2001

This is one of those immortal days when we all remember where we were... But not only were the events of 911 globally significant, I believe they also had a considerable impact on my time as Mayor of Doncaster.

I am in no way trying to trivialise what happened – just recognise that they provide a record of how individuals grasp the magnitude of such an incident and respond to it in the early stages.

ooo

2.40 pm – The Ivanhoe Centre, Conisbrough

Meeting of South Yorkshire Forum
Meeting of South Yorkshire Objective 1 Programme Monitoring Committee
Meeting of South Yorkshire Objective 1 Performance Management Board

These meetings are turgid affairs – and only really serve to provide minutes of agreed decisions that will satisfy external audit requirements. The real work is always undertaken outside such fora, by the officers so charged.

The meetings consist of representatives from a combination of local and sub-regional groups [all lobbying for their pet transactional projects to be funded]; senior politicians and staff from Barnsley, Doncaster, Rotherham and Sheffield Councils [struggling to work together on a transformational agenda]; and regional, national and European bureaucrats trying to encourage a strategic intervention programme of international significance and impact.

They are always a nightmare to Chair and Martin Havenhand, the Chief Executive of Yorkshire Forward, the Regional Development Agency, is the man with the task.

Phil Coppard, Chief Executive of Barnsley MBC [looking down at his Blackberry]:

"*Chair... I'm sorry to disturb the meeting... but I've just had a text message informing me that the twin towers in New York have just been bombed – as has the Pentagon – and that planes are attacking key destinations across America... it would seem that, to all intents and purpose, World War III is about to start!*"

Martin Havenhand looks quizzically at the members around the table, saying falteringly:

"*Okay... well can I thank you for that intervention Phil... can I err... can I suggest that... that we just finish this agenda item first... and we can then consider the implications of what you're saying, Phil*"

Since I have already arranged to leave the meeting early, I choose to head off immediately – I have a pre-arranged appointment to collect my children from school.

ooo

3.10 pm – Our House at Kirk Sandall

Having switched on the TV, I watch the astonishing scenes unfold. Knowing that my Chief Executive is at the meeting in Conisbrough, I telephone one of our Senior Officers in the Civic Office who has offered me excellent advice on several issues during the early weeks of my leadership.

"... I don't know if you've seen a television or not but these scenes from America are quite extraordinary and I am concerned that we need to be doing something urgently... I don't really know what we should be doing – but we need to be on standby or something. This will have massive ramifications for us and we need to be ready".

"Okay – thanks Leader – I'll get access to a television and come back to you as quickly as I can."

"Thanks ▮▮▮▮ if you need me to come in, send a driver to come and get me – and I'll get somebody to have my kids."

ooo

3.15 pm

▮▮▮▮ calls me back "Yes I've seen the images Leader, it really is quite appalling. But I've spoken to one or two of my colleagues and we are having a letter drafted right now and we will send this with a condolences card to the Mayor of New York straight away."

Even my children slammed the door to block-out my language!

ooo

Friday September 14th 2001...

10.00 am

Jeff Ennis calls *"How do you feel about the Mayoral referendum next week?"*
"Well I'm looking forward to it – but I wonder what effect 911 will have?"
"What do you mean?"
"Well for the last 54 hours all we've seen, every minute, is Rudy Giuliani taking charge of New York after the Twin Towers were destroyed – and Bush running for cover, of course!"
"Do you think that will have an effect?"
"Well Aidan certainly does – I think having had corrupt bastards running the place for the past few years will probably have more of an effect"
"Well that's not a problem is it? Kev seems to think you'll make a good Mayor as well" he smarms me.
"Well... let's cross that bridge if we get to it."

"Malcy's calmed down now has he?" he fishes.

"He has thanks – and "old Jockey's" been at the races all week for me. Will you be coming on Saturday?"

"I will – I'll be going as a guest of Ladbrokes thanks. But I'll pop in at some point with Dick Caborn. Tony's just made him Minister of Sport."

ooo

Monday September 17th 2001...

I pen a letter to Martyn Doughty, Chair of Natural England, asking for a meeting to consider how we might end the extant Mineral Extraction permissions on Thorne & Hatfield Moors.

ooo

Thursday September 20th 2001...

10.30 pm – the referendum result

25% turnout:

35, 453 [65%] vote in favour of a Mayor.   19, 398 [35%] vote against a Mayor.

ooo

11.45 pm – Kevin Hughes House, Bentley, Doncaster

Aidan and I have gone to Kevin's house to discuss the referendum result. Kevin opens the door for us – he has a cigarette already lit, which he bites between his teeth so he can speak.

"Well... the people have chosen – a Mayor for Doncaster eh?" and he closes the door "... the people have chosen eh... did you see that one coming?"

He takes us into his kitchen, where he already has a bottle of red wine open. He pours us both a glass.

"Well I didn't – well I don't think I did, but Aidan certainly did. Didn't you?"

"The Giuliani effect" says Aidan prophetically.

"But the question was very leading, wasn't it?"

"What was it?" asks Kevin rhetorically... **"Would you like Doncaster Council to be run in a different way..."** he pauses for effect... **... that includes a** *directly elected Mayor?"*

"We've invaded countries for less than that" he says, in masterful overstatement.

"Would you like Doncaster Council to be run in a different way..." he pauses again "... that includes a directly elected Mayor?"

"YES – we're desperate for Doncaster Council to be run in a different way! Of course they're going to say fucking YES!" he shouts in a kind of mock rant.

Kevin looks at his wine, checks we each have a glass and drinks his full down.

"Ahh..." he says loudly, wiping his lips with the back of his hand "Still... the people have spoken..." and he pours himself another glass. "Democracy has prevailed... So what's your plan B then?"

"We haven't really got one... have we?" I say looking sheepishly at Aidan.

"You haven't fucking got one?" he shouts exasperatedly before Aidan has chance to respond.

"Whoa... We can't be held to account for 911" says Aidan – equally exasperated.

"And you can't realistically be blaming it on 911, either" despairs Kevin.

Sensing the mood is getting a little tense, I look at Aidan and add dismissively: *"He's only fucking joking. He didn't see this one coming either – did you?"*

Kevin turns to me: *"No... You're right, I didn't see it coming."* He smiles – and draws heavily on another cigarette: *"That doesn't mean you didn't need a Plan B though..."*

"So what's your Plan B then?" asks Aidan.

"I haven't fucking got one...." and we all laugh. "But I'll fucking get one" and he tops up our drinks.

ooo

05.30 am – Kevin Hughes House, Bentley, Doncaster

Aidan and I are leaving Kevin's. We are both 'tired and emotional'.

"Well at least we had a plan B" he slurs.

"When?" I ask him.

"At about 3.00 o'clock – but I can't remember what it is now"

ooo

Friday September 21st 2001...

Several TV and radio stations want to interview me about last night's historic referendum result. To be honest, I am suffering terribly from the previous night's over-indulgence and the interviews are a real struggle.

ooo

3.30 pm

Always predictable in its pessimism, Doncaster Star runs with the story "You Vote For History in the Mayor-Making – poll chooses new way to run borough and end to ceremonial role"

The paper also goes with the linked story "Cabinet shake-up set to be unveiled – face-lift for services" and says running Doncaster's schools, transport network and social services will change forever next week when the authority unveils its new cabinet system – a reference to Local Government Act 2000 and the new democratic structures which prompted the mayoral referendum.

ooo

Tuesday September 25th 2001...

The Finningley Airport Public Inquiry is postponed for two weeks "after protest groups, Friends of the Earth, Finningley Airport Network [FAN] and a consortium of international airports claimed they did not have enough time to read the case papers" reports the Doncaster Free Press.

The Doncaster Star's article says an attempt to change the venue for the Public Inquiry was thrown out by the Inspector, Mr Graham Self, who also threatened to eject a campaigner from the hearing.

"Balby man John Hammond clashed with Mr Self when he asked him to read out a letter from FAN member Ray Nortrop, claiming he was not allowed into the Earl of Doncaster."

"Good old Ray" I exclaim *"He never misses an opportunity to try to do Doncaster down".*

ooo

Tuesday September 25th 2001...

"£60,000 a Year For New Mayor" cries the Doncaster Star and brands the independent advisory panel's recommendations as "obscene".

ooo

Friday September 28th 2001...

The Star runs with a follow up story "Cabinet Door Still Shut – Opposition Group Stay Out In Cold" and slams me for picking an "...all Labour Cabinet to run the town despite losing a referendum to scrap the system just a week ago".

Forever desperate to prompt fate – and parade their anti-Labour stance – the newspaper continues [hopefully these] "Labour councillors could lose their new roles... when a mayoral leader is elected in a poll next year."

ooo

Monday October 1st 2001...

South Yorkshire Police announce Operation Danum ["Donnygate"] has ended. Aidan and I are elated and keen to see what line the media take. Generally speaking, they have been supportive since we took charge in May; although we put this down to the huge charm offensive we have been on for the past five months. The Doncaster Star puts it on the front page.

> DONNYGATE inquiry ended
>
> The long running Donnygate expenses fraud inquiry has finally ended, South Yorkshire Police announced today. A statement issued from police headquarters said that Operation Danum was "now complete" and no further arrests were expected.
>
> The police probe has lasted over four-and-a-half years and resulted in more than 20 former and serving councillors being convicted of offences relating to expenses fiddling, with a few serving jail sentences...

The Yorkshire Post fails to cover it – despite winning awards for the way its staff "uncovered and investigated" the story previously, which is irritating to say the least. Both Aidan and I are furious. How dare they give such an important story for Doncaster, such a low profile?

"*Do they not know what a big story this is?*" rages Aidan.

Staff in our communications unit, are much more philosophical, arguing the important thing is that the inquiry is over and we can move forward once again.

"We invested so much fucking time in getting the police to draw the line" I moan.

"Think politically" says Aidan — and I can see him moving over to the comm's team's point of view. *"Everybody knows we've ended it Martin — and that's mainly down to me and you"* he reasons.

"I know you're right but we've wanted this for so long — and so have a lot of other people — that's why it hurts that they dismiss it when it comes."

"Just look at the Poulson scandal in the North East — the media will never let that go, so why should they let Donnygate go?"

He drives home his point: *"It's not in their interests to get rid of Donnygate. It's bad news and they sell too many papers on the back of it."*

ooo

Tuesday October 2nd 2001...

9.30 am

I have a meeting with David Marlow, where I express concern that he is unable to present me with a scoping paper outlining all the inward investment projects across the borough — mapped out in the context of short, medium and long-term and with a corresponding SWOT analysis for each.

David tells me he has charged the Executive Director of Development, with this task and assures me he will provide such information as a matter of urgency.

ooo

Monday October 8th 2001...

Although I've never been overly worried about what the papers say, they've been provoking a media storm about the "Mayor's pay" — recommended in a report before Council today — and it seems to have got a hold with the public.

The report, on all elected members' roles, responsibilities and remuneration levels, has been compiled by an independent panel of Doncaster business people, especially convened for that task.

I'm fairly relaxed about the issue myself. It's a large amount of money but not if you consider how much I was earning before I became the Leader of the Council — with a lot better hours and a lot less hassle!

However, I'm not doing the leader's job for the money and the way the media are spinning the story is making mischief.

Doncaster's councillors are being labelled the second highest "paid" in the region [after Kirklees].

My view is that we've not even got to the mayoral election yet and the general "members' salaries" position is pretty undefendable, so I suggest we kick the matter into the long grass until after the election and review it after a year.

Ever keen to avoid making an accountable decision, unless it's a decision they want to be seen to make, the Labour group [and Council] members delight in my proposed "non-decision" – and there is unanimous support when I move that we defer the report and revisit the matter after the election of the town's inaugural Executive Mayor.

ooo

Tuesday October 9th 2001…

"Mayor's pay is cut to £40,000" cries the Doncaster Star. The paper continues "…the cut was suggested [sic.] by the bookies' early favourite for the job, council leader Councillor Martin Winter. He also ordered [sic.] that councillors should lose a fifth of their takings for poor performance."

ooo

Friday October 12th 2001…

Doncaster's bid for city-status is sent off to the Home Office in London. In an attempt to get an unsupportive local press on board, we have asked Merrill Diplock [Doncaster Free Press Editor] and Rob Hollingworth [Doncaster Star Editor] to sit on the Doncaster City-status bid steering group.

The strategy appears to be working, as both newspapers are now publishing more encouraging stories.

ooo

Monday October 15th 2001…

7.30 pm – Dinner with George Holmes, Principal of Doncaster College, High Melton

George Holmes, the relatively new Principal of Doncaster College, has invited David Marlow, Aidan and me for dinner at the Stables, the college's catering and hospitality centre at High Melton.

George had previously been at the new Lincoln University Project – something I was involved with in its very early stages – and knows I am keen to explore a "big" project or statement with regard to education.

Over an excellent private dinner George pitches the concept of the Education Village [sic.]. All four of us are excited at the prospect of a large joint project and, potentially, an antidote to the previous leadership's aborted attempt to close many of the smaller sixth forms we have within our seventeen secondary schools.

We ask George to scope a broader Doncaster Education City project for further discussion.

ooo

Wednesday October 17th 2001…

The Doncaster Star runs with "New Order – a new-style cabinet of 10 Labour councillors began taking charge at the Mansion House today."

"The new cabinet system was today in action for the first time – adding another chapter to Doncaster's democratic history. But… may not be the last change to affect the authority along its road to regeneration."

In a mildly supportive article, the newspaper attempts to report objectively about the new democratic structures and how they will work; offering faint praise for our role in promoting the emerging new democracy and how we have championed the opposition's role in the overview & scrutiny function.

However, we have to run with a shadow system until after the mayoral election next May, with the "Cabinet Ratification Committee" legally making the decisions presented by the Executive Committee.

Completely ignoring our massive strides forward, Councillor Martin Williams is, as usual, quick to seize the opportunity presented by a press always desperate for good copy.

Despite my obsession with involving all parts of the [elected] Council and the public in the decision-making process, Martin has refused a position on any of the sub-committees – and is claiming he has been frozen out of the process.

Jumping on the convoluted model we are operating, the Star reports: "Having the Cabinet sit on the ratification committee means that they will be ratifying themselves, which is no more than a closed shop" and he pledges to put forward a candidate for the mayoral election next May. "It will probably be all change in May when we have a new mayor. We will run things more democratically if we get the chance."

Friday October 19th 2001...

2.30 pm – Meeting with Phil Blundell – Leader's Office, Mansion House.

Phil and I have one of our regular meetings with regard to his support for me and the intervention programme with our Education Directorate. Badged under the Public/Public Partnership with Warwickshire County Council.

Phil briefs me on the background to a conference planned for the beginning of November – specifically for leading members and key officers from the respective authorities. It will address issues in Section 3 [No. 27] of Ofsted's Grade Criteria for Inspection Judgements.

"Number 27" in the Strategic Management Section deals with crucial issues of member/officer responsibilities and relationships, and structures for members' strategic and scrutiny roles.

The SoS for Education, Estelle Morris, will be attending.

My Cabinet Member for Lifelong Learning, Tony Sockett, is to head up the event. Tony is the retired Assistant Director of Education for Doncaster Council and one of the year 2000 intake of new breed "novice" councillors. He is a sharp dresser and always looks well-manicured and turned out. But as a man employed by DMBC for most of his life, Tony sometimes has difficulty thinking of himself as a politician and not as an Officer.

Phil is very aware of Tony's limitations and says I should be under no illusions as to the need for me and my colleagues to perform well. *"This isn't about Doncaster's Education Directorate 20 years ago"* he tells me pointedly, *"Warwickshire County Council is a high performing Local Authority and you will do well to benchmark us against them."*

I ask Phil about the Director of Education. I believe that, with the appointment of Mark Eales as the Acting Director of Schools, his position is becoming untenable.

"What do you want me to say Martin?" Phil responds. *"You've seen how it works – you don't need me to join the dots. You're a superb intuitive politician Martin, you should always follow your instinct, because invariably it's right. You know what you need to do."*

I'm reminded of so many issues I've dealt with intuitively over the years – not least the road rage attack by the off-duty police officer two years ago, which, in my view, the Police Complaints Commission never dealt with satisfactorily.

ooo

Monday October 22nd 2001...

Adam Skinner, the Executive Director of Development, goes on long-term sick leave.

ooo

The Doncaster Star manages to get the story wrong again! Reporting on a National Apple Day at the Glass Park, it confuses what is a voluntary project with Doncaster Council, presenting it as a Doncaster Council Outdoor Services' event. I am seething – I see it as a conspiracy, a set-up, and I want to chastise the newspaper.

Our communications team calm me down – arguing that it's a reasonable mistake to make. I'm not so sure.

ooo

6.00 pm – Meeting with Aidan – Leader's Office, Mansion House.

I've asked for a diarised meeting with Aidan to discuss two issues:

Firstly, it's now four months since he began his lecturing at the college. I tell him I want to discuss whether he feels it's having any impact on his commitment to the role of deputy leader. Not for the first time, Aidan becomes very fuzzy about the benefits and drawbacks and is awkward, clumsy even, in his avoidance of the subject.

Secondly, I say I want to be clear about exactly what we want to achieve from the Stoke Rochford event.

This is a fairly big event for us, particularly for me, because it takes me back to my Baptism of Fire – the video conference with Estelle Morris the morning after I became Leader. It also marked my introduction to Phil Blundell and his support of me as an emerging political force. I have come to regard him highly and it's a relationship I think I can trust.

I have issued a three line whip on the conference and my Chief Executive, David Marlow, all Executive Directors and several senior education staff, are expected to attend alongside their counterparts from Warwickshire County Council. As such, it is being classed by DfES and Ofsted as the turning point in Doncaster's educational crisis.

I have been investing a significant amount of time and energy into turning around the Education Directorate and despite what Phil and our Officers are telling me, *we are going to be judged* against Warwickshire CC.

I tell Aidan I believe you can learn many lessons from sport and, to this end I've decided we're all going down to Grantham together on a "team bus". Call me hyper-competitive but we've got to intimidate the opposition. Let them see that we're a tight unit; that we're family.

Aidan tells me I've lost the plot; that I've misjudged this and my competitive streak is in danger of damaging our relationship with WCC.

"Let's be under no illusions here, Aidan" I say. "Of course WCC are supporting us as a sister Labour Local Authority; but we need to be very, very clear, they are gonna love being made out to be the big hitters – it's only natural."

"I still think your turning us out like a football squad is too competitive – we're going to look stupid. They're just trying to support us and you want to pummel them into the ground."

"It's nothing of the sort" I counter. "I want us to travel down together so I can talk to everybody individually and collectively. So we all know our individual and team objectives understand our roles and responsibilities and are very clear about what we want to get from the weekend."

"I want to get some motivation into the team – so they can see how much it means to me, to Tony and to you. So they feel proud about representing Doncaster – and they're in no doubt as to how important this event is for Doncaster."

"And when we get there I want them to see we're a close knit team – that you can't get a fag paper in between us!"

"You do talk bollocks" he tells me "You'll be getting us all kitted out in our team tracksuits next."

"Now there's an angle I haven't thought of... and we'd all look good in matching light brown eighties wool suits. Like that one you wear!" I smirk at him.

He feigns injury and sticks out his bottom lip.

"And if you want to carry the analogy on further" I continue "I suppose I can always drop you for poor performance."

"You see" he reminds me "You do talk bollocks! I'm the best team player you've got – and I'm the best individual you'll ever have."

"And don't you know it!" I close.

ooo

Wednesday October 24th 2001...

More than 1,000 new jobs are announced as part of motor breakdown and insurance firm Green Flag's expansion plans for Doncaster.

ooo

Thursday October 25th 2001...

11.30 am – House of Commons

The Secretary of State for the Department of Education and Skills, The Right Honourable Estelle Morris MP, responds in Parliament to oral questioning about Educational Standards and elaborating on the principles of support between local education authorities, states:

> *"... I am happy to go further than that and say to my Hon. Friend [Tony Colman MP for Putney] that our best authorities are needed to support our weaker local authorities. I take the pragmatic view that the education of children is too important to waste and we must use whatever source from whatever sector, as long as it is good quality, to raise standards in our schools. Yesterday I was in Leeds, where an external partner is helping to raise standards. Next week I am going to celebrate the connection between Warwickshire and Doncaster. Warwickshire, which is very strong, has helped Doncaster which is less strong. In both cases the Ofsted report shows that progress is being made."*

Hansard – October 25th 2001 Column 395

ooo

3.00 pm

The Doncaster Star runs with a City-status special feature "Reasons To Be Hopeful – why Doncaster should head the list of 42 UK towns aiming to be turned into cities".

In a hugely supportive double page spread, the newspaper really pushes our case and highlights several of the emerging economic regeneration projects; the Racecourse development, New Performance Venue, Airport and new job creation figures.

Aidan's really pleased with the article and seems to think we might have a chance. I'm less enthusiastic, fearing the "Dough-boy" scenario I'd warned of in August.

ooo

Tuesday October 30th 2001...

The Doncaster Star's front page headline is: "We're On Course For Glory – Town Moor set to be world class track" and reports very favourably on the proposal to create a world class racing stadium with conference and exhibition facilities at the Racecourse.

ooo

Wednesday October 31st 2001...

"Sick And Tired Of The Rumours" blazes the front page of the Doncaster Star and reports on a letter sent out to all staff and elected councillors from the Chief Executive David Marlowe.

The article reports that Marlow "circulated a letter which criticises 'unhelpful rumours' about development and transport chief Adam Skinner and education director Mathew Simpson's continuing absences on ill health.

I am apoplectic. These two issues should never have got into the public domain and have only done so because David insisted on sending out the letter following a question I took at Full Council. Sometimes I feel we are better off if we let issues gently fade away and don't over-inform...

In his defence, Martin Williams was right to ask the question – everybody knows there are some key changes in a couple of directorates – and he is quoted as saying *"I am entitled to ask whether Adam Skinner is on sick leave and if he will be back or not. Time will tell"*.

ooo

Friday November 2nd 2001...

2.00 pm – The Mansion House, Doncaster

We are ready to leave for the Public/Public Partnership Conference with Warwickshire County Council. It is being held at the National Union of Teacher's National Training & Education Centre, Stoke Rochford Hall, just south of Grantham in Lincolnshire.

There is an atmosphere of eager anticipation and Tony Sockett is fussing over everybody. He has a clip board with him and is checking everybody off as they arrive! Tony is an ex-PE teacher and I remark that he reminds me of "Mr Sugden", the thick-set, bald and comically overbearing sports coach in Ken Loach's film "Kes".

Despite the fact he is neither thick set, bald nor over-bearing, I decide he shall be known as "Mr Sugden" for the weekend!

ooo

3.30 pm – Stoke Rochford Hall

We arrive at the Hall, to be greeted by Ian Bottrill, the Leader of Warwickshire County Council, and Richard Grant, their Chair of Education.

Both are extremely pleased to see us as we disembark and make a joke about us all turning up on a bus together. In return I make a wisecrack about trying to keep expenses down and the added benefit of cutting the amount of CO^2 we are spewing into the atmosphere.

As we enter the reception, I am met by Ian Caulfield, the Chief Executive of the County Council *"Hello there Martin"* he enthuses *"is David* [Marlow] *not coming?"*

"Oh yes – of course he's coming" I blag, annoyed he's not here yet. *"It's just that with his family living in Lincolnshire he's making his own way, so he can travel home to see them when we finish on Sunday afternoon."*

It's a reasonable excuse but it's left me a little peeved in terms of the "team loyalty" I am trying to breed. I decide there's no need for unnecessary friction, however, and let it go.

David is proving to be a hard but fair taskmaster and a man with very high expectations of those working with him; and I wonder what stance he would take with his executive team in similar circumstances.

ooo

Saturday November 3rd 2001…

6.00 pm – Stoke Rochford Hall

The first day and a half has been very successful with members acquitting themselves well. Very importantly, they have not over indulged in alcohol, a behavioural issue raised during our team discussion on the coach on the way down – and a significant turn-around from the disgraceful behaviour of previous Doncaster councillors.

Having said that, I consider that Lib-Dem Edwin Simpson has consistently played politics and displayed poor political and intellectual capabilities in undertaking his role. Refreshingly, our colleagues from Warwickshire take the view he is a very "little picture" transactional politician.

Phil, usually quite dismissive about some of my Cabinet members individually, is very complimentary about their performance as a team. We are doing well.

We put together a skeletal development plan for each authority, with a timetable for implementation.

After dinner the previous evening there had been an excellent presentation from Matthew Taylor, the Director of the Institute of Public Policy Research. In later years Matthew, a former Warwickshire County Councillor, will go on to head up Tony Blair's Policy Unit at Number 10.

ooo

7.00 pm – Stoke Rochford Hall

We are to be joined for dinner by Education Secretary Estelle Morris, another former Warwickshire County Councillor. I am beginning to see how well-connected Phil is.

Tony Sockett is hosting tonight's reception and is completely in his element. As always, he is impeccably turned out, attentive to the Secretary of State's needs and seems to have the right degree of small talk as an entrée to wider discursive issues.

I watch him carefully. He is expertly involving his opposite number, Richard Grant, and both respectful, and deferential to my position as Leader/Mayor elect and that of Ian Bottrill as Leader. He is performing masterfully.

As we sit down to dinner the SoS delivers an excellent speech. As usual, she pitches it at exactly the right level for her audience, no mean feat given the vastly differing intellectual and political abilities of those present. I find it brilliantly informed, knowledgeable, complimentary, respectful, contemporary, supportive and, above all, challenging.

Whilst the SoS is speaking, I sit and admire the cut of the lovely woollen skirt suit she is wearing – although its hem has come undone and is hanging down slightly.

As my mind drifts, I begin to contemplate the magnitude of this event and how the future of education in Doncaster depends on how we perform this weekend. I consider my role, as Leader of the Council, and the pressures upon me at such a level.

I start to think about the symbiotic relationship we need for education to succeed in Doncaster; the butterfly effect – the chaos theory – of this extremely sensitive interdependence and the conditions in which a small change at one point can result in large differences later on.

Paranoia starts to creep in as I look down again at Estelle's skirt suit. If I were to reach forward now, while she is delivering such an important address, and pull the thread hanging from her hem... The ramifications are unthinkable – but I'm thinking them!

Would Estelle realise I was trying to smarten her attire? Or would she think I was making a grab for her leg? There would be complete uproar... We would be cast into the wilderness... I snap out of it – chastising myself. What the fuck are you even thinking about this for? And I focus on her presentation once again.

ooo

9.30 pm – Stoke Rochford Hall

The Secretary of State bids farewell and leaves. She makes some extremely supportive comments to me and says Phil has told her I am a very capable and exciting new political leader.

Tony walks the SoS to her waiting car.

When he returns I tell him I thought the evening went exceptionally well. I let him know I'm really appreciative of the job he has done and that the people of Doncaster should be very proud of him.

We adjourn to the bar where I buy him a drink.

ooo

11.55 pm – the Gardens, Stoke Rochford Hall

It's a beautiful moonlit autumnal evening – almost balmy – and Aidan and I are walking back from the Hall to our rooms. The evening, and weekend, is proving to be a huge success and we both marvel at the sensitivities and tolerance of such high-level relationships.

We agree that the tone we set, as leaders, appears to have a disproportionate effect on how others relate to the Education Directorate, including the head teachers themselves, who display their own values, ethics and behaviours in leading their schools and governing bodies.

I ask Aidan where he thinks the incumbent Director of Education fits in with all this, given that the appointment of Mark Eales as [Acting] Director of Schools has steadied the ship, on the one hand, but created significant ambiguities on the other.

"*You need to calm down a bit*" he advises me. "*You're obsessed with removing him*"

"*Not at all, but you need to read the mood music – can't you see that DfES and Ofsted want him gone.*"

"*Well even if they do – let David do it. And you've heard David's view. He thinks it'll be damaging to staff morale.*"

"*Well I think it could be more damaging if we don't deal with it – it needs to be sooner rather than later.*"

"*Well he's on sick leave at the moment – so it's in the long grass for a while. You're better off leaving it there.*"

"*Anyway – let me tell you what happened whilst Estelle was speaking*" and I tell him of my "chaos" moment.

Surprisingly, Aidan doesn't judge me, admitting he sometimes has similar thoughts himself. His view is that it isn't mischievousness, more a case of self-doubt creeping in; that it's actually a sense of paranoia fed by anxiety or fear of the circumstances.

I tell him *I am* anxious because other than Phil Blundell, I have nobody I can rely on to give me honest, constructive feedback on my performance.

Aidan seems taken aback – almost hurt "*What about me, you bastard?*" "*Aren't I good enough for you?*" he pretends to sob.

"*But that's just it Aidan. You don't give me objective feedback on how I might improve... We're doing that much that we're running around like idiots – and it's either all fantastic, as it is at the moment, or it's a fucking disaster. And then it's usually obvious that it's shite.*"

We sit there on the grass, under the beautiful starry night sky and have a fairly deep conversation about how I need good, reliable, objective feedback from a non-biased, experienced individual I can trust and respect.

"*It's nearly 1.00 o'clock*" I say finally.

And we agree to call it a night – and discuss it more in the future.

ooo

Monday November 5th 2001...

The Doncaster Star announces: "Winter To Stand For Council's Leader [sic.]" – and cites "... crucial projects [I have] been involved in, including negotiations to save Hatfield Colliery and the winding up of the operation Danum Expenses enquiry".

Friday November 9th 2001...

2.45 pm – Reflection

It's now six months since we became "the new leadership" and I have asked Aidan to sit in with me and reflect on what we have achieved [or not].

We are both pretty pleased with our progress "Reinventing Doncaster". We have engineered increased community political engagement – through the referendum on the mayoral model. We are seen [for a while] to be more accountable to communities and I point out that, if we get it right, the mayoral model will create greater accountability for the council and each and every councillor.

We have laid the foundations for better relations with ethnic minority groups in the borough – although there are some worrying emerging undercurrents of institutionalised racism within the authority.

We've encouraged the promotion of a [putting the] "Community First" agenda – trialled first in Edlington and Armthorpe. It's proving a huge success but our officers are reluctant to roll it out across the borough, without further "trials".

We've also developed our 'Making a Difference weeks' – where the community can see the impact if all agencies work together to deliver cleaner, greener and safer streets and communities.

We've staked a huge amount on prioritising and investing in education – mirroring TB's "education… education… education" mantra. Yet we need to develop this theme further, through the public/public partnership with Warwickshire.

We have agreed that now George Holmes has come back to us with a wider Doncaster Education City project we have our "big" project or statement to make with regard to education.

In terms of economic regeneration, many long planned projects are now coming to fruition and there is a greater sense of a "new" Doncaster emerging from the fraud and corruption of the past, with significant stakeholder "buy-in". The "completion" of the Lakeside seems to have been well received by investors, with significant interest in this project and the wider Doncaster area.

We agree that there is a great deal for us to feel confident about with significant economic and social progress. From an environmental perspective, my meeting with Martyn Doughty, Chair of Natural England, has also gone extremely well and I am working on a "Zero-waste" concept and approach for the borough.

However, there is still much to feel circumspect about – not least the opposition's reluctance to move on and the [sub-standard] media's obsession with reporting on past trials and tribulations as if they were live today.

Monday November 12th 2001...

08.30 am – Leader's Office, Mansion House

Aidan and I are going through our diaries with Alison, when Ian Spowart enters without knocking.
    "Morning chaps..." he greets us *"... well it's really hit the fan now..."* And he proceeds to tell us how John Ryan has attacked "councillors" over what he sees as a lack of progress with the new football stadium.
    "Well that's nothing new" I say. *"They're always fucking moaning about it."*
    "I know – but this is bad, it's the worse one yet."
    "Oh that's a bit Blade Runner" pipes in Aidan, acknowledging Ridley Scott's film.
    "No it is... he's threatening to kill people" says Ian rather menacingly *"... and he's shouting about there being blood on the streets".*
    "Where? Where did he say it? When did he say it? Who's saying he said it?" I question him rapid fire.
    "It's been published in a fanzine – it's supposed to be really bad."
    "Nah... I don't believe it – he's the Chairman of a Football Club, he's not gonna threaten to kill us. Get me a copy of what he's supposed to have said, Ian, and we'll take a view then."

ooo

11.30 am – Leader's Office, Mansion House

Spowie has returned with a copy of what Ryan has said and it is bad. He has condemned councillors in a 'Rivers of Blood' type speech, accusing "the council" of dragging its feet and reneging on promises made by the previous leadership.
    He is demanding we build a new stadium, threatening that supporters 'know where we live' and promising that there'll be 'blood on the streets' if we don't build them one!
    We have no option but to give the article to the Monitoring Officer to advise us on the legal position with regard to Ryan's threats.
    We agree that I need to make a public [non] statement about our "plans" for a new stadium.

ooo

Tuesday November 13th through to Friday 16th November 2001...

My sister is having increasing difficulty managing the behaviour of her eldest son, Luke. Although she has two boys and two girls, Luke is my only godson and she asks whether I will let him come and live with us.

I worry she's using me as some kind of a bogey man, who will "sort him out".

Luke proves to be just another teenager having problems adjusting to becoming a young adult. I enjoy the conversations we have but find the demands difficult to manage alongside my responsibilities as Leader.

After a long protracted conversation with Luke and his mother over many days, we agree he is better off going to live with my mum and dad – his grandma and granddad – at their house in Loversall.

ooo

Tuesday November 20th 2001...

Following the public outcry from John Ryan's extraordinary "Rivers of Blood" speech, the Football Association has launched an investigation into his behaviour, and he has resigned as Chairman.

The Doncaster Star is today reporting on a subsequent interview, and runs with the headline "Council's Pledge Over Stadium Plan" and continues with the sub-heading "Leader denies Racecourse development will harm scheme".

I refuse to be drawn into commenting on John Ryan's behaviour but the article makes it clear that Rovers' supporters feel the council somehow "owes it to them" to build a new ground; and that despite discussions over several years, they believe a new stadium is bottom of a "priority list" we have somewhere.

I have explained how the Town Moor [Racecourse] development is a public/private partnership, with the private sector providing the lion's share of the £55 million capital investment.

Yet neither the Rovers not the Star seem to understand the difference between private capital investment and [private] revenue expenditure.

Although I have previously explained this to Chaz Walker, Chair of the Rovers' Supporters Club – in an attempted to assuage his fears – it doesn't seem to have got home.

He is quoted as saying: "It's all very well to say that there will be private money coming into the Racecourse and that it will stand on its own two feet, but so will the new ground."

There is in terms of "entrance fees" but who's going to provide me with a £20 million capital receipt to build us a new stadium?

ooo

Saturday December 15th 2001…

The media seem to be pre-occupied with the concept of my apologising for the mistakes and misdemeanours of others.

One such – an organisation that was promoted and financially supported by the previous leadership – is the Miners' Yorkshire Compensation Recovery Service [YCRS] and we have now received a report into the scheme, compiled by former Housing Ombudsman, Roger Jeffries.

Although thousands of former miners clearly benefitted from the low-cost support YCRS provided, the report paints a picture of false information and "deeply flawed" council support in 1996 amid suggestions it was a "welfare trust", when it was actually a company run by the daughter of a former Doncaster Labour Party Chairman.

It's yet another example of our past dragging us down, but I am keen to distance myself and simply apologise stating:

"I have only been a councillor for two years and was not a councillor when this happened. I am very sorry for the people of Doncaster that this has happened and will take steps to ensure that this doesn't happen again".

Our communications staff go into free-fall, claiming I've fallen for the three-card trick of taking responsibility for others' behaviours and that, by doing this, I am likely to be sued.

I tell them to grow-up! And manage to avoid swearing… I'm learning!

ooo

Thursday January 3rd 2002…

Doncaster Free Press proclaims: "Setting the Standard for Improvement". The story tells how Whitehall is trumpeting our schools improvement drive – and particularly our [new] "Standards & "Effectiveness Unit" as "… the best way to train staff and improve schools".

ooo

Monday January 14th 2002...

Martyn Vickers, the President of Doncaster Central Labour Party and Head of Danum School Technology College, announces he will seek the Labour Party nomination to stand for Mayor.

ooo

Wednesday January 17th 2002...

The Doncaster Star runs with the Martin Vickers story...
   "The cheeky bastard" I shout. *"He's claiming he'll take a substantial drop in his salary if he becomes the Mayor."*
   "He'll fucking retire from the school with a massive lump sum and a big fuck off pension at half his salary" I bawl at the newspaper. *"He'll have a limit on what he can earn after he's retired – and it'll be £30,000. He'll have to limit his salary – or they'll take it from his pension."*
   "I am prepared to make a personal sacrifice to carry out this dream" he says... the cheeky twat...
   "The reward would be taking Doncaster forward"

ooo

Monday February 4th 2002...

"More Jobs On The Way – Employment rate rises as town's economy booms" shouts the front page of the Doncaster Star and goes on to report how Doncaster has hit its biggest economic boom since records began. Pretty good news only thirteen weeks away from the mayoral election.

ooo

Tuesday February 5th 2002...

9.00 am – En-route to the Education Conference, The Moat House, Harrogate

Today is the first day of the two-day "Sharing the Vision" Education Conference in Harrogate. Aidan, Mags and I are heading there in my car because we have a regional Labour Party meeting the following day. As usual Aidan is driving.

We have invested a large amount of energy into getting things "right" with our schools in terms of the relationships with governors, head teachers, the all-powerful Secondary Heads' Group, DfES and Ofsted.

The conference marks a key point in our reinvention of education in Doncaster and an important milestone in our new participative working; I have insisted all cabinet members attend.

Phil Blundell has been responsible for organising the conference, working closely with Tony Sockett. Phil has been very clear that I need to deliver a strong keynote speech from two perspectives:

- Firstly, the future of education in Doncaster relies on my building bridges with the schools.
- Secondly, Martyn Vickers will be working the conference for the whole of the two days so I need to deliver from a Labour party selection perspective.

When I tell Phil that the Labour Party selection process in two weeks is when the Vickers/Winter decision will be made, he agrees that there aren't many card-carrying and voting Labour Party members within the head teacher cohort in Doncaster. *"But if there's just one – it's enough"* he says.

Notwithstanding that, I recognise that there are a large number of what I call "Career Party Members" in Doncaster – individuals who have joined purely to show their support for the leadership and curry favour for their career aspirations.

ooo

Although I own an absolutely pristine, concourse 1956 Porsche 356A Cabriolet, a car that I have lovingly restored during the previous five years, my daily "run around" is a rather dog-eared white Ford Mondeo estate [or "skip"]; and it is this car we are travelling to the conference in.

Ever conscious of the need to create a good impression, I notice several high profile senior officers, head teachers and others mulling around the entrance to the conference car park.

As Aidan drives around looking for a parking space, I realise some of them are looking at us whilst, simultaneously, a very high profile head teacher has also arrived and is parking his particularly expensive E class Mercedes Sports Coupé.

"We're paying our head teachers way too much" says Aidan ironically as he allows the Mercedes in first.

"They certainly like to parade their riches" agrees Mags as we seem to wait a lifetime for the driver to manoeuvre.

"It makes us look good, arriving in this" I say, waiting for the painfully slow

parking process to end.

The Mercedes duly parked, Aidan simply nips in to his space and we get out and remove our bags from the back of the car.

I can see the group of heads watching us and commenting.

Embarrassed that I should have put myself in this position, I pretend to inspect the side of the car they can't see, then say loudly: *"You've got a really big scratch <u>on your car</u> here Aidan – have you seen it?"*

And Mags and I quickly enter the conference hall.

ooo

2.45 pm – The Moat House Conference Centre, Harrogate

The Changes in Doncaster, Councillor Martin Winter, the Leader of the Council

As I gather myself on the stage, I tell the audience how I have been preparing for the speech for some time – and that even my children know how important it is that I deliver a good speech that impresses those attending and helps to secure a new, revitalised relationship both within the LEA and with the schools themselves.

I tell them that I tend not to see my children as often as I would like, since becoming the new Leader; but that I try to involve them as much as possible in my career as a learning process.

I explain that while I was getting dressed this afternoon, I found a screwed up piece of paper in my suit pocket.

When I unwrapped the paper there was a note from my youngest child Marcey [7] which read:

"Good luck with your talk to the teachers Dad! Wear this – it'll make you look good."

And I reach into my pocket and produce the largest, most garish blue, plastic ring I have ever seen – given free in a "lucky-bag" or some other promotion. The audience laughs and laughs even louder when I put the ring on. I hold my hand up in mock admiration: *"Nah... it doesn't suit me – blue's not my colour... I'll put it here* [on my lectern] *for Good Luck".*

As the initial hilarity calms down, I begin my speech, opening with a quick joke about Chris Woodhead, the former Chief Inspector of Schools. It's a cheap shot but one that quickly relaxes everyone and seems to get them on my side.

In an enthusiastic and impassioned presentation I talk about how Doncaster LEA has been criticised and about the poor relationship between the political leadership and the schools themselves – and I assure them I will never let this happen again.

I tell them we are not here simply to criticise the past; but to learn from it and develop an ever-closer strategic relationship as an LEA, so we can look to the future with optimism.

I talk about education being critical to all our futures and although the conference is an important symbol – it must become a working reality with Councillors, Heads, Teachers and Officers all working together for a world class education service in Doncaster.

I praise them on last year's results and talk about the challenges in front of us – epitomised by the opportunities around the new airport – and that the way we plan for and respond to these challenges will be much more effective if we have a rejuvenated relationship between the schools and the LEA.

I finish by committing to 'passport' education at Government Standard Spending Assessment again this year – ensuring a growth of over one and a half million pounds within the LEA alone.

As I come off stage, Phil Blundell comes up to me and whispers *"Excellent Martin... Absolutely bloody excellent – you were brilliant Martin and certainly stuck it up Martyn Vickers."*

ooo

Now whether it really was a good presentation or not begs the question I keep asking – can a leader really get good, honest, constructive feedback on his or her performance?

But it seemed to hit the right note and I got a huge amount of support in the afternoon, during the dinner and in the networking that followed.

ooo

Saturday February 9th 2002...

"Council U-turn On Wage Cut Plan" reports the Doncaster Star, revealing how Doncaster Council's plans to remove holiday retainer fees from some of our lowest paid workers, such as school meals staff, cleaners and caretakers have been halted – after I intervened.

The paper quotes Unison Doncaster's Branch Secretary, Martin Warsama, saying: "This is an extremely positive step by the council's leadership. The leadership of the council has seemed to have listened to our views and I hope that this positive move will now continue."

Tuesday February 19th 2002...

Doncaster Star reports "2,000 Jobs To Be Created In Next Phase Of Luxury Lakeside Development" and links the investment to our earlier decision to invest £1 million in completing the Lakeside Development.

ooo

Thursday February 21st 2002...

Today marks the opening of an exhibition in the Frenchgate Centre to promote our new Borough Strategy – "Achieving Our Full Potential – The Changes In Doncaster".

ooo

Friday February 22nd 2002...

Private Eye No. 1048
Ever the purveyor of honest and decent reporting, the "Eye" attempts to damage my mayoral candidature in an article entitled "WINTERWONDERLAND" which mis-reports:
"His favourite project is the Twelve Million Pounds [sic.] Glass Park, which will transform a former Pilkington Glass factory site outside Doncaster…"

ooo

Sunday February 24th 2002...

10.00 am Mayoral selection Count – Doncaster Trades & Labour Club.

During the past two weeks I have completed and mailed out my "Mayoral Selection" leaflet to all Doncaster Labour Party Members. Subsequently, at every opportunity, I have been phoning around the membership of the four Constituency Labour Parties to secure as much support as I can.
    I have also been to as many Branch and Party meetings as possible and three pre-planned hustings meetings, which have been very well attended.
    Today marks the culmination of this activity in the count at the [old] Trades & Labour Club.
    The room is absolutely packed and all four local MPs – Caroline, Jeff, Kevin

and Rosie – are in attendance, Rosie's long-standing and loyal Election Agent Stuart Exelby, and several Regional Labour Party members are also there to oversee the process including Nan Sloane, the Regional Director, and Peter Box, the Leader of Wakefield MDC. Peter is a very astute political operator who has been very supportive of me since I became Leader ten months ago and we enjoy each other's company and humour.

Although the selection process and campaigns themselves have been clean affairs, with the debate about the vision for the future of Doncaster, the support has become tribal and split between the CLP boundaries and their MPs:

Doncaster Central CLP [Rosie Winterton MP] – a very well-organised constituency with a large membership. Central are keen to support "their man", Martyn Vickers, who is their President and Chairman and phenomenally loyal to Rosie. Also, they have never really forgiven me for beating John Wain to the Labour group leader position and want to "pay me back".

Doncaster North CLP [Kevin Hughes MP] – my own Constituency with a much smaller membership but one that is really keen to support my selection and subsequent election as "their" Labour Mayor.

Doncaster Don-Valley CLP [Caroline Flint MP] – a fairly ambivalent CLP with a similar sized membership to North's and, initially, frustrated that they didn't have a candidate in the selection process themselves. However, with Aidan, Gerry, Mags and Chris Mills all being Don Valley CLP members, I have a good number of councillors championing my selection. Kevin says he has convinced Caroline not to take a view on the candidates.

Barnsley East & Mexborough CLP [Jeff Ennis MP] – a partial constituency which straddles both Barnsley and Doncaster Wards; the membership is small, consisting of only two Doncaster Wards.

The participation rate is high, nearly 60%, and the voting is close – extremely close. Each CLP has nominated a teller from each Ward to count the voting papers and oversee the process.

As the votes are put into bundles of fifty and stacked up, both stacks look almost identical. As Nan and the officers compare and tally the figures, it's not good news. At the first count I've lost by four votes.

I immediately ask for a recount. Well, Chris Taylor, my *de facto* campaign manager, immediately asks for a recount. I am shell-shocked – absolutely devastated – although trying to remain dignified and calm. What the fuck is this? I didn't expect this. It never occurred to me that I might lose...

I glance across at Martyn Vickers who looks stressed. All I can think about is that, after all the hard work I've put in reinventing Doncaster, this jumped up little twat has ridden into town and stolen my fucking clothes.

As the tellers from each Ward begin to count the voting papers again, I glance over at Kevin – who's looking perplexed.

Fifteen minutes elapse and the bundles start stacking up again. Nan and the officers compare and tally the figures again... my heart is in my mouth.

Nan announces the numbers – and at the second count, I've lost by four votes again. What do I do? I look over at Martyn Vickers and he raises his eyebrows at me. *"It's a close one Martin"* he comments.

I just look at him – but say nothing... *"... but good for democracy"* he adds *"... good for democracy"* he says it again, clearly uncomfortable with the situation.

Nan and the officers go into close discussion with Peter Box.

Chris and I compare notes and agree that we need just one more recount – and as I look up to ask for it, Peter Box sidles up to me.

"Don't let this one go Martin" he whispers out of the corner of his mouth.

Jeff Ennis is now beside me. *"It's a tight one Martin – you need to make sure they're not trying to turn you over."*

I request one more recount – and there's a collective sigh from the room. I laugh at their response and announce that, if it's the same again, I'll accept the result.

Nan steps up and informs the tellers that we are counting right from the beginning again.

"But this time..." she proclaims, taking the "Vickers" bundles and distributing them on the "Winter" tables and allocating the "Winter" bundles to the "Vickers" tables... *"... I want you to count in pairs."*

"But I want you to make sure there are fifty ballot papers in each bundle."

As the tellers begin to count in pairs I look at Martyn Vickers, who's looking very red-faced and stressed. Having said that, I can't see how I look!

After about five minutes one of the tellers on the "Winter" table beckons Nan and Peter Box over and a brief confab takes place.

"That's it" says Chris.

"What is?"

"That is – they've found whatever it is" he adds in his sardonic black-country accent.

"Well that's not very fucking helpful."

"I know – let's just hope it helps us more than I'm doing" he laughs.

A further ten minutes passes by and the bundles start stacking up again. Nan and the officers compare their figures once more...

Nan announces the numbers – and at the third count, I've won by six votes!

I look at Chris… I look at Kevin… I look at Peter – but nobody's saying anything. I look at Martyn Vickers who's looking devastated.

This time it's Martyn Vickers' team that goes into a huddle.

Peter Box comes across to me *"The clever bastards"* he says *"They'd put a bundle of forty in as fifty"* he explains.

"That's a right union trick that is…" says Kevin.

Rosie has joined Martyn Vickers and now they ask for a recount.

There's another collective sigh from the room. I laugh at their response but this time with humour rather than nerves.

The tellers begin counting again. Nan and the officers compare and tally the figures yet again… my heart is in my mouth.

Nan calls Martyn and I over and explains that the figures are exactly the same again. She tells us that it would appear that a mistake had been made which has now been identified.

Martyn immediately offers me his hand and as we shake he states that he is happy to accept the result.

Nan announces that after four counts, I've won the Labour Party Mayoral Selection process.

ooo

Monday February 25th 2002…

With no notice whatsoever Central Government announces that it has agreed to pay £20 million compensation for the extant mineral extraction rights for Thorne & Hatfield Moors.

We have "saved" Thorne & Hatfield Moors.

ooo

Friday March 1st 2002…

We have a booked the Palace of Westminster's Terrace, overlooking the Thames, for a "Celebrating Doncaster" event. This is a shameless lobbying affair – aimed at promoting Doncaster before the results of the Golden Jubilee "City-status Bids" in a fortnight.

I am massively cynical of this whole process and pretty certain we don't stand a chance – particularly with the high-profile "Donnygate" court cases starting in Nottingham next week – but I have to admit that Aidan was right and the process has led to a huge buy-in from our many partner organisations.

We drive down to London with George Holmes, who has become a strong supporter of the City-status bid and with whom we are working closely on the Doncaster Education City project. This is proving to be a hugely exciting venture aimed at developing a new College Hub Building, several Area Based Campuses, stronger links with the business community, a borough-wide curriculum, Digital Knowledge Exchange, new University for Doncaster and new economic opportunities.

The discussion during the journey centres on the fact that, despite agreeing to it beforehand, Aidan hasn't written me a speech. He argues that I need to cut loose and simply present myself as an authentic, more natural, off-the-cuff speaker.

This doesn't help me at all. I'm very nervous that this is my first speaking engagement at Westminster and conscious that it will have significant ramifications with regard to the mayoral campaign, not least because the editor of the Star will be there, having been part of the "City-Bid" submission team.

I'm desperately trying to put some thoughts together for my presentation, but everyone in the car, including my driver Paul, is taking the piss out of me so I'm having trouble concentrating…

As we near the Houses of Parliament, I still haven't got anything tangible to say and both George and Aidan are playing down the significance of being "un-prepared for such a career defining meeting".

When we arrive at the venue, I'm really impressed – Caroline Newton, our Marketing Manager, and her team, have put together a fantastic "City-Bid" display and presentation. With a very strong attendance, including the Deputy Prime Minister [DPM], John Prescott, the event is looking good.

I disappear to the toilets before I have to make my address and, while I'm there, I notice that all the taps for the basins are made by Peglers [of Doncaster] – which gives me an idea.

To begin with I pitch my tried and tested speech about the massive regeneration portfolio Doncaster is sitting on:
- Doncaster Transport Interchange – the largest town centre retail development in the UK
- Finningley Airport – and that we are awaiting the outcome of the Public Inquiry [DPM]
- The Racecourse development and exhibition centre – with the St Leger being the world's oldest classic horse race
- Doncaster Education City – and our educational improvement figures
- Our plans for a new community stadium

I tell them things are already looking good for Doncaster but that, in addition to this massive regeneration portfolio, we have just "saved" Thorne & Hatfield Moors– thanks to the government buying out the extant mineral extraction rights [from Scotts] for £20 million. And there is a huge cheer for this decision.

The audience clearly love what I'm saying and so I tell them how Doncaster has a real shared commitment to a new, emerging, corporate vision for the city as witnessed by the fantastic attendance today.

As I wrap up, I describe how I've just been to the 'washroom'... and that within all the washrooms in the Houses of Parliament are taps and plumbing systems provided by Pegler of Doncaster – so the UK government can only function on a daily basis with the support of Doncaster!

I glance across at Rosie, a big supporter of Pegler – and she's loving it – so I tell them how Pegler is a world renowned manufacturer of plumbing, heating and engineering products and was first established more than a hundred years ago when, in Doncaster's glorious past, we led a world class skills agenda, with the manufacturing of trains like the Flying Scotsman and the Mallard...

... and I close the circle by telling them this is where our emerging vision sees us going in the future, with the support of our Education City, becoming a vibrant city that leads the world again.

ooo

As we travel home, we are self-congratulatory; the event was a huge success. I am exhausted having been networking particularly enthusiastically and in danger of wallowing in my own self-importance.

George is hyper. The event was such a success he's convinced we'll be successful in the city-bid.

Both George and Aidan are congratulating themselves on the "speech" they prepared for me as we journeyed down this morning; telling me everyone regarded it as a big success and that it defined me as a true leader.

This again raises the spectre of how I illicit objective, constructive and honest feedback on my performance?

And how do I get Aidan to understand my need for us to be an even stronger "team". I need him to be my "stoker" in the boiler room, making sure I'm fully prepared.

We've previously agreed our roles, responsibilities and tasks, but he keeps slipping on his obligations – and it's affecting my performance. We got away with it today but it's not the way I want us to work. He's happy enough to do the "schmoozing" but I need him to also help me with the preparation.

All these missed deadlines are affecting the message we're trying to deliver and it's beginning to worry me – but now is not the time to discuss it.

ooo

Wednesday March 13th 2002...

The so-called "Donnygate" court case starts in Nottingham, with all the attendant national publicity.

ooo

Thursday March 14th 2002...

City-status bid fails. The Doncaster Star runs with a four page post-mortem of the campaign and the strapline "Donnygate Cost Us Dearly".

ooo

Wednesday March 20th 2002...

Prime Minister's Office – The Palace of Westminster

Kevin has arranged for me to have an audience with Tony Blair – as the Labour Mayoral candidate – before the Mayoral election in May.

As we get closer to the date, it transpires that the meeting with the PM will last just three minutes – immediately after Prime Minister's Questions; nonetheless, Kevin informs me, I am the first on the list so he may be hyper from the adrenalin and theatre of PMQs.

I arrive well before time and am joined by Kevin. All the media talk and speculation for the past 48 hours has been when, not if, Tony will make the decision to send our troops to Afghanistan.

There are presently around 4,500 non-combative troops involved in security operations and Geoff Hoon, the Secretary of State for Defence, announced on Monday that up to 1,700 combative troops were to be readied for sending to the region.

A Number 10 spokesman stated *"... I don't think anyone is under any illusion. We are not talking peacekeeping here, we are talking warfare. It is dangerous terrain, testing conditions, and a very murderous enemy."*

As a result an emergency Commons debate has been called for today, by the shadow defence minister Bernard Jenkin, who says MPs should be allowed to discuss the implications of deploying Royal Marines to the war-torn region – and the future prospects of troops serving with the international security force – before the House goes into recess next week.

As we wait for PMQs to finish, we are ushered into a small rectangular anteroom. Lounging on the two-seater chesterfield sofa, watching the PM on TV is Alastair Campbell, Tony's Director of Communications; he neither acknowledges us nor removes his eyes from Tony's performance.

An aide enters the room: *"Can I have a quick word with you please?"* and Kevin and the aide move to the back, where she whispers into his ear.

Kevin returns. *"You – are going – to – 'ave – to – wait – before – the – PM – can – see – you"* he enunciates.

"He needs to speak to somebody before he can see you" he continues.

I roll my eyes as if to say I knew this would happen.

"... and the future Mayor of Doncaster cannot pull rank" he adds dryly.

Over the next fifteen minutes, another dozen or so individuals join us to wait for the Prime Minister and it becomes clear he is massively in demand.

As PMQs finishes, the office becomes a hive of activity, with several civil servant types marching into the admin office/reception area and lining up attentively, quickly followed by another half dozen staff. I recognise the faces of Geoff Hoon and Jack Straw as they too enter the room.

Geoff and Kevin exchange pleasantries and have a brief, private conversation while the office rapidly fills.

Just as the room seems to be reaching bursting point, the Prime Minister comes in, followed by a further cohort of civil servants. The PM, Geoff Hoon and Jack Straw quickly disappear behind a richly coloured, oak panelled door– followed by a staff member, who closes it urgently behind them.

Almost as if a pressure valve has been released, the myriad of civil servants, aides and staff also disappear back into the warren – leaving around a dozen of us still awaiting our audience.

Kevin and I are ushered through a further door and told the PM will be with us forthwith. I look around the room; it is a large oak-panelled room with built in sideboards, not dissimilar to the Georgian splendour of our own Mansion House meeting rooms. Down one side is a large oval mahogany table, inlaid with leather and capable of seating twenty or so individuals.

The table and adjacent sideboard are covered with bottles of House of Commons whiskey, wine, champagne, photographs of the Prime Minster, photographs of the House of Commons, copies of Hansard, House of Commons calendars, wedding anniversary cards and all manner of gifts and trinkets. Each has a note attached to it – an instruction, as to the purpose of the item and a small script to be written and signed by the Prime Minster.

I look at Kevin and nod towards the masses of gifts, raffle prizes and awards, fingering the labels as I say: *"I suppose he's taking a briefing from them on Afghanistan"* – It's probably the most idiotic piece of small talk I could utter, given the magnitude of the situation we are in.

"You'll see on the news tonight" he replies, clearly aware something big is going down.

As I glance at the clock on the wall, the PM enters the room. It's the first time I've met him and I'm ready to pitch my key messages:

i) Public/Public Partnership with Warwickshire County Council
ii) Operation Danum police inquiry closed
iii) a Mayoral Election in May;
iv) and a huge economic development portfolio;

But as I introduce myself, he appears quite distant. Launching into my first message, I realise he's not receiving me clearly at all – he's on auto pilot – so I fall back into inane "chit chat" making simple small talk.

We've been with him for about one and half minutes now and an aide is hovering at the door with the next person for him to "greet". I decide to cut my losses and get out early. Kevin takes a photograph of us together for my Mayoral Manifesto and we bid him goodbye.

As we leave the room, the aide ushers the next people in and asks Kevin if something is wrong.

"We don't normally see people leaving early."

"Aye well, it's an unusual day" replies Kevin.

When we get outside he tells me the Prime Minister had just made the decision to deploy the troops – with immediate effect.

ooo

Thursday March 21st 2002...

The following morning I read that the PM had physically made the decision during yesterday's discussions with Geoff Hoon and Jack Straw.

Hoon, the Secretary of State for Defence, and Straw, the Secretary of State for Foreign and Commonwealth Affairs had been with Tony for less than 5 minutes and he'd had to make probably the biggest decision of his life – no wonder he wasn't attentive to me!

ooo

Monday March 25th 2002...

I have a fairly intense discussion with David Marlow about getting feedback on my performance.

As a sculptor, I was used to giving and receiving it in the form of a "critique" and I am now searching for clear objective judgements on how I'm doing.

We discuss the search for feedback; how to construct a feedback sandwich – both giving and receiving it; and the art of active listening.

David agrees to critique on my performance but it doesn't work. We're too close to each other. I have to find a developmental coach who will be both non-directive and completely confidential.

ooo

"Leader In Legal Bid On Smear" reads the front page headline in the Doncaster Star. In a newspaper "exclusive", the paper reports that I have taken legal advice regarding an alleged smear campaign over my role in a "multi-million pound" [sic.] development.

In a sign of things to come, the paper reports on the Glass Park development and highlights that I was paid £10,000 by the Trust to project manage the £150,000 civil engineering works – which reclaimed the former cullet [glass] landfill site to make it safe for access as a public open space.

The article incenses me. I have worked on this project voluntarily for more than ten years – putting in huge amounts of effort and re-mortgaging our house to realise it. Now these tin-pot shitty little fuckwits have "suddenly" decided that all my work – all the community's work – is theirs to destroy for their political ends.

Remembering that I had warned the trustees that the project could become a political football and now having first-hand experience of what a nasty business politics – and journalism – is I simply comment: *"I have nothing to hide with this project. I am immensely proud of it – it has huge public involvement"*.

ooo

Thursday April 4th 2002...

Following on from my commitment to healthy eating, I am completing a food and nutritional skills qualification I began before I became Leader. I have to be assessed in a cookery demonstration, which has been hanging over me for nearly twelve months now. So I decide to run my demo [assessment] in the Mansion

House's 'Great Kitchen'. "Council Leader Wises Up On Nutrition Skills" heralds the newspaper article.

ooo

The "City-status Steering Group" have decided that the bid process and resultant promotion was so successful they wish to continue meeting to consider how best they can promote Doncaster. It would seem Aidan was right!

ooo

Friday April 5th 2002...

9.00 am

It's one of our reflection days and both Aidan and I are becoming extremely concerned that less than a month before the historic mayoral election, the Head of Paid Service or, perhaps more accurately, the Corporate Management Team [CMT], have still not identified new offices for 'The Executive Mayor'.

Despite tasking them more than six months ago to identify [new] mayoral offices preferably external to 'the council' and commensurate with the new position of Executive Mayor of Doncaster – they have failed.

I believe this may prove problematic. As we get ever closer to the mayoral election, Aidan and I have agreed we need to use the mayoralty as the step-change that's needed in Doncaster. The role isn't that of a "Super Councillor" or comparable to that of an MP, quasi-MP or Minister; it's something entirely different and we need to convey this message in the face of a media obsessing about civic robes and chains!

Having been 'The Leadership' for nearly a year now, we are both concerned by the latent conservatism within the Labour group and the Labour Party generally, and by their twin obsessions of 'process' and 'the past' as strategies for dealing with the future...

Assuming I am elected mayor, we are both clear that we need to grasp the mayoral model and run with it as fast as we can. We need to leave the 'others' straggling behind unable to catch up – so they can't obstruct our improvement agenda.

With this in mind, we agree to do some work on a model that connects the Doncaster electorate with the politician's accountability; specifically the 'mayor' but also with the ward councillors.

I tell Aidan that, based on my role as 'Leader', I've outlined what I think will probably epitomise what 'the mayor' does all day – and I read to him...

- *"Scarcely a minute of the day is unaccounted for; nevertheless, what the mayor does is not as important as what the mayor is...*

- *To be the Mayor of Doncaster is a responsibility like no other and the role must become a symbol of all that is best about Doncaster...*

- *He must communicate a vision for a better tomorrow... for the town and its citizens.*

- *He must be an embodiment of our history, our culture, our morality and our proud achievements...*

- *In short, our ideal of a civilised leader – the mayor must, in the harsh light of public scrutiny, exhibit all our virtues and none of our shortcomings...*

- *If we get it right, it will be a God's burden to bear – unfortunately it must be borne by us"*

I finish. *"That's decent stuff"* he replies *"It's a bit pretentious – but a good starting point – have you done it all on your own?"*

"You patronising bastard" I tell him... thankful that he's clearly never seen the 'low-brow' film 'King Ralph' starring John Goodman and Peter O'Toole!

ooo

David Marlow is also keen for us to have a clear understanding and, thereafter, a statement of the mayoral model we are seeking to achieve.

After a couple of structured discussions, we agree the mayor as a "radical change agent" and "serious politician" – a 'mayor of the borough' [as opposed to the council] pursuing a selective, radical agenda, strategic and external-facing, and with a strong "inner team" which will ensure the organisation delivers.

We agree we need to restate and refine precisely what we want to deliver. The deliverables all broadly contribute to four principles/purposes of a "Winter Mayoralty":
- to build the mayoralty
- to build the borough and its communities

- to build the "regional city"
- to build the "good" council

Under such a model the mayor would concentrate on a small number of key deliverables and "commission" cabinet members to support these, whilst also being responsible for the delivery of three or four each themselves.

The deliverables are not particularly new – and are already charted in the mayoral manifesto, the borough strategy and other commitments we have made. However, we agree I should aim to formally outline the agenda at the start of each new municipal year – through an annual 'state of the borough' type speech.

Although we have identified it as a desirable element of my mayoralty, I have my concerns; bequeathing responsibility to my cabinet members, though logistically attractive, might create difficulties depending on their individual political, managerial and motivational capabilities.

ooo

I am delighted when a former colleague agrees to operate as 'Campaign Communications Manager' for my mayoral campaign. Having worked as a freelance PR and Communications Consultant and also having headed up the Press Office at DMBC several years ago, they are dynamic, gregarious and an excellent communicator. We get on famously.

Having agreed to work voluntarily at the campaign stage, I understand they will apply for the full-time role created once the new mayor is elected.

ooo

A hugely important aspect of my work, as Leader [and hopefully mayor] is to promote Doncaster by getting the message out there that people should have confidence in me, in Doncaster *per se* and in the council and its operations.

To achieve this, we have identified a variety of audiences and how we can reach them:

1] **Our residents** – the electorate who put me into the position I now hold; physically getting out there, "walking-the-walk" "talking-the-talk" and developing a community-focused approach to policy development through a Green and White Paper system. In terms of the captive audience that is the Local Authority's 17,000 staff, physically getting out there and meeting and greeting our staff on a regular basis.

2] **Our businesses** – the companies, men and women who are driving Doncaster's economy forward; as above, and also by developing stronger relationships with the likes of Doncaster Chamber of Commerce, encouraging the Local Authority's Officers to have a more private sector focus/approach to dealing with them.

3] **Our Public Sector Partners** – the organisations, their staff and volunteers who are often working in close collaboration with us; mainly through networking and developing mutually beneficial policies and procedures.

4] **Our Non-Governmental Organisation [NGO] Partners** – their staff and volunteers, frequently delivering non-statutory objectives; as above and by encouraging an outcome-focused approach from the NGO services;

5] **Our Private Sector Partners and Inward Investors** – the massively important individuals and organisations who operate in Doncaster or have identified it as a possible investment opportunity; through networking and developing policies and procedures which will attract inward investors, and also by developing and encouraging a "can-do" attitude by Local Authority Officers.

6] **Government, External Decision-Makers and Opinion Formers** – the people, usually in positions of power, who can help change the perception of Doncaster as the grim northern town that's the very embodiment of council corruption; mainly through networking, punching above our weight regionally and internationally, and by striving to achieve recognition as the embodiment of what a successful mayoral system looks like.

In terms of communicating a consistent message, I have to encourage and develop "buy-in" to the 'Doncaster Vision' selling this to all our partners, mantra-like, at every opportunity-including going on a charm offensive with the local media!

ooo

Saturday April 6th 2002...

Mayoral nominations close and the list has seven candidates seeking office:
  Andrew Burden [Conservative];
  Jessie Credland [Independent];
  Shafiq Khan [Independent];
  Graham Newman [Lib-Dem];
  Mick Maye [Independent];

Terry Wilcox [Independent];

and myself – standing for the Labour party.

ooo

Tuesday April 9th 2002...

My birthday

Private Darren George, 23, from the Royal Anglian Regiment becomes the first British soldier to be killed in Afghanistan since the start of the mission.

ooo

Thursday May 2nd 2002...

I am elected as the Mayor of Doncaster. In a very disappointing campaign, I feel hugely demoralised by the mediocre level of debate promulgated by the mayoral candidates and encouraged by the local media.

On a progressive level, I have been impressed by the Conservative candidate Andrew Burden, who took the time to request a meeting with David Marlow, the Doncaster Council Chief Executive, in order to discuss his views on the roles, responsibilities and challenges presented by this new position.

Party	Candidate	1st Round	%	2nd Round	%	Total	First Round Votes	Transfer Votes
Labour	Martin Winter	21,494	36.75%	4,213		25,707		
Conservative	Andrew Burden	9,000	15.39%	3,707		12,707		
Community Group	Jessie Credland	8,469	14.48%					
Independent	Michael Maye	7,502	12.83%					
Liberal democrat	Graham Newman	5,150	8.81%					
Independent	Terry Wilcox	4,036	6.90%					
Independent	Shafique Ahmad Khan	2,836	4.85%					
	Turnout	58,487	27.02%					
	Registered Electors	216,097	4.85%					

Doncaster Mayoral Election 2002

Footnote

911

It is important to understand that this was 2001 – and there was no immediate access to information; no smart phones or tablets like there is today. Indeed, arguably this single event gave birth to the 24-hour rolling news culture and sparked the demand to be continually updated on news events.

After the mayor making…

"In the corner of my eye... I saw you in Rudy's... you were very high... you were high...
It was a cryin' disgrace... they saw your face..."

Walter C Becker
and Donald J Fagen

Saturday May 4th 2002…

"Labour in control – but stalwart Marshall goes in shock defeat" declares the Doncaster Star reporting on Bev Marshall losing his [Intake Ward] seat.

The story is less of a surprise to us, however, with Intake resident Ian Spowart briefing us well in advance about the Lib-Dems' Cliff Hampson, whom he describes as a nasty piece of work, a dirty campaigner and a man who will go to any lengths to get his message across – in this case, an 'anti-Labour' and 'pro-Lib-Dem' message. Clearly he has done this with some success in Intake and Ian expresses his further concerns that Hampson has now moved from Intake to Kirk Sandall – about 500 yards from my house – and "will become troublesome to me".

Although Ian is a good intuitive politician and a man whose judgement I trust implicitly, I am less concerned than he is about the activities of such a ne'er-do-well…

ooo

Monday May 6th 2002…

As I say, Aidan and I have always been clear that we need to use the election and the mayoralty itself as the step-change that's needed in Doncaster… in a manner reminiscent of the radical Blairite modernisation measures brought in when Labour came to power in 1997.

Notwithstanding the inauspicious start of the Corporate Management Team in failing to identify new mayoral offices, I take the interim decision to utilise two rooms at the Mansion House – the front and back committee rooms – and instruct that they are readied immediately.

ooo

Gerry tells me that Aidan wept when he realised Bev had lost his seat last Friday!

ooo

Thursday May 9th 2002…

The Government launches its White Paper 'Your Region, Your Choice: Revitalising the English Regions'. In his preface, Tony Blair writes that this White Paper is a great opportunity for the English regions. It delivers on our Manifesto commitment to provide for directly elected regional assemblies in those regions that want them. It gives people living in the English regions the chance to have a greater say over the key issues that affect them, as well as the power to devise tailored regional solutions to regional problems. And it builds on the success of devolution elsewhere in the UK – offering people more accountable, more streamlined, and more joined-up government.

This White Paper is about choice. No region will be forced to have an elected assembly. But where there is public support for one, we believe people should be given the chance to demonstrate this in a referendum.

ooo

I am less enamoured with the document. It proposes devolving only limited executive powers to elected regional assemblies and I would argue that the mayoral model just chosen in Doncaster provides the right framework for giving people a greater say.

One thing that does worry me is that the White Paper proposes that elected assemblies be required to meet 'ten high level indicators', promising additional funds if they meet these targets. This completely runs against the spirit of devolution – representing "devolution on a leash" – and will stifle innovation. Furthermore, no such regime exists for the devolved assemblies in Scotland, Wales and Northern Ireland.

I see a more favourable model being that of a directly-elected mayor working with a directly-elected assembly in a similar manner to that which Ken "heads up" in London.

But then I would say that – wouldn't I?

ooo

Friday May 10th 2002...

"Mayor Unveils New Face in the Cabinet" hails the Doncaster Star "But Opposition Says There Should Have Been More Change". The paper reports that I have brought in Councillor Ian Spowart to replace Bev Marshall with the 'Trade, Industry & Innovation portfolio'.

One week into the mayoral model and the Star has produced yet another disappointing article on the new administration. It misses the chance to celebrate the "dawn of a new era" and takes the shoddy journalistic "business as usual" route – focusing on opposition councillors being unhappy with those elected to lead...

But I view the newspaper's poor reporting in a much more critical and sinister manner. I judge the 'article' disappointing in its attempts to convey the singularly accountable mayoral model; referring to me as a councillor [twice] and also as the "mayor elect".

I respond determinedly: *"The people of Doncaster elected a Labour Mayor with a Labour Party manifesto. That's what I have delivered. I believe it is a strong, robust cabinet team that will deliver the requirements for me as elected mayor and a manifesto for Doncaster".*

To which the newspaper reports that "Mayor elect [sic.] Martin Winter was defiant when announcing his all-Labour cabinet to lead Doncaster yesterday".

Referring to me as "mayor elect" – meaning that I've been elected but not yet installed or officially taken office – just confuses the public further.

I may appear a pedant, but newspapers have a duty to report issues correctly. They wouldn't make the same mistake with a newly-elected MP.

ooo

Saturday May 11th 2002...

Continuing the newspaper's "business as usual" theme, the front page of the Doncaster Star announces : "A Winter of discontent – anger as Mayor takes up Mansion House space" and goes on to report that Doncaster's civic building has been branded the "Winter Palace" after critics of the elected mayor claimed he was turning committee rooms into personal offices.

I am livid. Our officers had enough time to get something organised and, as usual, Martin Williams has caught the press's interest with his jibe at me – a reference to the <u>Bloody Sunday</u> massacre when demonstrators marched on the palace in the Russian Revolution.

ooo

Wednesday May 15th 2002...

In what proves to be the first of several visits to Doncaster, Prince Andrew, the Duke of York, is here to see the work of the Doncaster Chamber of Commerce, in their "new offices".

When I say "new", I mean the offices I have encouraged Doncaster Council to provide for the Chamber at a low-cost rent as a statement of increased support for Doncaster's business community. Prince Andrew also visits the adjacent Doncaster Business Innovation Centre – an incubator facility for emerging Doncaster businesses.

Andrew is pretty impressive in his broad grasp of business development and support issues and the visit is a real success in terms of the many staff and supporters who work tirelessly to support the town's emerging dynamic business community.

He seems particularly interested in my role as the "elected" mayor and my enthusiasm for supporting emerging and established local businesses. As everyone gathers to say their final goodbyes, Andrew stands in the middle of a large horseshoe of about forty or fifty people, while he sums up his day. Intent on supporting my role, he thanks me as the 'Mayor of Doncaster' and asks:

"So how long before the next election, Martin?"

"Oh another four years, Sir" I respond, although it's actually foreshortened to three to dove-tail with future elections.

"Four years... and, presumably, that's it then... is it?"

"Oh no Sir – I can then seek re-election after four years."

"Oh," he seems surprised.

"And then is that it?" he's obviously unaware of the ongoing nature of the position.

"Not at all Sir... I can continue seeking re-election whilst ever the electorate is prepared to vote for me," I say, completely unaware at this point of the two-term clause the Labour party has imposed on the role.

He places his left arm across his mid-rift and supports his chin with his right hand pondering the ramifications of what I have just said.

Seeing an opportunity to have a little fun, I add:

"Having said that Sir... I cannot see myself seeking re-election term after term after term...I think the key to being a good leader..." I venture, smiling at him devilishly, "... is to know when you've been around for too long... and when you need to get off of the merry-go-round."

He lifts his head to stare at me, raising his eyebrows in mock surprise, opening his eyes as wide as he can – as if on stage at the Globe – and clearly getting my little joke.

"....*So I can't see a situation where I continue beyond one or two terms...ad infinitum... or, more probably, ad nauseum, Sir.*"

But he doesn't bite: "*Yes... well perhaps the less said about that, the better,*" he closes, to laughter all round.

ooo

Thursday May 16th 2002...

"Andrew Means Business – Visit of Duke of York to Chamber" cries the Doncaster Star and goes on to provide an in-depth report and pictures which are captioned...

"The Duke of York listens intently to elected Mayor John Winter [sic.] on his arrival... he is welcomed by... Councillor Winter [sic.] and Council chief executive David Marlow."

Now I know it's early days, with the mayoralty, but I'm pretty dis-chuffed that the paper can't comprehend that I'm not now a "Councillor"... and has also decided I am Mayor "John" Winter...

ooo

Tuesday June 25th 2002...

As a sign of what's to come, the Doncaster Star runs with the headline "It's a jungle out there – overgrown Glass Park beauty spot is more like Grass Park say campaigners" and quotes a "local campaigner" [part of an emerging Lib-Dem coterie] as being concerned that the grass is too long and that her children were nettled during a recent visit to the site.

I'm appalled that the Glass Park is becoming a political football – however I am no longer involved and need to stay out. This is clearly a smear campaign aimed at the new mayor's previous involvement with the project; it's a sign of greater things to come, and promulgated by Cliff Hampson, the Lib-Dem councillor who took Bev Marshall's seat in May.

Hampson is proving irksome through a strategy of gradual attrition; inveigling himself into the affections of individuals and groups through generally criticising "The Mayor" and reaffirming their prejudices, whether latent or overt.

To this end, Hampson has established the 'Kirk Sandall Community Group', which I see as an attempt to compete/confuse with the 'Kirk Sandall Community [Wildlife] Group' which we set up several years earlier to deliver the Glass Park project...

Glass Park trustee Liz Jeffress attacks the paper and "community group" insisting the project is designed as a wildlife area and not a formal "mown" park or "beauty spot" – but the paper still fills the front page with a real non-story that insinuates against me.

ooo

The malcontents are up to mischief again. One of their number is an ex-lecturer from Doncaster Art College and fancies himself as a bit of Ralph Steadman/Steve Bell type…

Suffice to say, they're unhappy – they're always unhappy [!] – but this time it's not because I'm "corrupt", it's because I'm majoring on a "big vision" for Doncaster – one we can get everyone to aspire to. As a result, this ex-lecturer's been distributing disparaging pictures of me around the town…

'VISIONS' for the FUTURE
MY GOD!
'MOSES' WINTER
RECEIVES THE TABLETS FROM ABOVE

To be quite honest it shows I'm getting the message out there and I think it actually does us more good than harm – these people are suggesting that to have big ideas is a bad thing worthy of their criticism…

Thursday June 27th 2002...

My concerns about "bequeathing" responsibility for delivery to cabinet members are proving correct... despite considering themselves "politicians" most prove not to be very good ones – and when I say "most" I mean at least five of the nine!

Individually they are quite pedestrian, weak even, something commented on by Phil Blundell at the Public/Public Partnership Conference at Stoke Rochford last November. Collectively, however, they are more capable with a greater sense of "group assurance".

Individually, though, is where they operate most frequently and I fear they are less than exacting in offering political direction for their cabinet areas.

Officer intransigence, manipulation and downright obfuscation, frequently prove too much for their political capabilities. Despite my constant insistence that "officers advise... but politicians decide" they are finding that difficult to grasp – with the result they are too willing to accept officer recommendations and not exert their political authority.

In my experience, this is symptomatic of officer/member relationships across UK Local Government and is similarly played out with the civil servants in Westminster – you just have to watch Jay & Lyn's superb 'Yes Minister' and 'Yes Prime Minister'.

With support from Phil Blundell, we prepare a performance management structure for managing the performance of [my] cabinet members based on the Nolan Principles of Selflessness, Integrity, Objectivity, Accountability, Openness, Honesty and Leadership.

ooo

Monday July 1st 2002...

Today is Full Council and I am really excited to be presenting one of the key tenets of my mayoralty – that of greater public participation in the development of [the mayor's] policies.

I see my mayoralty being based on a 'Realpolitik' model that puts community consultation and pragmatic and material considerations right at the heart of the decision-making process – not solely ideological premises and notions. Not that I am some kind of moralistic or ethical philistine, but I'm acutely aware of the cynicism of the Doncaster and wider electorate, and mindful of Mullany's dulcet tones as he forever told me you can't lead people where they don't want to go...

To this end, I see the introduction of a Green and White Paper system for policy consultation and policy-making alongside regular Mayoral Policy

Development Forums as being fundamental – presenting the opportunity for greater community involvement in the shaping of major policy initiatives, mirroring the language or process of Westminster.

I believe it represents the first real attempt at engaging the public in policy development and decision making in Doncaster, ever! Which is more a statement on Doncaster and its backwards or esoteric nature than a statement on my enlightened or progressive approach!

Nonetheless, I am introducing two papers today that convey both aspects of the scheme:
- **a Green Paper "Making A Difference In Your Neighbourhoods"** – which I characterise as a consultation or "listening" phase where I publicly state that I'm considering developing a policy on an issue; the areas I think it should consider; the ramifications and the time scale I am working towards... **what are your views?**
- **a White Paper "The Doncaster Development Direction – 3D"** – which I characterise as a policy intention or "checking" phase – where I publicly state that I have listened to what you have said [on this issue]; what I am thinking of doing as a result of what you have said and the new time scale... **what are your views?**

I am very keen for the written style of my Green & White Papers to be "conversational" – as accessible as possible and written in the active first person. These first two don't hit the "conversational" style I want– nonetheless, they are a huge step forward and I'm happy
with the general direction we are travelling in – the more subtle nuances can come later.

The two proposals council is considering today relate to increasing the neighbourhood focus on planning and delivering excellent quality services, and encouraging greater involvement and support in the delivery of transformational investment projects, through the creation of a development company for Doncaster.

Tuesday July 2nd 2002...

It's still very early days in the mayoralty and, despite my insistence that the front and rear committee rooms are readied as the temporary suite of rooms for the mayor, it's an on-going problem. Not necessarily with the opposition, whose anger is relatively short-lived, but with the staff!

Doncaster's elegant Mansion House has dominated the High Street for over two hundred and fifty years. It is one of only four surviving civic Mansion Houses in the country and is Grade 1 listed. Since the interior is quite magnificent and also listed, the staff member responsible insists he is having trouble locating filing cabinets that will prove acceptable to English Heritage!

Such a relatively minor resources issue is beginning to cloud the office's operation, and since no one, including David Marlow [!], appears capable of resolving the matter, my staff are having to stack often sensitive papers on chairs and the floor!

I decide to intervene, incensed that I have to allocate my time to "broker" the establishment of the office; however, we are now eight weeks into the mayoralty and there are still no filing cabinets!

I tell the office administrator to get his finger out. We are only using these rooms temporarily and to just get any cabinets – does he really think the computers and printers have to be Georgian style as well!

ooo

I explain the above because it typifies the resistance inherent within the system – we've always done it this way and see no reason to change.

In another example, a Yorkshire Post journalist rings my office to ask if I want to comment on the 'Chippendale table' that has been cut up so it can be removed it from the back committee room!

In mitigation, our officers had to remove the legs from a large meeting table, of no particular antiquarian note, but I instructed that it then be placed in storage to be returned as soon as we vacate the Mansion House.

One or more of our officers has clearly been making mischief. Consequently, I need to make sure anyone working closely with me is capable, diplomatic and, above all else, loyal to me.

ooo

Seldom do individuals and organisations get the opportunity to set up a system of political governance from new, but that task is ours in Doncaster.

Although I have consistently stressed that if we do not to use the referendum and mayoral model as the step-change Doncaster needs, we will have singularly failed the electorate, many of our councillors, and several of our officers, are less enthusiastic and seem to want to carry on as usual.

This is particularly the case with opposition councillors – all the Lib-Dems, several independents and the "old guard" Labour members – but, surprisingly a number of senior officers also see the mayoralty as a "bolt-on", which could allow previous poor practice to contaminate future activity.

With this in mind, David Marlow stresses to me that politicians and certainly executive mayors - don't get involved with appointing staff at anything lower than senior officer level. I explain that I am fully aware of this but that I do not have a political office established at this precise moment – and am nervous about officers establishing one.

I explain to David that I am less than enamoured by the overly bureaucratic manner in which the council's Human Resources Dept. sought to "oversee" the [political] appointment of Chris Taylor as my political advisor – advising me that I must advertise the job across Doncaster; that I could not put down membership of the Labour Party as a pre-requisite for the job; and that I must also be prepared to interview non-Labour Party applicants – absolute madness!

I tell him we have to be prepared to do things differently and not fall back into local government's obsession with mediocrity…

He is annoyed that I characterise [some] staff as protecting their pensions: "Oh I can't do that – it's too difficult and I retire in 20 years" but he tells me he does recognise the behaviour I describe…

I say I want my immediate team to be strong on capability, delivery and loyalty. Loyalty is an attribute we seldom give sufficient merit to in the recruitment process. We frequently talk of it being a virtue money can't buy but seldom attempt to recruit to it – probably because it is so subjective it can cloud our views and at worst lead to cronyism.

However, I would always prefer to employ a member of staff who was 75% of the finished article and loyal, than somebody who appeared to be 90% of the finished article but with questionable loyalty – more so for particularly sensitive positions.

Much to David Marlow's chagrin, I tell him I am looking to appoint my volunteer Communications Manager – knowing they will fit into the team I want to build.

The post is advertised.

"All roads – and investment – lead into Doncaster" shouts the headline on page 2 of the Doncaster Star and in a hugely supportive article, comments that "Work begins on £200 million industrial site".

All the same I continue to be disappointed that the newspaper's reporting is still very civic in its approach and that the press don't seem to understand the "mayoral model".

ooo

Tuesday July 23rd 2002...

3.30 pm – House of Commons

A statement from the Secretary of State for Transport:

> *The Secretary of State for Transport [Mr Alistair Darling]: I should like to make a statement about future air transport and airport capacity in the United Kingdom.*
>
> *We have built the fourth largest economy in the world on our ability to trade. Air travel is crucial to our expanding economy and we need to plan for the future. There has been a sixfold increase in air travel since 1970, and now half the population flies at least once a year. Demand is expected to continue to grow.*
>
> *The Government will next year publish a White Paper on air travel. As part of that, we will set out our concluded views on how much additional airport capacity is needed and where it should be sited. Before we do that, we need to canvass views on a range of options. So today, in advance of the White Paper, I am publishing six consultation papers covering the English regions, Scotland and Wales. A further consultation paper for Northern Ireland will be published shortly...*
>
> *Hansard – July 23rd 2002 Column 847*

The Transport Secretary has lit the proverbial blue touch paper today with regard to airport expansion plans [for the South East!]. He has presented a study to parliament which offers MPs a list of strategies for dealing with congestion – at

London's airports, which the aviation industry claims will face a doubling in air traffic within 20 years.

In the face of scathing criticism from environmentalists and local residents, the Transport Secretary doesn't state a preference but has called for consultation on proposals which include a new runway at Heathrow and two extra runways at Stansted!

In addition to the principal south-eastern study, he also makes reference to the long-term outlook for airport capacity in five other regions, including proposals in the form of Green consultation papers, to create new airports from military airfields, including Finningley.

To say I'm disappointed is a monstrous under-statement. Undoubtedly there are issues which I am not privy to, but by producing six separate consultation papers he's taken a "regional" approach to a national problem – with global ramifications! And he has certainly ducked the main issue, which is this government's obsession with over-development in the south-east, when it should be encouraging UK-wide development.

How could a Scot with a Scottish constituency be so London-centric in his view of his UK responsibilities and national transport brief?

By segregating the consultation process, he has underlined the predisposition to develop the south-east, which is now overheating, further widening the north-south divide.

If Alistair Darling wants to stimulate a real debate about UK aviation capacity, then it should be UK-wide. If he wants to develop a third runway at Heathrow or a second runway for Gatwick, then I will argue it's already built – at Finningley – some 90 minutes north of London and midway to Edinburgh on the East Coast Main Railway Line!

ooo

Wednesday July 24th 2002...

3.00 pm

The Doncaster Star leads with the front page headline "Darling offers clear skies to Finningley". Directly alongside it the newspaper screams: "Special Schools closure threat".

This article reports how, as part of the proposals in my White Paper 'Learning Together' on the provision for pupils with special educational needs, we have to consult on a range of options to provide an enhanced and more inclusive educational offer.

At the forefront of my deliberations is the provision of better opportunities for such pupils to learn and socialise alongside their peers and extend their educational opportunities further into adult life.

I have said throughout that the needs of the individual pupil and their family will come first, and that no pupil will be forced into provision against their wishes.

A key part of this process has been to consult on the closure of some outdated provision; the construction of new facilities, including the delivery of a new purpose-built school; and the delivery, and support, of mainstream learning opportunities.

Some opposition councillors, supported by the media, have, however been consistently hostile to the proposed closure of Rossington Hall School as part of this consultation process, despite a detailed parallel review by the overview & scrutiny function supporting my proposals.

Rossington Hall School offers a Dickensian-like educational provision – metaphorically speaking – being within the confines of a fantastic Georgian stately home which is totally unfit for a 21st century special educational needs provision and the demands of the modern curriculum.

The newspaper article quotes Councillor Martin Williams, asking *"What is the point in going out to consultation if you don't act on what you found out?"*

On one level, of course, Councillor Williams is correct. However, this is a time for strong leadership and I am clear that we do not simply go out to consultation to be "told what to do" – we go out to consultation to hear the different arguments and counter arguments to inform the decision-making process.

The electorate needs to see that we/I [the mayor] has listened – and acted – rather than that the electorate has been heard and ignored, as has so often been the case before.

Which is why officers advise – but politicians must be seen to decide.

ooo

The Doncaster Star announces that the former Civic Mayor of Doncaster, Ron Gillies, has died – with the headline "Former Mayor's death is a 'terrible loss". Notwithstanding the effect on Ron's family, who will have loved him dearly, I ask my staff if I'm missing something.

Above this piece, and I doubt by accident, the paper also reports on the 'Donnygate' corruption trial at Nottingham Crown Court with the headline "Top Tory 'received bribe' in land deal".

ooo

Tuesday July 30th 2002...

Former leader of Doncaster Council Conservative Group, John Dainty, is found guilty of
corruption at the Nottingham trial "Shameful end of a political big-hitter" says the Doncaster Star in a special report.

ooo

Wednesday August 7th 2002...

"It's a Walkover" reads today's Star headline followed by the sub-heading "Mayor takes up charity challenge from Barnsley".

The article reports on the friendly rivalry between the Leader of Barnsley Council, Steve Houghton, and myself and his 'challenge' for Doncaster to undertake a sponsored walk to raise funds for the South Yorkshire Children's Hospice – Bluebell Wood – which is to be sited at Balby in Doncaster.

ooo

Thursday August 8th 2002...

"Race lessons to be learned says Mayor" as the Star reports on the independent inquiry into the needs of black and minority ethnic communities in the borough – part of Doncaster's preparations for its Borough Strategy.

The inquiry was undertaken by Professor Gus John, Professor of Education at Strathclyde University and advisor to the Home Office on racial issues. Prof. John brought together a small team of people to help him with the work, reflecting a wide range of ages and life experiences; local people and national figures.

To ensure the Inquiry should be truly independent, no Local Authority staff were on this team; and, apart from financial and administrative support, the role of council officers and elected members was limited to speaking to the Inquiry Team when asked to.

To be honest, I am a little worried about some of the findings and see the whole issue of equalities as something of an Achilles' heel for the local authority – and my mayoralty – unless we undertake a significant amount of work on this area.

I agree that the report should form the preparation of a Mayoral White Paper that makes clear the strength of our commitment to improving race relations, equal opportunities, social inclusion and community cohesion; and ensures that this strategic commitment is reflected in the delivery of services by all council departments and its partners.

Notwithstanding the above, I agree with Chris that I need to have someone I can trust to advise me on emerging BME issues – someone close to my immediate team but who is not seen as a member.

ooo

Thursday August 15th 2002...

I attend Doncaster Royal Infirmary to have my Right Anterior Cruciate Ligament [ACL] reconstruction following a rugby injury in January 2000.

My staff are concerned I won't be able to do the sponsored walk to Barnsley but I am less worried – I can still walk on crutches!

ooo

Monday August 26th 2002...

Following John Ryan's remarkable attack on Doncaster Council and my leadership last November, the Football Association has found him guilty of bringing the game into disrepute and fined him £10,000 – with £8,000 of the fine suspended pending further conduct.

ooo

Tuesday September 3rd 2002...

Spowie comes to tell me that Doncaster Rovers' fans are holding a collection at tonight's game against Kettering Town, to raise the £2,000 to pay John Ryan's fine!

I am not happy. Firstly, the Chairman threatens that the streets will be covered with [my] blood if we don't deliver a new community stadium; then, when the FA punishes him for his abusive behaviour, the fans want to lord him and pay the fine for him!

I rant at Ian that we have never been so close to delivering a new stadium for the people of Doncaster – not just Doncaster Rovers – and these people still want to poke me in the eye!

ooo

Wednesday September 4th 2002…

"Fans fund row – supporters call off bid to pay ex-chairman's fine" reads the front page of the Doncaster Star.

The Star reports that I had a conversation with the *de facto* Chairman, Trevor Milton yesterday and suggests that I insisted the collection was cancelled. The newspaper states "Mayor Winter today stressed that at no time had he asked for the collection not to go ahead" – which is correct.

ooo

Sunday September 15th 2002…

Following an excellent turnout from more than one hundred Doncaster residents, I take on the 'challenge' to walk to Barnsley, raising funds for 'Bluebell Wood Children's Hospice'.

Carolyne and our children accompany us on the walk as do Aidan, Chris Taylor, Spowie and several other elected members.

I am still on crutches from my ACL reconstruction and do the walk through a combination of walking and wheelchair sessions [as rest periods] whilst being pushed by four day-release inmates from Hatfield Open Prison.

Four miles into the nine mile walk it becomes evident that Aidan is phenomenally unfit and struggling with the distance, much to our collective amusement.

My hands are badly blistered but I still manage the final mile unaided, meeting up with our colleagues from Barnsley Council at the Crown Inn at Barnburgh – the boundary between the two boroughs.

As I walk the last couple of hundred yards, I am surprised to see Nadeem Shah applauding our arrival.

Nadeem is a major investor in Doncaster – and a financial supporter of the Conservative Party!

Suffering from polio as a child, he has a severe limp and is unable to join us on the walk but still makes a significant contribution to the charity.

As Leader of the council I tended to stay away from property developers – but now I'm mayor I see it as a key part of my role to encourage them to invest in the borough. Consequently, I express my appreciation at seeing Nadeem supporting this fundraising event and make a fuss of him and his delightful wife Maureen.

ooo

Tuesday September 17th 2002...

"Waterfront scheme in Doncaster of future" is the headline in the Doncaster Star, reporting on a presentation I gave in Scarborough to a conference of Yorkshire Forward's Urban Renaissance Panel.

My 45 minute presentation focused on Finningley Airport proposals; Doncaster Education City; designs for a mixed-use Waterfront scheme; the Lakeside completion; Civic & Cultural Quarter including our New Performance Venue; Town Moor Racecourse development; and the markets revitalisation project; and was extremely well received, not least because I had to deliver it in a wheelchair!

ooo

Thursday September 19th 2002...

We are launching a consultation programme with regard to DEC. I am concerned that we are struggling to get business fully involved and this may prove to be a weakness with the project.

There is a huge disconnect. Businesses are quick to cry that colleges and universities are not turning out "job-ready" graduates and not delivering the correct skills, but they are also struggling to vocalise the outcomes they want from study programmes.

ooo

Friday September 20th 2002...

I'm getting a little frustrated with the furore over Doncaster Hockey Club's plans to create a further hockey pitch as part of its facilities – on the edge of 'Town Fields'. 'Town Fields' is a significant green space in the heart of the town centre and the club has stipulated that it needs a new water-based hockey pitch as a pre-requisite to competing in the National Premier League.

I have several concerns. 'Town Fields' are supposedly a public open space – the green lungs, if you like, in the heart of Doncaster – and were stipulated [in 1895] to be left forever open. They have, however, gradually been eaten into by the Planning Authority and council allowing piecemeal leisure developments on the periphery of the site during the previous ten years or so.

The whole of the area is a conservation area, with some quite superb Victorian and Edwardian Villas overlooking the 'Town Fields' themselves. There are also several quality Georgian buildings in the Bennetthorpe and Christchurch areas, including the Gilbert Scott designed Christ Church itself.

I'm fairly certain I am not going to allow the development, which will be an incredibly popular decision within the community, but I must be seen to be objective and considered in my deliberations whilst using the furore to assert my mayoral authority.

I instruct my office to call a public meeting as soon as possible, diary permitting.

ooo

Friday September 27th 2002...

"Public talks in pitch row – Mayor calls together all sides to meet over Hockey Club expansion proposal" reads page 5 of the Doncaster Star.

ooo

Saturday September 28th 2002...

Aidan and I set off in my car for the Labour Party Conference in Blackpool. It's our first Labour Party conference and we are very excited at the prospect of "selling Doncaster" [and ourselves!] to all and sundry.

As part of my leadership programme, Phil Blundell is also attending to enable my networking and act as my 'chaperone'!

I'm disappointed to find that my office has "booked" me in to attend the Public Meeting into the Town Fields Hockey Club facility on Wednesday 2nd October at 6.30 pm. I'll have to come back early from the Labour Party Conference – and miss Bill Clinton's speech!

ooo

Monday September 30th 2002...

4.00 pm

The Conference is going extremely well and we have just listened to John Prescott's speech. It's his usual mix of impassioned socialist pragmatism, humour and mispronunciations [!] – the perfect antidote to TB's "Big Picture" rhetoric...

Prescott warns that a third term, which we are all expecting, will not come easy – and the party will have to earn it.

And he delights many of those attending with an attack on the Countryside Alliance demonstrators who have just staged a mass rally in London opposing the ban on fox hunting.

"Isn't it a pity they didn't march in their thousands when the Tories closed rural schools, rural post offices and rural bus routes, and increased rural unemployment," he declares. *"That's far more important than foxes."* And the audience burst into applause.

I'm less ebullient to see Blair's populist meanderings emerging into government policy. Arguably this is exactly what governments should do but I am less sure and view it as an appalling piece of misguided legislation – an example of New Labour's desperation to be "popular".

ooo

6.00 pm

Aidan tells me he has to go back to Doncaster for an "emergency"; I see it as yet another example of his propensity for secrets and lies. He takes my car and says he will be back for breakfast tomorrow morning.

ooo

8.30 pm

As we network during the evening, I discuss my concerns about Aidan's behaviour with Phil Blundell. We agree that, at the end of the day, it has to be a trade-off – eccentricities come with being a bright young thing.

ooo

Tuesday October 1st 2002...

8.00 am

Aidan joins us for breakfast. He must have left at 6.00am but the early start has been good for him and he appears full of life.

1.00 pm

Phil Blundell and I have just sat in on a session at which Doug McAvoy, the NUT General Secretary is also speaking and I want to hear his views on Blair's innovative, and arguably contentious, proposals for education.

Having said that, I become pre-occupied that one member of the panel seems unable to mention their constituency town and avoids saying the town's name at all costs.

During a Q&A input the delegate describes their constituency as being "close to [another city]"; a "tactic" that really begins to irk me.

When I see them avoid mentioning their elected home town another two or three times, I lean across to Phil and say I'm going to ask them how far from their "home town" their constituency actually is. Phil suggests I don't and we sit there for a further 20 minutes as I become increasingly agitated.

After leaving the session, Phil quickly suggests we take a tram-ride along the seafront to Fleetwood for a traditional lunch. Dressed in our sharp suits and resplendent with our Labour Party Conference passes and lanyards, we have a wonderful ride on the tram, laughing and joking with many of the other passengers, who all seem to want to connect with us as a vision of 'New Labour'.

We reach the end of the line and go to the Corner Café, a lovely little spot on the corner of Pharos Street and Queens Terrace – overlooking the sea front – where we have one of the best fish & chip lunches I have ever had.

The good humour continues in the café and as I sip my third cup of tea I ask Phil why he's suggested we come to Fleetwood.

"Well I've known you for more than a year now, Martin..." he replies *"... and I know that you don't always think of your own safety as a politician... and I recognise when you're about to damage yourself."*

"Well thank you," I tell him, cheerfully tucking into another mouthful.

ooo

Wednesday October 2nd 2002...

6.30 pm – The Carr House Centre, Bennethorpe.

Having driven back from Blackpool, I arrive for the public meeting over the Town Fields Hockey Club development. To be honest, I'm pretty pissed off to have missed Bill Clinton's speech.

Mullany advised me never to go to public meetings unless you know you can

control them – or they can frequently get the better of you – but I'm looking forward to tonight's for several reasons:
- I enjoy speaking to large groups and particularly when they give me a hard time;
- The general feeling in the community is that of cynicism, that it's a done-deal and the development will be given permission;
- As 'mayor', I am intent on doing things differently from "the council" of the past;
- We have been briefed that the malcontents will be attending to disrupt the meeting as much as possible.

Since I am even more certain now that I will be turning down the development, I am very comfortable about attending – but I still need to be seen to be objective and considered.

The hall is packed with more than 200 people and press photographers working overtime. As I enter there are several boos, catcalls and a palpable level of aggression and tension. I look around and see Chris Taylor and Chris Stephenson, and a few others from the inner team but we are considerably outnumbered.

As the meeting gets underway I'm on top of my game. I'm calm, considered, relaxed and well in control, dealing effectively and with humour, with all the antagonism from the malcontents. There are several here, including Nortrop, and they are strategically placed around the room. I deliberately make eye contact with each of them as I address the entire hall.

After a fifteen minute presentation, during which I deliver a strong "community first" mayoral message, I say I want to hear the views of those present and we move to a Q&A session.

A key lesson with a meeting like this is to manage its length correctly. Leave too early and the public will feel short-changed and that you weren't prepared to listen; stay too late and they start to drift away and become crotchety and tired – although tonight I'm both very well-prepared and actually on the same side as most of those present.

After two hours nobody has left and I calculate that I've got the vast majority "on-board" with me as the mayor. Another half an hour later, and I can see Nortrop and his cronies getting frustrated with the way the audience is responding to my reasonableness.

One particular malcontent is very loud and belligerent and constantly attempting to agitate the room. I've known him for years and I know his limitations, so I make a high-risk call. I engage him directly in a question and ask that he is given the microphone. One or two of my advisors look terrified – even some of those in the audience look worried – but I'm fairly relaxed.

As one of our officers hands him the mic I can see the sheer excitement in his eyes – this is his chance!

Within seconds he's insulted me – for which I thank him. But the audience don't like it. They've watched me act graciously and with good humour all evening and now the malcontent is seen as both an agitator and a danger – a threat to the audience's new-found allegiance with the mayor.

A couple of those in the audience turn on him, making disparaging remarks themselves, and now he doesn't like it! My strategy has worked… he's blown it!

The meeting begins to descend into chaos as several people shout him down. My staff member takes the mic from him again, as he engages in a row with those near to him.

For my part, I have the upper hand – and I offer calming words to the meeting.

"*I suppose that's the problem with giving everyone a voice,*" I say… and I wrap-up, thanking everyone for attending and explaining the next steps as I see them; then reminding them there is still coffee and tea at the rear of the room.

As the meeting comes to a close a small crowd gathers around me and several people offer their congratulations and thanks for being open and accessible. I make my way to the back to get myself a glass of water, but more importantly to position myself so that people have to pass me on their way out.

I'm feeling great, the meeting went brilliantly and I'm getting a lot of support for my approach. I also have the advantage over the malcontents – who are now viewed as rabble-rousers.

I notice Ray Nortrop skulking off through the hall's double doors. "*Just a moment,*" I say to the couple I'm talking to.

And I lean towards him.

"*Thanks for coming, Ray.*" But there's no response!

ooo

Thursday October 3rd 2002…

7.30 am

Driving over the M62 back to the Labour Party Conference in Blackpool, I take the opportunity to call Martyn Vickers. Martyn is 'President' of Doncaster Central Constituency Labour Party, a titular position which I assume was created by Rosie to reward his loyalty. To be fair, Martyn has been fully supportive of me as mayor since I defeated him at the Labour Party mayoral selection in February, but I want to talk to him about encouraging Doncaster Hockey Club to build their new water-based Hockey Pitch at Danum School. Martyn is the Head at the school, which is less than a mile from Town Fields, and offers a potential win/win to the story.

He is very amenable to my suggestion in principal and we agree to talk again in the future.

ooo

9.30 am

Back at Conference Aidan is really hyper – apparently Clinton's speech was a masterpiece and JP had an open-top bus trip along the seafront last night promoting regional government and economic regeneration...

Despite my own triumphs, I'm envious of what I missed.

ooo

Tuesday October 8th 2002...

"£8m European grant puts Interchange right on track to create 1000 jobs" reads the Doncaster Star front page.

The very supportive article explains how £8.2 million of European Structural Funds are being invested in the Interchange scheme and in the innovative skills and training programme for Doncaster workers doing construction jobs on the site.

ooo

Thursday October 10th 2002...

Despite my reservations David Marlow has continued with the appointment of a very senior officer to support him with his work. Performing phenomenally well at interview, the successful applicant came from a high profile role at the ODPM – the Office of the Deputy Prime Minister.

David and I have our first real disagreement with regard to this appointment. I insist we should be focusing on 'mayoral delivery' not 'Head of Paid Service delivery'...and David maintains that if I want to be "guaranteed" on operational [mayoral] delivery, then we went for the wrong mayoral model and should have chosen the 'Mayor and Council Manager' option.

This – alongside the debacle over the Communications Manager appointment – puts another slight mark against David's performance where he sometimes seems to delight in opposing me...

David Marlow briefs me on the 'Core Cities Group' [Birmingham, Bristol, Leeds, Liverpool, Manchester, Newcastle, Nottingham and Sheffield]. This is a self-elected group of leading English cities working together to present a united local authority voice to promote the role of our cities in driving economic growth.

He says that Bob Kerslake, the Sheffield City Council chief executive, is keen to make overtures for Doncaster to be introduced as a new member. This is because, as part of the South Yorkshire Spatial Strategy, there is a general consensus about the emergence of a 'bi-polar' [Sheffield-Doncaster] model in terms of economic drivers for the sub-region.

I'm quite excited at this thought. Although not a politician Kerslake controls everything that happens in Sheffield, and arguably, the whole of South Yorkshire. David needs to keep working on this one…

ooo

Saturday October 12th 2002…

"Mass opposition to Hockey Club plans" screams page two of the Doncaster Star, highlighting the findings of the consultation exercise we have undertaken, which shows that 82% of Town Moor residents oppose the expansion.

To be honest I'm surprised it's as low as that; but what concerns me most is the photograph they've used from the public meeting last week, taken from the stage behind me…

… I didn't realise I was balding so much!

ooo

Monday October 14th 2002…

"The shadow of the past is fading" cries a full article, written by me, on page 5 of the Doncaster Star. The article is part of a series to celebrate Local Democracy Week.

ooo

Thursday October 17th 2002…

George Holmes has approached me with some whirlwind news that the college is having talks with the University of Huddersfield for a full merger, and that the proposal for the amalgamation is Huddersfield's. While I welcome the news, it doesn't quite seem right. Why would Huddersfield approach us with such a model? And with no previous overtures?

I'm nervous, although George is phenomenally hyper – even by his standards. It's a fantastic development certainly in terms of the overall DEC concept but I tell him to proceed with caution and obviously to make sure all due diligence is done. If it succeeds then it's absolutely fantastic news for Doncaster; but if it fails or falls through, it could rule out Doncaster's chance for a University for ten years or more.

000

Friday October 18th 2002...

"Back a winner – have a say in future of our enterprising town" reads another full page piece to celebrate Local Democracy Week.

Featuring an interview with Ian Spowart as my Cabinet Member for Trade, Industry & Innovation, the article reports that "Doncaster has undergone a major transformation over the past few years" and goes onto encourage the reader to become involved in the community through the many differing consultation events.

000

Wednesday October 23rd 2002...

"Bid for university – College plans merger to boost further education [sic.] in town" reports the Doncaster Star, revealing that the college is in merger talks as part of the Education City project which could bring the town full university status.

I'm a little annoyed that the newspaper has got hold of the story, which it says has come from a "joint statement" although I suspect instigated by George. We should be playing a much more political game and have considered how realistic such a merger is before spouting off about it.

Having said that, the newspaper states erroneously: "It would create a new institution and establish a university college in Doncaster." My understanding is exactly the opposite; indeed George briefed me that it would mean full amalgamation and not 'university college' status.

Nonetheless, the article adds: "Mayor Martin Winter welcomed the move and said "It is crucial that the model proposed is the best model for the people of Doncaster. I look forward to the proposals that emerge from the negotiations, which I will consider in due course".

Tuesday November 5th 2002...

I instruct David Marlow to inform our Corporate Management Team – given that today's date is particularly appropriate – that they have still not identified a solution to the location of new mayoral offices. This is more than eighteen months now!
    Remaining calm, I explain that I wish to see a report, with options, on my desk within two months.

ooo

Wednesday November 13th 2002...

9.00 am – Cabinet Brief – The Mansion House Ballroom

I have taken the decision to move today's Cabinet Meeting from the Priory Suite, where we normally hold it, to the Ballroom. This is because we are expecting a large attendance for the decision on Doncaster Hockey Club's expansion plans.
    I go through the choreography so that all cabinet are clear as to what we will be deciding and which aspects we should be stressing.

ooo

10.00 am

Approximately 100 people turn up and following a theatrical opening, where I welcome everyone, we move on to the business on today's agenda.
    I present a rehearsed speech - supportive of the community and their involvement in this issue, but also supportive of the Hockey Club – which culminates in my decision:
1) The request by Doncaster Hockey Club for the disposal of Public Open Space by means of a long term lease for the purpose of constructing a water based pitch on the Town Field site be refused;
2) The Council support Doncaster Hockey Club in identifying an alternative site for the pitch;

I am also keen to turn the large-scale objections into large-scale participation and speak of drawing a red line around the site to prevent future developments there – in line with the views of the residents, my own as mayor, and our forebears. Our officers interpret this as:

3) A policy and plan for the management of the Town Field be developed for recommendation to Cabinet incorporating the following:
   (a) No further encroachment which is detrimental to community use;
   (b) Addresses the issues identified in the consultation undertaken regarding the Hockey Club proposal and also in the consultation undertaken regarding the children's play area; and
   (c) A stakeholder group be established comprising representatives of all user groups, interested community/residents groups and Council representatives.

ooo

Thursday November 14th 2002…

"On course to learn – Deputy Mayor leads research into public sector" declares a full page article in the Doncaster Star, citing a new learning initiative linking up Doncaster College with the private sector.

The article reports that Management Consultants NTP Meridian have joined forces with Doncaster College to research changes in management in the public sector and explains that Deputy Mayor Aidan Rave will be carrying out the research, as part of working towards a PHD at the end of the programme.

Yet again Aidan has failed to stay on message and is promoting projects which further his career.

ooo

Monday November 18th 2002…

11.00 am – Sandringham Road Primary School

When people ask me why I entered into politics, I frequently tell them that "I never really recovered from having my milk taken away from me when I was at school, aged nine!"…

After the war, under Labour Prime Minister Clement Attlee, the 1946 Free Milk Act was passed, providing one third of a pint a day to all children under the age of 18. Research had linked poor nutrition, low income and underachievement in schools; and milk was identified as a key food that could help alleviate the problem.

Margaret Thatcher was Education Secretary in 1971 when Edward Heath's Conservative government had to find substantial cuts to meet election pledges on tax. Removing free school milk from the over seven's became the most notorious saving introduced, with the Labour education spokesman Edward Short saying that scrapping free milk was "the meanest and most unworthy thing" he had seen in 20 years. It earned Thatcher the nickname "Milk Snatcher" and haunted her throughout her career.

This morning we are launching my "Fruit into Schools" programme – one of the key areas of delivery within my new [2002-05] Mayoral Manifesto – in which I state:

"South Yorkshire has some of the highest levels of cancer and heart disease in the country and a better diet with more fresh fruit and vegetables can provide important long-term health benefits."

I pledge to develop healthier eating in our schools and communities, with today's launch part of a project to ensure every child in Doncaster's schools has free daily fruit provided as part of a healthier eating plan.

This pioneering scheme has been paid for by the Doncaster Children's Fund and, if successful, will be implemented across all Doncaster's schools and fully funded as a second term election priority.

On the basis that it is always easier to work with those who want to support you, I've chosen to launch "Fruit into Schools" here because Ian Spowart is the Chair of Governors and I know I am with friends.

I am welcomed by the head teacher and "Spowie" and I'm delighted to see that our educational staff and the schools' catering team are a hive of activity and tables are laid out with all manner of fruit and sliced carrots.

As I chat to Ian and the head about the health benefits of all this, I notice that each table also has a couple of plates full of chocolate biscuits...

I question the schools catering officer...

"Well, we thought that for the children who don't like fruit, rather than sitting there not eating anything..."

Sometimes the most transformational of polices are reliant on the most basic of transactions.

ooo

With a class full of schoolchildren now joining us, and after a particularly frantic operational U-turn, we pose for the promotional photographs.

The children are really enjoying the fruit and carrots and there isn't a single one who's not tucking in; but how many would've had a chocolate biscuit given the choice!

I am moved by one particular child, a small thin boy who seems to be enjoying it so much I remark on how much he is eating to the head teacher.

The boy tells me he has already eaten two apples and two pears! As I talk to the others I monitor his intake and I'm horrified to see that by the end he has eaten seven pieces of fruit…

When did this child last eat?

ooo

Thursday December 14th 2002…

"Donnygate days now in the past – Rapid improvement after dark legacy" reports the Doncaster Star, commenting on the authority's Comprehensive Performance Assessment rating.

We are all absolutely delighted with the Audit Commission's inspection report, which cites us as one of the most rapidly improving local authorities in the country – and marks the significant progress over the past two years since elected Mayor Martin Winter and chief executive David Marlow took the reins.

The article goes on to say that "Doncaster Council is dragging itself out of the Donnygate mire by moving up the local authorities' performance league… and that the borough is improving rapidly and putting the dark legacy of corruption and freeloading behind it".

"The report highlights the transformation since the cull of old guard councillors in the wake of the Danum police enquiry into fiddling and backhanders and 'there is now a growing sense and belief in the ability of the council to make a difference to the people of Doncaster'."

"One of the highlights of the Audit Commission report is the success in turning round a failing education service – which the mayor admitted was "in an awful state" – and development of the Education City vision."

I don't recall ever saying publicly that education was "in an awful state", but I am also quoted as saying: "This report draws another line under the past and once and for all closes the book on Donnygate. The challenge is to make sure that improvement continues."

This hugely supportive article concludes with a statement from the Audit Commission:

"Although the council has become more successful in engaging the citizens of Doncaster, it must continue to work to put the past behind it and focus on the future."

ooo

In the Star's 'Opinion' piece on page six they comment:

"Doncaster Council has had more than its share of bad publicity over recent years. So it is only right that the authority should be roundly congratulated when good news comes its way."

"Such an occasion presents itself today with a report from the Audit Commission which praises the council for making rapid improvements over the last two years. This fits in with what we have been told many times, that the past is finally behind the authority."

"Of course, such claims have been met with some scepticism. But this time it seems that there really is light at the end of the tunnel, though there will always be the critics and detractors who refuse to give credit where it is due."

"However, we are pleased to do just that and congratulate the current administration for steering us in the right direction."

Credit where credit is due – but they just can't bring themselves to say the word "mayor"!

ooo

One step forward and another step back. Cliff Hampson's stealth strategy is beginning to rile me.

My community C of E Vicar is a Lib-Dem supporter and freely associating himself with Lib-Dem councillors and their campaigns. Although there is nothing wrong with this in itself, Hampson has now inveigled himself into the local vicarage and the church's parish magazine…

… the "Shepherds Watch" is regularly trumpeting "local man Cliff Hampson", promoting the "Kirk Sandall Community Group" and launching mini "campaigns" to the detriment of the Glass Park project and – through this – the Mayor.

I decide I will take it up with someone higher up the ecclesiastical ladder.

ooo

Monday January 6th 2003…

Another of my mayoral pledges is delivered today. The Mayors FLAG [Fighting Litter Abandoned cars and Graffiti] scheme is launched.

I wish it were my idea but the reality is that Phil Cole, Caroline Flint's partner, gave me the idea, having seen it somewhere down south. It's a really simple concept; you see litter, an abandoned car or graffiti; you phone it in to the FLAG hotline and it's removed with 24 hours.

Wednesday January 8th 2003...

I have received a report and briefing with regard to potential solutions to the new mayor's offices, including costings.

I am absolutely apoplectic; they have actually come back with costings of £1.8 million for a reconfiguration of the chief executive's suite at the Mansion House! This is the price for no walls being moved but a complete redecoration and carpeting of the present building's footprint and the provision of new furniture and desks.

I tell the officer responsible that I adjudge his report a deliberate attempt to antagonise me. In effect, it's absolute rubbish. I tell him to bring me back something better – and to sharpen CMT's collective pencils in the process.

To be fair, office accommodation is at a premium across the council's properties and one of the reasons why we are looking to establish a new council house within an all-singing and dancing Civic & Cultural Quarter.

Aidan and I agree that we will attempt to source offices ourselves – how difficult can it be?

ooo

Thursday January 9th 2003...

5.30pm – The Mayor's Office, The Mansion House

Despite batting the issue of the "mayor's salary" into the long grass some fifteen months ago, the issue has come back to haunt us – like some bad penny.

The report on all elected members' roles, responsibilities and remuneration levels – compiled by an independent panel – was "deferred" to be revisited "after the election of the town's inaugural Executive Mayor". What members didn't realise was they weren't deferring the awarding of the mayor's wages *per se* – they were actually deferring their own wage rise and new wage structure – doh!

I'd like to say that I realised this at the time – but I didn't. I don't think anybody did, it was just a politically expedient decision to make.

So "they" went back to the independent panel – which, despite having seen its original work deferred, revisited it and concluded that, if anything, the demands on the town's inaugural Executive Mayor were greater than anticipated.

The report is to come back to Full Council on Monday.

The moral dilemma Full Council now faces is that, as we near the end of the inaugural mayoral year – when neither the mayor nor his deputy have been paid what the panel recommended – elected members are also nearing the end of a full municipal year and they haven't had their wage rise either!

The predicament for these upstanding self-righteous bastards is to have to accept a report that moves a holistic new remuneration structure, one that includes the mayor, in order for them to get at their enhanced salary – what a quandary!

For my part, I can see the writing on the wall. I have argued that I don't want the 'rise' within cabinet and Labour group, but the members want theirs.

Now I can forgive this from the Labour group and Tory members – who always accepted the independent report – but the hypocrisy of the likes of the Lid-Dems and Independent Councillors...

... 'twas ever thus.

ooo

Monday January 13th 2003...

2.00 pm – Full Council – Doncaster Council Chamber

I am not attending Full Council today, choosing to have an important meeting elsewhere, so as not to take part in the vote to give myself a wage rise. Only forty two of the sixty four council members are in attendance but they unanimously move to accept the report.

A new wage structure and future wage rise isn't enough, however, so they backdate the award from the beginning of the present municipal year – to get their ten month's back pay!

You have to have morals in public service.

ooo

Friday January 31st 2003...

Herten, Germany

After receiving an invitation from Herr Bürgermeister, Klaus Bechtel, Carolyne and I leave with two officers and Paul, as driver, for a civic visit to our twin town in Recklinghausen, Germany.

ooo

Saturday February 1st 2003…

Hotel Schloss

We are awoken to scenes of the Columbia Space Shuttle breaking up as it re-enters the earth's atmosphere, killing all seven crew members.

ooo

Thursday February 6th 2003…

I attend the launch of a new film, by Doncaster film maker Graham Oxby, entitled "Shotgun Dave Rides East".
 We have agreed, via a contra work exchange, to be a small-scale part funder of the film; another opportunity to promote Doncaster and its burgeoning presence after years in the doldrums.

ooo

Footnote

The Doncaster Mansion House "front" and "back" Committee Rooms did not have 'Chippendale tables' in them. After we moved out, all the furniture was returned and the rooms made up again in an "as found" condition.

ooo

Mayor's Priorities

Doncaster's Green and White Papers work on the same system as national Government. The mayor issues Green Papers when he wants to consult with citizens on issues where he intends to introduce new policies and legislation. When he has decided changes need to be made, a White Paper is issued.
 This clearly signals the mayor's intentions to the Borough and gives stakeholders the opportunity to comment on the more detailed proposals. The system provides for inclusive, transparent and decisive leadership of the council and borough.

Doncaster NHS Report – November 2003

"TACKLING DEPRIVED COMMUNITIES – NEIGHBOURHOOD WORKING IN DONCASTER"

Paul Fryers, Public Health Specialist – Head of Public Health Intelligence Unit
Arnold Drakeley, Head of Strategic Partnerships
Michael Geraghty, Research and Information Officer
Doncaster Primary Care Trusts

"The Mayor of Doncaster's White Paper on Neighbourhood Management [Winter, 2003] is the driving force in getting all our communities involved in issues that affect their lives. The neighbourhood structure outlined in the White Paper is based on natural communities that are defined and recognised by their residents. If the PCTs, Doncaster Strategic Partnership and the seven Key Strategic Partnerships are to support communities effectively, the focus of attention needs to switch away from the electoral ward level to a neighbourhood level."

Winter M [2003]. Making a Difference in Your Neighbourhood – Proposals for introducing a new approach to managing neighbourhoods. Doncaster: Doncaster MB.

One million people – a view from a hotel room

"Get up, stand up, Stand up for your rights.
Get up, stand up, Don't give up the fight"

Bob Marley and Peter Tosh

February 2003...

As Mayor I feel it's incredibly important to practice what I preach and what better example than to adopt strong work life balance policies and encourage staff to respect them.

What becomes clear, however, is that "the organisation" wants me to promote such policies and programmes to our staff and partners, but not to practice them myself.

For example, throughout my tenure I take the view that for me to function effectively, I need "down time" to reflect on issues – thinking time to consider the ramifications of my policies and programmes and how these inter-relate with government statute or other external social, economic or environmental indicators.

Consequently, I adopt Fridays as my "thinking" days. Thinking days are to be kept clear, with no meetings or visits booked in, to allow my personal reflection, political meetings and associated work to take place. Others, however, don't see it that way. And when I say "others" I refer to professional officers, colleague politicians, those from partner organisations etc. In short, everybody thinks they have a stronger call on my diary time than I do. To a certain extent this is fair enough. If you put yourself forward for election to public office, then you are making a statement that you wish to serve the people who put you there; not retire into solitude, claiming you need to spend more time with your family.

These demands on my time hamper my attempts at "Time Management". You can be the best prioritiser in the world but your prioritisation only works effectively if it's communicated clearly to others, who, themselves, respect your time management principles and procedures. For my office staff the policy becomes a nightmare; at the beginning of each week, they valiantly defend "attacks" on Friday's [free] "diary window", demands which are becoming ever greater for several reasons:

- As my profile grows and the public becomes more familiar with the [elected] mayoral model and my role within the borough, demand for my involvement increases.

- We are improving as a local authority. The Audit Commission has stated in it's 2002 CPA, that we are the most improved in England.
- South Yorkshire Police has ended its Operation Danum Inquiry.
- I am a political mayor and there is growing and widespread political support for the ideology I/we are promoting. As a result, my political advisor Chris Taylor makes sure I play a full role in the Labour party's political governance structure in Doncaster. This entails an annual programme of regular attendance at monthly District Labour Party meetings, 4 Constituency Labour Party meetings, 21 Ward [and several branch] meetings, as well as other, ad-hoc Labour Party functions and requests.

Additionally, the party nationally is promoting me as the only Labour mayor outside of London, with a commensurate programme of visits and support opportunities to sister local authorities and mayoral candidates.

As a result of all the above, we are gaining widespread public and partner support for our re-invention agenda.

We are winning the battles... and slowly the war.

ooo

Sunday February 9th 2003...

6.30 pm

I have now been Leader/Mayor for nearly two years and the demands on my time are really starting to impact on my children.

I have consistently stated publicly that being Mayor is not the most important job in my life; being a parent to three young children and a partner to Carolyne is the most important job I have to do. Carolyne is much more philosophical about it than me.

"It's the volatile nature of the job... The kids are fine if they know they're not going to see you, because they can accept it, plan it in to their routine and adjust, accordingly" she says.

"What they can't handle is being messed about – expecting you home at 6.00 or 7.00 and then you phone up last minute to say you're going to be late or not coming home tonight. They can't, or don't want to, deal with the uncertainty."

This particular weekend has proven as chaotic as many others, with a crammed diary of events and activities; consequently I have seen very little of my children. To compound matters, I am looking at an incredibly busy diary for the forthcoming week, with attendance at the Labour Party Spring Conference in Glasgow the following weekend. After arriving home at 6.30 again, I am acutely aware that I need to spend some quality time with the children; so I call them into the kitchen.

"I know it's Sunday and I've only just got in – but I've also got to go out again to a [Constituency] *Labour Party Meeting in an hour,*" I tell them.

"*I've also got the Labour Party Spring Conference in Glasgow next weekend...*"

"Well that's it!" I state definitively "*I am not spending all my time at work – we need to do*
something as a family".

"*It's not fair on me – and it's certainly not fair on you,*" I tell their expectant faces. "*So I'll tell 'them' that I'm going to finish at 3.30 on Thursday so I can do something with my kids ... and we'll go to the pictures to see the new Harry Potter – as a family*"

"*... and the chamber of secrets*" adds Joss helpfully.

"*Yeah... but something'll crop up – it always does*" says Marcey in her usual sardonic way.

"*No it won't – because I won't let it*" I reply. "*No deals... and certainly no excuses. Is that a deal? [!]*"

ooo

10.00 pm

Following the Constituency Labour Party Meeting, I ring Chris and ask him to gather my Office together for a quick meeting tomorrow morning.

ooo

Monday February 10th 2003...

8.30 am

I tell my Office team I understand the pressure they are all under to find space in my diary; but that I'm in great danger of being burnt out before I've even begun!. As a result, I want them to be firmer about protecting my "thinking" Fridays.

I also stipulate that I'm going to the cinema with my children on Thursday and under no circumstances are they to book anything for me after 3.00 pm.

Some three months into the due diligence tests for the college's amalgamation with Huddersfield University, a fairly colourless joint statement has been issued drawing an end to the negotiations. I have feared the worse for some time as George briefed me on "problems" they were experiencing on both sides.

I comment: *"Naturally I'm disappointed that these discussions have not been successful. However, in view of the Government's recent 'Higher Education White Paper', I have every confidence that the efforts of Doncaster College will achieve a university for the borough in the future."*

ooo

Tuesday February 11th 2003...

Following a question at yesterday's Full Council about my trip to Herten, an argument is brewing about whether Carolyne should have accompanied me. For the avoidance of doubt, I report:
- Carolyne paid for her own passage;
- We paid a child-minder to look after our three children for three days;
- Carolyne played a full role during the visit, including providing translation services;

I ask that members don't criticise someone who isn't here to defend themselves and who was invited to represent Doncaster and had done so at a not insignificant financial cost to herself.

Furthermore, I ask that on the basis of the mayoral model being new to us all, will council be so kind as to advise on the etiquette pertaining to the 'mayor's partner', the role of the 'mayor's partner' and what, if anything, the 'mayor's partner' should be known as...

She is not a 'Lady Mayoress' as with the civic mayors of the past; she is not the mayor's consort, and she is certainly not the First Lady!

ooo

Thursday February 13th 2003...

Life at work continues, as usual – but with staff continually referring to "keeping Fridays free" – and vocalising the adjustments this means to their work planning and my diary preparation.

ooo

1.00 pm

Chris comes in to see me; he is looking extremely pensive.

"I've just had the Prime Minister's Office on to me Martin... and we've got a problem. He'll be attending Cedar Court [at Wakefield] this evening at 5.00 pm and wishes to meet up with you and Aidan... And you're obviously going to see Harry Potter with your kids, aren't you?"

"Nah... it's bollocks, Chris. He doesn't want to see me – or us," I say, thinking about my children's reactions.

"The Party will just be making sure he's got an audience of admirers there ... I've seen it all before; there'll be about two hundred of us in a room..."

"No – I'm not doing it" I conclude. "He'll understand. Aidan can go – can't he – but you're gonna have to tell 'em, Chris." I am becoming increasingly annoyed as I think about the political repercussions and the ramifications for my children.

"Fucking four hours notice! Who do they fucking think they are?" I scream, oblivious to the idiocy of the question.

"Well, I suspect they're concerned about his security Martin," Chris replies sarcastically, in his delightful Wolverhampton brogue.

"I suppose they think someone might try and assassinate him; him being the Prime Minister [and singularly declaring war on Iraq] and all that... " he slaps me down.

It works though. "You know what I mean Chris" I legitimise. "My kids'll go fucking mad...

"... I promised 'em – Nah he can fuck off. He's got a family. He'll understand. He <u>must</u> understand. Get on the blower and tell 'em, Chris.".

"The Mayor won't see you, he's watching Harry Potter, Prime Minister... won't be particularly good for your career Martin... Why don't you have a word with Carolyne and the kids."

"They're gonna go fucking mad."

ooo

3.00 pm – en route to our house

"Hiyah Cazza – we've got a problem."
    There's no response – just telephone silence.
    "Can you hear me?"
    "Yes – I'm just waiting for it," she gambles.

"Obviously we're supposed to be going to see Harry Potter... in half an hour..." I begin.

"Well the PM's Office has just rung and said TB wants to see me in Wakefield at 5.00 – on his way up to Glasgow" I barely pause for breath.

"I don't want to go" I continue "There'll be hundreds of us in a room and he won't even miss me"

"Well why don't you have a word with the kids, Martin and see what they say" she suggests, chiming with Chris.

"They'll go fucking mad."

ooo

3.45 pm – Our House, Kirk Sandall

Beth, Joss and Marcey are with me in the living room. They're all dressed up and ready to go.

"We've got a problem kids," I say.

"We're not going then," interrupts Joss.

"Told you!" says Marcey, emphatically.

"Not necessarily" I respond. "It's just that the Prime Minister wants to see me in Wakefield, as he travels up to Glasgow. I don't want to go... because I've promised to take you to the pictures. But I want it to be your call... And if you say no then I won't go."

"We can go to the pictures next week" says Beth, incredibly maturely but with a hint of resignation.

"And he is the Prime Minister" says Joss.

"But it's important for you to know that if you want to go to the pictures, we can go – we can go right now" I add.

Silence.

"What do you think Marcey?"

"I think you should go... But you need to tell him..."

"... that we'll definitely be going to see Harry Potter next week!"

So we all have a big family cuddle and I leave for Wakefield.

ooo

5.00 pm – Cedar Court Hotel, Wakefield

Aidan and I arrived early and we're ushered in to a large anti-room – probably capable of holding two to three hundred people. As we enter, we are met by the Labour Leader of Wakefield District Council, Peter Box, and three others.

"What's the form Boxie?" I ask Peter.

"Well he's gonna rally the troops on his way up to Glasgow, if you'll pardon the pun..." replies Peter "... they're anxious about the ant-war demonstrations planned for this weekend."

"Well what do they fucking expect?" I respond. "But I meant with this?" I nod at the room.

"Oh he just wants to thank one or two for their work – and he wants to acknowledge what you've done in Donny" Peter replies.

"Fucking hell" I say looking at Aidan "That was a close call"

"What's that?" Boxie asks.

"Oh we were gonna blow 'im out"

"Whoa – less of the <u>we</u>" says Aidan "<u>You</u> were gonna blow him out"

"Like I said... <u>we</u> nearly blew 'im out... but I convinced Aidan we had to come," I give Aidan a wink.

"Fucking 'ell – you drive me fucking mad" says Aidan.

"I know – but that's why you love me," and I blow him a kiss.

ooo

We are put into a line to receive the Prime Minister and informed he will be with us in a short while.

On the way across to Wakefield, Aidan and I have discussed TB and the tough call he had to make over the war with Iraq. I ask him if he's every met him before?

"No not at all" he replies "That's why I was so keen to come and meet him."

"He'll totally amaze you" I say, playing the "old man"

"Oh I know he will," Aidan cuts across me "But you know I'm a massive TB fan."

"Nah – not for that reason" I respond. "They're working him to death – and he doesn't know what day it is; that's why I was so adamant about spending some time with my kids"

"Don't you remember when we met David Lammy in 2001 at the Labour Mayoral candidates' briefing event at Millbank – when Lammy said that [when you meet TB] he looks like a rabbit that had been blinded by the headlights of a car?"

At that point Nan Sloane enters the room from a small side door.

"Stalin's daughter," says Aidan nodding towards her "Have you got your three key points to deliver?"

"Operation Danum closed; CPA; most improved Local Authority; and Mayoral Accountability" I respond immediately *"But he won't receive them"*

"What do you mean?"

"Exactly what Lammy said" I say. *"You watch..."*

Nan sidles over to us. As always, she is slightly aloof.

"Martin... Aidan" she says. *"I presume you're going to Glasgow?"*

"Certainly are" says Aidan, suddenly coming alive in Nan's presence *"In fact, we're on our way up after this tonight,"* he lies, for no apparent reason.

"Have you got your three key points to deliver?" she asks.

"Operation Danum closed; CPA most improved LA; and Mayoral Accountability" Aidan jumps in.

"Thanks Aidan. I don't know what I'd do without him!" I say to Nan in mock respect.

Nan's pager buzzes; she looks at it, apologises and leaves us again.

Suddenly Tony is in the room; he has entered almost unnoticed, as part of a group with several aides but appears not to know where he is.

One of his aides physically holds his arm and turns him to face the line.

"You know Peter Box of course, Prime Minister, the Leader of Wakefield District Council," says Nan, who has positioned herself as his key consort, attentive to his needs and wishes.

"Yes of course, hello Peter..." and he shakes Boxie's hand...

I have positioned myself and Aidan towards the back and TB starts to work his way along the short line.

I try to listen to what's being said but despite the proximity, the conversation has become muffled; clouded by the number of aides surrounding him.

Finally it's our turn.

"You've met Martin Winter before, Prime Minister" says Nan, controlling TB's discussion pointers.

He looks at me and then glances to each side, confused and tilting his head slightly as if waiting for the next piece of advice.

"Martin's the Labour Leader from Doncaster" adds Nan, helpfully.

"Doncaster eh?" he slurs and rubs his hands together, while he considers what she's said.

"Do you know my mate Ron Rose?" he asked jokingly *"He's from Doncaster – and a good friend of Cherry's father, Anthony"*

Fuck me, I think, Ron would cream his pants if he knew TB had just said this...

"Yes, Prime Minister," I reply *"I know him well; he did a lot to expose the corruption, of course, that we were experiencing in the mid to late 90s..."*

"... This is my Deputy, Aidan Rave," I continue but the Prime Minister

doesn't respond, or acknowledge him.

"*Of course the police have concluded their investigations in Doncaster now*" interjects Nan.

"*Yes*" I say. "*We've put a huge amount of effort into getting the police to draw a line with the past. That's one of the reasons why I called the referendum on the Mayoral model.*"

"*Of course...*" he replies, remembering his brief "*Yes you're the Mayor, in Doncaster aren't you?*"

"*Yes Prime Minister... and the Mayoral model has helped us to turn a corner in Doncaster...*"

"*... and much to your friend Ron Rose's relief, if I may be so bold, Prime Minister*" I add – in my best Sir Humphrey Appleby voice.

The Prime Minister misses my lampoon – Aidan looks terrified – and one of the aides tries to usher him away; but Nan blocks him with her arm.

"*Being directly elected as the Mayor of Doncaster has allowed me to draw a line in the sand... and say that was then... or 'them'... Prime Minister and this is now. And we're going to do things differently*" I add.

"*Yes... the accountability it has given us has certainly been a key driver in the Audit Commission stating we are the most improved local authority in England,*" Aidan contributes.

The aide says he will have to be moving the Prime Minister on – and this time Nan yields.

As he is ushered towards the door he turns to us, almost staggering as he resists the directional encouragement of the aide; almost stumbling as he steps backwards, he struggles to speak...

"*You need to keep up...*" he says in a staccato, almost detached manner. "*... the good work...*" he labours "*... in Doncaster*"

And he smiles a broad proud grin almost as if he has remembered his brief once again.

"*And... you need to stick with the Mayoral model...*" as if we had an alternative.

"*It'll prove to be the right model...*" he concludes. And he's gone.

"*Well done,*" mouths Nan out of the corner of her mouth as she hurries after him.

"*Fucking hell*" says Aidan "*He was pissed. Fuck me, he was fucking smashed.*"

"He wasn't pissed," I say. "He was punch drunk – exactly as I told you he was."

"Fuck me" said Aidan again…

"Fuck me"…

ooo

"Thanks everybody. Now if you'd like to make your way to the Cedar Suite, the Prime Minister will be addressing the meeting shortly," says Boxie.

"Your seats are reserved on the front row"

ooo

6.00 pm – Cedar Court Hotel, Wakefield

We are led into the room and to our seats at the front. It's absolutely packed to the rafters with around 500 people or more.

"Fuck me… I can't believe they allow him to drink."

"And I keep telling you – he wasn't fucking pissed," I say. "He doesn't know what he's doing because they're working him so hard. He was fucking punch drunk. Haven't you ever heard the saying?"

No response.

Never one to shirk from hyperbole, I add: "He's the only thing that's stopping World War Three, at the moment!"

"He's flying around the world virtually every other day calming all the world's leaders down [after 911]; just think of the effects of jet lag alone…"

"Have you never heard of discombobulated? Well that's him! His body clock must be completely fucked." I'm on a roll…

But I'm cut off in my prime; the MC starts up, telling us the Prime Minister will be with us shortly.

The reception is a mixed one. There's the usual excited applause from those who idolise TB. But it isn't his usual reception and it's tempered by a sense of lethargy, with some booing, as the audience grapples with an underlying sense of unease over the impending war with Iraq.

Tony is unbelievably impressive. He reminds the Party membership that it [he] has secured successive landslide election victories after eighteen years in the doldrums; that we have sorted out the economy; improved public services beyond recognition; sorted out the Bank of England, Kosovo, Northern Ireland and more.

In terms of Iraq, he says there is no dispute with the Iraqi people, but one with Saddam Hussein; that it is up to him to show how it is to be resolved: by peace or by conflict. He talks about the failure of the economic blockade, the probability of Weapons of Mass Destruction and the challenge to the weapons inspectors.

He says the 911 attacks, and others, have created a new era of terrorism, where the terrorists don't care about the loss of their own lives as well as those of others. He explains the dilemma that confronts us and the strategy he proposes for addressing it.

He is humble, respectful, charming and funny but without trivialising such a massively important issue. In short, he is masterful.

The audience goes wild and Tony leave to tumultuous applause.

"Fuck me... that was brilliant" Aidan shouts above the deafening applause.

"Fuck me... I can't believe that was the same man who was stumbling around that back room just over an hour ago...

"I can't fuckin' believe it..."

"It was as if someone had just turned on his switch... and away he went."

ooo

8.30 pm

In the bar afterwards, Andy Sawford, the LGA Labour Group's Co-ordinator, approaches us. We know Andy well from his previous work as Rosie Winterton's Political Assistant and he questions us in detail about our views on the Prime Minister's speech.

ooo

Friday February 14th 2003...

2.00 pm – En-route to the Glasgow Spring Conference

Aidan and I are heading up to Glasgow in my car. Aidan is driving. Like a small boy going on holiday, he is incredibly excited; but more so as a result of Tony's speech the night before.

He keeps repeating that he can't believe the change he witnessed in a man, whom he'd thought was drunk, to the one delivering one of the best speeches he'd ever heard.

"He changed – at the flick of a switch" he keeps saying.

All he wants to discuss, for the full five hours, is a history of the world's leaders and the defining speeches they delivered.

After two hours I ask moronically: *"Do we have to keep discussing speeches that I've never heard?"*

"You're a fucking philistine you are"

"It's not a question of being a philistine" I protest, knowing it to be true. *"I'm just fucking bored of it."*

"Yes but unless we look at other great speeches... how will we ever deliver great speeches ourselves?" he asks.

"I like to think intuitively..." I reply. *"Look I know you're right – I'm just fucking bored with it."*

"Well how about playing Five Key Facts then?"

"Oh for fucks sake – the Blaggers Guide to Aidan's life."

"What?"

"You... Who do you think you are – John Cussack?"

No response.

"You're fucking obsessed with being Tony Sellars, you are," I accuse, referring to his predecessor in the Conisbrough & Denaby Ward.

"No I'm not... he just had – no he has got," he corrects himself, *"a very good general knowledge and can discuss salient facts on most subjects."*

"Has he bollocks, you thick bastard" I attack him *"He's just a good blagger..."*

"... and you – had – a – very – poor – general – knowledge" I enunciate to mock him.

"Sorry... that was then, this is now... you have a – very – poor – general – knowledge" I re-iterate.

"... and – you – couldn't – even – recognise – he – was – blagging you" I accuse further.

"Y'see I forget how young you are..."

"What you don't understand is that in the last century..." imitating Arthur Negus *"... the mid nineteen-eighties [I think]... there were a whole series of books, articles and abstracts written.*

"The Blagger Guides... I believe they were called... and these espoused the key facts you needed to know when blagging about every subject," I finish my Arthur Negus impression. *"Well that was Tony Sellars!"*

"Do I bollocks have a poor general knowledge!" he replies, *"... and why do you keep going on about John Cussack?"*

"Ah fuck off – I'm going to sleep"

And I pretend to be asleep.

ooo

5.00 pm – [still] en-route to the Glasgow Spring Conference

Having become bored with pretending to be asleep, Aidan and I are now having a more meaningful discussion about the fantastic regeneration the City of Glasgow has seen- particularly since its European City of Culture status in the mid-1980s and the opening of Sir Norman Foster's Armadillo Conference venue.

"*So where are we staying then?*" I ask Aidan.
"*We're staying in the Conference Hotel. The Crowne Plaza – Four Stars.*"
"*Oh fuck me... I'm not rooming with you again, am I?*"
"*Nah... we've got separate rooms. I've done a deal – and the Labour Party's paying for us... that's why you're doing that workshop on Sunday morning. That way we get our accommodation for free.*"
"*Yeah but you're not running it with me... are you?*"
"*No... er... I...*" Aidan isn't a very good liar. "*I'm running that session with the IDeA on emotional intelligence...*", as if I should know what he's referring to.
"*Ooh... you kept that one quiet... How did you get that gig?*"
"*Oh they just asked me,*" he replies.

I smell a rat. Things don't quite stack up. But I decide to leave it [again].

ooo

7.30 pm – The Crowne Plaza Hotel

Andy Sawford calls me.
"*Hi there Martin... where are you?*"
"*I'm in my room – we've just got here – where are you?*"
"*I'm in the Conference Centre, just finishing setting up the LGA stand for tomorrow...*"
"*Martin, you know John don't you – you've met him?*"
"*John who*"
"*Prescott... JP... you've met him before haven't you?*"
"*Yeah a few times Andy – why?*"
"*He's speaking at the LGA Labour Group Reception at 8.00, are you going?*"
"*Can do Andy – why?*"
"*Oh he likes to talk with people he knows when he enters a room – will you and Aidan greet him for me?*"
"*Yeah... 'course we will Andy, where and what time?*"

7.45 pm

I call Aidan and inform him we've been asked to "greet" JP when he attends the Labour Group Reception.

We congratulate ourselves on how far we've come – that we should now be classed as the first point of call for greeting the Deputy Prime Minister...

ooo

8.15 pm – The LGA Labour Group Reception, Crowne Plaza Hotel

"What time is he supposed to be coming in, Andy?"
"Any time Martin – glass of wine?"
"Cheers"
"So what are we doing?"
"Oh you know the score, Martin. Nobody likes to be kicking their heels with nothing to do... well JP just likes to know that they'll be somebody there who he knows... and who he can have a conversation with when he enters a room."
"If you just stand here, he likes to know there'll be somebody on his left as he comes in."
"That's a bit contrived, isn't it Andy?"
"Well you could say that... but he's a target isn't he [?]... and it's simply about covering all bases and eventualities."
"Well we've got dinner with Jeremy [Beecham] *and Brian Briscoe at 9.00; so we'll have to be gone by then."*

ooo

8.25 pm

In comes JP, accompanied by two security guards and his Office Manager, Joan Hammell.

Andy shakes John's hand *"You know Martin from Doncaster of course, John"*

Yes," replies JP, looking me up and down [whilst shaking my hand]. He sniffs disdainfully and immediately walks passed us.

Andy hurries after him.

Aidan looks me up and down and then looks at his shoes and the sleeves of his jacket.

"Well that went well," he says.

And we both burst out laughing.

ooo

9.00 pm – Orwell's Brasserie, Crowne Plaza Hotel

Aidan and I arrive at the small select dinner, to be welcomed by Kevin Wilson, the Labour Group Leader of Milton Keynes Council [MKC].

Kevin fusses around us, and impresses me with his knowledge of Doncaster, and then Aidan tells me he met Kevin whilst undertaking a CPA at Milton Keynes the previous year.

Less than a dozen people are in attendance and both Jeremy Beecham and Brian Briscoe make a complete beeline for us, insisting we sit next to them.

Although they have to welcome all new leaders of local authorities into the LGA fold, they are incredibly supportive of us, discussing, among other things, our plans for the town, the distance Doncaster has travelled in the past two years, the mayoral system, the CPA process, the Doncaster Labour group and, yet again, a blow-by-blow account of the detail of our takeover.

ooo

The conference is proving to be a huge success; Aidan and I attend every formal and fringe session we can. Everywhere we go people make a fuss of us; it seems everybody wants a piece of our action.

ooo

Saturday February 15th 2003...

8.00 am – The Crowne Plaza Hotel

Today marks the "One Million People March"; a co-ordinated day of anti-war protests across the world and specifically against the imminent invasion of Iraq. I've always assumed the day was so called after the "Million Man March" organised by Louis Farrakhan and the Nation of Islam in 1995 but very little is ever reported of this fact.

I've been on marches before, particularly following Thatcher and Heseltine's pit closure programme of the late eighties and early nineties; and there is to be a march on the conference today in Glasgow.

It's hard to describe [now] the massive outcry of public opposition to the war

[then]. Certainly the great and the good are attempting to have their voices heard; and Harold Pinter makes an extremely rare public speech, describing America as *"a country run by a bunch of criminal lunatics"* and Tony Blair as *"A hired Christian thug"*.

The likes of Tariq Ali, Tony Benn, Jesse Jackson, Bianca Jagger, Ken Livingstone, Mo Mowlam, and Vanessa Redgrave all take part in the UK demonstrations.

The actor Tim Robbins, speaking on the BBC News says the crowds are...

"What democracy looks like" and that if Bush and Blair ignore them... *"they are not rightful leaders of democracies"*.

I question Aidan as to whether we should attend the March...

"Not if you value your political career" he says...

To my chagrin [now], I take an incredibly dispassionate, process-orientated view of the situation. I attempt to see it objectively as a leadership conundrum; a stance more understandable if you consider that my Myers Briggs type is an ENTP.

The "T" in an "ENTP" suggests that when making decisions I'm a "Thinker". In this context, Thinkers use impersonal means of reasoning, such as logic, empirical data and verifiable experience; as opposed to being an "F" or a "Feeler" as they are known. Feelers prefer to use personal reasoning, value judgements and emotions when making decisions.

T types [Thinkers] often find Feelers muddle-headed; F types [Feelers] often find Thinkers cold and inhuman.

I find that frequently, as a leader, I have to make decisions that are borne of pragmatism and the need for greater corporate gain rather than deferring to or defending my values. That doesn't mean I have no values – just that I have to decide if my values are deal breakers or not!

My view therefore is a simple one, from a starting position that no right-minded individual would ever want to go to war. But having elected Tony Blair as our Prime Minister, we have to support him in leading us and in making and taking the difficult decisions.

And there is only one decision to make – do we invade Iraq? No decision is still a decision and we have to consider the consequences of non-intervention; we've seen what happened in Rwanda and Bosnia. TB has access to the intelligence reports and dossiers; he must be allowed to assess the risks and make the value-call himself.

Leaders have to lead – they cannot lead by referendum – quite simply, if we don't support his decision to invade Iraq, then we do not support him as Prime Minister; which opens up a whole new can of worms with regard to unity, discord and loyalty within [and to] the Party. As big a call as it is, it's TB's to make, that's why we elected him.

I ask Aidan what his view is and he fudges his answer, true to his media skills training.

ooo

11.30 am

Aidan has asked me if I'll do some work with him, to prepare for the IDeA fringe event seminar he is speaking at on emotional intelligence.
We adjourn to his room.

ooo

12.30 pm

After we have finished his preparation, we walk to the end of the corridor to take the lift down to the hotel lobby. As we reach the lift we can see the Armadillo building below and literally tens of thousands of people massing for the anti-war march.
Men and women of all ages, children, able bodied and disabled, all creeds and colours; all brought together through a belief in a common goal. I stand for an age, transfixed by the demonstrators and their greater sense of purpose and moral legitimacy… and I begin to cry.
I wipe the tears from my eyes.
"Are you crying?" asks Aidan.
As it's patently obvious, I don't reply straight away: *"Just look at all those people"* I say. *"This is massive Aidan… there's fucking thousands of them."*
"Yeah but there's no need to cry about it," he says awkwardly.
"Sometimes that's all you can do Aidan…"
"You fucking wuss"

Silence.

"That's about it Aidan… I'm – a – fucking – wuss…"

Silence.

"I'm – a – fucking – wuss – as you so eloquently put it…"

"... but I'm not crying about the war... and I'm not crying for those bastards down there..." I nod at the protestors.

"I'm crying for those poor bastards on your emotional intelligence seminar this afternoon."

ooo

Footnote

Although I report that TB was punch drunk at our meeting with him, I had seen this behaviour on previous occasions and heard other people comment as such. Consequently, I do not think his behaviour was in any way unusual; more a result of constantly having to function at an extremely high level and, as a result, having to be fully briefed on the simplest of issues.

ooo

The BBC reported that co-ordinated protest marches were held in upwards of 800 cities around the world estimating that between six and ten million people took part; others estimated as many as thirty million.

The number marching on the Conference in Glasgow was estimated at 25,000. Police said the London demonstration was the UK's biggest ever with at least 750,000 taking part, although organisers put the figure at two million.

In his article, **First, let us stop calling it a "war"** published on 14th February 2003, John Pilger prophetically wrote: "*The power of public opinion, both moral and political power, is far greater than many people realise. That's why Blair fears it and why, through the inept Tessa Jowell, he tried to ban tomorrow's demonstration.*"

"*It is all a charade. The Americans want Iraq because they want to control and reorder the Middle East... There is no issue of "weapons of mass destruction". That is a distraction for us and the media.*"

Favourite car journeys of the world

"It is far better to foresee even without certainty than not to foresee at all"

Henry Poincaré

Saturday February 15th 2003...

11.30 pm – The Crowne Plaza Hotel

The fringe meetings and receptions continue until well after 11.00 pm and Aidan and I try to cover as many as possible. As a result of these events, two specific youth related issues resonate with me:

Firstly, following a workshop on the Middle East; the hypocrisy of the politicians warning our young people off knife crime and violence, whilst simultaneously preparing to bomb communities in several countries.

Secondly, following a workshop on alcohol, anti-social behaviour & violent crime; the same politicians instructing the same young people not to binge drink whilst the vast majority of those politicians are binge drinking all weekend.

Indeed, excessive drinking is positively encouraged with all fringe meetings and receptions offering complimentary wine and nibbles; as a consequence, we are certainly "relaxed".

Having met up with Rosie Winterton, Paul Clark MP [for Gillingham], Andy Sawford, Gill Morris and the staff from Connect Communications [the parliamentary and public affairs company]; we position ourselves for a full evening of networking and socialising.

There is a gradual but never-ending "flow" of people stopping to have a chat, mainly with Rosie, Gill and Paul. Of real note is a particularly select series of individuals dropping by after having completed their "stint" writing JP's now traditional, end of conference closing speech. The likes of Rodney Bickerstaffe, Barbara Roche, Ian McKendry, and finally, at about 1.30 am, John's PPS Phil Hope, who declares: *"That's it... I can't do any more. We're just reinserting pieces that we took out three hours ago now – I'm off to bed."*

We go on networking into the early hours and eventually crash out at about 2.30 am.

ooo

Sunday February 16th 2003...

8.30 am – The Crowne Plaza Hotel

I take my place on a panel considering the accountability of the [elected] Mayoral model of Local Government Act 2000.
LGA 2000 has several key effects:

i] To give powers to local authorities to promote economic, social and environmental well-being within their boundaries.

ii] Requiring LAs to shift from their traditional committee-based system of decision-making to an executive model, possibly with a directly elected mayor and a cabinet.

iii] To create a consequent separation of functions, with backbench councillors fulfilling an overview and scrutiny role.

iv] To introduce a revised ethical framework for LAs, the adoption of codes of conduct for elected members, and standards committees to implement the codes of conduct.

v] The introduction of a national Standards Board and Adjudication Panel to deal with complaints and oversee disciplinary issues

vi] To require each local authority to produce a publicly available constitution.

The introduction of directly elected Mayors was the most radical innovation within LGA2000, with about twenty local referendums taking place, the majority of which decide against the elected Mayor option.

This really is the graveyard spot; nevertheless, I'm impressed by the number of people turning up and, despite the delicate constitution of many delegates, the quality of the discussion is high. Having said that, I'm surprised at how animated people are getting – blaming the mayoral model [and Mayors] for the very introduction of Local Government Act 2000.

ooo

11.30 pm

I attend a Mayor's Forum, with the other three Labour Mayors, Steve Bullock [Lewisham], Jules Pipe [Hackney] and Sir Robin Wales [Newham].

ooo

Sunday February 16th 2003...

1.30 pm

Rosie calls *"Where are you Martin?"*
"We're just getting ready to get a flyer Rosie – why?"
"Are you not staying for John's wrap up?"
"Of course we are" I gamble again. *"Loyal customers me and Ade are... especially after he blanked us last night!"*
"Yes... I think that was a bit of a cock up"
"How?"
"Well... he said you just had tee shirts on and looked a bit suspect... or something."
"Nah... did we bollocks – as a matter of fact, I thought I was looking quite good – I had my good blue suit and a nice navy blue turtle neck on. You saw us afterwards."
"Oh well... he was worried with the way you were dressed... or something" she waffles.
"D'you know, I wear my good suits and shirts all the time... and as soon as I wear something slightly less formal it backfires on me."
"Well I thought you looked nice... but there's probably a lesson there isn't there? Anyway... I'll see you in front of the Costa Coffee stand at half past two."

ooo

4.30 pm

Rosie, Aidan and I leave the Conference Hall after listening to JP's wrap-up. Both Aidan and I are pleased and impressed by the way he speaks to the membership and the humour he puts into his speech.

We particularly like the comedy pledge card he uses. He holds this up to signify the 5 Labour election pledges we are delivering on; then allows it to drop down revealing a further dozen or so pledge cards as he recounts all the other areas this socialist government is delivering on – excellent!

Rosie asked if we are in a rush and invites us to JP's suite, for a post-speech discussion.

We take the lift to JP's floor; specially reserved for those requiring a higher level of security or privacy than the hotel can ordinarily provide. As we exit two of JP's security guards move their bodies to the corridor side of their doors so we can see they are clocking us.

Wearing shirts and shoulder gun holsters, they occupy rooms on either side of JP's suite. As we approach them they acknowledged Rosie, her attendance seemingly signifying our legitimacy.

We enter JP's suite where he is sat on his bed, watching Andrew Neal's choreographed critique of his wrap-up speech. JP's Office Manager Joan is there as is Barbara Roche the MP for Hornsey & Wood Green – Minster of State for the ODPM, and his wife Pauline. A couple of minutes later, John's PPS Phil Hope joins us – issuing a suitably dismissive analysis of a particular nuance of Andrew Rawnsley's commentary.

"Anybody want a drink?" asks JP.

"I'll have a water please John," I say.

"Well get yourself one then," he reacts, with mock annoyance that I should assume he's going to get it.

"I'll do it John" says Joan, fussing around us.

"It's this bit here..." says JP to Barbara Roche, referring to a point they have been discussing earlier.

She doesn't even respond, but just leans back on her chair watching the TV.

[Pregnant Pause]

"You liked the Pledge Card... didn't you?" says Rosie, clearly uncomfortable with Barbara's ignorance – and opening the door for our discussion with John.

"You liked that did you?" asks John in response.

"Absolutely classic" says Aidan, practising his sycophancy.

"It took us all fucking night to get it working properly," interjects Phil. *"I was petrified it wouldn't fall properly,"* he addresses the room.

"I was" adds Joan, nodding to the room.

"Y'mean it might not have worked?" questions John, in mock annoyance.

"We were worried you might compress it together as you fiddled with it, John" adds Phil.

"They love these little gimmicks and jokes," John acknowledges, referring to the audience.

We spend a further 15 minutes, chewing the fat with John and his colleagues, as he winds down from delivering the speech.

"These are all those towels" he says to Rosie, holding a huge pile of soaking wet towels.

And Joan regales us with the story of how John flooded out the bathroom less than an hour before his speech and how she had to mop and bucket the room while watching him on TV.

We leave to return to Doncaster.

6.00 pm – en-route to Doncaster

Aidan and I congratulate ourselves on a successful conference and our "arrival" on the Labour Party scene.

We both agree that it represents a turning point and we are no longer *persona non grata* in the world of local government.

Aidan is driving again. He loves driving, which is useful because I loathe it, and since I have a self-diagnosed "night-time myopia", Aidan has to drive again. Having said that, I am navigating and decide to take the M8 across to Edinburgh and then go south on the A68 through Jedburgh, before taking the A696 through to Newcastle and then back to Doncaster.

I choose this route because it's one of my favourite car journeys. It's certainly one of the most beautiful I know and reminds me of when I was a kid, travelling up to Scotland every Easter with my Dad. We'd spend some real quality time together, bird watching, poaching, egging and generally connecting with nature.

I remember one particular year, when I'd "disappeared" for more than a fortnight, making my way up the West Coast en route to the Summer Isles and Handa [looking for Storm Petrel and Great Skua].

But Aidan doesn't want to discuss the great outdoors, ornithology or zoology! Aidan wants to discuss how much he adores politics; how he thinks he is destined to become a great politician, delivering some of the greatest speeches. It's his assessment that we've arrived and he wants to talk about his chances and opportunities for election as a Labour MP.

So there we are, driving through some of the most beautiful countryside the UK has to offer, through the Scottish lowlands, to the mountains and moorlands of the Northumberland National Park and on to Newcastle.

"Well you know I don't particularly want to be an MP... So why don't we use this journey back to explore some of the models that are open to you," I say to him, in my best coaching mode.

"Why don't you want to go to Westminster?" he asks.

"Well... if you want to know the truth... I can't stand a lot of the members of the party...You know 'em..." I add. *"Every Ward, Branch and Constituency's got 'em. The fucking idiots like Ted and John."*

"And, to be honest, Ted & John aren't that bad. They're just self-serving fucking idiots... and you can legislate for that... you know what drives 'em."

"No it's the fucking idiots that just drive you mad... and we all need them because they put a lot of the slog in that helps you to win the elections..."

"But I've watched Rosie and Kevin... how they have to keep the fucking idiots happy... and warm..."

"... and I don't want to do it."

"It's not that I can't do it" I defend myself "It's just that I don't want to do it"

"Because being mayor is different... look at Livingstone... he couldn't hack it as an MP and he'd only been in charge of the of GLC before [at that time]"

"If you want to deliver... as we need to.... as we're starting to... you've got to rattle cages... and that [invariably] means you've got to piss people off..."

"I know that... and I'm good at that [!] But I don't think you can mix the two"

"And because of my accountability [to the electorate]... well to every fucking one. Every... fucking... one," I enunciate in mock tmesis...

"... I expect every other fucker to be accountable to me – and they don't like that. Look at the palaver over the performance management of cabinet [my fucking cabinet!]"

"And with no disrespect to you Aidan... unless we have a really good Tough-Cop/Soft-Cop routine [which we don't]... well then I'll always come over as the bastard – because it's the way I am"

"So if I went to Parliament, as an MP, well I'd lose my core support fairly quickly..."

"That's why Chris is so fucking good – he's like an Agony Aunt to them all and he keeps 'em warm and tells me when I need to cuddle 'em!"

"To be honest... that's why I've been thinking about the House of Lords. It's an easier gig... its permanent... and I could still do a real job for the Party"

"And... we're the fifteenth biggest urban conurbation in the fucking country... and besides Harold Walker and Lord fucking Kirkham, who's never fucking attended, we don't have anybody in the other place"

"Well I suppose that's clear then" Aidan responds.

"Hey... don't knock it... it leaves the path open for you" I tell him.

"So c'mon let's use this journey back to look at getting you there..."

"Have you thought, first of all, that you need to put your name forward for the Parliamentary Panel" I ask him. But in true style he isn't listening.

"You see I'm absolutely knackered. Especially with Women Only shortlists," he comments. "Basically, I'm the wrong sex and the wrong colour to become a Labour MP."

"Well yes... if you want to look at it that way... but you need to get on the Panel first... You've got to contest your unwinnable."

But he isn't listening.

"You're not listening... are you?"

"Yes... it's just very fucking annoying. I'd be fucking brilliant"

"Where do you want to represent?" I asked him.

"Well Doncaster of course"
"But you'll really struggle if you're that choosy – you've got to contest your unwinnable first, which means spending a lot of time in some godforsaken place where you don't really want to be...?
"And if you look at the MPs in Doncaster..." I continue.
"Kev's relatively young and healthy – despite trying to kill himself smoking...Rosie's young and healthy – mind you she's trying to kill herself smoking as well"
"Caroline's young and healthy – probably the healthiest of the lot of them..."
"... and Jeff's relatively young and healthy. So... basically... you're fucked"
"You won't get the opportunity locally"
"You don't want to go and work an area as your unwinnable..."
"... and, besides that, Maria wouldn't understand, or accept you working away for such a long period of time..."
"You don't want to be parachuted in to an area that you have no connections with do you? So what options have you got left?"
"What d'you mean?"
"Well... as far as I can see... the only real option is that you kill one of them off."
[Pregnant pause]
"Which you haven't got the bottle to do" I add [as if I fucking have!]
"Or one of 'em becomes ill... and dies suddenly..."
"So that's it... that's what will happen"
"What d'you mean?"
"Exactly what I say... One of them will die suddenly"
"Just trust me Aidan... I see things like this... and that's how I see it. One of them will die suddenly – and you need to be ready for that day... Just as others have in the past."

And we drive on into the night, oblivious of the truly prophetic nature of our conversation.

ooo

Loyalty is a two way street

"If you can make someone laugh who's dead set against you, that's the first step to winning them over to your side"

John Waters

Friday February 21st 2003…

It's a reflection day and, as preparation for next week's mayoral conference Aidan, David and I have been doing a stock-take against the "four principles of the Winter mayoralty":

Building the mayoralty – we agree that mayoral governance is now a distinctive feature of Doncaster, arguably giving us an edge over other comparable areas; making the most of that and proving the mayoral system works, should continue to be the primary purpose of our "inner team".

Building the borough and its communities – we agree that our political positioning in several policy areas – Finningley, public health, crime etc. – has led to an emerging mood that I am here for the people of Doncaster and their local communities.

Building the "regional city" – we agree that unlike most other places in the UK we are now carving out a distinctive economic and geo-political niche. Together with the support of our many partners we are creating an exciting new vision for Doncaster. We are destined to be a regional and national player, and the mayoralty will not be perceived as fully successful unless we achieve our destiny.

Building the "good" council – whatever I feel about being the "Mayor of Doncaster", the main instrument of the mayoralty is the council, and how it performs will be a major criterion for judging the success of "The Mayor". Therefore, achieving a "Good" CPA score, or equivalent measure of improvement should remain one of our key themes and purposes.

ooo

We have had many discussions in recent months on the future mayoral agenda and re-clarifying the respective roles of the mayor, deputy mayor, chief executive and other key players. This has been in the context of:
- my frustration that colleagues, officers and other stakeholders have such a poor understanding of the mayoral model

- the slow pace of change and capacity to deliver it
- dissatisfaction with the effectiveness of the mayor/chief exec' partnership – such a key feature of the council's 2002 CPA success

In a paper to me David Marlow writes that I probably have "THE MOST" difficult job as a politician in UK local government today; having to prove, one way or the other, whether a mayoral system has a place in the future, and doing this against a backcloth of:
- This being the first term ever of UK local authority mayoral governance.
- No thought-through government guidance as to what a successful mayoral system looks like – and, therefore, no significant incentives, rules and procedures against which to assess the performance.
- No real enthusiasm for a mayoral system from the established local government community – indeed, more probably, some opposition.
- Being the only mayor outside London from a majority political party, with most other mayors being too maverick and idiosyncratic to seriously test or "prove" a model.
- The mayoral system being super-imposed on a local government system where, most local authorities have very limited autonomy or influence over the major outcomes that concern local people – such as crime and disorder, health, even education...

To deal with the first of those bullet points, the fact that most people don't understand the mayoral model is hardly surprising... THERE IS NO "MODEL" in the accepted sense of the word.

The challenge and responsibility for Doncaster, and especially for the two/three of us, is to develop, clearly articulate, "prove" and thereafter popularise a mayoral model as a coherent way of thinking – to provide a basis for values, behaviour and standards in UK local government in future terms and different mayoralties.

ooo

Monday February 24th 2003...

3.00 pm – Doncaster Racecourse – Mayoral Conference – "Changing and Growing"

This two-day conference marks a key point in embedding mayoral governance in Doncaster.

The main thrust is to bring together a wide range of stakeholders to consider the future of the town and our improvement agenda.

Those attending include all political groups, council officers, and local partners such as health and police. I also make sure there are representatives from regional government and the New Local Government Network [NLGN], which is supporting the "Mayoral Forum".

ooo

7.00 pm – Dinner

Earlier today I was approached by one or two councillors wanting to know if I would, in essence, "sanction" the positioning of several televisions around the room during dinner; they wished to watch "Coronation Street"...

Tonight's episode is a particularly exciting one – and will become the most watched TV programme of the year with just shy of twenty million viewers!

It's the moment Richard Hillman confesses to a stunned Gail. He admits to leaving Duggie for dead, killing Patricia, attempting to kill Audrey and convincing her she was going mad, attempting to kill Emily for her money, killing Maxine and framing Ade.

ooo

Tuesday February 25th 2003...

2.15 pm

Before Rodney Bickerstaffe sums up the conference with his final thoughts, it's time for me to deliver my "State of the Borough" speech.

I tell delegates that, during last night's meal...

"I was thinking about the role of "A Mayor"; about the need to agree a shared vision, build consensus and to take bold and difficult decisions."

"Which led me to reflect on what power a mayor really has..." and I tell them how decisions can often come when you least expect them...

"Such as last night – when I had a deputation from the majority Labour Group... who asked me if I would sanction switching the televisions on... so they could watch Coronation Street..."

There is mild amusement from the room.

"So I thought about it... and I thought yes... this is exactly the type of decision a mayor can, and should be making..." a little more amusement.

"So I said... No!" which earns a big laugh.
As the room settles, I explain myself:
"Having made the decision, I thought to myself..."
"Should I have taken it to Group first?"
"Should I have consulted the opposition?"
"What role did overview & scrutiny have in the decision?"
"And scandalously... I ignored the views of our partner organisations – I didn't even consult them..."
And they were loving it.
"But a mayor also has to be innovative... to be entrepreneurial," I tell them...
... and I hold up a VHS Video I have brought with me for the speech.
"So I recorded it...
"And I'm selling the recordings at £2.99 each... with all proceeds going to the Bluebell Wood Childrens' Hospice..."

And it brings the house down.

ooo

March 2003...

During the previous few months, I have been frustrated by the limited success of certain aspects of our regeneration programme; particularly the fact that the first thing people do when they get a job, can be to leave the community.

I have been ruminating on the challenges of encouraging businesses to "recruit" staff from specific neighbourhoods – streets even – offering direct benefits to deprived communities, and to businesses that work with us, to address issues like employment levels, educational attainment, housing condition, health and crime.

Following these discussions, Rosie invites Aidan and me over to Hull for a Labour party bash. The event, at JP's favourite restaurant, the China Palace [Mr Chu's] is organised by East Hull Constituency Labour Party to celebrate eight members' 50 years in the Labour Party. John and his wife, Pauline, are guests of honour alongside Gordon Brown and his wife, Sarah.

Before the event Rosie takes us to JP's house where the Browns are staying and we have a personal audience with the Chancellor of the Exchequer, to discuss exactly these issues and governmental freedoms for a more accountable mayoral authority.

I am captivated by Gordon's friendliness and compassion and pitch to him a model of greater flexibility with respect to fiscal instruments such as income tax, national insurance, corporation tax, VAT, business rates, even a "greenfield development levy" [given that we have had a moratorium on greenfield housing development for several years!]; and how these might be used to incentivise the private investor to contribute to one or more priority outcomes.

For his side, Gordon is incredibly supportive – telling us much of what we want is already available – and asks me to put together a paper for Chief Economic Advisor, Ed Balls...

After a couple of sessions with David Marlow, we draft a paper which proposes a unique central-local partnership between Doncaster and Central Government in order to accelerate the transformation of Doncaster over the next five years in line with the government's priorities for development and regeneration.

The partnership will build on a number of existing and proposed government policy instruments, – and also trial a small number of new policies in a model of "joined-up" local-government, which may, if successful, be applicable in other areas.

"Central-Local Partnership and the Doncaster Mayoral Model" makes the case for a serious dialogue between central government and Doncaster, based on a "once in a generation" confluence of:
- strong political direction and legitimacy; a Labour Mayor, Labour Council, 4 Labour MPs and a Labour Government;
- a rapidly improving council;
- an enthusiastic buy-in by public sector partners;
- a case for need which already attracts and justifies considerable public investment;
- major development and regeneration opportunities to attract the private sector and have benefits well beyond the borough boundaries.

Topics or issues that could comprise the initial dialogue might include – and I summarise:

A Borough Budget –how the government might look at public finance allocations to Doncaster and pilot a genuine "Borough Budget" presented jointly by the mayor and central government to Doncaster citizens and stakeholders.

A "Super-LPSA", "Delivery Contracts" and "outcome budgeting" – Developing the LPSA [Local Public Service Agreement] format into a "Delivery Contract" between, central government and Doncaster Local Strategic Partnership [LSP] – on which all major public service organisations and Government Office are represented – to deliver a small number of high priority outcomes/improvements.

Joint Commissioning, pooled budgets, and a "Local Invest to Save" prudential regime – to move to the next level of sophistication with joint commissioning, pooled budgets and a multi-annual "prudential" financial regime.

Incentives for the private sector to become further engaged in the development, regeneration and skills agendas – Doncaster's development agenda is very ambitious and progressive [Airport, University, Stadium, Waterfront development, Urban renaissance etc.] but fragile because of the poor perception and low market values of the area. There are immense benefits to engaging new investment but this requires incentives if it is not to erode Doncaster's already relatively weak market position.

We finish the paper by summarising that turnaround in Doncaster over the last two years has been quite remarkable – "exceptional" was the term used by the Audit Commission in the CPA Corporate Assessment. However, the most profound changes are yet to come. Doncaster has the potential to be a major role-player both nationally and regionally.

The elected mayoral model, coupled with rapid improvement, a strong LSP, significant public funding and major opportunities for development and regeneration is too good to miss. This paper suggests that a central-local partnership "pilot", of innovation in public policy and public finance management, is worth exploring.

The hope is that this resonates with colleagues in central government.

We never receive a reply!!

ooo

Tuesday March 11th 2003...

The shit's hit the fan again!

George Holmes has appointed Martyn Vickers as Doncaster Education City's Director of Learning. Martyn retired as head teacher at Danum last term and Martin Williams has started kicking off about the appointment, which, even I have to admit has a certain smell about it…

When George called me to say he was considering making the appointment – after a full recruitment & selection process – I said I didn't think it was the brightest of moves, being an explicitly political appointment to bring on-board a waning secondary heads cohort.

Martin Williams has been quoted as saying: "Doncaster Council is a partner in Doncaster Education City, along with Doncaster College and South Yorkshire Learning and Skills Council.

"I am very concerned about the appointment of Director of Learning at Doncaster Education City.

"To me it all stinks of Labour patronage. Is this a consolation prize for having come second in the Labour mayoral candidate election?"

I have to defend the appointment and respond: *"Someone who was a head teacher of one of Doncaster's secondary schools and chairman of the borough's Secondary Heads Association was always going to be considered when the project was looking to appoint someone to pull together the borough's schools".*

ooo

Wednesday March 12th 2003...

Part of the back story to the 'failed' city status bid last year, is that it actually succeeded in many ways – and that's not mayoral spin. The whole idea of putting forward a 'borough-wide' bid, rather than a Doncaster Council bid, allowed us to say to people "get behind Doncaster and its emerging vision as a new regional city".

In fact the City-status Steering Group decided that the bid process and promotion was so effective they wished to continue meeting in order to promote Doncaster. As part of this they have been developing proposals for a new 'Doncaster Brand Identity' to "Define a new, lively, energetic and enterprising Doncaster".

I have kept out of the process, other than speaking to the Steering Group and offering whatever support and advice I can, which includes keeping newspaper editors on-board.

The group has launched the 'Discover the Spirit' brand and guidance, which has received fantastic support from Doncaster's businesses with more than five hundred of them taking information packs in the first three months.

Despite the brand's unquestionable success, however, and their own involvement in the Steering Group, the press have attempted to hang it out to dry, reporting:

"The controversial £30,000 Discover The Spirit logo is under fire despite it taking off with Doncaster businesses".

Why should I expect anything different?

ooo

Monday March 13th 2003...

We have had overtures from DfES over the funding of a completely new secondary school – a city academy – to the tune of approximately £20 million. The city academy programme aims to completely re-focus a community's educational prospects by creating a new school with a new governing body and a completely new approach to promoting learning and achievement.

I have been advised to consider three sites in and around north-east Doncaster and have decided Thorne is my preferred location – because of its out-dated facilities, abysmal exam results and need for a significant economic investment.

Following meetings with a potential sponsor – a Monaco-based philanthropist keen to provide the £4 million funding which will trigger the government's £20 million investment – we have decided to go live on the "possibility" of the project and submit our 'Outline Expression of Interest'.

ooo

Friday April 4th 2003...

It's official. We have received the result of the Public Inquiry into Finningley Airport and it's YES! To be frank, I have never doubted we will succeed with this significant phase of Doncaster's renaissance.

ooo

Sunday April 13th 2003...

2.15 am – Our House, Kirk Sandall

Nobody likes phone calls in the early hours of the morning; they are either wrong numbers or bad news...

My sister has just called to say she is at Doncaster Royal Infirmary. Her son Luke – my godson – has just been killed in a car crash near our mother's home in Loversall – and only a hundred yards from the scene of my near-fatal crash in July 1988.

Thursday April 17th 2003...

'£30,000 for logo 'was a waste of cash' screams the Doncaster Star in response to promptings from an opposition councillor.

ooo

Thursday April 24th 2003...

6.30 pm – The Earl of Doncaster Hotel

Doncaster Youth Jazz Orchestra [DYJO] and their compatriots from Limonest in France perform
our bi-annual Limonest/Doncaster Exchange Concert, which is also attended by the Mayor of Limonest, Monsieur Maire Max Vincent.

My French is pretty poor despite the fact I'm a massive Francophile, but thanks to Caroline Newton, our French-born Marketing Manager, I deliver a welcome speech… in French.

ooo

Thursday May 8th 2003...

The Regional Assemblies [Preparations] Bill receives Royal Assent.

The Local Government Chronicle reports "Within a year of the publication of the White Paper 'Your Region, Your Choice' which first set out its proposals, the government today made good on its promise to give regions a real say in the way they are governed.

This is the next step towards establishing elected regional assemblies in those regions that want them.

Local government minister Nick Raynsford says: "I am delighted that today we have taken a major step to deliver our promise of devolution to the English regions. With this Bill the government has sought to give power and responsibility back to the people. To make our politics more open, more accountable and more inclusive".

I am not as convinced – the electorate in the north of England are a pretty cynical bunch and I can't see them buying "another tier of government" as it will be portrayed by the media and opponents.

ooo

JP [via Rose] asks me to head up the "Yes Vote" campaign for the regional assembly. It's an excellent opportunity to create a significant regional profile for myself, explaining what regional government would mean to the people of Yorkshire and the Humber so they can make a more informed choice in the referendums due to be held next year.

But it might also confuse the mayoral message – I'm the Mayor of Doncaster, not of Yorkshire – with the media and the electorate already struggling to understand the emerging mayoral model.

Additionally, my intuition is screaming at me not to get involved – with everything pointing to JP getting a massive slap in the face in the referendums.

Despite my personal commitment to devolution, I don't want to associate myself with a losing campaign so I decline JP's [Rosie's] request – but suggest they might want to consider Aidan.

They grab it with both hands!

ooo

Saturday May 10th 2003...

2.30 pm – Roland & Mary Hunter's House, Pocklington

Doncaster Rovers are in the Football Conference Play-Off Final today against Dagenham & Redbridge. The winner will be promoted back into the Football League.

The match is being played at the fantastic new Britannia Stadium in Stoke-on-Trent but I have chosen not to go. I have watched them twice this season and they lost both games! So I've told John Ryan that I don't want to jinx them…

Despite a standing invitation from John, who has become very supportive of "The Mayor" since I pledged to deliver a community stadium, he says he agrees with me!

Aidan, Ian Spowart and Eva Hughes have gone to the match, along with Rosie Winterton, but I choose to visit my father-in-law, Roland Hunter, with Carolyne and our children to watch the game on Sky with him.

I call John Ryan half an hour before kick-off to give him and the team my best wishes.

After a tense 90 minutes the sides are drawing 2-2 and extra time is needed – the only time in UK football that promotion has been decided by the controversial "golden goal".

Francis Tierney scores that golden goal for the Rovers and the pitch is invaded by Doncaster fans.

Six years and one day after being condemned to the Nationwide Conference, Doncaster Rovers' promotion to Division 2 of the Football League is confirmed.

I call John Ryan again to congratulate him and wish the team every future success – and he agrees it's a good thing I didn't go!

ooo

Friday May 23rd 2003...

10.00 am – The Mansion House, Great Kitchen

Cherie Blair is coming to the Mansion House. On one level it's a completely worthless visit with a 'presidential first lady' feel to it. But she's well-respected, loved even, within the Party and we're expecting a good turnout.

Since the event is completely political, I ask Carolyne to the Mansion House early doors to look over the arrangements. She has a lot of experience in event planning and has a very good eye for detail.

Whilst checking over the plans and the layout of the rooms she asks if a presentation bouquet has been ordered. After all, our guest of honour is the Labour Party's 'first lady' – our 'Queen', if you like – and we need to show that Doncaster can do protocol and do it well!

Chris Taylor says he would like to get the flowers sorted himself, as he really admires Cherie...

"Do you know where to get the best flowers and what you want the bouquet to look like?" asks Carolyne helpfully.

"I just thought I'd go up to "Tom Woods [Interflora]" and ask them to do something nice," replies Chris.

"I could help if you want Chris... because I am quite good at that sort of thing ... you know... all the girlie details."

"Yes please, Carolyne – that would be really useful, thanks."

So off they go to the local florists, around the corner.

Chris is both excited and sheepish – for all his awkwardness with all things soft and fuzzy he obviously wants to give this a personal touch from him.

As they walk, Carolyne asks him again what he wants from the bouquet... what he thinks it should look like and what colours he prefers.

Chris says he doesn't really have much of an idea and would appreciate any help she can give him; as they near the shop they decide it's best not to say who the bouquet is for... just in case...

They go in: *"Umm... err... I'd like some flowers please?"* says Chris, accentuating his brummie accent.

"*Are they for a special occasion and have you any idea of the price range?*" asks the florist.

"*Err... yes it is a special occasion and no I don't know how much I want to spend.*" Chris, looks at Carolyne with the eyes of a drowning kitten – 'help me!' they seem to say.

"*It's ok...*" intervenes Carolyne. "*I can help!*"

"*We would like a hand tied bouquet for lunchtime today, please,*" she takes charge of the situation.

"*We want to create something elegant with some sculptural flowers and leaves... and no fillers like carnations and chrysanthemums please...*

"*We want the main colour to be red, so a few red roses... and no blues thank you.*"

Carolyne asks the florist if it's okay for her to pick out a few flowers she thinks would work and begins selecting a handful of structural stems...

"*And we're thinking of the £50 mark if that's possible please?*" she turns to look at Chris, who just gulps hard and widens his eyes.

"*Don't worry Chris...*" she adds "*... that's not too much – and this florist will do us proud.*"

They say they'll return to pick up the bouquet just before noon.

On the way back to the Mansion House, Carolyne reassures Chris we will be giving Cherie a magnificent 'thank you' present – one that shows that we support the Labour party, that we recognise Cherie's role in supporting the PM and, most of all, that the people of Doncaster have flair and panache – something not often associated with this part of Britain!

ooo

12.15 pm

Chris comes back to the Mansion House's Great Kitchen with the flowers – and with the biggest beam on his face. In a very animated manner he tells us how he has already had compliments about the flowers whilst walking down the street and knows this is a magnificent thing to present to Cherie.

We place them in a cold room until the visit.

ooo

5.00 pm

Cherie joins us and the whole event goes wonderfully. Carolyne has collected our children from school so they can meet Cherie, as has Spowie.

Cherie is on top of her game: professional, political, respectful, thankful and fun! And we ask if any of the staff at the Mansion House would like to come down to meet her as well.

She is presented with her bouquet and everyone comments on what a fantastic display it is.

ooo

After waving Cherie off, Chris, Carolyne, Spowie and I tidy up, while the children finish off the last of the cream cakes. Chris sidles up to Carolyne and, clearly emotional, thanks her for all her help saying he's amazed at how simple it was for her to come up with such a stunning present.

"Well it's one thing you should always know about yourself," says Carolyne. *"If you are good at something or have a talent in a specific area, then use it – and make sure you do it to your best ability..."*

"But if you haven't got a clue about something," she continues *"then stay clear and leave it to those who do have that strength..."*

"...And Martin and I are good at building teams and knowing how to play to each other's strengths."

ooo

Wednesday May 28th 2003...

Another of my manifesto commitments is launched today – as part of the 'A healthy and sporting chance' theme.

The "Champion Sports Pass" is a fantastic scheme to allow all our young people, from five to eighteen, half-price admission to the town's Leisure Centres and we have already distributed more than 55,000 of them through the schools.

Such programmes make me proud to be mayor and as you might expect it is fantastically well received...

By everyone, that is, except the staff managing the economics of the system who seem unable or unwilling to grasp the meaning of 'half-priced' reduction or 'a swimming session for under a pound'.

[Manifesto excerpt images omitted]

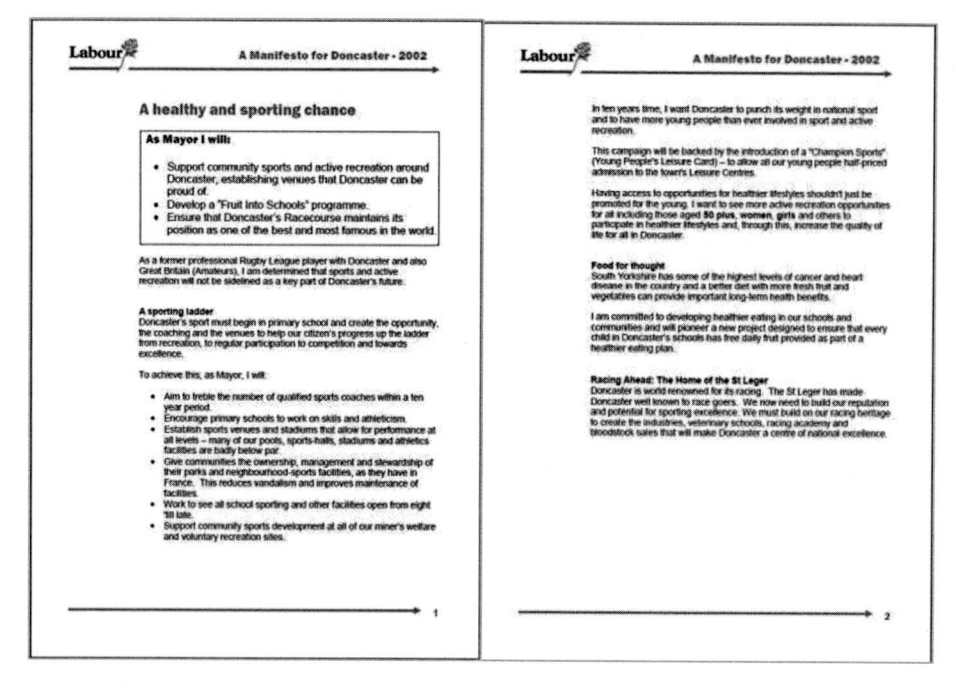

The media seem equally flummoxed – despite hailing "an innovative new sports scheme" they simply report that "The Champion Sports Pass will be unveiled... by the mayor" in a "civic duty" kind of way; not that it's a scheme which the mayor [you elected] has introduced...

Nonetheless I'm heartened by the speed with which we are delivering the changes in Doncaster – running with them as fast as we can, leaving the 'others' straggling behind and unable to catch up and obstruct our improvement agenda; so we may be going too fast for them – we may be [I may be] victims of our own success...

ooo

Wednesday June 4th 2003...

Aidan and I have found our new mayoral offices! We were walking down the High Street on the way back from a meeting when we saw them advertised in an estate agent's window.

It's a large office suite, over two floors, at 55 High Street, Doncaster – immediately opposite the Mansion House – and will accommodate all my inner team and the whole of the council's communications department as well.

After viewing the suite and seeing that the rent is forty times lower than any comparable scheme the Corporate Management Team has proposed, we decide to go ahead.

ooo

Speaking of Communications, I still don't have somebody I feel confident with managing my PR – despite last year appointing a "Mayor's Communication Manager" – or "Spin Doctor" as the press reported it.

My former colleague applied for the post and, following the interviews, David Marlow told me they were minded to offer the job to another applicant. I was mortified. I told David this was not the way I wished to proceed. I was looking to appoint my volunteer Communications Manager; that they were qualified for the role and would fit into the team I wanted to build.

David said that *if that was what I wanted*; and if I was instructing him to do so, then he would see to the appointment.

Sensing a future problem, and knowing the integrity of the person in question, I told David we don't work like that and he must make sure we appoint the person he feels is most capable and best suited to the job.

We did not appoint my preferred candidate.

ooo

Friday June 6th 2003...

9.00 am – Harrogate Conference Centre

Today I am attending the Yorkshire International Business Convention [YIBC] at Harrogate Conference Centre.

Doncaster is fast becoming a real hub of investment and there is significant interest in the borough and the new mayoralty.

The Convention has developed over recent years into one of the leading business events in Europe. Bill Clinton delivered its key-note address in 2001 and it has always attracted world-class speakers and delegates from around the globe.

I am particularly keen to attend this year because Rudolph Giuliani is speaking and I judge it my opportunity to schmooze with the big boys!

Giuliani pitches his speech about leadership to coincide with his newly released book "Leadership" and contextualises many lessons from the management of New York City and its recovery following the September 11 attacks.

As we move into Q&As, I am asked to put a question to him as to what advice he might give me – as the region's only directly elected mayor. Naturally, Giuliani knows nothing of me or Doncaster and offers some pragmatic political advice about accountability, then finishes off with a banal statement about British mayors wearing civic chains.

I turn to Aidan and tell him it's yet another case of someone who doesn't understand the mayoral model!

ooo

7.00 pm – Harewood House

Aidan and I attend a private dinner at Harewood House with Rudolph Giuliani as special guest. Harewood is a Georgian Country House built in the 1760s for Edwin Lascelles, designed by John Carr and Robert Adam and with grounds by Capability Brown. This superb building, with a great deal of Thomas Chippendale furniture, is still in the Lascelles family. Viscount David Lascelles, the Queen's cousin, is the present owner.

With catering provided by Michael Gill – whom I'd met at the Earth Centre some five years previously – the evening promises an excellent dinner with Mayor Giuliani.

As we tuck in to our gazpacho starter, Aidan leans across and complains his soup is cold – and he isn't joking!

Nonetheless, as we moved through the courses, the event is proving a great success. Although we are two tables from Giuliani, John Ashcroft, RDA Board Member and Vice-Chair of South Yorkshire Investment Fund is sat next to us and wants to discuss all things racing as well as Doncaster's improvement agenda and emerging development portfolio.

Giuliani is wonderfully impressive for the second time today and offers me some real nuggets of advice as we smoke a cigar together on the terrace… I laugh that my Villiger Export is more like a cheroot compared to his La Gloria Cubana – made in the Dominican Republic [not Cuba] of course – and he regales those present with his story that in the 'cigar aficionado' magazine's "Top 100 Cigar Smokers of the Twentieth Century" he is ranked at about 50 – below Whoopi Goldberg!

Aidan is phenomenally hyper and spends a lot of time with some developers at our table.

For the second time tonight, his immaturity hits home when he announces he's going to ask my driver, Paul, if he'll drop his "new friends" off in Leeds on our way home where Aidan will be joining them for a night out in the city.

I tell Aidan I think it's a bad idea on the basis that one of them has offered me a "line of fluff" [cocaine] in the toilets earlier in the evening. But Aidan is having none of it and becoming infatuated by his 'new friends'.

ooo

11.30 pm – the Forecourt, Harewood House, Leeds

As Paul picks us up for our journey home Aidan asks him about a lift …True to form Paul says that if he wants a night in Leeds with his friends, he can share a taxi with them.

ooo

Monday June 9th 2003…

8.30 am – Doncaster Train Station, Platform 3

I have been asked to give a presentation to the Local Authority Social Exclusion Network on 'Promoting Social Inclusion – the role of elected representatives' – at their conference at Dublin Castle in the Republic of Ireland.

As I wait at Doncaster station for the train to Birmingham Airport, I hear the announcer say it's due in two minutes... Whilst trying to sort out my Euros I drop them on the floor... and a lady comes over to help.

"Here you go you've missed this one... they're them Euros aren't they?"

"Oh thank you," I say. "Yes they are Euros... I'm on my way to Dublin..." And there's a slight, pregnant pause...

"It is you, isn't it?" she says.

"Well it's certainly me... it all depends who you think 'me' is..."

"Yeah... you're that politician aren't you? Yeah – I saw you on telly last week..."

"Oh, did you?... What was I talking about?"

"Oh I can't remember... but I think you're doing a really good job"

"Well that's very nice of you to say so..." I reply.

Then: "Do you mind me asking for your autograph?"

So... after a momentary [slightly embarrassed] pause, I start to sign on a piece of card she's found in her bag...

"What name is it?" I ask.

"Elsie" she said... very proudly.

So I write... "Best wishes Elsie... thanks for all your support... Mayor Martin Winter."

And Elsie says to me "Do you mind me asking you a question?"

"No... no that's what happens all the time... fire away Elsie!"

"Do you think we'll ever have Euros over here?"

"Well it all depends whether TONY wants to listen to what GORDON tells him... and whether he wants to have a referendum on it or not, doesn't it..." I said...

By this time my train's just pulling in.

"Yes I suppose so..." she says.

"Look... I've got to go... this is my train... nice meeting you and thanks for your support," and I hold out my hand to shake hers.

"Oh that's alright..." she says, shaking my hand as the train stops next to us, "... but can I just say... I think you're better looking in real life..."

"Well thank you very much," I mutter embarrassed... and open the train door...

"But you haven't got anywhere near such a strong Scottish accent as you do on telly, Mr Brown."

ooo

9.00 am

Because I still have no Communications Manager working with me on a regular basis, I draft my own press release to communicate the significance of Rudolph Giuliani wanting to discuss matters with the only elected mayor in Yorkshire...

World's Greatest Mayor praises Doncaster

Rudolph Giuliani, the former Mayor of New York offered words of advice and guidance to Doncaster at the Yorkshire International Business Convention at Harrogate last Friday.

In an exclusive meeting with Mayor Winter, the former New York Mayor discussed how the new mayoral model was working – taking time to personally compliment Mayor Winter and the people of Doncaster for having the confidence to embrace this new experiment in Local Government.

Mr Giuliani who so courageously led the city in the aftermath of the attack on the twin towers on 11th September 2001 said *"Having a directly elected Mayor is the best way of delivering local government..."*

"... Mayor Winter knows, better than anyone here today that there's no hiding place – if he fails to deliver for the people of Doncaster they know where he is – and the electorate don't give you second chances!" He continued.

After the unique meeting of the two, Mayor Winter commented *"I was honoured to have several discussions with Mr Giuliani both during the day and over dinner. I think the two key messages he gave me were issues I've been aware of for some time. The first was his zero tolerance approach to issues that disrupt people's quality of life – and this is precisely why I'm determined to create cleaner streets and safer neighbourhoods during my first term of office. The second is a fundamental that I've always understood – that you should never forget your accountability to the people of Doncaster".*

The press office refuse to send it – claiming it is too specific to the mayor!

ooo

Monday June 16th 2003...

The DPM, John Prescott, announces that Regional Assembly Referendums will be held in the north-east, the north-west and Yorkshire and the Humber. He directs the Boundary Committee to make recommendations about the structure of local government in these regions; stipulating that the reviews cover the existing two-tier areas of Durham, Northumberland, Cheshire, Cumbria, Lancashire and North Yorkshire county councils.

ooo

Saturday June 21st 2003...

The Regional Labour Party holds a Parliamentary Panel Training day in Leeds. Gerry McLister is attending and tells me he had to make a presentation at short notice in the afternoon session. He says Aidan failed to attend and it was reported that he was at a Regional Government Event with Martin – which he wasn't.

ooo

Thursday June 26th 2003...

The Doncaster Star takes great delight in running with the line that I was at Glastonbury festival with my children. I don't know where or how they got the story, but they've done a "mock-up" photograph of my head superimposed on the body of someone sat in the middle of a load of mud, in a rubber ring!

ooo

Monday July 28th 2003...

2.00 pm – Full Council, Mansion House

The members have been rumbled. When they granted themselves their "wage rise" at the Full Council in January, unanimously accepting the report – with member's remuneration "hidden" in the calculation of the Council Base for 2003-04 – they only made a decision for that year.

We are now in a position where they have to formally debate and decide on the Independent Remuneration Panel Report in to Members' Allowances. For whatever reason, they are clearly still worried about this report and bat it into the long grass again:

> "Members noted the report; however it was felt that further consideration was required before fully debating the issues before them. RESOLVED that this item be deferred until 1st September, 2003 to enable Members to digest the proposals fully before debating the issues.

Wednesday July 30th 2003...

10.30 am

Following the Huddersfield University amalgamation fiasco, we have strengthened our existing relationship with Hull University and George has now announced plans for a new University Centre at Doncaster College's High Melton Campus.

There's been a lot of media interest and the BBC's Aeneas Rotsos has asked for a radio interview about our plans. Aeneas has just returned to Doncaster as BBC Radio Sheffield's Doncaster Producer, following a stint in London working for the BBC's Regional Political Unit.

I quite like Aeneas. He's a bright young man who once had the temerity to "correct" Jeremy Paxman on University Challenge! He clearly has designs on a much bigger career than local journalism and is always looking for a controversial story to report:

I give him the usual Doncaster Education City storyline, that industry will not wait for Doncaster residents to "up skill" themselves, recruiting their capable and qualified workforce from wherever they can...

"So will your children be going to Doncaster University, Mayor Winter?" asks Aeneas.

And he's got me... I have been enjoying the conversation so much I've forgotten the golden rule of being interviewed – don't lower your guard!

What I should say is quite simply – well that's for them to decide at the time. But I don't. I want to move the debate on to what "going to university" is for...

"Well, I actually think 'going to university' is more than simply a period of educational study," I say. *"I think it's an opportunity to learn to live away from home, to deal with your finances, utility companies and make new friends and have new experiences... so I will draw a line fifty miles around Doncaster and say you can find a university further than fifty miles away..."*

As I finish the interview, I'm happy with the way it went and tell Aeneas I'm glad to see him back and wish him well for the future.

ooo

1.30 pm

Our Communications Team come down to see me. Apparently Aeneas is in the town centre running live voxpop interviews with people along the lines of "Mayor Winter says Doncaster University is not good enough for his children – what do you say?"

The one I hear has somebody saying: *"Well it just shows you – he's an idiot isn't he."*

Lesson learnt!

ooo

Thursday July 31st 2003...

"Now is the winter of our discontent – Doncaster Mayor is to undergo lessons at acting school" reports the Doncaster Star. In a pretty damaging report it slams Aidan and I for attending a one day "Improving your communications" course with RADA - at a cost of £464.

The only problem is we haven't attended it yet, due to our heavy work commitments!

We have, however, booked on to it at the recommendation of Paul Bettison, the Tory Leader of Bracknell Forest Council, a delightful individual whom I first met on the IDeA Leadership Academy programme in Warwickshire.

The article reports light-heartedly how Doncaster-born graduates of RADA, such as Diana Rigg, Brian Blessed and Keith Barron, have done all right by the "school" and juxtaposes my face [apparently striking at theatrical pose!] alongside contemporaries.

It's another example of the media's determination to fill column inches, whatever the cost, and regardless of the ramifications for my massively increased profile as "Mayor of Doncaster".

A spokesman for RADA says the course was designed for senior councillors but denies it's aimed at simply improving their ability to spin. "We don't teach anything about the message. It's about the way they are coming across" he says.

ooo

Friday August 1st 2003...

Following on from the launch of my White paper on the Doncaster Development Direction [3D], both David and I have been trying to encourage the Regional Development Agency, Yorkshire Forward, to work with us and establish an Urban Regeneration Company [URC] in Doncaster – like they have in Sheffield, Hull and Bradford.

But all to no avail. Despite conceding that Doncaster has one of the most dynamic and exciting regeneration agendas in the country, Yorkshire Forward will not sanction a new URC. After considerable frustration I decide that the new Doncaster Development Company, for all intents and purposes, will operate as a *de facto* URC, with its independent board advising the mayor directly.

Although clearly linked to the council, 3D will be a lean and mean, arms-length company, working closely with the mayor but operating as a private sector business, in order to capitalise on Doncaster's success.

Plans for this new-style partnership have moved forward swiftly and private sector inputs from KPMG and DTZ Pieda have already been identified. The shadow board I have established is chaired by Rob Wilmot, who made his fortune as co-founder of communications giant Freeserve, and includes a wide range of Doncaster, national and international business people from a variety of backgrounds.

ooo

Saturday August 2nd 2003...

Following a 2nd Round Interview at the Labour Party Regional Office in Wakefield, Gerry McLister is placed on the panel of candidates with the Labour Party NEC. Aidan is unsuccessful at interview - but doesn't tell me!

ooo

Monday September 1st 2003...

2.00 pm – Full Council, Mansion House

Back it comes again! The members have to now "fully debate" the independent report into members' remuneration and agree it or otherwise. Of particular note is the subject of performance management, which members are having difficulty grasping.

After a full and frank debate, they unanimously agree twenty three of the report's twenty five recommendations.

Recommendation 2 – the scheme for the "Demonstration of Commitment" be rejected at this stage as being too narrow, although it was noted that elected members would have to come to terms with performance management; and…

Recommendation 4 – consideration of the level of Special Responsibility Allowances for the Elected Mayor and Deputy Mayor be deferred in order to provide an opportunity to reflect on the future management structure of the

Authority and its impact on the Mayor and Deputy Mayor. [In deferring this item, the SRA's for the Mayor and Deputy would continue at the present level];

It would appear elected members can have their cake and eat it!

ooo

Wednesday September 10th 2003...

Bob Kerslake is named in the Guardian's list of the "100 most influential people in the public sector".

ooo

Friday September 12th 2003...

Yet again I am phenomenally disappointed by the quality of newspaper reporting. Today we have a major article in the Times Higher Education Supplement [THES], written by Claire Sanders and one of a series exploring the impact of universities on their local towns/cities.

As part of this THES has also been looking at cities without universities – to examine the implications of not having one – and this is why she came to Doncaster. Having been furnished with our "Doncaster Education City Strategic Plan" she signposted some areas she would like to cover, including:

- Doncaster has a poor staying-on rate for HE. Given that many people now study at a local HE institution as getting a degree is so costly, how crucial is it for Doncaster to have a university or university-link?
- Who are the principal employers in Doncaster and what are their skills needs?
- What would you define as Doncaster's key social and economic problems and how will HE provision help with these problems?
- How important is the role of the directly elected executive mayor in the plans for Doncaster Education City?
- What can Hull University offer Doncaster?

I agreed to the interview because I saw it as a huge opportunity to get our message across about Doncaster's massive regeneration agenda and our poor educational record, which is jeopardising that economic revival.

"Donny set for take-off" begins the article and reports that Doncaster is undergoing a massive economic regeneration, yet the local population doesn't have the skills to take advantage of the new opportunities… all good so far…

"For Martin Walker [sic.], Doncaster's executive mayor, education is key to its survival. *"We have high unemployment but are importing workers,"* he said. "Mr Walker [sic.] has real power…"

"What the fuck is going on here?" I blaze – *did we not have copy approval? Clearly not!"*

Despite having email exchanges with Claire Sanders, being introduced to her as Mayor Winter, and having given her a business card, she still decided my name was "Walker".

ooo

Monday September 22nd 2003…

The Liberal Democrats have adopted "zero waste" as party policy following a debate at their party conference in Brighton today.

It includes targets of 60% recycling by 2010, 75% by 2015 and zero waste by 2020. The UK currently recycles about 13%, and has a government target to reach 25% by 2015.

Norman Baker, the Lib-Dem shadow environment minister, says the zero waste policy shows the party at the "cutting edge" of political thinking in the UK!

ooo

Thursday September 25th 2003…

Doncaster Film Director Graham Oxby releases his new film "Shotgun Dave Rides East".

The 10 minute comedy is about two unlikely friends from Doncaster who attempt to canoe from their home town to the Ukraine, and stars Martin L Evans, Peter Capaldi and Tim Dantay.

It is critically well received and as a result, Chairman of Doncaster Rovers, John Ryan agrees to fund a future feature-length film about a French footballer who comes to live in Doncaster.

ooo

I have negotiated a new mayoral car.

Eighteen months into my role, I am constantly frustrated by some of our senior officer's capabilities. This time they have "struggled" with the instruction "to agree a sponsorship deal that provides a mayoral car at no cost to the people of Doncaster".

I have asked one of the members of my 3D Advisory Board, Paul Dixon, if his company will agree to a three year sponsorship deal – without prejudice to any future interactions his company may have with Doncaster Council.

His company has come back with a three year deal to provide a mid-range Mercedes C220 CDI Elegance Saloon, supplied, maintained and fuelled – at no cost to the council.

But the Doncaster Star reports that the deal has been condemned by opposition councillors with Martin Williams commenting that the mayor is *"cutting himself off from the public, in a veneer of luxury"*.

ooo

The Mayors FLAG scheme is now well and truly embedded into Doncaster's psyche. Eight months since we launched the programme, it's proving a massive success with local people and early focus group sampling shows it has high recognition amongst the public.

Even so it's been a hard slog to convey the "within 24 hours" aspect of the scheme to those higher up the managerial structure. Senior officers just don't believe we need to set or achieve this target!

Nonetheless, the public love it and people are commenting that they don't see abandoned cars anymore.

ooo

George Holmes has been pestering me for some days now to attend a meeting of the British Waterways Board [BWB] in Rotherham at the beginning of October.

He wants us to pitch to them the benefits of supporting the DEC project to achieve dual objectives in terms of the project's Hub being an anchor tenant for the Waterfront scheme to revitalise the canal and riverside in Doncaster town centre.

I've explained to George that I can't be there because of the Labour Party Conference but he's insistent I must, as Chair of the DEC Board and Partnership.

"What about if we fly you back?" he ventures in desperation. But I decline the offer. It seems a little extreme as a solution and I'm not a good flyer [despite previously establishing an aerial photography company] and usually avoid it if I can. I tell George I'm not convinced my attendance is so crucial and anyway it'll cost us a fortune...

It won't cost us anything, he says, because we have the use of a [significant Doncaster employer's] private helicopter. When I question him further, he tells me the college runs a management development programme for them and they have use of the helicopter as part of the company's "business support" for the college; which is then contra'd against the college's operational costs.

I quiz George some more on the finances of the trip. Seeing that I'm coming round and, knowing I'm a fan of this particular entrepreneur, he delivers the killer punch:

"And he's a massive fan of yours as well, Martin," he closes.

I acquiesce and accept the philanthropist's benevolence.

ooo

Friday September 26th 2003...

10.00 am – Full Council, Mansion House Council Chamber

Today is David Marlow's final Full Council meeting. He is leaving to become the chief executive of the East of England Regional Development Agency [EEDA].

Having worked with David for more than two and a half years now, I can honestly say he's the most capable professional I have ever had the pleasure of working with, in any field.

I will be sad to see him go and would welcome him back at any time in the future, which I think is always a good testament of a person's employability.

In his reference I state that David is an exceptional strategic thinker and change management strategist. Equally, he has a real ability to articulate aspirations and turn them into deliverable plans and programmes. His key strengths are rooted in his professional capacity as an economist and, in particular, he is strong in the fields of economic regeneration and investment planning.

Above all, David's strongest personal quality is an uncanny ability to capture the essence of an organisation and an area, and to translate that into a readily understandable concept, including the definition of critical success factors.

David is, without doubt, an exceptional professional leader and his contribution to the Doncaster Council of today is nothing short of remarkable.

But life must go on and, as result of David's departure, today's Full Council must consider a report with regards to the "Appointment of Head of Paid Service and the Senior Management Structure from 1st October 2003".

We appoint Roger Taylor, the former chief executive of Birmingham and Manchester City Councils, on an interim basis.

3.00 pm – Mansion House, Great Kitchen

In an emotional goodbye to David, I present him with some solid silver "Discover the Spirit" cufflinks which I have had specially made.

ooo

Saturday September 27th 2003...

Aidan and I attend the Labour Party Conference at the Bournemouth International Centre [BIC]. We are booked into the Durley Dean Hotel along with several other MPs and colleagues from Connect Communications – the political public affairs company. Stuart Exelby, Rosie's Agent, is also at the conference, as are one or two other members of Rosie's CLP, including Eva Hughes.

ooo

Whilst Aidan and I are away, we are quietly moved into our new High Street offices and the Mansion House front and back committee rooms are returned to their former glory.

ooo

Tuesday September 30th 2003...

6.00 pm – SERA event "Greening the Reds".

I am attending the Socialist Environment and Resources Association [SERA] "Greening the Reds". There's a Q&A session afterwards and I have been desperately trying to find Elliot Morley to get a brief to him – a response from the Labour Party to the Lib-Dem's Zero Waste Policy announcement last week.

Elliot has been an absolute nightmare to find, despite me asking Rosie to get a message to him – and I regard Rosie as one of the best connected MPs in Westminster! Finally, I am signposted to his "box" but nobody seems to know where he is…

Briefing for Elliott Morley – SERA "Greening The Reds" Q&A [Tuesday]

Question re. a Zero Waste Policy for the Labour Party

Dear Elliot,

You are speaking at the SERA event "Greening the Reds" on Tuesday [6 - 7.30pm]. May I suggest that I ask you a question about Zero Waste at this event so that you can respond with a position statement from the Labour Party. This would counter the Lib Dem's "Zero Waste by 2020" policy [60% by 20110, 75% by 2015] which they adopted at their conference this week [paper attached].

I am hoping that you will agree with me that the Labour Party needs to make a quick response to this since recycling has massive popular support and we would not want the Lib Dems to steal a march on us in this respect.

The Lib Dems have proposed what I would argue is the equivalent of an "O" level Policy; if we move quickly, the Labour Party can claim to have already adopted and begun to implement the "degree" level version.

I am particularly interested in this because, <u>as the elected Mayor for Doncaster, I commissioned</u> "Zero Waste UK Trust" to carry out a community consultation to produce <u>a Zero Waste Strategy for implementation in Doncaster starting on April 1st 2004</u>.

<u>I announced a Zero Waste Policy for Doncaster in October 2002 at a major public event</u> and this formed <u>a key tenet of my Mayoral Manifesto</u>.

Additionally, we are hosting the English leg of the Zero Waste International tour at the Earth Centre, Doncaster on November 3rd and 4th as part of our awareness raising campaign with regard to this Zero Waste strategy [publicity attached]. So, as you can see, that the Labour Party can [justifiably] claim to have been actively pursuing a Zero Waste agenda for several years.

Zero Waste is not simply a "waste" policy [as the Lib Dems have announced]. Zero Waste is about the creation of a new sector in the economy, which will bring massive public benefits right across the board – and reaching every person. Zero Waste is a maximising recycling issue - turning all "wastes" into new resources for further use.

Zero Waste International [the campaigning arm of our Zero Waste consultants] will put out a Press Release, if required, saying essentially that recycling is not a party political issue - it has had over 90% popular support in every survey since 1990.

May I suggest that you respond to my question – maybe referring to the fact that the Labour Party's Zero Waste position has higher quality – perhaps using the O level/Degree level analogy.

Martin Winter – Mayor of Doncaster   Tel: 07900 ▓▓▓▓ [if required]

The evening, chaired by the actor Tony Robinson, proves to be a pretty pedestrian affair which doesn't really excite any of the delegates. As they leave I wait to have a word with Elliot and explain I've been trying to get hold of him for a couple of days.

"*Yes...*" he says in his emotionless manner "*I received your brief Martin, thank you,*" leaving a long silence, waiting to be filled.

"*And you never saw a reason to call me?*" I say, trying not to sound too aggressive.

"*Well it's a flawed concept, I didn't think you were serious,*" he proffers, fundamentally questioning both my intelligence and judgement as a politician. "Tosser", I think to myself – but where do I go with this one... when the Minister of State for the Environment doesn't grasp the magnitude of a significant environmental movement? The supercilious shit!

"*In what ways is it flawed?*" I ask him, being careful not to sound annoyed or sneering.

"*Well it's simply impossible to get to those levels – the likes of 75% recycling targets are simply unachievable,*" he says condescendingly, fumbling a badly rehearsed [and poorly understood] civil servant briefing.

"*Well firstly... the targets are aspirational,*" I clarify, trying not to sound too exasperated. "*But secondly... I believe we can realistically get to figures of 80% plus if we fundamentally change waste management from a disposal problem to an employment creation opportunity.*"

I sound pretty lame; am I so easily beaten? The answer is yes, in this case I am that easily beaten. Morley is a lazy, sub-standard apology for a politician who clearly doesn't have a hold of his brief and takes his advisors' words as gospel.

ooo

Wednesday October 1st 2003...

6.30 pm

George Holmes calls to confirm I'm still okay for the BWB meeting tomorrow. He tells me the helicopter is too weather dependant, so the company's jet will be flying me.

ooo

Rosie always spends a lot of time with me at conference. Indeed she usually checks in with me at least once a day and we have developed a very close working relationship with no secrets [on my side].

Tonight is a fairly long evening; Rosie has taken it upon herself to introduce me to as many of her contacts as possible and we are attending a number of newspaper soirées. Delighting in parading her extensive network of contacts, the evening is only spoiled by a fairly well-known northern political journalist making a fuss of me and asking if Rosie is my 'wife'…

One event she is particularly keen for us to pop in for is the ASLEF Dinner in one of the sumptuous ballrooms at the Marriott Hotel, immediately to the rear of BIC.

The left-wing General Secretary of ASLEF, Mick Rix lost his election in July and is presently serving out his commitments before the more right-wing [surprise victor] Shaun Brady formally becomes General Secretary in October. Mick is also staying at the Durley Dean with colleagues including the ASLEF President, Doncaster-born Martin Samways.

I expect to see a packed ballroom but am greeted by the sight of a single large dining table positioned in one of the huge bay windows overlooking Bournemouth Beach and Poole Bay.

I make the long walk to the richly-set, candelabra-adorned table, stunned by the bizarre image of a dozen or so diners eating silently and a certain miserable atmosphere to the proceedings; it's a scene redolent of the Peter Greenaway film 'The Cook, The Thief, His Wife & Her Lover' – "The outgoing General Secretary and his President received their guests".

After some twenty minutes of polite conversation, primarily commiserations and comforts, we bid goodbye and go on to our next engagement.

ooo

11.30 pm

Rosie and I arrive back at the Durley Dean Hotel to a packed bar area and an atmosphere thick with political dialogue.

We join our colleagues who are seated near to Mick Rix, Martin Samways and company. They have been talking to Aidan, Stuart Exelby *et al* for quite some time.

The evening's revelry continues.

ooo

Thursday October 2nd 2003...

0.45 am

At this point the evening takes on a rather more sinister tone with Aidan and Martin Samways involved in a heavy conversation about socialist values and capitalist ideals.

Suddenly there's a disagreement. No punches are thrown – unlike the well-publicised ASLEF barbeque brawl some eight months later – but the air is full of aggression. I remove Aidan from the room. He is clearly upset and emotional at what Martin Samways has said but I can't get any sense from him.

After twenty minutes trying to calm him down, we agree he's better off retiring for the night. I tell him I'll see him in the morning and re-join those in the hotel bar.

As sensitively and carefully as alcohol allows, I ask Martin Samways what happened.

"*Not a great deal really...*" then in magnificent understatement: "*I just told him he didn't have a socialist bone in his body and he didn't like it.*"

"*Well that would piss you off slightly,*" I say.

"*That's not my problem – but it will be yours,*" he tells me. "*He's one to watch that one. And for good reasons – you need to watch your back.*"

"*I hear what you say... but he's only young and still finding himself,*" I defend Aidan, not for the first time.

But not for the last time has someone with real emotional intelligence fired warning shots across my bow.

ooo

6.20 pm

After a taxi ride to Bournemouth Airport, I check in and am immediately taken across the apron to a small private jet, where I am welcomed by the plane's two pilots.

I'm relaxing into one of the eight sumptuous seats, preparing for take-off, when one of the pilots informs me there are drinks and snacks in the cold box.

As we reach a cruising altitude of 22,000 feet, I open the cold box and see a bottle of champagne, ice, but no soft drinks – which seems strange – so I just close it again.

ooo

7.00 pm

Landing at Retford Gamston Airport, I am reminded that this is the airport Jamie flew from some five years previously – shortly before being killed in the mid-air collision. As I disembark, both pilots stand attentively by the steps. Shaking their hands I ask them to convey my thanks to the aircraft's owner. Both of them seem puzzled by my words but bid me a safe journey.

In the car, I tell Paul about the pilots' bewilderment when I asked them to thank the owner and that I may well live to regret tonight's 'act of generosity'.

ooo

10.10 pm

Leaving the meeting I tell Paul I believe it was a bit of a dead loss; there was such huge support from those present that I couldn't really see the need for me to be there.

ooo

October 2003…

Carolyne and I have made the decision to sell my beloved Porsche 356 Cabriolet. There are several contributory factors:
- it's only a small 2+2 and our children are getting too big for 'her' now;
- my godson Luke was killed in a car crash earlier this year – Luke was wearing a seatbelt;
- the car has no seatbelts in it and couldn't easily have them fitted – especially in the rear;
- we only managed 500 miles in her last year;
- despite me having an extremely successful career before I became mayor, and having restored the car myself over several years, I have heard one or two people suggest I received it as a "bung";

ooo

Friday October 10th 2003…

I am devastated to hear the news that Herr Bürgermeister, Klaus Bechtel, has died of a heart attack – ten days after retiring as the mayor of our twin town in

Recklinghausen, Germany.

ooo

Friday October 17th 2003...

7.30 pm

Nadeem Shah has invited Carolyne and I as special guests, to his "Bollywood" themed fancy dress ball, raising funds for the South Yorkshire Community Foundation and South Yorkshire People Against Crime.

As a Conservative, Nadeem has become a huge advocate of my mayoralty, praising my passion and commitment to Doncaster as something above party politics. He has also told me privately that the manner in which I finished the charity walk on crutches in 2002, particularly impressed him and made him feel I deserved his support.

ooo

Sunday October 19th 2003...

Eighteen months after being elected as mayor, briefings are becoming a huge problem. I frequently have to read up to twenty a day and the straw that has just broken this camel's back is a twenty four pager from colleagues within Economic Development.

Essentially they amalgamate several notes and papers they are familiar with but which I have to decipher before I can extract the key issues.

It's making my job much harder and, on the basis we have now entered a post David Marlow era, I decide to deal with the issue once and for all.

I speak to Rosie who as Minister of State for Health agrees to arrange a visit to her offices in London, so that Chris Taylor and another of my officers can see how ministerial briefs function.

I also send Chris an email attaching an exemplar briefing note which is less than one page long and majors on Rudyard Kipling's – 'The Elephant's Child' – who, what, where, why, when and how memory jogger:

> *"I keep six honest serving men:*
> *[they taught me all I know]*
> *Their names are What and Where and When*
> *and How and Why and Who"*

Tuesday October 21st 2003...

"Tolerance plan for town's vice-girls – Mayor proposes way to deal with town's prostitutes" reports the Doncaster Star in an excellent article by Richard Heath. He really does seem to grasp the mayoral model.

I am very keen to work with South Yorkshire Police in developing managed zones for prostitution – to take the trade away from residential areas where it blights the lives of those living there.

This moves prostitutes to a non–residential "Managed Zone" for soliciting, with purpose-built areas within it to accommodate sexual activity.

Developed in Utrecht, it means everything is contained in one area, keeping the women as safe as possible and deterring violence or sexual assault. It enables tighter controls on the prostitutes and the punters and reduces antisocial behaviour, litter and drug paraphernalia in residential areas.

Caroline Flint, as the Home Office Minister, is also keen to see such pilot schemes trialled.

ooo

Wednesday October 29th 2003...

10.00 am – Cabinet, Mansion House, Priory Suite

Today I make the decision on the new 10,000 capacity Community Stadium at Doncaster Lakeside.

The report includes an estimated cost to the council at today's figures and instructs that a further report – outlining the final financial position and covering *inter alia* grant funding, revenue streams and third party contractual agreements – be presented back to Cabinet at a future date.

Importantly, it also demands that an appropriate professional team be appointed, in conjunction with 3D, to deliver the Stadium and that 3D ensure tenderers provide a fixed price for the project.

ooo

Friday October 31st 2003...

Private Eye No. 1092

Under a feature entitled "EDUCASHUN NEWZ" the Eye reports: "The Times Higher Education Supplement ran a long piece in September, talking up the prospects of Doncaster College [Eyes passim ad nauseam] metamorphosing into the University of Doncaster by the year 2010.

"Education was key to the town's regeneration, said Doncaster mayor Martin Winter, who made such a big impression on THES hackette Claire Sanders that she referred to him throughout as "Martin Walker"...

They're completely correct of course, how unimpressive must I have been? But I now have a huge dilemma – I've always been a fan of Private Eye, even though I've been pretty pissed off by the war they seem to have waged on me over the last two years.

If I were Private Eye editor, Ian Hislop, I would have relied on the Eye's deliberate misspelling to come up with a much better jibe or insult... along the lines of: "Mayor Wanker... sorry Walker... sorry Winter..." or "Mayor Wanker [shurely shome mistake Ed.]..."

It's all I can do not to contact Hislop about his poor editorial control!

ooo

Monday November 3rd 2003...

10.00 – The Earth Centre, Denaby Main

Today and tomorrow we host the English leg of the Zero Waste International Tour as part of our awareness-raising campaign for my Zero Waste strategy. Elliot Morley has declined our invitation to attend or speak at the event.

I am particularly pleased to welcome to Doncaster Mr Tachi Kiuchi, the Managing Director of Mitsubishi Electric Corporation and the Chairman of The Future 500.

ooo

Thursday November 6th 2003...

John Prescott mounts a campaign to raise awareness and spark debate about an elected regional assembly for the three northern regions.

He launches a year of debate on the 'Great North Vote' and 'Your Say' campaigns to explain what regional government would mean for people in the North West, North East and Yorkshire & the Humber.

ooo

Saturday November 8th 2003…

Doncaster Rovers' fans begin a campaign for [their] new stadium's capacity to be increased from 10,000 to 20,000!

ooo

Tuesday November 11th 2003…

9.00 am The Mayor's Office, 55 High Street, Doncaster

A letter from a constituent – threatening me with significant harm and describing himself as "Le cinquième cavalier de l'apocalypse".

It's the second or third letter I've received from "The Fifth Horseman" as I call him. They have all been hand-written in French, on very specific coloured paper, and in a very distinctive script. I ask my office to file it with the others.

Wanting to make light of a stressful situation, Chris says he will file them under "French letters!"

ooo

Lord Harold Walker dies. Despite the tragedy of the loss of this fantastic statesman, this leaves Doncaster with no representative in the House of Lords….

ooo

Saturday November 15th 2003…

1.30 pm – My Parent's House, Loversall

BJ's not been very well just lately and once again Carolyne and I have taken our children to my parent's house for the day.

Today is the second rugby league test match, between Great Britain and Australia at the Kingston Communication Stadium in Hull. In the first test match last week, Great Britain forward Adrian Morley was sent off after just seven seconds and GB had to play the entire game with only twelve players – before narrowly losing 22:18.

This time everyone is expecting a British victory; not least my father, Joss and me! Carolyne joins us in front of the fire as we sit down to watch and my mother, Beth and Marcey – who are cooking in the kitchen – pop in intermittently as well.

After an exciting game, which we all enjoy, Great Britain narrowly lose again 23:20. Naturally, we are disappointed and, as a life-long rugby league fan, I look at my father and say: *"I don't think you'll ever see Great Britain win another test series against Australia, Dad."*

"Aye... I think you might be right there, son..." he replies.

ooo

Sunday November 16th 2003...

8.00 am

My mother calls to say BJ passed away last night. I go over to console her and stay with her until she asks me to leave – so she can have some time alone.

ooo

3.00 pm – Doncaster High Street, Clock Corner

I have to switch on the town's Christmas lights.

ooo

Monday November 17th 2003...

4.30 am

I finish drafting the Housing Green paper. We have been having difficulty getting the language, tone and syntax correct and, having lost my father yesterday, I decide to stay up and get it right.

ooo

Saturday November 22nd 2003...

11.00 am – The Earl of Doncaster Hotel

I am invited to attend the Doncaster Rovers Supporters Club meeting. They are a pretty cynical bunch and want me to speak to them about the new community stadium; but they're also cock-a-hoop about winning promotion back into the football league and the good start they've had this season.

While I'm addressing them the supporters are fairly well behaved, but there are one or two slight grumbles, and even now a certain level of scepticism, so I decide to stir them up a bit.

In answering a question about the vexed issue of the [proposed] stadium's capacity, I say 10,000 is more than sufficient for a club that has only just been promoted.

"It's all very well but crowds of nine and ten thousand won't pay the mortgage on a 20,000 seater stadium," I tell them. *"... and it will be built in a way that allows it to be expanded as and when the Rovers get promoted up the leagues. "But I'm doing my best for the Rovers... I mean... I got you promoted back into the league – didn't I?"*

One or two are clearly annoyed *"You can't say that!"* shouts one.

"Of course I can... I just did! I get blamed for things I haven't done, so I'm claiming I contributed to getting them promoted."

But there's still a little unease in the room.

"Don't forget... John Ryan asked me <u>NOT TO GO</u> to the play-off final at Stoke... in case I jinxed 'em," I declare.

"And we won!"

ooo

Tuesday November 25th 2003...

It's BJ's funeral today. I have to admit it's been a pretty difficult week because I've been trying to support my mother and still carry out a full diary as mayor.

We've also had to source a new car for my mother; my dad had a Motability car and they turned up to take it back within twenty four hours of him dying! There's efficiency for you.

Chris Taylor, Paul and Aidan are coming today and I'm really thankful for their support. We're expecting an extremely good attendance and have rigged up some speakers for those who can't get into the church.

I decide I want to have a bit of fun so I deliver a candid eulogy explaining that he died peacefully, having never really recovered from Great Britain's 2nd Test defeat by Australia – he would've appreciated that.

I remind them that he loved my mother dearly and that today is not about sadness but about celebrating a man who had a fantastic life and lived it to the full; who died in his sleep, peacefully, after spending his last day with those he loved most – his family.

To finish we remind people of BJ's love of jazz and play an albeit poor recording of BJ's brother, my Uncle Roy, on saxophone.

ooo

Monday December 8th 2003...

The Audit Commission releases its annual Comprehensive Performance Assessment [CPA] ratings. We have been given a 'fair' CPA rating with a strong narrative.

I am slightly disappointed we haven't been rewarded with a 'good' rating, having been designated one of the fastest improving councils in the country last year.

However, there is much to praise, with the report specifying: "New initiatives introduced by the mayor are having a positive impact, including community safety wardens, the FLAG initiative and Community First neighbourhood management". And we are still on course to achieve a "good" rating within the first mayoral term.

ooo

Thursday December 11th 2003...

I draft a letter to Elliot Morley – with regard to his support for Doncaster's bid to the National Waste Minimisation and Recycling Fund – "Zero Waste and the Doncaster Exemplar".

The letter explains that I have placed DMBC in a unique position – showing a lead to other UK local authorities in delivery on government waste strategy; that under my stewardship, DMBC has improved its domestic waste diversion from 3.5% to 9% in one year, and we can be very sure of extending our recycling capacity well beyond merely achieving the national recycling targets.

If successful, the project will increase our domestic waste diversion to 20% within two years; furthermore, because of the significant political commitment I have given to this area, I am confident we will achieve a combined waste diversion figure in excess of 50% within three years.

ooo

Monday December 15th 2003...

With papers being prepared for next month's Full Council Meeting, the Yorkshire Post reports "Council to reconsider 'fat cat' pay". In a fairly perfunctory article, the paper reports:
"Under the proposals, the chief executive role would be redesignated as managing director with a salary increasing from 103,000 to up to 145,000."
"Coun Martin Williams, leader of the independent Community Group, said: "I think they already receive enough money. This is public money we are talking about and if we are just going to attract people for money, we are going to get the wrong kind of people".
"But the officer who recommended the increases, Roger Taylor, interim chief executive, said in a report prepared for the mayor, that Doncaster needed to keep pace with other authorities to ensure it attracts good quality staff."
Councillor Winter [sic.] said Mr Taylor's report would be widely consulted on before a final decision was taken.
Two years into the mayoral model, the Yorkshire Post shows it simply does not understand that I am not a councillor – it's hard not to think they are conspiring to undermine my role.

ooo

Monday January 12th 2004...

10.00 am – Full Council, Mansion House

Following Roger Taylor's appointment as [interim] chief executive, I have asked him to bring forward a report on embedding lessons from the first two years of mayoral governance and proposing a senior management model reflective of, and responsive to, the primacy of the mayor.
Roger presents his paper to Full Council today: "Managing Doncaster 2004 – Sharpening the Focus on Performance", which details his views and recommendations to the mayor on the top level operations of the council, and suggests steps for improving performance. The report focuses on:
- Clarification and strengthening of the pre-eminent role of the elected Mayor to reflect more accurately, in the definition of the role and the

support framework to discharge it, mayoral accountability to the electorate of Doncaster.
- Clarification of the role of the Head of the Paid Service [chief executive] within the context of mayoral governance prior to making a permanent appointment.
- The organisation of the corporate centre and clarification of the position of the council's Statutory Officers [chief finance (151) and monitoring officers].
- The further development of a performance based organisation exploring the links between performance monitoring, performance management, appraisal, succession-planning, organisational development and remuneration.
- The interface between the Mayor and Deputy Mayor, the Cabinet and the Paid Service.
- The position of Economic and Development Services in the transformation of Doncaster.

Given the positive CPA rating and narrative announced before Christmas, in which it clearly states that the council risks losing its best officers if it doesn't address the issues of senior officer pay, the report is broadly welcomed and unanimously accepted – with it "minuted" that it is acknowledged the council has to move forward.

Following this extremely mature and positive discussion, however, members slip back to their tribal patterns of behaviour when the vexed issue of the mayor and deputy mayor's allowances and the recommendations of the Independent Remuneration Panel are debated again, in the context of the previous "Sharpening the Focus on Performance" debate.

Members are reminded that that the council must have regard to the recommendations of the Independent Remuneration Panel but is not bound by them.

After a fractious discussion, it is moved by Councillor Gerry McLister and seconded by Councillor Ted Kitchen that:

The Special Responsibility Allowance for the mayor and deputy mayor be set at the level recommended in the report of the Independent Remuneration Panel and backdated to 1st May, 2003. Only three Councillors do not vote to accept the report:

Councillor Carol Williams	– voted against
Councillor Martin Williams	– voted against
Councillor David Hughes, JP	– abstained

Thursday January 15th 2004...

MAD Week – Mexborough

I have introduced "MAD Weeks" within our communities. A Making a Difference [MAD] week is a week of multi-partner activity with the community where we establish a minimum standard of cleanliness and community activity with the mayor's office on which the community can depend.

ooo

Wednesday January 21st 2004...

David Miliband gives us the government go-ahead for Thorne Academy.

ooo

February 2004...

Deputy Prime Minister, John Prescott, launches 'The Northern Way' – as a way of countering the North-South Divide.
    A collaboration between the three northern regional development agencies [RDAs] – Northwest Development Agency, One North-east and Yorkshire Forward – the strategy aims to specifically address the £30 billion output disparity between the North of England and the average for England as a whole.

ooo

Thursday February 5th 2004...

Despite having been in our new offices for more than four months, the rent has now come into the public domain through the budget-setting process where members have to consider the ramifications of the budget I am presenting for the following year.
    "Mayor's Office Rent Slammed" reports the Doncaster Star – having sought out the costs of the new offices and then asked for responses from opposition councillors.
    The whole problem of town centre accommodation is becoming severe now and we are planning for a new "Council House" as part of a huge "Civic &

Cultural Quarter" mixed-use development on the old college site to the south-east of the town centre.

Having criticised us for using the Mansion House temporarily and labelling it the "Winter Palace" Martin Williams, god bless him, feels impelled to say something disparaging. But even he is struggling to "slam" the rent, as the newspaper desires.

They "report"; "The move was criticised by independent community group leader Martin Williams as a waste of money. He would prefer to see Mr Winter move to council premises such as Council House. But a council spokesman said there was no room there".

Presumably the cost of finding new accommodation, for the staff we displace at Council House, wouldn't be a waste of money!

Disregarding the political expediency of Martin Williams' comments, I actually think the costs are remarkably low; equating to about £24 per week per member of staff and some eighty times less than the only scheme the CMT proposed!

The council spends millions each year providing office accommodation for its 17,000 plus employees, yet the newspaper is trying to create a row about a £25,000 per year cost for offices which house just twenty plus staff.

I wonder how much the newspaper pays for its accommodation?

ooo

As I say, the issue of town centre accommodation is providing a real challenge to my mayoralty. The existing Council House is an absolutely appalling building. It was designed and built as "Coal House" by the infamous John Poulson in the 1960s, as the South Yorkshire area headquarters of the National Coal Board. It was passed to the council after the Tories decimated the coal industry.

The building is in a terrible state of repair, with its metal framed windows condemned as needing replacing at a cost of several million pounds. Additionally, our town centre master plan identifies a desperate need to develop the south-east area to protect the Waterdale precinct from the pressure of the Frenchgate Interchange development, which will pull visitors to the north-west of the town centre.

As a result I have agreed we will rent my new offices for a maximum three year period by which time we should have freed up space for the mayor in the Council House, pending the construction of the new civic offices in 2010.

ooo

Tuesday February 10th 2004...

Roger Taylor and I attend the SOLACE Dinner in London. After an enjoyable evening, where he delights in demonstrating how incredibly well connected he is in the local government world, I stay overnight in the spare room of his flat in Farringdon.

ooo

Wednesday February 11th 2004...

3.30 pm

I am enraged. I have just endured the most ill-conceived interview of my life. Newsnight are in town, seemingly at the behest of the malcontents, who are on the streets collecting signatures for their petition against the mayor.

The interviewer, Paul Mason, and I have just nearly come to blows! His questions, which appear to have been fed to him by the malcontents, all relate to the Glass Park; a project I have not been involved with for nearly three years.

I initially refuse to give the interview it's such an appalling piece of pre-judged, subjective and biased reporting and not worthy of the BBC's supposed focus on being objective and fair.

Nonetheless, our Communications Manager is desperate for me to comply, terrified of what they may report if I do not...

Having kicked seven bells out of Paul Mason for the previous half an hour, and against my better judgement, I agree to the interview.

ooo

Friday February 13th 2004...

Two years into the first mayoral term and I'm feeling a little jaded.

The programme of general attrition waged by the likes of Cliff Hampson and the Lib-Dems; Ray Nortrop and the malcontents; all manner of waifs and strays, aided and abetted by local media desperate for column inches; and a staff [still] unfamiliar with the mayoral model, is beginning to get to me.

Chris Taylor is much more philosophical and sees it as an indicator that we're winning the war to re-invent Doncaster. He tells me he thinks I am suffering from a bit of a lull in my energy levels; the result of a huge amount of overwork and not having had a day off since last August.

11.30 am – The Mayor's Office, 55 High Street, Doncaster

Part of the reason I'm feeling a little weary is that there has been quite a backlash from some residents to the "Sharpening the Focus on Performance" report which council agreed on January 12th.

One woman has been particularly vociferous during the past month or so, as is her democratic right, but her dissatisfaction has been promptly backed by Nortrop and his cronies and, to a certain extent, by newspapers wanting stories.

Ably supported by many of the usual suspects, Ruth Bacon's anger is quickly translated into the "Doncaster Fair Deal Campaign" – and campaigners are marching on the Mansion House today to show their anger at the report.

Mrs Bacon states: *"I want a peaceful protest march, and a non-political one. I am just angry that when we voted for a mayor we didn't vote for all this."*

She might say this is non-political but when one of the key malcontents – Joan Moffat, wife of Central CLP Labour Party member John Moffat – has inveigled herself in as "Secretary to the Doncaster Fair Deal Campaign" it makes it political.

As does the fact they are collecting signatures on a petition "demanding the mayor's resignation"!

ooo

11.45 am – Mansion House

One of the benefits of our new offices is that they are right next door to the Mansion House, so I pop next door.

I have decided to receive the marchers on the Mansion House steps and invite a deputation in to consider their complaint. To that end I make sure I've asked the Chair of Council [previously the civic mayor] if we can have use of the mayor's parlour and he makes it available for me.

As we get closer to the marchers' arrival at 12.30, the Mansion House becomes a bit like the Marie Celeste; very quiet with nobody about at all.

Not that I can't handle situations like this, but I'm concerned that there are no senior executive officers near to hand. The Interim Chief Executive and Head of Paid service, Roger Taylor, only works three days a week so he is not here today and every member of the CMT [Corporate Management Team] seems to be elsewhere…

ooo

12.15 pm

Suddenly the Executive Director of Education & Culture, Mark Eales, joins me.
"Hi there Mark, how are you?" I greet him.
"I'm fine, Mayor Winter," he responds. "I've come across to make sure you're alright with this march, in case things get out of hand"
"Oh, I'm fine Mark but thanks for your concern. It's always helpful to have a senior officer present, particularly at times of stress!" and I brief him on how I intend to welcome our guests.

ooo

12.20 pm

The marchers arrive outside of the Mansion House and, taking position on the Mansion House steps, ex-councillor Terry Wilde begins to address them with an impassioned political speech about democracy.
Paul, who also functions as a Mansion House attendant when he isn't driving for me, peers through the huge Georgian door's spy hole.
"Ooh... there's a lot of them, Martin," he taunts me in his usual ribald manner; and never one to miss an opportunity to wind me up, he adds. "Shall I let them in?"
He smiles at me. I haven't bitten.
"No... let's listen to what they have to say and then we'll invite a deputation in," I tell him.
To be fair to the marchers, we have already agreed that will be the protocol in our discussions with them before today.

ooo

12.30 pm

The huge brass knocker bangs twice on the door. I open it to a few boos and jeers from the fifty or so marchers – fewer than I expected.
I note that the usual malcontents are nowhere to be seen, although I spot Nortrop's face near the back of the "crowd".
Four of them come in and I welcome them to the Mayor's Parlour, introducing them to Mark Eales and to Paul. I have asked for a pot of tea and I try to be charming but the marchers are having none of it and are quite brusque.
Whilst Paul pours the tea, I ask if they would like to tell me their concerns.

They jump about from "mayor's pay" to "officers' pay" to anti-mayor statements, to parking and the condition of the roads, and I realise what a disorganised bunch they are. Meanwhile Ruth Bacon is trying to keep the focus on delivering a consistent "anti-mayor" message.

After listening to them for five or ten minutes, I ask if I can respond and offer my first overtures about democracy and my delight at welcoming them to the Mansion House...

"But... in terms of what you've just said, " I continue... *"Well if I can just explain a few facts..."* and I start to run through the usual things, the huge amount of investment we are seeing in the borough...

"We don't want to hear facts," one of them shouts, cutting me off.

I laugh: *"Well... I would've thought that's exactly what you should want to hear."*

But despite Mrs Bacon's efforts otherwise, the meeting disintegrates into a meandering rabble. I smile at Mark, as they argue amongst themselves, and quickly lose interest in listening to them. I thank them for attending and bid them a safe journey.

As we close the door after them, there are even fewer people outside – and there isn't even a cheer when they leave.

ooo

1.00 pm

I decide I've heard enough about this being non-political and I go on the attack in an interview with the Doncaster Star.

"People have a right to voice their opinions and I certainly do welcome that. This is what democracy is all about. But what should be remembered is that the pay rise decision was also taken democratically by a council of 63 elected representatives and not by me; and I only remember three councillors not supporting it. Indeed, some of the people who supported it are marching with the 'campaign' today. Equally, council took that decision on the basis that the last District Auditor's report clearly stated that the council was in danger of losing its best officers if it didn't address the issues of senior officer pay. Taking side swipes at me is easy – the easiest thing in the world to do is to criticise. But I have to point out that I am mayor because that's what the people wanted. They voted for a referendum on how this local authority should be run."

"We need to be clear that this campaign is now political and there are a number of people whose only goal is to halt the undoubted progress this borough is making. Progress that has created thousands of jobs, millions of pounds of investment and a host of major projects which other towns and cities are envious of. It is many of these politically motivated people that wanted an elected mayor in the first place, in fact they started a petition in favour of it, and now because the result didn't suit them, they appear to want to get rid of the system.

So what I am saying is let's get this out in the open and engage in the democratic process. Ultimately it is the ballot box that will decide the direction of this town. If some people want to take up valuable time arguing about structures that is fine. But as mayor I remain preoccupied with making sure we continue to increase levels of educational attainment, better services and more jobs through new initiatives like Doncaster international airport and my cleaner streets and safer neighbourhoods' initiative."

The Doncaster Star prints what I have said practically verbatim on page 3 but also "taunts" the electorate with the headline alongside a half-page image of my face:

"Why I'm happy for people to protest at my 50% pay rise"

Thanks for that one!

ooo

Monday February 16th 2004...

We have advertised the new Managing Director's post. I am very pleased with the recruitment pack provided by Veredus Executive Resourcing.

ooo

Wednesday February 25th 2004...

10.00 am – Local Government Centre, Warwick University

I am attending a two-day New Local Government Network and Improvement & Development Agency [NLGN/IDeA] Mayoral Forum event. I enjoy these events from a networking perspective and have also become attached to Judi Billing, the Head of Leadership at the IDeA for whom I have great respect. Judi has become a huge supporter of the Doncaster improvement agenda Aidan and I are promoting.

Nick Raynsford, Minister of State for Local Government, is joining us for dinner tonight.

ooo

10.45 pm – BBC 2 Newsnight

After an enjoyable dinner with Nick Raynsford, I adjourn with my mayoral colleagues to watch Newsnight, who are running the attempted expose [?] on me in tonight's show.

Paxton begins by telling viewers: *"Ten thousand people sign a petition calling for the Mayor of Doncaster to resign – but he's refusing to go. Is this what the government had in mind when it said elected Mayors would reinvigorate local democracy?*

Paul Mason reports..."

This unbelievably poor feature opens with images of Joan Moffat and the malcontents encouraging people to sign "the petition" to get rid of the mayor. The reporter declares: *"...some of these campaigners are veteran thorns in the side of the Doncaster Labour Party and in the past they have had lots to campaign about..."* before going onto explain "Donnygate".

Deciding now to criticise me over the sponsored mayoral car, the feature shows images of a "lookalike" black Mercedes – which the BBC has clearly "hired" for the feature – screeching away from the backstreets of Hexthorpe to background music from the gansta rapper '50 Cent' !

The reporter then asks questions about the Glass Park, its un-cut grass [!] and a local food network project that struggled... firstly because the foot & mouth crisis in 2001 meant it had to re-profile its outcome to deliver a community allotment, and secondly because the project could no longer access the funds committed to it – following my becoming mayor.

Paul Mason then comments: *"Mr Winter's partner who he describes as the first lady of Doncaster..."* despite my actual words being *"What, if anything, the 'mayor's partner' should be known as... She is not a 'Lady Mayoress' as with the civic mayors of the past; she is not the mayor's consort, and <u>she is certainly not the First Lady!</u>"*

The piece finishes by returning to Donnygate, the past and all the court cases... then me, once again, appealing for people to allow Doncaster to move on...

ooo

Friday February 27th 2004...

It is now official. The malcontents have officially launched their insurgency campaign against the mayor, so they have a twelve month run-up to the mayoral elections next year.

I say "officially" because they have handed in a petition demanding the resignation of the mayor to the Chair of Council, Mick Jameson. Handing the petition to him is an interesting tactic in itself. The position of "Civic Mayor" disappeared on May 2nd 2002, when I was chosen as the town's first elected "Executive Mayor". The civic mayor then became "Chair of Council"; and it's become public knowledge that Councillor Jameson and I have had a disagreement because he wanted to be known as "The Mayor" and I would not agree to it.

In fact my role as mayor has become something of a "bête noir" for the councillors, who blame me for the introduction of the whole of Local Government Act 2000 and the new democratic structures which replaced the old committee system.

"Petition calling for mayor to go" reads the headline on page two of the Doncaster Star, and continues: "Campaigner Ruth Bacon said more than 5,000 people had signed during the march on February 13th and they want the mayoral system scrapped. She said she was not sure people realised what they were voting for".

Never mind how insulting such a statement is to all those who voted for the mayoral system and did understand what they were voting for; but to claim 5,000 signatures in a morning is what I really would call political spin!

ooo

Sunday February 29th 2004...

John Hardy's wedding day. As my Cabinet member for Older People, John asked me if I would be his "Best Man" but I declined, citing my current workload and the furore over the new management structure and pay.

The truth is I turned him down because I thought he was trying to use me to avoid making a decision between his two best friends [!] and also because I don't want to be beholden to John if I want to discipline him in the future.

ooo

Tuesday March 2nd 2004...

7.30 am – Mexborough Montagu Hospital

I have a ganglion cyst removed from my left wrist under general anaesthetic – then head home to recover from the op' under a duvet on the settee

ooo

12.30 pm – Our House, Kirk Sandall

Roger Taylor, our Interim Chief Executive, calls and asks me if he and Paul Evans, our Head of Legal Services and Monitoring Officer, can come to see me.

I explain that I am less than four hours out of anaesthetic, but he appears very keen.

"You know I'm not supposed to make any important decisions or sign any important documents for twenty four hours after a general – don't you?" I laugh...

But he isn't amused and his demeanour is so serious I say they had better come as soon as possible.

ooo

1.00 pm

Carolyne brings Roger Taylor and Paul Evans into the living room. I ask them if they don't mind that I don't get up to greet them.

Carolyne asks if she can sit in on the meeting since it's clearly so serious. Roger looks worried but smiles politely. Paul won't make eye contact with me, which is surprising given the high esteem I hold him in and the strong working relationship [I think] we have.

Roger says they have something very serious to tell me; the sim card allocated to my laptop has been used to access "premium rate sex lines" and ran up costs of £2,500 in the three months up to Christmas, and £3,000 so far since Christmas.

I'm completely gobsmacked! I look at Carolyne and she looks horrified. I look at Paul and he still won't look me in the eye.

"Well the first thing I'll say... is this is obviously a 'set-up'... and has nothing to do with me. But you would expect me to say that... wouldn't you? "The second thing is..." and I gesture to the end of the settee *"There's my lap-top there,"* and I reach down, pick it up and hand it to Roger.

"That's what we'd come for..." he ventures. "So thank you for volunteering it."

"But the third thing is..." I cut across him, and I look deep into his eyes *"If you've been monitoring it [me] since before Christmas, why the fuck haven't you done something before now? And why have you let it run up another fucking big bill?"*

For the first time, Paul looks me straight in the eyes and gives me a half-smile because I'm giving them a gentle bollocking.

"You can take it with you now and do whatever tests, or analysis, you need to do..." I tell them. *"But I can tell you categorically,"* I'm having to think quickly... *"that I have never used my lap-top to access anything I shouldn't have... I don't even do that with my own machines! Do I?"* I turn to Carolyne, but she says nothing and looks stunned by the events.

I'm also wracking my brains. What could I have accessed that's led to such ridiculously high costs? Could my children have been using my laptop? [I doubted it very much]. What about Carolyne?

I need to assert my innocence, so I re-state what I've just said. *"Right... I can tell you 100%... that I have never used my laptop to access anything I shouldn't have..."* I pause, look deliberately at both Roger and Paul and then swallow hard as I add, horrified that I should even be thinking such thoughts:

"However, I cannot speak categorically for my children [who are 9, 11 and 14] *or for Carolyne – but I'm pretty sure they won't have been using it either."*

"I've never used your laptop," says Carolyne *"I have my own."*

I go on: *"This is clearly a set-up. You've both seen how the malcontents have been preparing for some time and they've now launched a 'full-on' insurgency campaign – starting with the march on the Mansion House last month."*

And then I spot my out.

"Right," I state. *"I've got it. I stayed at your flat in London last month Roger, when we attended the SOLACE Dinner,"* and he nods in acknowledgement but looks quite confused. He doesn't know where I'm going with this one.

"Well that's my alibi" I say, almost ceremoniously.

"When you analyse my lap-top, look at that evening, when I was with you for a good twenty-four hour period Roger..." I'm like a Raymond Chandler dime detective.

"...and if the sex-line was accessed then, well it can't have been me because I didn't have it with me, did I?"

Paul smiles at me. It would appear I've given them both something to focus on.

We agree they will take my laptop away but that, as Monitoring officer, Paul Evans will make sure it isn't given to simply anybody to analyse for fear of what might be said. I know I haven't done anything wrong and I'm not going to be killed by hearsay!

As they head for the door I call after them: "*Can we also attach a high priority to this one please? I don't really want it hanging around for days…*"

Carolyne hugs me – what with surgery as well, I'm really under the cosh at the moment!

ooo

3.40 pm

I am woken from a snooze by a call from Roger Taylor who tells me there is nothing whatsoever incriminating on my laptop. I am not relieved – just annoyed that such an incident has ever taken place. Roger assures me he has commissioned a full investigation into how the situation has arisen.

ooo

Friday March 5th 2004…

Good news – we have distributed our one millionth piece of fruit this week as part of my "Fruit into Schools" initiative. And the resulting newspaper article – a good three quarters of a page – seems to recognise that the scheme wouldn't have been introduced without the mayor.

ooo

Tuesday March 9th 2004…

2.00 pm – Full Council – Doncaster Council Chamber

A pedestrian, though emotional Full Council. The 1984/85 Miners' Strike began 20 years ago this week and I speak about the devastating effects it had on the local mining communities in Doncaster, before moving a minute's silence in remembrance of the suffering they endured.

Barbara Hoyle asks a question about the Newsnight story – concerned that they criticised Doncaster's "Overview & Scrutiny" function.

In response, I point out that some members seem unable to move on from the "innuendo politics" emanating from past misdemeanours when Doncaster experienced fraud and corruption. I suggest that she might like to walk in my shoes for a while and that I bitterly regret the way the media has tried to attack my partner and our children.

Aidan presents the General Fund Budget for 2004/05, the three-year financial strategy for years 2004/05 to 2006/07, and the capital programme for same three-year period.

ooo

4.00 pm – Mayor's Office, 55 High Street

Roger has briefed me on the matter of the sim card allocated to my laptop. The police are now involved and, having monitored the card's use – it was still being used last Friday[!] – have arrested a man in the Wheatley area, who had it in a phone.

It turns out that this man has been given a formal caution and "claims" he purchased the phone and sim for £50! I am appalled that the police and council appear to be dealing with an important issue of theft/fraud in such a flippant manner; surely we should be seeking to be compensated for the £6K loss to taxpayers and commissioning an internal investigation into how we allocate, monitor and record the distribution of such resources.

I refuse to accept that any of this is pure coincidence and refuse to take my laptop back, preferring to buy my own rather than rely on such poor internal controls. Roger tells me he has asked for a full report on the matter, which again makes me nervous. I stress to him that this is an unbelievably sensitive issue and that any such report needs to be "highly restricted".

ooo

Wednesday March 10th 2004…

I have been referred to the Standards Board for England [SBE] with a complaint *"that [I] have or may have failed to comply with Doncaster Metropolitan Borough Council's Code of Conduct"*.

The complaint is that in sending out a letter [to Labour Party members] on my mayoral headed paper, inviting them to a "Mayoral Policy Forum", I have utilised council resources for political purposes and, through this, breached the council's code of conduct. The SBE has asked me to provide a letter in my defence [?]; from which I quote:

Under the Local Government Act 2000, the Mayoral model is succinctly different to the Leader and Cabinet [or other] models of governance; in that I am an explicitly political elected mayor, elected to deliver a political manifesto for the benefit of all people of Doncaster – regardless of political preference or democratic involvement.

This fact is often difficult for people to understand, in terms of the work I am undertaking to raise peoples' awareness of the Mayor's responsibilities <u>vis a vis</u> policy making and how key decisions are now made in Doncaster. As a result, I have undertaken a whole range of activities, for example:

- **My "Green and White Paper" approach to policy development** – giving the public an opportunity to both contribute to the policy and hold the Mayor and Council to account in ways they have never been able to do before.
- **Visits to Communities** – travelling around the borough talking to people about the issues facing Doncaster, its villages and its towns. Visiting each community forum at least once and also town and parish councils, community groups and Tenants and Residents Associations, so that Doncaster residents can put their concerns to me in person.
- **Mayoral Conferences** – held in January 2003 and looking to take stock of the mayoral model, its impact, strengths and weaknesses and agreeing ways in which all political parties and senior officers can contribute to its further development. <u>Opposition political group's involvement in policy making was highlighted as an outcome from this conference.</u>
- **Mayor's Policy Forums** – opportunities for all sections of the community to give feedback on the Mayor and Doncaster's policies and contribute to developing new ones.

Further to the above, my Manifesto pledged to deliver "A new style of government" – where I explicitly stipulated: *"You voted for a Mayor to have things done differently... to see Doncaster governed differently... I want to encourage as much participation and engagement, as possible, for all of our communities in the running of the council... You will have more say... No community will be ignored... A voice for all...*

If elected Mayor, I will establish a frank and open dialogue with all sections of the Doncaster community"

The allegations, therefore, need to be seen in this context. It is definitely not about promoting me personally, but about the promotion of the Office of Mayor and the related decision making process under the Mayoral form of governance we are pioneering in Doncaster. With this as the background, I will outline the process and approximate cost implications preparing and despatching the letter that the complaint has been against:

3 letters drafted – at home and using my own computer, outlining three options for delivering "Mayor's Policy Forums":

Letter 1 – Labour Party Policy Forums [Copy enclosed]
1 copy printed on "Office of the Mayor" paper and sent to the Labour Group offices. Subsequently photocopied on Labour Office photocopier and distributed through the Labour Party's postage system. Approximate cost to Doncaster Council – £ 0.05

Letter 2 – Opposition Party Policy Forums [Copy enclosed]
3 copies printed on "Office of the Mayor" paper and sent to the Liberal-Democrat, Conservative and Independent Community Group offices. Subsequently distributed through my office's postage system. Approximate cost to Doncaster Council – £ 1.00

Letter 3 – Community Forum Policy Forums [Copy enclosed]
7 copies printed on "Office of the Mayor" paper and sent to the Community Forums. Subsequently distributed through my office's postage system. Approximate cost to Doncaster Council – £ 2.33

I am quite mystified by this referral to the SBE. The complainant is someone whose name I do not recognise and I can only assume this individual has made the referral to hide the identity of the true complainant...

Consequent to this, the referral can only have come from a Labour Party member! It would appear everything in the garden isn't rosy and I ask Chris Taylor to do some fishing, to see if we can find out who or where the disquiet is coming from?

ooo

Thursday March 11th 2004...

Roger has given me a copy of the "highly restricted" report into the "sim-card incident", which Chris Taylor is calling "sim-cardgate". Thanks Chris!

I am astounded at what has been written. I explain to Roger that, having read the report, even I think I'm guilty [!] such is its construction. How on earth can such a report have been drafted when all those involved in the process, including the police and crucially Paul Evans, the Head of Legal Services and Monitoring Officer, know the mayor's involvement is completely coincidental? My paranoia is running wild...

Roger agrees and says that he will have it re-drafted. I give him back my copy and ask him to confirm its restricted circulation – which he does. There are five individuals involved and all have been made aware of its sensitivity and restricted status.

This whole affair is fast becoming a farce...

ooo

Wednesday March 17th 2004...

10.00 am – Executive Board, Mansion House Priory Suite

Cabinet meets every other Wednesday – and on the interim Wednesday, Executive Board meets to consider all matters.

ooo

11.30 am – Mayor's Office, 55 High Street

Exec' Board has finished and I am back in my office going through various issues. Having been at Exec' Board, Chris Taylor always waits to make sure nobody has left anything before leaving the room...

He comes into my office to show me a black diary that one of the Corporate Management Team has left behind. It's clear whose diary it is and in the back is a copy of the restricted "sim-card incident" report.

ooo

1.30 pm

Chris tells me that the officer in question has asked if anybody has handed in his diary. We say no. But by 4.30pm, he's been asked the question again...

ooo

Thursday March 18th 2004...

Mayor's Office, 55 High Street

Chris says the office has been asked twice today if anybody has handed in a diary.

ooo

Friday March 19th 2004...

4.30 pm – Mayor's Office, 55 High Street

Chris tells me that this particular officer is at their wit's end over the "lost diary"; and wonders if we should admit we've found it. I say we'll let them worry over the weekend and hand it to Roger Taylor after that.

ooo

Thursday March 25th 2004...

12.30 pm – Mayor's Office, 55 High Street

I sit down with Roger and show him the report we found. He is naturally apoplectic and agrees that it might be classed as gross negligence on the officer's behalf.

ooo

Thursday April 1st 2004...

3.00 pm – The Mayor's Office, 55 High Street, Doncaster

Rosie contacts my office to ask if Aidan and I would like to have dinner with her and John Prescott. We are certainly not going to pass up the opportunity to have some quality time with the Deputy Prime Minister and agree to go over to Hull this evening.

ooo

On the way I ask Aidan how his wife Maria is. She recently collapsed and has been having medical tests to ascertain the nature of the illness/episode. Aidan says she has had tests but nothing is clear at the moment.

ooo

8.00 pm – China Palace [Mr Chu's], St Andrew's Quay, Hull

Rosie, Aidan and I join John Prescott, his wife Pauline, his Chief of Staff, Joan Hammell, and his Office Manager, Della Georgiason at "Mr Chu's".

During a very enjoyable evening we get to brief John on all things Doncaster and he asks for our opinions on a wide variety of regional and national government policy; Aidan and I both see the invite as a massive sign that we have "arrived".

ooo

Tuesday April 6th 2004...

After several days of interviews and meeting candidates, we appoint Susan Law as our new MD. She is presently the World Bank's "strategic management advisor" to the Mayor of Cape Town, South Africa, and the former Chief Executive of the City of Adelaide, Australia.
    I am keen to hear how she has been involved in rolling out a neighbourhood management model in the South African townships. Having said that, I don't think she's the most impressive candidate at interview compared to another with a very good pedigree. She does, however, have an air of quiet confidence about her.
    It's a comment from Hamish Davidson, the Chairman of Veredus, that seals the deal, if you like, for me. In summing up the applicants he states: *"... the logical appointment is [a candidate]... and that would be an excellent appointment for you... but the potentially inspirational appointment could be.... Susan Law"*
    He plays to my propensity for taking risks... Sometimes, you have to take a chance. If you want to be a great leader, you have to be prepared to make the decisions that will make you a great leader... You have to be prepared to make a risky decision... to weigh up the pros and the cons and take a chance...
    I live by the maxim that 'If you want to win... you have to be prepared to lose...' and surely we certainly wouldn't lose – we had both Hamish Davidson and Roger Taylor advising us on this appointment...

What could go wrong?

ooo

Wednesday April 7th 2004...

11.00 am

I draft letters to all the candidates and tell Aidan to make sure we source Susan's references. One of our policy advisors, a very bright young man called Chris Stephenson asks me about her appointment.
    "I'm really pleased," I tell him, explaining why I think it's a strong appointment, in terms of her world player pedigree, experience working with high-profile mayors, reluctance to conform to stereotypes etc.
    "It's quite frightening – she can be more like me than I am," I say, then prophetically: *"So it'll either end in glory – or disaster all around!"*

ooo

I also draft a letter to Ruth Bacon of the "Doncaster Fair Deal Campaign" drawing her attention to the following points: *"During 2003 the Chief Executive and 2 Executive Directors left the Council. In our annual letter from the Audit Commission, they stated that:*
    Substantive appointments are expected to be made after a review of the structure and pay levels for senior executives. It is crucial that Doncaster acts decisively to ensure that its momentum is not jeopardised by a failure to attract and retain senior officers.
    In December 2002 the Audit Commission recognised Doncaster as being one of the fastest improving authorities in the Country. As part of the Commission's Comprehensive Performance Assessment [CPA] of the Council, it stated that:
    "The council has shown a high degree of self-awareness in recognising the problems of the past. The rate of improvement, particularly in the last year has been exceptional. The transformation has been ably led by an effective partnership between the newly elected Mayor of Doncaster and the Chief Executive. They are now supported by rapidly growing capacity among senior politicians, a good executive team of officers, and, increasingly throughout the organisation.
    In December 2003, as part of the second CPA, the Commission stated that the council has continued to improve and that "new initiatives introduced by the Mayor are having a positive impact, including community safety wardens, the 'Fighting Litter, Abandoned cars and Graffiti' initiative, and Community First neighbourhood management...
    In terms of other ways the public are benefiting from the mayoral model, I will simply refer you to the following:

- FLAG scheme [Fighting Litter Abandoned cars and Graffiti] and 6 new Community Litter wardens
- "Community First" approach to delivering neighbourhood services
- 50 Community Safety Wardens
- 45,000 households receiving kerbside recycling collections, to be extended to over 100,000 by the end of my first term
- 1 million pieces of Fruit Into [Doncaster] Schools
- 8 Skateparks
- Champion Sports Cards available to every young person under 19 - leading to a 20% increase in young people using our leisure centres
- Decentralised services of the council [into our communities] through "One-stop" and "First Stop Shops"
- Every community in Doncaster having its own "Community Action Plan" by the end of 2004 - with 70% prepared already
- New sports halls in Intake, Conisbrough, Rossington & Askern
- "Job Shops" in Stainforth and Edlington

All of which are direct mayoral pledges that have benefited the borough's residents in my first two years.

In addition to these, we are witnessing a massive economic regeneration programme in Doncaster – with exciting projects underway or ready to begin, such as Doncaster International Airport; a "top twenty" retail complex and transport interchange; Doncaster Education City [£80 million of investment into a new town centre learning hub and Area Based Campuses in our communities]; a new Community Stadium and a New Performance Venue.

Many of these are coming to fruition after several years work and specifically because of the confidence investors say they now have in Doncaster after years of decline – citing a visible, high profile mayor as the single point of contact they can now deal with...

Obviously I am experiencing several negative comments at the moment, however, I am even more determined to stay focused on the journey we have begun – I believe it is the right one for Doncaster and, ultimately, the people will decide whether Doncaster is a better place because of my mayoralty or not.

As such, I have no intention of resigning my position.

ooo

Monday April 12th 2004...

Doncaster Rovers are promoted into the in the Second Division of the Football League, with a two nil home victory against Cambridge United – the first time in the club's history they have gained promotion in consecutive seasons.

ooo

Tuesday April 13th 2004...

The new name for Finningley Airport is announced as Robin Hood Airport – Doncaster-Sheffield – by the airport's owners "Peel Airports". The name sparks a media furore over what it might have been called or should have been called, as well as a side argument about who actually owns the airport and, therefore, has the right to name it.

Having been involved in earlier discussions – including one where *another name* was proposed in a way which compromised me terribly – I explain to Peel's senior management that I will have to voice my opinion but will try to be as diplomatic as possible.

The Doncaster [Sheffield!] Star reported: "But Mayor of Doncaster Martin Winter said "I am, bitterly disappointed that the name of the airport does not focus primarily on Doncaster. The majority of people in the borough supported the re-opening of Finningley as an international airport and will be very dismayed to see that Sheffield is being used in the name.

But he added he understood the crucial role the name of an airport had in ensuring it became a commercial success and understood Peel's choice of name."

Interestingly, this is exactly where the people of Doncaster "get" the mayoral model, or indeed, their expectations of it, and fully expect me to be able to over-rule the company's choice of names.

ooo

April 15th 2004...

"Fury over council decision to appoint overseas MD" reports the Yorkshire Post. But the elected mayor of Doncaster, Martin Winter, praised the appointment:

"Doncaster is the emerging city of Yorkshire and the Humber and our ability to attract top class executives such as Ms Law is testament to how far we have come in the past two years," he said.

A spokesman for the Society of Local Government Chief Executives said the association welcomed Ms Law. He added: *"It is ironic that when councils appoint the most senior officer from within their own ranks they get criticised and when they look abroad they still get criticised".*

ooo

Saturday May 1st 2004...

I have never made any secret of the fact that I don't aspire to be a Member of Parliament and only see myself being the Mayor of Doncaster for a maximum of two terms. I have spoken in some detail with Rosie about Doncaster having no representatives in the House of Lords and the natural progression, if you like, of a successful Labour mayor finishing his two terms and then moving into "the other place". To this end, I have presented her with a paper which I have entitled "Local Authority Leaders as Working Peers"; in which I have espoused the benefits of my becoming a working Labour Peer, whilst functioning as the Mayor of Doncaster:

Firstly, the appointment would confirm Doncaster's recovery and enable it to be presented as a place of some stature.

Secondly it would provide a worthy affirmation of the Government's increasing support for, and interest in, the sharper accountability of a mayoral system.

Lastly, it would enable legislators to benefit from my experience at a time when there are many new and developing interactions between central and local government eg:
- development of regional government.
- issues around security and immigration.
- the de-centralisation of government offices.
- improvement in local government performance, and
- the critical challenge of making all local public service provision more joined up, coherent and cost effective.

ooo

Monday May 10th 2004...

"Mayor in plan row rumpus" screams the front page of the Star; reporting that "The Mayor of Doncaster was today dragged into a planning row after being accused of "meddling" by a mum." This is absolute madness. I know this family from their son having worked with the Glass Park project as a young boy. They asked my opinion about a planning application that had been granted for an extension being built next door to them.

I explained I was not allowed to get involved with the planning process but that they had three options open to them: they either accept the decision and get on with their lives, object to the decision, or move house.

I told them that, on a quality of life issue, it was my opinion that they should either accept the decision or move house. The rationale being that they could, very likely, get involved with something that might take years to resolve, cost them a lot of money and ruin their lives.

ooo

Tuesday May 11th 2004...

Work on the new Community Stadium gets underway

ooo

Tuesday May 20th 2004...

7.30 pm – Mansion House, Drawing Room

Paul Bettison and I have become quite good friends. I first met Paul in 2001 after we did the IDeA Leadership Academy programme together. Paul was an extremely knowledgeable and admired member of the programme and became very well respected by the many other leaders in our cohort.

After we graduated the Leadership programme, he becomes my trusted advisor [mentor even] in mapping out a vision and future for Doncaster and I always find him supportive whatever the subject or occasion.

As my earliest political mentor, Pat Mullany, taught me to think that all politics is tribal and you should always hate the Tories; I am surprised, that a Conservative Leader should show such willingness to advise and support me but Paul is always capable of seeing the big picture – over and above the barrier that can be party politics.

Paul has rung me to ask for my support for a colleague of his, Annette Howard, who is riding a horse the six hundred mile trek from Edinburgh to London, to raise money for MacMillan Cancer Relief. We have assisted as much as we can and have invited Annette, Paul and Paul's charming wife Jean, to join us tonight at the Mansion House.

ooo

Tuesday June 1st 2004...

A Minster for Doncaster – St George's Church, which stands in the heart of the town and was designed by Sir George Gilbert Scott, is re-designated as the Minster Church of St George, Doncaster.

ooo

Wednesday June 2nd 2004...

11.30 am – The Mayor's Office, 55 High Street, Doncaster

Chris comes in to see me worried about some item of minutiae, as usual. Having said that, Chris doesn't miss a thing and his antennae often tip us off about emerging issues...

This morning, amongst other things, he's concerned about a rumour that is seemingly being pushed around by Ted Kitchen, the Labour Group's well-known rabble-rouser. *"Somebody over in the Mansion House has supposedly said that they can see into your office, from a window opposite; and that they've seen the mayor having sex with his PA over his office desk,"* he tells me.

"Well I'm not particularly bothered about that Chris... it certainly beats some of the more mundane rumours people are peddling!"

"Well I am," he comes back quick fire and very droll *"... being as I am your PA!"* He underlines his role as my *political advisor*... and we both laugh.

"How do you know this?" I ask him, and he tells me that Ted was seen shouting it from his car at my PA as she left my office the previous night.

Chris says she was a little surprised that he should be bawling such accusations in the street; but that others in the office had said that nobody takes Councillor Kitchen seriously.

"I also explained," Chris added *"That the window opposite your office is actually bricked up because of the 18th century window tax – one of the first examples of 'daylight robbery'. So nobody can see into the mayor's office from the Mansion House."*

We both chuckle that it's one of the funnier urban myths circulating with regard to the mayor; but agree that we'll have to keep an eye on Ted and his propensity for swimming against the tide.

ooo

Wednesday June 9th 2004...

I have been reported to the Standards Board for England [SBE] for the second time in three months – for "interfering" with a planning decision. This is absolutely preposterous. One of my constituents had asked me what their options were on a planning decision that had been already been made!

However, the complaint does highlight the malcontents, nay generic opposition's, strategy twelve months before the next mayoral election: to keep referring matters to the SBE on the basis that one will eventually be upheld. To this effect, the "word on the street" is that I am being investigated on two separate counts by the Standards Board for England.

ooo

Thursday June 10th 2004...

For the first time, all 63 councillors are up for election this year. Local elections have been delayed one month to coincide with European parliamentary elections and an "all-postal ballot" pilot. The night that sees Gerry McLister stand down as a councillor, proves disastrous for Labour with the number of Party seats on Doncaster Council plummeting from 45 to 27.

Aidan has also had a pretty torrid time. With the person getting the highest poll receiving a four-year term of office, the second highest a three-year-term and the lowest a two-year term, Aidan has polled poorly and gets the minimum two-year term.

ooo

Tuesday June 22nd 2004...

You win some… you lose some…

"Mayor Winter cleared in planning probe" shouts page 2 of the Doncaster Star; and reports that [Standards Board for England] "Investigators have rejected allegations that Mayor of Doncaster Martin Winter broke planning rules."

The result does not surprise me and I am quoted: *"It is ridiculous to suggest that an elected mayor is not able to advise a constituent about their options, especially when it related to a planning decision taken six months previously."*

What does surprise me, however, is that I'm found guilty on another issue. The investigation into the complaint *"that* [I] *have or may have failed to comply with Doncaster Metropolitan Borough Council's Code of Conduct"* has found in favour of the complainant. The SBE has decided that, in sending out a letter on my mayoral-headed paper – inviting Labour Party members to a "Mayoral Policy Forum" – I utilised council resources for political purposes and through this breached the council's code of conduct, at a cost of £0.05p to the taxpayer! Although in mitigation the SBE added that there were no policies or codes of conduct in place relating to such a communication process from a directly elected mayor.

ooo

7.00 pm – The Lounge Restaurant, Bradford Row

Aidan and I are having dinner together at the Lounge – a really nice new bistro restaurant with a very good menu. We need to talk about him coming third in the election earlier this month but also to discuss the type of deputy mayor I want him to be.

As we begin our second course, it's clear Aidan is very stressed about the election result and we agree he will have to put the hours into his ward responsibilities over the coming two years. Notwithstanding that, I explain that I am not happy with the level of support he is giving me. That he appears to be more involved in things that further his own career or pay additional allowances.

"*I can't support you the way you want me to support you Martin...*" he sighs, and begins to tell me how much stress he is under at home.

I know Aidan too well, he's a chronic dissembler and I can see him bluffing a mile off.

"*Don't give me that crap, we're all under stress,*" I tell him – forcefully but quietly, conscious of other diners – and I remind him of the "deal" we did to support each other and my on-going loyalty to him.

But shockingly, he suddenly begins to cry. "*You don't know how much stress I'm under at home...*" he insists again. And then he tells me "the lie". It's not just any lie, a "little lie"; or a little "white lie"; but a monstrous lie... It is an outrageous lie with massive implications for our relationship...

"*I can't support you the way you want me to support you Martin...*" he sobs "*Because Maria's dying...*"

It would be laughable – if it wasn't so tragic.

"*Oh! ... What's wrong with her?*"

And he starts to ramble about an "illness" she has which is terminal... but he's so vague and uncertain, it's outlandish to think I might even consider believing it.

"For fuck's sake Aidan," I say. "I cannot believe you are stooping so low. Do you think I'm that fucking stupid? Do you really expect me to believe such a story?"

But I don't want to create a scene. So quietly, through gritted teeth, I tell him:

"Carolyne has been supporting Maria, Aidan..." and I pause to calm myself "... and she's told Carolyne that there's nothing seriously wrong with her!"

He just stares blankly into space.

"Let me tell you this, Aidan," I begin again. "What you have just told me is a heinous fucking lie – and I don't believe you"

"And what's more... Not only do I not fucking believe you, but there'll come a time when I'll remind you... that you said this – and I'll tell everybody that you told me such a heinous fucking lie."

And I put £25 on the table as my contribution to the meal and leave him alone with his thoughts.

ooo

Thursday June 24th 2004...

It's announced that Meredydd – 'Med' – Hughes is to be appointed the new Chief Constable of South Yorkshire Police – and will take up his post officially in September. It's no surprise as he has been the Deputy Chief Constable for two years now and has been doing the rounds letting everybody know that he will become Chief when Mike Hedges retires.

There's a general level of comfort with the appointment across South Yorkshire, with Med being known as a "safe pair of hands". He started his career at South Wales Constabulary in 1979, was transferred to West Yorkshire in 1995 in the position of Superintendent, promoted in 1999 to the rank of Assistant Chief Constable of Greater Manchester Police and became the Deputy Chief Constable of South Yorkshire Police in 2002.

I ask my office to set up a dinner with Med so we can get acquainted.

My staff book "The Lounge".

ooo

Monday June 28th 2004...

Following the "loss" of overall control of the council at the all-out elections earlier this month, the "mayoral opposition", nay majority council groups, take great delight in appointing themselves to chair and vice-chair of every committee they can control.

Fortunately, because I hold all the [executive] cards, we manage to limit the financial impact on several Labour councillors; however, having lost their positions as Chair and Vice-chair of Overview & Scrutiny, John Mounsey and Ted Kitchen have a lot more time on their hands… which is never a good thing!

ooo

Thursday July 1st 2004…

10.00 am – Mansion House, Ballroom

My Zero Waste Strategy is launched.

ooo

Wednesday July 7th 2004…

2.00 pm – Telephone discussion with Bryan Gladstone

Bryan is a freelance consultant working for the RDA Yorkshire Forward on the emerging South Yorkshire Spatial Strategy. He wants to discuss the key points with me from a Doncaster perspective, which is, quite simply, that we want a bi-polar city region model and not a "Sheffield centric" city region.

ooo

Friday July 16th 2004…

11.25 am – West Moor Park, Armthorpe

We have been invited to a special event to celebrate Priority Sites' 2 millionth square foot of small business accommodation. Priority Sites is a joint venture between the Royal Bank of Scotland [RBS] and English Partnerships which provides sites and develops premises for small and medium sized companies throughout England – about two thirds are in former coalfields.

The event is one of the first our new MD Susan Law is attending with me and, with Rosie also in attendance, JP has been well briefed to bull me up as the mayor.

At around 12.15 pm, we all gather outside for a fireworks display to mark the occasion. My cynicism for central government is underlined when none of the fireworks are visible – and at 12.30 pm I have to ask who sanctioned a daylight fireworks display as part of the celebration?

You couldn't make it up...

ooo

3.00 pm – The Mayor's Office, 55 High Street

Call me paranoid, but I wonder why the first decision the new MD has made is to overrule the council's alcohol at work policy and install a fridge in her office *"To keep the beers cold"*. She is also insisting that all senior officers join her on a Friday afternoon *"For a de-brief on the week's activities... over a tinny"* [!]

ooo

Wednesday July 21st 2004...

Westminster

I am in London to brief ministers on Doncaster as part of our lobbying for the Lyons review into Civil Service relocation outside the capital. Whilst I'm here, I take the opportunity to meet up with Kevin Hughes [at his request] and we go out for lunch together.

Kevin is still limping quite badly and explains that the problem with his gait, which developed several months ago, isn't diminishing. Consequently he seems quite downbeat, certainly not his usual jovial self.

As we talk, Kevin reminds me how he asked me to sort out the mess in Doncaster by becoming leader some three-years earlier, and the marvellous progress we've seen since then. He wonders if I still want his seat [!]... one of the issues I threw into the mix at the time. But I tell him no – that I've never really wanted to become an MP and I see MPs as glorified social workers and clearing houses for local government bureaucracy. No disrespect to social workers.

Kevin says he's glad I have such high regard for his profession! But I explain that, having functioned as a mayor, it would be difficult to then function as "just" an MP, with all the frustrations that would bring.

Sensing I have insulted him, I implore: *"Look at Ken Livingstone; he couldn't hack being an MP after being the Leader of the Greater London Council –*

could he!"

So I ask him outright *"Why do you ask – are you standing down Kev?"* He cleverly turns the issue away...

"No... not at all... although none of us can go on forever... It's just that I'm conscious that you're good at your job – and I wanted to know if you still wanted to come to Westminster... so we could start looking for a seat for you."

"Nah... no fears Kev – but I wouldn't say no to a peerage... so we've got somebody in "the other place"... but the answer is no... I don't want to become an MP, thanks, Kev"

And we agree that I'll give him a copy of the "Local Authority Leaders as Working Peers" paper that I gave Rosie a couple of months ago – she having spent two years in the Lord Chancellor's Department, as Derry Irvine's Parliamentary Secretary.

After a very enjoyable afternoon, I bid Kev goodbye and journey back to Doncaster.

ooo

Tuesday August 10th 2004...

12.30 pm – Toast, Priory Walk

Aidan and I have been struggling to get together for our Friday reflection days, so we're having lunch together at a small bistro just around the corner from our new offices. I remind Aidan that I went down to London a couple of weeks ago and met up with Kevin Hughes.

"You know he's not standing next year," I tell him in a sage-like manner.

"What? What d'ya mean?" he pricks up his ears.

"What I say... he asked me if I wanted his seat."

Aidan goes very quiet and serious.

Filling the silence I add: *"I'm reading between the lines [of course] but that's the key point..."*

Still silence.

"I don't know whether it's because he's ill, or somebody in his family is, but he's become very solemn in his deliberations."

Personally, I think Kevin is very aware of his loyalties to me and wants to honour them. But having said that, I see it as a bargaining chip to get Aidan to be more supportive of me as mayor.

"So it's yours... if you want it?"

Aidan looks like a startled rabbit.

"But you have no profile in Donny North, so I'll give you as much time off as you want and we'll start to build you a profile," I continue – but I don't think he's listening – and we agree that we'll leave it for now and speak in the next couple of weeks.

We never discuss it again.

ooo

Monday August 23rd 2004...

I unveil a "University Centre Doncaster" sign at Doncaster College's High Melton site to formally open our university centre, in partnership with the University of Hull.

I have found Hull's Vice-Chancellor, Professor David Drewry, both charming and supportive of our HE aspirations – despite the hiccup over the amalgamation with Huddersfield University eighteen months ago.

ooo

Wednesday August 25th 2004...

9.00 am The Mayor's Office, 55 High Street, Doncaster

Another letter threatening me with violence – this one is written in English and the writer calls himself "Shotgun Dave". He says he intends to kill me, and talks about having shot somebody previously in a very public arena – hence the name. I note that the letter is hand-written, on coloured paper, and in a recognisable script.

I ask my office to pull out the previous threatening letters from "The Fifth Horseman" – so I can compare them.

"Now you can call me a genius," I announce to Chris Taylor. *"But I think 'Shotgun Dave' and 'The Fifth Horseman' are one and the same person"*

"That's interesting, Sherlock... So there's only one person trying to kill you [not two!].

"But yaouw still down't know who it is," he delights in emphasising my fecklessness and his Black Country ancestry.

"Arr," I concede – imitating Aynuk and Ayli, the mythical Black Country characters.

"Oid bedda file it agen then," Chris laughs.

"Yes, but file them all under "D" – for Death Threats then!"

ooo

3.00 pm

The front page of the Doncaster Star has a "mock-up" picture of me with an Oscar under the headline "... and the winner of this year's Oscar for spending your cash goes to... Martin Winter"

ooo

Friday August 27th 2004...

The shit hits the fan yet again!

Whilst I am away on our annual vacation in France, the issue of the RADA public speaking course has blown up again with national daily newspapers cranking it up. It is the "silly season" of course, so I shouldn't be surprised.

"His Loviness the Mayor" declares a half page article in the Daily Express, before reporting "A Mayor has controversially taken centre stage – after using taxpayer's cash to fund his private acting lessons."

Alongside the article is a [nice] quarter page photograph with the caption "Trained Voice: Mayor Martin Winter who went to RADA".

Now I know newspapers never let the truth get in the way of a good story but I would've thought a better [or comparable] tale would be how entrepreneurial RADA is delivering the "Improving Your Communications" course.

ooo

Wednesday September 1st 2004...

Med Hughes is formerly appointed as Chief Constable of South Yorkshire Police.

ooo

Monday September 6th 2004...

2.00 pm – Full Council, Doncaster Council Chamber

Today's Full Council is a good one. Firstly I have to concede that the stadium should have a capacity of 15,000 and secondly, we have developed more exciting design proposals that incorporate a synthetic running track.

As such, today's agenda asks council to note the changes incorporated in the Lakeside Sports Complex, namely that the capacity has increased to 15,000 seats, a better quality design in terms of a stadium bowl with curved roof, the inclusion of a full suite of athletics facilities; and a further budget allocation of £12 million for this scheme.

But before we get to the stadium report, I have to deal with further questioning from the malcontents' insurgency campaign – part of their strategy of gradual attrition.

Ray Nortrop poses the first question – on a bus services issue – and knowing full well that I don't control the buses, more's the pity, however, there's nothing wrong with that.

It's this second question from the malcontents, in their guise as "Doncaster Council Watch", which annoys me. The question has been submitted but the questioner does not even give us the courtesy of attending to hear my response, knowing that newspapers will report the answer and keep the issue "alive":

> 33. QUESTIONS FROM THE PUBLIC
> IN ACCORDANCE WITH COUNCIL PROCEDURE RULE 12
>
> [b] *The following question had been received from Mr. Dunlop Griffith, Doncaster Council watch, 3 Roberts Road, Balby, Doncaster, to Mayor Martin Winter:*
>
> *"A special Police investigation into the 'Donnygate' scandal, Operation Danum, resulted in some 68 arrests and 40 convictions, the last of the sentences being handed down on the 24th June 2004 to three contractors and a former Council Officer. It is a matter of Council and media record that, in parallel with the Police investigation, a team of senior officers was commissioned to conduct an internal Council Inquiry and write a report. The only information ever published about the Internal Inquiry was its cost to the tax-payers being £285,000. The reason given for not publishing the report was that matters were subjudice.*
>
> *Now that matters are no longer subjudice, will Executive Mayor Martin Winter put the full report, paid for by tax-payers, in the public domain before the next Inspection of Accounts, so that members of the public and press can question the District Auditor?"*

I respond: *"It is really quite interesting that some people continue to raise this issue and seem intent on re-visiting Doncaster's past, because that's exactly what* it is, the past. We all know that Doncaster's recent history is nothing to be proud of and I, for one, intend to ensure that we never go back there.

But we really must, and this is crucially important, stand up and hold to account individuals and groups such as Doncaster Council Watch, who are constantly conspiring in an attempt to stop Doncaster from moving forward.

This is a time of massive economic regeneration – where the future of Doncaster is being built now – based on an international airport, a top 20 retail complex, a Lakeside Sports Complex *[hopefully]* and the visionary Doncaster Education City amongst others.

The Internal Inquiry Report referred to was indeed published on 2nd September 1997, and made freely available to all, including being placed in every Council reception area. Not only that, but in December 1997, the District Auditor published a comprehensive report noting the publication of the Internal Inquiry Report and commenting on improvements that had already been made at that time.

I have a copy of the Internal Inquiry Report here. It details the 31 recommendations and I am more than happy to distribute it to Doncaster Council Watch or obtain copies for anyone else who wants one. But I must once again stress, this report has been available publicly to anyone who wants it for the last 7 years. Frankly, many of the recommendations have now been superseded by improved structures and processes.

It is time to draw a line in the sand. We must not allow people to talk Doncaster down, it is time to talk up Doncaster and all of us, politicians, Action Groups and the media, have a responsibility to drive this message forward."

ooo

As we move to the Stadium agenda item, Councillor Edwin Simpson [Lib-Dem Leader] begins outlining various concerns, trying to position himself as some kind of a *de facto* decision maker… He moves an amendment as follows:

> "The Council requires the Overview and Scrutiny Management Committee to ensure robust consideration of management and contractual arrangements prior to any binding commitments being entered into and report back to full Council."

This motion is purely and simply aimed at undermining the excellent work 3D is undertaking – and making the council the decision-maker – but many members don't [or can't] understand what Edwin is doing.

On being put to the vote, the Chair declares 27 votes in favour of this amendment, 26 against and 2 abstentions. Then all hell erupts as members question the number of votes recorded and the number of members present. Subsequently, 2 votes cast in favour of the amendment are found to be invalid. The amendment is LOST.

Soon after the meeting, it becomes apparent that two invalid "yes" votes have been registered from empty desks belonging to Councillor Monty Cuthbert and Councillor Sue Phillips. [both Lib-Dems]. Neither was there at the time of the vote.

Somebody has been naughty and cast votes for people not attending, so we commission an investigation.

ooo

Monday September 13th 2004...

After more than six months of sensitive negotiations, IKEA has announced it is coming to Doncaster, opening a new "city centre" store as part of the "Catesby Property group" Firstpoint Business Park site – off White Rose Way.

ooo

11.30 am – International Convention Centre, Birmingham

Following my attendance at the SOLACE Dinner with Roger Taylor in March, I have been invited to deliver a speech at the Standards Board Conference in Birmingham "The Code of Conduct is Good for Local Government".

I talk about the challenges rebuilding public confidence in the council and in Doncaster – and I explain that it's proving to be a long haul. The reality is that once confidence in the ethical behaviour of the council has gone, it takes many years to rebuild.

The speech goes down fantastically well and I have many people congratulating me on it for the rest of the conference.

ooo

1.30 pm – Not Enough Leaders?

I am sitting on a Q&A Panel, chaired by David Prince, the Standards Board CEO, and alongside Paul Croft, the President of SOLACE, and Barry Quirk, the CEO of Lewisham. The session looks at the role of chief executives and council leaders in promoting an ethical environment and getting the culture of an authority right.

ooo

Tuesday September 14th 2004...

After a 40% fall in visitors, the Earth Centre closes its doors. I am bitterly disappointed at the news and tell the press: *"The Earth Centre is a large asset for the people of Doncaster, but in terms of financial sustainability, the project has failed".*

ooo

Friday September 24th 2004...

Planning Resource Magazine

Doncaster's elected leader has formed a strategic partnership to develop key sites, reports David Dewar.
    Racing fans, bookies and gamblers flocked to the Town Moor course in Doncaster this month for the St Leger, the fifth and final classic of the British flat racing season. But at the start of September it was the great and the good of the regeneration world that held forth with the launch of a strategic partnership for the borough.
    Doncaster Development Direction [3D] is the brainchild of the South Yorkshire borough's mayor, Martin Winter. One of the first wave of directly elected mayors in England, Winter models himself more on Ken Livingstone than Hartlepool's former football mascot Stuart Drummond, while stressing that he has no plans for congestion charging in Doncaster.
    Winter has been proactive in the three years since his election. He has his own website and produces his own green and white papers. One of these, published two years ago, outlines his vision of a strategic partnership focused on delivering renewal in Doncaster, establishing it as a regional city with a knowledge economy and a gateway to Yorkshire and the North East.

ooo

Wednesday September 29th 2004...

We're at the Labour Party Conference in Brighton.
    Bono, the lead singer with the Irish rock band U2, delivers a speech which urges Labour to "get real" and deal with the problems of world poverty and the Aids crisis. Describing Tony Blair and Gordon Brown as the John Lennon and Paul McCartney of the global development stage, he praises their achievements but

urges them to "finish what they started" and end world poverty.

The media make a huge fuss of Bono's speech and his initial appearance in sun glasses: *"Hello... my name is Bono..."* to rapturous applause.

Knowing that JP is always good for a laugh as he wraps up the conference on the final day, Aidan has bought a pair of plastic Brighton wraparound sunglasses, suggesting JP should walk up to the lectern, put them on and introduce himself: *"Hello... my name is Johno..."*

JP's advisers think it's too high risk. I think it's genius and would have endeared him to the nation...

ooo

Thursday September 30th 2004...

After JP's wrap up speech [minus the sunglasses] Rosie takes me and Aidan up to his suite. The usual mix of people are helping him wind down but, after about half an hour, he takes a call from TB and goes off to see him.

When he comes back John is shocked, frustrated and hyperactive explaining Tony has just told him he' going into hospital tomorrow for minor heart surgery and that he is going to announce he will also be completing a full third term in office if he wins the next election.

Clearly JP wants to discuss these and other issues with his people, so we bid our goodbyes.

ooo

Aidan drives us back to Doncaster, and we discuss all manner of things: TB, his health, the "deal" with Gordon [or not] and who will challenge for leadership if and when TB stands down.

Rosie takes several calls, including one revealing that Tony is to make a statement on TV in half an hour; we park up at a services to watch.

Later I tell Rosie I believe she is in a phenomenally strong position, that her standing amongst MPs is excellent and that she needs to be ready, when the opportunity arises, to capitalise on it.

As I speak I'm reminded of a similar discussion I had with Aidan as we came back from the Glasgow Conference in February last year, and how Aidan appears completely unprepared to take up the opportunity.

ooo

Monday October 4th 2004...

Following our meeting with Gordon Brown in early 2003 and our [unanswered] paper proposing a unique central-local partnership between Doncaster and Central Government, we have been invited to pilot the government's new Local Area Agreement [LAA] scheme.

But beggars can't be choosers and I am simply happy that we have been asked to be one of seven local authorities involved. The scheme promises greater flexibility and less red-tape, allowing the local authority's strategic partnership to decide on the outcomes it wants, rather than be dictated to by central government in a cumbersome "top-down" manner.

Several years on, the reality of the LAA process [and what should have been a move towards greater devolvement of powers and responsibilities] is that it has become yet another layer of government bureaucratic performance management for local authorities.

ooo

Tuesday October 5th 2004...

After the furore of the "double-voting" scandal over the community stadium at September's Full Council meeting, an investigation has been carried out to ascertain what exactly happened.

Councillor Edwin Simpson, the Lib-Dem Leader, and Councillor Patrick Wilson, have admitted casting electronic votes for absent colleagues, although Councillor Wilson says he did so by accident whilst rearranging papers on his desk.

The Leader of the Lib-Dems, however, is guilty of vote rigging – having pushed the button of his absent colleague, Monty Cuthbert!

"Fury over vote scam – Leader admits voting for absent colleague" reads the front page of the Doncaster Star and goes on to report: "Their confession sparked Labour Councillor Ted Kitchen to call for them both to resign" [!].

ooo

Tuesday October 19th 2004...

The Lib-Dems have sacked Edwin Simpson as their Leader over the "double-voting" scandal.

The Doncaster Star reports that Councillor Simpson described his action as "schoolboy foolishness" and that the matter has been referred to the Standards Board for England for investigation.

Dead man walking!

ooo

Thursday October 21st 2004...

Following my speech as host of the English leg of the Zero Waste International Tour last November, I have been asked to deliver the keynote speech at the CLYCH Zero Waste Wales Conference in Cardiff.

I have refined it to concentrate on a "waste into wealth" strategy; which aims to look at waste not as a problem but an opportunity to create jobs, training and employment opportunities. I tell delegates that [as the elected mayor]...

"*Last year, I was responsible for burying more than 180,000 tonnes of waste in Doncaster – an average of three-quarters of a tonne of waste for every man, women and child in the borough...*

Around 30 per cent of that waste is capable of being recycled, generating an income of £40 per tonne, which is more than £2 million a year!

So we are encouraging people to throw valuable resources away. And we're charging them for throwing it into our bins... And we then pay [somebody else] to collect it for us... Who we then ask to bury it.

And, if this wasn't bad enough, we then pay up to £30.00 tax for every tonne we bury.

So when people talk about my accountability [as Mayor] for this appalling waste of public money... Well it's alright – because the public don't really care [ironically enough] as long as their bins are emptied!

The delegates seem to love it and Member of Scottish Parliament, Shiona Baird is very keen on our approach in Doncaster, commenting: "*If Doncaster Council can take this challenge on, then what is stopping the Scottish Executive?*"

ooo

Saturday October 23rd 2004...

Fundraising Ball for Nadeem Shah – "Jungle Fever Theme" – raising funds for the South Yorkshire Community Foundation and South Yorkshire People Against Crime.

Tuesday October 26th 2004...

6.30 pm – Rossington All Saints School

Rossington is an interesting community of approximately 5,000 households and I have known it intimately for a long time having captained the amateur rugby league side for several years before and after my professional rugby playing days.

There is only one road into Rossington. Entering at the north-eastern side of the village, it leads straight to the colliery gates at the north-west side and there comes to a dead end. Because of this, the only reason to go to Rossington, is to "go to Rossington" so the area does not benefit from passing trade in the way other communities do.

I am attending a meeting tonight with regard to choosing a route for the link road to Robin Hood airport. Our engineers' modelling work has suggested a variety of potential routes, with none really beneficial to Rossington, in terms of "opening the village up" to new jobs and investment; and the issue of "northern route" and "southern route" is becoming a real hot potato within the community.

More than three hundred people are there and it's the usual format. Passions are high and the regular malcontents are there agitating; although the community is wise enough not to let them have their "say".

The meeting goes well but I am not happy that the route with the most public support – the "southern route" – is not really a goer as far as the modelling our engineers have done, being both significantly longer and more expensive as well as a potential minefield of protected habitats and landowner issues.

A MORI opinion poll, commissioned by Rossington Development Trust has found that 76% of people favour "any route" as long as it connects the community with Junction 3 of the M18.

As a result I tell the community that I believe the options open to me are the wrong options; that the northern route is about the Rossington [and Doncaster] of today; but that the southern route is about the Rossington of tomorrow. However, my hands are very much tied with regard to being able to deliver a "southern route" through public sector funding alone and the road will have to be incrementally delivered through private sector development.

ooo

Wednesday October 27th 2004...

Evidently I didn't communicate my support for the community and my difficulty with the funding mechanisms clearly enough… "Referendum call on airport link road bid – village residents split over northern or southern route" declares page 5 of the Doncaster Star.

If the village is "split", why call for a referendum? Surely, this would simply exacerbate the situation... and exactly when you need an elected individual to take a difficult decision.

ooo

Tuesday November 2nd 2004...

10.00 am – Parliament Street, Westminster

Today I am meeting with Richard Caborn, as the Chair of the Millennium Commission and Minister for Sport. Richard is keen for the Millennium Commission to transfer its ownership of the Earth Centre to the council. I have to be careful here, not only because the Earth Centre is "my bag" but also because the Earth Centre Chief Executive keeps referring to me and my company as one of its [historical] creditors...

ooo

Thursday November 4th 2004...

Election Day in the North East. The vote concerns the question of devolving limited political powers from the UK Parliament to elected regional assemblies in North East England, North West England and Yorkshire and the Humber respectively.

Devolution referendums in Northern England were proposed under provisions of the Regional Assemblies [Preparations] Act 2003.

Initially, three referendums were planned, but this turns out to be the only one that takes place; arguably because the vote was 77.9% against regional government on a 49% turnout...

ooo

3.00 pm

"FALL TO EARTH – Tourist attraction looks doomed after rescue plan fails" screams the front page of the Doncaster Star; and reports that the Mayor "abandons Earth Centre talks". In a broadly supportive article, the paper explains I wasn't prepared to have the site and operation transferred to the council without the

Millennium Commission underwriting the financial risk of transferring staffing liabilities.

ooo

Friday November 5th 2004…

3.00 pm

It seems everybody has a view about the link road to the airport. My ex-councillor colleague, Ian Spowart, is now working as the manager of the Rossington Development Trust and is vociferous that the "southern route" is the Trust's favoured option.

Spowie became manager after losing his seat in the "all out" elections last June and it is he [they] who commissioned the MORI poll on the subject. However, I have also commissioned an opinion poll – and the findings have now come in:
- 34% want a route from Junction 3 of the M18 and south of Rossington – the so-called southern route
- 21% want a route from Junction 3 of the M18 and north of Rossington – the so-called northern route
- 26% want a route from Junction 4 of the M18 and via Armthorpe

ooo

Monday November 8th 2004…

2.00 pm – Full Council – Doncaster Council Chamber

Under "Questions by Elected Members to the Executive", Councillor Barbara Hoyle quizzes me over recent discussions in the media regarding new gambling laws and wonders whether the Council will be advocating a casino for the town, where it would be and whether members would be consulted?

In my response, I mention several investors who have recently contacted the Council with regard to establishing a "super casino"; and cite one particular option – offered by what I can only describe as "Las Vegas gangsters" – which would deliver us a "Community Stadium" free on the back of it.

I say I'm not convinced that such a development would create jobs in the short to medium term, however, and would be more likely to displace them from the town centre. Since that would affect the night time economy of public houses and restaurants, I would not be encouraging the "super casino".

Councillor Hoyle then congratulates me on the way in which we have dealt with the Earth Centre issue, making, in her opinion, the correct decision.

ooo

Friday November 12th 2004...

Councillors Ted Kitchen and John Mounsey present a petition they have organised against the name of the airport. Signed by more than 12,000 people, it asks for the name to be changed.

ooo

Sunday November 14th 2004...

After a solemn start to Remembrance Sunday at the Bennethorpe war memorial, I spend an enjoyable day, at the "Deliciously Yorkshire" culinary conference at Doncaster Racecourse and Exhibition Centre. I am invited to cook alongside James Martin and tell the audience of my commitment to healthy eating, balanced and healthy school meals, and the fruit into schools programmes.

ooo

Thursday November 18th 2004...

12.30 pm – The Mansion House Ballroom.

Prince Andrew visits Doncaster as part of his role as 'UK special representative for trade and investment'. The visit includes a meeting with McCormick Tractors on Wheatley Hall Road; B&Q at Firstpoint Business Park site off White Rose Way; a private visit to Redhouse Interchange, plus a visit to DFS to thank Lord Kirkham for the work he does for the Outward Bound Trust.

A short lunch at the Mansion House is followed by afternoon visits to Paragon Foods and Fellowes on the Westmoor Park industrial estate at Armthorpe.

ooo

Friday November 19th 2004…

3.00 pm – Doncaster Star

The natives are getting restless… Councillors Ted Kitchen and John Mounsey are said to be "… fuming after they only heard about the Duke of York's visit on the day it happened".

However, South Yorkshire's Lieutenancy officer David Fisher, who organises Royal events in the county, tells the paper the visit to Redhouse was private and not a civic occasion. He adds that rules set out by the Queen mean only elected Mayor Martin Winter and Civic Mayor Margaret Ward were on the list of civic dignitaries for the Mansion House.

"*It is not normal to invite councillors to visits of this nature, The Mayor was not invited to Redhouse.*"

ooo

Tuesday November 23rd 2004…

Caroline Flint has done a huge amount to deliver Robin Hood Airport and has now helped me decide over the siting of the link road.

"Residents back link road plans – MP's survey backs southern route to new airport" shouts the Doncaster Star and reports that "Caroline's survey" had a 22% return rate of about 1,200 questionnaires, breaking down as 67% for the southern route and 23% for the northern route; with 10% presumably favouring neither of these two.

ooo

Thursday November 25th 2004…

7.00 pm – Discover the Spirit Awards Ceremony, Mansion House Ballroom

Despite the local media's attempts to scupper it, the "Discover the Spirit" brand is proving a real success.

Doncaster Youth Jazz Orchestra has entitled its new CD "Discover the Spirit" and tonight's event marks the first of my "Discover the Spirit" awards ceremonies, where I reward those who have been nominated for their achievements in their communities.

Friday November 26th 2004...

9.00 am The Mayor's Office, 55 High Street, Doncaster

After the ecstasy always comes the agony, and following last night's celebrations I am brought back down to earth again...

In with my papers is a signed and addressed letter from a member of the community, praising me for a particular initiative; nothing unusual about that but this letter is written in a very distinctive script and on vibrant coloured writing paper.

I call Chris Taylor. *"Now this time you can call me a genius,"* I inform him... *"because I know who 'ShotGun Dave' is and where he lives"*. And I pass the 'fan letter' to him and ask him to compare it with the letters from 'ShotGun Dave' and 'The Fifth Horseman'.

Five minutes later Chris joins me in my office. He's carrying several coloured letters and looking very serious *"Yes... I think you're right Martin... they all seem to be written by the same person. Do you want me to pass them on to the police?"*

"Nah... he's been threatening us for more than three years now and never done anything – just file them again."

I can see he doesn't agree – but he still has mischief written on his face. *"I'll file it under 'Death Threats – pending' then."*

ooo

7.30 pm

I am joining Rosie for dinner, along with Aidan and Chris; she shows me a short report. Rosie has asked Philip Gould, TB's polling guru, to do some work in central Doncaster to ascertain where the voters are positioning themselves some six months before the general election.

Rosie won't let me have a copy of the report but it's fairly damming; in summary Gould's findings show the Doncaster electorate as extreme in their views, right wing in their tendencies, and with an underlying sense of racism.

He predicts that if a credible candidate came forward, pedalling an extreme agenda, they would be well-received in the constituency.

ooo

Wednesday December 1st 2004...

The natives are still restless. Now 'they' [Ted & John] have written to the Doncaster Star – in the guise of a letter from their [Adwick] Ward Labour Party member, David Hatt – complaining they are not consulted enough on policies.

There is not enough discipline in either the Labour party or council in general and The Star is lapping it up. Certainly, the whole issue of group discipline needs dealing with since Ted & John constantly kick off over issues, regardless of the effect on Doncaster's improvement agenda. In the last month alone, there have been stories about their campaign over the name of the airport; their failure to be invited to the royal visit; a call for Edwin Simpson to resign; and now an open letter stipulating that the Mayor doesn't consult. And that's not to mention the stories the newspaper doesn't run, such as the mayor having sex with his PA in the office!

Now the Star is reporting on the issue of a "trigger ballot" challenge to the mayor and reveals *"another candidate has been lined up for the post,"* but that *"he will not be named until after the initial ballot of branches"*.

Chris isn't concerned and neither am I. I attend at least one or more ward branch Labour Party meetings on a monthly basis, so have attended all 21 in the previous two years... some more regularly if they have invited me to speak on a particular theme or issue.

At all these sessions I speak of Doncaster's renaissance being not because of me... but because we have a Labour mayor, working with four Labour MPs, a Labour council and a Labour Government, to deliver socialist policies and programmes. One large [socialist] community driving the emergence of Doncaster as a city of national significance.

ooo

Thursday December 2nd 2004...

After a great deal of soul searching, I have chosen the "northern route" for the link road to the airport. Whilst acknowledging that the southern route would be much better for the village, the simple fact is that it may, very possibly, not be built. Having opened up southern route land for development, the government would be less likely to utilise taxpayer's money to build the road – and would expect the development process to deliver it at minimum cost to the taxpayer.

Clearly there is nothing wrong with the concept of the private sector being forced to fund the scheme, [and I have considered a toll road to serve the airport]; but the road might then be delivered in a much more piecemeal manner, if at all.

Developers could attempt to cherry-pick the infrastructure to serve "their" development land, rather than strategically, and more expensively, serving the airport.

Although I am disappointed that I am not in a position to bid for the funding for a southern route, I believe I can encourage a "win-win" scenario by constructing a "spur" from the motorway roundabout across to the Rossington Colliery site, which will then encourage such investment to open up the village.

ooo

Tuesday December 7th 2004...

"Mayor accused over airport link road" reports the Doncaster Star, quoting "angry" Rossington Councillor, John Cooke who accuses me of failing to take any notice of public opinion in the village. To which I respond:

"The right decision might not be the most popular decision but I am here to make the right one for the people of Rossington and Doncaster. Seventy five per cent of people who responded said they would support a route via Rossington regardless of its specifics."

ooo

Wednesday 15th December 2004...

11.30 am – Press Briefing, Mansion Hose Rear Committee Room

We are briefing the press on the Audit Commission's Comprehensive Performance Assessment [CPA] for 2004. In line with our "first term" mayoral plan, we have achieved a CPA "Good" Rating for the council. The reports comments:

"Doncaster Council has changed from being fair to good. It has made significant improvements in street cleanliness, waste recycling and housing repairs over the last year. Neighbourhood management and community consultation and participation have improved. Educational attainment is improving from a low starting position and remains a challenge to the council.

Access to services has significantly improved through Community First, streets are cleaner and customer satisfaction with recycling is high. The housing repairs service has also improved although the council recognises that further improvement in housing services is necessary.

The council has a clear vision for the area and the mayor is pursuing his executive power to implement council priorities and encourage greater community involvement. The new Managing Director is improving the council's ability to manage change.

The Council works well with other agencies through the Doncaster Strategic Partnership. This will be critical in establishing new joint working arrangements under the recently announced Local

Area Agreement pilot. Based on Doncaster MBC's current plans, the Council is well placed to continue to improve the way it works and the services it provides to local people."

To thank our staff for all their hard work in achieving the "good" CPA rating, I decide they shall all be given an additional one day holiday in the next financial year; but that such holiday should be managed though the flexi-process and that schools *in particular* should not close to allow staff to take the extra entitlement.

Despite this explicit instruction, Hungerhill School, where I am a governor and where I send my children, closes for a full day later in the year. A letter from the head informs parents this is as a result of the mayor giving staff an extra day's holiday!

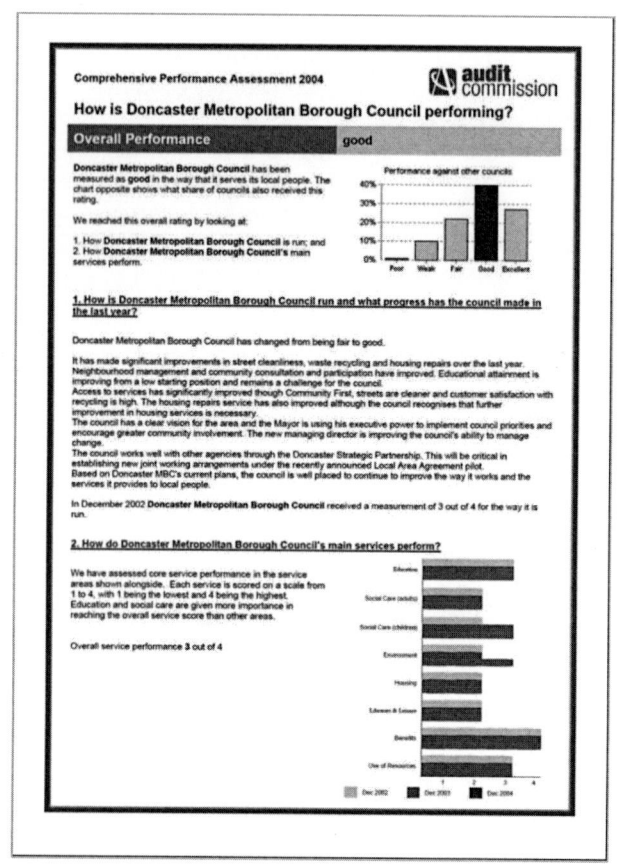

Thursday December 23rd 2004...

"Who will challenge Martin's Winter Wonderland?" cries the Doncaster Star in a full page three feature prompted by our own press release on the outcome of the "Trigger Ballot" process, which has been taking place during the past few weeks.

Despite visiting ward branch Labour party meetings on a regular basis, Chris has arranged for a hectic month of such visits – having been "invited" to attend and address members as part of the branch's "Mayoral Trigger Ballot" processes.

As well as the borough's twenty one Labour party ward branches, there are eight union branches with a vote in the process and I need to have more than fifty per cent of the collegiate votes; although guidance does not state whether "more than 50%" means "15 or more of the branches voting" or "more than 50% of the votes cast within the 29 branches".

Regardless of this ambiguity, in most cases I secure unanimous support from voters; only failing in one of the ward branches and one of the union branches:

Adwick Ward Branch Labour Party – John & Ted's ward – where they voted 17:1 against me [!] and in favour of the trigger; and one of the Unison Branches [with John & Ted as members] where they voted 4:3 in favour of the trigger!

As such, Chris's press release states that 92% of Labour Party members who voted, voted for my selection as the Labour Party mayoral candidate for a second term.

ooo

Chris and I are cock-a-hoop over the support shown for me and feel it only emphasises what a strong team we are. Having said that, one further ward branch meeting did come close to voting for the trigger. It's a particularly small branch where a very disagreeable councillor lives; but I'm told that after an acrimonious meeting his proposal for the trigger was defeated – though not before he had mentioned the "mayor having sex with his PA in the office" allegation...

We agree that I need to make overtures towards John & Ted, who are clearly "unhappy" with my mayoralty, and get them on-board with our agenda.

ooo

Why did he just call me Jim?

"Truth and love will overcome lies and hatred"

Vaclav Havel

Saturday January 1st 2005...

"Education Landmark Taking Shape" heralds the Doncaster Star as it gets the new year off to an optimistic start; reporting on the bright future for education in the borough, with the new Doncaster Education City 'Hub' building being speedily built during the previous six months.

ooo

Sunday January 9th 2005...

Heavy rainfall on Friday 7th January has led to flooding in Carlisle on Saturday 8th and Sunday 9th. Coming in the wake of a prolonged period of rain over the previous three weeks, floodwater from three rivers and localised flooding from sewers and road drainage have combined to cause disaster.

Three people are killed, many homes and businesses are flooded and schools are closed. There is widespread transport disruption with all Carlisle's buses damaged.

The Minister for the Environment, Elliot Morley, goes on TV and gives an absolutely perfect jargon-ridden technical response to the floods; you would think he worked for the Environment Agency!

ooo

Wednesday January 14th 2005...

1.30 pm – The Mayor's Office, 55 High Street, Doncaster

Chris has been talking with "John & Ted", so Ted has joined me for a meeting to discuss how we might allay some of *his* concerns...

This is a little disconcerting, given that Ted & John always work [hunt!] in pairs, however John insists there's nothing particularly concerning him...

Suffice to say, I have agreed with Chris that I will be utterly charming. Ideally, I would have asked Aidan to deal with this but it needs my personal touch.

Ted tells me he is unhappy that we are building a new £32 million stadium for Doncaster Rovers and the penny drops immediately; Mounsey is a huge Rovers fan and so doesn't want to criticise the new ground.

I ask Ted about the "rumour" about me being seen having sex in my office. Ted laughs and says what I get up to is up to me – so I ask him to look across the street and point out that the window opposite is bricked up.

He moves the subject back to the new Rovers' ground and our conversation becomes quite terse, as he claims all I'm bothered about is the Rovers. I tell him that the stadium is a "community stadium" and will host other sports and events.

He demands to know why we are not building an athletic track within the development and I explain that I fully intend there to be one, but that we can't do it until a submission lodged with Sport England Lottery Fund [from DuPont Sports & Social Club] is withdrawn.

I tell him how it was my company, MWC, which submitted the bid some four years previously, having undertaken the work *pro bono*, with the agreement that we would be paid if the outcome were successful. Consequently, I am financially tied into a successful "DuPont" bid, to the tune of around £30-40,000, which limits my activity because of a declared interest.

However, I tell Ted that Doncaster Athletics Club is in discussions with DuPont [as their partner in the bid] and that I expect DuPont to withdraw their submission in the near future. At a not inconsiderable cost to myself!

This seems to appease Ted somewhat and he tells me an athletics facility at the stadium would make it more acceptable to him...

But just when I think he's with me, he launches into a tirade and says he will be telling everybody that we shouldn't be building the facility and that it's all just part of "A Winter Wonderland" – the malcontents' contemptuous strapline for "the mayor" and his manifesto projects.

I say all the manifesto projects have the full support of the Labour group and that I'd appreciate him not peddling such a story – four months before the mayoral [and General] election.

But he's having none of it, insisting he doesn't care whether it has the support of the Labour group or not. *"I shall be telling everybody that it's all just part of a winter wonderland,"* he reiterates, knowing it riles me.

I begin to see red. Now I would like to say that the diplomat in me massaged Ted's ego and the problem went away; or that, like a charmer playing his *pungi*, I hypnotised this particular poisonous snake...

But I can't – and I didn't... suffice to say, Ted left the building much earlier than he probably anticipated.

Monday January 17th 2005...

2.00 pm – Full Council – Doncaster Council Chamber

We [I] must be doing something right – here we are at Full Council, four months before the mayoral elections and Councillor Martyn Williams is being a pedant, correcting how the minutes have recorded my response to his question:

> 68. **MINUTES OF THE MEETING OF COUNCIL HELD ON 6TH DECEMBER, 2004**
>
> **RESOLVED** that subject to the amendments set out below, the Minutes of the Meeting of the Council... be approved as a correct record and signed by the Chair:
>
> [2] Page A8 - Reply to Councillor Martyn Williams, the word "would see" be replaced with "are seeing" on the last line of the page, the sentence now reading:
>
> "Doncaster was booming and people are seeing a difference."

I suspect this pedantry has a lot to do with the mayoral election in May and Martyn's veiled support for my leadership. In a fractious Q&A session at the previous Full Council meeting I had taunted him about whether he would be standing for Mayor himself.

A question was put to me by Mr George [Jock] Ross. Jock Ross is the piper who plays outside the Mansion House for any event Doncaster Council Watch wishes to promote. He is here to ask the question wearing his full Scottish piper's uniform.

> 70. **QUESTIONS FROM THE PUBLIC IN ACCORDANCE WITH COUNCIL PROCEDURE RULE 12**
>
> [e] The following question had been received from Mr. George [Jock] Ross, 17 Don Street, Doncaster, to Mayor Martin Winter:
>
> "I am 77 years of age and I was born in Balmoral, Scotland and, I came to live and work in Doncaster almost 48 years ago. I am retired and a Council Tax Payer and, entitled to benefit from local services. It has been brought to my attention that there is to be an event in Doncaster Town Centre between 10 am and 4 pm on Saturday 26th February, 2005, at which buskers will be able to perform. I am informed by **Doncaster Council Watch** that buskers will be coming from Edinburgh, London and Paris. **Council Watch** tell me that whilst the performances are likely to be on the street, the exact locations are not yet known. I have attempted to trace leaflets and posters at the usual places... but nothing is available. It seems that with this event being less than two months away, there appears to be something lacking. **Doncaster Council Watch** have told me that there is always a problem with adequate publicity for cultural events in which the Council is involved.

Therefore, I would be honoured if Mr. Winter, the Elected Mayor, could address these points immediately in order to secure the guarantee of a good attendance for the event which should assist shops, stalls and market traders."

This question, clearly written by Ray Nortrop, is typical of the general attrition exacted on my mayoralty and the Council by Nortrop and his cronies. While it's their democratic right to hold me to account, the demands on council officer time dealing with such mischievous queries are onerous.

Thanks to a sub-standard local media desperate to fill column inches, however, their strategy always gets plenty of coverage.

ooo

Wednesday January 19th 2005...

Doncaster Star runs with the story "Council Leads the Way on Recycling Targets" and relates how we are now recycling 13% of our municipal waste, up from 2% and compares it against our South Yorkshire neighbours in Barnsley, Rotherham and Sheffield. Given that it's just six months since I launched my Zero Waste strategy, I'm very pleased with the progress.

ooo

Friday January 21st 2005...

9.00 am – The Green Tree Hotel, Hatfield

I'm speaking today at the launch of the Humberhead Levels and [Thorne, Hatfield, Crowle] Moors Partnership.

The Environment Minister, Elliot Morley MP, is launching this partnership of twelve organisations – three Wildlife Trusts, the RSPB, three Local Authorities, three Drainage Boards and two Government Agencies – all of whom have agreed to work together tackling the environmental problems of the area.

I have to be careful today on several levels; firstly, I used to work for the Yorkshire Wildlife Trust and also the Wildlife Trusts' National Office in Lincoln; secondly, I steered the Glass Park project to working closely with the Countryside Agency [before its amalgamation into Natural England] on exactly this partnership.

As we arrive there is a demonstration outside the hotel over local planning applications for wind turbines and the government's national policy. I am pleased to see the demonstrators but sad that I've been discouraged [by our Monitoring Officer] from having a public view on something so close to my heart.

The Minister arrives and deals with the demonstrators with some mealy-mouthed platitudes that seem to appease them. He greets me in his usual disingenuous way, saying he knows he's got to Doncaster when he sees my recycling posters at the train station.

In the large function room to the rear of the hotel more than one hundred people are in attendance and, following an overview and suitable introductions, the Environment Minister is invited to give his address.

I already have a pretty low opinion of Morley, not least because of his ignorant, yet immovable, stance on Zero Waste *per se*; his refusal to come to the launch of my ZW Strategy for Doncaster last July; and his inability to operate as a politician – constantly subservient to DEFRA's officers.

Even by Elliot's standards the speech he delivers to launch the partnership is poor, mechanistic, slightly cursory and apolitical.

"What a load of bollocks," I whisper to Chris Taylor. *"Here we are 16 weeks before a fucking general election and that twat doesn't even mention that it was the fucking Labour Government that bought out the peat cutting rights from Scotts!"*

"Ah – but he's not a politician, is he Martin?" replies Chris.

"You're telling me… what did he used to do?"

"He's an ex-teacher"

"I should've realised. I thought he was an ex-civil servant but it makes sense – he always wants to tell people he knows best – but it's not borne of any expertise – he's just repeating what others have told him!"

So that is it; I take it upon myself, 16 weeks before the General Election, to deliver the political message to those in the room. This had been the Minister's opportunity to hail the Government's commitment to the environment and Morley's just given a politically neutral speech that's been drafted by fucking Whitehall mandarins!

It's a relatively simple task; instead of delivering my prepared speech, I speak from the heart.

I highlight my background in the environmental movement; playing on the moors as a child; the RSNC peat campaign and its "Tomorrow is Too Late" and "Losing Ground" reports; William Bunting and "Bunting's Beavers"; and I say I'm proud to be a directly elected Labour mayor and that I can be politically explicit – that it was the Labour Government that committed the £17 million for the removal of the extant mineral extraction rights on the moors – and that I'm proud my Government did so.

"*Well that stuck it up him*" says Chris as I sit down again *"You reminded him he's supposed to be the politician – you're always much better when you play to your convictions."*

Morley however is less convinced and almost churlish towards me for the remainder of his visit.

ooo

12.30 pm

I am speaking at the Doncaster College Graduation Ceremony.

ooo

Thursday January 27th 2005...

"Official Red Light Plan for Borough" cries the Doncaster Star and, in a broadly supportive story, reports how I have been pushing for Doncaster and Liverpool to pilot a 'Utrecht style' prostitution park. I say we need to find radical solutions to such problems, which are blighting one part of the Doncaster community.

The report includes the fact that Home Office Minister, Caroline Flint, is presently putting together a report on prostitution and is similarly keen to see such pilots.

ooo

Thursday January 27th 2005...

I have launched an official "managed zone" consultation process, to try to manage the ongoing problem of prostitution in the central Doncaster area.

ooo

Friday January 28th 2005...

Work starts today for the new community stadium; stripping vegetation and preparing the site for the commencement of construction work. Given this, Chris is understandably concerned about my disagreement with Ted. His antennae are telling him it was a bad move.

It clearly was, but I am emphatic that I cannot and will not put up with such behaviour – where the fucking hell is the Group Whip on this one?

With the elections fast approaching, we agree Chris will try to broker some kind of a meeting between us.

ooo

7.30 pm – The Rockingham Hotel, Doncaster

I host a campaigning evening for all four constituencies – with all four Labour MPs in attendance – which proves a huge success. As part of the evening, we ask members to pledge their support to see me re-elected at the mayoral elections in May.

ooo

Monday January 31st 2005...

"The Shape of Things to Come" declares the Doncaster Star in a double page spread on the fantastic future Doncaster can now look forward to. Parroting HG Wells it tells how "A changing skyline of new offices, stores and developments heralds the dawn of a new era around the borough".

Citing projects like Education City; Trax Park; the Lakeside Sports Complex; Transport Interchange; the Racecourse Re-development; Catesby Business Park and others, the article is very supportive of Doncaster's rejuvenation.

Although I'm pleased with the general tone, with only three months to go before the election, I'm somewhat dismayed by the implication that these developments have just happened "by accident" and are not the result of any greater provocation such as a "mayor" or "3D [Doncaster Development Direction]" – the development company I established for Doncaster.

ooo

Tuesday February 1st 2005...

MAD Week – Tickhill. The "Making A Difference" [MAD] Weeks I introduced in our communities have been really well received. This is a week of multi-partner involvement where we establish minimum standards of cleanliness and activities with the Mayor's Office, which the community can expect throughout the year.

Saturday February 5th 2005…

MAD Week – Hatfield/Stainforth.

ooo

Monday February 7th 2005…

6.30 pm – [Labour Group] Mayoral Policy Forum – Mansion House

As an outcome of my Mayoral Conference in February 2003, I have held several 'Mayor's Policy Development Forums' – specific meetings where I ask the community for feedback on Doncaster's undoubted rejuvenation and seek advice on the direction of travel for the future.

As well as meeting all the community forums, I have held individual [political] meetings with the Conservative Party and the Community Group [the Lib-Dems refused to meet me!]; and tonight's meeting with the 'Council Labour Group' is one of several with my own party, including individual constituency policy development forums.

ooo

Wednesday February 9th 2005…

1.30 pm – Meeting with Councillor Stuart Exelby and John McHale

I have a meeting today with regard to implementing the first of my 'Un-adopted Roads' programme. I have been developing this as a second term Mayoral priority for some time, ably assisted by the promptings of Caroline Flint MP and her Office Manager Phil Cole.

It's proving controversial – particularly with our own Labour Councillors. They argue that residents have often purchased cheaper properties because of the condition of unadopted roads and work to bring them up to adoptable standards can add considerable value to their homes.

Nonetheless, I am moving ahead with the policy – these roads drag our communities down, look appalling [to inward investors] and often attract fly-tipping and other anti-social behaviour.

We have been looking at a variety of options including consulting with the residents themselves; exploring whether they will commit to paying for the work;

and the possibility of placing a charge on the house, to be redeemed when it comes to be sold.

I want to get the first road undertaken before the Mayoral/General elections in May and, as usual all three MPs have been kicking off about the number, and state, of "their" un-adopted roads – demanding we start with the ones in their constituencies.

Consequently, I have made a purely political decision to tackle the first of the roads under this policy in Rosie Winterton's constituency – in Central Ward. This is because of one specific road in Belle Vue, opposite the Racecourse and Doncaster Bloodstock Sales, which local man John McHale is actively campaigning on. It now appears he will be standing for election as the Labour party councillor for that ward because the incumbent independent councillor is extremely ill.

ooo

4.00 pm – Mansion House

I have a meeting with Aidan, Susan Law and others, regarding John Prescott's 'The Northern Way' strategy which is supposedly a collaboration between the three northern regional development agencies [RDAs]. It's JP's baby and its fundamental tenet is the encouragement of and investment in successful city regions. I have significant concerns about the Northern Way:

Firstly, the principal conclusion of the strategy is that 'a city region' can come together to act as one. My own view, from looking at research into European models, is that the best way to proceed is by constructing 'informal strategic alliances between willing partners'. I contest that this can only happen if all players, including the core cities, take a truly city-region view, recognising that every part has assets that benefit every other part.

Secondly, the Northern Way is still emerging and in a state of flux and should not be seen as the definitive prescription for the region's investment over the next twenty years. There is no doubt that a successful Northern Way will be based on city-regions – but whether these are city-regions 'driven' by their core cities remains to be settled.

The 'bi-polar model' set out in the South Yorkshire Spatial Strategy is a case in point. Put simply, the 'wrong' city region model could be adopted; and, indeed, the RDA is attempting to force Doncaster into the Sheffield City region. I contend that the RDA's proposal that 'informal strategic alliances between willing partners' should be restricted to the city-region's boundaries is pure folly – especially for Doncaster with its fantastic geographical location. Links with Leeds and Hull are obviously important as too are links with York, whose status as a major tourist attraction clearly adds to the potential of the new airport. As the most southerly outpost of the 'North' – at its quickest we're a mere 90 minutes from London – both Doncaster and indeed the sub-region should always consider themselves in international and national terms, not just 'Northern' alone.

Lastly, and arguably most importantly, at no point have the Yorkshire and Humberside Leaders come together to debate the rationale for 'The Northern Way'; let alone met with our north-west and north-eastern counterparts! Yet we are being bullied into accepting it as the correct strategy for the next twenty years' investment priorities. On this last point, the whole concept has become the catalyst for a quite bad-tempered debate between the northern leaders and the whole issue is becoming divisive.

RDA Officers are treating the Northern Way as an instruction from Whitehall rather than the beginning of a debate. Indeed, because of their completely inflexible approach, I have started to make explicit my strapline for dealing with government dictats "Treat it as a challenge to rise to, rather than an instruction to follow".

Consequently, I have been ruminating for some time over a new approach that can be seen as a unification model for all the northern leaders. Today's meeting is to discuss my thought processes with Peter Kenway of the New Policy Institute before drafting my response to the Northern Way – 'A Doncaster perspective'.

ooo

Thursday February 10th 2005...

9.30 am – The Mayor's Office, 55 High Street, Doncaster

Gerry McLister says part of the reason for his standing down as a Councillor was managing the dichotomy of the officer/member relationship.

"The officers will tell you I am getting in the way of their professional futures..." he says. *"Well I say they are constantly getting in the way of my political future".*

Aidan does not differentiate at all. Although patently capable as a politician, he frequently sees himself in competition with the officers. Forever obsessed with parading his "intellect", he views them as stepping stones to his "future career", whatever and wherever that might be.

The senior offices have been quick to take advantage of this, praising him on his "intellectual grasp" of situations as cover for seeking advice on technical aspects of their work rather than looking for any political steer. Aidan just enjoys ratifying their *de facto* policy decisions.

Susan Law has been particularly quick to exploit this situation and it's become the bedrock of her political manipulation of Aidan. It may seem paradoxical, but like many senior officers in local government, she wants rid of the politicians whom she considers a burden to *her* operation of *her* council.

She is rabid in her desire to be completely "in charge" and is attempting, through Aidan, to force the removal of the elected members' from the Member's Appeals Panel, a sub panel of the Employee Relations Committee. In effect it will allow her to be both judge and jury with regard to staff dismissals.

Susan has primed Aidan to deliver the Labour Group for her when the issue comes to the next Full Council on 21st February.

I ask Susan why she thinks Aidan will succeed. That, in my opinion he will fail on the basis that he's lazy, lackadaisical, and never covers his bases.

With the Council being in "No Overall Control" since the all-out elections the previous June, the Labour group doesn't control non-executive decisions like this – therefore he'll need the opposition's support as well, which won't be forthcoming.

Both Susan and Aidan are disdainful of my comments.

ooo

12.30 pm – Wakefield

Meeting of the Yorkshire & Humber Association of Local Authorities Leaders. This is another opportunity for me to promote the unification model as the antidote to the Civil Servants' Northern Way implementation model.

ooo

Friday February 11th 2005…

The opposition have got wind of Susan and Aidan's attempted "manipulation", with the husband and wife team of Martyn and Carol Williams putting forward the following counter motion:

> *21st February Full Council*
>
> *"This Council insists that the Employee Relations Committee should exercise the power for decisions in respect of appeals by staff against dismissal and that this function should not be delegated to the Managing Director or any Officer."*

Monday February 14th 2005...

MAD Week – Askern.

000

Wednesday February 16th 2005...

MAD Week – Edlington & Warmsworth.

000

The penny has apparently dropped with the media and the Star's headline "Winter Freeze on Tax levels – Mayor announces NO increase in Council Tax months before election" seems to grasp that it's the 'Mayor's Budget' that I put forward each year.

But always keen to "create" an argument, the newspaper reports that the 0% increase "could be bank-rolled with job cuts" and says Lib-Dem leader Monty Cuthbert has raised concerns over jobs and highlighted the fact Mr Winter will be fighting an election in May.

I point out that budget-setting is about making choices – prioritising our resources to deliver outcomes that the people of Doncaster require. I explain there is unanimous support for my budget proposals within the Council Chamber [including from Councillor Cuthbert's party], which the paper ignores.

"But concerned Councillor Cuthbert said: "It's an election year, the mayor's an unpopular guy and he's got to do something to hold his place."

It gives Monty a final opportunity to poke me in the eye!

000

Thursday February 17th 2005...

"No Job Cuts vows Mayor" cries the Star, reporting the political ping pong it has generated outside the [public] budget setting consultative process. The article goes on to describe how my neighbourhood re-structuring aims to create a Local Authority which is closer to the community in its responsiveness and delivery.

000

Monday February 21st 2005...

8.30 am

Kevin Hughes MP announces he is suffering from motor neurone disease and will not be standing in the forthcoming General Election in May. I ring Aidan to let him know.

ooo

9.45 am

I discuss the day's extremely unusual event with Aidan.
 He is due to lead the debate in opposition to the motion. As I predicted, he hasn't covered his bases within the Labour group, and is relying on his rhetorical ability to "convince" Labour colleagues on this hugely important issue.
 Although the group will follow the whip, several are unhappy that Aidan is insisting on the further removal of their powers. As they see it, it compounds the damage already done by the Executive [Mayoral] Model being implemented through Local Government 2000.
 I tell Aidan he needs to think carefully, and politically, about his position. *"Kevin has just announced he is not standing in May – and you need to understand that you shouldn't antagonise the Labour group, Aidan"*
 "Why?"
 "Because – as – of – exactly – fifteen – minutes – ago" I enunciate *"You will be wanting to stand for Parliament in May"*
 He looks at me quizzically. *"And in the next four or five weeks you'll need several of the group's members to support you. Do – you – fucking – under – stand?"* I spell it out again.
 No response – he just looks at me as if I'm the devil.
 "I can't be any clearer," I tell him *"Do you want to be selected for Kevin's seat?"*
 No reply.
 "Then think what you are doing... and turn on Susan," I order him. *"Tell her that this is just politics. She'll understand – and quite frankly who gives a fuck if she doesn't... Just tell her that this is politics – explain what's happened with Kevin and tell her you'll be supporting Martyn Williams's motion not opposing it – but that you'll deliver it another day for her."*

But the absolute idiot that he is, he won't listen. He seems more concerned with letting Susan down than with playing the politic; or maybe he's delivering to a different political paymaster!

I write in my Full Council papers' margin...

AR – STUPID FUCKING BASTARD!

Big Brain – No Nouse – [and certainly] ***no bollocks!***

And it is here where I begin to develop my understanding that, pragmatically speaking, there are three facets to leadership:

i] You need a good level of intelligence
[You must be able to have an intellectual grasp of what is in front of you – but not too much of an insight or you can over analyse the situation and move into seizure]

ii] You need a very good standard of emotional intelligence – what I call political nouse or intuition. [You have to be able to read the situation as it arises and understand all its ramifications]

iii] You need bollocks – metaphorically speaking and certainly not gender specific! [You have got to have the courage of your convictions – to be able to physically make, and take, the decisions that are required of you]

But Aidan can't see the politic of the situation and because of this he is still attempting to garner support for his [Susan's] proposal. Or maybe he can see it but doesn't have the courage to say no to her? If that's the case, why doesn't he ask me to get him out of it?

ooo

12.30 pm

Labour Group Pre-meet – Mansion House, Priory Suite

Aidan has a particularly rough ride in the Labour Group, even though he finally gets them to agree to his amendment to Martyn and Carol Williams's counter motion.

ooo

2.00 pm

Full Council begins and, very quickly, Aidan takes a huge public kicking. As a result, he loses the vote on his own amendment.

> Agenda Item 7a]
>
> In accordance with Council Procedure Rule 15.1, a Notice of Motion was submitted by Councillor Martyn Williams
>
> "This Council insists that the Employee Relations Committee should exercise the power for decisions in respect of appeals by staff against dismissal and that this function should not be delegated to the Managing Director or any Officer."
>
> The Motion was Seconded by Councillor Carol Williams.
>
> An amendment to the Motion in the following terms was Moved by Councillor Aidan Rave and Seconded by Councillor John Mounsey:
>
> "This Council recognises the important role of the Employee Relations Committee in respect of appeals by staff against dismissal. Therefore, following specific concerns about the current process at a recent Employee Relations Committee meeting, this Council:-
>
> a] Retains the right to oversee staff dismissal appeals through its Employee Relations Committee;
>
> b] Establishes a Member/Officer Working Group to conduct further study into the potential for streamlining of the current appeals process ensuring that a fair and transparent but more effective process is developed; and
>
> c] Requests that the findings of this Working Group are reported back to Full Council within six months."

This first amendment, which Aidan moved, is a cynical attempt to vicariously steal the populist glory from Martyn and Carol's own motion and kick it in to the metaphorical long grass for six months – at which point, Aidan won't have to deal with it [because he'll be in parliament!].

But, despite the Labour Group being conned by Aidan, Full Council don't buy it and unceremoniously kick it out – voting it down by 32 votes to 22.

For good measure Terry Wilde and Jessie Credland, two Independents, then make their own attempt to steal the Williams's clothes – but lose 34/19. The vote then comes back to the original motion which "Aidan" loses 33/20.

Aidan looks absolutely devastated – Council has twatted him and he didn't see it coming!

I do not vote at all. I can see we're in for a kicking and that this issue will become a political hot potato; it's one I don't want to get hold of at this particular moment.

ooo

12.30 pm

Aidan asks if he can take me to dinner this evening to discuss the emerging situation regarding Kevin's seat.

ooo

8.00 pm – Mount Pleasant Hotel, Bawtry

Aidan and I sit down for dinner together. In our overtures, we cover all manner of subjects; not least the kicking he took at Full Council this afternoon.

I know it's a serious meeting because he orders a bottle of Châteauneuf-du-Pape – at restaurant prices! Aidan is one of the tightest people I know and never freely dips into his own pocket without calculating the true cost of his expenditure first.

I begin to regale him with the papal history of the wine but he's much too focused; I think he's looking stressed again. He waits quietly until we both have a full glass in front of us.

"*It's amazing isn't it Martin...*" he begins as if we are two long-lost brothers "*... how right you were two years ago when we were coming back from the Glasgow Conference.*"

"*Yes... I told you I see things Aidan – but, just like Cassandra's prophecies, you never want to hear them.*"

"*What do you mean?*"

"*Well you can't be that bloody bright...*"

"*What do you mean?*"

"*What I say... for all your fucking brains, you can't see how important it is to listen to me... Like this morning*" I continue "*You shouldn't have tried pushing that motion, less than an hour after Kevin's seat came onto the market – but you wouldn't listen... and it might prove costly to you – they might turn around and bite you on the arse!*"

"*No... they're not that bright*" he says, incredibly disparaging about his fellow party members.

"*Clearly...*" I smile at him.

"But the thing is Aidan... I told you Kevin's seat was coming up last August... didn't I?"

No response.

"And you did fuck all. You could be sitting on a done deal here. No..." I correct myself *"You should be sitting on a done deal here!* But what have you done about it? Sweet Fanny Adams!"

"I'd like to think I can rely on your support Martin?" he says breaking a long painful silence.

"Well *I'd like to think* you could rely on my support Aidan. And I intend to support you... But I have to be seen to back the winner [whoever that is] so let's see the short list first."

"It would mean so much to me, if I could have your support."

"We need to keep our powder dry on this one..." I say "... and there's nothing to be gained from jumping to support people too early, which is what I'll be advising Cabinet to do. What does Maria say?"

"Oh... er... she's... fine," he replies, clearly uncomfortable I'm raising the issue.

"But it can't be easy for her... if you go to London... what with her illness and all that"

I'm reminding him of the discussion we had when I asked for his unconditional support over dinner at the Lounge.

"No... she's... she's fine with it," he dismisses the notion clumsily. "But I need you to understand Martin how important it is to me to have your support."

"I know... that's three times you've said it... but I'm not sure you understand yourself how important it is."

No response.

"Anyway, I haven't decided whether I'm throwing my hat in the ring or not yet," I announce.

"But you said you didn't want to go to Westminster." He sounds like a forlorn child.

"I don't. But that doesn't mean I can't try and negotiate something with the party – they owe me big style for sorting out all the shite that I have."

"Anyway... a sitting Mayor, can't stand for election as an MP... even though sitting MPs and MEPs, can stand for election as Mayors..." I add helpfully.

"So you've got nothing to negotiate with then," says Aidan.

"Of course I have – I can be outraged that I'm not allowed to stand. It's an infringement of my human rights and all that."

"Private club"

"*Private clubs still have to adhere to European Legislation... Anyhow... I might be so outraged that I choose to stand down as mayor and stand independently for Kev's seat.*"
"*The Party wouldn't buy it*"
"*Oh I don't know... I think they know not to try and second guess me.*"
"*Have you spoken to Kev?*" I ask him.
"*No... not yet*"
"*Well you need to – ASAP.*"
"*Anyway... if it's any consolation... I think you'll make a fucking brilliant MP,*" and I take a hearty mouthful of wine. "*But you've got to be able to see it from my perspective. What'd happen if I jumped in to support you... and they don't even put you on the short list?*"
Silence.
"*Rest assured Aidan, you can rely on the same level of support that you've given me over these last few years*"

ooo

Tuesday February 22nd 2005...

"Borough 'shining example' on tax" reports the Doncaster Star and continues with the sub-heading "Prescott praise for freeze".

In a comment on national trends in council tax increases, the Deputy Prime Minister is quoted as saying: "The difference is shown when you look at Labour controlled Doncaster. They are proposing an increase of zero per cent and promising a very low increase next year as well."

I am pleased he has singled us out nationally; particularly as I am planning a "zero per cent increase for the entire four-year second term" election pledge.

ooo

Wednesday February 23rd 2005...

8.30 am Cabinet Brief – Mansion House, Priory Suite

Cabinet Brief is a political meeting which takes place every week before either Cabinet or Executive Board, which themselves take place on alternate weeks.

In attendance are Stuart Exelby [Central]; John Hardy [Doncaster North]; Eva Hughes [Central]; Glyn Jones [Central]; Ken Knight [Don Valley]; Chris Mills [Don Valley]; Bill Mordue [Doncaster North] and Tony Sockett [Doncaster North].

As usual, Aidan is late; in fact Aidan is now known as "The Late Aidan Rave" because of his propensity for bad time-keeping.

"Before we start, this morning... can we have a quick word about Kevin's seat? Obviously it only really applies to you John [Hardy], Bill [Mordue] and you Tony [Sockett]; with it being your constituency... but my advice to you is to keep your powder dry.

"There'll be a lot of people wanting your support as members of cabinet, but there's nothing to be gained from jumping in to support people too early... it's probably best to wait until you see who's on the short list... and I say this with no-disrespect whatsoever to Aidan, who tells me he will be throwing his hat in the ring."

"Well... if I can just say, Martin," says John Hardy "It's my opinion that Kevin has not been a good MP and I think Aidan will make a fantastic MP for Doncaster North."

"And that's your opinion and you're right to express it, John" I reply. "But that's exactly why you should keep your powder dry... It's very early doors and it will have to be a quick selection process. I have suspected Kevin wouldn't be standing for some time as his health has been deteriorating... and I'll bet he's declared late in an effort to avoid a Women Only shortlist – so he may have somebody in mind."

"Are you saying you're going for it Martin?" asks John "Because that would be disastrous for Doncaster – you're doing a fantastic job and we need you as Mayor."

"Well... again... that's your opinion John... and it's very good of you to say so. But no... a sitting Mayor, cannot stand for election as an MP... even though sitting MPs and MEPs, can stand for election as Mayors."

"But that's why you need to keep your powder dry... we need to see how the picture develops. Because we will have to work with whoever wins... so it's important we are seen to back the winner – whoever he or she is. I've said this to Aidan – and I've also told him I intend to support him."

"But this is about politics... not necessarily friendship... and it's about doing the best for Doncaster North and Doncaster."

Aidan comes in late.

"Just so you know Aidan. We've just been talking about Kev's seat... and support for candidates... and I've said the same thing as I said to you on Monday evening."

"Er... yeah..." he grunts.

"Do we know anybody else who's throwing their hats in, Aidan?" I ask.

"Oh yes..." he replies with glee "Michael Dugher... the jumped up little twat."

Chris Mills raises her head so people can see.

"Has he really?" she says, in an effort to hold the room's attention. "*I saw his mother yesterday... and she never said anything*"

"He's from Conisbrough is he?"

"Well Edlington... but he's got family in Conisbrough..." she responds.

"And he's a complete pillock," adds Aidan. "*He was Geoff Hoon's Special Advisor – on Iraq*"

"Ah... that's it then," I say.

"What is?" asks Chris Mills.

"*Well Kevin and Geoff Hoon are big buddies... they were in the Whip's Office together. So that's the deal, that's who Kev's going to be supporting – Geoff Hoon's Special Advisor on Iraq...*"

"Have you spoken to him Aidan?"

"No... not yet"

"Okay..." I sigh.

"*Well... we've got a full Cabinet Agenda this morning... so let's go through it. Can you introduce this first item on education please Tony?*"

And I lean over and whisper to Aidan: "*Are you fucking stupid or something?*"

"Why... what do you mean?"

"*You need to start listening to me... or you're gonna blow it. It's two days since I told you to speak to Kev and you've done fuck all about it. I'm beginning to think you don't want this seat.*"

ooo

1.00 pm

I take a pre-arranged telephone call from Ruth Redfern. Ruth now works for the RDA, Yorkshire Forward, and used to be a Labour councillor at Bradford City Council; she wants to discuss tomorrow's Yorkshire & Humber Assembly Meeting.

Ruth is a petite, good looking woman with very short black hair; we meet on a regular basis but she's worried I'm making too much noise about the flawed concept of the Northern Way and the lack of any political dialogue or involvement; its approach being tantamount to politically-motivated funding of [favoured] northern authorities.

I explain that I don't buy the concept of "trickle-down". The RDA is promoting the concept of investment in and around the core cities – with the surrounding areas benefitting by any successes 'trickling down' to them!

3.00 pm

Chris Taylor gives me an update on possible candidates. So far three have formally announced they're "throwing their hats in the ring":
      Michael Dugher   – the ex-SpAd to Geoff Hoon
      Sandra Holland   – the ex-Office Manager to Caroline Flint

And... Aidan

ooo

Thursday February 24th 2005...

Storm clouds are beginning to form... Liz Jeffress has been acting as the Company Secretary to the Glass Park Development Company [GPDC], which is additional to her role as a trustee of the Glass Park Millennium Green Trust.
    She tells me that officers within Doncaster Council's finance and audit section are concerned, that one of the key malcontents, Secretary to the "Doncaster Fair Deal" campaign, Joan Moffat, has been "camped out" at their offices for several weeks now. She has been trawling through everything Glass Park project related and is constantly making accusations to the Audit Commission.
    They have told Liz they simply don't know what to do, such is the tenacity of this woman.

ooo

12.00 pm

I attend a Yorkshire and Humber Assembly Meeting to discuss the Northern Way. Despite Ruth Redfern's attempts to assuage my fears, I use it as another opportunity to promote my unification model.

ooo

3.30 pm

Chris rings to let me know he's been talking to a contact at Wakefield [Labour Party Regional Office] and they are going to announce it will be an open shortlist – not Women Only. The contact has also told him that there is another candidate running – a woman Councillor from Derbyshire County Council.

5.30 pm

I ring Andy Sawford, who is now working for the parliamentary and public affairs company, Connect Communications. Andy was a candidate for the Labour Party, Leicester South by-election last July [2004] following the sudden death of Jim Marshall, so I know he is keen to find a parliamentary seat.

Andy lost the Labour nomination narrowly to Sir Peter Soulsby, who subsequently lost narrowly to the Lib-Dem, Parmjit Singh Gill, in a by-election that was dominated by the invasion of Iraq.

In an extremely intense conversation Andy tells me he has looked at Kevin's seat but doesn't want to be considered for it, although he's flattered I've rung him. I express my concerns over the quality of the candidates coming forward and ask if he is aware of any "names" on the horizon.

He tells me David Miliband's younger brother "Ed" is looking for a seat but may be going for Plymouth – although this looks like it might be a women only short-list. He also mentions Alison Seabeck, Nick Rainsford's SpAd, and also thinks she may be going for the Plymouth Seat.

We agree that he will "ask around" and come back to me if he hears anything.

ooo

Friday February 26th 2005…

6.15 pm

Chris Taylor rings to say Nic Dakin has announced he will be standing for Kevin's seat.

Michael Dugher	–	the ex-SpAd to Geoff Hoon
Sandra Hollands	–	the ex-Office Manager to Caroline Flint
Nic Dakin	–	the ex-Leader of North Lincolnshire Council
Elizabeth Donnelly	–	a TUC rep on the East Midlands Assembly

And Aidan… Things are not looking great

ooo

6.25 pm

Michael Dugher calls – he has obtained my 'phone number from Kevin Hughes and wants to know if he can come and speak to me. He tells me he views obtaining my support as fundamental to securing the selection for this seat.

I tell him he is the first candidate I have spoken to, other than Aidan of course, and that I will gladly meet him. I check my diary commitments and we arrange to meet.

ooo

Sunday February 27th 2005...

7.00 pm

I ring Rosie Winterton before her Constituency Meeting tonight and express my "considerable discomfort" that firstly, as a sitting mayor, I am not being allowed to stand for Kevin's seat and secondly, that I class the potential candidates coming forward as "fairly pedestrian".

Rosie knows my position with regards to Westminster so she isn't really going to buy any fake claims that I'm being excluded from the process, though she does acknowledge the principle of my argument.

I slowly build to a rant, making sure she is in no doubt that I'm looking for a "name" for Doncaster North's next MP, somebody who will really be able to deliver.

She says she will ask around and come back to me.

ooo

Monday February 28th 2005...

6.20 pm – Christ Church, Thorne Road

I have arranged to meet Michael Dugher outside Christ Church, a beautiful neo-gothic church with a chancel designed by George Gilbert Scott, who also designed the rebuilt St George's Church, now Doncaster Minster.

I suggest here because I have a meeting at 8.00 pm with the management team and I want to take the opportunity to look at the church on my own – on a dark evening; firstly because I am keen to illuminate several landmark buildings in and around the town, and secondly because I have been told the area suffers from a significant amount of anti-social behaviour linked to sex worker activity.

ooo

6.30 pm – Meeting with Michael Dugher, Central Park Bistro

Michael arrives at exactly 6.30 and I suggest we have a drink at the nearby Central Park Bistro. I tell him that, within reason, he can ask me anything.

We have an amicable discussion about his political beliefs; his family background; knowing Aidan from school; the transformation Doncaster is now undergoing and, very tellingly, his work as Special Advisor to Geoff Hoon on Iraq. On this topic, Michael is very candid about the support Kevin Hughes has given him – alluding to a deal between Geoff and Kevin to declare as late as possible to avoid an all women shortlist.

The meeting reaches a fairly natural conclusion at 7.50 pm – and I tell Michael that, in order to be fair, I will give all the candidates an hour and twenty minutes of my time.

ooo

8.00 pm – Meeting with Friends of Christ Church

I meet David Craven and John Leaske, part of the Church management team; refreshingly, they are both officers of the council and I remark that I'm delighted to see the work they are putting into the community.

During a very enjoyable evening's tour, they tell me that over the years the building deteriorated and by 1989 was declared redundant because it became too expensive for the congregation to maintain. It was purchased in 1994 for £5 by Reachout Christian Fellowship and at a cost of almost £1 million it opened again for public worship in 2004.

I express my support for the work these volunteers are doing and tell them I will seek to put together a package of support they will be satisfied with.

ooo

8.50 pm

John Healey, the MP for Wentworth & Dearne [Rotherham] rings me. I have always got on well with John and find him a refreshingly honest and genuine politician who connects well with people. He has been appointed to the position of "Economic Secretary to the Treasury" so I know he will know Ed Miliband.

He's rung me under the ruse that he wants a chat about our progress with the "Gershon Report" and savings. I know this isn't why he's calling but I enjoy answering his many questions, knowing he's leading up to something else. Finally he stops procrastinating and gets to what I consider the real reason for his phone call – Kevin's vacant seat.

But now it's my turn to procrastinate – I can hear the division bell ringing and I start waffling over issues to see how direct he really wants me to be. After what seems like a lifetime, he finally mentions Ed by name and asks for my views on the likelihood he would secure the constituency's support.

I answer encouragingly and suggest that in order for John to get to the division in time, he should give Ed my phone number so we can have a chat.

ooo

9.25 pm

Ed Miliband rings me – and after a short intense conversation, we agree he will call again at 2.30 pm tomorrow, but on my home office number, so we won't be disturbed.

ooo

Wednesday March 2nd 2005...

8.30 am

I brief Chris Taylor on the previous evening's discussions and we agree Chris will come home with me for my telephone call with Ed. I also ask one of our Policy Assistants to see what she can find on David Miliband's brother.

ooo

11.00 am

Our Policy Assistant brings me a briefing on Ed Miliband. She says there is very little about him, but what she has found is quite disparaging; she tells me he prepared the way for Gordon to bring in new, more demanding inheritance tax legislation, but allegedly benefitted by making sure his mother's property was transferred to him and his brother before the legislation was introduced. I dismiss it as political tittle-tattle.

ooo

2.20 pm – Our House, Kirk Sandall

Chris and I are preparing for the telephone conversation/interview I am to undertake with Ed Miliband. Although from completely different moulds, Chris and I have an uncanny understanding of each other, knowing intuitively what the other thinks. I am more than happy for him to listen to my discussion with Ed. In fact, such is my respect for his judgement, that I want and need him to sit in.

We connect a set of headphones to my phone so Chris can hear and I give him a pen and pad for him to jot down any observations or questions he wants me to ask.

ooo

2.30 pm

Ed calls me on the dot. After 40 minutes we agree I should go to London the following day, with Chris, so we can meet up with Ed and talk further.

As I put the 'phone down I look at Chris. *"Well I think yes... what do you think Chris?"*

"Well I think yes as well – he really impressed me."

"He impressed me too. My only misgiving is that he kept referring to Gordon and I don't want him to constantly be playing the GB card."

"No, but it's a pretty good card to play," replies Chris, accentuating his sardonic Brummie twang.

In terms of where we are to meet, Ed prefers the Treasury, clearly wanting to roll GB out to support his case. I explain that I already have to be at the Cabinet Office for a "Customer Focused Public Service Leadership" event and would prefer to meet there. Although this isn't complete fabrication, I only insist on it so I have the upper hand.

Ed agrees to a 2.30 pm meet at the Cabinet Office.

ooo

4.30 pm

Aidan and I have a meeting with Mike Bower, the former [Labour] Leader of Sheffield City Council, who now works for the RDA, Yorkshire Forward; I'm obviously rattling their cage because they keep sending people to talk me down – they obviously don't know me!

Mike is a very pragmatic operator and tells me he is concerned I am making too much fuss about the Northern Way and the RDA's obsession with Doncaster being part of the Sheffield City region. I tell him that, quite simply, the 'wrong' city region model is being promoted and that the "bi-polar [Sheffield-Doncaster] model" set out in the South Yorkshire Spatial Strategy is more likely to get my support.

I explain how I don't buy the concept of "trickle-down economics" and that we've seen this approach before – with Reagan's tax reduction policies being offered to those at the top in the hope they would somehow trickle down to those in greater need; it was also tried at the time of the Wall Street Crash, which led to the Great Depression. Aidan then jumps in, to explain in even more detail, waxing lyrical about Franklin Roosevelt promising the New Deal that would help the economy from the bottom up rather than the top-down – and the birth of Keynesian economics.

I tell Mike that the city region model is completely unacceptable to Doncaster, as is the regional government reorganisation which I expect will surely follow, where we will be governed from Sheffield.

I explain, yet again, that I am not attempting to destroy the Northern Way but that, paradoxically, I'm actually trying to encourage a stronger unification model worthy of John Prescott's legacy. Furthermore, I say, Sheffield has no real predisposition to working with Doncaster – but is "having to" because of the model being forced through.

I launch into a comic rant and tell Mike I believe Sheffield has turned its back on the South Yorkshire coalfield communities of Barnsley, Doncaster and Rotherham; is obsessing about Manchester and Leeds and having better trans-Pennine transport links with Manchester; and that, rather than opposing my high speed rail connectivity model, Sheffield should support it or simply concentrate on becoming a suburb of Manchester itself!

ooo

6.30 pm

I ring Andy Sawford who tells me Ed has rung him and that he has briefed Ed on Doncaster. I tell him how Ed was desperate to meet me at the Treasury so he could wheel GB out.

"Do you know," says Andy, "he's a fucking idiot – I could scream. I told him not to try and dazzle you, that you don't do starstruck!"

ooo

6.45 pm

Steve Houghton, the Leader from Barnsley Council calls to seek my advice.
"What's the crack with the Donny North position then Martin?"
"There is none Steve"
"Well is it a done deal?"
"Not at all – it's really wide open. As a matter of fact, I'm really pissed off with the quality of candidate that's come forward so far."
"I thought Aidan was going for it?"
"He is – that's what I was referring to! I don't think – and more importantly most other people don't think – he'll get it. He's lazy and a lot of people know that."
"Well I know that he likes to toss it off... But I didn't know it was as serious as that. Is it worth while throwing my hat in?" he asks.
"Of course it is Steve," I say. "I think your approach would go down well with members"

ooo

Thursday March 3rd 2005...

7.30 am – Doncaster to London Kings Cross Train

Chris and I are excited by what the day offers. Although my business in London, at the LGA Recycling Conference and the Cabinet Office event, would legitimise Chris's attendance with me, he insists on paying for his own ticket; such is his level of integrity.

As we travel, we analyse the discussion with Ed the previous day and both agree he appears to have a healthy leaning to the left. Chris is very familiar with the writings of his father Ralph and we discuss our nascent understanding of the Miliband brothers' more polarised politics.

I tell Chris how I expect Ed to attempt to roll Gordon out; and how I have been toying with him, suggesting I would prefer to meet at the Cabinet Office rather than the Treasury because I have a "Customer Focused Public Service Leadership" event there.

"You'd better put him out of his misery then," says Chris

ooo

8.30 am – Doncaster to London Kings Cross Train

I call Ed to let him know our progress and that we will be on time; we also agree it would be better to meet at the Treasury after all!

ooo

2.30 pm – HM Treasury, Horse Guards Road, London

We arrive at the Treasury for our early afternoon meeting. Ed comes down to meet us almost immediately. He is unbelievably gracious, charming even, and leads us into a small ante-room overlooking a quiet side street.

My first impression of him isn't good. He is incredibly young looking with the most beautiful soft olive skin, but he looks like a sixth former – a mere boy and with hands that are so velvety it's obvious he's never done a hard day's "graft" in his life.

But it's his speech that really shocks me! He is so unbelievably nasal that it starts to get in the way of what he's saying. I keep thinking he needs to have his adenoids removed.

I introduce him to Chris Taylor and we continue the previous day's discussion; I repeat what I have already said, that if Chris and I wish to support Ed [as king makers] it is practically a done deal and he will become the next MP for Doncaster North.

Ed says Gordon wants to "pop in and say hello". How predictable I think, but I'm not going to miss having a private discussion with the next Prime Minister.

I have met GB once before, at John Prescott's house in Hull shortly before a Labour Party function at Jack Chew's [Chinese] restaurant. Aidan and I had a private discussion with him about a relaxation of the interpretation of tax laws to favour businesses employing workers from specific, priority areas within a community. Gordon was very supportive of my stance, insisting Whitehall would back such a scheme.

The door suddenly opens – and sure enough, in walks Gordon. He is friendly, warm-hearted, relaxed and incredibly impressive.

He pulls up a chair, swinging it into place at our table, sits down and says he's ordered some cream cakes to go with the pot of tea we are having. "Tea & Cream Cakes with Gordon Brown at the Treasury," I think; that's one to tell the grandkids!

Now then Martin, he begins excitedly, Ed's been telling me about some of the fantastic work you're doing in Doncaster; tell me all about it and what the USP is for the town.

Well I wasn't going to pass the chance up, so I outline my usual pitch about Doncaster achieving its destiny. I've done this a thousand times before and I give him my usual marketing patter that we are witnessing the birth of new city. I tell him of the huge economic regeneration we are witnessing; our transformational projects; our schools investment programme; the opportunity to link Doncaster into the Lyons review and a devolved civil service; and the fantastic opportunity Doncaster is, in terms of its connectivity and the myriad opportunities presented by the new airport.

As I go along I highlight the specifics as they relate directly to Ed's prospective new constituency.

Pitching Doncaster as the emerging strategic metropole for the North of England, I tell him we need to capitalise on the airport's capabilities <u>vis a vis</u> the new Super Jumbo, the A380 Airbus being built jointly with France, in Toulouse, which can only land at three runways in the UK – Heathrow, Prestwick and Doncaster.

I tell him we need to loosen the stranglehold Manchester and the north-west exert on the North of England, demonstrating this in terms of my own vision for the "Northern Diamond": a big, strategic regional unification model, as the antidote to JP's laudable [though flawed] "Northern Way" concept. High-speed rail connectivity between all the cities, towns, airports and seaports in Northern England – from Nottingham to Newcastle and Liverpool to Hull – and mirroring the London, Lille, Paris triangle is what is needed, I repeat; creating a new self-standing "Northern-England" region, which would be globally competitive in its own right and not forever subservient to, and reliant on, London and the south.

I look at Chris and he gives me one of his admiring looks, telling me I'm on fire. What's more, I think, GB's actually receiving what I'm saying. He is responding, commenting, disputing and counter-arguing the thesis I'm putting forward; what a difference compared to the sheer exhaustion that characterised similar opportunities with TB.

Not only does Gordon appear enthused by what I am saying – he sends Ed out to arrange for a fresh pot of tea! As we get our second cup of tea, we start to focus on the 'real' business and he thanks me for the "level of support" I am giving Ed.

I repeat that with my support as mayor, it's practically a done deal and Ed will become the next MP for Doncaster North. I also tell the Chancellor that such a deal could clearly be very costly to me personally – in terms of the damage it will do to my relationship with my deputy, Aidan.

"Yes... that is a big call..." says Gordon. *"Well you need to let me know what support you need from me... because Ed's delighted that you are offering this*

level of support. And I, of course, will be delighted to see him elected to Parliament.

"I've told him he can have the time off... but you need to let me know what you want from me," he says again.

"Well let's get him selected first," I reply. "I know I can deliver him for you Chancellor, but let's see that I deliver my part first"

"Please call me Gordon, Martin"

"Thank you – I might not want anything, Gordon... and I might want everything..." I say, tellingly. But the fact is I've already had many discussions with Rosie regarding a potential Peerage and I've parked that one, on the understanding it's my exit strategy after my second term, and I want to keep my powder dry with regard to any potential payback from Gordon.

"So let's just get him selected first."

"Well, I just want you to know..." Gordon continues "... that it's incredibly important for me to have Ed elected in Doncaster... and you'll need to let me know what you require, in return."

"What's the plan now?" he asks.

"Well Ed needs to hit the ground running... so he'll be coming back up to Doncaster with us this evening so we can get him out there meeting people as of tomorrow."

Gordon thanks us once again and leaves.

ooo

As we depart for Kings Cross, I reflect on the meeting and its success. Could I really see myself getting that sort of air time with TB? I think not. GB will be the next Prime Minister and Ed his right hand man. With Ed as our newest MP – and indebted to me as king maker – we/I will be able to access the PM to pitch our development programme at him – a programme for Doncaster and the north of England...

The strategy makes the utmost sense.

ooo

4.30 pm – Kings Cross to Doncaster Train

One of the things that impresses me about Ed Miliband is his eagerness to get involved. In our 'phone discussion the previous day, I'd said he could stay at our house. As the meeting with Gordon finishes, Ed has already got a bag packed so we could get the earliest available train back to Doncaster.

As we sit on the train, I explain to Ed that I have a 7.00 pm meeting with my Youth Council, which I have to attend for about an hour.

I notice the man opposite me prick up his ears up at the content of this discussion. Both Ed and Chris seem oblivious to this fellow traveller but I begin to struggle to speak meaningfully in code.

I text Carolyne: *"Guess who's coming to dinner?"* As we journey back, Ed questions us about everything he can. I am very clear that, as mayor, I will be seen to have "supported" the winning candidate, whoever that person is; but Ed should make no bones about it – he will be the winning candidate!

As I speak, I become increasingly concerned that the man opposite is at pains to seem disinterested in the micro drama playing out at his table; nonetheless he is clearly absorbed by it. As we get off the train he smiles at me knowingly.

ooo

7.00 pm – Mayor's Youth Council – Mansion House, Priory Suite

Ed and Chris sit in as the Youth Council holds me to account for delivering on the youth agenda in Doncaster. I always enjoy these sessions because the young people are so honest in their questioning. As I answer, wherever possible I refer to the MP whose constituency it is if I think it has relevance to Ed's attendance.

ooo

8.30 pm

After the meeting finishes, the three of us walk across to the Council Car Park, where I left my car earlier in the day. I have been winding Ed up on the way back from London about Carolyne doing the real "interview" with him when we get back to Doncaster.

"She's been a card carrying member of the Labour Party since she was 18, so you'll do well to pass muster with Carolyne," I tell him.

As ever, Chris supports me, telling Ed she's a fearful woman – so assertive she is like a Dominatrix and known to make grown men cry!

As we drop Chris off he shouts: *"Good luck with Carolyne, Ed!"*

ooo

9.00 pm – Our House, Kirk Sandall

When we arrive home, I introduce Ed to Carolyne. I explain that I have to see my children first but Carolyne will make a brew and have a chat with him!

I have a quick word with my children Beth [14], Joss [11] and Marcey [10] who are in bed now. Joss has been moved out of his room to bunk with his siblings – as a result they are very hyper about our "special guest".

ooo

9.15 pm

Carolyne is having a cup of tea with Ed.

"Thank you for allowing me to stay here Carolyne... it really is very good of you, for you to be so supportive."

"That's okay... it's fine Ed. But what you need to understand... is I don't [necessarily] support you... And I'm not doing this because I like you... In fact whether I like you or not doesn't even come into it... I'm doing it... we're doing it... because Martin has brought you here to Doncaster. And he's done so because he's seen something in you... or he thinks you can do a job for Doncaster, or for him..."

"You do understand that though, don't you? It's just politics."

"Oh yes... of course I do... but I just think everybody is being so nice and supportive... and I want you to know I appreciate it."

"We're being supportive Ed... because Martin's decided he wants you as our MP in Doncaster"

ooo

9.30 pm

I explain to Ed that I have to deal with several emails in my office and I'll be back shortly.

ooo

11.30 pm

Having shown Ed his bedroom for the evening [Joss's room – bottom bunk], we say good night.

Friday March 4th 2005...

7.45 am

As first impressions go, Ed has a strange induction into our family. He tells me what a bizarre breakfast he's had this morning. Having been introduced to all three children over coffee, they then proceed to have a vicious row as to whether the painting "The Bathers [at Asnières]" by Georges Seurat is an example of Pointillism or French Impressionism.

As ever, each thinks they're correct and they want an arbiter – *"What do you think Ed?"* they ask proceeding to involve him in their row. He says he found it all quite bizarre and not what he'd expected at all.

As he appears to have very little cultural awareness, I find it incredibly patronising that he should assume a level of academic superiority, so I ask him if he considers it an example of Pointillism... He looks completely flummoxed – so I tell him most young people in Doncaster like to debate the history of art over breakfast!

ooo

8.30 am – Mansion House

I have an early meeting at the Mansion House and tell Ed that Carolyne will take him to "Olivers", a local eatery, and Chris and I will join them there at 10.00 am.

I am meeting with Aidan Rave and Ian Spowart over a Doncaster Chamber Celebration of Success event – celebrating McCormick Tractors expansion and new assembly lines. Aidan is fairly quiet – and to be honest he's been very reserved since Kevin announced he was standing down two weeks ago. He doesn't appear to be handling the stress very well.

I feel slightly uncomfortable about the deceit that has entered my life.

ooo

9.00 am – Olivers, Edenthorpe

Carolyne takes Ed to Olivers for breakfast, *"I need to ask you Ed – are you Jewish? Because you certainly look Jewish..."*
    "I am" replies Ed *"Is it a problem?"*
    "Not at all – I just wanted to know if you are alright eating pork."
    "Oh I'm fine. I'm not that committed – I'm fine eating pork, thank you."

As they settle down for breakfast, Ed asks Carolyne if she's on flexi time – and she explains she is a freelance Community Development Consultant and has taken two months from work to concentrate on the operational side of my campaign.

Ed thanks Carolyne once again for being so supportive of him.

"As I said last night Ed – we're being supportive because Martin's decided he wants you as our MP in Doncaster. But you also need to understand that we're all part of a big team. And getting you selected is about us all being very clear about what needs doing."

"Sometimes we just have to do what's asked of us and not question the rationale – on the basis that Martin and Chris have covered all the bases."

"Oh I appreciate that – they seem incredibly certain that they'll get me elected."

"Oh they'll get you elected alright – it's as Martin and Chris have told you – they weigh the Labour votes in sacks in Doncaster North..."

"But it's the selection process we've got to win first – and, to be quite honest, Martin and Chris are an unbeatable combination... but make sure you listen to them – and do what they say"

"Oh I will – I'm delighted that they're helping me."

"They're not helping you Ed. They are going to do it for you – <u>just listen to what they say.</u>"

ooo

Ed moves the conversation on and asks Carolyne which university she went to. She tells him she chose not to go to university but to secure a job with prospects at General Accident in York, enrolling on work-placed learning opportunities. She describes which courses, qualifications etc. and goes on to explain how different types of learning work for different individuals and how she feels she would have enjoyed university life but for all the wrong reasons; she tells him how her dad always said 'the school of life' worked better for her and university worked well for her younger sister who got a 1st from Leicester.

Ed tells Carolyne he agrees with her views on apprenticeships and work-based and vocational learning being equally valid; moreover, he agrees that academic learning doesn't work for everyone.

As they chew the fat waiting for us to appear, Carolyne secretly congratulates me on the synergy of views between me and Ed.

ooo

9.45 am

As I drive to our rendezvous, Chris tells me that when we were at the Youth Council event the previous night, Ed had whispered to him *"He's very good..."* nodding at me *"... isn't he?"*

This makes me nervous. Why did he need to offer such unsolicited praise? I suppose he's wanting to create a good impression but I'm reminded of how disingenuous those within [local] government are – constantly fawning over the elected members with apparent humility and general insincerity.

ooo

10.00 am – Olivers, Edenthorpe

Chris, Carolyne, Ed and I spend the morning mapping out a strategic operational plan aimed at Ed meeting with, and securing the support of, as many constituency members as possible. We have copies of each Branch membership list, complete with contact details, which we make available to Ed, having highlighted the key players and prepared pen portraits of each member known to us.

Initially we identify the key players in each Ward – the ones Ed needs to make contact with but whom Chris will approach in the first instance. Ed will then follow up that discussion with a meeting asking them to function as "champions" for him, espousing the virtue of supporting him to other members in a cascade effect.

I explain I still have the day "job" to do and, although Friday's are less frenetic "thinking days", I still have a full diary culminating in a dinner date with Rosie Winterton and Sir Patrick Duffy this evening at the Catholic Church in Doncaster town centre.

Ed uses this as an opportunity to offer to stay at John Healey and his wife Jackie's home in Rotherham this evening, before going back to London to work on some matters with GB, including the Budget briefing for next week.

From this point Ed stays with John and Jackie in Rotherham on a very occasional basis, to offer Carolyne and I respite from the intensity of it all. He probably also wants to give himself the chance to catch up with what's happening in "Westminster Village", check in with John on his election strategy and escape the low-brow discussion and rowdy family life Chez Winter.

ooo

11.30 am

On a housekeeping note, I have spare keys cut so Ed has access to our house and to my extremely well-equipped office, complete with two brand new computers bought especially for the election period. I loan Ed my car until he has hired one and we give him a company card so he has access to my business account at STAPLES and can pick up any stationary he needs.

Ed must be self-sufficient. We encourage him not to stand on ceremony – and to come and go as he needs, taking whatever food or sustenance along the way. Carolyne has converted the children's playroom into a bedroom for Ed; purchasing a new single bed and a wardrobe for him. He is to use the laundry bin we have put in "his room" and our housekeeper Pam will do his washing.

Pam thinks it's hilarious that not only has she had her hands in the Mayor of Doncaster's underpants but the future Prime Minister's as well!

Having said that, I am still incredibly careful for [the more militant political] people not to know Ed is living at our house; publicly I have to play a very straight bat, backing no one and offering all candidates the same level of support and time.

But the reality is we aren't particularly fooling people – and the fact that Chris Taylor is seen to be taking the lead in Ed's campaign [and mine] says a huge amount.

ooo

7.00 pm – St Peter in the Chains, Chequer Road, Doncaster

Dinner with Sir Patrick Duffy, Father Gus O'Reilly and Rosie Winterton

Ever since the public meeting over the Town Fields development at the Carr House Centre in 2002, Sir Patrick Duffy has been extremely supportive of me as mayor.
 Patrick was born in 1920, educated at the London School of Economics [LSE] and Columbia University, and served in the Fleet Air Arm in World War II. Injured in an aeroplane crash, he underwent pioneering plastic surgery and was a member of Sir Archibald McIndoe's famous Guinea Pig Club. He became the Labour MP for Colne Valley [1963-66] and for Sheffield Attercliffe [1970-92] where he was succeeded by Clive Betts. He was a Minister of the Navy in the 1970s; President of the NATO Assembly in the 1980s; Opposition Spokesman on Defence 1979-81 and 1983–84, and Under Secretary of State for the Royal Navy in Jim Callaghan's Government 1976-79.
On the Right of the Labour Party, a staunch pro-European, opponent of unilateral nuclear disarmament and fervent Pro-Life campaigner, Patrick has become very

attached to Carolyne, whose father was also a member of the Guinea Pig Club [also see Chapter 8]. Sometimes opposites attract!

This evening is a chance to catch up on all things Doncaster and much of the discussion is on the selection process for Kevin's replacement. Rosie and I have a full weekend together at walking surgeries and other events. We speak regularly and she knows my position with regard to Ed and that he is living at our house; but, as you would expect, she doesn't mention it, choosing to play her cards very carefully.

Sir Patrick, however, is less diplomatic and an enthusiastic advocate for the only Catholic he can see at this point in time – Michael Dugher. Having worked with Ralph Miliband when he was at both Leeds University and the LSE, Sir Patrick is vicious in his criticism of Ed's father – and therefore Ed.

"What about Aidan?" Rosie asks Sir Patrick [deliberately naïvely] and we receive a fairly aggressive, though accurate, deconstruction of Aidan as both a politician and person.

ooo

11.30 pm – Our House, Kirk Sandall

Carolyne has printed out a card sign and blue-tacked it to the children's playroom door.

"Future Prime Minister's Bedroom"

---

ooo

Saturday March 5th 2005...

10.00 am – Walking Surgery at Armthorpe [with Rosie]

12.30 pm – Cheque presentation [with Rosie]

2.00 pm – "One Blood" Ethnic Communities [with Rosie]

ooo

Sunday March 6th 2005...

2.00 pm – Walking Surgery at Lakeside [with Rosie].

ooo

Monday March 7th 2005...

9.00 am

The whole subject of the M18 Link Road to the airport is becoming a massive issue in the community of Rossington with factions wanting a "northern route"; a "southern route"; and "no route"! I have a meeting with Rossington M18 Link Group.

ooo

12.00 pm

I instruct Susan Law to identify a pot of money that will allows us to illuminate Christ Church and other landmark buildings in and around the town, and also to provide some new railings in a sympathetic style to the architectural vernacular of the Church and its environs.

ooo

12.30 pm

I am preparing for the Secondary Heads' Conference at Wetherby next week – 'Raising Standards' – where I have a speech to deliver about my schools' investment programme and where I'll announce my Partnership Agreement with the Heads.

To tell the truth, I'm pretty pissed off with them as a group – I have been massively supportive of education throughout my four years in charge, yet all I seem to see from these Secondary Heads collectively, is their bickering, individual disenchantments and general impatience over the 'building schools for the future' process and their school's position in our construction time-line.

The head teachers are acting more like project managers and what sometimes seems quite childish behaviour is manifesting itself in the form of obstruction and outright hostility to the DEC concept and George Holmes' activity. Some are operating like Robber Barons and I need to get them on their own to read them their futures – to "divide & conquer".

I intend to deliver a broadly supportive speech to them but, at the same time, [gently!] read them the riot act about some of their individual behaviours.

ooo

2.15 pm – Our House, Kirk Sandall

Ed has been very active during his first weekend with us and is calling to check in with Chris and me on a fairly regular basis. This evening Chris and I have a meeting at The Salutation pub with Russ Ballinger, a Trotskyist Unison Convenor, with regard to the restructuring that Susan Law is attempting to bulldoze through.

Because this is a political meeting, I don't want to be reliant on my driver to take me home afterwards, so I've asked Carolyne to pick us up after they've finished in Carcroft – she thinks they will be with us by about 7.30 and says she'll text me when they are outside.

Ed is excited and wants to attend the meeting with me but I say no – I think it might be a little dodgy for him to sit in on a meeting with the Unions. He's not impressed, so I explain my rationale. The game is now on to get Ed selected in Doncaster North and even though he's relatively unknown, Russ is a fairly sharp operator and might rumble us.

Russ knows most people and is also aware that there's a Parliamentary selection process imminent; my analysis is that he might smell a rat if we turn up with a polished "young man" who looks like David Miliband.

Ed's not keen to be kept out and keeps questioning my paranoia. I'm getting a little irked by this, he's constantly questioning why we need to do things, and it's starting to slow us down.

"We can't have a referendum on every decision we need to make Ed," I tell him *"And it's irrelevant anyway because you and Carolyne will be in Carcroft."*

Ed feigns injury because I've dismissed his "enthusiasm". However, we agree that "my paranoia" has raised a rather serious issue. We need to agree a pseudonym for Ed when he is with me, at least until it becomes more public knowledge that he is seeking selection for the seat, and preferably until he has been selected and becomes the official PPC [Prospective Parliamentary Candidate].

I suggest he should be a friend of mine called James or "Jim" and that if possible he should refrain from speaking!

"Jim – I don't particularly feel like a Jim," says Ed.

"No but you're definitely a James," I respond.

"Yes... but 'Jim'?"

"Fucking 'ell you awkward bastard... I've just told you we can't have a referendum on everything! What d'you want to be called? Butch? Woody?" I'm on a roll.

"Or what about Vladimir?" Chris laughs, joining in. "What about Karl – with a K of course... or Ralph?" he asks sardonically.

"Okay... okay... I get it!" says Ed.

"Or Friedrich... what about Friedrich?" asks Chris, disappearing into his own world.

"Okay... okay... I get it!"

ooo

6.00 pm – Salutation Public House

I quite like Russ Ballinger and enjoy a fairly open and regular discourse with him. Not unpredictably, whatever I do is never enough for Russ and his union colleagues – and as a result, prompted by Mounsey and Kitchen, Unison pushed for the trigger ballot on my candidacy for mayor last year.

Russ has requested the meeting to discuss the restructuring and its implications on my emerging 2nd Term Mayoral Manifesto, due to be published in five weeks. The reality is that Russ and his colleagues are quite ebullient, bullish even, over the discomfort they think they caused me when trying to force the trigger ballot.

With the Mayoral election due in eight weeks, they want to flex their muscles again, raising the spectre of the lack of Unison support for me.

Predictably, the unions are expressing their concerns over the restructuring and its potential impact on their members and on service delivery. I take completely the opposite view but it's not borne of rational political thinking:

- Firstly, these bastards tried to give me a rough ride and I'm going to make sure they suffer because of it;
- Secondly, there have been some absolutely appalling examples of linear thinking, obstructionism, cronyism and nepotism which the restructuring aims to address through its strong neighbourhoods focus.

Chris, on the other hand, has been smoothing the relationships with the unions [Unison!], highlighting how fatuous their opposition had been in view of my excellent working relationships with them; particularly my "no compulsory redundancies" policy.

Despite the fact that Aidan's Corporate Management portfolio covers internal operations and corporate services, and I'm not well briefed on progress with the restructuring [!], we are having a positive discussion. After about an hour Russ breaks off: *"Is that yer Gert'* [wife or partner] *over there Martin?"* I glance over at the bar and am horrified to see Carolyne with Ed. *"Looks like she's pulled,"* he adds acknowledging Ed stood next to her.

"Ha..." I laugh nervously *"That's Jim... who she's been working with. Well... at least we'll be able to get a lift home now, eh Chris?"*

Chris looks horrified.

"We'll be getting off then Russ," I try to wrap up the discussion.

"Aren't you gonna shout her over then?" he asks me, beckoning Carolyne.

Over she comes with Ed following like a gimp – Carolyne looks quite annoyed.

"Hi there... we've just finished," she says passing the ball to me and leaning forward so I can give her a kiss.

"Yes I was just saying to Russ" I nod *"We'll be able to get a lift home now, wasn't I Chris?"*

But Russ interrupts us laughing:

"Martin wants to get away... quickly... 'cos I've just criticised his manifesto and the restructuring – 'ant I Martin?" he adds with his broad South Yorkshire twang.

"Aye... you 'ave," I laugh nervously again. If only you knew you sanctimonious twat, I think to myself.

"Sit down... Carolyne [?]... " Russ stands up to make room for her.

She nods: *"At least he knows how to pronounce my name,"* she says, making reference to the strange spelling.

"Yeah... sit down... sit down Carolyne... " he repeats, smugly.

I jump in as a smokescreen: *"Well despite Russ trying to goad me... "* I smile at him *"I was just saying... that we're really happy with the way the manifesto is coming together... aren't we?"* and I look towards Carolyne, rather than Chris or Ed.

Carolyne nods again.

"Anyway..." I waffle *"... how are the kids?"* and I notice Chris has side-tracked Ed into a discussion.

"They're fine. Obviously they miss you – so we could do with getting home soon," she embellishes.

We make small talk for what seems like an age, but is probably only ten minutes *"Well... let's be getting off then,"* and I drink up my drink – motioning to Ed and Chris.

"Are we dropping Jim off?" I ask furtively gesturing towards Ed.

Carolyne mouths "yes".
But I notice Ed has become uncomfortable.
"Did he just call me Jim?" he asks Chris.
And I jump up quickly to divert attention.
"Well we'll be going then Russ," I say and we start to say our goodbyes.
"Why did he just call me Jim?" I hear Ed ask Chris again.
And I hurry us towards the door – just managing to get outside without any further problems. *"Fucking 'ell..."* I say *"... that was a close one... I thought you were supposed to be waiting outside while you texted me?"*
"We were... but you didn't respond to my text – so I came in to get you and I couldn't see you. Ed followed me in... and said he wanted a drink... [of orange juice!]"
"Well I'm glad we covered that base this afternoon then." And I laugh looking at Chris. *"Why should England tremble eh Chris? "Why should England fucking tremble?"*
As we manoeuvre ourselves into the car, Chris asks in his best Birmingham accent *"I don't know if you've ever seen a colony of ants – moving sticks – Martin?"*
But Carolyne is ahead of him *"I know... I know..."* she shouts with glee. *"...where they all work together... with every one of the ants knowing what the other one is doing..."*
And we all know where this one's going.
"That's right" says Chris.
"Well I don't think we'd get the ant hill built." And we all laugh in exasperation.

ooo

Footnote

Steve Houghton never did put his name forward... and I never asked him why...

ooo

After he was elected as MP, Ed told me that a fellow MP approached him in the House of Commons and told him it was no surprise to see him become the MP for Doncaster North. He described an occasion when he had been sat at a table on a train from King Cross and had been listening to the Mayor of Doncaster plotting [with Ed] to secure the newly vacated seat – it was Hugh Bayley, Labour MP for York Central.

A long Good Friday…

> *"Between notes, he had contemplated means of destroying her but had reached no satisfactory conclusion. His most promising scheme had involved getting a book on munitions from the library, constructing a bomb, and mailing it in plain paper to her.*
>
> *Then he remembered that his library card had been revoked."*
>
> John Kennedy Toole

Tuesday March 8th 2005…

7.45 am – Our House, Kirk Sandall

We've always been pretty keen on security in our house, fitting burglar alarms and front and rear door sensors which alert us when a door is being opened by emitting loud electronic "ding-dong" alarms. Marcey has joined Carolyne and me in our bedroom and, as we laugh and joke, she ventures:

"Y'know that fella that's living in the play room."

"Ed… " responds Carolyne.

"Yeah Ed… Well he's not very bright is he?"

"Well actually," Carolyne falters. *"He's actually really intelligent. Why do you say that?"* she's worried where this might be leading.

"Well yesterday morning" says Marcey. "When you were in the Office and Dad had gone out… I was laid in bed half asleep."

Carolyne and I look at each other, clearly concerned now with what she is about to say.

"And I heard him going out the front door. And you know how it beeps… Well I heard it beep… and I heard it beep again" she explains. *"And he kept opening and closing it over and over again. You know how it goes when the doormat gets trapped under the door as you go out… well it kept beeping… and he must have done it about ten times so, in the end, I got out of bed to do it for him.*

"As I went down stairs, I could see him on his knees trying to look under the door – he couldn't work out why it wouldn't shut properly. Anyway… as I went downstairs, he looked up at me – really helplessly – and I said it's alright I'll get it for you. And he went… Oh thank you Marcey – I think I've broken the door and it's

going to make me late for my meeting. And I said – it's okay I'll sort it and he said thank you and went. So I moved the mat, closed the door and went back to bed!"

ooo

11.45 pm – Our House, Kirk Sandall

I have just arrived home after a particularly long day. The children are in bed and Carolyne is in the living room. I ask where Ed is and she says he's in the office at the bottom of the garden, working on his selection strategy.

Ed has fitted into our routine quite easily now; during the day he is out and about meeting Party Members, and liaising with Chris and me, and from roughly 9.00 pm onwards, he comes back to our house, grabs a bite to eat and uses the office facilities until the early hours of the morning.

Having worked for myself for the seven years before I became Leader/Mayor in 2001, my office is a purpose built brick "Summerhouse" with a veranda; and has desk space, computers, telephones, a photo-copier, bookshelves, filing cabinets and seating for two workers in comfort – on swivel office chairs with wheels – three at a push.

It's a bitterly cold evening and I tell Carolyne I'll take him a coffee down and see how he's doing. I open the house door and see him slumped in the large swivel chair, which takes main stage in the office. I wave and signal that I'm making a brew but he appears deep in thought.

As I walk down the garden path with two coffees, I can see he looks exhausted; he must have had a hard day I think, as I near the veranda. I nod and smile at him, lifting the two coffees so he can see them but things just don't appear right. He doesn't acknowledge me and, although the chair is facing away from the door, Ed is slumped in it yet twisted so he is facing back towards the glass door and windows – as if he is trying to look towards me and the house without getting up.

As I step onto the veranda I can see his eyes look terrible, as if I have awoken him from a snooze. Resting the two coffees on the top rail of the veranda fence, I make a fuss of him as I open the door *"Fucking hell... have I woken you up?"* I joke. But things are definitely not right. He stares at me with the most terrible eyes which, if I didn't know better, would suggest he's drunk or drugged!

My mind is racing; something is very definitely not right and there's the most disgusting acrid smell. *"What... oh it's you"* he finally greets me as he appears to realise who I am.

"What the fucking hell have you done?" I shout and, as I look down, I can see exactly what he's done. For reasons known only to Ed, he's moved a large

convection heater, which stands on two building bricks [so it fits under one of the desks] out into the middle of the room. Presumably, so the heat is more directed at him, he has taken it off the building bricks and it is now melting through the synthetic carpet; releasing toxic chemicals into the room.

"*For fuck's sake, get out!*" I shout – but he's not listening – he's really lethargic. "*Get out!*" I shout "*You'll fucking kill yourself,*" but he doesn't respond. I kick the convection heater onto its back and reveal a metre long hole burnt through the carpet and its underlay.

"*You're gonna fucking kill yourself*" I shout again and, grabbing the back of his chair, I swing it round and drive it towards the door. As the chair's feet hit the threshold and bottom frame of the door, the chair stops dead catapulting Ed onto the veranda. He's clearly dazed and I throw the chair into the office and then run back to the house.

"*Carolyne – I need your help*" I shout, as I get him a glass of water. She joins me and we sit with Ed in the garden – calming him down and watching him for signs of poisoning – whatever they might be. We wonder whether we need to take him to hospital for a check-up.

"*I think you're over reacting a tad here, Martin*" says Ed, clearly now more <u>compos mentis</u> than he has been.

"*Well I don't at all Ed – what if tomorrow morning you're dead?*" I say, like an overprotective parent.

"*Yes – because he's not even living here... officially. Is he?*" adds Carolyne in her typical helpful manner. "*What would you do if he died?*" She continues as if he isn't here.

"*Well he wouldn't have died here!*" I reply smugly – amusing myself.

"*Well what would you have done with me?*" asks Ed, rather pathetically and feigning upset.

"*Well 'they' wouldn't have found you here,*" I say marvelling at how callous a scenario I'm painting. "*Just think of it from my perspective – I've got to support the winning candidate, not that comatose former Gordon Brown SpAd they've just found dead at the side of the road!*"

And we agree it will probably be safe for him to go to bed without a medical examination.

ooo

Wednesday March 9th 2005...

7.00 am

Ed joins us over breakfast – me, Carolyne, Beth, Joss and Marcey – so we haven't killed him. Or should I say, he didn't poison himself!

ooo

Both Chris and I have been incredibly clear about what needs doing both strategically and operationally. To be frank, it isn't difficult and I could do it standing on my head. However, last night's fiasco has underlined what a walking disaster Ed is turning out to be; and he seems completely unaware of how serious it could have been. I'm not regretting my decision to bring him to Doncaster [yet!] but I do worry what other disasters might befall us.

Although campaign-wise things are running unbelievably smoothly, it's in spite of Ed. He hasn't been communicating with us and doesn't function very well as a team player. He may be an excellent leader [arguable in itself] but one of the hard lessons I learned from playing rugby is that all team members, at all levels, need to be able to take direction from those up in the stands – they have a much clearer picture of the game. If only Ed realised, knowing one's weaknesses is actually a strength.

I can't fault Ed's work rate – he's out and about everywhere, every day, visiting the members arranged through Chris by a network of "champions"; but he isn't telling us where he is and when, so we are frequently having to make appointments blind and then struggling to get hold of him to tell him.

I am adamant that I want Ed as the MP for Doncaster North – that he will be a future Prime Minister – and that I have both his destiny [and mine] within my hands. But in pulling my own campaign together I have the logistical nightmare of dove-tailing it with Ed's – once he's selected – otherwise we will both suffer. Ed, however, certainly doesn't see the need to dovetail his campaign with mine; despite the fact we've agreed Chris will act as Election Agent for both of us and that Ed will share my campaign Headquarters [at Doncaster Trades & Labour Club] and my team of volunteer workers as well!

He's proving to be phenomenally arrogant and holds very clear views on most issues, which isn't a bad thing – but annoyingly he's taking standpoints on matters he doesn't understand or has never been involved with before.

Chris and I have made sure all our bases are covered, underlined them *and* put agreed contingencies in place wherever they are needed.

But Ed and I have now spent more than a week in each other's pockets and he is beginning to really grate on me.

ooo

7.15 am

Ed is procrastinating over breakfast about everything *he* has to get done; in particular his "Candidate's Address" letter which he has to mail out to all Doncaster North Constituency members before Sunday [13th]. As our children finish their breakfast and go upstairs to get ready for school, I take the opportunity to put him straight;

"Will you stop worrying about your mail out, Ed – either sort it out yourself or accept that I've got it covered. "But for fuck sakes stop going on about it – because you're not changing anything, you're just pissing people off. "I've told you 'till I'm sick of telling you – we have a system for mail outs – Beth, Joss and Marcey do them all the time for me. They've been doing it since they were tiny and they have a production line better than Henry Ford's."

"You keep saying this," he replies. "But can I rely on them?"

"Well first – don't let 'em hear you questioning them, Ed, or you'll have your first strike to deal with – and they're incredibly militant, they've had Carolyne to teach 'em"

"But second – and it's actually very simple. Make a fucking decision to use them... Because, if you don't... you – haven't – actually – got – a – campaign..." I spell it out. "It's as simple as that!

"Look." I'm exasperated. "One of them folds the letters... the next one stuffs them in the envelopes and the last one puts the label and stamp on the envelope... It's as simple as that. But you'll have to pay 'em – Thatcher's Children and all...!"

"Naturally – why would I expect any different – with you and Carolyne as parents," Ed replies sarcastically.

"Depending on how much packing needs to be done, I usually pay 'em £1 a sheet... when there's about 20 addresses on each sheet..."

"If they motor they can do five sheets in an hour – which is 100 addresses – you need 750 doing, which means about seven to eight hours work for them...

"... so that's two nights [ideally]... as we have to make sure we comply with the European Working Time Directive... " I add in my best Sir Humphrey Appleby voice.

"But that's why you – need – to – fucking – listen... [Minister]"

"*Because I've told you three times now... they – are – not – fucking – mind – readers... and you'll need to have a chat with them about it, because they've got school... homework... ballet... dance... football...*"

I pause to exaggerate that I'm taking a breath.

"*... and all 750 need to be posted out on Saturday at the very latest... which is <u>tomorrow</u> I state in hyperbole.*"

"*Assuming [of course] that you've metaphorically signed off the draft letter*" [knowing he hasn't]. And then literally signed off all 750 letters – because you need to make every one of 'em feels special – with it hand written from you.*"

"*Hand written!*" he replies aghast.

"*Not the entire fucking letter*" I shout, irritated by his stupidity.

"*Just the names – 'Dear John or Joan' and the 'Many thanks... Ed' bits.*"

"*Unless you want to print it – like Aidan does on his Christmas Cards,*" I laugh, thinking of the many arguments I've had with Aidan about the impersonal way he "signs" his Christmas Cards with a rubber stamp.

"*Oh god... I didn't realise,*" says Ed.

"*No... cos you're not fucking listening to us... you're just pretending you're listening. So we'll need to put a team together to do that as well.*"

"*No it's okay – I'll do it... it's probably best if I do it.*"

"*Don't talk fucking bollocks Ed. Have you ever watched GB doing his Christmas Cards?*"

"*Well no... but I know it becomes a massive problem each year.*"

"*Exactly... so trust me Ed – and for once in your fucking life listen to somebody who knows! There's about six hours continuous writing there – and that's if you can write them at two a minute – which will take some doing.*"

"*Nobody knows your script Ed – you've actually got a good script to forge – it's more of a scrawl! So Carolyne, Chris, you and me should just about do it in about one and a half hours. But you need to sign off the final draft letter – so I can print 750 of them... And you need to sign off your final draft CV – so I can print 750 of them... as well!*" I'm on a roll.

"*Which means tonight Ed. Tonight!*"

"*Can you hear me? Tonight! <u>Wednesday March 9th!</u>*" I underline, pausing so he can compute what I've said...

"*So if you can sign off your CV tonight – I can start printing tomorrow morning – tomorrow morning Ed! And then...*"

I pause for effect again.

"*And only then... can we start signing... Which means – if you take you thumb out of your fucking arse – we can start signing tomorrow afternoon!*"

Ed looks horrified.

"*Clever fucking bastard,*" I mutter as I leave the room.

ooo

7.45 am – [Fifteen minutes later]

Ed says he wants to have a word with my children. I shout the three of them down – Beth, Joss and Marcey. I've already primed them a few days earlier so they know Ed will need the work doing. But more importantly, having watched his behaviour for more than a week now, they are ready to negotiate with him.

I sit down with Carolyne on the foot of the stairs and the trio stand in the entrance to their play room – now Ed's Bedroom.

"*Ed wants to have a chat with you about his mail outs... so you need to think about what's a realistic and fair pricing structure,*" I warn them.

Ed stands in the hallway and starts to address them.

"*So your Daddy tells me you have a system for undertaking mail outs... will you undertake a 750 run for me?*" he asks, patronisingly.

"*Yes*"

"*Now... you do know what that entails... don't you?*" he patronises again.

"*Yes... we do it all the time Ed,*" says Beth [14]

"*How much will you charge me?*"

The three children go into a huddle at the back of the room – and then move into the "Bat Cave", the corridor which connects the playroom to the downstairs washroom and garage.

They return. "**We'd like Marcey to be our negotiator,**" announces Beth smiling at Marcey and glancing at me.

Marcey [10] smiles a big grin under her big, blue, almond-shaped eyes. "*What do you want mailing out and when for?*" she asks.

"*Well there's a letter and a CV... and they need to be posted for Saturday lunchtime,*" says Ed sheepishly.

"*How many pages in the letter and CV?*" asks Marcey expertly.

Ed looks at the wall... then at me "*The CV's three pages... and the letter's one*"

"*I think we need to reduce the CV to a two pager Ed,*" I interject "*So it will be 1 page each.*"

"*No staples then?*" Marcey states rhetorically, like an old hand.

"*No... apparently not,*" says Ed falteringly, clearly out of his depth.

The three go into another huddle at the back of the room.

"*Right – we'll charge you £5 a sheet*".

"What about £2 a sheet," he responds hair-trigger like.
Comically, all four turn and look at me.
"Don't look at me," I laugh. *"I'm keeping out of this"*
"What about £2 a sheet" Ed repeats.
"£5 a sheet" says Marcey. At which point Ed makes his first mistake.
"I think that's a lot more than you normally charge your daddy."
"Its £5 a sheet," says Marcey *"That's what we've agreed,"* she looks at the other two for support.
"Yes and I think that's a lot more than you normally charge your dad," re-states Ed, dropping the daddy bit now he realises he's in for a harder negotiation than he first thought.
"Yes... but he's our Dad" says Joss *"And we use his equipment."*
"And he gives us more than 24 hours' notice..." adds Beth.
"What if we were to agree to £3 a sheet?"
"We wouldn't" says Marcey, and Carolyne nearly chokes on her coffee.
"Sorry... sorry about that" she laughs. *"It went down the wrong way"*
"It's still rather a lot..." says Ed, clearly annoyed at Carolyne's laughter.
"... And it goes up the closer we get to Friday," adds Marcey.
"Four pounds a sheet is my last offer," says Ed nervously.
But Marcey knows she's got him.
"That's okay... because we've got to go to school now anyway" she says masterfully; and she leads the troop out of the room and upstairs so they can continue getting ready.
"Well that went well," I laugh to Ed.
"They're like hard bitten business men" he laughs.
"Nah – that's just Marcey. She's like a baby-faced assassin. I'll have a word with them, they'll come round."
"No it's alright – I'll pay them the £5 and learn a valuable lesson."
As we go back into the kitchen Carolyne says: *"I can't believe Marcey's just turned over the Chief Economic Advisor to Gordon Brown..."*
"Cup of tea, Minister?"

ooo

8.00 am – [another fifteen minutes later]

"So we're clear then Ed? You need to sign off the final draft letter... so I can print 750 of them... and preferably today. And you need to sign off your final draft CV... [at a maximum of two pages]... so I can print 750 of them as well... and the sooner the better... That way I can print them through the night and we can start signing

them tomorrow afternoon."

"Now we are going to be up against it... and colour takes about four times longer per page to print than black & white... So I suggest your letter is printed in colour, so they can see how pretty, and young, you are Ed! And we print your CV in black & white – particularly with it being double sided."

"Oh yes!" Ed reminds himself "I've been looking in STAPLES... and I thought it would look really nice... if we printed my CV on this card..." He goes into his room for a sample and brings out some beautiful 140-lb density card-stock.

"I agree Ed – it would look beautiful if you were printing two or three – but 750 of them and the printer will struggle."

Ed pauses – swallowing hard and looking at me ruefully. "But I've already bought it – eight packets of it."

ooo

After an unprintable conversation about Ed's predilection for quality printing materials, all paid for on MWC's business account, I agree that I will attempt to use the 140-lb density card-stock.

ooo

10.00 am – Campsmount Technology College

I am invited to the ground-breaking ceremony at Campsmount Technology College where we have agreed a new sports hall, additional learning and new community facilities. The Head Teacher, Peter Trimmingham, describes it as *"a new bridge... a bridge to the community"*.

ooo

3.15 pm

In a "catch all" article on the Mayoral and General Election, the Doncaster Star runs with the story "Labour should look locally for candidate".

"A high profile Labour councillor is urging Party bosses to look locally after reports linked a Gordon Brown advisor with a Doncaster Parliament seat. Councillor John Mounsey, who represents Adwick... wants to see a list that includes candidates from the Doncaster North area."

"Councillor Mounsey, who says he will not be applying, said: 'There is some great potential, especially in Doncaster North and they should have at least a fair representation on the shortlist'."

ooo

11.15 pm

Ed agrees the final draft letter and CV. I take it from him and he retires to his room for the night.

ooo

Thursday March 10th 2005...

3.50 am

At 4 pages per minute [4 PPM] I finish printing 750 colour "Candidate's Address Letters". I commence printing 750 double-sided black & white CVs on 140-lb density card-stock. Printing at a speed of 22 PPM this should take a maximum of two hours.

ooo

4.30 am

Having managed to print less than 100 single sides of Ed's CVs, the printer burns out.

ooo

8.30 am

I source a new HP Laser jet 4650 printer – to pick up today – in Leicester.

ooo

9.30 am

I attend a meeting with Susan Law and Barry Hearn from Matchroom Sport, with regard to holding a series of televised sporting events in the Doncaster area.

ooo

11.30 am

I attend the launch of the Doncaster Resettlement and Aftercare Provision Initiative.

ooo

12.30 pm

I leave to attend the Secondary Heads' Conference at Wetherby. I deliver a hugely supportive speech, in which I praise the progress we've achieved together over the last four years, celebrating the 13 specialist colleges we now have; a greatly improved OFSTED assessment; year on year gradual improvement; and significant improvements at two ends of education – Key Stage 1 and 'A' level.

But sadly improvements in GCSE results are in points of percentages. I tell them gradual improvement isn't enough – we all want transformational improvement. This is why I've established a single focus Directorate of Education Standards tasked with driving, supporting and facilitating significant leaps in standards – 4% per year over the next 3 years! This will take us above the national average so that together we will deliver "world class skills" for the young people of Doncaster.

I remind them of the programme I'm in the process of agreeing – more than £200 million of taxpayers' money invested in Doncaster's secondary schools. Together, with my on-going commitment to passport educational spend [from government] direct to the schools and with no top-slicing, it will really make a difference.

I point out the absurdity of the government's support for an "on-message" Labour mayor in Doncaster. We already have four prisons, yet we had to fight to stop RAF Finningley becoming 'Sangatte 2' – a new national refugee camp – following the closure of 'Sangatte' a couple of years ago. We can have a new prison built in Doncaster tomorrow, yet we have to wait until 2011 for our place in the "Building Schools for the Future" programme!

I tell them I need their support – to welcome the Education Standards Team [EST] into their classrooms and to heed the EST's carefully researched advice.

Citing my own experience within schools and my work with the Qualifications and Curriculum Authority and several awarding bodies and standards authorities, I explain why I think we may be forcing young people down incorrect learning routes – to satisfy schools' objectives rather than those of the learners' themselves.

I explain my own learning style preferences and how I believe we need to help students identify theirs and tailor their personal development plans to take account of these preferences. I tell them I'm setting up a new team within the Standards Division, the "Doncaster Careers Service": seventeen professional senior officers across the borough's schools providing the highest quality careers advice to students, and starting in year 6 to ensure we don't try and put square pegs into round holes.

I begin to crank up my presentation slightly, reminding each of the Heads of the investment made and needed, in each school. I tell them I want to be able to invest in our schools but must be able to so with confidence. It must be in the sure and certain knowledge that the schools will not then "go it alone". I cannot invest the money, to find that the assets are then "removed from DMBC" and therefore the taxpayers of Doncaster.

As I begin to [gently] read the riot act about some individuals' behaviour – I stress we are all part of a team, with collective responsibilities, and will benefit from collaborative working. As I do so, I'm reminded of the scene in The Long Good Friday when Harold Shand [Bob Hoskins], the old-fashioned kingpin of the London underworld has all the city's gangsters hung upside down on meat hooks in an abattoir...

"In the past four years I have tried to look after each and every one of you..." I begin, restating the massive investment programme taking place right across education & training in Doncaster.

Now I know that I've just compared myself to a London gangster but they do need to understand who's in charge – and so I announce a "Mayoral Pause". This is a stop to any new development proposals, while we [I] get a proper hold of the whole area of secondary and further education investment; the needs, requirements & priorities and the often competing demands being created between schools, public sector organisations such as prisons and across the borough.

I tell them the findings of this "review" will be published in "The Mayor's Education Strategy for Doncaster, with particular relevance for young people aged 14-19". To this end, I emphasise the need for them individually, and collectively, to sign up to a "Partnership Agreement" with me and I inform them that I will be holding a series of 1:1 meetings to discuss the individual implications with them and their schools.

The reality is that some of these Heads have been operating like Robber Barons and I need to get them on their own to read them their futures.

ooo

4.30 pm

Carolyne returns from Leicester with a new HP 4650 Laser Colour Printer at £987.00.

ooo

5.00 pm

Ed, Chris and Carolyne begin signing Ed's "Candidate's Address Letters".

ooo

5.30 pm

Having returned from Wetherby and having had to purchase a 180 mb RAM extension facility, I finally begin printing 750 black & white, double-sided, CVs – but choose to print them on 80-lb laser printer paper!

ooo

6.30 pm

I attend the AGM of the Doncaster Federation of Tenants and Residents and deliver a speech about my proposals to establish an Arms-Length Management Organisation [ALMO], which will also provide local solutions to deliver sustainable, decent homes for the people of Doncaster.

ooo

7.30 pm

Having finished a first run of 200 CVs, Beth, Joss and Marcey begin production-line packing Ed's Candidate's Address Letters and CVs.

ooo

9.30 pm

Printing at 22 PPM, I finally finish 750 black & white, double-sided, CVs on paper.

ooo

9.45 pm

Ably supported by Liz Jeffress; Ed, Chris, Carolyne and I finish signing Ed's Candidate's Address Letters.

ooo

Friday March 11th 2005...

11.30 am

The Labour Party National Executive announces the short-list for the Doncaster North Constituency Labour Party Seat.

ooo

8.30 pm

After a total of more than eight hours, over two nights [after school], Beth, Joss and Marcey finish packing Ed's Candidate's Address Letters and CVs – at an agreed price of £5 per sheet!

ooo

fall out   A long Good Friday...

Edward Miliband
Tel: ███████

Labour 🌹

13ᵗʰ March 2005

I am writing to you to seek your support to become the Labour parliamentary candidate for Doncaster North.

I'm hoping to meet every party member individually before the selection, but to introduce myself, I'd also like to ask you to spend a few minutes reading this letter, where I hope to show you I have the passion and dedication to represent this constituency.

I first campaigned for the Labour Party at the age of 13 in the 1983 General Election. I marched with my parents in support of the miners during the 1984 strike and joined my local Labour Party at 17. I've been a member of the TGWU since 1994 and for the last ten years, I have worked as a senior adviser to Gordon Brown, first in Opposition before 1997, then in Government.

So I've been brought up in the Labour movement. I've experienced many of the campaigns and battles that are a part of our history and I believe I can represent you in Westminster. But to do this, I know I need to become a key part of this community. So I will live here, work here and establish a fully staffed office in the heart of the constituency.

This community deserves an MP with clout at the highest level. If selected as your candidate, I will use my national experience to hit the ground running for Doncaster North. I would use all the knowledge and experience I have gained working for Gordon Brown for one purpose - to win the best deal for Doncaster North.

After two terms of the Labour government, Doncaster is on the up and we have seen some change in Doncaster North. But we all know that it is not yet enough to undo the damage done by eighteen years of the Tories. That is why we need an MP who can work with you to develop a vision for every part of this constituency – a vision that will win the argument for more resources.

You have a once in a generation opportunity to select your next Member of Parliament, who will represent your views in Westminster. I would fight the constituency's corner and wield the influence we need, working with your Labour Mayor and Labour Councillors to deliver for Doncaster North.

Over the past months, I have been working on Gordon Brown's Budget, which will be delivered on Wednesday, as I have worked on his previous eight Budgets. I hope and believe it will deliver on the priorities that matter to you.

Next Sunday, it will be for you to choose the new MP. I hope to be able to transfer the energy, commitment and drive I have shown working for Gordon Brown to working for you.

I hope to have the chance of meeting you in the coming days if I have not done so already – you can contact me any time on ███████.

I thank you for your consideration.

Ed

Friday March 11th 2005...

I email Susan Law to express my concern about the manner in which the "One Stop Shops" and neighbourhoods' agenda is being implemented – and the lack of preparation time for meetings and quality of the briefings.

I never get a reply!

ooo

Sunday March 13th 2005...

3.30 pm

Taking advantage of the respite from Ed's Campaign, Liz Jeffress has asked me if I'll move some rubbish out of her garage for her, as she needs to create some room.

This all sounds very altruistic of me – until you realise it's my rubbish! I'm a terrible hoarder, collecting all manner of articles and objects – architectural antiques, house furnishings, old books, auto-spares, fairground ephemera, objets d'art – you name it and I've got it, either in my own double garage, Liz's garage, my mother's double garage or elsewhere. Indeed, I have a well-developed network of *de facto* storage facilities across the town!

She never really expects me to throw anything away, so I am re-arranging her garage to create some more space. As a result, her back garden is strewn with parquet floor tiles, cast iron drainage hoppers and large glass roof domes – all salvaged from the former Pilkington Glass Company's Offices when they were demolished for housing.

As we work our discussion is around Ed and the selection process. The general feeling is that he is being very well received and creating a great first impression – something I've noticed Ed is obsessive about. Michael Dugher is getting around too, and while we are obviously not as well informed about how he is being received, there does appear to be a certain level of support for him.

Otherwise, there has not been a great deal of activity around any other particular candidate. Nic Dakin is out and about around the constituency but as a deputy head he has less "spare time" – although he lives less than 15 miles away in Scunthorpe.

Liz is aware that Ed is living at our house and I tell her that to ensure fairness, I have made sure I've spoken to all the candidates and offered to meet them for the allocated one hour twenty minutes; the time set by my first meeting with Michael Dugher at the end of February.

"He's certainly been active for some time" she says of Dugher. "But I think Kevin got him well primed so he could hit the ground running early on."

Liz is a very astute politician and speaks to Kevin on a regular basis so she is very well tuned in to what's happening on the ground. Having said that, it's becoming common knowledge that Kevin is supporting Michael Dugher; "sponsoring" him may be too strong but that's what Dugher is telling everybody.

"I think the Kevin link is beginning to damage him" she proffers.

"In what way?"

"Well Kevin is Marmite, isn't he?" she says. "As many as love him, hate him..."

"But I suppose that's Donny North politics – isn't it – Ted & John have been calling him from a pig to a dog for the last ten years... so it's no surprise people don't like him... is it? So, as a strategy, telling everybody that Kev wants you as his successor isn't too clever then." I gesture for her to move...

"... which is why I've kept my powder dry," I roll one of the 3 metre wide glass roof domes to a new position against the back of the garage wall.

"Why?" asks Liz.

"Because everybody loves to hate me as well – and I can help Ed more by not being too closely associated with him... In fact, I was telling Ted Kitchen last week that I don't know what all the fuss is about – that I'm not particularly impressed with Ed."

"Uh – future Prime Minister says Ted," she grunts, imitating Ted's gruff Yorkshire accent.

"Well it's worked then – because that's the message we've been sending out"

"And if Ed's Ted's bastard – then everybody's got to love him," she imitates again.

"Exactly."

"That'd make a good slogan for him..." laughs Liz "Vote for Ed – he's Ted's bastard..."

"Don't you know it!" I agree.

" Anyway... they've all taken up the opportunity to speak to me as Mayor, other than Aidan, of course, and Sandra Holland who seems astonished that I should have contacted her with the offer. It was almost as if she was saying – well who do you think you are?"

Liz: "Well what did you expect? – That's because she knows it all. And Aidan's got Ken Knight working for him – so that's a done deal"

"What?" I ask in amazement, sitting down on a box of Brazilian mahogany parquet floor tiles.

"Exactly what I said – Nora Troops told me. Ken rang her and asked if he could bring Aidan round to meet her and Derek."

"*The stupid fucking bastard. I told him not to get involved – well I told all of Cabinet not to get involved. The stupid fucking bastard.*"

"*Mind you, Ken's a big supporter of Aidan – he really rates him.*" I justify of their twin stupidity.

Liz: "*Apparently Aidan just sat there, looking nervous, saying nothing, while Ken told them how good he is.*"

"*So are Nora and Derek voting for Aidan then?*"

Liz: "*Nah – are they bollocks – Nora's voting for Ed and Derek thinks he'll be voting for Dugher*"

"*Well getting Ken involved worked then! The stupid fucking bastard,*" I say it again.

"*Well that's the best bit,*" she laughs "*Nora and Derek can't stand Ken Knight!*"

"*Good strategy...*" I summarise "*Get somebody from outside the constituency – who's not well liked in the constituency – to be your sponsor!*"

"*Absolute fucking genius*"

ooo

Monday March 14th 2005...

8.30 am – the Mayor's Parlour

8.30 am – Meeting Mrs Campbell, Mexborough School

9.20 am – Meeting Mr Morley, Edlington School

10.15 am – Meeting with Mr Johnson, Don Valley High School

ooo

As we enter the final week before the candidate selection evening there is a calm air of optimism about the place. Ed is almost self-sufficient now, particularly since I purchased the new colour laser printer which even an idiot can operate – Ed's nearly worked it out as well!

He is concentrating on 'keeping his supporters warm' and travelling around the constituency on a daily basis – making sure those who have pledged their support remain his supporters.

Once or twice a day, Chris or Ed might get a call from one of Ed's "champions" about a potential new supporter or asking for help with someone who is "wobbling". Usually this means they want to try and negotiate something for themselves or their area or just want a visit from those in power, to feel they are being courted.

In most cases such "wobbles" are addressed by a visit from Ed or Chris, or from another of the "champions" if they know them better; *in extremis* Chris and I might go to see them but in such cases, we always assess the risk first and if we need to visit, we do so from a customer care perspective [as the mayor] and deal with any MP selection issue peripherally.

ooo

10.00 am – Mayor's Office, High Street

Aidan is looking terrible. Never one to cope well with stress, he is really struggling and people are beginning to comment on it. They are also commenting that he's not doing a great deal to secure the seat and that this is starting to damage him. For the first time, people can see that he's lacking in ideas, has little energy and seems to expect the seat to be gifted to him as of right.

I still love Aidan dearly and am trying to support him as best I can. *"Look – I know it means a lot to you... but can you not see that this time it's just not your time?"*

Nothing – no response.

"What about if you do a deal to pull out and support Ed."

"No I can't! People will say I bottled it – that I've got no backbone and can't stand the stress." It's plain for anyone to see that he can't take the stress.

"They won't," I tell him, but he isn't really listening. *"Look Miliband's on a journey – he's a future Prime Minister and you're gonna have to accept that it's just not your time."*

Again, no response.

"Look at Bev Marshall. When Prescott wanted Rosie in Central, everybody thought it was a done deal and was Bev's seat as of right. But he didn't get it and everyone thinks he did a deal, even now"

"Did he?"

"I don't fucking know! But what I'm saying is that sometimes it's just not your time – and if you're half the clever politician you think you are – well, you'll realise and wait for the next one"

"But there won't be a next one. This is it – this is my time – and if I don't do it this time..." but I've started laughing and interrupt him.

"What are you laughing about?"

"You... it's like watching Mikey in the Goonies: Come on, guys, this is our time. Down here it's our time. It's our time down here. Up there it's their time," I quote from the film.

"Bastard – I'm baring my soul to you and you're fucking laughing at me!"

"I know... and I'm sorry I'm laughing Aidan... but it's funny! You're only 31 and you're throwing a teenage strop."

"<u>They are not going to just gift it to you</u> – I told you when we came back from Scotland – they're not going to gift you a seat – and definitely not when they've got a Miliband wanting it!"

"You're gonna have to contest your unwinnable first – get some experience and then you can look for a safe[er] seat. It might be different if you'd got a massive profile in Donny North – but you 'aint. You had that chance and you blew it."

But he says nothing – because he knows it's true. Aidan realises he's had his chance and blown it. I'd told him more than six months ago that Kevin's seat would be coming up and he did nothing about it. In essence, his laziness has been his undoing and, like a teenage boy, he wants to blame everyone but himself.

I'm now trying to show him how to use it to his advantage – but he doesn't want to see that either. "Look – ask for a meeting with Ed – or Gordon even. You're an unknown quantity at the moment and nobody knows how well you're gonna do. Tell him you can see his undoubted capabilities and you're prepared to stand aside for him and publicly support him... but, as a result, you'll want his or GB's support for the next, northern-based safe seat that comes up."

He is studying me – and for a moment, I think I've got him – that I'll be speaking to GB, to tell him that this is what I want [for delivering Ed]; a safe seat for my deputy.

"But you can only do this now, from a position of strength – that's what a clever politician would do... don't wait 'till you've lost – because at this moment you've not lost – but it's looking as if you're gonna get the biggest butt-fucking anybody's seen for a long time. And if you wait 'til then – then you're dead!"

No response. He is thinking.

"No I can't. People will say I bottled it – that I've got no backbone – and I've got to prove them wrong."

ooo

3.00 pm

"Snub Row as Labour Names Shortlist" cries the front page of the Doncaster Star; with the sub-heading "Lack of local candidate stinks".

"Councillor Ted Kitchen, who represents Adwick, said members were disgusted nobody from the Doncaster North Constituency had been chosen," the newspaper reports before going on to quote Ted as saying: "I don't have any gripes with the candidates on the shortlist – some are very good".

ooo

8.00 pm – The Sun Inn, Scawthorpe

Tonight I've been invited to speak at Scawthorpe Ladies Group – and in a compact meeting room I count twenty three in attendance.

Chris has done his homework – asking around – and he's been reliably informed that they're looking forward to giving me a hard time; par for the course these days. For my part, I always enjoy speaking at events like this and he knows I thrive when the audience is against me!

I deliver my usual pitch but tailor it to suit their interests and questions, with a suitable degree of self-deprecation as the circumstances demand – and the result is a real humorous but educational evening.

I keep my eye on the individual and group behaviour and dynamics and involve as many as possible and, after two enjoyable hours, my analysis is that I've got them all "on board". Not only have I got a previously cynical group of potential supporters with me, but they are all aware of Ed's name and the success we're collectively engineering for Doncaster.

Furthermore, because I enjoy group interactions like these – flirting as much as seems polite and decent – I have invited them on a follow-up visit to the Mansion House in June for cream teas, depending on my successful re-election of course!

ooo

10.30 pm – Our House, Kirk Sandall

Ed has called Carolyne into the living room. His brother David is being interviewed on Newsnight and Ed wants Carolyne's perspective on it. David is acquitting himself quite well, countering the interviewer's points and asserting a strong Government line. Ed is suitably complimentary.

"My father used to get so frustrated with him when we were young..." he ventures completely unprompted. *"Because all David wanted to do was to play football all the time; in fact, I think he wanted to be a professional footballer for quite some time"*

"Is he athletic? Because he looks athletic," says Carolyne.

"Well he's certainly more athletic than I am – I spent a lot of years undergoing operations on my feet because they weren't functioning correctly." he replies.

There is a pause for a few seconds whilst Carolyne and Ed watch David's performance, until Ed breaks the silence: *"Do you think he's better looking than me?"*

Surprised by such an undignified question, Carolyne keeps her eyes fixed on the TV, buying herself some time to consider her response...

"... Does he normally wear glasses?"

"Yes he does – he's wearing his contacts now, which he doesn't like doing."

"Yes... he's got that look of someone who normally wears glasses," and Carolyne smartly moves the conversation on to the problems I had finding a pair of spectacles that a] suited me and b] I liked.

ooo

Tuesday March 15th 2005...

10.00 am – The Mansion House, The Mayor's Parlour

Meeting with Mr Coady, Hatfield Visual Arts College

ooo

11.30 am – Mount Pleasant Hotel

Susan and I have been at a Local Area Agreement event and afterwards I take the opportunity for a coffee and a chat with her about Aidan, because I'm worried. I paint the picture as I've done the previous day with Aidan. Susan seems to grasp it straight away, summing up our discussion with:

"I know exactly what you mean, Martin – he needs to start pissing or get off the pot; and he's doing neither. He's inexperienced and he needs to get some battle scars on his back – I'll have a word with him."

ooo

1.30 pm

I have a lunchtime appointment with Ruth Redfern, who tells me she's still worried about the lack of support I am giving the Northern way. More worryingly, she admits she agrees with my analysis and unification model!

ooo

3.00 pm – The Mansion House, The Mayor's Parlour

Meeting with Mr Pattinson, Armthorpe School

ooo

Wednesday March 16th 2005...

8.30 am – The Mansion House, The Mayor's Parlour

8.30 am – Mr Blackledge, Thorne Grammar School

9.20 am – Mrs Lawrence, McAuley Catholic High School

10.15 am – Mr Storey, Hayfield School

11.10 am – Mrs Price and Mr Marfleet, Balby Carr Community Sports College

ooo

12.30 pm – House of Commons

In a 48 minute speech, the Chancellor presents a Budget of *"tax cuts that are reasonable; spending that is affordable; and [economic] stability that is paramount"*, that is *"the prudent course for Britain"*.

There are few surprises that had not already been indicated in his 2004 pre-Budget report. The increase in the threshold on stamp duty is greater than that forecast by commentators, as is the amount of the Council Tax rebate to households with pensioners.

ooo

fall out   A long Good Friday...

1.30 pm – The Mansion House, The Mayor's Parlour

1.30 pm – Dr Simmonds, Danum School Technology College

2.00 pm – Mr Rowsell, The Rossington All Saints Church of England Aided School

3.30 pm – Mr Blakemore, North Doncaster Technology College

4.30 pm – Mr Wakeling, Hungerhill School

ooo

6.30 pm – Our House, Kirk Sandall

Ed has drafted a "Budget Briefing" paper, to explain its implications for Doncaster North, and to be sent to all Doncaster North Labour Party members. Plus, having previously "negotiated" a fee of £5 per sheet for a system he now knows he can rely on, he has willing workers ready to prepare his mail outs.

I think this could prove to be a master stroke for Ed. The members will receive a personal budget briefing the day before Sunday night's selection meeting – from Gordon Brown and Ed Miliband. Ed has put a photograph of himself with GB on the front *'... discussing the Budget with the Chancellor Gordon Brown on the night before the Budget – 15th March 2005'* – nice call!

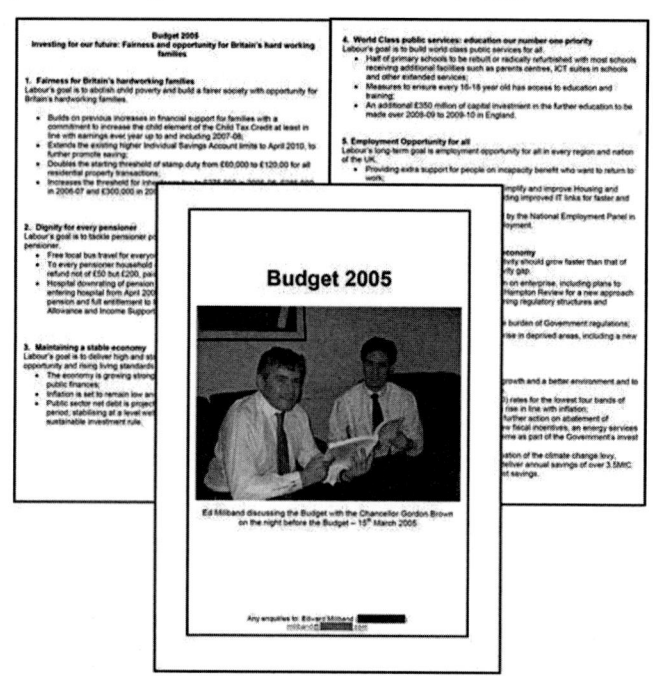

11.30 pm – The Old Summerhouse, Our House

Ed's been working pretty hard during these past few weeks, getting to know a new Labour party constituency and its members' idiosyncrasies; the town's economic, social and environmental drivers; and the exacting nature of the selection strategy Chris and I have put together for him.

In addition to this workload, however, he's had to be constantly "on-call" for Gordon Brown, particularly with regard to his budget preparation work and following today's Budget at Westminster Ed appears de-mob happy and the most relaxed I have seen him since I brought him to Doncaster.

We are working late in my office while I put the finishing touches to my "Mayoral Manifesto" and Ed is looking at whether he can dovetail any of the bigger picture national and global issues with my city initiatives.

He's now concentrating his energies on preparing his candidate's address for Sunday – his support base is fairly strong and appears solid. I suspect that between 150 and 200 people will attend so we need to focus on getting around 100+ supporters there. Ed remarks that Chris is putting in some sterling work to make sure all his supporters are clear about the time they have to be there and, if needed, they have a lift to take them.

He's been rehearsing his speech with me but is getting annoyed because I'm fairly ambivalent about its content.

"The thing is..." I argue in my defence "... people don't actually listen to what you're saying – it's the syntax, diction and tone that matter..."
They want to have confidence in your delivery – not necessarily what you're saying – although if you tell 'em you want to bring back hanging they'll carry you out above their heads!"

"A good speech won't win you the selection – but a bad speech will certainly lose it for you."

"People want an authentic leader. They don't want to think you're making a speech to them, they want to think you're having a conversation with them; a discussion even. So you've got to relax and engage with them."

Ed tells me he's very worried about the war; whether those attending will give him a hard time over Blair's decision and whether Hans Blix and the weapons inspectors should have been given more time to look for the weapons of mass destruction.

"Just answer as a politician Ed – not an officer"
"In what sense?"
"Very simply – you need to forget you're an ex-SpAd."
"Do you really think I'm stupid? Do you have such a low opinion of me that this is the level of advice you are giving me?"

"It's a simple message but one that's sometimes hard to grasp."

He looks at me as if I'm the devil.

"Let me give you an example – in January, when the floods hit Carlisle, Elliot Morley went on TV and gave a perfectly technical, intellectual defence of the floods rather than a political response"

But I can see that for all his intelligence he still doesn't get what I'm saying.

"Let me explain further, Minister," I use my best Sir Humphrey Appleby voice "Perhaps a less eurocratic, less dispassionate, less objective, less technocratic, more emotional response was what might have been required by the viewer."

He looks at me with disdain this time.

"The public were looking for a more simplistic, less academic response that commented on the scale of the disaster, warnings given, response times, lives lost, businesses damaged, community impact... a more emotional response – one that physically related to their lives."

"Yes, but you've just got a downer on Elliot Morley," he says dismissively.

"Yes – but that's because he's a TWAT!"

Ed laughs: "You really don't take prisoners do you?"

"Look – that bastard conned us out of £500,000! As he and his officers kept asking us for more information and more work – placing us on a "suspension list" for nearly a year. And he was more interested in promoting Lib Dem and Tory projects than a socialist authority on his doorstep" I begin to rant. "The man doesn't have a political bone in his body – and never did! I knew him when I worked for the Wildlife Trusts in Lincoln – I detested him then and I fucking hate 'im now."

"All he's after is what's good for Elliot Morley – and he just does and says what his Civil Servants fucking tell him."

"That's all very well Martin," he cuts me off mid-tirade, "but how does it relate to Sunday's selection process?"

"Look, I'm not going to draw you a map Ed, you're gonna have to do your own navigating on this one."

He smiles knowingly.

"Last week you asked me to come and look at David debating climate change on Newsnight with a climate change expert – remember?"

And I can see he remembers our discussion immediately.

"I told you then. He didn't have a political debate, as he should have done as a politician... he got involved in an intellectual joust with another academic... didn't he?"

He smiles knowingly again.

"Well fucking learn from it then."

Thursday March 17th 2005...

8.15 am – Mansion House, The Mayor's Parlour

Meeting with Mr Trimmingham, Campsmount Technology College.

ooo

10.30 am – Our House, Kirk Sandall

Ed has asked Carolyne if he can go through his speech for Sunday's selection meeting with her. She listens to what he's saying and comments on a couple of issues. Ed is quite hyper about presenting to Carolyne and tells her how he is in awe of Robert Kennedy.
"Who's Robert Kennedy?" she asks sarcastically.
"He's an American politician who was assassinated!"
"Really" gushes Carolyne, annoyed that he actually thinks she doesn't know. "Because I thought..." she continues "... that everyone in the world knows him as Bobby Kennedy and you need to be aware of that before Sunday – because you're talking to people in South Yorkshire not a set of intellectuals in a lecture theatre"
"Well I'm not going to dumb it down for them," he replies.
"It's not a case of dumbing it down," she retorts. "It's more a case of blocking people's attentiveness – if everyone knows him as Bobby, then call him Bobby. Otherwise you're introducing a distraction into their listening patterns – a barrier you don't need."
But Ed is clearly irked that she has a view about his beloved Robert or indeed his interpersonal skills. "Have you thought about what you'll be wearing when you address all these people?" she asks, expertly changing to a subject she knows he can't [or won't] question her opinion on.
"Well I thought I'd wear my brown corduroy suit and a blue shirt."
"The blue shirt with the button-down collar?" She's seen it several times over the previous few weeks.
"Yes," he answers enthusiastically.
"Oh! – you'll look a music or science teacher in that outfit – have you got anything smarter?"
"Well I like that suit," replies Ed, clearly hurt that she should be so frank with him. "But yes – I have another smart jacket with patches on the elbows."
"Oh my God, no!" she gasps. "You'll look like a geography teacher in that!
"Look – I'm sure that you understand how first impressions count... These are

good, honest, South Yorkshire people you are talking to – asking to vote for you. You need to look the part as well as saying the right things"

"Well, what should I wear then?"

"You need to be wearing classic, good quality, business attire – like I dress Martin in"

"So do I have to buy a new suit?"

"Yes, you most certainly do" she says, exasperated that he should be such a skinflint.

"Unless you want to borrow one of Martin's?" she giggles. "In which case you'll look like that small boy playing Tom Hanks in BIG!"

"No – I don't think that would do my chances any good," Ed concedes.

"But stop worrying – you've no need to worry – you'll get your wear out of it... if you get selected!" she laughs, delighted at the opportunity to throw him a morsel of doubt.

"Can you help me then?" he asks pathetically. So she agrees she'll dress Ed as well, and they will go to the Yorkshire Outlet, to "Suits You" a shop that sells decent quality, marked down, last season's suits.

ooo

2.00 pm

I attend the funeral of Henry Green [Lib-Dem].

ooo

Friday March 18th 2005...

8.00 am – The Mayor's Parlour

Meeting with Mr Hoyle, Ridgewood School

ooo

12.30 pm – The Yorkshire Outlet

Carolyne takes Ed shopping for either a charcoal, or navy, classic-cut suit and a white shirt with double cuffs. As they enter the shop Ed's like a fish out of water; Carolyne likens it to shopping with a five year old boy. When she turns she finds he's disappeared and is meandering aimlessly around the store.

Having managed to extract his measurements, they chose a suit for him to try on, but Carolyne bursts out laughing when she sees him. It's much too tight in the crotch area making him look as if he has padded pants on. Like a mother getting her son ready before the start of a new term, she tells the assistant she thinks the cut of the trouser isn't right and asks if they can see something less 'streamlined'.

The second suit is a classic navy single-breasted style with single pleat trousers – this works fine but Ed almost chokes at the price tag. Moving him on, she gets him a bright white shirt, which she says will complement his lovely olive skin and black hair and make him look healthy and smart.

Like a bad actor in a 1950s B-Movie – he smiles to himself smugly.

ooo

2.30 pm – Our House, Kirk Sandall

When they arrive "home", Carolyne realises her mistake – that when he said he was okay for ties, she shouldn't have trusted his judgment. Thankfully, she's made sure I have lots of really nice ties Ed can borrow and chooses a red silk tie with small dark red ovals/spots in the pattern.

ooo

4.00 pm – Our House, Kirk Sandall

Despite keeping his supporters warm and everyone remaining extremely confident, Ed's getting jittery; he's now worried he doesn't know the cost of a typical shopping trolley. As a result, he's decided he must know the price of a pint of milk and other staples and is checking various items with Carolyne.

ooo

Saturday March 19th 2005...

10.00 am – Coffee morning with Caroline Flint

12.00 pm – Question time event at Barnardos

7.00 pm – St Patrick Day's Dinner – Earl of Doncaster with Sir Patrick Duffy and Rosie

Sunday March 20th 2005

5.00 pm – Our House, Kirk Sandall

The evening of the Labour Party selection is finally upon us. It's a month now since Kevin announced he was standing down and the activity has been frenetic in some quarters, calm and considered in others. Chris and I are very relaxed and extremely positive about Ed's chances. He is less confident.

Ed has arranged to make his own way there from our house – having been given everybody's best wishes for the evening. Carolyne and I are taking Liz Jeffress with us and have arranged to meet Chris Taylor there; however, Chris and I will sit apart from each other [just in case!].

ooo

6.00 pm – Bullcroft Memorial Hall, Carcroft

Nobody does process like the Labour Party and, as you would expect, tonight is a very formal affair. The Constituency Chairman, retired head teacher David Oldroyd, is running it like a well-ordered school assembly. For their parts, the members are both excited at the evening's prospects and conscious of their responsibilities in selecting their next Member of Parliament.

With two hundred seats laid out, the Chairman is expecting a bumper attendance. The chairs are arranged in two phalanxes – a hundred on the left of the room and a hundred on the right – with a central aisle between the two. At the head of the room is the stage area, where a microphone and lectern stand adjacent to a table and a seat with a carafe of water and a glass for each of the candidates.

After receiving nearly fifty applications, the Labour Party's National Executive has eventually produced a short list of six preferred candidates for this evening's selection process:

- Dakin, Nic — the ex-Leader of North Lincolnshire Council;
- Donnelly, Elizabeth — the TUC rep on the East Midlands Assembly;
- Dugher, Michael — the ex-Special Advisor to Geoff Hoon;
- Holland, Sandra — the ex-Office Manager to Caroline Flint MP;
- Miliband, Edward — the Special Advisor to Gordon Brown;
- Rave, Aidan — the Deputy Mayor of Doncaster.

The Chairman proclaims that this is the last chance for everybody to use the lavatories before the meeting commences and the door is [metaphorically] "locked".

After a last flurry of activity, he formally pulls the meeting to order and, with great aplomb, announces that the doors will now be closed. Anybody arriving late will not be allowed to take part in the evening's activities.

I finish counting the room and look at Chris – "a hundred and fifty five" he mouths at me – I'd made it a hundred and sixty, so we need about 80 votes then.

The Chairman begins explaining the format the evening will follow and that they must decide how much time the candidates are given for questions. This is immediately followed by a proposal from ▓▓▓▓▓▓▓▓▓▓▓▓, an active, very militant member who always seems to take a skewed view of issues;

"I'd like to propose, Chair," begins ▓▓▓▓▓ in his harsh Irish drawl, *"ten minutes for questioning sir,"* he looks around at the meeting smugly.

"Thank you for that ▓▓▓▓▓*,"* replies David Oldroyd, barely concealing the pre-ordained nature of their interaction. *"Are there any further proposals?"*

None are forthcoming, so David immediately moves to a show of hands and decrees that the motion is carried and candidates will be given ten minutes for questions.

Lots are drawn to establish the order of presentations and the candidates are then led to an ante-room to ready themselves.

The Chairman asks if he can have nominations for the positions of "tellers" – to supervise the distribution and collection of completed voting papers after the presentations.

ooo

Michael Dugher is one of the first to speak and delivers a fairly predictable presentation, using his notes and delivering from the lectern.

As we move to the questions and answers, they focus, unsurprisingly, on the war and the advice he has given [or not given] to Geoff Hoon.

Michael is doing quite well – taking a particularly firm stand-point in response to one question insisting: *"it's fundamental that a country controls its own borders"*. It seems rather xenophobic to me and geared towards some of our more extreme members, but it's working; there are quite a few nods in the audience.

ooo

7.30 pm

It's Ed's turn now – the first couple of candidates have made their presentations, which were fairly pedestrian, and the audience have been very gentle with their questioning. Thanks to Carolyne, he's looking good, modelling a classic-cut navy suit, a white double-cuff shirt with collar stays and cuff-links, and the defining point for the entire ensemble, one of my best silk woven red ties.

Ed walks purposefully to the front of the room, where the microphone and lectern are. As he readies himself for his presentation, he makes himself comfortable by taking off his jacket– throwing it onto a table at the edge of the stage.

Pouring himself a glass of water, he begins speaking to the audience, all very much as planned, without referring to his notes. But instead of standing at the lectern, he becomes more animated and walks to the front of the stage and then physically into the audience – up and down the central aisle.

I look at Carolyne, who seems perplexed, then make eyes at Chris who returns my look of surprise: What the fuck's he doing? Where's he going?

"This is a bit off script," I whisper to Carolyne.

"And a tad contrived," she returns.

Contrived or not, this might be too much for a fairly conservative constituency, I think to myself – it's either gonna blow it or make it for him.

I begin to worry. He's left his microphone on the stage and the acoustics aren't brilliant – what if the rest of the audience can't hear him?

But as I look around it seems to be working. He's projecting himself well and the audience seem to be engaging with him. He's using all the right words and the delivery's working as well; he's engaging with both sides, making eye contact with as many people as possible; he's turning around and around so he's speaking to the front and the back and the sides – nobody's left out.

Seven minutes later it's over and to a very enthusiastic applause from the audience. What could have been a nightmare approach, had he got it wrong, turns out to have been a master stroke...

Phew! Now let's just get through the question and answer session.

The questions are pretty mundane. As expected, one asks for his view on invading Iraq. Ed gives what I consider to be a perfunctory answer – clearly stating that it was Blair's decision to make.Deliberately appealing to the anti-war feeling, he tells us we would all have wanted to give Hans Blix and the weapons inspectors more time...

Then comes a fairly left field question, typically it's from Ted Kitchen, asking if Ed will be buying a property in the constituency and living here with his constituents – unlike his brother David, who simply rents a property in South Shields as a front, when it's actually his Constituency Office.

This isn't entirely unexpected as Ted has asked it with monotonous regularity for the previous three weeks. Ed is very clear that, although he can't be his brother's keeper, if selected, he will definitely be buying a property in the constituency and looks forward to getting to know all the members. As an addendum, he says he would like to target new members and, if elected, he hopes to get the Doncaster North membership up to more than 350 in his first year!

"There's a target he didn't need to set," whispers Carolyne.

"It can be the first one he fails to hit..." I answer.

It's Aidan's turn now.

As he steps up to the lectern I make eye contact with him and smile. He looks terrible; he's in a cold sweat and appears petrified. His actual presentation isn't bad but his whole demeanour is defeatist; there's no spark, no humour, and certainly no passion.

ooo

9.15 pm

After nearly two and a half hours the presentations have finished and David Oldroyd announces we will now move to the vote.

There are one hundred and fifty six members present, he instructs. He explains that the vote will be an exhaustive ballot. Each member will cast a single vote for his or her favorite candidate; if no candidate has more than 50% of the votes cast at the end of the first round, then the candidate with the lowest number of votes will drop out and we will move to a further round of voting. This process will be repeated for as many rounds as necessary until one candidate has a majority.

"Seventy eight is what's needed then..." I say to those around us.

"What for?" says a voice behind me... [!] I make my mark for Ed and show my paper to Carolyne and Liz, so they can see who I have voted for; and then hold it above my head so a teller can come and collect it. As I do so I look around the room and many people are holding their papers up.

The Chair asks if there are any outstanding – but they've all been handed in. The meeting is getting restless so the Chairman decrees that there will be a fifteen minute adjournment, while the tellers count and reconcile the papers; there's a mad rush for the door as everyone races for the toilets. As I make my way there, everyone wants to talk about the candidates. Nic Dakin is in front of me and I congratulate him on his presentation.

"What on earth are you talking about Martin?" he says. "It was bloody awful!"

I smile at him: *"Well I thought you did well, Nic,"* I lie.

I continue on my way but now Aidan's in front of me.

"How do you think it went?" I ask him.

"Shite!" he responds.

"Are you alright?"

"No – I feel fucking terrible"

ooo

9.25 pm

As I make my way back from the toilets, I share my thoughts with David Oldroyd, who observes that there's a huge sense of excitement and anticipation in the air.

While I'm speaking to him I notice a slight disturbance at the entrance – central to which is a long-time member of the party and an ex-rugby playing friend of mine. More worryingly, Ed is on the periphery of it.

I grab Ed's hand and shake it: *"Well done Ed – a good presentation – good luck with the vote,"* then I steer him away from the argument.

ooo

As I shepherd Ed back into the main room Pat Hall makes an immediate beeline for him. *"Let me look a' you Ed, sweetheart,"* she commands in her delightfully honest Glaswegian [Gorbals] drawl. *"Well y' dae look awful nice Ed…. Ach – that's a brammer bit ay clootie,"* she says, delighting in her native tongue.

Ed looks confused – and smiles politely.

"Ah said… that's lovely piece of cloth," she repeats [in English] caressing his jacket cuff with the back of her hand. Pleased she's now holding court, she bellows to the onlookers: *"Aye… I've seen him many times ower th' past few weeks an' he has ne'er looked sae stylish!"*

But they are clearly having difficulty understanding her as well… Frightened she might lose her audience, she now adopts her version of the Queen's English *"But you haven't been honest to us – have you Ed dearie?"* she turns round, very pleased with herself for rumbling him. *"You haven't dressed yourself tonight have you?*

"Eh… look at his shirt, it has collar stays and he's wearing some lovely cuff links…" she stops herself mid-flow and leans towards him. *"Carolyne's dressed you hasn't she!"* she whispers *"Because you're dressed like she dresses Martin…"*

Although he's laughing with her, Ed beats a hasty retreat.

"In fact, that's Martin's tie you're wearing," she hollers after him.

"Aye, I rumbled him…" she says to those still bothering to listen *"… I rumbled him…"*

ooo

fall out   A long Good Friday…

I've gone back to the argument. It's a Party Member claiming he's been delayed on his way home from work and has now been told he can't enter the meeting or the main hall nor take part in the vote.

He is extremely agitated and begins shouting that he wants to vote for Ed Miliband – insisting he'll be resigning from the party now. He appeals to me for assistance.

I manage to assuage his anger somewhat – partly by telling him Ed's got it in the bag anyway – but I promise I'll call him tomorrow to have a chat.

ooo

9.35 pm

With a great deal of satisfaction David Oldroyd formally pulls the meeting back to order and announces that we will now move to the first count and that the doors are to be "locked" again.

He declares the first round of votes as follows: *"Ed Miliband 100 votes…"* and he pauses slightly, knowing that means Ed has "won". That's it, I think to myself, he's done it – we've done it. *"Michael Dugher 38 votes; Sandra Holland 9 votes; Aidan Rave 7 votes; Nic Dakin 1 vote; Elizabeth Donnelly 1 vote;"*.

But the audience is too busy cheering and celebrating.

Milband	100
Dugher	38
Holland	9
Rave	7
Dakin	1
Donnelly	1
Spoilt	0
Total	**156**

ooo

10.00 pm

After a suitably triumphalist introduction, the Chairman congratulates Ed on his victory and asks him to make his inaugural speech as the Prospective

Parliamentary Candidate for the Doncaster North Constituency Labour Party.

Ed delivers his acceptance speech with due deference to his fellow candidates – and the audience rewards him with a huge round of applause. I give him a hearty handshake and congratulations, saying I hope we can develop a strong working relationship.

As you might expect there is a huge throng around him for some time with several members keen to get in early with their on-going grievances, grumbles and requests for parliamentary assistance. Others simply want to congratulate him and discuss the forthcoming campaign[s].

The room is a hive of activity and Chris and I exchange glances.

He sidles over to me. *"Job done,"* I tell him.

"It's interesting," he exaggerates his accent again, *"that most of the other candidates are more magnanimous in their defeats,"* and he nods at a thoroughly dejected Aidan skulking away at the far side of the room.

"Arr..." I return – imitating Aynuk and Ayli, the mythical Black Country characters. Chris starts to analyse some of the finer points in our strategy. *"Fucking 'ell Chris"* I tell him *"Let's 'ave an hour or two off."*

"Ahh... I'd better get a round in then," he replies

ooo

10.30 pm – Carcroft Village Working Mens' Club

Chris and I manage to extract Ed while relocating the more enthusiastic members to the Working Men's Club over the road. Carolyne has already texted me to tell me several members have gone there for a drink and, as I open the door for Ed, we are greeted with a huge cheer from a now packed club.

John Healey and his wife Jackie are in attendance – wishing to support Ed again – and John offers to buy Chris, Ed and me a drink. Despite being an ex-rugby player I have never been a particular big drinker but even I see the need for a communal glass of beer in celebration. Not Ed though – he is either teetotal or, worryingly for me, he doesn't see the need to celebrate.

ooo

11.30 pm – Our House, Kirk Sandall

Back home Carolyne is mildly dejected by Ed's refusal to have a glass from a newly opened bottle of bubbly.

Monday March 21st 2005...

10.30 am – Meeting with Mr Jones, Hall Cross [Upper] School

ooo

In readiness for my Mayoral campaign I have booked two rooms at the Doncaster Trades & Labour Club for three months to use as my Campaign Headquarters. It is clear Ed has no infrastructure in place over and above the Party's campaigning infrastructure and we have decided he will use both my Campaign HQ and my volunteer workers.

Although he has been party to this decision, and agrees to it in principle, Chris is slightly nervous about the administrative requirements of our "sharing" an office together and the accountancy demands on him as our Election Agent. But knowing Chris as well as I do I trust him implicitly and am confident he will complete the correct paperwork as required under the Representation of the People Act 1983.

ooo

Tuesday March 22nd 2005...

10.00 am – Bentley Sure Start Centre

This morning I've been invited to officially open the Bentley Sure Start Centre and because it's in Ed's prospective constituency I have taken him with me, as I dovetail his campaign with mine. Ed has already told me how he played a major role in the design and implementation of the Labour Government's Sure-Start programme and is keen to see how the policy is working on the ground.

I have always been a massive supporter of Children and Early Years Centres and see educating people on pregnancy, child-care, good parenting, parent & family support and health & nutrition as key tenets of successful and healthy communities. I have run several cooking sessions at such establishments, demonstrating low-cost, healthy and tasty meals for families. Jambalaya is a speciality of mine that seems to go down great guns when I show people how to prepare and cook it, before giving them the ingredients to cook it for their families at home afterwards.

It's a fairly run-of-the-mill opening with a plaque unveiling, commemorative tree-planting and bouquet presentation photo-opportunities. I introduce Ed to those present as the prospective new Member of Parliament [after the elections in May of course]; he delivers a pretty innocuous speech about his policy experience and duly takes an *ad hoc* position in the proceedings.

The most significant aspect of Ed's appearance is his clothes. He is wearing a poor quality grey pinstripe suit, which is crumpled, dirty shoes, poor quality shirt and one of my [badly tied] ties – but what do you expect now Carolyne's not dressing him!

ooo

Thursday March 24th 2005...

Today marks six weeks until the Mayoral and General Elections [Thursday May 5th 2005]; as a result, Doncaster Council enters a period of election purdah.
Purdah is the time in the UK between an announced election and the final election results. It offers government departments the chance to develop guidance and policy. It also prevents central and local government from announcing any new or controversial schemes which could be seen as advantageous to any candidates or parties in the forthcoming election, or might commit any incoming administration to policies it wouldn't support.

ooo

6.30 pm – Stainforth 'Old Folks' Centre'

Ed and I have been invited for an evening of bingo at the 'Stainforth Old Folks' Centre' – well, what I actually mean is that I have an invite to play bingo and I've taken Ed with me.

I actually have a standing invitation to bingo from Stainforth Labour "Town Councillors" Julia and Ken Keegan. In fact, I have functioned as a *de facto* 'bingo caller' on previous evenings at the Old Folks' Centre! Both Julia and Ken are stalwart community organisers and ask if I want to say anything to the audience – I take the opportunity to thank the couple for all their hard work and to introduce their prospective new Labour Party MP.

We sit down at a table with a dozen or so others, exchanging pleasantries as we ready ourselves for the first game. Once it begins a deathly hush falls on the room, only to be broken by a successful *"'ere y'are"* cry as one of the competitors gets a winning number.

In one such breather, one player tells us how she had been *"sweating on six forever just then"*. As I translate to a confused Ed, I remark that they take their bingo seriously in Doncaster and tell him that on no account should we disturb their game. One lady is playing eight bingo cards – and still finds the time to point out when I fail to mark a called number!

After half a dozen games Julia announces that we will now have a fifteen minute 'comfort-break' – and I buy tea, coffee and biscuits for those sat at our table.

I notice Ed is struggling to have a meaningful conversation with anyone and seems to be favouring very low–brow, almost bland discussions. I hear him tell one lady how much difficulty he is having keeping up with the numbers being called and that he is struggling marking his bingo-card. I take the opportunity to mention the lady's winter fuel allowance with coalfield regeneration – and Ed's involvement with the drafting of such policies – giving him an entrée into a more purposeful conversation with her.

As the second bingo session begins the evening has a nice sense of comradeship to it, and Julia has already briefed me that we are among Labour supporters. After a further couple of games Ed suddenly surprises us all… *"Yes – that's me!"* he cries.

I find it difficult to hide my surprise – doesn't he know that we aren't here to win! The teller comes out to our table and begins to count the numbers off Ed's card back to the caller.

"Three…" yes.
"Twenty eight…" yes.
"Fifty seven…" yes.
Things are looking good.

"Seventy three..." No!
"NO" No?
"And eighty seven..." Yes.

There's a collective expression of dismay from the room... disappointment that someone should have made the call wrongly, but also excitement that we are still in the middle of a game.

Ed looks horrified. No? NO? He's made a huge fool of himself. The mood is unsettled and I sense the need to make light of Ed's *faux pas*...

I stand up: *"I'm terribly sorry about that..."* I begin, garnering their attention. *"Can I apologise for our new prospective MP's behaviour..."* and I bow, for some reason!

I look towards a suitably embarrassed Ed *"... but he's not very good with numbers y'know"* – and there's a ripple of amusement around the room.

"He's only Gordon Brown's Chief Economic Advisor at the Treasury."

"Oh that's alright then," says Julia, joining in. *"There's no need to panic – as long as my pension's safe,"* and there's a good laugh in the room.

The bingo caller announces that now we know our pensions' are safe, he'll do a recap of the numbers called so we can begin anew... As he does so, I lean across and whisper: *"My fault Ed – I should've told you... we're not here to win – even if your cards full!"*

ooo

10.15 pm – Our House, Kirk Sandall

Ed and I have returned and, whilst he nips down to the office, I regale Carolyne with his prowess with a bingo card! We are sat in the living room with the TV on. Ed comes back and joins us, sitting next to Carolyne on the big settee.

The TV is showing something about the forthcoming Easter celebrations and the fact the Jewish religion does not observe Easter because it does not recognise Jesus as anything more than a mortal man.

Using this as a prompt, Carolyne asks Ed:

"Do you celebrate Christmas or Hanukkah Ed?"

But before he has chance to answer her *"Anyway – what's Hanukkah about then?"*

Ed seems surprised by the question. *"Well,"* he begins cautiously *"Hanukkah is a Jewish holiday. It's the celebration of a miracle... years and years ago there were these people called the Maccabees. And they go into the desert..."* but then he starts to trail off and mumble a little.

"Well... it's all got to do with the festival of light... and that's when we sing... Dreidel, Dreidel, Dreidel, I made you out of clay."

Carolyne looks at him bemused – he clearly doesn't know or understand...

"You've just quoted Ross from Friends!" she exclaims.

Ed smiles, giggles a little and changes the subject – starting to talk about Ariel Sharon.

I give him a knowing smile...

ooo

Friday March 25th 2005...

9.30 pm – Good Friday – Our House

Chris, Ed and I are having a 'sweep up' meeting to make sure we are happy with the 'joint' campaigns we are running.

Chris tells me he thinks we need to find Ed somewhere to live; not least because he needs an address to register at if he wants to stand for election. Ed seems more than happy to continue with the arrangement we have, but I point out, gently, that the tensions of having us all living under the same roof are beginning to drive us [all] mad! I suggest he gives Carolyne a specification for his new house and she can draw-up a collection of houses he may wish to view.

ooo

11.00 am

I spend most of the rest of the day pulling together the images for my Manifesto and finalising the designs for my leaflet campaign, ready to begin printing them. To be honest, it's more for the benefit of the Labour group, the MPs and their constituencies and Wards than for the public. Having said that, we have produced a brilliant document [again] and I am really proud of its content and appearance.

Ed is playing around with the idea of developing a Haiku type poem to stimulate our thought processes and as a strapline to encapsulate my campaign – and his. After a relatively short period of time we come up with:

Doncaster's on the up
It didn't happen by accident
Just think what might be possible
With the additional strapline of 'Don't put it at risk'.

I'm really pleased with this and, to be quite frank, it's the first time I've seen Ed as less of the liability I've been beginning to think he is [!].

A Haiku for Ed poses more of a challenge – how do we develop something around the man and his accomplishments or values when he has none [accomplishments that is!]. We play around with ideas for what seems like hours until he finally settles for:

The Labour Government's working
Never forget what the Tories did... [and would do again]
The risks are too high not to turn out

I think it's bloody awful and could probably even be harmful – but Ed seems desperate to find his own Haiku and appears wedded to it.

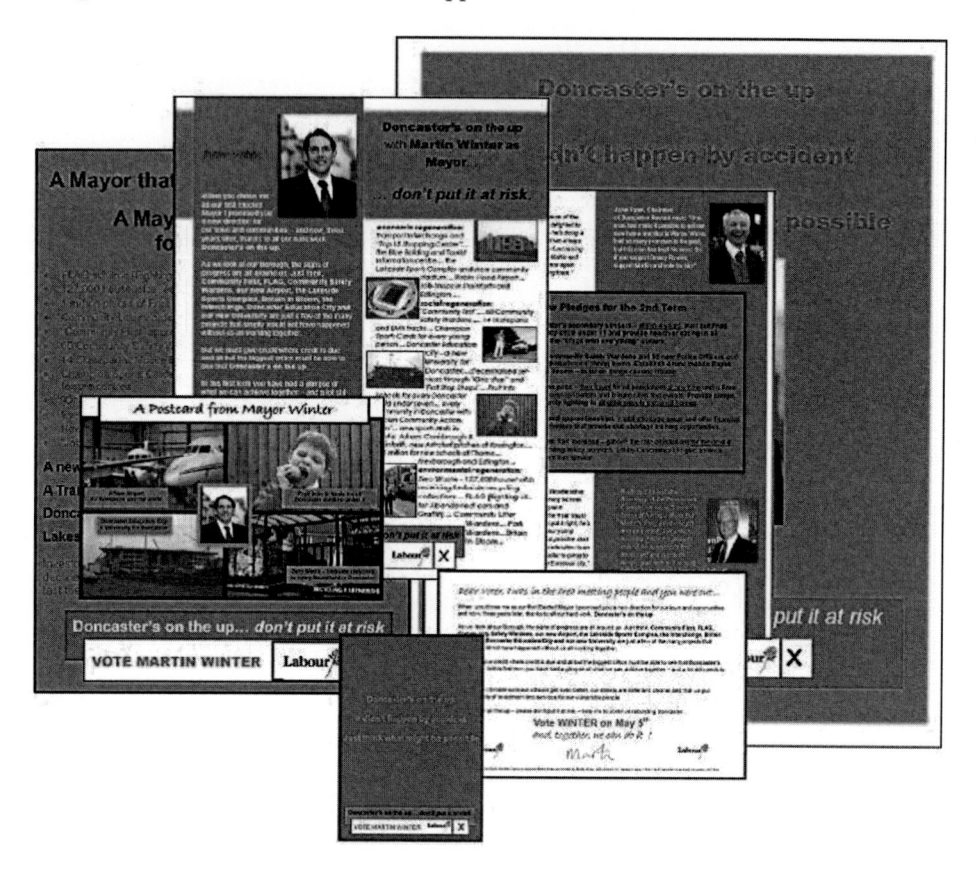

Having said that, I've found the whole process illuminating in terms of Ed's way of operating and his intellectual grasp of situations – he is unbelievably naïve about the world's workings and the motivations of individuals and organisations; he is also culturally immature, which I find strange for an Oxbridge graduate. Yet he has an incredibly sharp mind and quickly taps into an extensive filing cabinet of historical lessons or equivalents.

Following on from our earlier discussion, and very much from left field, Ed suddenly begins asking me about what drives me, questioning my beliefs, my political ideals, principles, heroes and heroines.

I tell him I have no over-riding doctrine that drives my behaviours, other than a desire to change people's lives for the better – and to take a pragmatic approach to finding solutions to problems. But I find his questioning slightly insulting given that many political leaders seem to be only concerned with self-preservation; by now he should have realised that I am more concerned with delivery.

"Well you certainly don't worry about upsetting people," he says.

"That's why I have no aspirations to become an MP, " I tell him *"The majority are just glorified social-workers; they're mostly insincere little shits, ever beholden to the party-machine and too busy trying not to upset people because they have to feed their families and myriad hangers-on."*

"Hee hee! Like I said..." he laughs in response *"But that's a suicidal approach – you have to be part of a larger family with greater responsibilities."*

"Of course I do – and I am – so I suppose I class myself as a proper, socialist, although a pragmatic one – so I won't live or die by my beliefs, if that's not too simplistic."

"But you must have some kind of underlying belief or ideals" he asks again, almost in desperation.

"Of course I do... it's just that sometimes you have to make sacrifices to achieve what you want to achieve – that's how the world operates, you can't be too wedded to a particular approach, otherwise you'll never succeed. Politics has to be about compromise."

"To be a leader, a 'Mayor', you have to be the 'General' – the one that leads from the front, the one that leads them into battle, and that means that you have to be prepared to be injured. "But we avoid injury – and train our politicians in the art of how to avoid accepting responsibility!"

"Being a mayor isn't about ability, it's about responsibility – and that means being responsible for the bad decisions as well. Just wait until they send you on your media skills training – and you'll be congratulating people on how they've just avoided answering the questions!"

"That's why I'm in a rush," I continue *"I like to do things in sixes and sevens and I only see myself doing two-terms – I usually only last five or six years before I*

go stale."

"So I have two terms to deliver the transformation of Doncaster. The change must be exponential. It can't be incremental change – I haven't got time."
[Pregnant pause]
"Or, if you like, I have two-terms before they've had enough time to be disappointed in me! You're a fan of American politics – the two term limit seems to work for the presidential elections and even Thatcher only managed 11 years!"

"Well, yes," he looks uncomfortable "Firstly I hope you're not classing yourself alongside the likes of Robert Kennedy? And secondly, she was the Leader of the opposition for four years before she became Prime Minister," he corrects me.

"Okay – bad examples – pedant!" I tell him. "Clause IV was about the fruits of our collective endeavour – but a mayoral authority is about individual accountability, individual responsibility for policies and activity and you [I] have nowhere to hide."

"That's why they [the malcontents] whipped up the petition to get rid of me. It's just too easy – the public can see exactly who makes the decisions and who they want to get rid of... People love to demonise 'the bloody council' – well the Mayoral system is about the personification of 'the bloody council' as 'the fucking Mayor' – and it's 'that twat Winter'!

"It's hard enough to deliver when you've got capable politicians, but we have 'militant', dysfunctional politicians in Doncaster, constantly working against you and trying to feather their own nests."
"Don't forget I came out of Donnygate – and I've seen some horrendous examples of what 'The Labour Party' has done in Doncaster. I've watched 'The Labour Party' with Kevin Hughes – eating itself with jealousy; jealous of his 'power' and ever desperate to destroy him."

"These people take great delight in swimming against the tide; and they'll come for me [prophetically] and they'll come for you too!" I tell him.

"Just look at what nasty bastards the likes of Mounsey, Kitchen, Blackham et al are. That's why we had to play the strategy we did with them – because if they'd have found out I was promoting you as the MP, they would've tried to destroy you."

But he's not really listening – he's not particularly computing the words I'm saying. "Maybe that's it," he adds excitedly "Maybe you're like Thatcher – everyone dislikes you but they'll still keep re-electing you." He offers it as some kind of a comfort blanket.

"Oh, I'll have no problem getting elected – you don't need to worry about that. But I doubt I have a third term in me. That's why I'm impatient to deliver."

My conversation with Ed has worried me on several levels:

Firstly, it all appears to be an academic exercise to him. His questioning is like that of an academic or university lecturer, forever obsessed with acquiring the underpinning knowledge and understanding of an issue – the theory of the activity rather than the experience to perform it. I'd prefer somebody with more of an interest in activity than theory.

This is exactly why I feel the education system fails – too frequently we "teach" people by academic analysis of case-studies, which they then have to re-learn through the application of the theory in the real world. Ed appears never to have existed in the real-world and constantly refers to theoretical and historical parallels.

Consequently, Ed is a career politician – but I have to accept that he's "my" career politician – and I have to take responsibility for bringing him to Doncaster. Every time I shake his hand I marvel at the baby-like softness of his skin. He's never done a real day's work in his life, so what am I doing?

I have always taken the view that we need MPs who have done real-life [normal] jobs before entering politics; MPs who have a better understanding of how the real world works. I now have to accept that I am contributing to the ever-increasing chasm between politicians and the people, the government and the governed.

ooo

Saturday March 26th 2005...

11.00 am – Craganour Tara Coffee Morning, Denaby

Gerry McLister has booked me in to attend a coffee morning at the Craganour Estate's Tara. James Leo Tierney [Jim] is the 70 year-old community organiser here and he's both a stalwart Labour-man and a big 'Mayor Winter' supporter.

Jim's health has not been good lately and in an *ad hoc* speech I thank the "real Mayor of Doncaster – the Mayor of Craganour – for inviting me to come to meet you and listen to you today".
Gerry says he's always thought of Jim as the Mayor of Craganour and the residents love it!

ooo

4.00 pm

Ed tells me Kevin [Hughes] has been pressuring him to continue employing one of his staff – a young woman who has been working as his researcher/office manager in London. He asks me what I know about her capabilities, which is very little given her base in the capital. Ed says he needs some assistance with his campaign and will agree to bring her up to do some work once we have the Campaign Office established at the beginning of April, with a view to keeping her on after the election in May.

ooo

Sunday March 27th 2005...

Carolyne and Ed are viewing houses for him to rent – on a temporary basis.
    She tells me she has concerns about his emotional immaturity, clumsily flirting with her and constantly wondering out loud whether people might think they're a couple – looking at houses together.

ooo

Monday March 28th 2005...

9.30 am – Bank Holiday Monday – Doncaster Trades & Labour Club

Most of the morning is spent shuttling between our house and the Trades & Labour Club as we finish readying the office suite for the forthcoming Mayoral and General Election.

ooo

3.30 pm – Poulton Close Community Centre, Stainforth

We have been invited to a Bank Holiday Monday Easter Fayre in Stainforth – complete with pie and peas!
    Councillor Nora Troops has invited us – she became the councillor for the Stainforth Ward after my 'Councillor' seat became available when I was elected as the 'Mayor of Doncaster' in 2002. Nora has developed a pretty strong and loyal base of Labour supporters. It's important we attend events such as these to show support to our councillors, our Labour party ward members and, perhaps more

importantly, to speak to the people living with our local and national policies and find out their views and concerns.

As the afternoon's event progresses, I notice Ed again struggling to have any meaningful level of discussion with people. He likes to tell you how he can connect with folk but the truth is his conversation is entirely superficial and he finds it difficult to make real connections with them.

He seems more like a member of royalty than an MP – visiting his minions and preparing to bestow his favours upon them. Chris and I are working the event and using every opportunity to bring Ed into our discussions. As the food is served Ed tries to catch my attention, at the same time as he tucks into his pie & peas.

He has a disdainful look on his face and his toothy grin is reminiscent of the cartoon character Wallace – from Nick Park's Wallace & Gromit films. Holding a piece of pie on his plastic fork, as if posing for a photograph, he shouts across to me: *"Do you know... I've never had one of these* [pies] *before! And what's this – guacamole?"* gesturing to the mushy peas.

Now I find it quite amusing and it would go down extremely well in the Village of Westminster – echoing the urban myth that Peter Mandelson once mistook mushy peas for avocado dip. But at an Easter Fayre in Stainforth?

ooo

When we get home, Ed goes down into the office and I take the opportunity to share my concerns with Carolyne. I tell her how he is forever obsessing with academia and the 'Westminster elite' and simply doesn't understand what life is like for the people out there in Britain.

Ed doesn't seem able to share a real community's aspirations apparently only concerned about them as an academic conundrum to be understood from an intellectual perspective; because of this he is actually holding his nose to their lifestyles; metaphorically and physically.

ooo

Tuesday March 29th 2005...

9.30 am – Doncaster Trades & Labour Club

Ed is bringing GB up for a rally on Sunday and we are having a meeting to make sure we have covered all the last minute preparations for the visit.

Before he joins us I voice my concerns about Ed to Chris. Unsurprisingly, he is fairly ambivalent and asks me what I expected? We agree that he's exactly what we wanted; someone who's capable of sitting and operating at the big table – and we shouldn't criticise him for that.

ooo

Thursday March 31st 2005...

Ed finally secures a rented property in Adwick-le-Street. It's a nice, clean part-furnished property and, the best of all, it's ready to move in to and he'll soon be gone!

ooo

Friday April 1st 2005...

A bit of a disaster – GB's visit for Sunday has had to be called off! As a result, there has been much activity in the "Campaign Office" getting notice out to those coming and changing the venue for the hastily re-arranged visit – now the following Sunday [April 10th].

These things happen.

ooo

3.00 pm – Mayor's Office

"Protesters back Maye for Mayor" runs the Star; and continues to report that "A group which organised a protest march against Doncaster Council 'fat cat' pay rises is backing an independent candidate for Mayor."
    "Doncaster Fair Deal Campaigners is backing Councillor Mick Maye in the election next month, but their support is conditional on him campaigning to abolish the post if he is elected."
    "The group which describes itself as non-political..." the article continues "... says it wants Doncaster to be governed in an open, accountable and democratic manner."
    "That sounds like a political campaign to me," I argue to myself, and anyone else who'll listen; which, by now, is Mags, John Hardy and Tony Sockett. "I thought it was a fucking April Fool!"
    "It still might be," says John Hardy.
    "Do these people not understand how well Doncaster's doing?" I say, irked that the newspaper is giving them column inches.

"For fuck's sake – first they campaign for a Mayor and then, having got one, they're campaigning to get rid of him within three years."

"Yes Martin but don't take it too personally..." says Mags sagely. "It's not 'the Mayor' they want rid of – it's you they want rid of!"

"Dead right," I agree with her *"We want a Mayor... We want <u>our</u> Mayor – and if we can't have <u>our</u> Mayor... we want NO FUCKING MAYOR."*

And in a final nod to the smear campaign they've been waging against me since I was first elected, I read out:

"Fair Deal Secretary Joan Moffat [wife of Ted Moffat and the <u>*de-facto*</u> queen of the malcontents!] said they had decided to offer their support to independent Councillor Mick Maye. We are hopeful that the people who supported the march and petition will again support us in this decision and turn those signatures into votes."

"Fuck me," I cry *"We hope to convert signatures into votes – yet they say the campaign is non-political."*

I throw the newspaper down in mock exasperation.

ooo

Sunday April 3rd 2005...

7.30 pm – Doncaster Trades & Labour Club – Election 2005 Campaign Launch

Even though Gordon cancelling on us today, tonight's event marks the formal launch of the Doncaster North General Election Campaign and Rodney Bickerstaff is speaking. Rodney is a wonderful orator and loves to address such gatherings. The event is a big success.

ooo

Thursday April 7th 2005...

Despite having rented a house, Ed is still reluctant to "move". Following a forceful discussion with Carolyne, Ed packs his bags.

ooo

Saturday April 9th 2005...

2.00 pm – Ed's [new] House, Adwick-le-Street

Everything is going swimmingly and Ed has asked friends of his from London for help with his campaign and attend Brown's rallying speech tomorrow morning. To this end, he has asked me to help him move some beds and a wardrobe upstairs so it's more homely for their stay.

I tell him that, despite the fact it's my birthday, I'll come around with Carolyne after the morning's election campaign stand outside the Asda Supermarket in Carcroft. When we arrive at his house he says he is awaiting a phone call from Gordon.

It's the day of the Grand National and, as usual, Carolyne's father Roland has been giving her tips on the most likely winner. The racing at Aintree aside, within ten minutes of arriving it becomes very clear that we are going to achieve very little. Ed has no strength in his arms – or legs, no co-ordination and no spatial-awareness – consequently, moving furniture is proving to be a nightmare.

I remove him from the equation, telling him to make the drinks – while Carolyne and I shift the furniture. Despite having switched the kettle on, however, Ed now insists on supervising and is physically obstructing progress as we attempt to manoeuvre the items upstairs.

It's half an hour to the start of the Grand National and, as we rest for a couple of moments, with the wardrobe firmly stuck at the top of the stairs, Carolyne regales Ed with her family's historical links to the great race.

"Are you putting a bet on?" she asks him.

"No – not really" he says. *"I don't usually have much success with betting."*

And Carolyne takes great delight listing her successes over the years... *"So you need to take advice from someone who knows,"* she says finally... *"Just look at the signs – Hedgehunter – it's got Ed in it [for you]... and Hunter... [for my surname]"*

"Oh... I don't know."

"Well you make the teas... while we finish with this," she orders him, gesturing at the wardrobe.

Afterwards we head downstairs to find Ed still making the drinks. *"I'm just waiting for a phone call from Gordon,"* he apologises again, as we sit down.

But Carolyne's already got her head in the newspaper: *"Well if you think that's going to get rid of us... ten minutes before the start of the big race?"*

"After we've just re-arranged your house," I interject.

"You can tell him to bollocks!" completes Carolyne, with the expert timing of a music hall gag-man. And we all laugh.

"No," replies Ed *"I don't think he'll buy that one – I'm sorry Gordon... can we speak after the Grand National... I've got some money riding on it... It could be very career limiting"*

"Not if your horse won!" laughs Carolyne *"Look... take advice from someone who knows. It's ridden by Ruby Walsh... the ruby red of the Labour Party... And it was foaled on 25th January – my last born's birthday,"* she finishes triumphantly.

Ed's phone rings – it's Gordon.

"Do you want me to put you a bet on Ed?" asks Carolyne *"Ask Gordon if he wants me to put him a bet on?"* she laughs.

We settle down to watch the 2005 Grand National from Aintree – in the bizarre position of cheering the race on in silence whilst Ed conducts a conversation with Gordon Brown.

History will show that the race is won by the nine-year-old Hedgehunter – the 7/1 favourite.

Ed, however, didn't have any money riding on it!

ooo

As we travel home later I tell Carolyne I'm becoming increasingly concerned that we have made a mistake with Ed, that he doesn't appear to have any kind of a 'hinterland' – no interests or knowledge outside of politics.

This worries me because it means he actually exists in a vacuum – simply as a member of the 'political class' – the 'entitlement class'. He's been brought up as one of two 'princes' with no real-world experience outside of an academic discourse and seems to have an absolute ignorance [abhorrence even] of the real values of ordinary working class people.

Carolyne agrees and sees it even more starkly: *"It's as if he's looking down on us – as a member of the establishment – the elite,"* she says.

"And it's not that he just disagrees with you – but that he tries to make you feel as if you're intellectually, and morally, inferior..."

ooo

Sunday April 10th 2005...

9.30 am

It's the morning of Gordon Brown's visit to Doncaster where he is delivering a speech at the Trades and Labour Club. Gordon is arriving on the 11.30 am train from London, with his wife and son, and we've been asked to make sure there's a room available for Sarah and their boy, John. As usual, Carolyne has everything under control and has readied the meeting room adjacent to my Campaign Suite, which we share with Caroline Flint's Office, as a 'playroom' for John and Sarah.

ooo

10.00 am – Our House, Kirk Sandall

It's a relatively normal Sunday at our house and we are getting Joss ready for football and his transport to the game. Beth, Marcey, Carolyne and I are preparing for the meeting with GB. Ed calls Carolyne.
"Carolyne – can you help me as I seem to have locked myself in the house."
"What?"
"Can you help me please? I've locked myself in the house."
"IN the house?" Carolyne questions "In the house? How've you locked yourself IN the house?" she drills him. But there's no reply – just an embarrassed silence.
"Look – I'm really busy and still have to set up the playroom for Mrs Brown and son John – can't you just climb out of the front window?"
"I tried to get out, via the back of the house, by climbing out of the back window..." Ed begins "... and then I was then going to climb over the fence by using the garden bench... but I hurt my leg when I climbed out of the window as I over stretched it..."
"... and when I stood on the bench, to try to climb over the fence, my foot went through the seat and now I've scratched all my lower leg and I'm stuck here in the back garden."
"Oh my God, it's like a scene from Monsieur Hulot or Mr Bean! Where are your house keys?"
"I have the house keys in my hand."
"Okay – well, can't you shout for your neighbours to help?"
"I'd rather not and would like YOUR help please."
"Okay but this going to have a real knock-on effect for me... I need to get Joss to footy, the girls dressed and I need to be calm and get myself looking presentable. It'll take me about 20 minutes to get to yours and I'll need another few minutes to rearrange my plans," She's like a well-drilled sergeant-major. "So I'll be with you in 25 minutes".
"I've got to go to Ed's" she tells me "Don't ask!".
She calls some friends to ask if they can take Joss to footy and lays out the girls' clothes for me to supervise. My clothes are hanging up on the outside of the

wardrobe ready for me to put on. She puts all the toys, drinks etc. that she has gathered together to make the room fun and comfortable for baby John Brown, into a bag and finally she lays out all her clothes and make-up for her return.

ooo

10.30 am – Ed's [new] House, Adwick-le-Street

As she arrives at Ed's house Carolyne shouts to him from the front garden – but he can't hear. Having knocked on the door of his next door neighbour with, thankfully, no reply, Carolyne goes around their garage into their rear garden where a six foot wood-panelled fence stands between Ed and freedom...

"*Right Ed,*" orders Carolyne "*Throw me your house keys.*"

She stands back, readied like an expert wicketkeeper, and is disappointed to hear a dull thud as they hit the top of the fence.

"*Once more – with feeling,*" she encourages him.

"*Sorry... they caught on my finger but I did try,*" he whines nasally.

"*For fucks sake Ed ... just throw 'em. We haven't got all day!*"

At the second attempt, the keys come over the fence, and she picks them up, opens the front door, and storms to the back of the house. Entering the kitchen, she can see Ed in the garden waiting for her like an attentive meerkat.

As she opens the back door, he begins to relay his woeful story once again: "*I've hurt my leg here,*" he says, touching his inner thigh like a forlorn child, "*While I was climbing out of the window. And here...*" he adds rolling up his trousers leg "*climbing on that garden bench over there!*" he points.

"*Yeah, yeah! You'll be ok,*" Carolyne replies, like a dismissive parent. "*Anyway, hurry up 'cos I have things to do and you're making me late.*"

She ushers him into the house, making sure all the doors and windows at the back are locked; then, brushing Ed down, she straightens his tie and shoves him out the front door, locking it behind her.

"*I can't stop and talk now Ed, I've got to go. See you later!*" and she's gone, throwing him the keys as she jumps into her car.

ooo

11.05 am – Our House, Kirk Sandall

Having driven like Winston Wolf, the problem fixer played by Harvey Keitel in Pulp Fiction, she arrives back at our house 10 minutes later, runs upstairs and gets changed into her red linen suit [from Hobbs], makes up her face, brushes her hair, and then takes a long, deep breath to calm herself down.

The girls and I have already gone to the 'Trades Club', so Carolyne just picks up the bag of toys and makes her own way there.

ooo

11.20 am – Doncaster Trades & Labour Club

Carolyne arrives at the Trades & Labour Club. With no time to wait for the Trades' 'temperamental' lift, she races up three flights of busy stairs to be met by a locked 'playroom' door.

"*Does anyone know where the key is please?*" she asks an overly-populated corridor.

"*Yes, I've locked it,*" says Sandra Holland.

"*What?*" asks Carolyne in disbelief "*I need access to it. We've got it ready for Sarah and Gordon's son*"

"*Well you can't have access to it,*" says Sandra, the perfect gatekeeper. "*Caroline says nobody should be let in*".

"*Well it's not Caroline's room – it's our collective room – and I need the key now.*" Carolyne is struggling to stay calm.

"*I'll have to ask Caroline,*" says Sandra and disappears down the hall.

For the second time in an hour, Carolyne takes deep breaths to relieve her stress levels.

ooo

11.30 am

Sandra returns. "*Caroline says you can have the key,*" she says, handing it over. Then legitimises herself: "*But she didn't want just anyone in the room.*"

Biting her lip, Carolyne goes in and begins strategically placing the toys around the room, in relation to type and activity, in readiness for Sarah and John's arrival.

Ten minutes later she comes to find me and asks me to take a look to check it's alright.

Entering the 'playroom', I'm surprised to find four or five of Ed's 'cronies' [including Justine Thornton, whom he has brought up from London for the launch] playing with the football, jack-in-a-box, 'Tickle Me Elmo' and other toys laid out for John. The room is in disarray!

Conscious that they are Ed's helpers, Carolyne avoids swearing at this ramshackle bunch of friends and SpAd's, but demands: "*Who's let you in?*"

"*Ed told us to wait here,*" says one of the cronies nervously, "*so we weren't in the way*" and, one by one, each starts to slowly and carefully place the toys back on the floor.

"*Well we wouldn't want to question Ed's judgment would we?*" says Carolyne rhetorically, as she ceremoniously re-positions the play equipment.

"*Please leave the playthings alone and as you found them*" and she walks out the door.

Like a faithful terrier I follow her, saying nothing.

ooo

11.45 am – Doncaster Trades & Labour Club – Gordon Brown's visit

Looking up the street from the Trades towards the train station, I can now see GB, with a buggy type pushchair and Sarah beside him, on the pathway leading to the Club. Ed and I walk towards him and I marvel at the simplicity of the scene unfolding before me;

Here is, arguably, one of the most powerful men in the world, casually strolling along one of the backstreets of Doncaster. There are no security men, no advisors, flunkies or hangers-on – surely here is a man and a family, who appear completely at peace with themselves.

As we near each other, he slows down, safely positions the buggy by the building's wall and then checks to make sure his wife is safe and comfortable. Then, and only then, does he turn to address me. Besides being remarkably attentive to his wife, he appears genuinely pleased to see me and, placing an arm on my shoulder as he shakes my hand, he is the epitome of friendship, warmth and gratitude.

"*Delighted to see you again, Martin…*" he greets me "*… and can I just say, before the madness begins Martin, that I really do appreciate everything you've done for Ed. He's been telling me how he really does want for nothing…*" he tells me as we walk.

Once at the club the madness begins as everyone wants a piece of Gordon. We are first met by the MPs and their partners.

Introducing [my] Carolyne to Gordon, I'm startled to witness Caroline Flint desperately laying claim to the preparation of the 'playroom' – I can see Carolyne is furious!

Dreading what she will say, I have visions of Flint lying prostrate on the floor. But I shouldn't have worried, for a second time Gordon is the epitome of attentiveness [to 'my' Carolyne] and I swear he sneers at the MP's claim.

As I shepherd them into the building we leave Carolyne, who takes Sarah and

John up to the 'playroom' along with Marcey, our youngest.

ooo

11.55 am

The three MPs, Ed and I then enter the Ballroom with Gordon, where we are met with rapturous applause from what is unquestionably a 'full house' of more than 200. As we take our seats on the stage, I can see our daughter Beth sat right in the middle of the front row.

Brown is magnificent; statesmanlike, humble, funny and self-deprecating; global in his reach yet local in his relevance. As I sit listening, I congratulate myself on the rationale and strategy that Chris and I have formulated. We've never been able to get Tony Blair to come to Doncaster and here we are, six weeks after developing the strategy, welcoming GB for the first time.

Gordon's speech is admiring of the Labour MPs, the Labour Mayor and the Labour Councillors; he praises the audience for their membership of the Party and paints a picture of the Labour party delivering a bright new future for all.

He speaks of our global responsibilities and obligations, of global citizenship, famine relief, access to clean water and education; and, as he does so, I glance down at Beth who appears spellbound by him, focusing on his every word.

He moves on to talk about a global immunisation programme for under-fives, one which will lead to a future drive against malaria, HIV and Aids. I glance again at Beth and think how often we have spoken to her about such issues, particularly in the run up to Glastonbury each year, and my eyes began to water. This is what politics and parenthood are about – leaving our children a future which is better than the past – and I quickly wipe the tears from my eyes.

ooo

After posing for photographs we bid our goodbyes to Gordon and his family as they are picked up by his driver. Carolyne helps Sarah put John in the car and then takes the buggy to the rear of the vehicle. *"Can I thank you Carolyne for everything you have done for Ed,"* says Gordon as he helps her put it in the car boot.

"You must be glad he has moved out now," he says. *"What was it like having him living with you for several weeks?"*

"Well... it was like having an unruly teenage boy staying."

"I know exactly what you mean," replies Gordon, laughing as he leans towards her, holding one of her hands and patting her warmly on the back.

"You have my complete sympathies."

At an immediate de-briefing we all agree it's been an undoubted success. Gordon has captivated and charmed the audience and delivered some very strong supportive messages. Conscious that I now have to pick up our son from football while Carolyne wraps up the event, I gather Beth and Marcey with me and we quickly make our way to the car.

"I know what I want to do now, Dad," says Beth as we journey home.

"What's that sweetheart?" I ask, expecting her to say something like working for Oxfam, Save the Children, or Voluntary Service Overseas.

"I want to move into politics."

"Oh... that's fantastic sweetheart..." I say, quite shaken by her assertiveness. "But do you really think that's a good move... when you see on a daily basis all the shit these bastards throw in their campaign to destroy me?"

"Oh... I mean real politics," she replies dismissively.

"Not this Micky Mouse shit that you do!"

ooo

Monday April 11th 2005...

3.00 pm

"Brown drops in to back Miliband" reads the front page of the Doncaster Star. "He voiced his support for Doncaster's Labour candidates at the general election and also the re-election of Labour Mayor, Martin Winter. "Mr Brown said 'Doncaster is really on the up and the Mayor's vision is delivering for Doncaster with projects like the airport, the community stadium and Education City'."

ooo

Tuesday April 12th 2005...

Ed welcomes one of Kevin's researchers to Doncaster and informs us she will be working on his campaign for a few days.

ooo

Wednesday April 13th 2005

10.00 am – Mansion House, Priory Suite

Doncaster Council Labour Group AGM [Part 1]

ooo

11.15 am – Campaign Office, Doncaster Trades & Labour Club

As I expected, Carolyne has got the Campaign Office working like a well-oiled machine.

Over the previous eighteen months, we have been asking Labour party members and others to pledge their support to see me re-elected at the mayoral elections. Now the office is functioning as a seven-day-a-week 'Campaign Office' and Carolyne has daily and weekly rotas set up which identify the individual working, mapped against their support 'pledges' for the Mayoral campaign.

With an all-singing and dancing data-base for such volunteer time, she has a very strong handle on the staffing needs for the office, cross-referenced against leafleting and mail out timings and requirements for both the mayor and the MP's campaigns.

Carolyne has created a routine for herself – attending at the start of the working day to agree work responsibilities with the day's volunteers, before going on to any other meetings and appointments she may have for the day. She has also provided me with specific times to 'pop in' and/or make phone-calls to thank people for their time and help.

Around mid-morning Carolyne returns to check how far the volunteers have got with their workloads and if there is anything else they need.

This particular morning there are three people in the office including Liz Jeffress and Pat Hall; Carolyne is re-planning their work with them. Ed's new worker comes into the office and they all exchange pleasantries before Carolyne continues instructing her volunteers.

"No, you won't be doing that now," interrupts ▮. *"You'll be doing Ed's work now and I want you to concentrate on folding and enveloping his letters ready for the mail out at the end of the week."*

"Firstly, I was talking... and you interrupted me," says Carolyne *"And secondly, we already have designated tasks for today, thank you. But we have time this afternoon for Ed's mail out – and I intend to put a couple of workers on to it then."*

"Well that's no good – and won't do at all," replies ▮. *"We have to get*

Ed's leaflets ready as soon as possible so they make Friday's post – and it's more important that we get the MP elected than the mayor, because he's more important," she bumbles.

"So we need to prioritise Ed's leaflets over the mayor's,"

"Well hang on a minute there ▬▬▬?" says Carolyne, checking her name disdainfully "If the MP's work was more important, then he would have sorted out his own office... his own staff... his own volunteers... and his own plans."

Ever mindful of the knock-on effect such behaviour can have on staff; Carolyne apologises to them and asks them to continue the work as planned at the beginning of the day.

Turning back to Ed's worker, she tells her: *"This is Martin's Campaign Office and his work is the priority – Ed is just camping here – and the volunteers can do work for Ed after they have finished Martin's work. We have plans for this which are being implemented."*

Ed's worker's face looks like a baby's slapped backside and Carolyne whispers in Liz's ear: *"Don't take any shit from her and call me if you need to."*

With that, she asks if everybody is clear and tells them she'll be back in about two hours.

ooo

6.30 pm – Our House, Kirk Sandall

Despite having now moved to Adwick, Ed is still using my office facilities.

Carolyne has made a family tea and is washing the pots. I am playing with the children in the living room. There's a knock at the door and as I open it I see it's Ed, who says he'd like to have a word with Carolyne.

"That's a bit formal, given that you have your own key..." I tell him; but he's looking very serious, so I take him into the kitchen and close the door as I re-join our children.

"Hi Ed," says Carolyne, continuing to wash the pots, but Ed just nods to her with a tense smile.

"I'm wanting to have a word with you to ask you what went off this afternoon?" he questions her nervously.

Carolyne finishes the item she's washing, reaches for the tea towel, begins to dry her hands and smiles at him. With an intake of breath, Ed summons up courage and declares: " ▬▬▬ says she was stopped from carrying out work for me today – by you Carolyne... and that you were bawling and shouting at her."

Unsurprised by Ed's questioning, Carolyne replies calmly: *"Well the first* thing is... I wasn't shouting at her. I didn't shout at her – but I suggest you go and ask the volunteers what happened – that's an unbiased view."

"Well I want to hear it from your side," he asserts.

"Well okay then," says Carolyne, annoyed she is having to justify her behaviour to Ed.

"I went into the Campaign Office at half past eight to set the work up for the day with [my] workers... I then went on to my other duties... and came back late morning, much as I do each day. Then ▮▮▮▮▮▮ came in – we all said 'hello' to her– and I continued talking to the volunteers, until she interrupted me..."

"She interrupted you?" Ed interjects.

"Yes"

"Oh!" Ed has physically worked himself up to fettle Carolyne, who is quite a formidable character in her own right, and quickly realises all is not as he has been told.

"She interrupted me," clarifies Carolyne once again for effect, "which I find extremely rude... I simply told her <u>what you seem to have forgotten</u>. These are the Campaign Offices for Martin and they are merely yours by grace and favour, Ed."

"Oh!" repeats Ed – less confidently now as his body language weakens; his face physically changes as he becomes deflated, adopting his cartoon-like 'Wallace' smile. "She interrupted me last week when I was talking..." he says.

But Carolyne isn't really bothered what Ed has to say. "What you don't seem to understand..." she begins "... is that I've told you before about getting an unbiased view before taking sides." and she begins to manoeuvre herself onto the opposite side of the kitchen, forcing him slowly back into the corner of the kitchen worktop – trapped at the apex of the 'Sink, Hob, Fridge work triangle'!

"How dare you?" she says. "How dare you come into my house... into my kitchen... and spoil my family's tea time..." she starts to rage at him.

"On the say-so of some jumped up twat from Westminster who was a second rate operator in Kevin's office before yours."

Having heard the crescendo building I enter the kitchen. "Is everything alright?"

"Is everything alright?" asks Carolyne, in return, glaring at me.

"I'll be going then..." and I turn around and leave the room.

Carolyne swings back to Ed: "Martin has diffused this" she says. "Just remember that I am loyal to him first. You... are only here because Martin wants you here... and he and Chris have put you here – and you'll do well to remember that. I have taken time off work to manage Martin's office, not your 'hot-desk' in Martin's office."

"Understand?" and she moves to one side to give him a way out.

"Right – you can go now!" she orders.

And he goes.

ooo

Tuesday April 19th 2005...

My Mayoral Manifesto for 2005 – 2009 is published.

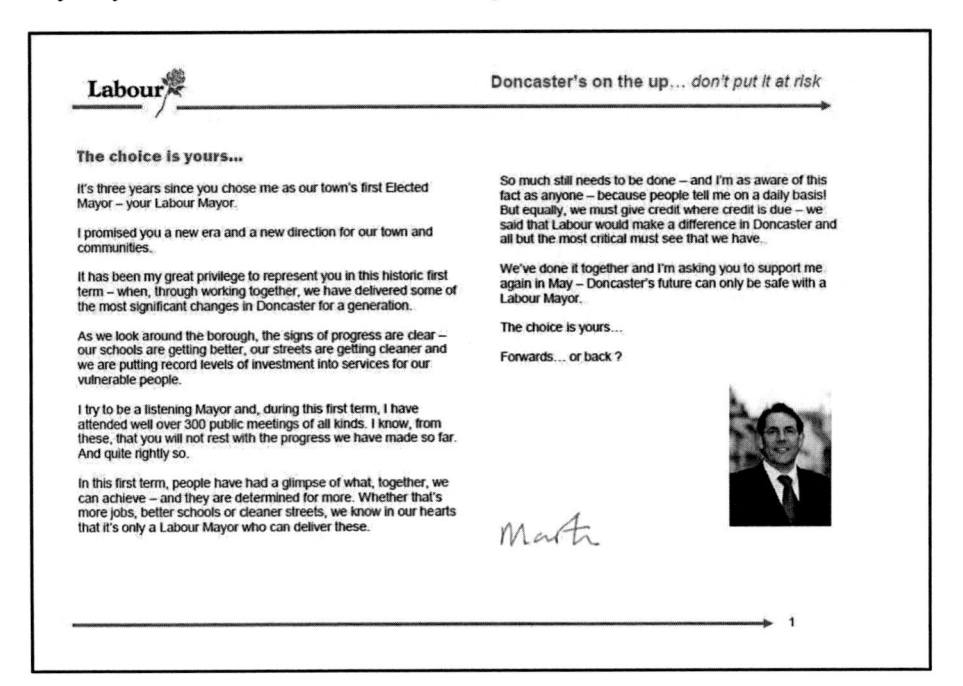

> **Labour**
>
> **Doncaster's on the up**... *don't put it at risk*
>
> **The choice is yours...**
>
> It's three years since you chose me as our town's first Elected Mayor – your Labour Mayor.
>
> I promised you a new era and a new direction for our town and communities.
>
> It has been my great privilege to represent you in this historic first term – when, through working together, we have delivered some of the most significant changes in Doncaster for a generation.
>
> As we look around the borough, the signs of progress are clear – our schools are getting better, our streets are getting cleaner and we are putting record levels of investment into services for our vulnerable people.
>
> I try to be a listening Mayor and, during this first term, I have attended well over 300 public meetings of all kinds. I know, from these, that you will not rest with the progress we have made so far. And quite rightly so.
>
> In this first term, people have had a glimpse of what, together, we can achieve – and they are determined for more. Whether that's more jobs, better schools or cleaner streets, we know in our hearts that it's only a Labour Mayor who can deliver these.
>
> So much still needs to be done – and I'm as aware of this fact as anyone – because people tell me on a daily basis! But equally, we must give credit where credit is due – we said that Labour would make a difference in Doncaster and all but the most critical must see that we have.
>
> We've done it together and I'm asking you to support me again in May – Doncaster's future can only be safe with a Labour Mayor.
>
> The choice is yours...
>
> Forwards... or back?
>
> *Martin*
>
> 1

ooo

Thursday April 21st 2005

8.00 pm – "Going4It" Rally, Doncaster Dome

Doncaster's economic regeneration is now well underway with several key transformational projects such as the Racecourse Development; the Frenchgate Interchange; Robin Hood Airport; Doncaster Education City [and new University]; and the Lakeside Sports Complex.

The media is generally supportive, referring to *"the changes that Doncaster is undergoing"*; very little is reported about the mayoral system being the stimulus for such a recovery however. Significant progress is being made with the plans for the new community stadium, within the branded "Lakeside Sports Complex", although there is little to actually see "on the ground".

Doncaster Rovers have had another good season and are really pushing for promotion into the Championship. As a result, John Ryan has asked me as his special guest at his end of season bash.

This is a fairly celebratory evening with the Rovers' Chairman acting as MC/host, and follows a format he used the previous year, where he introduces fans to the new signings for the following season, shows them the new kit and takes questions from the floor.

It's packed with more than 2,000 Rovers' fans and as I walk to my seat on the stage, I notice a couple of key Lib-Dems in the audience, including one elected councillor and a man who used to teach my children at the local primary school.

The event gets underway and, after some 45 minutes of general housekeeping and Rovers- centric fun and frivolities, John introduces me and asks if I wish to address the meeting. Never one to miss an opportunity to promote Doncaster, I deliver a suitably impassioned speech, asking the audience to look out of their windows today, where they will see the birth of a new city.

During the Q &A session, I again promote many of the economic, social and environmental regeneration initiatives – telling the audience I believe successful towns and cities need successful sporting teams and that I see the Rovers' success as a fundamental piece in Doncaster's recovery. They seem to like this, so I dwell for a while on the fact that Doncaster's recovery is not due to me, not due to my policies; but that the introduction of the "mayoral system" has proved the catalyst for many individuals, groups and organisations to "buy in" to a vision for a successful Doncaster. Again, they seem to like this more low-brow, self-deprecating approach.

But the fans are still quite restless and clearly want "their stadium" built tomorrow. We're close to seeing work start on the project, but I'm still a little worried that the fixed-price quotations coming back are way above what I've [previously] allocated for this development within my annual budget setting.

After a particularly well-informed question from the audience, no doubt from a fan close to one of the bidding construction companies, I decide to take the high ground. *"I've recently had a very frank discussion with the [successful] company about their project costs and, quite frankly, they're having a laugh!"*

"I've told them they need to have another look at their figures and sharpen their pencils – otherwise I'll be going out to tender <u>again,</u>" I stress *"... to find somebody who does want to build this landmark facility in Doncaster."*

But it isn't enough, and the fans want more, increasingly frustrated by a perceived lack of delivery. By now I'm getting pretty pissed off with them for not accepting my assurances – the ungrateful set of bastards, I think, I'm going to have to show them how committed I really am to delivering for Doncaster.

"I have been in charge for less than four years now – and look at the amount of activity that's taking place – the whole town is booming," I tell them *"It really is very simple. I am telling you tonight..."* and I pause for effect *"that we will have a new community sports complex for Doncaster... built within two years..."*

"In fact, I'll go further and tell you now – that if it's not built within two years, I will resign."

The audience begins cheering and after a few further questions I conclude my address to strong applause. John Ryan gets up and joins me on stage and, as the audience starts cheering and applauding him, he takes the microphone from its stand.

"I think you can see..." he says. *"That we are going to deliver a new stadium for the Rovers"* The audience cheers and screams and John waves at them like a member of the royal family – I'm a little more circumspect and concentrate on smiling.

Taking to the microphone again, John says: *"I don't know whether you are cheering for the new stadium... or at the thought of Martin resigning?"* and John and I laugh like hyenas as there's an even bigger cheer.

Thinking he might have set me up somewhat and ever the showman, John puts his hands on my shoulders: *"This man delivers..."* he says *"He is a man of his word. He's delivering for Doncaster... and he's delivering for the Rovers."*

The audience is ecstatic – John is really whipping them up.

"You need to vote for him – and if you don't, well you're stupid!" he concludes.

Whoops! That's going to get us into trouble…

ooo

Friday April 22nd 2005…

3.45 pm – Campaign Office, Doncaster Trades & Labour Club

As we near election day, tensions are rising. It's a joint election for both the MPs and Mayor – so we're looking at an increased turn-out; and, here in Doncaster, all are sitting Labour party candidates. Clearly this means we are all working together to ensure that after the election we have <u>status quo</u> – a Labour Mayor and 4 Labour

MP's.

I am busy electioneering; meeting and greeting as well as carrying out my "day job" as the mayor. Chris Taylor is heading up both mine and Ed's campaigns, acting as "Election Agent" to both of us, and Carolyne is in charge of the day to day running of the campaign office.

Carolyne has been advised that the mayoral leaflets have not reached a number of residents she knows in the Conisbrough, Denaby and Mexborough areas, even though she gave a box of them to Caroline Flint's office some time ago. It's only a week before the postal votes are due to be cast and these leaflets should have been distributed along with the MP's campaign material a while back. She checks with locals in the other 3 constituencies and all is fine, the mayoral campaign leaflets having already landed on their doormats.

Carolyne says she will investigate further and get back to me. By investigate further, she actually means going next door to Caroline's campaign office to have a word with her staff!

She knocks but no-one replies. Conscious that the occupant might be on the phone, she quietly opens the door and puts her head around – but the office is empty. Since she hasn't got time to waste waiting for staff to return, she "pops in" and has a cursory look around. None of my leaflets are visible, not one! Ever the conspiracy theorist, Carolyne decides there is mischief afoot and heads for the best hiding place – the far corner behind the desks and under all the detritus. Lo and behold ... there they are... three full boxes of my leaflets!

Just as she is digging them out, the door opens and in strides Sandra Hollands, Caroline Flint's Office Manager.

"What do you think you are doing?" she demands.

"Just getting back some of my property!" replies Carolyne.

"If it's in Caroline's office, it doesn't belong to you!" She insists, moving ever closer to Carolyne.

Carolyne stands up to her full 5ft 2inches and faces her. "It's the mayoral leaflets that Caroline and Phil agreed would be delivered as per the united Labour front."

"Well I don't know anything about that, but if Caroline said she would get them delivered then it will happen," replies Sandra.

"They were hidden under all that crap, so maybe they had been forgotten about... or not..." and Carolyne bends to pick up all three boxes, adding sarcastically: "Don't worry, I'll deal with it"

Sandra moves to block the doorway saying she wants to check what Carolyne is taking out of the office.

"Move!" Carolyne says loudly.

Sandra steps aside and Carolyne carries the boxes back into my campaign office and calls me. I speak to Gerry McLister and agree to drive the boxes of leaflets to his house at Conisbrough within the hour. Thanks to his hard work and organisation, ably supported by Martin Warsama, Jim Tierney [the Mayor of Craganour] and a group of loyal Labour supporters, all the leaflets are hand-delivered over the weekend. Disaster averted!

ooo

Tuesday April 26th 2005

Today marks the first flight from Robin Hood Airport and I am invited to say a few words about Doncaster's transformation and the role of the Airport and Peel Airports' support.

ooo

Tony Blair comments: "Today is a significant day for Doncaster. The opening of Robin Hood Airport is a sign of the renewal of Doncaster and South Yorkshire".

ooo

Wednesday April 27th 2005

9.15 am

I'm driving to a campaign meeting in Edlington, but the traffic is bad so I take the M18 at Armthorpe and go around to the south. As I pass the village of Rossington, I catch sight of an aeroplane taking off from Robin Hood Airport.
    One of the first flights, I think, and I'm suddenly so overcome with emotion at the magnitude of the event, I begin to cry.
    I pull over onto the hard shoulder to watch it bank overhead and then disappear over the horizon. Composing myself, I continue on to my meeting.

ooo

Tuesday May 3rd 2005…

Chris and I are attending the opening of the postal votes. From our sample, Mick Maye seems to be doing quite well. After about an hour we leave and calculate what the numbers are telling us. We anticipate that we will poll at 38% – slightly better than in 2002.

More worrying is Maye's showing – he seems to be polling consistently well and if he has a second choice preference strategy we could be in trouble. However, there is nobody here from Maye's camp...

ooo

Friday May 6th 2005...

9.00 am

We are all pretty exhausted today. The count didn't finish until very late last night and we didn't get in until gone half past five this morning.

The mayoral count doesn't start until 10.00 am but I try and fail to grab an hour's sleep. Instead, in an attempt to look more alive, I head to a beautician's for a facial. As I walk from my car, someone tells me Mick Maye has been parading the market this morning – telling everybody he's won!

ooo

The history books will show he didn't – although he did come a commendable second. With 45,742 votes, [36.72%] I won; Maye received 37,308 votes [25.06%].

Interestingly enough, I beat Maye comprehensively on first choice votes – by 13,000. I was concerned we could be in trouble if he had a second choice preference strategy. But he didn't need one; he scored consistently there – beating us 2:1 on second choice preferences.

I picked up a lot of Tory, BNP and Green Party second choice preferences and very few of the "Independent" second choice preferences – which is exactly as we anticipated, with the independents' insurgency campaigns aligning themselves very much "against" the existing leadership.

What is interesting is Maye's comment that he *"... could have won if rival candidates "on an ego trip" had not taken a share of the vote"*. How unbelievably arrogant; everyone should have stepped aside to allow the great pretender to stand! That's the trouble with democracy...

Nonetheless, Chris and I had done the numbers pretty accurately and polled some 36.72% of the vote – slightly below our "38%" calculation – and only 0.03% below our achievement in 2002.

fall out   A long Good Friday...

But this time on a turnout of 54.46% – more than twice the turnout in 2002.

ooo

1.30 pm

Fast-forward from the "leaflets fiasco" to the mayoral count. The whole place is a hive of activity with all the interested parties buzzing about the tables and eyeing up the opposition. All four Labour MPs were returned last night and I've just been returned for my second term as a Labour mayor – so there's a fair sense of optimism in the place!

Resplendent in our victory, Carolyne and I are chatting with some of the Labour party members when we almost bump into Caroline Flint and her husband Phil Cole – clearly delighted with her victory last night. We exchange a few friendly words with Caroline and then start to leave... Phil pipes up:

"*About those mayoral leaflets we didn't manage to get out...*" he looks directly at Carolyne. But before he is able to continue, she takes charge:

"*Yeah, yeah you forgot all about them didn't you and couldn't get them delivered?*" she says. "*Don't worry about it... Phil. We have a really loyal team from your constituency who got them all delivered in time...*"

"*So we cud... you c'unt !*" And she spins on her heels, leaving Phil open-mouthed. Carolyne plays up her Yorkshire accent a bit too often in my view!

ooo

4.00 pm

"Winning smiles as Labour stand firm," cries the front page of the Doncaster Star.

On page two of a sixteen-page "election special" is a lovely photograph of Rosie Winterton and her election agent, Stuart Exelby; next to one captioned "New Doncaster North MP Edward Miliband".

He looks sharp in his new suit... wearing my tie... But he does look somewhat like Wallace from 'Wallace & Gromit'!

ooo

Footnote

Ed always made sure he made a great first impression – something I noticed he was obsessive about.

ooo

Ed is not a good team player – but he is very good at pretending he's a team player! Being a team player, amongst other things, requires clear communication lines and good listening skills; Ed doesn't listen, he just pretends he is listening to placate people and then carries on doing what he was doing originally, often displaying complete disrespect for an alternative opinion. Carolye told about discussing with Ed my pledge for 'A University for Doncaster' and the subject of academic and non-academic study.

ooo

Ed said he thought traditional education and gaining degrees was the way forward. Carolyne disagreed, insisting there were many people in this borough who could be helped through apprenticeships, particularly in the building trades. She reminded him that he had once told her he thought non-academic forms of learning were just as valid. Ed replied that he had never held that view and only agreed with Carolyne because it was the first time he had met her and he wanted to make a good impression. He emphasised that he thought academia was much more important than vocational experience – as was coming from a 'good college'.

ooo

The Long Good Friday

Harold Shand: *For more than ten years there's been peace – everyone to his own patch. We've all had it sweet. I've done every single one of you favours in the past – I've put money in all your pockets. I've treated you well, even when you was out of order, right? Well now there's been an eruption. It's like fuckin' Belfast on a bad night...*

fall out   Between the wars…

hated & abused…

Between the wars

> *"I paid the union and as times got harder, I looked to the government to help the working man...*
> *I kept the faith and I kept voting, Not for the iron fist but for the helping hand...*
> *For theirs is a land with a wall around it, And mine is a faith in my fellow man...*
> *Build me a path from cradle to grave, And I'll give my consent to any government...*
>
> *Desert us not, we are between the wars"*
>
> Billy Bragg

Friday May 13th 2005...

11.00 am – Our House, Kirk Sandall

Carolyne hears the letterbox go and collects the mail. Along with the usual junk are a number of envelopes addressed to the Mayor; since being elected for my second term last week, I have received many congratulatory cards and emails both to home and work...

As per usual Carolyne opens the post and is pleased to see more cards and lovely handwritten comments thanking me and wishing me 'all the best' etc. But as she opens one brightly coloured envelope, with matching brightly coloured paper, she is stunned to find a handwritten note promising harm will come to Martin; that he and those around him will be hurt; and that pain will be felt by all!

It's signed "The Fifth Horseman of the Apocalypse".

ooo

11.10 am – The Mayor's Office, 55 High Street, Doncaster

Carolyne calls me. She is clearly perturbed by the threat, especially when I tell her I have received several death threats from one particular man over the past few years and that I know who he is!

"Well you need to get it sorted out once and for all," she says firmly. And she's right – this is now getting extremely serious – particularly with letters coming home. Carolyne is very worried that the family are now under threat so I tell her I'll come home immediately to calm her – and to collect the letter as

evidence.

I tell Chris, asking him to brief Susan and, through her, the Police.

ooo

12.00 pm – Our House, Kirk Sandall

Paul waits for me in the car outside while I give Carolyne a hug and put on a pot of tea. Carolyne's mobile rings – it's Susan and she wants to talk to her about the letter.
Carolyne is surprised that Susan has her phone number; but thankful that she's taking this seriously. She seems to empathise with the situation – the protecting mother.

She tells Carolyne she sounds upset, which, in itself seems to make her a little tearful; and then – in what I consider a complete over-reaction... she proposes that Carolyne and our children fly out to New Zealand, where she says she has a beach house, and stay there until the issue has been dealt with; she says she wants to put them all in a hotel over the weekend while the flights are sorted out!

Always quick to spot a ruse, this seems to jolt Carolyne back to reality... the woman is trying to take of advantage of her as soon as she displays the slightest weakness. What a witch!

She is actually trying to get something on us – by giving her house free *gratis* as a place of refuge for Carolyne and the kids. Carolyne brushes aside the monstrously over the top reaction, saying she wants the family to be kept together.

For my part, I am not particularly worried... I reckon I am more than capable of protecting myself and my family.

ooo

Asking to speak to me, Susan then tells me of her 'kind offer'; and says this is a very serious issue and that I should take her advice. I stand firm – does she think I was born yesterday?! Susan has contacted the Chief Constable and they are coming to the office to pick up the letter and the myriad others we have.

Afterwards Carolyne and I discuss the situation. We agree this is getting worrying. I have always tried to keep such cranks away from my family and home-life. Having said that, I did notice that my home address was on last week's election papers, which was odd. He has probably taken his lead from there.

The thing is we know where he lives," I tell Carolyne. *"So the police will sort this..."*

1.30 pm – The Mayor's Office, 55 High Street, Doncaster

I arrive back at the office having agreed with Carolyne that she should call me immediately if anything strange happens or if anybody turns up at the house.
    The Police are very quick to arrive and take away all the letters from 'ShotGun Dave', 'The Fifth Horseman' and the man I believe to be both of the above.

ooo

5.45 pm

Susan calls to tell me they have locked him up and he won't be out for some time! There's efficiency for you. Apparently, the man has some previous and was on a suspended sentence. I'm not sure whether this makes me feel relieved or [more] worried.

ooo

Monday May 16th 2005...

Launch of 'The Northern Way; a Doncaster Perspective'

After asking Peter Kenway of the New Policy Institute to do some work on the unification model, we have launched our response to the Northern Way – 'A Doncaster perspective'. Within the document I comment that *"Doncaster wishes to promote a discussion on how best to identify and promote truly pan-northern transformational projects."* And that:
    "This is an approach that requires northern stakeholders to put to one side local interests and local initiatives in favour of pan-northern initiatives taking centre stage.

The term "Northern Diamond" might be a better description as a label for the north of England and proposals to accelerate its economic regeneration. The Northern Way primarily presents a linear east-west focused image of the north, stretching from Hull to Liverpool. A Northern Diamond also reflects the importance of the north-south axis too, with Newcastle at the diamond's apex and Sheffield at the base."

MOVING FORWARD: THE NORTHERN WAY	THE NORTHERN DIAMOND: WAY FORWARD
Since publication of the Northern Way, work has progressed with a core Northern Way Implementation Group who have prepared an Action Plan and Progress report. A wide range of partners are involved in the preparation of City Region Development Programmes for each of the eight city regions.	Returning to the original principles of the Northern Way is a sensible approach and Doncaster wishes to promote a discussion on how best to identify and promote truly pan-northern transformational projects. This is an approach that requires northern stakeholders to put to one side local interests and local initiatives in favour of a pan-northern initiatives taking centre stage.
ISSUES Doncaster is very supportive of the original Northern Way agenda, recognising that the health and vibrancy of the Borough, and therefore the quality of life of its residents, is inextricably linked to the strength of the northern economy. There is a unique opportunity to respond to the Government's invitation to put forward a radical programme that would close the output gap. Doncaster does not wish to waste this opportunity through an approach which: ■ is based on the dissipation of effort and impact through support for a plethora of projects and initiatives that should more appropriately feature as part of the Regional Economic Strategy; ■ focuses on core cities in the mistaken belief that a focus on core cities will "trickle down" and improve the wider city region. There is no evidence that trickle down has been at work to date, and therefore it is not likely to be at work in the future; and, ■ fails to identify the extent to which the Northern way proposals, including the City Region Development Programmes, would contribute to the £29 billion output gap.	The term "Northern Diamond" might be a better description as a label for the north of England and proposals to accelerate its economic regeneration. The Northern Way primarily presents a linear east west focussed image of the north, stretching from Hull to Liverpool. A Northern Diamond also reflects the importance of the north-south axis too, with Newcastle at the diamond's apex and Sheffield at the base. This diamond provides a useful framework for identifying examples of the kinds of pan-northern projects that are likely to be needed if we wish to achieve a step change. Possible pan-northern projects include: a) Linking the North East to the Motorway Network. A key pre-requisite if the North is to become a single and efficient market; b) High Speed Rail Links to the South and Scotland. Developing a high-speed rail link (300km/hr) network linking London, the Midlands, the North and Scotland. Construction costs are estimated by the government's consultants at £32 billion, although this is only five years worth of the amount by which investment in the North falls short of the national average. The initial analysis also demonstrates that benefits would exceed costs. Whilst the amount required is large, it is not unachievable and would substantially reduce the perceived peripherality of the North; c) Linking the Diamond: Internal Connectivity The Northern Way identifies connectivity as one of the keys to achieving its economic goals, based on "Premier Transit Systems". Across the north, 75% of all journeys to work are made by car. What is needed is a twin track approach promoting and investing in Premier Transit Systems but recognising that most journeys are going to be made by car. Therefore the project needs to address both the capacity and quality of the road network and the use made of it (e.g. favouring High Occupancy Vehicles);

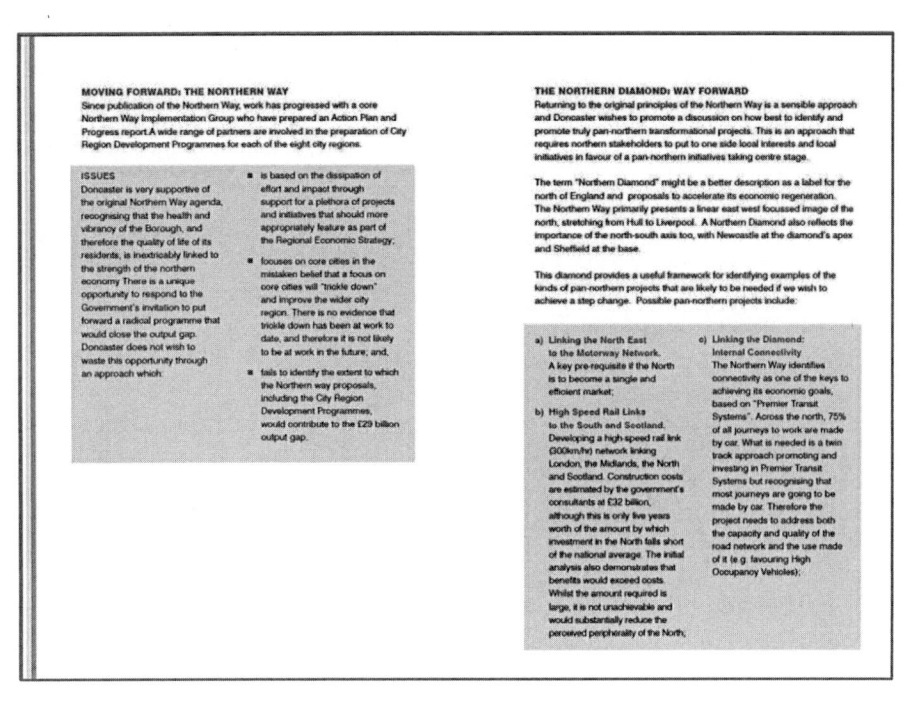

ooo

Tuesday May 17th 2005…

2.20 pm – Mayor's Office, 55 High Street

I have had to make a decision I am not particularly pleased about or proud of. Despite instructing all cabinet members "do not get involved", after Kevin announced he was standing down last February/March, Ken Knight became Aidan's sponsor, introducing him to constituents as part of the selection process.

After the kicking Aidan received, many people have been questioning Ken's judgement… and mine. I like Ken, I always have since working with him many years ago; his wife works in the mayoral office as well, so it makes my job doubly difficult. Having said that, Ken is unbelievably gracious about leaving cabinet and says he knew it was coming; he understands that he left me pretty much no option.

But it's sliding doors and it gives me the opportunity to bring John Mounsey into cabinet and to tweak some of the cabinet portfolios; particularly with respect to the greater recognition we have given to transport and the re-regulation of the bus service in Doncaster.

So John takes responsibility for the [new] portfolio of "Transport & Connectivity" but is reluctant to get involved in anything to do with the South Yorkshire Passenger Transport Executive [SYPTE]! Which might give me a problem in the future...

ooo

Thursday May 19th 2005...

10.00 am – City Mayors and Urban Regeneration

I have been asked to deliver a keynote speech at the Centre for Cities event at Carlton House Terrace in London. The Centre for Cities is an independent urban research unit taking a fresh look at how cities function, focusing on the economic drivers behind urban growth and change. It is based at the Institute for Public Policy Research [IPPR] and today's event is literally a hundred yards across St James Park from the Treasury.

Ed has told me he will pop along to support me – and Dermot Finch, the Director of the Centre for Cities, is very excited that I have "secured" Ed as our new MP. Maybe I am being unfair but I judge Ed's attendance as more a case of he's still spending an inordinate amount of time with Gordon at the Treasury, and so can pop in for half an hour; or that he wants to link up with another key speaker, Bruce Katz, the Director of Brookings' Metropolitan Policy Programme at Washington...

The event goes well as I deliver my tried and tested pitch about Doncaster's regeneration, whilst imploring those civil servants attending for a greater devolution of Whitehall powers. During the Q&A session, I again deliver my critique of JP's 'Northern Way' concept and the need for greater connectivity and a 'Northern Diamond' unification model.

ooo

Monday May 23rd 2005...

8.30 am – Mayor's Office, 55 High Street

Telephone interview with the Public Servant magazine re. the Northern Way – a Doncaster perspective.

11.30 am – Robin Hood Airport

The "Discover the Spirit" brand is going from strength to strength and today I have the honour of attending the dedication ceremony at Robin Hood Airport, where one of the 'Thomsonfly Boeing 737' aeroplanes flying out of Doncaster has been named "The Spirit of Doncaster".

ooo

Monday May 30th 2005…

"Miliband will be 'breath of fresh air' for Doncaster" reports the Doncaster Star and continues:
"Adwick councillor Ted Kitchen – one of the leading sceptics when Mr Miliband was appointed as candidate for the seat – today said the new MP had won over his critics. Councillor Kitchen said he's turned out to be a breath of fresh air for us. If he continues as he has started, he will definitely be an asset for Doncaster North."

ooo

Tuesday May 31st 2005…

3.00 pm – The Mansion House, Mayor's Parlour

Aidan and I are meeting Hamish Davidson to discuss Susan Law's first annual appraisal. Hamish was the Chairman of Veredus Executive Recruiting, and the reason why we used them for the recruitment process which led to Susan's appointment. Hamish has now left Veredus to establish a new company "Rockpools".

Aidan has been badgering me about this session with Hamish for two or three weeks now and I am not sure why – other than Susan's been badgering Aidan about it. It seems strange to involve a third person in the appraisal process but it can help it be more objective; although I do have several qualifications in objective assessment and appraisal.

Nevertheless, I agree to the meeting which, for some reason Aidan has set up in the "Mayor's Parlour". This is a beautiful little Georgian parlour room that we only use *in extremis* and/or when we don't have access to any other room. I would have thought today's meeting met neither of these criteria…

Hamish is not as business-like as I expect and doesn't focus on Susan immediately, preferring to spend a good hour discussing associated issues before drilling down to specifics related to the MD's performance. I usually cannot contain Aidan's enthusiasm when talking about organisational performance issues but when it comes to Susan, he is surprisingly silent. For my part, broadly speaking, I am satisfied with her but there are some niggling little areas beginning to creep in, not least a poor grasp of UK local government and governance, and a very direct, confrontational management style.

I agree to put together a paper "2nd Term Delivery Priorities" which will provide a [mayoral outcome] base for a performance management process.

ooo

4.20 pm – The Mansion House, Mayor's Parlour

Hamish has now left us to prepare for his meeting with Susan. I ask Aidan what the fucking hell that was all about? He seems confused...

"*I mean exactly what I said... How much did it cost us to get Hamish here for that?*" and like a small child he mumbles something about not really knowing.

"*What was it all about? It seems to me that the only reason you got him here was for you to parade your intellect and capabilities!*" and I ask him once again:

"*How much did it cost us?*"

But he just looks sheepish.

"*I assume you've just wasted upwards of £1,000 to make sure that you've got a foot in the door for a future career with Hamish then...*"

ooo

NOTE: The Public Interest [PIR] Report, published on May 14th 2008 stipulates that some two months prior to this meeting "*In April 2005, the then Deputy Mayor, Aidan Rave, discussed the performance of the Managing Director with the then Head of Human Resources, Mandy Coalter.*

The Deputy Mayor decided that the Managing Director should receive a performance increment of £5,000 leading to an email dated 13th April instructing payment to be made."

I was never made aware of this "bonus payment" to Susan [until two years later] and, interestingly, was not copied in to the email. Having said that, at that particular moment in time, I wouldn't necessarily have refused to approve it...

The Public Interest Report also states: "*On 13th April 2005, the Head of HR started to set up a proper process for the Managing Director's performance* management for 2005/06 involving the Mayor, Deputy Mayor and Managing Director with facilitation by Hamish Davidson of Rockpools".

Thursday June 9th 2005...

The newspapers still do not understand the mayoral model and continue to flip-flop between the "strong, dynamic, statesman championing Doncaster" type and the "mayor attends civic opening" type reporting...

Now we've got past the election they are celebrating two huge mayoral initiatives under the strapline "Shaping Up Nicely – two major constructions illustrate town's redevelopment".

They feature Doncaster Education City's £47 million hub building, being constructed on the waterfront, and the £250 million Frenchgate retail complex; although they fail to mention its integral transport interchange!

ooo

Friday June 10th 2005...

4.30 pm

I have got away from work early and am play fighting with my children in our garden. Beth and Marcey have me pinned on the floor, tickling me! Simultaneously my phone rings. It is on the marble-top washstand in our hallway.

Carolyne answers it. *"Hello... Martin Winter's phone."* There is a mumbling and a muffled comment. *"I'm sorry... I can't hear you – this is Martin Winter's phone... can I help you."*

With more clarity now: *"Can I speak to Martin?"*

Thinking how impolite the caller is being, Carolyne says again. *"Yes... I can get him for you... he's just busy at the moment... who's speaking please?"*

"John," says the man curtly.

"John who?" asks Carolyne, slightly annoyed.

"Prescott," comes the response... more obsequious now... almost embarrassed that Carolyne doesn't know who he is.

"Oh... I'll get him for you," and she brings the phone into the garden...

ooo

By this point, I am screaming because my children are all wrestling with me... Carolyne approaches. Phone in one hand she motions at me – but I haven't a clue what she's saying...

"*It's John, Martin,*" she says, motioning again – but it's no good the kids have got me pinned!

"*John who?*" I ask, laughing at the children's fighting.

"*John Prescott...*" for some reason she is whispering.

"*Oh*" and I beckon for the phone, asking the kids to get off me.

ooo

"*Hello John... this is an unexpected call...*" And the Deputy Prime Minister proceeds to scream down the phone, tearing strips off me for my "failure" to toe the party line over the "Northern Way" – his northern way – his beloved northern way...

As I wander around the garden, sometimes having to hold the phone away from my ear, he shouts me down over my criticism and specifically my comments "*... at the IPPR event in London the other week... whatever fucking good the IPPR is...*" I give as good as I get – as they say – but he isn't really listening; he just wants to call somebody up [me] and give them a bollocking.

I explain, or try to explain [!], that I am actually very supportive of it, just that I want a greater political dialogue... In the end, I lose my temper and shout [at him] that he isn't listening. It works... he seems to calm down somewhat, as I tell him that the Northern Way should be looking to unify the north, not create greater division through encouraging cities and towns to "compete" over their slice of the [undefined] pie... and I try to explain that we can achieve this if we concentrate on major pan-northern transformational projects such as high speed transport and connectivity and my Northern Diamond model.

But he isn't having it – his attention doesn't last for long – and he begins screaming at me for criticising Yorkshire Forward for not getting the political leaders together and for simply trying to implement a "civil servant led" Whitehall instruction; one which is consequently undefined and unsupported.

"*Well we might as well scrap all the bleeding RDAs then!*" he shouts. "*I'm trying to keep them alive when everybody's saying they want to scrap them.*"

But it's my turn to lose attention now. I'm bored... and he simply wants to hear his own voice... plus he has been shouting at me for a good half an hour and I want to continue playing with my kids!

I suggest I write to him, and to Yorkshire & Humber Labour leaders.

ooo

Having reflected on JP and my disagreement, I am [people are] gradually becoming disillusioned with the poor support for the north of England – Labour's heartlands. What we need is one big, joined up transformational project that connects the north; but what the Government wants to support is a whole series of small, parochial projects.

With this as a preferred strategy, "they" can reward locations – conducting transactions with individual councils, keeping them divided... and conquered!

ooo

Sunday June 12th 2005...

I complete a paper for Susan Law entitled "2nd Term Delivery Priorities" within which I state:

"As we begin the second term of Mayoral Governance in Doncaster, there are several areas requiring attention:
 1] An Increased Local and National Profile
 2] Assuring Local Operational Delivery

Within *'1] An Increased Local and National Profile'* I specify four areas of intervention including:

"The strategic use of the Chancellor of the Exchequer to publicise and promote Doncaster's renaissance and Mayor... Position ourselves as a key player within the North of England and influence the Northern Way agenda".

Within *"2] Assuring Local Operational Delivery"* I specify twenty six outcomes relating to the five mayoral pledges, for example:
 "Pledge 1 – A Better Start For Our Young People
 1b] An extended "Fruit into Schools" scheme for every child within Key Stage 2 – <u>identified for immediate expansion and to roll out in September 2005.</u>"

ooo

Monday June 13th 2005...

4.00 pm – Mansion House

True to my word from my visit to the Scawthorpe Ladies Group in March, today is their "follow up" trip to the Mansion House. Chris joins us and we have a very enjoyable half an hour tucking into cream teas and chatting about their guided tour around the Mansion House with Paul.

ooo

Tuesday June 14th 2005...

Susan tells me she received a report from the Audit Commission into the Glass Park project. It has been drawn up as a response to the on-going war of attrition being waged by the malcontents, specifically Joan Moffat, and some opposition councillors. To be honest, I understand why the Audit Commission has produced it – it's an attempt to kill off the disquiet and I expect it to report that the project was an exemplary one. However, these people will not accept it, whatever it says; it will only antagonise things.

ooo

I draft a letter to JP following our "disagreement" over the Northern Way:

Thank you for taking the time to telephone me last week. I am sorry that you thought that my comments were not supportive of your concept for the Northern Way.

In Doncaster, we are fully supportive of your original model for a Northern Way, and in particular that the economic performance of 'city regions' is key to the success of the North. However, I have concerns about the complete lack of political debate in the Northern Way and its very literal interpretation. Consequently, your original aims will not be achieved because the current proposals:
- *Duplicate existing regeneration initiatives such as previous economic programmes and the core-cities work.*
- *Do not address the fundamental infrastructure requirements for a competitive North.*
- *Only seek to enhance the performance of the core cities, yet merely offer 'trickle-down' benefits to the Core Cities' surrounding regions and, because of this, will not result in an increase in the economic performance of the city regions.*

We believe the Northern Way should:
- *Focus on the elimination of competition between cities and city regions.*

- *Concentrate on major pan-northern transformational projects.*
- *Use existing City Region Development Plans to help identify what can be achieved and exploited by the development of these pan-northern projects.*

I am pleased to say that the Chair of the Yorkshire and Humber Assembly has now agreed that this debate should take place at the YHA AGM on 21st July 2005.

However, the majority of the 6 remaining Labour Leaders in the Yorkshire & Humber region [out of 22!] remain extremely concerned, and we are keen to have a meeting with you as soon as possible. I hope this proves to be achievable.

ooo

Thursday June 23rd 2005…

Wakefield – The Yorkshire and Humber Association of Local Authorities [ALA] Annual General Meeting.

Pre-AGM "political group meeting" – another chance to try and sell the unification model, so I propose that I convene a meeting in Doncaster.

ooo

Friday June 24th 2005…

8.00 pm – Our House, Kirk Sandall

Anyone in a position of responsibility or in the public eye will always become a target for lies and mischief making… The rumour mill has been working overtime with regard to the mayor.

One of the reasons I chose to sell my Porsche was because of comments that I must have received it as a "bung".

Carolyne and I have become used to hearing how each and every large detached house being built in Barnby Dun is "the mayor's new house".

ooo

Carolyne suggests I speak to Marcey about something that happened at school today.

Marcey tells me that at lunchtime one of the "dinner ladies" approached her and asked if she was okay. She then asked how her mother and father were keeping. Being polite, Marcey responded to the lady's idle 'chit-chat'; so she then asked her:

"Where's your dad living now, Marcey?"
"At home."
"Yes but where's he really living...?"
"At home with us."
"Oh is he? I thought he'd moved out and was living in a new house in Barnby Dun..."
"Well he was living with us when I saw him at breakfast this morning."
"Oh"

ooo

Marcey's conversation with the dinner lady perturbed me greatly. Firstly, a member of staff shouldn't be interrogating a child, any child, about their parents' behaviour; and secondly, the rationale behind this lady's questioning can only have been vexatious – bent on propagating the irritating urban myths being built up against "The Mayor".

I speak to Mark Eales, our Director of Education, about my concerns and he agrees we will have to deal with the matter sensitively.

ooo

Monday June 27th 2005...

I draft a letter to all Labour leaders for Yorkshire and Humberside...

I am sure that as Labour leaders in the north of England you, like me, welcomed the Deputy Prime Minister's initiation and pursuit of the Northern Way growth strategy. After the economic vandalism of the Tory years, with its associated destruction of many of our communities, it is indeed good to know that there is someone at the very top of government prepared to fight our corner.

It may surprise some of you to know, but I am a huge supporter and advocate of this initiative – coming from Doncaster, which bore the brunt of those Tory years, I can clearly see the need for us to be more competitive, higher skilled and better connected.

Indeed, my only real criticism of the process so far is the lack of local political involvement and leadership within this very important initiative.

While I think it will be advantageous for northern leaders to have some sort of collective position on the Northern Way, I believe it to be much more important for Labour group and council leaders to have a view in order that we can make the maximum possible impact across our northern communities.

This is a unique opportunity for us – if we are unable to grab hold of it, I fear that the Northern Way could become just another wonderful plan that never quite reached its original potential.

To that end, and following such a discussion and proposal at the ALA Leaders Meeting AGM pre-group meeting last Thursday, I would like to invite you to a meeting of Labour Leaders to be hosted in Doncaster... in order that we can share our views and perhaps come to some degree of consensus on our position.

ooo

Monday July 4th 2005...

10.00 am – The Local Government Association Conference – Harrogate

This week we are attending the LGA Conference in Harrogate. I am particularly keen to attend because Karen Cooper is working on our stand before she starts as my new Executive Assistant next week. Karen is an extremely efficient and gregarious woman who later proves to be a loyal, hard-working, committed, and conscientious member of my immediate staff.

ooo

Wednesday July 6th 2005...

10.00 am – Doncaster Crown Court

I have had to come back from conference today to give evidence in the 'ShotGun Dave' court case.

It transpires that he has also been threatening John Ryan, the Chairman of Doncaster Rovers, and Graham Oxby, the Doncaster Film Director who made "Shotgun Dave Rides East". Oxby and the rest of us are all guilty of stealing his life story, he claims. The man has been behind bars since he was locked up in May.

After giving my evidence, I listen to the judge sum up... and hear him sentenced to six months and given a restraining order "not to contact Mr Winter directly or indirectly wherever he may be".

I send bouquets of flowers to the staff members who had to give evidence and attend court. Interestingly, although there are several journalists there and my name is clearly on the court board and papers for the day, no newspaper covers the story. It would appear a real life true story about the mayor and his family being threatened with death isn't newsworthy...

ooo

6.00 pm – The Majestic Hotel, Harrogate

I arrive back at the LGA Conference and meet up with Susan in the hotel's reception/bar area. Aidan has inveigled himself into the position of Deputy Leader of the LGA Labour Group and has gone down to London "for a Local Government Association meeting" tomorrow... which seems strange, given the LGA's annual conference is taking place up here in Harrogate... Nonetheless, I order a bottle of wine and tell Susan how the court case went, thanking her for all she has done.

Our Marketing and Communications Manager joins us for ten or fifteen minutes to ask me how today went. As she leaves us, Susan asks me: *"Why does she attend these events?"*

Thinking I'm stating the bleeding obvious, I reply: *"Well, given that she's our Marketing & Communications Manager, I assume she wants to make sure that our stand is a good one and that we're getting the message across..."*

"Well of course..." she responds *"But I mean... why does she really attend these events?"*

"Well... that and she's a bit of control freak," I address Susan's tenacity for a definitive answer.

"Yes. But she doesn't need to be here for the full week," she goes again, like a dog with a bone. I feel slightly nervous now:

"Well... I also think it's a bit of a blowout for her... It's her birthday this week and she always likes to relax in the atmosphere of a job well done," I explain unnecessarily. *"But you'll have to ask her, if you don't think she should be here."*

"It's not a question of whether I think she should be here," she counters. *"It's if you want her here..."*

"... because you are close – aren't you?" she insinuates.

"No – not particularly.... if you're trying to suggest there's something going on between us..."

"No – I'm not saying that," she responds quickly.

"But... if there is... I can help you hide it."

"Well – I can assure you that there isn't," I state for the second time.

"No – I don't think you understand what I'm saying" she repeats. *"If you are... I can help you... I can help you to cover it up..."*

"Right," I'm annoyed now. "Let me make it clear to you, because you don't seem to get it"

"I am not having an affair with ▮▮▮▮▮▮▮▮▮▮▮▮. Furthermore, if I was having an affair with her, then that would be between me and her... and I certainly wouldn't tell you," I rage.

"This is three times I've told you now... If you ever ask... or insinuate this again... then there will be hell on!"

And I stare deep into her eyes – she's clearly shocked.

"Do you fucking understand?"

I get up and leave the room.

ooo

6.40 pm

Now that wasn't the cleverest decision I've ever made – and I may have given Susan an opportunity to cause me difficulties, having arguably threatened her. I need to create an audit trail; something that records the circumstances of the discussion Susan and I have just had.

Consequently, I make another not so clever decision – and call the Marketing & Communications Manager!

"Where are you?" I ask her, and she tells me she is in her room, just along the corridor from Aidan's and mine.

"I need to speak to you urgently," I say. "Can I come up?"

ooo

6.45 pm

Her room is dark because the curtains are closed and it's littered with display boards, files, gifts and all manner of marketing giveaways and bumf. She apologises for the mess but I can see she has been working extremely hard.

I explain that I think we have a problem and that Susan is clearly wishing to "get something" on me. Moreover, I describe the scenario that played out down stairs after she left us.

I explain that as well as her, there are another two or three female staff members that I am very close to. I tell her that we are going to have to be very careful about the amount of time we spend together; and we must always make sure other people are present.

I name the three other staff members and tell her I'll be speaking to them all and, in essence, "severing" the niceties of our close working relationships. To be honest I don't think she knows what to say – I've certainly surprised her with my "revelation".

ooo

As I reflect on Susan's behaviour, I see she is beginning to exhibit many of the classic signs of a sociopath:
- insisting that all my briefs go through her – and that I am never briefed directly;
- having an oversized ego – and tending to blame others for her own failures;
- using deceit and manipulation on a regular basis;
- having few friends;
- being charming – but only superficially – sociopaths can be very charismatic and friendly because they know it will help them get what they want;
- showing a complete disregard for societal norms – breaking rules and laws because they don't believe society's rules apply to them.

ooo

It's announced London will host the 2012 Olympic Games after a bid that highlighted the city's multicultural reputation.

ooo

Thursday July 7th 2005...

8.50 – 9.47 am – London

Several suicide bombs have been detonated in London – three in quick succession aboard Underground trains and, later, a fourth on a double-decker bus in Tavistock Square.
As well as the four bombers, fifty-two civilians are killed and over seven hundred more injured in the attacks. It's the United Kingdom's worst terrorist incident since the 1988 Lockerbie bombing, as well as the country's first ever suicide attack.

10.25 am – The Majestic Hotel, Harrogate

I receive a call from the Labour party. Because of the bombs there are no trains coming out of London. Will I stand in for David Miliband at the New Local Government Network [NLGN] seminar in an hour's time…?

ooo

11.30 am

"NLGN seminar – What now for local government"

The session is more of a plenary discussion, based around Q&As after short introductory speeches from those on the "top-table". This is very impressive – Sir Sandy Bruce Lockhart [Chair of the LGA]; Sir Jeremy Beecham [Vice-Chair of the LGA] and Leader of the LGA Labour Group; and Mike Storey, the Leader of Liverpool City Council [presently embroiled in a power struggle with his Chief Executive David Henshaw].

I begin my presentation… *"I'm honoured to have been asked to stand in for David Miliband at today's important debate on accountability in Local Government… But I have to say that, like all of us here today, I wish the circumstances were better… and I know that all our thoughts are with those and their families who have suffered injuries or death this morning".*

And I begin my intro proper:

"I'd like to think that it is testimony to the recovery that I have led in Doncaster during the last four years, and the distance we have travelled from the bad old days of Donnygate… and I trust that I can do the Minister of State for Communities and Local Government justice today… in terms of my contribution as his stand-in…

Many people ask me what is the position of [executive] Mayor of Doncaster like… how do you handle the accountability…?

… many people say it's akin to being a gangster [!]… or it's like the mafia…

… and they say that I am the "Don" in "Doncaster…"

There is a chuckle throughout the room – they like that one.

"… to which I always reply – well, it could be a lot worse…… I always thank god I'm not the Mayor [or MP] for Scunthorpe…

… because Elliot Morley is…"

The room is in uproar – they love that one. Even Sir Sandy can't contain his laughter.

7.00 pm

There is a distinct calmness to proceedings because of this morning's bomb blasts in London. But tonight is the main Labour Party Dinner and, in that context, delegates are looking forward to it.

Aidan is still not here and Barbara Hoyle is going to the Conservative Dinner. Margaret Ward is attending the Labour Dinner with me, as is Stuart Exelby.

The difference between the two parties; the Labour Dinner is free, sponsored by the Labour Party; the Conservative Dinner costs £28 per head!

We meet first in the hotel bar. Barbara Hoyle is the Leader of the Conservatives in Doncaster, and the only Tory attending the conference with us. She is concerned that she won't know anybody at the Tory event, and resents paying the £28 ticket price!

"Why don't you come with us Barbara?" asks Margaret Ward innocently.

"I can't do that" answers Barbara *"Can I?"*

"Of course you can" says Margaret. *"Nobody will know and you're more supportive of Labour than some of our own members!"*

And so they agree that Barbara Hoyle, the Leader of the Conservative Group on Doncaster Council, is to attend the Labour Party Dinner!

ooo

Mags asks me what I think. To be honest, I'm a little frazzled by the court case and Susan's attempted manipulation yesterday; but it will be quite amusing, in a potentially career-limiting kind of way…

Barbara is a good woman, and very supportive of Aidan and I – so why not!

ooo

7.30 pm – Ballroom, the Majestic Hotel, Harrogate

Once in the main ballroom it becomes clear there are several northern MPs in attendance; not least Rosie Winterton, who's hosting our table!

As everybody greets each other, preparing to sit down, Rosie gives me a kiss on my left cheek. As she does so, she sees Barbara who she knows, of course.

"What's she doing here?" she whispers, kissing my right cheek.

"She's joining us for dinner," I answer, as I overplay the melodrama of the scene, kissing her left cheek for a second time.

"She's Mag's dinner guest," I tell her, lingering with the kiss *"It's a bit of*

harmless fun... and it's not as if we'll be laying out any big strategic political plan over dinner – is it Minister?"

So there you have it. Barbara joined us at the Labour Party Dinner; and sat at the same table, knowing she was a Tory, was Rosie Winterton, later to become the Labour Party Chief Whip in Ed Miliband's opposition government.

ooo

Monday July 11th 2005...

For the past twelve months I have been sitting on a steering group for the Joseph Rowntree Foundation – advising on a research project "Local political leadership in England and
Wales".

This is an academic report on how local political leadership has been changing as a result of the Local Government Act 2000. LGA2000 introduced four new forms of executive government into local authorities:
- 'elected mayor and cabinet';
- 'elected mayor and council manager';
- 'cabinet and leader';
- a streamlined committee system [available only to authorities with populations under 85,000].

The focus of the research is on how local political leaders are responding to external and internal pressures and opportunities under these new conditions; and the Government has placed particular emphasis on the following aspects of leadership:
- clarity of vision – the capacity to identify and focus on clear priorities for action;
- community leadership – the capacity to develop connections with local stakeholders and local communities;
- visibility – the capacity to generate recognition on the part of the local population and so strengthen accountability.

In its summary, the report comments that *inter alia*:

There is no uniform political leadership. Elected mayors generally recognised the need for a high degree of visibility and responsiveness to the public and stakeholders. Most elected mayors saw external networking and community leadership as key roles. Where authorities had adopted the 'cabinet and leader' model there was little evidence of party pressure or adversarial party politics having diminished. Leaders with a strong power base did not necessarily behave like strong leaders. Strong individualistic leadership did not necessarily equate with effective leadership. Strategic ability, personal effectiveness, political intelligence and organisational mobilisation marked out political leaders.

ooo

For all their paraded stupidity, newspapers sometimes manage to hit the nail on the head by accident… The Doncaster Star runs with the strange headline "mayor defends system after critical report" despite the report being ambivalent.

The Star focuses on one specific aspect of the report's findings that *"Some mayors or council leaders had been tied down in politics rather than leading their communities, while others had been unable to pursue long-term goals"*.

"Independent Councillor Mick Maye, who stood for mayor on the premise of scrapping the [mayoral] *system in Doncaster…"* the newspaper continues *"… said he did not think the mayoral model was democratic"*. Which is a strange view from a man who was democratically rejected from the post before claiming that there were too many people standing for election!

However, the paper's take on it points to a more sinister emerging malaise… This report and study compares and contrasts the approaches taken by mayors and council leaders. The Doncaster Star takes one generic comment with regard to "both" types of leadership and aggregates it up; firstly, to become a comment on "mayors" *per se* but more worryingly to then, *ipso facto*, become a comment on the Doncaster mayor…

… There's objectivity for you!

ooo

Tuesday July 12th 2005…

I am getting a little frayed around the edges! It is now a month since I presented the MD with my paper "2nd Term Delivery Priorities" and Susan is proving a little difficult to pin down with regards to a response.

She is beginning to display a real lack of respect for anyone involved in UK Local Government and constantly seeks the views of overseas "experts". I am concerned she is encouraging a culture of cronyism, which may create motivational issues within our existing workforce.

Notwithstanding the above, Susan and Aidan have now come up with the concept of "Doncaster Values"…

We dare to be different;   *We are winners;*   *We take responsibility;*
We are one council;   *We are proud;*

… and they want to put together a series of "values workshops" to promote them to all our staff. I am not convinced at all – but the Corporate Management Team seem to like it!

ooo

Wednesday July 13th 2005…

10 .00 am – Mansion House, Priory Suite

Meeting of Y&H Labour Leaders to discuss the Northern Way.

ooo

Friday July 15th 2005…

2.30 pm

It's a beautiful sunny day and as I look out of my office window, I see Susan and Aidan returning from lunch. The three of us frequently pop out for something to eat together. I may be overly suspicious, jealous even, but I can't see why they didn't ask me along…

ooo

Monday July 18th 2005…

"We've got the money" screams the front page of the Doncaster Star, reporting that £135 million pounds worth of investment has been ploughed into Doncaster in the first six months of the year. This, of course, underlines the Haiku type poem I adopted to encapsulate my campaign three months ago:

Doncaster's on the up
It didn't happen by accident
Just think what might be possible

Well they are encouraging their readers to "think what might be possible"; as they highlight the many regeneration projects being delivered at the moment, citing the likes of Debenhams, Ottakars and Ikea waiting in the wings...

but despite my election campaign strapline of 'Don't put it at risk', they are doing just that by encouraging political unrest through their naïve reportage...

ooo

Thursday July 21st 2005...

Yorkshire & Humber Assembly AGM

I give a presentation to the members and officers ... damp squibs come to mind!

ooo

Friday July 22nd 2005...

2.00 pm

Ed is going on patrol with my Community Safety Warden's "Rapid Response Team" today. It's exactly the type of "visit" MPs do – attaching themselves to successful local authority operations – in this case part of our wildly successful "Community First" operation, one of the main tenets of our "good" CPA rating.

I'm a little concerned that Ed wants to link himself with what is clearly a mayoral project and one that is [now] being replicated across the country. In essence, he is trying to "hijack" my successful project and confuse the mayoral delivery "brand".

I have explained *ad nauseum* how community safety is one of my key mayoral pledges and that this must be communicated at every opportunity...

ooo

Monday July 25th 2005...

The Doncaster Star has asked me for a quote with regard to Ed's patrol. Not wishing to muddy the water that Ed has already muddied, I simply comment: *"I am delighted that Ed has had the opportunity to see the work of the wardens at first hand."*

ooo

Thursday July 28th 2005...

11.00 am – The Mayor's Parlour

Following my presentation to the Yorkshire & Humber Assembly AGM last week, I have a diarised meeting today with Ed Balls and Les Newby from the RDA, Yorkshire Forward.

ooo

Friday July 29th 2005...

4.30 pm – Doncaster Star

I've just got back from a special South Yorkshire Leaders Meeting on the "Northern Way". I'm pretty pissed off because they all see it as an opportunity to try and get more resources than their neighbour!

Our Comm's staff have brought in tonight's Doncaster Star. They are concerned about how the newspaper has reported on Ed's patrol with the Community Safety Wardens last Friday:

"MP goes on patrol with wardens to see fight against young yobs" reads the headline.

"I thoroughly enjoyed patrolling with community first on Friday evening where I saw first hand how antisocial behaviour is being tackled in Doncaster," says Ed. So far, so good; and then, surprise, surprise, he goes off script.

"... I am determined to support the local authority and the police in working with the community on safer streets and cleaner neighbourhoods [sic.]"

"Twat!" I shout out *"He's not only got the message the wrong fucking way round... and he's not mentioned the fucking mayor!"*

My staff look dismayed. To be honest, they are not all that enamoured with my "selection" of Ed as the new MP for Doncaster North and this sort of thing underlines that – as well as "my" poor judgement.

It might appear pedantic but the message has to be consistent: "a Labour Mayor who is delivering cleaner streets and safer neighbourhoods"... and what's more, Miliband knows this!

I am reminded of one of the key findings of the Joseph Rowntree Foundation research project on political leadership:

Elected mayors generally recognised the need for a high degree of visibility and responsiveness to public and stakeholders' concerns; non-mayoral leaders varied more in the extent to which they recognised this.

Thursday August 4th 2005...

Edgbaston, Birmingham

My Policy [political] Assistant, Chris Taylor, functioned as election agent for both Ed and I in May. As a big "thank you" to Chris, I suggest to Ed that we buy him tickets for the first two days of the Ashes Test Match in Birmingham.

What had seemed like a good idea almost backfires when we have to pay £680 for two tickets with a face value of just over £100! But it's worth it to see Chris's face. In what turns out to be an excellent game of cricket, Australia lose the toss and, foolishly opt to put England in to bat; England take full advantage and become the first team to hit 400 runs in a first day of Test cricket against Australia since 1938!

ooo

Friday August 5th 2005...

All day

To coincide with his second day at the Edgbaston Test Match, Chris has now left my office to manage Ed's office permanently. I love Chris dearly and am sad to see him go. I owe him a huge amount but have become increasingly worried about his health over the last year, as he committed himself tirelessly to my mayoralty.

I wanted Chris to go part-time, in view of his tendency to overwork, but we've now agreed he is better employed managing Ed's new Doncaster North office [!]. It's a huge challenge and an honour for Chris, as both he and I know that Ed is destined to achieve great things in the Labour Party.

Nonetheless, life goes on and I now have the unenviable task of replacing Chris. The obvious person is Ian Spowart who is currently Manager of the Rossington Development Trust – if I can get him…

ooo

Susan's behaviour is really beginning to concern me. It is now two months since I presented her with my paper "2nd Term Delivery Priorities" and she has still not responded! I am meeting her with Eva Hughes, the cabinet member responsible for the delivery of the extended "Fruit into Schools" scheme;

Susan says the September "roll out" will not be possible because *"nobody had planned for it… and there is no budget for it"*.

She refuses to acknowledge the political will of the executive – and uses them as scapegoats for her failure to deliver.

I make it very clear to Susan that I expect the scheme to be ready for the beginning of the September start of the school year.

ooo

Friday September 12th 2005...

6.00 pm – Central Park [bistro], Lazarus Court, Doncaster

Aidan, Chris and I are meeting up with Rosie for a drink tonight. We've got into a vague routine where we work late on Fridays and usually end up somewhere having a meal whilst we talk politics.

ooo

Monday August 15th 2005...

9.30 am – Our House, Kirk Sandall

The landline rings: *"Hi, Carolyne – it's me, Maria* [Aidan's wife]*"* Carolyne is surprised at the call... she's been very supportive of Maria during her "illness", the previous year but Maria has been really busy since then, establishing her new business "A tempo" – a music shop on South Parade.

"Hi... I'm fine thanks Maria... how are you? How's everything going with the shop? Is everything okay with you and the kids?" asks Carolyne.

"Yes all is fine thanks... the shop's going really well..." and Maria continues to dance around a few "housekeeping" niceties.

"The main problem is Martin & Aidan," says Maria, manipulating the conversation. *"I mean, what are they like coming home at four in the morning again?"* she's referring to [our] propensity for late Friday night working.

"Yes... they enjoy their Friday nights don't they..." Carolyne gambles [and giggles] thinking... what the hell is Aidan up to – Martin was in bed next to me snoring by 11.30 on Friday night!

ooo

6.30 pm

As I arrive home, Carolyne tells me about this morning's phone call from Maria – she's not happy. *"This is the third time Maria has called me to talk about you and Aidan being out 'til all hours... And you've only stayed out really late that time you, Aidan and Kevin* [Hughes] *got really drunk at Kevin's house,"* she reminds me of the night of the mayoral referendum result.

"You need to tell Aidan that I am not lying for him again... If he's up to something, then he's not bringing me into it! If you want to lie for him you can. But I don't like him and I never have so I don't see why I have to be compromised by that twat."

I agree to have a word with Aidan about his lies.

ooo

Friday August 19th 2005...

Carolyne and I leave for our annual break in France.

ooo

Monday September 5th 2005...

When I return from my summer holidays my staff have quietly moved us into our new offices at the Council House – we're getting quite good at this!

ooo

2.00 pm – Full Council – Doncaster Council Chamber

Full Council today and the Leader of the Lib-Dems Councillor, Patrick Wilson, asks me about the recent cancellation [for a second time] of a briefing to elected members on the council's restructuring. No reason has been given for the cancellation and Councillor Wilson says he believes the Managing Director is treating elected members without any respect or due regard. He asks if I can explain, on behalf of the MD, why the briefing has been cancelled again.

I actually agree with Councillor Wilson. Susan is becoming a bit of a liability treating both members and staff with contempt and disdain. However, on the basis that I have only just returned from holiday, I say I am unable to answer the question immediately; buying time to find out what's been going on...

David Hughes questions me about the appointment of Ian Spowart... He wants to know who will be paying his salary – the Labour Party or the Council Tax payer. He also wants to know, as indicated in the recruitment pack, when my Political Assistant will be speaking to the public and publishing work – and how can this be right?

I explain, again, that [my] Political Assistant will be "free" to publish material "if he so wishes" – his post not being politically restricted as other council officers are.

Again, I emphasise that he has been appointed to assist and develop the mayor's policies within the confines of the Local Government Act 2000, which is in keeping with any other mayoral authority in the United Kingdom.

Councillor Simpson asks if the mayor can indicate how widely, when and where he has advertised the post of Political Assistant, to which Ian has been recently appointed?

To try to draw a line under this political appointment I explain succinctly that the post was advertised widely [by word of mouth] within the Labour group/party in Doncaster; and that I'm delighted Ian is working with me and working effectively.

ooo

Wednesday September 7th 2005...

The new Vardy-sponsored Trinity Academy opens in Thorne today. Run by the Emmanuel Schools Foundation [ESF], the project has been controversial in that the school sits outside Local Education Authority control and has been criticised because the ESF teaches creationism.

Despite my insistence that the academy route is the best solution for this community, I choose not to attend the opening.

ooo

Thursday September 8th 2005...

"Ousted Councillor in Mansion House return" screams the Doncaster Free Press and proceeds to report how "A former Labour councillor who lost his seat in last year's elections has returned to
the Mansion House – as the mayor's £25,000-a-year policy advisor."

To be frank, I don't see what the fuss is about – this is a political officer appointment like many made within local authorities up and down the country. I need to have somebody I can trust, who understands the mayoral system… However, I need to be on my guard. The press are now openly fuelling the political unrest they so desire…

The paper reports: "Ian Spowart held two positions in DMBC's ruling cabinet [sic.] but became a high-profile casualty of 2004's election, moving to Rossington to run the village's Development Trust".

Not only are they poking me in the eye about a day-to-day political appointment, but they are guilty of extremely shoddy journalism; they have [deliberately] confused the model again – it is not "DMBC's ruling cabinet" but the [elected] "mayor's cabinet"!

The confused rag continues: "But news that Mr Spowart – who ran Martin Winter's 2002 mayoral election campaign – has again become the mayor's right hand man has led to claims of 'jobs for the boys' from opposition councillors."

ooo

Friday September 9th 2005…

6.00 pm – Central Park [bistro], Lazarus Court, Doncaster

Aidan, Chris and I are meeting up with Rosie once again to wrap up the week, over a meal, whilst we talk politics.

ooo

9.30 pm

As the evening moves on we find ourselves visiting a senior national political figure at his home in Doncaster.

ooo

10.00 pm

Rosie makes her excuses – telling us she is leaving for an appointment first thing in the morning.

ooo

10.30 pm

Aidan makes his excuses – which is even stranger, saying he'll get a taxi out on Thorne Road, one of the main roads into Doncaster.

ooo

10.45 pm

Chris and I finish off and get a cab on Thorne Road. I drop Chris off first at his house before heading home for about 11.15pm.

ooo

Saturday September 10th 2005...

7.30 am

I tell Carolyne about last night's meeting and we talk about how strange it is that Rosie left at 10.00 pm and Aidan half an hour later... Carolyne suspects Aidan may be 'playing away from home' and we speculate that the woman in question could be Rosie, before quickly dismissing the idea.

Rosie wouldn't do that and certainly not with Aidan for a number of reasons – not least because he is far below her on the status scale.

ooo

Monday September 12th 2005...

Carolyne pops round to see Maria as she is passing that way. Maria confides in Carolyne that yet again Aidan didn't arrived home until 4.00 am on Saturday morning. Carolyne can't help but raise her eyebrows: *"I don't think Martin was home that late..."*

"Oh yes, I heard the door go at about 4.00 ish but Aidan didn't come upstairs," Maria responds. *"So after a couple of minutes I went downstairs to confront him. He told me he had walked home from town after the meeting with your Martin and Rosie, and he needed to have a good think about the conversations and the implications for him and his family."*

Carolyne tells me she just nodded but wondered how Aidan had taken six and a half hours to walk approximately 3 miles?!

Maria: *"We then talked about many other things and I got quite upset, but we managed to get through it all... Aidan was so lovely and kind..."* and she begins to tell Carolyne some rather intimate details of their time together.

Carolyne is used to getting 'too much information' from Maria and moves the subject on. When I arrive home later she tells me all about their meeting and their sordid conversation...

ooo

4.30 pm

I am livid. Susan has unilaterally halted both the September roll-out of the borough-wide green waste collection and the move to fortnightly waste collections. The cabinet and I have expressed our concerns that Susan made this decision without any discussion with either of us. As a result, I commission a series of actions to examine the effect of the delays and the associated cost implications.

I never receive a response!

ooo

Thursday September 15th 2005...

9.00 am – Toll Bar

In an effort to address the communication cock-up that Ed created patrolling with my Community Safety wardens in July, I have suggested we work together – alongside our Community First staff – during a Making A Difference [MAD] week entitled "operation deep cleanse".

To keep hold of the message, I have suggested Ed joins me for the day and we have an enjoyable time. He surprises me on many levels; his enthusiasm, but also his complete lack of common sense, coordination, fitness or any ability to move bulky household waste items... Although, having banned him from moving furniture when Carolyne and I moved him into his house last April, I don't know why!

After several hours, where we undoubtedly slow down the refuse team, Ed and I bid them farewell and congratulate ourselves on a good morning's work.

ooo

Monday September 19th 2005…

3.00 pm – Doncaster Star

Our Comm's Team staff have brought me tonight's Doncaster Star. They are concerned about how the newspaper has reported on my MAD activity with Ed last Thursday:

"MP and mayor back big clean-up blitz of village" reads the headline – not a good start, I think, with the mayor playing a [lower-case] subservient role to the MP.

"A Doncaster MP and the town's mayor rolled up their sleeves to support a Community First Initiative cleaning the streets of a local village." Not a good start in terms of mayoral messages – but compounded by a sole image of the MP, caption "Ed Miliband: On the bins".

"What the fuck do we have to do?" I ask our comm's team *"These bastards are doing it deliberately"*. The rest of the article reports, in a civic responsibility way, how the mayor appears to have muscled in on the MP's photo-session in his attempt to court public recognition… Not the message we conveyed:

The MP has been invited to join the Mayor in specifying the level of cleanliness the Mayor [and community] expect within their neighbourhood; as part of the Mayor's drive to deliver cleaner streets and safer neighbourhoods across Doncaster!

This constant inaccuracy, mendacity even, on the part of the newspapers may yet prove to be the most significant of threats to my mayoralty… I ask the Comm's Team to organise yet another meeting with the local newspaper's editors and that we undertake an independent analysis of its reporting of Doncaster and "The Mayor".

ooo

Saturday September 24th 2005…

6.00 pm – Lakeside Apartments, Kentmere Drive, Doncaster

Nadeem Shah has invited Carolyne and me as special guests to his charity event to raise funds for the South Yorkshire Community Foundation and South Yorkshire People Against Crime.

Beforehand we are meeting up at Susan Law's apartment at the Lakeside for drinks; Carolyne and I, Susan and her husband, and our new Director of Development, Peter Dale and his wife.

Aidan and Maria are supposed to be joining us as well but Aidan phones Susan to say they are running late and will go straight to the ball.

ooo

7.00 pm – Old Cantley

When we arrive at the ball, Aidan and Maria are already there. Tonight's "Speakeasy" theme encourages guests to dress as 1920s gangsters & molls and many have made the effort – even sporting violin cases and tommy-guns. It builds on the success of previous charitable fundraisers organised by the Shahs, not least the hugely successful Bollywood party two years ago.

These events are extremely well run and held in a large marquee in the palatial grounds of Nadeem's home. They have become widely supported and admired in the region and as a result, all Doncaster's great and the good are in attendance as well as many from further afield.

The marquee has been transformed into a prohibition era 'Speakeasy' with approximately thirty circular cabaret tables laid out around a large sprung dance floor. Around the room are many images of Al Capone, Dillinger, Bonny & Clyde, and others, such as Billie Holiday, Cab Calloway and Duke Ellington. A large self-service food area is at the rear of the room with a separate bar; there is a band area to the fore of the dance floor and stage, where there is also a display of raffle prizes and auction lots.

The new Chief Constable, Med Hughes, is here. To be quite frank, I find the man deplorable – as do many in the sub-region – and I try to avoid him wherever possible. I'm not a fan of South Yorkshire Police having witnessed their brutality at the 'Battle of Orgreave' in 1984; the deaths of the 96 at Hillsborough in 1989; and the way they were complicit in covering up the road-rage attack on me in 1999. But I've made every effort with Med, including having a romantic dinner with him some twelve months ago!

Nonetheless, I find him unbelievably arrogant, manipulative, cynical of politicians [and particularly the mayoral model] and a self-confessed admirer of Thatcher – despite acknowledging the damage she inflicted on our coalfield communities, not least in South Wales!

For this evening, sporting a sharp pinstriped tailored suit, I am the epitome of 1920s networking respectability and enjoy speaking on micro and macro levels with a great many guests, about all manner of local and global issues.

As the evening moves on, representatives from the South Yorkshire Community Foundation and South Yorkshire People United Against Crime are invited to make presentations before the new Chief Constable is due to speak.

Then Med gathers himself to address the event:

"Good evening ladies and gentlemen. Can I first of all thank Nadeem Shah and his wife for organising this excellent charity fundraising event... The last time I was in a room with as many criminals as are here tonight, I was in a meeting with Mayor Winter and Doncaster Council."

You could hear a pin drop – and Med hurriedly moves on, delivering a short, nervous, speech. After a perfunctory round of applause, he makes his way back to our table and the Speakeasy Band strike up again. He smiles nervously at me.

"Thanks for that one Med," I say as he bends to take a sip of his drink.

"What's that Martin?" he asks in his Welsh Valley [Rhonda] accent, smacking his lips.

"Four years I've been struggling to distance Doncaster from the allegations of fraud and corruption."

"And you decide to call us all gangsters – and me Al Capone!" I tell him in exasperated hyperbole.

"Oh you're too fucking touchy Martin," he defends himself. "You need to lighten up – it was only a bit of fun"

"Only a bit of fun... Oh that's alright then – it you were only joking.... If you were only joking, you won't mind apologising then?" I'm mindful not to swear, keenly aware that Med has crossed this line.

I look across and can see Nadeem and Maureen Shah and other guests looking decidedly uncomfortable with the situation and Med's behaviour. I look at the guests, mindful of my moral supremacy. "I spend all my time, trying to move on from the corruption of the past and you see fit to destroy it in one swoop," I address him and the guests around the table.

"Ok fuck off" he exclaims at me. "You sanctimonious cunt!" and he walks away.

Well I am shocked. Genuinely I am shocked – to use the 'C word' so instantaneously. Ordinarily, I would have chased after him and remonstrated over his behaviour – but this is a very public spectacle and several of the guests who heard his outcry are similarly shocked.

"It seems strange he should sink to the 'C word' so quickly..." I say to those present. "But I suppose we should be grateful that he's graced us with his attendance." I change the subject to the Ricky Hatton signed boxing gloves that are to be auctioned; but while I'm calm on the outside – internally I am raging.

How dare he speak to me like that in public? How dare he accuse all Doncaster politicians of being crooks? And how dare he use such appalling language – does he have no sense of decorum...? Evidently not.

ooo

As the evening proceeds, Carolyne remarks that Maria, who is sat with Aidan at a separate table to ours, has been blanking her all evening – there's maturity for you!

ooo

Thursday September 29th 2005...

Despite problems with Susan Law, who has constantly prevaricated over the funding and delivery of this mayoral commitment, today marks the rollout of my Fruit into Schools programme to all under elevens across the borough.

Teachers, children and parents who have already taken part in the pilot project have reported a better atmosphere in class with more attentive pupils, improved behaviour and children eating more fruit at home.

ooo

Aidan is becoming increasingly difficult to manage and won't toe the line. He has now inveigled himself into so many external appointments that he is earning more than I am! Whilst I am not concerned about remuneration, there is a massive issue about whether he is capable of applying himself to the job in hand...

Having said that, after the kicking he took last March over the MP position, he's been seriously disenchanted and I have to accept that our relationship is probably on the way out...

In the interim there is a good piece in tonight's Doncaster Star under the strapline "Donnygate Change a good example to others" – on the downside it's a piece promoting Aidan, who has been speaking at the Northern Personnel Conference in Harrogate [!].

ooo

Monday October 3rd 2005...

2.00 pm – Full Council – Doncaster Council Chamber

Due to a family funeral, I arrive late at today's Full Council. But when I subsequently look at the draft minutes, I see that during the questions on notice to the mayor, which Aidan took, he stated that he wanted to respond to a question submitted by Councillor John Cooke, outside of the timescale for inclusion on the agenda for this meeting...The question asked about the cost of the 'Values Workshops' being held for Council staff.

He confirmed that the council was conducting a series of 'Values Workshops' for its entire staff and that this would be at a total cost of £115,000, equating to £19 per head. He felt this was a modest and sensible sum in the context of the council's overall annual turnover of £0.5 billion, and given that the workshops would define and engender in staff the standards and values which this council was currently driving forward and aspiring towards.

This seemed strange. Clearly the question aims at making trouble – but I don't understand Aidan's maths – £115,000 divided by £19 per head would mean we only have around 6,000 staff. Now it may be we have omitted the several thousand staff across our many schools, although I don't see why; but the numbers don't seem to stack up when you consider we have around 13 - 16,000 staff - depending how you calculate it.

I need to stay away from this one!

ooo

Thursday October 6th 2005...

12.00 pm – Doncaster Racecourse

Today we are launching "St Leger Homes" – the Arms Length Management Organisation [ALMO] we have established to deliver on the decent homes programme. I am fairly pleased with how the process has operated and put some of that down to the Housing Green Paper I drafted the night my father died.

ooo

2.00 pm

After two aborted attempts, Aidan and Susan finally run the Members Seminar on the Corporate Plan's Implementation, including their briefing on the council's restructuring.

ooo

Friday October 7th 2005...

Ian, Aidan and I have been reflecting on a conundrum I have over my new mandate and the reluctance of government to devolve powers to mayoral authorities, despite talking a very good game...

South Yorkshire has four "joint authorities" which operate on a sub-regional basis across the boundaries of the four local authorities.
- South Yorkshire Police Authority;
- South Yorkshire Fire & Rescue Authority;
- South Yorkshire Pension Authority;
- South Yorkshire Passenger Transport Executive – SYPTE.

Control of membership of these "outside bodies" is very much a "closed shop" affair, controlled through the South Yorkshire Leaders who, themselves, are controlled by their elected members [councillors].

All positions on the "joint authorities" carry a Special Responsibility Allowance [SRA] and each has a chair and vice-chair role, which commands an enhanced SRA.

Although nominations are controlled through majority group processes, the South Yorkshire Leaders apportion the roles through the allocation of one chair and one vice-chair to each of the local authorities. Doncaster has the Chair of the SYPTE and the Vice-chair of South Yorkshire Police Authority.

ooo

For the past three months I have been embroiled in an internal Labour Party argument about who has the executive control of appointments to outside bodies; and whether an [elected] mayor can legally sit on such a body since the legislation only specifies elected councillors!

The legislative guidance is vague but I am clear that because these are executive functions, the executive mayor has responsibility for such allocations through his election.

This has never been too much of a problem previously because I have tended to run with the incumbents and/or use the process to "reward" the loyalty of those supporting me.

However, the times they are a changin' and I have become preoccupied with taking charge of transport and the re-regulation of the bus service in Doncaster. My mandate being my manifesto commitments to introduce the "Free*Don* Pass" and "lobby Government for the re-regulation of the bus service in Doncaster"; stipulating *"If they can do it for Mayor Livingstone, then they can do it for Mayor Winter"*... and to achieve this, I need to Chair the SYPTE.

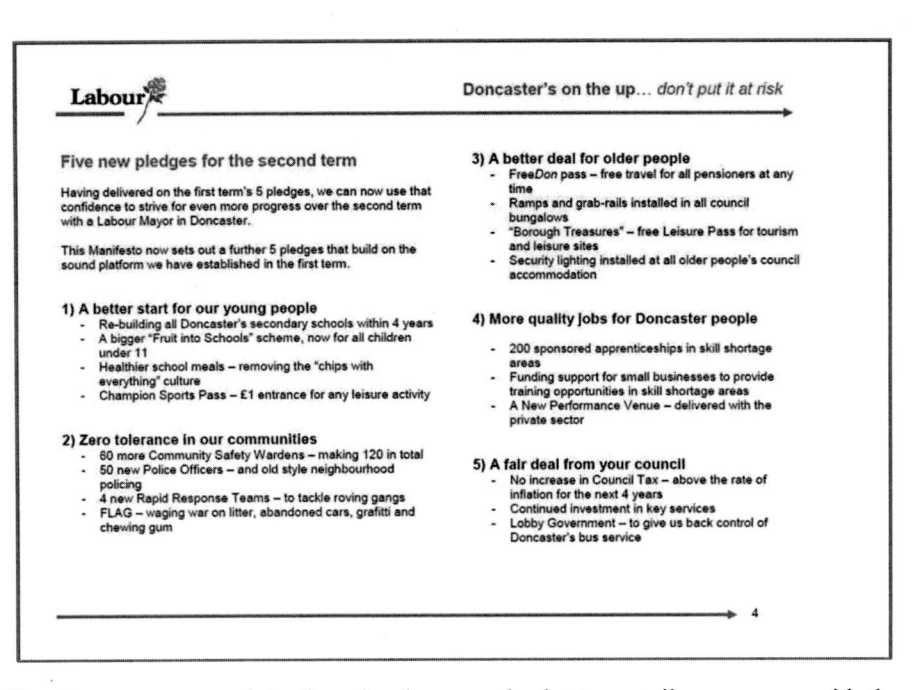

> **Labour**
>
> **Doncaster's on the up... *don't put it at risk***
>
> **Five new pledges for the second term**
>
> Having delivered on the first term's 5 pledges, we can now use that confidence to strive for even more progress over the second term with a Labour Mayor in Doncaster.
>
> This Manifesto now sets out a further 5 pledges that build on the sound platform we have established in the first term.
>
> **1) A better start for our young people**
> - Re-building all Doncaster's secondary schools within 4 years
> - A bigger "Fruit into Schools" scheme, now for all children under 11
> - Healthier school meals – removing the "chips with everything" culture
> - Champion Sports Pass – £1 entrance for any leisure activity
>
> **2) Zero tolerance in our communities**
> - 60 more Community Safety Wardens – making 120 in total
> - 50 new Police Officers – and old style neighbourhood policing
> - 4 new Rapid Response Teams – to tackle roving gangs
> - FLAG – waging war on litter, abandoned cars, grafitti and chewing gum
>
> **3) A better deal for older people**
> - Free*Don* pass – free travel for all pensioners at any time
> - Ramps and grab-rails installed in all council bungalows
> - "Borough Treasures" – free Leisure Pass for tourism and leisure sites
> - Security lighting installed at all older people's council accommodation
>
> **4) More quality jobs for Doncaster people**
> - 200 sponsored apprenticeships in skill shortage areas
> - Funding support for small businesses to provide training opportunities in skill shortage areas
> - A New Performance Venue – delivered with the private sector
>
> **5) A fair deal from your council**
> - No increase in Council Tax – above the rate of inflation for the next 4 years
> - Continued investment in key services
> - Lobby Government – to give us back control of Doncaster's bus service
>
> 4

Despite my new mandate, there has been a sub-plot to curtail my powers with the increasingly more militant members of the Labour group attempting to wrestle power back from the mayor.

Central to this particular plot has been Councillor Mick Jameson who has never forgiven me for refusing his plea to be known as "The Mayor" during his tenure as "Chair of Council" the previous year; it's a squabble not lost on the malcontents who delight in presenting him their petition demanding my resignation.

Mick was the Chair of SYPTE until I removed him three months ago. With its membership drawn from the four South Yorkshire authorities, it was an appointment with a not insignificant SRA attached to it.

Since I mooted the issue of providing the "Free*Don* Pass" – free bus travel to all pensioners in Doncaster – as part of my 2005 Manifesto – SYPTE and the South Yorkshire Leaders have been a little circumspect about me and my policies.

Consequently, I have become embroiled in a wider South Yorkshire row as Councillor Jameson solicits the support of his SYPTE colleagues and, through them, the South Yorkshire Leaders who fear the unrest may spread.

Monday October 10th 2005…

There are always at least two different sides to an argument – and this battle over who appoints the Chair to the SYPTE is taking up a lot of time, so I need to consider my options.

One area to consider is that I have a huge popular mandate, having been elected less than six months ago by nearly forty six thousand people on a fifty five percent turnout.

Another is that, despite being so early into my second term, there is still quite a lot of disenchantment over my mayoralty… this I put down to three things;
- a rabid opposition continually waging its insurgency campaign;
- an immature and mendacious press eager to create a regular news stream;
- and the tribal and increasingly militant nature of the Labour group, blind to the implications of LGA 2000.

I'm reminded of a scene from a George A Romero film… you can only fight one, maybe two or three "zombies" at any one time; otherwise, they come one after another in waves, until they finally engulf you.

In a similar manner, and if I'm not mixing my metaphors, they act like vampires, sucking your enthusiasm and draining your energy and drive…

I have to acknowledge that I'm fighting on a lot of fronts. If I'm not careful, the battles will engulf me; I decide to concede defeat… for today.

000

Wednesday October 12th 2005…

The Doncaster Star runs with the headline "Mayor faces call to quit – Labour councillor tells him he must go over transport wrangle". You can always rely on Ted!

Even so, I have to concede that losing this particular battle, on the basis of the South Yorkshire Leaders' reluctance to deal with their councillors for fear of repercussions, has certainly damaged me.

This is an area I need to consider in more detail. To quote David Marlow's extremely perceptive insight from three years ago: *"There is no thought-through government guidance as to what a successful mayoral system looks like – and, therefore, no significant incentives, rules and procedures against which to assess the performance".*

000

Thursday/Friday October 13th/14th 2005...

Today and tomorrow I am working with the Improvement and Development Agency [IDeA] on a peer review at the London Borough of Hackney. This is to enable a fellow mayoral authority to prepare for its Comprehensive Performance Assessment [CPA] next year.

ooo

Monday October 17th 2005...

It's that old issue of discipline again. Despite seventeen secondary heads appearing to be on-board with my "Partnership Agreement", which was presented to them last March, they are clearly not. One of the teaching unions' secretaries has gone to the press accusing me of trying to bring the schools under political control.

"Row over £300m Schools Deal" shouts the front page of the Doncaster Star and criticises my six point "Partnership Agreement" with the schools.
- Do not opt out of Local Education Authority [LEA] control;
- Welcome the Education Standards Directorate into schools and heed their advice;
- Welcome independent careers advisors into schools;
- Give parity of importance to academic and vocational study;
- Support DEC and allow presentations from the college and "taster days";
- Back my healthier school meals initiative;

I would have thought the very nature of being part of an LEA means there's "an element of political control".

It's really quite simple. If we are going to "up-front" the investment needed in these schools, investing Doncaster taxpayer's money in advance of the government's support, then I want to make sure we are all singing off the same hymn sheet – and that the schools aren't going to snatch the cash and then "cut-and-run".

ooo

Thursday October 20th 2005...

9.00 am – Mansion House Priory Suite

Change for the sake of change... The Corporate Performance Assessment [CPA] process that I have been so looking forward to has changed this year. It now consists of a "Corporate Assessment" and "Joint Area Review".

This morning I am leading the "CA/JAR" presentation to the visiting Audit Commission team. I must say, I am a little irked to see my Fruit into Schools programme on the front slide of my PowerPoint, given the difficulties I have had getting it extended. Nonetheless, I lead off, explaining how Doncaster has changed significantly over the past five years, inspiring a renewed confidence in local people.

I talk about our industrial past, the decline of which contributed to many deep-rooted economic and social problems and how the opportunities presented by our strategic location, transport infrastructure and external funding, are now being harnessed to deliver an economic revival which is helping to deliver outcomes for residents.

A new international airport has now opened and the urban renaissance of the town centre will take a significant leap forward with the opening of our new £200m transport interchange/retail complex and Doncaster Education City in 2006. A new Community Sports Complex and stadium, a racecourse and conference centre revamp will soon follow and we have just started a "competitive dialogue" with three major developers on the redevelopment of our inner-city Waterdale area into a Civic and Cultural Quarter.

But fundamental challenges remain in terms of tackling deprivation and improving educational attainment. Our radical remodelling of the council through the 'Winning Council' agenda is aimed at delivering the services people want and need. Working with our partners and with Government we aim to transform the lives of Doncaster residents and lead the move towards Doncaster becoming a dynamic, vibrant European city.

As I summarise, I explain how "the Council" is leading these changes – and how the Mayoral system of Governance has been key to establishing clear accountability for delivering against the transformational goals we set ourselves four years ago. Our success in improving the Council and rebuilding confidence following the well-publicised problems of the 1990s was recognised through a "Good" CPA rating in 2004; and building on the success we achieved the previous year, our self-assessment for the Corporate Assessment for the "Five Key Lines Of Enquiry" [KLOE] is:

Theme 1 – Ambition   4

Theme 2 – Prioritisation   3

Theme 3 – Capacity	3
Theme 4 – Performance Management	3
Theme 5 – Achievement	3

ooo

12.00 pm – Mansion House, Ballroom

Following David Moody's appointment last year as the new Lord Lieutenant, he has been holding a series of South Yorkshire Business Luncheons to celebrate business in South Yorkshire. Central to this is Prince Andrew, in his *de facto* role as Business Champion. After similar events in Rotherham and Sheffield, today it is our turn to host a 'Lord Lieutenant's Business Luncheon', at the Mansion House.

I have met Prince Andrew several times now and he knows I am always good for a laugh, letting him use me as his stooge. I don't mind playing this role, because I want the Prince to accompany me on a trade visit I am proposing to Memphis, where I am attempting to court Fed-Ex with regard to the opportunity that is Doncaster Robin Hood Airport.

The Prince is on "fine form", regaling everyone with the history of the Mansion House paintings while "testing" me on my memory of which canvas sits where on the walls of the Mansion House Salon.

I give a very powerful presentation on the huge business opportunity Doncaster has become and the community buy-in for the big Doncaster vision. I cite particularly notable projects such as Robin Hood Airport; Doncaster Education City Hub Building and University Centre; the Town Moor Racecourse, Exhibition & Conference Centre; the Frenchgate Interchange and Retail Complex; the Community Stadium; and the New Performance Venue, Civic and Cultural Quarter.

It goes down fantastically.

ooo

Friday October 21st 2005...

Ian Spowart has asked me to have a meeting with Peter Thompson from Dantom Homes. I initially refuse, but Ian says Mr Thompson wants to make a complaint against the Head of Planning so I agree to hold the meeting to discuss the complaint.

I instruct Ian to speak to the Executive Director of Development and set it up.

11.00 am – Mayor's Parlour

In attendance are Peter Thompson; a person I believe to be a planning consultant for Mr Thompson; Peter Dale; and myself.

Opening the meeting, I stipulate that the only basis on which I am here is because there is a complaint against the Head of Planning. I state extremely robustly that in no way am I going to get into a discussion about the specifics of any planning application and everyone seems happy.

Mr Thompson, whom I know, paints a pretty appalling picture of customer care from several members of staff – but not particularly from the Head of Planning although as "Head" he is ultimately responsible for his staff's behaviour. Specific mention is made of an officer who has left the council's employment but taken "a file" with him – which Mr Thompson seems to think is the main issue.

I ask Peter Dale to sort it out and take it up with the appropriate officer.

Mr Thompson then starts to talk about whether or not some land is being used as a garden. I tell him I feel he is nudging at the planning application which I'm not prepared to discuss, and that we are best ending the meeting.

ooo

11.20 am

When everyone has gone, Peter Dale and I have a quick wrap up meeting to discuss a course of action. I again point out to Peter that I'm not concerned whether we pass the application or not... and stress that I am not being dragged into a planning application issue... But, stating the bleeding obvious, I ask why the officers haven't simply looked at the original application for the site to see what its designation was then?

I tell Peter that when the original plan was passed, in either 1999 or 2000, I was on the Planning Committee that conducted a site visit. I said I was against it then because of the orchard on the site – and I didn't want to lose another Victorian orchard. Surely, the application then would have stated whether it was an orchard or a garden.

ooo

Thursday October 27th 2005...

2.00 pm – Platform 1, Doncaster Train Station

In 1960 John Connell lobbied the Noise Abatement Act through parliament making noise a statutory nuisance in the UK for the first time. I am attending an event in London today – because our joint project between Environmental Health Officers [EHOs] and South Yorkshire Police, has used the noise abatement act to combat the problem of off-road motorcyclists, and been given an award.

I have just met the EHOs on the platform at Doncaster Station and the whole team is going down, alongside Ian Chorlton, representing the police.
Trevor McDonald, one of the senior EHOs is a barrel of laughs and we have an enjoyable journey down.

ooo

6.00 pm – Portcullis House, Westminster

At the venue, we are joined by Ros Jones and Hilary Caunt, the officers' managers, and I suggest I take them all to China Town afterwards for a celebration meal paid for by the council.

ooo

8.00 pm – China Town

The event was a huge success and I am really proud of this team, which has confiscated more than 300 nuisance, off-road motorcycles.

I explain that the meal will be paid for by Doncaster Council, as thanks for all the hard work they have been putting in but that I'd like to personally pay for their drinks for the evening. It's not very often some of these staff get to go to London, so I want to thank them and make the evening a bit of a celebration, for them having won such a prestigious national award.

ooo

Friday October 28th 2006…

1.20 am – Doncaster Train Station

Having just caught the last train, we finally arrive back in Doncaster and as I wave everyone off, we all agree it has been an excellent team-building event, great for staff morale.

ooo

2.16 pm

A copy of an email sent out by Susan Law, as a direct response to an officer suffering under a "deluge" of information requests from Councillor Margaret Pinkney. The officer talks about the inordinate amount of staff time spent responding to such requests and states *"If these were FOI requests, we would be charging, as the costs of compilation are more than £450. These are, however, simply queries from a Councillor – she is not sending them in as FOI."* The officer requests advice and states *"... but I also feel the need to stem this tide"*.

Susan responds:

From:	Law, Susan
Sent:	28 October 2005 14:16
To:	▅▅▅▅▅ Rave, Aidan; ▅▅▅▅▅
Cc:	▅▅▅▅▅ [Legal services]; ▅▅▅▅▅
Subject:	RE: Councillor Pinkney
Sensitivity:	Confidential

Aidan [in particular]

I think we should develop a clear policy and procedure for dealing with such requests. They are time consuming and what is worse, they are fishing expeditions. What would be the Councillor response to a policy that includes say, in responding to Councillor requests for information, that if it impacts significantly on time of staff, we can ask them for the purpose for which they are seeking the information? Also, the policy could include that information will not be given in respect of particular employees unless it is being sought for the purposes of raising performance issues or issues of impropriety with the MD.

Susan

Note – I have included the above "diary" entry for chronological correctness. I did not receive a copy of this email thread until several months afterwards.

ooo

3.00 pm

"Air Freight Capital of Yorkshire" screams the front page of the Doncaster Star, reporting on Robin Hood airport's first six months of operation and stating that with "… half a million passengers and 900 tonnes of goods" it has earned a place in the record books "as the fastest growing airport in the country's history".

ooo

Tuesday November 1st 2005…

"SCHOOL POLICY SLATED – council rapped for contract demand" declares the front page of the Doncaster Star and reports how "Council chiefs could face a caning…" after the newspaper sought the views of DfES officials.

It goes on to report that the DfES "… slammed the contract [my letter] as "unreasonable" and "not in the spirit" of its current proposals to make all schools independent of local authority control".

I suspect if they took the time to discuss what we are trying to achieve, they may be more supportive rather than responding to a mischief-making local rag.

ooo

Wednesday November 2nd 2005…

Susan still hasn't responded to the "2nd Term delivery priorities" paper which I presented her with four months ago; as such I have no action plan against my manifesto.

Susan is becoming increasingly belligerent within her work; refusing to acknowledge the political will of the executive and, paradoxically, Full Council; meanwhile the political executive are increasingly being used as apologists and scapegoats for her failure to meet expectations.

ooo

I express my concerns to Aidan. Susan has become fixated with the restructuring she has been bulldozing through, with apparently no real tangible results for me, the executive or wider councillors and certainly not for the Doncaster community.. He seems ambivalent to the whole issue; so I explain that I have decided we will need to performance-manage her through a series of [evidenced based] interventions during the next few months.

I feel I need to register my concerns and ask Susan if we can sit down together and talk about the emerging situation – because it certainly isn't working for me, or arguably most politicians.

Aidan agrees he will sit in with us but doesn't turn up! So at our next weekly discussion, I sit down with Susan and explain that I am beginning to have real concerns over her performance. I tell her I expect to have a full action plan and implementation strategy for my manifesto, as the response to my "2nd Term delivery priorities" paper, before she goes to Australia for Christmas. When she comes back, I tell her, we will be agreeing monthly, and weekly [if necessary] performance actions and targets.

She looks at me with puffy, bloodshot eyes almost as if she has been, or is about to start, crying. *"Well I don't suppose there's a great deal I can say [is there?]"* she replies in her inimitable arrogant antipodean manner. *"I suppose I must be really bad then..."* she continues, which really stuns me as a professional officer's response to a fairly exacting and serious statement.

"So you wanna get rid of me?" she asks in a hard Aussie accent.

"No," I say. *"Not particularly... I just want you to do your job"*

"I suppose... if you're that disappointed with me... you should sack me..." she taunts.

Then: *"I really can't be bothered to deal with this now – why don't you just sack me then...?"* And she leaves the meeting.

Clearly we have real problems here.

ooo

I try to discuss Susan, with Aidan, who makes one of his many excuses that "something has cropped up at home" and is then extremely evasive and non-committal about performance- managing the MD [or not!].

ooo

I email Susan Law about my Zero Waste policy and strategy. Within the letter I stipulate that "municipal" [domestic] waste only accounts for 14% of the UK waste stream and ask her to focus officer research on the wider waste stream; that is, the remaining 86% of construction/demolition [43%] and commercial waste [43%] not featured in the local authority recycling rates.

This email contains five action point requests, including:

"To request a report that clarified the financial implications of not moving to fortnightly collections; with the kerbside green waste"

The MD never responds.

Monday November 7th 2005...

2.00 pm – Full Council – Doncaster Council Chamber

Unison has organised a protest outside today's Full Council meeting against the restructuring plans for the Council.

ooo

5.00 pm – Mayor's Office, Council House

I have a debriefing with two of the CMT members who are leading on the CA/JAR process. It would appear the process isn't going as well as we expected.

ooo

Tuesday November 8th 2005...

9.30 am – Mayor's Office, Council House

Interview for the CA/JAR.

ooo

3.00 pm

The Doncaster Star features a front page report on yesterday's protest. The article says that protestors "...also raised concerns over £150,000 spent on council "values" seminars which have caused controversy within the authority after it brought in Australian consultants".

It continues: "A question was also raised over the seminars by Councillor Martin Williams who asked how much it has cost "to bring in a consultant from Adelaide to give a pep talk on being a winning council".

ooo

Thursday November 10th 2005...

I am getting seriously pissed off. The interim feedback from the JAR and CA is not good – although I believe we can furnish the Audit Commission team with further evidence to address some of their concerns. Having said that, I have a slight worry that several staff members, unhappy with the restructuring Susan is bulldozing through, may be taking the opportunity for a little payback.

ooo

Thursday November 17th 2005...

4.23 pm – Holyrood, Edinburgh

During the Scottish Parliament's Waste Strategy debate today, Mark Ruskell MSP [Green] cited Doncaster as a "best practice "exemplar project for zero waste.
    "If the minister adopts in full a zero waste policy, he will not be alone in doing so, because New Zealand has adopted the concept and the Labour mayor of Doncaster is mad keen on zero waste. We should all be working together on such issues".

ooo

Friday November 18th 2005...

8.30 am – Mayor's office, Council House

Second interview for the CA/JAR and the Peer Inspector wants to drill down on some of the issues identified earlier.

ooo

2.00 pm – Mansion House, Priory Suite

Feedback from JAR and CA. Things are not good. The Audit Commission is proposing to award us a "3 Star" rating... I am not happy. We should have achieved a "4 Star" rating – the "excellent council" status we [I] have put so much store by.
    In the feedback from JAR, they say they are not happy about children's services, citing "piles of unallocated cases" they have seen in offices.
    I express significant concerns and Susan starts to rant about the process being unsafe suggesting we should consider challenging it – and our rating.

ooo

Thursday November 24th 2005...

10.00 am – Sustainable Communities Overview & Scrutiny Panel [Minutes].

Under Agenda Item 12, the Doncaster Local Development Framework Core Strategy Update – as part of the discussion, the Audit Commission report into the Glass Park was produced.

Resolved that:

2. a copy of the recently produced Audit Commission report on the Glass Park Project be circulated to all Members of the Council for information;

ooo

Monday December 5th 2005...

The shit has hit the fan again. Following circulation of the Audit Commission report, eleven days ago, members are claiming a cover up.

I talk to Liz about the situation. This is a project I am incredibly proud of, having given more than ten years of my life – and re-mortgaged our house twice – to deliver it.

To be honest, I half expected I would be nominated for some kind of an honour, in and around 1999-2000, given my huge commitment to this project. But I always knew it would become a political football when I took over as leader and then mayor.

Whilst I was involved– as "Project Director" – it was the epitome of probity and integrity. Everybody knew it was a brilliant project, and wanted a piece of the "action"; and I bent over backwards to keep it away from Doncaster Council.

The Glass Park was a massive success and the embodiment of 'community-led' in terms of transparent consultation processes and accountability over decision making. All the decisions and expenditure were scrupulously recorded and audited.

Nonetheless, the project is becoming damaged and I am distraught that its name is being dragged through the mud by malcontents rabid in their attempts to find the means to discredit me.

ooo

2.00 pm – Full Council – Doncaster Council Chamber

You should never underestimate the enemy and it is clear that the malcontents are working with several opposition councillors. They have also coordinated their activity with reporting on the issue in today's Yorkshire Post…

Under "Questions to Mayor Martin Winter" Councillor Patrick Wilson suggested that as a Millennium Project the 1st Phase of the Glass Park at Kirk Sandall appeared to have been a success. Do you not agree with me that if the 67% of grants, which had been spent solely on administration, had been spent differently, the project would have been more successful?

In reply, Mayor Winter thanked Patrick Wilson for his questions and indicated that he didn't agree, the Millennium project was a successful project with which he was proud to be involved. He stated that it had provided the local area with 25 acres of sports ground and a millennium green nature reserve. He indicated that it was unfortunate that, as he was involved with the project, a political smear campaign had been undertaken, but he was incredibly proud of the project.

Councillor Mick Maye asked whether Mayor Winter would agree that the best way to deal with the revelations and accusations made in today's Yorkshire Post, along with the rumours of further revelations to follow... would be to call an extraordinary meeting of this council to discuss the funding given to the Glass Park Company in addition to any further funding applications currently pending. He suggested that at the same time council could examine the recommendations in the auditor's report.

In response, Mayor Winter thanked Councillor Maye for his question and indicated that Councillor Maye would understand the situation as Councillor Maye had recently also stood down as a representative on the Market Traders Association [with similar allegations having been made]. *Mayor Winter reported that he had made his public statement and the article was a politically orchestrated attempt to discredit the Mayor. He indicated that he had not read the report yet* [genuinely] *but would look forward to reading it tonight.*

Following this, under "Questions to Councillor Barbara Hoyle, the Chair of the Overview and Scrutiny Management Committee", Councillor Jessie Credland referred to a request made some time ago for a report on the Glass Park to be submitted as an item for Scrutiny to look at.

In an effort to provide Members with an opportunity to discuss the report, Councillor Hoyle agreed that the Audit Commission report be placed on the Overview and Scrutiny Management Committee's Work Programme to be discussed at a future meeting.

ooo

Notwithstanding the above, and operating slightly schizophrenically, the meeting then unanimously agrees to support two motions backing my manifesto:
 I submit a motion with regard to our concerns over the third price increase this year for users of public transport – a motion "seconded" by Councillor Mick Jameson [!] and agreed unanimously.
Councillor Tony Sockett submits a motion [in support of my partnership agreement with schools], which condemns government proposals to reduce the role of LEAs – which is agreed unanimously. Additional motions worthy of note include:
- Councillor Edwin Simpson [Lib-Dem] submits a motion to scrap ID Cards – which is defeated;

- Councillor Patricia Schofield [Tory] submits a motion to adopt a policy of using renewable, sustainable energy sources in council-owned property – which is carried;
- Councillor John Mounsey [Labour] submits a motion condemning the Lib-Dems national conference for suggesting that congestion charging be introduced in towns such as Doncaster as a means of dealing with increased traffic flows – which is carried;

ooo

Tuesday December 13th 2005...

There appears to be a theme emerging here... Councillors Cliff Hampson and Tony Brown have reported me to the Standards Board but more importantly, they've notified the newspapers as well!

The Doncaster Star delights in giving its front page to the headline. "Mayor faces polls probe – Standards Board investigates claims over latest election campaign" and explains how Councillor Hampson said "I believe there has been a breach of the statutory conditions of the Local Government Code of Conduct and therefore I was obliged to report it to the Standards Board for England".

Politics can be a very dirty game but it's gratifying to know he was "obliged to report it"; duty-bound rather than malicious.

ooo

Thursday December 15th 2005...

3.00 pm

"Auditors praise efforts of council" reports page four of the Doncaster Star, completely missing the opportunity to kick a man who is stumbling [thankfully!].

"Improving but still more to do – that's the verdict of the Government auditors in their annual assessment of Doncaster Council..." before reporting that we have been given three out of four stars and that the CPA/JAR "... praised neighbourhood services as "good".

Partnership working with organisations such as the police and community groups was "strong". And the use of white and green papers by elected Mayor Martin Winter – similar to those created by national government – were highlighted for doing "a lot to promote public involvement in council policy and service delivery".

Susan is quoted as saying: "We are pleased with the three star rating. The process is more rigorous this year and we are still showing improvement."

I am more concerned that we have failed to achieve the excellent, four star rating I wanted. Certainly, the JAR process asked some very exacting questions of our children's services provision and commented on "hundreds of allocated cases" but Susan insists this is merely an administrative or procedural disagreement...

She is adamant that the whole process is corrupted, flawed, and needs challenging. She's done the business and has several people from our partner organisations making complaints about the preconceived and leading nature of the questioning.

Though I agree with her thought process, I wonder if this is to distract me from a "train crash" elsewhere...

ooo

Footnote

In seven years as the Mayor of Doncaster, I had to withstand three police investigations; three internal audit investigations; one independent external investigation and thirteen Standards Board for England investigations.

The only case I was found guilty of, was the SBE investigation into the complaint *"that [I] have or may have failed to comply with Doncaster Metropolitan Borough Council's Code of Conduct"*.

The SBE decided that, in sending out a letter [to Labour party members] on my mayoral headed paper, inviting them to a "Mayoral Policy Forum" alongside invitations to all other political parties, I utilised council resources for political purposes and, through this, breached the council's code of conduct – at a cost of £0.05p to the taxpayer!

Although, in mitigation, the SBE stipulated that there were not any policies or codes of conduct in place relating to such a communication process from a directly elected mayor.

ooo

Local political leadership in England and Wales by Steve Leach, Jean Hartley, Vivien Lowndes, David Wilson and James Downe, is published by the Joseph Rowntree Foundation:

There is considerable interest in the role of effective political leadership within local authorities in achieving the goals of the Government's modernisation agenda for local government. This agenda is intended to improve service performance and strengthen community leadership and democratic renewal.

Central Government has legislated for executive or cabinet government in the majority of local authorities to strengthen clarity of vision, community leadership and visibility. This study, by researchers from De Montfort and Warwick Universities, explored this agenda's impact on local leadership priorities, behaviour and skills, and found that:

- The introduction of local executive government [mayoral and non-mayoral] has not led to more uniform political leadership. Leaders have interpreted their role in diverse ways.
- The new political management structures and powers have had less impact on political leadership than expected: context and personal capabilities have been equally influential.
- Elected mayors generally recognised the need for a high degree of visibility and responsiveness to public and stakeholders' concerns; non-mayoral leaders varied more in the extent to which they recognised this.
- Most elected mayors saw external networking and community leadership as key roles. However, in general, political leaders have yet to give these roles the importance implicit in the Government's agenda.
- Where authorities had adopted the 'cabinet and leader' model there was little evidence of party pressure or adversarial party politics having diminished.
- Possessing a wider range of formal powers [as in the mayoral option] has not necessarily led individuals to exploit these powers proactively: leaders with a strong power base did not necessarily behave like strong leaders.
- Strong leaders could emerge without having either a strong power base or, sometimes, a formal leadership position.
- Strong individualistic leadership did not necessarily equate with effective leadership. Shared or collective leadership was also effective.
- Strategic ability, personal effectiveness, political intelligence and organisational mobilisation marked out political leaders. Several of these skills are acquired through work as a leader. This finding has important implications for the development and support of political leaders.

ooo

The "Free*Don* Pass": it is my contention that Ed Miliband unceremoniously "filched" this policy for Gordon to announce as part of his 2005 election campaign. He was very surprised to see that I had written it into my mayoral manifesto and took a great deal of interest that an [elected] mayor might want to deliver such a patently populist policy.

A very English coup d'état

*Even my close friend, someone I trusted,
one who shared my bread, has turned against me – Psalm 41:9*

Thursday December 15th 2005…

South Yorkshire Constabulary, Doncaster Division, College Road.

Susan Law, Paul Evans [as Monitoring Officer] and a senior communications officer attend Doncaster Central Police Station.
 Susan Law, as Managing Director of Doncaster MBC, asks the police to investigate [her allegation of] potential fraud within the Glass Park project.

Note – I have included the above "diary" entry for chronological correctness. I did not find out about who attended this meeting until six months later.

ooo

Friday December 16th 2005…

Susan Law requests a meeting with Mark Eales, Executive Director of Education. During the meeting she informs Mark that, whilst she is going to Australia for Christmas, she is appointing him Acting MD. In terms of a brief, Mark has a good hold of most strategic and operational issues but Susan tell him that she has drafted a short "key issues" paper she wants him to peruse so they can discuss it in more detail this afternoon.

ooo

1.30 pm – Full Council EGM

The members have now called for an EGM over the Glass Park… to be quite frank, I would've expected a strong Head of Paid Service to have fettled them for mischief-making but here we are…

The councillors calling the meeting reject my claims that it is a politically orchestrated smear campaign, and Councillor Mick Maye [defeated mayoral candidate] states: *"This has nothing to do with Mr Winter being the mayor – this issue goes back several years before then"*. This is my point entirely... they are trying to take a project – which [admittedly] is now being maintained poorly, and been so damaged it cannot "trade" or secure maintenance funds – and tie it in to the incumbent mayor.

It's a boisterous meeting, but nothing I can't handle and my main point is that whilst ever I was involved with the Glass Park, there was nothing untoward happening.

In fact, it was entirely the opposite; I was obsessive that the project should be delivered in an openly accountable and fully auditable manner and made sure the trustees involved had eminence and were protected from accusations of wrongdoing.

But I'm also reminded of what I said to the trustees when I stood down back in June 2001... *"I'm leaving the project in a very strong position, both financially and from a capacity perspective.*

... they should be under no illusion as to the pressure they will come under during the forthcoming months and years. I believe the Glass Park will become a political football, as individuals and groups attempt to destroy my credibility as the senior Local Government representative in Doncaster."

That prophecy, it appears, is now coming true.

ooo

5.50 pm

Susan has her follow-up meeting with Mark Eales.

"Finally Mark..." she tells him *"you need to be aware that whilst I'm away... something really bad will happen...*

"I can't tell you what it is [now]... but as soon as it happens you will know."

And with that prophetic statement she leaves for Heathrow and the flight to Australia.

Note – I have included the above "diary" entry for chronological correctness. I did not find out about that she had said this until six months later.

ooo

Saturday December 17th 2005...

12.30 pm – Our House, Kirk Sandall

Ed has rung asking if he can pop in to see Carolyne and me. He arrives with a Christmas card and two wrapped presents, one a heavy box [for me] and the other something more flattened and heavy, which he says is something for Carolyne – as compensation for the burnt carpet!

ooo

1.15 pm

We wave Ed off and then open our "presents":
Mine – a pair of two boxed "House of Commons Whiskey Glasses". A lot of thought went in to that, given that I don't drink!
Carolyne's – a small silk rug, supposedly to put over the "accident damaged" burn-hole in my office carpet; it's not in line with our décor and looks to us more like a prayer mat. This seems a really strange present, given that it is to be "used" to put our dirty feet on.
Having visited a number of mosques and temples over the years, it looks remarkably similar in size to the markings on the floors in such places. With this in mind, rather than use it disrespectfully, we decide to store the mat with some of our other cherished possessions.

ooo

Monday December 19th 2005...

Mark Eales tells me that South Yorkshire Police has announced it is to investigate my role in the Glass Park project.

ooo

Tuesday December 20th 2005...

9.00 am – Our House, Kirk Sandall

I speak to Susan [in Australia] about the police investigation. She seems more surprised than me that the police are involved and offers to fly back straight away.

I tell her not to be so stupid – this isn't anything serious, just a bit of mischief-making from the members!

ooo

3.00 pm

We should all be thankful for small mercies, I suppose, but my, how they are communicated...

"Mayor broke rules claim: No action" reads the headline in the Doncaster Star in a "bad news – good news" kind of way. It then reports that the Standards Board for England [SBE] complaint – first reported in the Star last week [!]– has been thrown out and that an SBE spokesman said "we have decided not to investigate either of the complaints".

What's clear here is that the newspaper has been chasing bad news with the SBE! And when the SBE treat the "complaint" with the contempt it deserves, and dismiss it... the newspaper still feels duty bound to lead with the negative angle... Mayor broke rules claim... have you got that message into your psyche? Oh! and we almost forgot to say, there was no action... but the damage has been done.

ooo

Friday December 23rd 2005...

Aidan has been difficult to pin down all morning. Each year we purchase Christmas gifts for the staff; smellies and things for the girls in my office, Quality Street for the reception staff, alcohol for the attendants at the Mansion House etc. Every year he tries to avoid paying and this year is no exception – he is really trying to dodge me today.

I have bought him a bottle of House of Commons whiskey, which I tell him I had to "order" several weeks ago. I write on it *"Best wishes Tony"* and I take it round to his house and tell him thanks for all his support this year!

ooo

Friday January 13th 2005...

The front page of the Doncaster Star reads "Mayor urged to go" and follows with the sub-heading "Fraud squad officers' investigation into £500,000 Glass Park scheme".

Ouch – this one hurts. The article says both an internal investigation and an Overview & Scrutiny investigation "have been called for". This cry will become common place over the next few months as a variety of police, internal and external "investigations" all get underway.

What's the best way to damage somebody who ended "Donnygate"?... Create a sequel... "Donnygate 2– The Return"

ooo

The newspaper also reports how the College needs to quadruple its student numbers as part of its plans for full university status. I have a two stage cunning plan to help with this:

Firstly, I have been working with a councillor from Newcastle to bring the "Relate Institute" to Doncaster; Relate employs nearly 2,000 counsellors and psychotherapists, who will be enrolled for courses through Doncaster College's university centre.

Secondly, I am keen to allow our staff to have access to an additional one half day per month flexi-time if they commit to a learning programme with the university centre; using the 1½ days per month for studying. This would be funded through the college's access to "train to gain" funding.

ooo

Susan is now back from Australia and explains it was she who took "a file" to Doncaster Police! Apparently, *"because of Councillor Margaret Pinkney obsessiveness with her claims that the mayor is corrupt"* she instructed an officer to go into the archives and get out all the files on the Glass Park – to *"make sure everything's okay with the project"*.

Why you would ask somebody to "retrospectively audit" a previously audited and signed-off project remains a mystery. Nonetheless this is what Susan told me she instructed the officer to do. Having done that she says, the officer "found something" and therefore she had no option but to go to the police.

I tell her I would have thought her first "duty" was to raise the matter with me, as mayor, to see if I could clarify it. If she was still unhappy, then she should have told me that she remained concerned and had no option but to go to the police... But all this seems a little underhand.

I say the police will find nothing wrong with the project and that I am one hundred and ten per cent certain about that. But that her actions have severely damaged our relationship and I doubt we will be able to work closely together again.

Friday January 27th 2006...

Susan is really causing me difficulties. I clearly stated in my manifesto that I would: *"Limit the increase in council tax – for the whole of the second term. There will be no increase above the [RPI] level of inflation for the preceding 12 months."*

The RPI set the level last autumn but Susan is trying to get it to a different rate of inflation – the monthly rate – and as such we have brought forward budget scenarios and papers showing a proposed 3.2% rise!

I am not happy.

ooo

Saturday February 4th 2006...

It's increasingly difficult to think it's not a conspiracy against "the mayoral model" and the "mayoral brand", when the Doncaster Star is reporting on the "Council's Green Paper" consultation document!

ooo

Supposedly in preparation for the Overview & Scrutiny Management Committee [OSMC] investigation, Susan Law has commissioned another [independent] inquiry into Glass Park. It feels like war out there.

"Council sets up project probe – Controversial Glass Park scheme to be investigated again" reports the Doncaster Star.

ooo

Tuesday February 7th 2006...

5.00 pm

I have just discovered that Aidan is doing a CPA all week at Hackney, as part of an Audit Commission team. This is the first I know of this and, to be quite frank, I am livid. We have a Budgeting Seminar on Friday and Aidan leads on the whole of the budget-setting side of things...

I text him, bollocking him for not notifying me he is away – and the fact that I now have to present his portfolio. I tell him this is just one of several areas he has lapsed on and that I want to see him first thing Monday morning to discuss the situation.

Friday February 10th 2006…

10.00 am

I present Aidan's portfolio area as part of the Budgeting Seminar at OSMC!

ooo

Saturday February 11th 2006…

I attend the spring Labour Party Conference at Blackpool. Oh how the times have changed… after five years of being lauded, it would appear I have become *persona non grata*!

I have long discussions with Nan Sloan about the onslaught I am having to withstand; she appears to be very supportive of me.

I also have a good discussion with Judi Billing from the IDeA; and also Jules Pipe, the Mayor of Hackney, about Aidan's work there last week.

ooo

Monday February 13th 2006…

7.00 am – Grand St Leger Hotel

Paul picks me up at 6.45 am to take me to one of my regular breakfast meetings with the Chamber of Commerce at the Grand St Leger Hotel. This morning's meeting is with Chief Executive, Neville Dearden; President Sue Scholey and Vice-President Stephen Shaw.

As we approach the hotel, we pull up at the Racecourse roundabout, waiting to turn right.

"*Is that Aidan there in his new BMW?*" asks Paul.

"*Aye… it is… well he must've shit the bed to be up this early*"

And it concerns me that he is out and about so early…

ooo

8.25 am – Executive Office, Council House

As we park up later at the Council House, I am preoccupied with an action point from the meeting with the Chamber, which I want to discuss with one of my

Cabinet members. Approaching the office I glance over to see if they are in. None of them are but movement sensitive lights are on in all four ante rooms.

I go into my office and ask Karen if she knows where they are.

"I don't know where they are now... but they were in earlier on – in fact they've all been in since seven o'clock..." And I'm reminded of a conversation I had with Aidan once:

"But you're NEVER in early Aidan..."

"I am when I have a reason to..."

I smell a rat.

"How did they appear Karen?"

"Well... to be honest Martin... Aidan looked terrible and so did Glyn and Chris Mills.

"I was going to have a word with you about it because they looked really worried... You know... as if they were up to no good."

"I do... and they are" I reply. "Do you know... that stupid bastard thinks I'm gonna sack 'im... after all that shit last week"

"You ought to!" she responds.

"I know I should... that's half the problem. Where's Spowie... is he in yet?... I'd better ring Chris T."

ooo

"Hi Chris – it's me Martin. What do you know about Aidan and cabinet, Chris?" But before he has chance to respond I add: "Because they're up to no good... There's a coup going down."

"No... there's not a coup going down..." he says "... but they are very concerned and worried about you..."

"Nah... that's bollocks... this isn't about loyalty and support Chris... I'm telling you there's a coup going down here... right now as I'm talking to you."

"I think we should have a chat Martin... things aren't good... but there's no coup"

"I'm telling you Chris... that little fucker [Susan] has put Aidan up to it... and the stupid bastard's fallen for it – he's bit..."

At which point Karen interrupts me. "Oops... just a minute Chris..."

"Sorry to disturb you Martin – but Aidan wants a meeting with you... and cabinet" and she lifts and rolls her eyes to warn me she thinks it isn't good.

"Okay... can you ask them to give me five minutes Karen please?"

"And get hold of Spowie... and let him know something's going down" I whisper.

"Yes... it's going down now Chris... I'll have to get back to you."

8.45 am

I gather my thoughts – now's not the time for irrational thinking. I need to remain calm and avoid swearing. Aidan knocks on the door. He won't look me in the eye.

"Can we have a discussion with you please Martin" he asks rhetorically, entering my room followed by the other eight cabinet members: Stuart Exelby; John Hardy; Eva Hughes; Glyn Jones; Chris Mills; Bill Mordue; John Mounsey; and Tony Sockett.

"Sure... You're all looking very serious – you're not going to sack me are you?" I ask out loud, as they troop in. Letting them know that I know they're up to something. One by one they sit around my table. Nobody speaks so I decide I'll have fun with them.

"Well I've never seen you all looking so glum. Shall we sort out some cups of tea?"

"We need to talk Martin" says Aidan. He looks terrible and is struggling to look at me.

"Serious shit is it?" I ask, looking at each of their faces.

Only Eva and Stuart can look at me. Aidan peers down at the papers he's put out on the desk in front of him. *"We've had a meeting..."* he begins *"... and we're concerned about the allegations... and how you're standing up to them."*

I look around the room and most of them are still incredibly uneasy, so I start smiling. *"Well thanks for your concerns..."* I interject... *"But I'm not suffering at all ...well I don't think I am. I've always said that proving the truth is easy... but proving a lie is more difficult and I've done nothing wrong – it's Susan trying to set me up... It's obviously difficult for Carolyne and the kids... but we're bearing up thanks."*

"Well, if you'll allow me to continue" Aidan wrestles back control. *"We're concerned... you're not thinking straight... And we are so concerned that we want you to resign."*

He quickly grasps a paper in front of him *"... and if you won't resign... we've all signed this letter saying we'll all resign"* he finishes in a flourish.

"Whoa... " says Tony Sockett immediately *"... that's not what we agreed at all."*

"No it's not" adds Stuart Exelby *"Give us that paper here Aidan... I want my name taking off it. We just talked about you taking 'Gardening Leave' Martin..."* says Tony Sockett.

"... about you taking a month off... and Aidan [and us] covering for you" he continues. *"We are concerned about your health Martin... I want my name taking off the letter [as well]"* he finishes.

I look at Aidan and all the others around the table, smiling and making eye contact with each and every one individually...

"You know..." I begin calmly. *"When I got up this morning, I took my cup of tea out into the garden and I breathed in the cold fresh air... And I thought to myself... I can smell treachery ..."* and I look at Aidan.

"Don't you just love the smell of treachery... in the morning Aidan?"

[No response]

This is it, I thought. This is the moment when the young buck challenges the stag – and I better make sure I'm good.

"You see... I knew this was coming... I knew it would come to this... This isn't about my health... it's about you wanting to be in charge... isn't it Aidan?"

And I look around the room once again.

"But you all need to be really careful here... because Aidan's not being honest with you."

"He's in cahoots with Susan here."

"Let me just read you what I said in my texts to Aidan last week..." And I take out my phone read out my text, where I gave him a bollocking over Friday's Budgeting Seminar and ask to see him first thing Monday morning to discuss the situation.

From:	MJW
To:	Rave, Aidan;
Sent:	Tue Feb 07 22:29:29 2006
Subject:	Budget Presentation to OSMC

Aidan

I am extremely perturbed to have found out at 5.00 pm this evening that you will be in Hackney for the next few days – this will be 3 days out of the office this week in addition to the 4 days out of the office last week. I don't think I need to remind you of how tense the situation is at present – in fact I shouldn't have to – this is in addition to the fact that we had not spoken for 11 days prior to this Monday, despite my leaving answer phone messages and my request for you to set up a meeting with the Editor of the Free Press on the 20th January.

I say perturbed because I now have to present a session for you at the Budget Presentation to OSMC, which is your portfolio responsibility – I am totally unbriefed for this.

I also now have to present the Annual Inspection Letter at Cabinet tomorrow morning – I have had no notice or brief on this whatsoever and the Press will be there apparently.

We must discuss this totally unacceptable situation at the beginning of next week.

Thanks

Martin

"So that's what this is all about..."

"Aidan was wanting to get me first... weren't you Aidan?"

[No response]

"And he's dragged you all in with him. But you must be really stupid Aidan... because you know me... and you know never to give me an ultimatum... Because all I'll ever do is... tell you to shut the door on your way out..."

And I pause for the drama... and to pile the pressure on Aidan.

"I don't do ultimatums..." I say quietly... "Do I Aidan?" I whisper to him.

"But you're only ever as strong... as your weakest link Aidan... [Aren't you?]"

[No response]

"And it seems to me that your plan is full of weak links... You don't appear to have all that much support here, have you Aidan?"

[No response]

"Come on Aidan...let's go and have a chat in your room – and let these good people have a chat about what you've done."

[No response]

"C'mon Aidan... I think we should leave these good people to have a chat about what's happening – because I think you've been rumbled lying to them haven't you?"

"I'm not lying... it's what we agreed" he was becoming pathetic; he was like a small child; pitiful [and he knew it].

"Is it Aidan... is it really what you agreed? Because that doesn't seem to be what some of your colleagues are saying"

I hold out my hand for the letter – but Aidan won't let me have it.

"It's not what we agreed at all Aidan" says Tony Sockett once again. "And I've told you... I want my name taking off that letter. I am not going to be part of this."

"Aye...and me" says Stuart Exelby.

I hold out my hand for the letter again – but he still won't let me have it.

"We agreed we'd stay together" he volunteers. "We're not going to be split up."

Presumably, he's convinced them I will somehow shoot them one at a time or, more accurately they'll realise he's set them up.

"You see Aidan..." I patronise him. "You've been lying... and you've been rumbled lying... Here you go... I'll tell you how he lies..." I address the room.

"Because I told you when you said it that you were lying Aidan..."

"*And you know what I'm going to say – don't you?*" I goad him – and he just sits there knowing what's coming. "*I told you I'd let people know what a heinous lie it was you were telling me [then] didn't I?*"

"*He told me that Maria was dying... didn't you Aidan?*"

"*He told me that Maria was dying... When I told him that he wasn't supporting me [like I wanted him to support me].*
He told me he couldn't... because Maria was dying... didn't you Aidan?" But he doesn't say anything – he just sits there in a cold sweat – and appears to have gone into paralysis again; just like when we were first elected and Margaret had to hold him up to stop him falling from the table.

And I look at him with such utter, utter contempt. He is beaten – and he knows it – and he starts sending a text. "*You know he's got a job...*" I declare – and one or two eyes grow big with this revelation. "*He's been setting up a transatlantic leadership programme with the Leadership Centre – he's gonna jump ship on you. He won't be standing in May... he'll be away to his new job.*"

"*No I won't*" he protests like a small child – interrupting his texting. You can see it in his eyes, I think – surely they can see it as well?

"*He won't be standing in May*" I repeat. "*He's never intended to stand in May – ever since he came third in 2004 at the all outs. Because he's got no bottle – have you Aidan?*"

Aidan's whole argument is falling apart around him; so I ask him once again. "*Come on Aidan... let's you and me leave these good people here to talk about what you've done... and you and I can have a chat in your room.*"

His face is bright purple – and I'm loving it.

"*We agreed that we'd stay together*" he growls out of the corner of his mouth.

ooo

11.00 am

After nearly two hours it's apparent Aidan is beaten. But Mounsey is sticking to him like glue; how predictable...

My final comment to Aidan is a plea to be careful about what he says to the media – that he must put the party first and discuss everything with the Regional Labour Party. He insists he isn't going to, doesn't need to...

John Hardy doesn't know which way to go and keeps threatening to walk out, to avoid having to take sides, the bottleless bastard! Poor old John just wants to be on the winning side, to protect his "wages" but without all this arguing!

Stuart Exelby, Eva Hughes and Tony Sockett are the only three that really escape undamaged, having realised straight away they've been conned, they side with the mayor very early on.

Glyn Jones, Chris Mills and Bill Mordue are with me, but less so. They know they've been conned – and are embarrassed by their fecklessness. But there's still an air of distrust about them; they are only with me for the moment.

ooo

Tony Socket says he and the others want to put down in writing their record of events. So they spend a couple of hours [!] composing a paper explaining their side of the attempted *coup d'état*. How stupid are they – surely they could see that Aidan is phenomenally self-serving?

I issue a press statement on my deputy's resignation:

"Aidan has been a valuable member of the council's executive for the past five years and also my deputy during this time. I am sure he will continue to work hard for his constituents and the Labour party, continuing to play a role in delivering Doncaster's new-found success".

ooo

5.00 pm

Cabinet meets with Susan Law. I draft the resultant letter to cabinet members:

Please find attached a draft note of our discussion with Susan on Monday evening. We discussed the need to reorganise portfolios as a result of Aidan and John Mounsey's resignations. Consequent to this, I thought it important to confirm the basic structure and content of the discussion.

During Aidan's resignation discussion with cabinet he had highlighted his and the cabinet's concerns that the organisation was not functioning as he, they, or Labour group wished. As a result, we discussed that though we are undoubtedly making progress with the area-based model, we felt that this new approach was understandably taking time to bed in. Nonetheless, when considered alongside three new areas of executive operation – namely...
  i.   *the new decision making process/financial limits;*
  ii. *the new Cabinet structure with the "operational/strategic" split between the deputy mayor/mayor;*

iii. the new "corporate" approach to collective cabinet decision making;

... *this was resulting in a cumulative effect of disenfranchising cabinet members and Labour group members alike. Cabinet expressed concern that this was evidenced in a lack of respect for cabinet [and wider] elected members and a generic lack of involvement or consultation.*

ooo

6.30 pm

Aidan and John have resigned from my cabinet. The news is full of it and the BBC Look North programme screens a press conference they attended at lunch time. I deduce this must have been what Aidan kept texting about.

However, clearly visible on TV, orchestrating this political event is MD Susan Law. I would have thought this is a case of senior officer misconduct! Indeed, Susan's contract of employment states *"... any breach would be regarded as misconduct and would lead to the disciplinary procedure being activated".*

And when you look at the emails I had passed to me several months later...

From:	Law, Susan
Sent:	13 February 2006 07:34
To :	▮▮▮▮▮▮▮▮▮
Subject:	Urgent meeting

▮▮▮▮▮▮▮

Can you please ask all CMT members to meet me in the Mansion House at 11.30 this morning? It is very important that they are there but they are not to discuss this with anyone. Can you please ask ▮▮▮▮▮▮▮▮ for a room for us? Any problems, please give me a call.

Thanks

Sent from my Blackberry Wireless Handheld

ooo

From:	▮▮▮▮▮▮▮
Sent:	13 February 2006 08:53
To:	Law, Susan
Subject:	Noon today

I have contacted the top 5 local and they will attend ...did we want TV? If so I would have to give a reason as otherwise they won't attend.

▓▓▓▓▓▓ Information and Communications

Judging by the number of TV channels that covered the press conference, they must have been "given a reason"...

Local authority officers orchestrating a political press conference – colluding with politicians surely not...

Note: in a later Audit Commission Public Interest Report the Audit Commission states: *"... the MD's support of the Deputy Mayor compromised her political neutrality"* and I can assure you, they were not just talking about her organising a press conference!

ooo

Tuesday February 14th 2006...

"Crisis over leadership – Cabinet split as two quit over the way the Mayor runs the council" announces the front page of the Doncaster Star. Ouch!

Aidan continues along the same lines as yesterday, positioning himself as the "wronged man" he says his own values were "about honesty, integrity and accountability" but that the mayor's style of leadership was one he didn't recognise and didn't want to be associated with.

It's a pretty good move – it feels as if the whole world's against me.

ooo

Margaret Pinkney, leader of the "Alliance of Independent Members" on the council, said Mayor Winter should have been the person resigning. *"Aidan Rave and John Mounsey are people with integrity and the moral courage to do what's right. We hope Mayor Winter's time in power is coming to an end..."*

Careful Margaret, people will start to think you're part of a campaign!

ooo

Aidan's behaviour reminds me of the lyrics from the 'Disposable Heroes of Hiphoprisy's' song 'Music and Politics': *"Sometimes it's easier to desire, and pursue, the attention and admiration of hundreds of strangers, than it is to accept the love and loyalty of those closest to you"*

I trusted him… even when I knew I couldn't and shouldn't trust him… the 'Pizza Hut' prophecy realised.

ooo

Wednesday February 15th 2006…

The Labour Group is leaking like a sieve but it's been a problem for some time now. Nan Sloane came over last night, as Director of the Regional Labour Party, and basically read the riot act to us all. Of course, instead of washing our laundry indoors, somebody leaked the meeting to the press!

I have no option but to go on the attack and insist I will not be quitting. "I won't quit says Mayor – Defiant Winter confirms he is staying after crisis meeting" reads the front page of the Star.

ooo

Thursday February 16th 2006…

The Star runs with the story that the "Alliance of Independent Members" is putting together a "no confidence" vote in the mayor. The newspaper polls leaders to see if they would support such a motion.

I always thought the basic tenet of British justice was that a person was innocent until proven guilty – the Magna Carta and all that…

Very helpfully, Nan Sloane has issued a statement: *"We have every confidence in the elected mayor's ability to continue to take the borough forward"*.

ooo

I put in a call to speak to Peter Box, the Leader of Wakefield Council. I like Peter and have a lot of time for him. He is the Chair of the regional assembly and well respected in local government. Peter has a legal background, as a probate and trust manager, and I need his advice.

His basic advice is very simple, and concurs with my own values: *"If you've done anything wrong Martin – resign immediately. If you have not done anything wrong – don't – why should you resign if you haven't done anything?"*

ooo

Friday February 17th 2006...

It never rains but it pours... "Mayor in Homes Row" reads the front page of the Doncaster Star; and goes on to report "Now fraud squad detectives have been notified and Doncaster Council has launched an internal inquiry".

I wonder who "notified" the police?

ooo

"Chill in the air as Winter fights for political life" reports a full page 3 feature.

ooo

Saturday February 18th 2006...

"Mayor "witch hunt victim" – Winter hits back in planning row" reads the Star front page.
"The Doncaster politician spoke as police revealed detectives will decide next week whether to launch a full inquiry into the latest allegations against him.
In his first official statement since the double resignation, Mr Winter said he totally rejected what he described as "the latest in a long line of inaccurate reports". He claims the allegations form part of a "politically orchestrated witch-hunt with the aim of destroying him, his family, and the position of Mayor of Doncaster."

ooo

Thursday March 9th 2006...

I announce that Margaret Ward "Mags" is to be my new deputy, following Aidan's resignation. We agree to bring Patricia Haith into cabinet, following Mounsey's resignation.
Pat is a well-respected member and we have agreed a "portfolio" aimed at addressing the damage Susan is wreaking– entitled "Supporting Front Line Councillors". I hope it will calm members down – particularly those within the Labour group!

ooo

Friday March 10th 2006...

"Mayor fears axe threat" screams the Doncaster Star and goes on to report how the Chair of Council, sometimes referred to as the "civic mayor", when undertaking certain duties, has "launched a blistering attack on Doncaster's elected Mayor Martin Winter amid fears he wants to axe her 800-year-old role."

What the paper doesn't report is how some councillors are desperate to keep muddying the water over the two titles and roles, to continue smudging the "elected mayor" issue.

I thought the people of Doncaster "voted" to get rid of the old style mayor in favour of an elected mayor in the referendum in 2001?

"Pair sign up for inquiry into community project flop" reports the Star in error, as it tells how Stewart Dobson, a solicitor and former Chief Executive at Birmingham City Council, has been appointed to carry out the Independent Inquiry into the Glass Park.

I am seething at the "report". Firstly, the paper has confused Dobson's two roles as two people. And secondly the project is not a "flop". It was never a flop and remains a project that I am immensely proud of.

It has become a political football and, because of this, has struggled to sustain the levels of volunteer support and goodwill it enjoyed whilst I was its driving force. This has demoralised the trustees and the project is now experiencing difficulties with its maintenance programme. But it is five years since I stood down as project director.

ooo

Wednesday March 22nd 2006...

"Ex-deputy Mayor to stand down – Race to quit council after fall out" says page 2 of the Doncaster Star. The newspaper then reports how "... a month after resigning as Mayor Winter's right hand man... Aidan Rave announced he is not seeking re-election in May, when his term... expires"

I could have told you that in 2004 when his electorate voted him least popular councillor in Conisbrough & Denaby!

ooo

Thursday March 23rd 2006…

1.00 pm – Mayor's Office, Council House

I am interviewed by a member of Doncaster Council's Internal Audit function team; alongside a further officer and a witness for me. The investigation is over allegations I interfered in the planning application for "80 Doncaster Road".

ooo

Friday March 24th 2006…

1.00 pm – Mayor's Office, Council House

Susan has informed me that our "appeal" against the CPA/JAR assessment has been upheld – the process was corrupted but the judgement remains. I always thought the "appeal" was a diversionary tactic – to distract me [us] from a "car crash" elsewhere… but to be quite honest, this is the least of my concerns at the moment… Let's see how it affects our CPA/JAR scores in October!

ooo

Monday March 27th 2006…

Breaking news: Doncaster's ex-Deputy Mayor is to join Rockpools!
    Rockpools is a relatively new recruitment company, headed up by Hamish Davidson. Doncaster Council has used Rockpools to recruit several key staff in the previous twelve months. Who would have expected that? It's insulting that people can't see what's been going on. He will be responsible for developing Rockpools' leadership intervention offer, a brand new concept in leadership development.

ooo

Friday March 31st 2006…

The Standards Board has announced it will investigate me over "80 Doncaster Road".
    "Standards board to probe plan row – Mayor to face investigation into 'interference' by Mayor" reports the Doncaster Star.

Wednesday April 5th 2006...

The Star: "Plans for £8m hotel at Robin Hood Airport."

ooo

Friday April 7th 2006...

8.00 am – The Mayor's office, Council House

I have a meeting with Ed and, quite frankly, I am not the happiest bunny in the land.

"*It's all going a bit Pete Tong*" I tell him complaining that eleven months after Ed's election he's not really communicating with me, unless he wants something; he's not done anything with regard to the Coal Gasification Project at Hatfield Colliery; and he's certainly not discussing the issue of "payback" with Gordon...

Having said that, he has smoothed the path for me to become a founder of Progress, the magazine which aims to promote radical and progressive politics – why should England tremble eh?!

He knows I'm right in the thick of it at the moment with allegations, accusations and enquiries taking place on what feels like a daily basis. Since the attempted *coup d'état* two months ago, it's beginning to feel a lonely place with officers unsure who to side with – "right" or "wrong"...

"*You're looking good, though*" Ed tells me "*Considering the stress you must be under.*"

"*Well, that's because I haven't done anything wrong...*" I tell him "*And proving a lie is a lot more difficult than proving the truth. So I'm 110% certain that I've not done anything wrong... but I'm only about 90% sure they won't get me!*"
Several of Ed's councillors are clearly now actively working against me and supporting the malcontents' campaign and I tell him to get them in-line or back on-side.

Ed simply says "*they're not my councillors*" and refuses to challenge their dysfunctional behaviour. Kevin didn't accept this type of behaviour, although he did tell me "*you need to watch yourself, because they'll be coming for you Martin, now I'm dying*"...

Also, Ed doesn't seem to think Aidan's behaviour is anything to do with me having supported him for MP; the stupid twat! I am giving him a pretty tough time. My "exit strategy" [if you like], is looking pretty ropey now and I tell him that, despite having "banked" this previously with Rosie, I want Gordon to deliver my peerage.

Ed starts equivocating: *"It's not as simple as that".*

"It is" I tell him in exasperation, feeling it begin to slip away. *"Gordon said to let him know what I wanted... well I'm telling you, that's the deal – that's what I want."*

"It makes obvious sense as the natural transition as I finish my second term" Ed's sweating: *"I'll have a word with him but it really isn't that simple."*

"It is – you know Ed that I always said... let me deliver [you] *first and then I'll let you know... but if you're telling me that Gordon's going to fail to deliver his part of the bargain... well then that's just fucking immoral."*

"No... No... don't say that" replies Ed with an air of desperation. *"Gordon hates to let people down; he can't abide it when people tell him he hasn't delivered."*

"Well that's exactly what he's done – <u>what you've done</u> – however else do you want me to see it?"

But Ed's gone; I can see I've lost him.

"You don't seem to understand the first thing about payback, Ed. I brought you to Doncaster. I chose you to come to Doncaster... into my house... with my family. We fed you – we even clothed you! You set my fucking office on fire; you burnt my fucking printer out – that cost me nearly a grand!"

And I pause for effect.

"You abused my STAPLES account; you stole my fucking tie; and destroyed my relationship with Aidan."

But that was too much for him: *"Your relationship with Aidan was already broken"* he counters.

"It was struggling... but I was managing it. It was smashed after I supported you" I tell him. *"And what did I get for all that shit? Correction – what did we get? Because you can't forget the support Carolyne gave you... can you?"*

" Fuck all – that's what we got – fuck all."

I'm on a roll – he needs to know I'm pissed with him [and with Gordon!]. *"You never even had the courtesy to take us out for dinner... although you were always telling us you would... weren't you?"* I look at him disdainfully.

"Well how much do I owe you?" he asks scandalously.

"What? What are you saying?"

"How much do I owe you? Will £3,000 cover it?"

I'm raging. How inconsiderate can you be? How completely oblivious to one of the most fundamental social interactions in life can you be? *"This isn't about money"* I tell him. *"This is about payback and you need to have a discussion with Gordon about it. How fucking much? Do you think it's as easy as that?"*

And I tell him we should end the meeting; that I've got another meeting to go to. I sit down to calm myself...

I broke bread with this man. He was someone I trusted. He of all people should understand the implications of that... But even shit has its own integrity as my old mate Gore [Vidal] used to say!

ooo

Friday April 26th 2006...

7.00 pm – Labour Progressives 10th Birthday Anniversary Reception

I attend the reception in London. To be fair, Ed does quite a bit of introducing and networking with me.

ooo

Friday May 5th 2006...

"Labour defy all the odds" shouts the front page of the Star. "Sleaze, scandal and a mayor under scrutiny held little sway with borough voters as Labour increased its share on Doncaster Council – by one seat."

I comment *"The people of Doncaster can clearly see that having the Labour party's national policies implemented by a Labour mayor and council in Doncaster is working. They're very happy with the way things are going."*

ooo

"Embattled Mayor breaks his silence on 'smears' " reports the Yorkshire Post. "Doncaster's beleaguered Mayor, Martin Winter, has finally broken his silence about the storm surrounding him, dismissing it as a "political smear campaign".

For the past six months the elected mayor has been at the centre of a number of allegations and is currently being investigated as part of three separate police inquiries [sic]. They include allegations over election expenses and a separate inquiry into the Glass Park regeneration project he helped to run.

He has also faced calls to stand down, including from former members of his own team. Earlier this year his former deputy mayor Aidan Rave quit over his leadership style. But speaking for the first time at Thursday night's election count in Doncaster, Mr Winter told reporters the controversy surrounding him was "politically motivated" and said he expected more allegations in the future.

He said: "Politics is a very dirty game. I think what we've seen just recently, in the last six months, are some very nasty allegations against me. What we'll see in the future, I think, is even more of those."

Note: There were never "three separate police investigations" as the Yorkshire Post claimed. The police received "allegations" attempting to prompt a "third" police inquiry into the so-called "80 Doncaster Road" issue; but these were quickly ruled out.

ooo

In Blair's Cabinet reshuffle, Ed is appointed Parliamentary Secretary to the Cabinet Office, Minister for the Third Sector, responsible for voluntary and charity organisations.

He never tells me!

ooo

Thursday May 18th 2006…

"Mayor faces third probe" reports the Doncaster Star revealing how "An official report into a planning row involving Doncaster Mayor, Martin Winter, has been delayed after a third investigation was launched…"

"The findings of Doncaster Council's internal probe… is now on ice… after the local government ombudsman… started a separate inquiry following complaints from residents." The article reports that: "It means taxpayers are now forking out for three investigations, with the Standards Board also gathering evidence".

Councillor Pinkney is quoted as saying "It could have been done a lot quicker… there are too many irons in the fire."

Whose fault is that then Margaret?

ooo

Tuesday May 23rd 2006...

"No charges for mayor – police end probe into alleged election expenses irregularities" reads the Star splash. The article reports on the absolutely preposterous allegation that the Doncaster Rovers' "Going4it" rally at the Dome last April should have been declared on my election expenses. It says a complaint was made to South Yorkshire Police by Lib-Dem Councillor Kevin Abell and reports "The CPS has sent a letter to Councillor Abel declaring the matter closed."

I am quoted: *"I am very pleased with this announcement and I would like to take this opportunity to thank both South Yorkshire Police and the Crown Prosecution service for the professional and rigorous manner in which they conducted the investigation."*

ooo

"Plan to change waste collection" reports the newspaper detailing the roll-out of the borough-wide green waste collections, which Susan damaged by unilaterally halting the move to fortnightly collections last September.

ooo

Thursday May 26th 2006...

"End of an era" declares the Star and pictures me standing on the rubble of the former "Old Yorkshire Stand" at Doncaster racecourse, it having been demolished as part of the £32m racecourse redevelopment.

ooo

Monday June 5th 2006...

"Glass Park cost public £165,000" says the Star, commenting on Stewart Dobson's report to Overview and Scrutiny, which shows it as a cocktail of Section 106 money and regeneration funds.

When you consider this was the local authority's total contribution and that the project also got a further £500,000 worth of funding and in-kind support to secure and restore a 25 acre redundant sports ground for community use; restore a 25 acre former waste glass dump as a publicly accessible informal recreation and wildflower area; and also create several acres of community orchards and informal grasslands; I think it's bloody good value!

On a much more positive note, the Star features the opening of the £250million Frenchgate Centre and Transport Interchange – "Doncaster's big answer to Meadowhall finally launched".

ooo

On a less positive note, on 'World Environment Day', I am delighted to see the headline "Why we should go green to save the environment" but it's above a report that reads:
"They're the vanguard of Doncaster's efforts to save the planet. And today the workers of North Doncaster Kerbside recycling were left with no doubt how much their work is valued... Ed Miliband, Labour MP for Doncaster North, launched a campaign" on a visit to the project.
That's nice to know. The mayor's Zero Waste strategy and the very community recycling companies that the mayor insisted were set up, is now being promoted by an MP who had nothing whatsoever to do with its establishment.
Thanks for that one Ed – I'm glad you are on message and that we are all working together!

ooo

Wednesday June 7th 2006...

Stewart Dobson's interim report is presented to the meeting of the Overview & Scrutiny Management. When he sat down with me for his initial interview, I told him to beware that this whole issue and local authority is a nest of vipers!

ooo

Monday June 12th 2006...

It really is unremitting! Our senior officers insist we go out to consultation to consider the closure of two of our care homes, to allow us to rebalance the percentage of beds purchased in the independent sector as part of my budget agreed at full Council in February.
This is a political minefield and will further antagonise Labour councillors; not least because one of the homes we are being urged to close is in Stainforth. If we go out to consult on its closure – even if we then keep it open – we will significantly damage Labour councillor, Joe Blackham's election chances for next May.

If we go out to consult on the closure of our best care home in Armthorpe, which has recently been refurbished, knowing that we will not close it [!], it will have no effect on the election next May, where the sitting independent councillor Margaret Pinkney is already assured of a handsome victory.

It's not an acceptable strategy but it's a no-brainer! I need to calm the Labour group down. It's the only way we, the politicians, can keep control of the whole process, keeping the homes open that we wish to keep open whilst minimising political fallout.

"Fury as Council target elderly" screams the Star front page.

ooo

Thursday June 22nd 2006...

South Yorkshire Police have contacted me with regard to their investigation into the Glass Park. I prepare a press statement.

South Yorkshire Police Authority today announced that the Crown Prosecution Service [CPS] has notified them of its decision on allegations that Martin Winter [whilst a volunteer worker with the Glass Park project, Doncaster in 2000] "... *made a false claim for a grant and misappropriated monies obtained from these grants*".

The CPS's decision is that Mr Martin Winter had *not* misappropriated [any] monies and that neither he nor the Glass Park project had made any false claim for a grant or operated illegally in any way.

Mayor Winter said, "I am very pleased to have been vindicated by today's CPS announcement. My whole family have in the last twelve months withstood intense personal and public investigation into our lives and into a project with which I have always been proudly and publicly involved.

I would like to thank both the South Yorkshire Police and the Crown Prosecution Service, for the professionalism and rigour with which they conducted the investigation.

These are exciting times for Doncaster and its people. Despite the vexatious accusations and the need for such lengthy investigations not helping the borough, I now call on those responsible to work with us on the main agenda – the regeneration and future of Doncaster. We need to focus on delivering the services that our residents expect and deserve and not waste public money on unfounded allegations.

Furthermore and finally, I would like to invite the media to work with us and support us, on the undoubted renaissance of an up and coming city".

Friday June 23rd 2006...

"Cleared" screams the front page of the Doncaster Star, with the sub-heading "Mayor won't face prosecution after police probe into Glass Park scheme fraud claims".

Pity they could only give me half the front page though, after all the entire front pages they devoted to the allegations recently...

Nonetheless, it's good to put this one to bed. I never had any concerns whatsoever and, when I attended the police station with my solicitor to be "interviewed" by the police, I was completely happy that we clarified one or two issues within about half an hour of being with them. However, I was definitely not happy that the police had a "false" copy document they wanted to ask me about, which we also soon put to bed in terms of any criminal activity.

I was, and remain to this day, concerned as to what that "false document" actually meant; but for ease, I will simply enclose the statement Stewart Dobson made in his final report:

> 5.63. Turning to my comments on this particular query, it is obviously very troubling that [a] the Council's file relating to this project has been shown to contain a "false" copy document and [b] despite all inquiries, it has proved impossible to establish or explain where this document came from or how it finished up on the Council's file. This is a most unfortunate "loose end".

ooo

Friday June 30th 2006...

Everything should be put into context. Today's Doncaster Star has a quarter page feature "Go-ahead to revamp ailing recreation area – and reports on a £750,000 makeover of the spot.
I think that puts the "£165,000 for Glass Park" article into perspective.

But underneath this article, surely not by mistake [?], is another – "Campaigners plea for donations over park rejuvenation". This is a redundant council-owned play area in Kirk Sandall, 50 metres from Councillor Cliff Hampson's home and one which he has decided to "save"...

ooo

Thursday July 6th 2006...

I have received a letter from the Standards Board for England [with reference to case number SBE14374.06.]; to confirm an interview with them next Wednesday. The letter makes clear that the complainant is Councillor Margaret Pinkney – but I have no idea which case it is!

ooo

Wednesday July 12th 2006...

10.00 am – Cabinet Meeting

After several weeks of very bumpy meetings, where the residents of Rose House and their families have made their feelings extremely clear to me, I make my decision over the care homes closure consultation programme.

1. That neither St. James Court, Town Centre nor Rose House, Armthorpe be closed and that savings for 2006/07 and reinvestments into older people's services for 2007/08 on-going be sought elsewhere. To note and support the Mayor's proposal to draft a Mayoral Green Paper in respect of formulating a strategic plan for older people in Doncaster.

In an opening statement made at the meeting, I outline my reasons.

"In reaching a decision today, we must consider the strength of feeling expressed through the representations I received, as Mayor, and by the Council as part of the consultation.

We must also take note of the additional information we were not initially aware of but have subsequently received, regarding the planned changes to health care provision; the independent sector's provision in the East; and the possible need for an increase in Elderly and Mentally Infirm [EMI] beds in the short to medium term as a result of these.

I think we must similarly be mindful of the comments made by our colleagues in health, about the provision at Rose House and the relationship we enjoy with these partners".

Susan is seething…

ooo

After the cabinet meeting a senior officer tells me that at a recent Corporate Management Team meeting, Susan Law told them, words to the effect that 'we didn't get the mayor on the Glass Park issue so we need a plan B' – if this is true, it is absolutely outrageous.

ooo

Somebody has passed me a copy of an email sent to Susan Law from Councillor Margaret Pinkney. It is self-explanatory...

> From: Pinkney, Margaret
> Sent: 3 July 2006 06:48
> To: Law, Susan
> Subject: meeting
>
> Susan, I am sorry but I will have to cancel the 3.30 pm meeting with you today Mon. 3/7/06. I have a Scrutiny meeting at 4.00 pm. And I really need to be there. Could I ask that now the Police have "backed out" of their inquiry you could give officers a push in answering my FOI questions, it is weeks since I asked and still I wait. Could you also please give me a "yes" or "no" answer to my query of "Have you got a Plan B?"
>
> Regards Margaret.

I believe the content of this email clearly suggests a wider campaign against the mayor...
 Local authority officers colluding with politicians surely not...

ooo

Several senior officers are now freely discussing their concerns about Susan's attempted *coup d'état* her complete disregard for rules and procedures and the fact she is constantly blaming them for her failures...

ooo

2.00 pm – Interview with Standards Board for England

I am interviewed by two members of the SBE, with a further officer as witness and Karen my Executive Assistant as note taker; she is phenomenally supportive of me and has been throughout the last twelve months.
 The investigations Manager and Chief Investigator are interviewing me as part of their investigation into "80 Doncaster Road". It's the first time I've been aware that it's Councillor Pinkney who has made the allegation against me. No surprise there then. But it clarifies that I don't suffer from paranoia. They are out to get me!

At one point in the investigation, the SBE officer asks me a very leading question.

"Mr Thompson is a very good friend of yours, isn't he Martin?"

"Not particularly – I know him quite well because he is a Labour party member and business supporter. Oh... we have been given information that you dine with Mr Thompson regularly and attended a barbeque at his house last year."

"That's correct... but you have to take things in the context of my job as Mayor of Doncaster [and where everybody wants a piece of me]."

I was invited to Mr Thompson's for dinner, with a former leader of Doncaster Council and my deputy leader, in 2001. In total, there were approximately ten or twelve guests at this dinner. In 2004, to commemorate twenty years since the start of the 84-85 Miners' Strike, I had a series of fundraising dinners at my house, when a number of "Labour supporters" attended – at one of those dinners, Mr Thompson and his wife were guests along with approximately a dozen others.

"I did attend a barbeque at Mr Thompson's last year – there were at least thirty or forty individuals in attendance and it was a Labour party barbeque. It is my job to be friendly with all residents in Doncaster – and particularly those who are investors in the borough. I am sure that if you asked Mr Thompson if he knew the mayor, he would tell you that the mayor was a good friend of his – that's my job!"

"But I hardly think three meals in four years is "regularly" – do you?"

And before he can even think to respond...

"In the last four years I have had lunch or dinner with the Duke of York four or five times."

" Whenever he comes to Doncaster, or sees me [elsewhere], he remembers me and always uses me as his "stooge" for having fun..."

"If you ask me if I know Prince Andrew, I'll tell you he's a great friend of mine...

"If you ask Prince Andrew if he knows Martin Winter... he'd probably say... who?"

ooo

Friday July 14th 2006...

The Relate Institute has announced it is to move its entire operation to Doncaster.

ooo

Sunday July 16th 2006…

Kevin Hughes died today. We knew his death was imminent and I managed to visit him a couple of weeks ago. We both knew it was the last time we'd see each other.

We spent an enjoyable few hours together, at his bungalow in Campsall. He showed me the newly built paths he'd had constructed to allow him to move more freely in his wheelchair around the garden.

"Do you know who built them?" He asks me, nodding at the new paths. *"Ted and John"* he laughs as he says it.

"Fucking 'ell" I'm shocked… but almost apologetic that I should've sworn. We don't swear now. Now that our discussions are more finite… it doesn't seem appropriate.

"It must've killed them…" I'm still surprised.

"It nearly did…but they're that guilty about how they've treated me over the years…" he tails off.

"What? They're trying to buy their way into heaven – are they?" I laugh.

"Something like that…"

"Y'know they'll come for you now – don't you?"

"They already are doing" I say in resignation.

"Aye… they've called me from a pig to a dog…" and he starts coughing, as he struggles with his breathing *"… over the years"* he finishes.

"They're never happy… unless they're swimming upstream – against the consensus" and he coughs again… *"hee… hee… it nearly fucking killed 'em… it did…"*

ooo

Wednesday July 19th 2006…

Alongside all our MPs, Caroline, Ed, Jeff Ennis and Rosie, we are meeting the Transport Minister Stephen Ladyman to try to expedite the construction of the airport link road.

I am not enamoured about the meeting. The advisors were very pessimistic and told me they wanted to see we were committed to the scheme through providing the funding for the much needed "White Rose Way" widening scheme and improvements, which also link to the Junction 3 of the M18.

I come away feeling very frustrated – four Labour ministers present and we are not going to get it. They seem to think otherwise, or perhaps they're just more adept at playing the "Yes Minister" non-delivery game than I am.

Wednesday July 25th 2006...

Kevin's funeral – I tell all my cabinet I would like to see all of them there.

ooo

Wednesday August 9th 2006...

Well it's official now. The Doncaster Star reports on a new petition to get rid of the mayor. The newspaper reports on a meeting of "The Fair Deal group, which is made up of councillors and residents who want an end to the current system... It quotes Kevin Abell: "Councillors are side-lined by the system." And Margaret Pinkney: "The system is diabolical".

ooo

Wednesday August 16th 2006...

"Mayoral referendum campaign takes to the streets" says the Star, picturing Joan Moffat collecting signatures alongside a Lib-Dem councillor.

ooo

Thursday 31st August 2006...

"The cloud over Doncaster's elected mayor has lifted..." begins an inside half-page feature in the Star under the headline "Mayor cleared in planning investigation". Alongside it is a photograph of me, with a five-o'clock-shadow, captioned "Councillor Winter" [!].

ooo

Wednesday September 5th 2006...

10.30 am – Mayor's office, Council House

I am interviewed by Stewart Dobson [SD] as part of the independent report Susan Law commissioned. In attendance is an officer making notes and a member of the council's internal audit team, as support for Mr Dobson. I quote from the interview transcript:

MW started by saying that he intended to speak extremely frankly and that he wondered about the implications of this for ▇ and ▇. Both ▇ and ▇ then confirmed that this was not a problem for them and that they would respect the confidentiality of whatever was said.

MW explained that, despite the advice from his Solicitor [which was to the effect that, because MW had already been questioned by the Police about certain of these matters, he should decline to participate], he had been very much looking forward to this meeting. He saw it as the opportunity to provide SD with a full explanation and understanding of the Glass Park projects – of which he was very proud. MW wished in fact that this meeting could have taken place much sooner, although he recognised [as explained in SD's letter of 26 June] that SD had been advised by the Police not to approach MW until the outcome of their investigation was known.

4.25 pm – The meeting finished

ooo

It became clear at the meeting that Susan Law took a file to the police, accompanied by the Monitoring Officer and also a senior communications officer. I am particularly disappointed to find this out because the senior communications officer is the staff member Susan accused me of having an affair with in Harrogate five months before.

When I ask her [some eighteen months later] why she went along with this "charade" – given that I had told her Susan was out to "get me" – she was most concerned that I should question her loyalty.

You don't know what she was like Martin – she was evil, frighteningly evil, and I had no option.

ooo

I am reminded very much of the Churchill quotation…

"It is not enough that we do our best; sometimes we must do what is required" a quote bastardised in the film Body Heat, when it is used to justify murdering someone.

Although such behaviour is alien to my sense of right and wrong, I can understand the fearsome way Susan seems to be controlling people.

Monday September 11th 2006...

The Doncaster Star covers a story where, alongside Barnsley and Rotherham councils, we are working on a sub-regional waste facility. I am using my Zero-Waste strategy to force up the recycling rates of the other two authorities and refuse to be party to a joint incinerator with Barnsley Council.

"Mayor Snubs Incinerator with Barnsley" runs the headline and quotes me: *"As long as I am mayor, I will not allow an incinerator to be introduced here"*.

ooo

Tuesday September 12th 2006...

I have been tipped off that, much as expected, both SBE investigations are soon to announce that there is no case to answer. I need to prepare for being given the "all clear" so we can then concentrate on what I started last November; dealing with Susan's underperformance.

I need to be careful though, for fear it looks like vengeance. Susan has really done a number on me but she has inveigled several more militant members of the Labour group into her *harem*. It is very clear. I am very clear. What does an underperforming Managing Director do to get at an overzealous mayor [intent on addressing her failures] off her back? Become a whistle blower; that way she is forever protected!

ooo

Friday September 15th 2006...

"Investigation clears Winter" reads the quarter page – page 13 [!] story in the Doncaster Star. It reveals I have been cleared by the [SBE] Investigation into "80 Doncaster Road" and rightly criticises the council on its handling of the application.

And in a frighteningly economical piece of reporting, it "tacks" on to the end – in the final paragraph: "Meanwhile, the Standards Board also cleared Mr Winter of any wrongdoing on his election expenses following similar findings by South Yorkshire Police.

The Mayor told the Star: "I am very pleased to have once again been vindicated by today's announcements".

ooo

Wednesday September 20th 2006...

10.00 am – Cabinet Meeting

One of the most important projects for Doncaster in many years needs pushing through: The initial works to agree and prepare for the major improvements needed on the A6182 White Rose Way. We also need to show we are committed to providing the money for this work, as part of the conduit for releasing the funds and support for the airport link road from central government.

Without this critical work, all future construction in and around the urban centre will be hamstrung; particularly the town's transformational projects, such as the Civic & Cultural Quarter and further development of the Lakeside. It has to be delivered.

But we haven't, as yet, identified a developer or public agency to help us bankroll the scheme; so in a worst case scenario, we may have to cancel other programmes to deliver this priority.

At this morning's cabinet, we decide: To agree the preferred option for major improvements to the A6182 White Rose Way in order to:

1. Approve the proposed design approach to deliver the wider scheme with associated sustainable transport measures as set out in this report; approve funding of between £26m and £33m;
2. Note that the precise mechanism for securing the additional £24m-£33m is not yet in place.

ooo

Thursday September 21st 2006...

3.00 pm

I'm not a mayor anymore. Tonight's Star reports that "senior councillors" made yesterday's decision. Five years after the referendum to change the system and they still don't get it!

The newspaper also reports "Services threat from £31m plan" even though we are talking about the funding of a capital expenditure programme here and services are fundamentally delivered through the revenue programme.

Nonetheless, several Labour group members are constantly working with opposition councillors and leaking to the press. With two and a half years of my second [and final!] term to go, the relationship is developing into open warfare and I need to plan for the next campaign, to develop a strategy.

I could do with talking to my father – he'd know what to do. And then it comes to me, as I remember lying on the grass as a child, watching a lapwing walking to and from its nest.

The closer you get to the nest, the less interested the lapwing pretends to be – displaying complete nonchalance the nearer you get. The further away from its nest you are, the more it attempts to distract you, plunging earthwards with a drunken spinning and turning fall, as if mortally wounded, in order to draw you away.

I need a "Lapwing Economics" strategy. I keep quiet, play dumb if need be over my favoured projects, and I make a fuss about those I'm not particularly wedded to; thus giving the opposition [the Labour group!] the opportunity to destroy the projects that aren't a priority.

ooo

Friday September 22nd 2006...

4.00 pm – Mansion House

It is now apparent that the issues I have been wishing to discuss for more than twelve months, and some which have recently arisen, are substantive. Cabinet, rather than I, have taken the matter forward, and involved the correct local authority officers and external specialist advisors throughout.

Because Margaret Ward Chairs the Chief Officer Appointments and Conditions of Service Committee [COACSC] and Pat Haith also sits on it, neither has attended cabinet meetings considering the way forward.

As a result, the MD has been granted "extended leave". I insist she should be suspended pending a full investigation, but all advice says that a special sub-committee of this Committee should be convened to consider the issues and advise council.

Today's meeting is to consider the report and establish the sub-committee – the Chief Officer Investigatory Sub-committee [COISC].

During the meeting, John Mounsey becomes extremely abusive of Margaret Ward, in front of several council officers. Ted is there in support, and this seems to give Mounsey more strength.

He is clearly working in support of Susan Law, and acting on very specific advice... Mounsey moves:

"That this matter, in accordance with the Council's Constitution, specifically Article 4.01 [f] and 4.02 [b] be referred back to Full Council with reasons for the complaints and who had instigated them for Full Council's further consideration".

This is seconded by Lib-Dem Councillor Paul Bissett.

Whoever is advising Mounsey is desperate for the whole matter to be considered by Full Council – thereby pitching it as the "council against the mayor". I suspect this is Susan herself, probably through Aidan; knowing the damage I have sustained during the last twelve months, a character assassination onslaught will count in her favour.

Because the debate and Mounsey's comments are both abusive and covering confidential issues, the Chair moves the meeting *in-camera* to consider further external professional and legal advice. The minutes record:

> "Following the receipt of professional advice and discussion thereon, the press and public were invited to re-join the proceedings of the meeting. Following the receipt of professional advice, Councillor Paul Bissett withdrew his seconding of Councillor Mounsey's motion. There being no other Seconder, the motion fell."

It was a clever attempted move, but clearly in complete disregard for rules and procedures.

NOTE: Margaret Ward was mortified with Mounsey's behaviour at this meeting and asked that the Regional Labour Party intervene. They did nothing.

ooo

On September 22nd 2006, the COACSC approved the establishment, membership and terms of reference of a Chief Officers' Investigatory Sub-committee [COISC]. The Sub-committee met that day to consider the issues of conduct and capability.

ooo

Friday September 29th 2006...

The District Auditor, Sue Sunderland, writes to Doncaster Council to ask what it considers its powers are to extend annual leave rather than suspend the former Managing Director.

Note: I only became aware of this letter when the DA's report was published in May 2008.

ooo

Monday October 16th 2006...

We have been notified by the Audit Commission of a fall in our performance – from 3 star to 2 stars out of 4. It's hardly surprising given the war that has been raging between the MD and the mayor and the Labour group and the mayor during the last twelve months.

ooo

Thursday October 19th 2006...

I attend a meeting at Number Ten with Tony Blair, Ken Livingstone and Mayor Daly, the Mayor of Chicago, to discuss all things mayoral and the devolution of powers. I make my usual pitch for the re-regulation of buses in Doncaster!

ooo

November 2006...

The Stewart "Dobson Report" is delivered. I am completely happy with it and, if you are prepared to read what it says, rather than interpret what you want it to say, it's actually very supportive of me...

"I was aware from the outset of my investigation that "the Glass Park issue" had become something of a political battleground. This awareness was only heightened when, during the course of my investigation, I was faced with widely differing views about what had or had not happened in relation to the various Glass Park projects and, even more particularly, about how the value of those projects and the conduct of those involved in promoting them should be judged.

Aside from telling me that my final report, whatever it might say, was highly unlikely to please everybody, this also told me:

- *that my approach towards establishing the facts of the matter would need to be as rigorous and thorough as I could make it; and*

- *that any views or opinions that I might express in the final report would need to be rooted in my own judgement, based on the facts that I had been able to establish.*

I believe that this final report reflects the approach outlined above. I very much hope that it will be helpful to the Council. If nothing else, I hope that the report will now enable judgements to be made on the basis of the facts, rather than on the basis of anecdote or rumour."

ooo

Friday November 3rd 2006...

"Fears over costs of Council row with Law" reads the headline in the Star – and comments that it is now three months that the MD has been on "extended leave".

A separate report comments on a letter I received from the Minister of State for Children and Families, Beverley Hughes, and the School's Minister, Lord Adonis, which congratulates us on the improvements seen in our primary schools since 2003.

ooo

Thursday November 9th 2006...

The District Auditor, Sue Sunderland, writes again to Doncaster Council to ask what it considers its powers are to extend annual leave rather than suspend the former Managing Director.

Note: I only became aware of this letter when the DA's report was published in May 2008.

ooo

Wednesday November 29th 2006…

I attend the "topping out" ceremony at the racecourse development.

ooo

Monday December 4th 2006…

9.00 am

It's Full Council and I am expecting a bumpy meeting with regard to the "Dobson report" into the Glass Park.

As I said, I am pleased with it. It clearly stipulates that when I was involved, everything was completely above board and correct:

4.17. Before dealing with the circumstances of Martin Winter's withdrawal from all Glass Park activities in 2001, it is relevant for me to refer to the impression that I have gained, from my meetings and discussions, of how the Glass Park Millennium Green Trust operated, from its creation in 1998 up until about 2001.

4.18. The clear impression that I have gained is that, during this period, the Trust was, by any standard, very successful. This was not only in terms of successfully completing the major task of establishing the Millennium Green, but also in terms of involving the local community [including the local schools] in a wide range of well attended events and activities. It would certainly appear that, during this period, the Trust enjoyed widespread support and interest from the local community. Another impression I have gained is that, during this period, the affairs of the Trust were well conducted and organised, with proper attention being paid to matters of probity and accountability.

4.19. These impressions are certainly consistent with what I have been told by those "independent" persons [Inspector Lomas, John Housham & George Boot] who served as Trustees at this time. For example, some of the things that they have said to me include:

- "my impression of the core group was that they were local people who were genuinely committed to improving the environment of their area by providing a new leisure facility that would be of benefit to the whole community, but particularly to young people"

- "I was impressed by the enthusiasm and involvement of a very large number of local people...there was a real buzz about the project"

- "there was a strong culture of openness and honesty, which I always found re-assuring...I admired the professional manner in which the quarterly meetings of the Trust were conducted"

- "the meetings were well managed, with full accounts and reports being provided to the Trustees"

- "it was a real pleasure to be involved with the Trust at this time"

4.20. In May 2001, Martin Winter became the Leader of DMBC. Although he had remained actively involved with the Glass Park project during the 2 years since he had first been elected to the Council [in May 1999], he decided that, once he had become Leader, the potential for conflicts of interest was so great that he should withdraw from active involvement with the project. He explained this to the Trustees of the GPMGT and then relinquished all his positions as [a] the Secretary to the GPMGT, [b] the Company Secretary of the Glass Park Development Company and [c] the *de facto* "Director" of the whole project.

4.21. Over the years following Martin Winter's withdrawal from active involvement, the fortunes of the project appear to have steadily declined. How much this has been due to the loss of what has been described to me [by one of the "independent" Trustees] as the "vision, organisational skills and drive" of Martin Winter or how much to other factors, I cannot be sure – although a number of people have identified Martin Winter's withdrawal as the main cause. Whatever the causes, it is clear that the number of local people who have been willing to volunteer for activities such as helping to maintain the Millennium Green and organise activities & events has declined. The Green and surrounding area are now in a somewhat overgrown and apparently "uncared for" state. Similarly, the number of Trustees serving on the GPMGT has declined to 7 or so.

It is sad fact but I have to admit that I sacrificed the Glass Park project when I was elected to head up the council; and I shall be forever regretful that this was the result.

ooo

10.00 am – Full Council – Doncaster Council Chamber

Despite my thorough "preparation" *vis a vis* the "Dobson Report", the meeting is very pedestrian. I receive a written question from a gentleman who attends to ask it himself:

> "In view of the on-going saga with the Glass Parks Scheme, would you please inform the public at the full Council meeting... as to whether or not taxpayers have or are likely to be paying your legal expenses in connection with any or all investigations or matters related to the Glass Parks Scheme that are already in the Public Domain?"

I respond: *"Thank you very much for your question Mr ▉▉▉. In answering your question, it gives me an ideal opportunity to comment on the costs, expense and indeed damage to Doncaster of what will soon be seen to be a malicious, spiteful and politically orchestrated campaign to dishonour me and through this hinder Doncaster's undoubted renaissance.*

    I look up expecting a rise... but the malcontents are taking it... I expect them to be outraged, to be booing, but nothing, no response at all, neither from them nor the opposition councillors.

    "So, the simple answer is that I can categorically state "No" Mr ▉▉▉. Taxpayers and the Council have not, and would not be making any payment for legal expenses incurred by me in connection with either the Police or Council investigations into the Glass Park project. But it does raise the question of what are the estimated costs of such investigations?

    In terms of the police inquiries... The so called Rovers Rally, commissioned by Councillor. Kevin Abell – £70,000 – <u>no case to answer</u>. The Glass Park inquiry commissioned by Susan Law – £140,000 – <u>and no case to answer</u>. Planning inquiry commissioned by Susan Law – £10,000 – <u>no case to answer again</u>.
With regard to Standards Board inquiries in respect of allegations by Councillors Margaret Pinkney, Monty Cuthbert, Tony Brown and Cliff Hampson – <u>no case to answer in any of these cases</u> – and at an estimated cost of £35,000.

    In relation to internal inquiries... all commissioned by Susan Law: The Glass Park – £85,000 – <u>and no case to answer</u>.

And I look up at the chamber *"And Stuart Dobson's report proves my innocence Mr* ▓▓▓▓*..."* but nothing – no response again... *The Planning Inquiry – £30,000 – <u>and no case to answer</u>.*

So a total estimated sum of £370,000 of public money has been used; probably closer to £500,000. My own costs have been almost £10,000, and I am currently seeking further legal advice.

There has been no case to answer in every one of these cases Mr ▓▓▓▓... because I haven't done anything wrong.

However, there are other costs which can't be accounted for – mental anguish, humiliation, physical and emotional distress and loss of reputation.

Also, damage to democracy – having been beaten twice at the ballot box, <u>there has been a politically orchestrated campaign to destroy public confidence in Doncaster's governance structure.</u>

And this has been done with complete disregard for the damage this may do to Doncaster but more importantly with the single objective of destroying me and my family.

I say to those individuals *"shame on you"*, for spending nearly £½ million and putting Doncaster's future at risk in pursuit of your own political objectives."

And as I wrap up I look intently at the likes of Pinkney, Cuthbert, Brown and Cliff Hampson. *"But perhaps more importantly I say to those individuals, I shall be seeking my costs from you."*

I sit down to applause.

"Brilliant... well done" said Mags *"Has it really cost you £10,000 Martin?"*

"Nah – has it bollocks" I tell her *"Less than a twenty quid [for petrol]... but let's not let them bastards know that"*

ooo

Tuesday December 5th 2006...

Aidan's been sticking his oar in and commenting in the press that we need to sort out the Susan Law affair and get on with delivering for Doncaster; I couldn't agree more.

I wonder why he has become vocal now?

ooo

Friday December 8th 2006...

"Secret bid for pay-off" cries the front page of the Star, with the sub-heading "Council MD rejects £150,000 offer to go as costly legal battle looms." I don't know where this story has come from but her union representative is quoted in the article.
It says Susan Law has rejected the pay-off and wants to clear her name!

ooo

Wednesday December 13th 2006...

Sue Sunderland writes for a third time to Doncaster Council to ask what it considers its powers are to extend annual leave rather than suspend the former Managing Director.

Note: I only became aware of this letter when the DA's report was published in May 2008.

ooo

Sunday December 17th 2006...

5,000 Doncaster residents attend an open day to have their first look at the new stadium.

ooo

Monday December 18th 2006...

I want to send a Christmas message to a few of my opponents so I contact Ian Spowart.

> *Ian – Can you please send a copy of this advice letter from my solicitor as follows:*
>
> *Letter from Martin Winter to be sent as "Recorded Delivery" – Letters on "Martin Winter" [not mayoral] headed paper to the following:*
>
> *All Independent Councillors [13?]*

All Liberal Democrat Councillors [8]
Jesse Credland, Joan Moffat, Ted Moffat, Ray Nortrop, ▮▮▮ *and also* ▮▮▮

Ian – *also consider those posing potentially slanderous questions at Full Council.*

Content of letter as follows:

To [named addressee]

Please find enclosed an advisory letter from my solicitor.

Yours sincerely

Martin Winter

ooo

Friday December 22nd 2006…

Well… the letter to potential defamers certainly stirred things up! "Opponents hit out at Mayor's legal 'gag'" cries the Star and then runs with the sub-heading "Letters with legal warning 'a way of silencing democracy' say critics".

The newspaper then comments "Mayor Martin Winter was today accused of trying to gag some of his political opponents with a letter warning them of the legal implications of continuing to question his role in the Glass Park controversy".

This is an interesting way to report on a letter which referred to several issues – but I'll once again remind [the newspaper] of what the "Dobson report" said: ***"I hope that the report will now enable judgements to be made on the basis of the facts, rather than on the basis of anecdote or rumour."***

Has the paper not read the report?! Or maybe it still wishes to peddle and trade on anecdote and rumour… The Star comments that my letter "… refers to the investigations by various bodies, the Police Fraud squad, the Council Audit Department, the District Auditor, the Government Audit Commission and a private consultant regarding Glass Park [sic.]. They all concluded the Mayor had done nothing wrong during his dealings…"

So the Star [and other newspapers] seem to support the opponents "right" to make all manner of vexatious, frivolous and libellous accusations against me, simply because I am the mayor. They believe it is right that I suffer 'the slings and arrows of outrageous fortune' – because they want to sell papers! And when I take arms against a sea of troubles – then they err on the side of the aggressors!

The letter adds: "We consider it would be difficult for anyone making a defamatory statement against you about the above to defend successfully any court proceedings you issue against them for defamation."

It goes on to warn that people should not hide behind the general protection given to people making potentially damaging remarks in public meetings such as council sessions... what is known as qualified privilege... but the solicitor says that "this privilege is lost if there is found to be malice on the part of the defamer".

My legal advice concludes "if however, the allegations continue... we advise you to take court proceedings against the person[s] making the defamatory allegation."

That certainly stirred up the malicious set of jobsites!

This approach, however, is not just the Star's... and begs the question why do we need to keep spending hundreds of thousands of pounds each year advertising council jobs in newspapers that constantly report that the council is crap and the mayor is shit?!

My advisors tell me we shouldn't confuse editorial and commercial. I tell them I'm not. I need to commission a best-value review of our media advertising; and how we may better use the council's free newspaper, the internet and emerging forms of social media, to promote recruitment opportunities.

ooo

Saturday December 23rd 2006...

"Council Chief on way out – MD set to reach agreement to leave after row" reports the front page of the Star. The article quotes Councillor Mick Maye saying: "I understand a deal has been struck. It's a shame Susan's leaving, she's exactly the sort of person you'd want as managing director".

But earlier this week the Chair of Doncaster Strategic Partnership, Colin Jeynes, himself a retired Doncaster Council chief executive, urged Ms Law to go. In an open letter he told her "You must recognise that if you can't work with Martin Winter then your career in Doncaster is over, so make a deal to leave".

I, on the other hand, take a different view – those who live by the sword should die by the sword. I believe Susan Law should be sacked. That she is guilty of several counts of misconduct and, as such, should be suspended [as a neutral act] until a full investigation has taken place into the allegations that have been made...

I'll take the risk to see how her behaviour stands up to rigorous criminal, legal and operational scrutiny; as I have had to endure for the last twelve months.

Let's look at what one of "several" Designated Independent Persons [DIP], working to advise the sub-committee said; and while we're at it let's see what the Audit Commission is saying; because I believe that they are both saying that these allegations are neither borne of vengeance nor malice [on my or anybody else's part].

The DIP is also saying that these are serious issues and warrant the MD's suspension, as a neutral act, while a full investigation takes place. Indeed, the Audit Commission has now written three times to the Council/Panel informing them of the need to take such decisive action.

On a different hand though, you could argue that the sub-committee ignored the advice they were being given [on "considering the evidence before them]; and considered themselves a *de facto* "investigatory" sub-committee, undertaking an "investigation" themselves. Because of this, they deliberately ignored some of the most compelling of evidence, I imagine, possible to put to such a panel.

When the sub-committee "interviewed" me as the mayor, Councillor Ros Jones actually asked me *"If Susan Law returns to work, will you leave?"* What an outrageous question. The advisory officers should not have allowed her to ask it. It hardly concealed her political objective; which I told them and asked for the question [and my response] to be specifically minuted.

It is common knowledge that the sub-committee, under Councillor Ros Jones' direction, functioned politically. This was clear to the Audit Commission and prompted the entry in their [later] Audit Commission Public Interest Report [PIR – published May 14th 2008], which stated:

> **20.** Most members of the Sub-committee clearly understood that their role was not to be political; to act impartially and make decisions only on the basis of the evidence presented to them but, in my view, not all members adhered to this… In addition, some COISC members did not appear to be sufficiently clear on when they were exceeding their remit by conducting an investigation, which is a matter for a Designated Independent Person.

ooo

For what it's worth, my analysis of the perverse behaviour of the Sub-committee's seven members is divided into three groupings:

Firstly, those who were completely aware of what was going on – but were powerless to stop it. Councillor Barbara Hoyle [Tory], Councillor Ken Knight [Lab].

Secondly, those who were vaguely aware of what was going on – but were too frightened to act or contradict elected members or officers [Councillor John Cooke [Ind], and Councillor Patrick Wilson [Lib-Dem].

And lastly those who knew exactly what was going on – because they were driving it [Councillor's Jones [Lab], Councillor Stuart Hardy [Lab] and Councillor Margaret Pinkney [Ind].

There were, in reality, more permutations, with further analysis showing that:

There were members who thought they were driving the agenda – but who were actually being politically manipulated by Councillor Mounsey, Aidan Rave and the MD [Jones, Hardy and Pinkney].

However, there is also another dimension, in that there were members who clearly didn't care what was going on – as long as it destroyed the mayor [Councillors Pinkney and Jones].

ooo

24. Despite being repeatedly advised on the need for confidentiality, Councillor Pinkney disclosed confidential details to a third party from whom she has frequently sought advice. The Council should establish whether Councillor Pinkney now understands the need for appropriate confidentiality. If not, I recommend that the Council should consider whether she should be replaced as a member of the standing Investigatory Sub-committee. This matter is also being investigated by the Standards Board for England following a referral by the Council's Monitoring Officer.

25. At least two members of COISC spoke to Susan Law by telephone during the investigatory process. Former Councillor Cooke also met Councillor Mounsey and former Councillor Rave during the process and discussed the case. I acknowledge that former Councillor Cooke disclosed his contacts at that time. However, it is entirely inappropriate for members to make, or agree to, such contacts during a hearing. Clear guidance should be issued to members and the employee at the start of each case so that they understand that unauthorised contact would make them liable for disciplinary action.

26. The Monitoring Officer repeatedly advised members on the need for confidentiality but he then disclosed some information in broad terms to a few people at the SOLACE conference [Society of Local Authority Chief Executives]. He has acknowledged that he made an error of judgment. Sound governance starts with individuals recognising and adhering to their responsibilities – all staff need to uphold the principles and values of good governance and senior officers need to lead by example.

71. Former Councillor Cooke met Councillor Mounsey and former Councillor Rave at Mr Rave's house and discussed the case. He also alleges that Susan Law telephoned him... I acknowledge that Susan Law strongly denies that she rang any member of the Committee although her representative has stated that *'It is true that some members of the Committee have telephoned her'* [Susan Law]. While the facts are contested, it is agreed that there was contact. It is entirely inappropriate for members to make, or agree to, such contacts during a hearing. Likewise an employee should not be involved in unauthorised contacts.

72. Council officers repeatedly stressed the need to maintain confidentiality yet this did not happen...

73. Councillor Pinkney told the COISC that she "accidentally" phoned Susan Law during the investigation. Councillor Wilson, as Chair of the Sub-committee, decided that Councillor Pinkney should remain on the Sub-committee as exclusion may have caused more damaging publicity, the political balance of membership may have been undermined and replacing her with a new member would have taken time to acquaint them with the evidence.

74. When I interviewed all seven members of the COISC, they all said that they had no contact with the press and had not disclosed anything to other third parties. When asked again, Councillor Pinkney disclosed her contacts with a former Labour Party member. She admitted that she spoke to him as a [political] adviser and she had forwarded details from COISC meetings to him... Councillor Pinkney agreed that this was contrary to being told not to disclose information but said she did so because she wanted advice.

ooo

I believe the above highlights the complete collapse of ethical governance in Doncaster. Members of the COISC displayed complete disregard for rules and procedures.
　　Members of the sub-committee, with support and advice from existing elected members and former elected members, conspired in an attempt to force

Susan Law back, regardless of what she had done, in an effort to force the mayor from office; what a nest of vipers.

Having said that, the sub-committee was always going to seek some kind of a compromise. I always questioned how quickly they appointed Wragge and Co. [Mark Greenburgh] as advisors to the sub-committee.

From my first meeting with Mark Greenburgh, I became extremely concerned that he appeared only to want to negotiate a compromise agreement [a "cover up"] rather than deal with the issues presented to him.

I believe the only reason Wragge& Co. were appointed, was to secure the "compromise agreement" everyone [sic.] wanted – it was "best" for everyone – but not a good advert for openness, transparency and the truth.

ooo

Tuesday January 30th 2007...

"Donnygate Unlocked" screams a huge headline in the Star. And reports how it has partly-won its two year Freedom of Information [FOI] battle to access the details of those paying money back under the "Donnygate" Inquiry; the so-called "Name the Names".

It appears we will never be allowed to move on.

ooo

Friday February 2nd 2007...

"Council row ends in £120,000 pay-out – Top officer will leave job with authority admitting she was correct".

ooo

Monday February 5th 2007...

The Star reports on the "£100,000 bill for council chief leaving" and cites the specific costs of the external legal advice the sub-committee received.

The new leader of the Independent Group of Councillors, Garth Oxby is quoted as saying *"I wouldn't be surprised if it ends up costing nearer £300,000 and I think it is a sad waste of money which would have been better spent on services for children and the aged and improving the highways"*. He's right of course.

Thursday February 8th 2007…

"Councillors' anger at 'gag' on pay-off deal – letters warn of 'no comment' over departure of former managing director" reports the Star. Although not a "councillor", I have always been clear I do not and will not accept a gagging clause.

ooo

Tuesday February 13th 2007…

"Mayoral referendum call by campaigners" – stuff and nonsense about a motion being debated at Full Council on calling a referendum on abolishing the mayoral system in Doncaster.

ooo

Monday February 26th 2007…

2.00 pm – Doncaster Council Chamber

The pipers are piping as the malcontents present their petition for the abolition of the mayoral system in Doncaster.

In an extremely bad tempered meeting, with appalling behaviour witnessed by members, the council agrees to call a referendum on the mayoral model; voting 31:27 in favour of Councillor Tony Brown's [Ind] motion.

Councillor Edwin Simpson asked a question of the mayor…

> "On page 13 of the Dobson Report it is stated that once you became Leader of the Council in May 2001 that you withdrew from active involvement in the Glass Park Projects. Could you supply me with the exact date in 2001 when this withdrawal became effective? Can you also say if the statement 'that up to 2000/01 when your consultancy was paid, that all of your time on the Glass Park Project had been given free', is true? i.e. neither you nor your consultancy received any money from public sources before that time."

I respond: *"Thank you for your question Councillor Simpson, which I view as yet another clumsy attempt by you and your party to discredit me. I must also inform you publicly Councillor Simpson that I judge your continuing questioning as harassment and I am taking legal advice. In answering your question, perhaps you will be so kind as to allow me to also quote from the "Dobson Report" particularly, pages 12 and 13".*

"Before dealing with the circumstances of Martin Winter's withdrawal from all Glass Park activities in 2001, it is relevant for me to refer to the impression that I have gained, from my meetings and discussions, of how the Glass Park Millennium Green Trust operated, from its creation in 1998 up until about 2001.

The clear impression that I have gained is that, during this period, the Trust was, by any standard, very successful. This was not only in terms of successfully completing the major task of establishing the Millennium Green but also in terms of involving the local community [including the local schools] in a wide range of well attended events and activities. It would certainly appear that, during this period, the Trust enjoyed widespread support and interest from the local community. Another impression I have gained is that during this period, the affairs of the Trust were well conducted and organised, with proper attention being paid to matters of probity and accountability.

These impressions are certainly consistent with what I have been told by those "independent" persons [Inspector Lomas, John Housham& George Boot] who served as Trustees at this time. For example, some of the things that they have said to me include...

"my impression of the core group was that they were local people who were genuinely committed to improving the environment of their area by providing a new leisure facility that would be of benefit to the whole community, but particularly to young people"

"I was impressed by the enthusiasm and involvement of a very large number of local people… there was a real buzz about the project"

"there was a strong culture of openness and honesty, which I always found re-assuring… I admired the professional manner in which the quarterly meetings of the Trust were conducted"

"the meetings were well managed, with full accounts and reports being provided to the Trustees"

"it was a real pleasure to be involved with the Trust at this time"

"So the simple answer to the first part of your question Councillor Simpson is NO! NO! I will not supply you with the exact date in 2001 when the withdrawal became effective.

You had many opportunities during the almost 9 months that Mr Dobson took to undertake his extremely rigorous enquiry, to ask that question. You could have asked it of him, or indeed me, at the OSMC meeting in November. You can of course request that information from the Trustees or indeed from the Charity Commission itself – I will furnish you with contact details of these following today's Council meeting.

The reason I take this stance is that I understand that the "Dobson Report" [or an independent investigation anyway] and I will quote your own words Councillor Simpson, "will draw a line once and for all under this issue".

In terms of the second part of your question, I don't know if you are trying to be subtle with your confused questioning or whether it is something else, but during my work as a consultant, I worked for hundreds of organisations, some of them public, some private, some voluntary and some of them charities, so undoubtedly, there will have been some public money involved at some time, but I see no point in this question other than a further clumsy example of how you will seek to keep referring issues back in furtherance of your own political objectives, regardless of the continuing damage it does to the council and Doncaster.

Now we do need to move on, of course Councillor Simpson, and I and this council should be allowed to move on, having been totally exonerated by a whole series of investigations. Just as you Councillor Simpson, were allowed to move on despite being found guilty of bringing your office and authority in disrepute and being suspended for 7 weeks."

The meeting goes into uproar – the Lib-Dems are shouting me down. They seem to think it outrageous that I stoop so low!

As the meeting calms down, I try once again… *"So you are allowed to move on but you want to keep dragging up the fact that I've been totally exonerated. You are allowed to move on, having been found guilty and having admitted that your actions were "a moment of madness, borne out of frustration that a fellow member had left the room."*

And the meeting is in uproar again, as the Lib-Dem's try to drown me out… *"Let us agree to move on together, Councillor Simpson, for Doncaster's sake and concentrate on the regeneration of this great town".*

ooo

Friday March 9th 2007…

12.35 pm – Full Council – Doncaster Council Chamber

Today is a special EGM called to consider a motion put forward by Councillor David Hughes.

> *"The terms of settlement concluded to secure the release of the Managing Director, Susan Law, from employment with the Council on the March 31st, has provoked serious concerns throughout local government institutions.*
>
> *Described by the highly respected Municipal Journal, 'as a messy struggle that does local government no favours at all', is a statement that should concern every elected member of this Council as participants in this lengthy and costly dispute.*
>
> *Recognising the damage inflicted on the standing of this Council, both locally and nationally, this Council establish a cross representative committee to investigate in detail the procedures and circumstances that prevailed, which created causes for concern".*

He wants another kangaroo court!

I say that it would be a much stronger piece of work if we amended his motion and asked the Audit Commission to come in and undertake an investigation and prepare a Public Interest Report [PIR]. Now I know you can't request a PIR but there is no way on earth that, having been invited in to look at what has taken place, that they will not prepare a PIR!

As such I get them to amend paragraph three of the motion to read:

"Recognising the damage inflicted on the standing of this Council, both locally and nationally, the Audit Commission investigates in detail the procedures and circumstances that prevailed, which created causes for concern, as a public interest report."

ooo

Friday March 16th 2007...

I am really worried about the way the council has handled the Susan Law affair. Firstly, I am concerned that the payment may be fraudulent. Members colluded with officers in an attempt to force the mayor from office and, when this strategy didn't work, then conspired to pay off the MD, rather than deal with the real disciplinary issues inherent in the case.

Not only am I worried about the corruption of this process, I am fairly certain that the Audit Commission will crucify us on the "use of resources" scores at the next CPA.

Consequently, I am putting a motion together to call for an Emergency Meeting of Full Council to debate the issue.

ooo

Rather than simply relying on the Labour vote to drive it, I have discussed the issue with Councillor Ray Bartlett, the leader of the Conservative group, and also his fellow Tory Councillor Alan Jones.

Both agree to be signatures to the EGM Motion.

ooo

Wednesday March 21st 2007...

My cabinet members are petrified by the Labour Group's behaviour and specifically the likes of Mounsey, Kitchen, Blackham and their "henchmen".

Consequently, I have asked the Labour Party Regional Director, Barrie Grunewald, for his advice.

From:	MJW
To:	barrie_grunewald@newlabour.org.uk'
Date:	21/03/2007 14:39:00
Subject:	Fw: Emergency Full Council Meeting and Resolution
Attachments:	Emergency Full Council Meeting - Motion.doc

Barrie

Further to our earlier discussion – attached is the motion I am proposing to move at an Extraordinary Full Council Meeting.

This is an issue of probity and I have several key opposition politicians signed up to it with me – hence I do not need the "support" of the Labour group to call the EGM.

Labour cabinet members are worried about signing it with me as it has been intimated that they will be disciplined by group if they don't agree it with the Labour group first.

Can you confirm our discussion last week – i.e., that it is your understanding that they would not be in breach of the Labour Party Rules for supporting such a motion without first seeking Labour group's "permission".

Cheers

Martin

Following Barrie's email response, I have called an Extraordinary Labour Group Meeting. I have decided that from a Labour Party perspective, it would be best if Mike Jameson signed the motion as Labour Group Chairman.

ooo

I take the motion to a hastily arranged Labour Group, and have practically unanimous support, with only two objections – John and Ted! As such, we agree that Mike Jameson should sign the motion on behalf of the Labour group.

ooo

I draft the final motion after a great deal of discussion with legal officers...

Emergency Full Council Meeting and Resolution

This Council recognises that within the "Compromise Agreement", imposed on this Chamber [by the Members of the Chief Officer Appointments & Conditions of Service Sub-panel] the Managing Director accepts that the Council acted properly when it convened a meeting of a cross party committee of members to consider the allegations made against her by the Mayor and Cabinet – and to refer these issues to a Designated Independent Person [DIP].

This Council believes that some Members of the Sub-panel have ignored the most compelling of evidence put before them; these having warranted the most serious of consideration and responses from this Council Chamber.

With respect to this, Full Council recognises Cabinet's repeated requests for advice, support and a direct intervention from the Audit Commission regarding the soundness, integrity and indeed legality of the investigation into the Managing Director's capability and behaviour; and significantly the Sub-committee's inability to make a decision. Many of these concerns having been expressed by the Audit Commission itself.

So grave is the situation that this Council now finds itself in, that it is left with no option other than to take the most serious course of action itself. It therefore asks the Sub-committee to reconsider the "compromise agreement" and that the DIP be requested to undertake a full investigation into the Managing Director's capability and behaviour.

It is with great regret that we take this proposed course of action but we do so in the furtherance of open, transparent and democratic governance. And because the people of Doncaster deserve to know the truth of this matter and the behaviours and motivations of all the individuals involved in the process.

Failure to do so would be to shirk our responsibilities as Elected Members. We would be acting in the most irresponsible manner possible and be failing in our duty to promote the highest possible standards of public behaviour in protecting the public purse.

The request for the EGM is signed and the meeting is arranged for next Friday, March 30th.

ooo

4.00 pm

Mark Eales our Director of Education has told me he is leaving. It's a real blow as he has been massively supportive of me as the mayor, through all the turmoil of the previous eighteen months.

ooo

I recently received a letter from a senior member of staff naming a Labour group councillor who threatened them saying "you should be sent back home", with reference to the staff member not being born in the UK.

I am now dismayed to receive another letter from a senior member of staff claiming they are being bullied and harassed by Labour group councillors:

From:	
Sent:	26 March 2007 07:42
To:	Winter, Martin
Cc:	▇ ; ▇ ;
Subject:	Formal expression of concerns

Dear Mayor Winter

It is with great sadness, and some reluctance, that I submit this e-mail to you. I feel compelled to do so because of the appalling treatment of me by my employer over a number of months. You will appreciate that I have held back from submitting a grievance in the hope that common sense would prevail and certain Members would stop behaving against the Code of Conduct and treat me as a hard working committed employee. Unfortunately they have not.

There are a number of incidents I could raise but for now I will sum up my concerns with the following five examples:

1. I was coerced into giving evidence to the Investigatory Sub-Committee despite advising strenuously that the Sub-Committee had sufficient grounds to make a decision to investigate without the need for officers' evidence. Subsequently, as predicted, my evidence found its way to the newspapers which led to me being ridiculed and a loss of reputation. Nothing was done.

2. Members of the Sub-Committee openly made derogatory remarks about me and one even did so at a ▇ meeting. Nothing was done.

3. I reported to the Monitoring Officer a meeting with three Councillors [together with a member of the public] at which I was abused and my job threatened. This followed an incident at a Members Budget seminar when my job was threatened by another councillor.

4. The ▇. However, that was closely followed by a letter to the ▇ signed by the Independent Councillors in the most derogatory and unacceptable terms. Again nothing has been done. You will recall that I had written to the ▇ promoting the Borough in terms agreed by yourself.

5. At the ▇ a report had been written recommending ▇ I was asked seconds before the meeting to confirm that I would not ▇.

Please be aware that if I do not receive a satisfactory response to this e-mail, both in writing and in actions, then I will have no choice but to take this matter further through the grievance procedure.

I have copied this letter to the Monitoring Officer and my employment adviser.

Yours sincerely

███

ooo

Wednesday March 28th 2007...

2.15 pm

The notice of the _in-camera_ Extraordinary Full Council meeting has been posted and, predictably, the Star has taken Susan Law's side! What price democracy?

The paper leads with the headline "Secret talks over pay-off questioned" and takes the opportunity to bring the Glass Park into the equation again. Nonetheless, the opposition are getting ready for the battle, with the Lib-Dems saying they will boycott, and Edwin Simpson saying he thought it was outside the constitution of this authority!

The meeting and the Alliance of Independent Members question how the meeting was called, and indeed its legality!

ooo

4.00 pm

I've been shafted – and by the Labour group! To avoid litigation, I will quote from the subsequent report to Overview &Scrutiny Committee.

> 15. The [Acting] Managing Director contacted each of the five named members personally, to talk through the impact the motion was likely to have in terms of negative publicity and potentially endangering the council's legal position. Each of them confirmed that they wished to proceed with the meeting.
>
> 16. Bearing in mind the fact that the meeting of the Labour group was on the afternoon of the last day on which an extraordinary meeting could be called without the legal basis for the meeting being questionable, officers were on standby to issue the summons if required. When the Mayor confirmed that the Labour group had overwhelmingly supported the motion, the [Acting] Managing Director instructed officers to proceed with issuing the summons.

Despite being mandated to sign the motion on behalf of the group, Mike Jameson withdrew his support for the motion last night!

As such I have no option but to withdraw the motion – the EGM is cancelled.

ooo

Thursday March 29th 2007...

"Mayor takes on own council" reads the front page of the Star and continues with the sub-heading "Winter complains after being forced to ditch secret meeting".

"The meeting was cancelled after Councillor Mick Jameson, who had initially seconded the motion, withdrew his support following claims from opposition councillors that the meeting was illegal."

In its article, the newspaper "reports" that it has seen leaked confidential papers – thank you! and adds that "following our story, letters to the council from independent and Liberal Democrats warned they believed the meeting was outside the council's constitution".

There's a good piece of impartial reporting!

I am quoted: *"Many councillors share my concerns that the whole sorry mess has not been investigated properly and the motion sought to encourage the council to undertake such an investigation.*

We are in danger of using public money to pay for what could be seen to be a cover up... The people of Doncaster have a right to know the truth – and I for one will not be prevented from upholding honesty and decency. As a result, I will be writing to the Audit Commission and Local Government Association separately to register my objections to this pay-off."

ooo

Friday March 30th 2007...

My EGM is cancelled

ooo

Tuesday April 24th 2007...

"Donnygate cash scam – we reveal seven councillors who had to pay back expenses" reads the headline in the Star and reports: "Doncaster Council has named seven councillors who paid back cash after making fraudulent 'Donnygate' expense claims, The Star can reveal."

"They were members of the authority who were ordered to pay money back by the courts after making fraudulent expense claims – and the council has only released their names after The Star fought using Freedom of Information laws."

"Today, we can reveal the details of the repayments the council has been ordered to release."

"They totalled £1,927 and were ordered from former councillors by courts when they were prosecuted."

"The highest was £664.10 from Tony Sellars. The others were Terry Sellars, £544.60; Steve Judge, £289.00; former council leader Peter Welsh, £169.00; Michael Farrington, £137.60; Gordon Jones, £74.00, and Danny Buckley, £49.25."

This is appalling – It's a story that pre-dates my first being elected in 1999! And, as if that isn't enough, the newspaper finishes the article by saying… "The information has finally been divulged by the council after a two year battle by The Star through the Freedom of Information Act. But the authority is still refusing to tell who else paid back cash."

ooo

Wednesday May 2nd 2007…

Doncaster Star runs with the headline "Fears mayor an election liability" and reports on a story about a Labour candidate "denying" [a Lib-Dem] leaflet's claims she was one of my closest supporters" [!].

ooo

Thursday May 3rd 2007…

The Labour Party in Doncaster gains one seat at today's elections.

ooo

Friday May 4th 2007…

"Father and son make ballot history" reports the Star, featuring Paul Coddington and his son Stephen who are both elected for the Liberal Democrats.

ooo

Monday May 21st 2007...

Work will start next month on the £45 million build of two new secondary schools in Edlington and Mexborough.

ooo

Wednesday May 23rd 2007...

"Mayor puts weight behind Lakers" says the front page of the Doncaster Star and reports on page 3 and the back page that the "Civic leader puts body on the line to help rugby league survival".

During a training session, one of the players [whose father I used to play with!] decides to make a big hit on me as we play "touch-and-pass". He bounces off me and I laugh with him that he tried it!

The photograph is captioned

"Mayor Winter's glasses are knocked sideways after a heavy tackle by members of the Lakers' squad"

ooo

Friday May 25th 2007...

In a Doncaster Star special feature, the newspaper headline states "Mayor Martin a real sport!" and follows with a sub-headline "Ex-Dons player Winter feels the force as he tackles a Lakers training stint"

A hugely supportive article reports: "Like any politician, Mayor Martin Winter has his critics. But the town's sports fans have little cause to criticise him. He pledged that if he became the town's first elected mayor he would deliver a state of the art community sports stadium. He was elected and proved true to his word.

Rugby League has always been close to the Mayor's heart. He played semi-professional for Doncaster Rugby League. Consequently, I was not surprised that he was keen to show his support for the club. But I was surprised how far he prepared to go to illustrate that support in addition to talking to potential investors.

When I heard he was going to 'train' with the Lakers squad I thought it would just be a case of posing for the cameras with a few players with a ball in his hand. But the Mayor quickly dispelled any doubts that it was a PR exercise, by joining in with the players during a gruelling training session.

And he didn't appear to be joking when offering his services if the club, who had struggled to raise a side last week, were short for the home game against Batley next Sunday."

I need all the supporters I can get!

ooo

Footnote

As part of the internal "investigation" commissioned by the Designated Independent Person [DIP] via the Chief Officer Investigatory Sub-committee [COISC], I had sight of some compromising text/email "threads" and exchanges.

All were "dismissed" by the COISC but they do make very interesting reading.

The message I sent to Aidan on February 7th 2006, was forwarded to Susan Law within seconds of it leaving my phone and the subsequent response from Susan was extremely telling…

The email exchanges between Councillor Pinkney, Susan Law and others are extremely haphazard and show her leaking papers to third parties, including newspapers!

In search of FLO [the calm before the storm]

"I always like walking in the rain, so no one can see me crying"

Charlie Chaplain

Monday June 25th 2007

6.30 am

Today is Full Council – and yet another question about "naming the names" is on the agenda; again I'm being asked to release the report which identifies the individuals asked to pay back the [Donnygate] expenses following Operation Danum.

It's a pretty gloomy day as the rain shows no sign of abating; if anything it's getting heavier. Carolyne has already left for work. She is away for three days, in Daventry today and then driving down for a further two days in Bristol on Tuesday and Wednesday. As a result, I have to get all three children, Beth, Joss and Marcey, off to school before I head off myself. This isn't particularly challenging because they are all very self-sufficient and have always liked to organise themselves.

Nonetheless, the house is pretty chaotic as everyone goes about their business; an added complication being that Beth's asked if I can give her a lift to school because the rain is coming down so hard. She's seventeen now and in the sixth form at Danum Technology College where she is studying 'A' levels in English Language, English Literature, Media, Politics and Sociology.

My driver Paul is on holiday this week, so I have a replacement – he's Keith Parkes, a genial man who drives for North Bridge Depot. He reminds me of the actor John Candy, in his size, his demeanour and his voice patterns.

ooo

8.00 am

Joss [14] and Marcey [12] have now decided they'd also like a lift to school because of the rain. This is going to be almost impossible because I won't have time to take all three to two separate schools and then get back to be picked up by Keith at 8.15 am…

Beth agrees she'll get the bus, whilst I take the younger two to Hungerhill School, which we pass on my way to work. So we agree that we'll drop them off as Keith takes me to the Mansion House. I don't like doing this but sometimes it's the only way I'm able to fulfil my conflicting duties as both mayor and parent.

ooo

8.15 am

Keith has pulled up outside and I quickly get my papers together and my umbrella before shepherding the children out of the house. As we rush out of the front door I slam it shut, immediately recognising the dull thud-like locking noise it sometimes makes to signify that I've trapped the doormat under the door.

I look at the door in dismay. Joss and Marcey look at me, realising straight away what I've done *"Oh bollocks,"* I say.

"Stop swearing," says Marcey in exasperation and, as she does so, the heavens open.

"Oh bollocks," I repeat as I open the umbrella; and all three of us laugh as we squash next to the front door, sheltering under the porch while the wind blows buckets of rain at us.

I have to think fast. *"Right, run and get in the car,"* I tell them, nodding towards Keith waiting patiently at the roadside. As they run, I turn and try the key in the lock, knowing all too well, because of the many times Ed Miliband trapped the doormat under the door, that it won't work. We will not be able to get in easily, if at all, when the children come home this evening.

I run to the car. *"Bollocks... bollocks... bollocks!"* I say as I get in.

"Stop swearing Dad," giggles Marcey.

"Right let's go Keith," I laugh, joining in with her amusement *"Can we drop these two off at Hungerhill on the way... and no swearing please Keith"*.

The rain is now so torrential that traffic can only travel at about 10 miles per hour, with the roads becoming more like rivers. As the windows mist up, I explain what I've done to Keith and he laughs at my predicament.

"Let's just drop these two off and get to the Mansion House," I say. *"I'm gonna have to deal with the door later..."*

ooo

10.00 am – Mansion House

Full Council offers a fairly ponderous agenda with little of real substance required from me. Mags is presenting both the Food Plan and the Performance Plan at

Agenda Items 5 and 6 and then it's Questions from the public and Questions by Elected Members. It would appear to be a fairly mundane day with nothing particularly controversial.

As she comes to the end of the Performance Plan, and is summing up the Members' comments, the heavens open again; it's raining so violently that it interrupts the meeting and we can see from the windows that it's an absolute deluge out there.

Agenda Item 7 comes and goes – it's the Lib-Dems fannying about again, replacing one member of Overview and Scrutiny with another – riveting stuff!

As the Chair is introducing "Agenda item 8a, Questions from the public in accordance with Council procedural rule 12", I get a text from Marcey: *"Dad, school is being closed because of flooding – can you come and get us please? Marcey X"*.

"Ah bollocks!" I whisper to Mags *"I'm gonna have to get away – they've shut the school and I've got to go and pick the kids up"*.

"Can't you get Paul to get them?" she asks me.

"Nah – there'd be hell on. He can take me home so I can pick them up on the way – but I can't send him to collect them. Anyway he's on holiday – he's gone to Herten."

I text Marcey back: *"I'm in a meeting – I'll be half about an hour – get Joss and wait for me! Dad X"*.

In accordance with Council Procedure Rule 12, the following question had been received from ▮▮▮▮▮ of ▮▮▮▮▮ ▮▮▮▮▮ to Mayor Martin Winter.

"Freedom of Information. The Star newspaper report captioned "Donnygate Cash Scam" published 24th April stated Doncaster Metropolitan Borough Council are being obstructive in disclosing details of all council members and employees, who have paid cash back as a consequence of Operation Danum's investigations. The Council frequently claims to be open and transparent but the actions reported would reflect an opposite view. The lack of cooperation with the newspaper is undermining the council and does nothing to restore the confidence of the public at large.

To satisfy the public interest, announce when the veil of secrecy is going to be removed?"

Having asked the question in writing, Mr Tetley has not attended so Paul Hart reads it out.

"But there's a fair number of 'malcontents' who could've asked it!" I tell Mags. I give a disdainful but perfectly perfunctory answer and move on to Agenda Item 8b, Questions by Elected Members to the Executive and the Chair of the Overview and Scrutiny Management Committee.

None of this has been notified beforehand, so it could be a quick session or a very long one.

After responding to elected members on the issues of a total ban on the consumption of alcohol in public places; the introduction of congestion charging; Designated Public Place Order boundaries; the introduction of Multi Use Games Areas; the provision of supplementary 'wheelie bins' for large families and households; my Zero Waste policy; and my views on the political beliefs and convictions of others, there are no further questions.

I ask the Chair if I may be excused from the remainder of the meeting as I have been notified that we are in the process of closing schools because of the flooding; the Chair consents and asked that it be recorded that:

> At this point in the meeting, Mayor Winter sought the approval of the Chair to leave the meeting to attend to a personal matter.

ooo

11.35 am – Hungerhill School

The school is utter bedlam, it's raining heavily and there are cars everywhere as parents, guardians, friends and helpers arrive to evacuate the pupils. I've been a governor here for about ten years, so I'm interested on many levels [both operationally and strategically] – as a parent; as a governor; as a member of the LEA; as the mayor – but perhaps most importantly as an individual who likes dealing with logistical challenges.

There are dishevelled and wet pupils everywhere. I can see where staff are attempting to rope off areas and provide restricted access and emergency exits. Teachers and children are physically brushing water out of the hallways and classrooms next to reception. Others are trying to register who is waiting to be collected or who has already left.

I spot Marcey with her friend Jessica straight away – both are soaking. Marcey goes to get Joss, his friend Bradley, and Bradley's younger brother Harry.

The school's head teacher Graham Wakeling spots me and tells me the situation is very testing for all concerned; not least because the school is struggling to contact parents and get them to pick pupils up at such short notice.

"*Is there anything I can do at all Mr Wakeling?*" I ask him.

"*Well you could help by taking Brad and Harry,*" he nods at the two of them.

"*My mum and dad can't get away from work,*" says Brad.

"*And me as well, Mr Wakeling,*" pipes up Jessica, raising her hand "*Neither can mine Martin*".

"*That's fine – no problem...*" I say, secure in the knowledge that all three know me well "*... and the single thing you don't want at this moment in time is a pedant Mr

Wakeling... but have you thought about the child-safety implications?

"*I will take them – yes – but with the proviso that it's because you've asked me to...*"

"*Yes – that's fine Martin,*" replies Graham, distracted elsewhere.

"*Are you okay with that?*" I ask the kids, who are all clearly excited at the prospect of being evacuated from school for the day.

ooo

12.05 pm – Our House, Kirk Sandall

As we approach our house, it's still raining but less heavily, and I ask Keith if he minds waiting for a while, with the kids in the car, to allow me to break in through the back door!

The irony of the situation doesn't escape Keith and he says he didn't realise he'd be aiding and abetting the mayor's criminal activities when he got up this morning. Knowing I won't be able to get the front door open, I walk around to the side of our house, climb over the fence into the rear garden and smash a small pane of glass in our Georgian style stable door; the burglar alarm starts ringing!

I walk through the house, switch the alarm off, give the front door an almighty jolt inwards – and it opens straight away. As I walk to the car, all five children are getting out and I shout them to get inside quickly, get dried off and for Joss and Marcey to sort their friends out with dry clothes.

"*And don't go into the kitchen...*" I yell after them "*... until I've cleaned the glass up.*"

I open the car door to thank Keith. "*Bloody 'ell – I didn't realise I was working for 'Raffles' today,*" he grins.

"*The gentleman cat burglar eh? Well I think that's a bit of an exaggeration – you wouldn't say that if you saw the state of the back door!*"

ooo

1.30 pm

I've spoken to Bradley and Harry's father and to Jessica's mother and they will come and collect them after work. Everybody's wet clothes are in the drier, I've cleared the broken glass up in the kitchen and I now have five children, all in dry clothes, tucking into fish & chips...

1.38 pm

I receive an email from Karen my Executive Assistant.

> From: Karen [MD's Office]
> To: MJW
> Sent: Mon Jun 25 13:38:37 2007
>
> Subject: Diary
>
> Just to confirm that the diary has been cleared now until Wednesday. Also, have just read on EPIC that Hungerhill is closed tomorrow.
>
> Cheers
>
> Karen

ooo

3.00 pm

It's still raining and the road outside our house is flooded with approximately six inches of standing water. Paul Hart, our Interim Managing Director has informed me that seventeen schools have been evacuated and there are many road closures and related incidents right across Doncaster – we agree that Emergency Control [Silver Command] should be established to deal with this incident.

ooo

Beth arrives home – she's absolutely soaking but really pleased we've saved her some fish & chips.

ooo

6.00 pm

It's still raining and, after seeing our three guests off with their thankful parents, I've settled down to monitor the emerging situation through both TV and phone conversations. It has become very apparent that the situation is playing out across South Yorkshire – with TV news showing images of significant flash flooding in Sheffield; a flooded Meadowhall shopping centre and helicopter rescues lifting people from the roofs of buildings.

Gold Command has been established in Sheffield.

ooo

9.30 pm

Since Hungerhill School has announced it will remain closed tomorrow I will have to take Marcey and Joss to work with me.

Emergency Control call and, amongst other things, tell me they are closely monitoring river levels. As we are downstream of all the rest of South Yorkshire, I know that whatever falls over Sheffield, Rotherham and Barnsley, will work its way through the river system and end up in Doncaster – it's going to be a long night!

Beth's studying so I ask Joss and Marcey if they want to come with me to see the River Don – and we drive the two miles to Barnby Dun where I can see for myself that it's high, probably about two feet from the top of the banks.

On the way back, we call into the local supermarket, where I buy eggs, bacon, sausages, forty bread cakes, a roll of 'Alcan Foil' and bottles of brown and red sauce.

"What are you buying these for?" asks Joss.

"So I can take bacon, egg and sausage butties to Emergency Control tomorrow," I tell them.

Before the children go to bed, I explain that I may not be here in the morning and, should this be the case, Beth is to make her own way to school and Marcey and Joss are to amuse themselves until I get back.

Marcey tells me Jessica's mother is taking the day off to look after Jessica, so she will go there for the day. Joss says he will watch TV! I tell him I'll be back by 8.00 am and I'll take him to work with me.

ooo

Tuesday June 26th 2007

3.15 am – Our House, Kirk Sandall

I am awoken by a phone call from Karen, our Communication and Marketing Manager, who needs to brief me on a situation which has emerged during the past two or three hours and about which I am not, as yet, aware. Karen is Canadian and uses a different vocabulary and syntax which, coupled with her accent, can sometimes lead to confusion.

"Is that you Mayor Winter? in her Canadian brogue. *This is Karen* ▬▬▬▬▬ *calling from Emergency Control."*

Sleepily: *"Yes... yes it is Karen – thanks for calling."*

"Morning Mayor Winter – I have been asked to call you with an update on the fishes in the Dam at Ulley reservoir."

[Pregnant pause, while I gather my senses]

Sleepily: *"The fishes in Ulley reservoir Karen? What about them? Is it a trout farm or something?"*

"No Mayor Winter – fissures... fissures in the dam wall – I've been asked to update you on the fissures in the Dam Wall at Ulley Reservoir."

Less sleepily now: *"Yes... yes sorry... I understand now – sorry about that..."* And Karen explains that during the night a potentially catastrophic situation has arisen with the torrential rain leading to unprecedented levels of water entering Ulley Reservoir. As a result, cracks have appeared in the dam wall and Environment Agency engineers are trying to reinforce the wall while fire crews pump water out of the reservoir in a bid to ease the pressure on the dam.

Karen also tells me that the M1 has been closed because if the dam bursts, it will create a wall of water that will rush down to the motorway and, potentially take out an electricity sub-station and pylons carrying 270,000 volts of power.

I look out of the bedroom window – it's still raining – so I tell Karen I'll come in.

ooo

Even though we are now five years into the implementation of Local Government Act 2000 – and the role of high profile executive mayors is more embedded than in the early days – the role, responsibility and function of this Gold-Silver-Bronze Command structure in dealing with major incidents is still undeveloped and unclear.

Consequently, my attendance at Emergency Control always seems to be treated more presidentially, even disdainfully, by some of the multi-agencies "on duty"; most notably those attending from the police. I have always put this down to the ambiguity of the roles and responsibilities rather than political reasons.

Having said that, rather than force a position on the matter I have taken a "hands-off" approach preferring to play more of a supporting role to those "professionally qualified" to deal with such scenarios; rather than create a debate, or any resentment, over my "interfering".

This "watching brief" role seems to work; and I always try to communicate it while I'm there.

4.15 am

Having been involved with Emergency Control on several occasions over the six years I have been leader/mayor, I know that, in the initial hours, sustenance is the last thing on the agenda but becomes the foremost thing on people's minds; so I set off with thirty freshly cooked rolls – a combination of bacon, egg and sausages – wrapped in silver foil to keep them hot.

I drive to Barnby Dun again to look at the river level – it's now less than a foot from the top of the banks.

ooo

4.30 am – Emergency Control

Emergency Control is a hive of activity as the multiple agencies come together to deal with the incident.

It is a large room measuring some six or seven metres square. I always think it's redolent of 'Bomber Command' during World War II. A large formation of desks forms one large table in the middle of the room and on the wall at one end, a large pull down projector screen gives a real time presentation of the council's Emergency Planning Information Centre [EPIC] while two 42 inch plasma screens play BBC and Sky 24-hour news channels. Around the other walls are further desks and PCs for the multi-agency attendees to utilise and all the usual filing cabinets and other office equipment you would expect.

Adjacent to this main room are several smaller syndicate rooms for partners and/or smaller groups to work in, Communications and Marketing; the office of Paul Reed the Council's Emergency Planning & Safety Manager; and a kitchen, toilets and shower facilities.

Upstairs is a large meeting room capable of accommodating twenty plus delegates, several "rest rooms" with beds and further toilets and showers.

I make a fuss of everybody, explain I'm here in a supporting role – and let everyone know there are hot bacon, egg and sausage rolls in the kitchen. The food goes down really well, as I expected, and Paul Hart and Silver Commander brief me on the present situation.

They inform me that "Gold Command" is now worried that, should the dam burst, the wall of water could hit the river Don, causing a potential "Severn bore" type wave which would travel down the Don towards Doncaster, breaching the flood banks as it went – with potentially catastrophic consequences.

Personally I think this is highly unlikely, but that the M1 electricity sub-station scenario is plausible.

ooo

6.00 am

After half an hour of briefings, I do a telephone interview with BBC Radio.

ooo

6.30 am

Finally it has stopped raining – and I arrive home and get Joss up so he can accompany me during the day.

ooo

8.00 am

Keith picks us up and we drive to Barnby Dun to look at the river level again. It's still very close to the top of the banks, which worries me because the water still has to work its way through the river system.

I'm joined by Mags and we plan to spend the day assessing the situation, visiting areas affected by the floods and working with Gold and Silver Command to get the resources deployed as needed.

The situation is not good. We are still on stand-by for Ulley Dam bursting and Gold Command is insisting on concentrating on Ulley and responding to the devastation in Sheffield last night.

I am fairly comfortable with this. Although we've had a fair amount of flash-flooding damage, there's nothing too demanding at the moment. However, Gold Command seems to be in denial about the deluge I'm expecting from upstream.

When I ask what the Environment Agency's Officers are advising, I'm told they appear to have nothing substantive to say and complain about their resources being stretched right across the region.
The picture being painted is one of confusion – masked by Gold Command's preoccupation with safeguarding Ulley reservoir, the evacuation of around 100 homes below the Dam [understandably] and the recovery of Sheffield City Centre [predictably].

I ask my Office to ring around the MP's constituency Offices to find out what picture of the floods they're recording in Doncaster. At this early stage they appear fairly relaxed with reports of some localised flooding in Conisbrough and Sprotborough [both in Caroline Flint's Constituency].

We agree we should visit Emergency Control and see for ourselves what is happening.

ooo

10.30 am

At Emergency Control [Silver Command], Paul Reed starts to brief me on the Ulley Dam and Sheffield City Centre again. I cut across him and ask about the picture in Doncaster but this is much less clear and very much an emerging situation.

I ask to speak to the Environment Agency officers but when I question them about the River Don, they seem remarkably relaxed over the levels they are recording. When I tell them I have been to see the levels myself – and am concerned that they are still rising – they mollify me, saying it's to be expected!

I ask them what their modelling shows for the next 24-hours and they appear both unsure and apprehensive about the model's reliability – it might be early doors but I'm less than confident about the performance of this key partner.

ooo

1.30 pm – Bentley Road, Tattersfield end

Even though the general picture within Emergency Control [Silver Command] is one of confusion, our Neighbourhood Management Teams are proving real stars and feeding information from their individual neighbourhoods.

Mags and I are in Bentley Road, at the Tattersfield end close to the town centre. It's a poorly drained area, and Bentley Ings Drain is in flood; more worryingly, however, water is now coming up through the roadside drains. Morrison's car-park has flooded quite badly and, as we assess the situation with the Neighbourhood Management Team, one or two residents take it upon themselves to start blaming me [the mayor] for the emerging disaster, becoming abusive over the "lack of action" from 'the council' and/or the emergency services.

The situation is not helping the Neighbourhood Management Officers so Mags and I decide our attendance is inflaming a difficult situation and make a tactical retreat.

2.00 pm

Emergency Control is still pre-occupied with the Sheffield and Rotherham scenarios but tells us that we're experiencing local flooding in Toll Bar as well as Bentley [both in Ed's constituency] Conisbrough, Denaby, Tickhill and Bawtry [all Caroline Flint's Constituency] and Mexborough [Jeff Ennis].

So as not to utilise a council vehicle, we hire a big Ford four-wheel drive Crew Cab.

ooo

3.00 pm

I brief Ed Miliband that the situation is proving difficult and that we are expecting significant flooding in his constituency. I recommend he comes back up to Doncaster this evening so he is seen to be helping us support his community. Ed tells me that with Gordon Brown's coronation as Prime Minister happening tomorrow, he is unable to come up today – but wants me to keep him briefed.

ooo

3.30 pm – Tickhill Mill Dam

Mags and I visit Tickhill Dam, where we are told houses are in danger of flooding from a local dyke that supplies the mill pond.

We are immediately surprised by the marked difference in approach; the Neighbourhood Management Team is working more closely [and productively] with the community, who have brought a JCB in from a nearby farm and are attempting to use bails of straw to block the rising water.

ooo

6.00 pm – Emergency Control

Back at Silver Command Paul Reed tells me we are now experiencing problems across a wider geographical section of Doncaster, with significant difficulties being reported in Bentley, Conisbrough, Denaby, Fishlake, Mexborough, Sprotborough, Stainforth, Sykehouse and Thorne.

ooo

Mags and I spend the remainder of the evening liaising between Silver Command and the Neighbourhood Management Teams. Our staff resources are being stretched across a very wide twenty mile transect of Doncaster; with transport infrastructure pretty much ground to a halt, bus and rail services are severely disrupted and many major roads are closed.

Paul Reed reports that a 68 year-old man and a teenage boy have died in separate incidents in Sheffield; a 51 year-old man has died near Chesterfield and a 28-year-old man was killed after becoming stuck in a drain in Hull.

The threat of Ulley Reservoir's dam bursting is still immediate but seems to be lessening as engineers stabilise the situation by pumping out as much water as possible via brooks and streams. However, Emergency Command is now really cranking up the 'Tidal Wave' threat – saying that, if Ulley Dam bursts, water will surge down the river Don and flood large parts of Doncaster.

Given my increasing concerns that we are failing to respond adequately to the general crisis in Doncaster, I believe this is scaremongering and designed purely to distract my attention.

ooo

7.30 pm – Our House, Kirk Sandall

I have to drop Joss off at home, so we take the opportunity to view an electrical sub-station at Thorpe Marsh [Barnby Dun], which has been identified as "at risk" from the River Don flood banks being breached.

The situation is pretty bad – worse than I've ever known it – with the river level now within a few inches of the top of the flood banks. However, it's the Ea-Beck [a tributary which feeds into the Don] that is causing the problems. There is a one-way [tidal] "gate" which allows the water to escape the Ea-Beck into the Don, however, with the Don in full flow the gate will not open and thus the Ea-Beck has nowhere to go. The Ea-Beck, therefore, is already flooding the area to the west of the Don and it's here that the pressure is actually being exerted on the sub-station.

ooo

8.30 pm – Bentley High Street, Cooke Street/Arksey Lane Crossroads

At Bentley High Street it's as bad as we've seen – the water is already a good eighteen inches deep and rising. The picture is pretty chaotic with council and emergency services attempting to sandbag properties whilst simultaneously dealing with traffic chaos and 'flood tourists' photographing and even swimming in the flood water!

I speak to our Neighbourhood Management Team, who are doing a fantastic job working with residents and fire officers to organise the sandbagging, whilst struggling in the face of the damage created by the wake, literally not metaphorically, of passing motorists.

The officers are desperate for one single identifiable individual to take charge – not least to control the traffic which is making on-going repairs almost impossible. I ask who the Forward Liaison Officer [FLO] is and everyone looks sheepish.

With a huge number of best endeavours seemingly going to waste, residents are becoming frustrated with the chaos and confusion and looking for someone to blame. As they recognise me, I realise my attendance is not helping [again], so Mags and I decide tactical withdrawal is required.

ooo

8.45 pm

I do a television interview with Sky TV.

ooo

Emergency Control informs us of problems in Woodlands and an emerging problem with the A19 at Toll Bar being blocked by flood water; I am also told that we are now evacuating people across the borough and that I need to consider instructing the opening of emergency centres as per the emergency plan.

My response is that we should not stand on ceremony; Silver Command has access to all the information, so must make the decisions it sees fit as and when required – and it's here that I determine my first strapline, or mantra, for dealing with this crisis:

Ask for forgiveness… not for permission.

ooo

9.00 pm – A19 Bentley [New Village], South of Toll Bar

We arrive at the railway bridge that signifies you have left Bentley [New Village] and are now entering Toll Bar. As we get to the foot of the bridge I am amazed to see water stretching as far as the eye can see into the village of Toll Bar – which is a good two hundred metres, before the road veers off to the right.

Judging by the many abandoned and submerged cars, the water must be at least three feet deep. However, the thing that really surprises me is the silence. Every area we have been to in the last 36 hours has been loud and chaotic, as residents, Neighbourhood Management Teams and emergency services battle to save their communities. But here, south of Toll Bar, it feels uninhabited; a discarded ghost town.

I'm worried that it's so quiet and we agree to try to access the northern end to see what the picture is like there.

ooo

9.30 pm – A19 North of Toll Bar

After driving to Woodlands to see how we are dealing with the flooding there, Mags and I are more relaxed. The Neighbourhood Management Team is well on top of the situation, which was more of a flash flood with the water now disappeared – and residents seem generally more pleased with the way we have handled the matter.

We drive through to Adwick Town Hall, where the Neighbourhood Management Team is based, then up Doncaster Lane towards Carcroft and east on Bentley Moor Lane. The road here heads slightly downhill to a low point in the surrounding area; the water gradually gets deeper, to a good eighteen inches before becoming shallower and dry again. At this point we join the A19 north of Toll Bar and then travel south to enter Toll Bar at its northern most point.

Here I am surprised to see an old caravan parked at the side of the road a few metres from the flood water's edge. Outside is a night watchman type brazier, glowing with bright red embers, and surrounding the brazier are half a dozen young men.

As Mags and I get out of the Crew Cab we are approached by two or three of the group, who want to know who we are and what we want. When we tell them, we are met with a hostile reception and aggressively "informed" that this community has been left to fend for itself 'with no assistance from nobody' [sic.].

They say "they" made the decision to evacuate the old people from the Sheltered Housing Complex at Hall Villa Lane and that they've seen no support or individuals from the council, police or fire service.

I like to think I'm in my element in situations like this and, after a good hour's conversation with them, I manage to assuage their fears, to some degree, by explaining that few people have had the support they would have wanted because we have been dealing with such a large and widespread crisis; that Gold Command is in charge and support for Sheffield and Ulley Dam has had to take priority because this is deemed to be where the most significant life threatening risks are.

Nonetheless, this all worries me – it's like a scene from a Mad Max movie, a vision of some kind of Armageddon. Nobody has communicated to me what we are now witnessing at first hand, and I'm concerned that Emergency Control are not aware.

Having said that, the mood seems calmer now the young men have vented their anger at me! They tell me they're protecting the community, making sure looting won't happen. We agree that I will make Bronze Command aware of what's happening and/or assess the community's needs.

ooo

Travelling back, I speak to Paul Hart and Silver Commander and brief them on the situation as I see it in Toll Bar. Paul tells me we are dealing with the threat of serious flooding in approximately thirty plus locations across the borough and that Bentley High Street and the Bentley North Road/Tattersfield areas are now identified as at risk of severe flooding.

He says we are evacuating residents in several communities and eight "Rest Centres" have been opened to cater for the evacuees.

Mags and I agree to meet at Emergency Control at 8.00 am tomorrow morning when we will aim to visit all eight centres.

ooo

11.30 pm – Our House, Kirk Sandall

Back home I call Ed Miliband and brief him on the fact we are expecting significant flooding in his constituency. We decide to speak again tomorrow and he agrees it's likely he will need to come back to Doncaster.

ooo

Wednesday June 27th 2007...

8.00 am – Emergency Control [Silver Command]

After half an hour of morning briefings, we have a clearer picture. By late last night, water levels were approaching the control and protection systems in the 400kV electrical sub-station at Thorpe Marsh. Sandbags have been ordered to protect the most critical parts of the site.

By early this morning, flood water has started to affect vital site controls and National Grid engineers have begun to de-energise the 400kV sub-station circuits in a controlled manner. When I ask what this means, I'm told it doesn't mean we are shutting the sub-station down [and losing the power supply] but "de-energising" it – shutting down all the periphery electrical circuits that are in danger from the flood water.

I speak to Gold Commander to request assistance from the Army – with specific reference to sandbagging the sub-station.

The situation at Ulley is much more stable now. More than a thousand individual residents, from several communities, have been evacuated into "Rest Centres".

I ask where we are with regards to Toll Bar and am told that Bronze Command and the Forward Liaison Officer [FLO] are monitoring the situation.

I'm also told that there has been an extraordinary reaction from the general public and we are being inundated with offers of humanitarian aid in the form of bedding, clothing, supplies of toiletries and food.

I do a telephone interview with BBC Radio and signpost the listeners wanting to donate.

ooo

9.30 am – Adwick Sports Centre [Rest Centre]

As Mags and I begin our visits to the evacuation "Rest Centres" she really comes into her own and is marvellous in offering support and empathy to those suffering.

We are absolutely humbled by the way local authority staff and our partners have got hold of the crisis, and, with one or two exceptions, the evacuees are thankful and appreciative of the support provided.

I say with one or two exceptions, because the nature of the mayoral model is that of an all-powerful, accountable, individual who makes things happen. These people want to see me respond to the disaster in a decisive manner; they want to see action – whatever that may mean.

If you've suffered significant flood damage to your home and its contents and you don't have home and contents insurance then my accountability can mean becoming the object of their anger.

For my part, I am becoming increasingly worried that those evacuated from Toll Bar are describing a picture of chaos and abandonment; when we talk to them, they tell of a "wall" of water coming up the high street.

I vaguely recognise a couple of sisters who make a fuss of me, saying they know me from my childhood, when they used to visit another of their sisters in Kirk Sandall.

Fully aware of how the mayoral model [and I] seems to polarise views, I latch on to this recognition and spend quite some time "befriending" the sisters and those around them who are full of praise for the "young men" who evacuated them and other old people from the Sheltered Housing complex at Hall Villa Lane.

Yet again, the story is of no support from anyone – not from the council, police, fire service or elsewhere. I challenge this perception and stress how all the agencies have come together in the "Rest Centre" today, but the public seem to expect some "higher" level of support that simply couldn't be achieved, such is the scale of the crisis.

11.30 am

I do a television interview for the BBC at the Adwick Rest Centre.

ooo

1.30 pm

Today marks Tony Blair's last day as Prime Minister and Gordon Brown's first. As Gordon steps into the role, he announces his inaugural cabinet:
    The surprise is that Ed Balls is not appointed Chancellor of the Exchequer – that position going to Alastair Darling. David Miliband is promoted to Foreign Secretary and his position of Environment Secretary is taken by Hilary Benn. Ed Miliband is appointed as a Cabinet Minister and Chancellor of the Duchy of Lancaster.
Ed's new appointment replaces his old position as Minister for the Third Sector – a Mickey Mouse ministerial responsibility that he never really understood and a position "created" for him by Blair.
    I call Ed, congratulate him on his appointment and brief him on the situation. I tell him it's now imperative that he comes back to Doncaster this evening; and if he can, he should bring Hilary Benn with him, because the situation is directly linked to Hilary's new ministerial responsibility.
    He agrees and says he will try to have a word with Hilary.

ooo

2.30 pm

We attend Emergency Control and I am immediately briefed that water levels in the Ulley Dam have dropped significantly and the threat of the Dam wall collapsing has been removed so the risk of flooding at the [Brinsworth] electrical sub-station is now considerably reduced.
    With regards to the electrical sub-station at Thorpe Marsh, I'm told that the National Grid field staff and emergency services crews are doing an admirable job but still struggling in their endeavours with the water rising at such a rate.
    Bentley High Street and the Bentley North Road/Tattersfield areas are subjected to severe flooding; however, with Ulley Dam now being down-graded, the large-bore pumps being used to remove the water from the reservoir can now come to Doncaster to pump the water from the Bentley area back into the Don at Marshgate.

Toll Bar has been conspicuous by its absence from the briefing and, when I ask for an update, I am told Bronze Command and the FLO are dealing with the situation.

Forty eight hours into the crisis I tell senior officers that I'm concerned our initial response appears to have been very haphazard, but that as we enter the consolidation phase we seem to be acquitting ourselves much more admirably.

Privately, Paul expresses concern that I have articulated this view to Silver Command; he thinks they will take it badly and it could be de-motivating.

"You haven't seen what I saw last night in Toll Bar..." I tell him "... you certainly wouldn't be saying that if you had. And these guys..." I gesticulate to the Silver Command team, "... will be gone as soon as we move from consolidation to recovery."

Paul still thinks I'm being a little harsh; nonetheless we agree that he will contact the Chief Executive at Carlisle City Council and see if we can speak to their top operational man, following their experiences with flooding in 2005.

I instruct my office to get hold of Carlisle's Council Leader so I can speak to him and maybe borrow their top operational man for a few days.

ooo

3.30 pm – North Bridge Depot

We attend for radio and television interviews as our officers fill sandbags. With so many staff out there in the neighbourhoods, we've put a call in to all departments asking for volunteers to help fill the sandbags, such is the demand for them.

As per usual, the result has been fantastic with hundreds of staff volunteering and a roster put together to cater for their support. When I arrive, there's a ' spirit of the Blitz' atmosphere to the activity.

Our 'Comm's' [and general] staff know I'm game for most things so I muck in with them for a good half hour before doing the interview.

ooo

5.30 pm – Doncaster Train Station

Mags and I meet Ed Miliband at Doncaster Station. He has Hilary Benn with him and we set off straight away to Bentley North/Tattersfield and the streets to the rear of Yarborough Terrace.

As we have two ministers with us, we have been allocated a brand-new Range Rover patrol car and officer/driver by South Yorkshire Police; he's a local man who I know quite well, as his parents live near to my house.

As we travel, Ed tells me they must get the 9.37 pm train back to London tonight.

I brief them on the situation and the fact that, because the water has gone from Sheffield and the threat of Ulley Dam bursting has receded, Gold Command appears not to recognise the emerging catastrophe here in Doncaster – 48 hours after the initial crisis – as the water works its way through the river catchment system.

ooo

5.40 pm – Bentley Road, Tattersfield end

When we arrive it is plain to see that the area is in significant flood with roughly two foot of water in the roads at their low-points. South Yorkshire Fire officers are now in attendance and installing a large-bore pump to begin attempting to remove some of the floodwater.

Both Ed and Hilary are extremely keen, as am I, to get out and speak to the residents and see what we need to do to help. They split up and Ed goes down one street and Hilary up another. I stay with Hilary.

Again, I am shocked at the reaction we get as one particular resident takes it upon himself to attack me [as Mayor] and the Minister for the disaster and "lack of action" from the council and/or emergency services.

Hilary also seems shocked and tries to calm the man – but it just makes him worse. He's a big strong fit young bloke and extremely intimidating and I try to find the police officer for his assistance. Steering Hilary away, I realise the officer is just sat in the Range Rover facing the opposite direction!

Beating a retreat, I manage to get Ed, Hilary, Mags and myself together again and in closer proximity to the patrol car. I suggest we aren't helping an already difficult situation and, once again, we make a tactical retreat.

As we climb into the car, the officer smirks at me…

"Aren't they happy Martin?"

"I think that's a bit of an understatement," I tell him.

"Yes – they're clearly, and understandably, upset," says Hilary in an unemotional, almost perfunctory manner.

Ed looks shocked and even Mags seems startled by the level of aggression we've just witnessed.

I suggest we have a look at Bentley High Street [again].

6.00 pm – Bentley High Street, Cooke Street/Arksey Lane Crossroads

At Bentley High Street it's bedlam. The water is much higher than yesterday and across a much wider area.

The picture is still one of chaos with council and emergency services sandbagging more properties, whilst simultaneously dealing with flood tourists and traffic. The cars aren't attempting to drive through the floods like yesterday – but they still arriving upon them and then having to be re-routed.

I speak to our Neighbourhood Management Team, who are continuing to do a fantastic job, and notice Pat Hagan, Chris Root and Trevor McDonald all struggling in the difficult conditions. Our driver takes one look at the situation and wonders aloud why there are no police directing traffic or shutting off roads? Nobody appears to know…

As the ministers get out of the car we are met by a tractor and trailer ferrying residents and evacuees to and from their homes; once again we face a torrent of abuse.

"What's he come for?" one of them shouts *"There in't a TV camera 'ere."* The local people are becoming increasingly aggressive – claiming they've either not been able to get sandbags or that they've been charged for them!

One particular man is doing all the spouting. He's the man driving the tractor and he's doing a good job of whipping up the residents claiming that in Toll Bar, where he says he's from, there's nothing happening at all – and they've been left to drown [!]

"Ar bet your fuckin' house i'nt flooded!" he shouts at me.

How do you reply to that?

"Well… no… I err…" I mumble, as I struggle for an appropriate response. *"No… fortunately it isn't,"* I answer carefully, so as not to create more of a scene. *"I do live on a floodplain… close to the River Don in Kirk Sandall… but at this moment in time we're lucky enough to be dry…"*

"Nah… you can stop the fuckin' water from getting to your 'ouse – can't yer'!" he screams *"I bet you've got plenty of sandbags 'ant yeh?"*

And whilst I am still thinking of a response: *"I've heard that all the fuckin' sandbags are in your garage!"*

But before he can finish his preposterous statement, Trevor McDonald jumps in to defend me… *"Woa… woa… I'm not 'aving that…"* he asserts, moving between me and the aggressor.

"This fella's doing more to try and 'elp than you'll ever know" – but I cut him off.

"No… no… come out Trevor," I tell him and lead him away.

"I can deal with this Trevor… [only half believing it myself] *… thank you…*

but we certainly don't pay you enough to take this shit."

ooo

6.20 pm

"It's getting crazy here," I say to Ed. Neither he nor Hilary, nor Mags are showing any signs of wavering, which is great but, to be honest, they seem to be getting nowhere near the level of grief I'm getting.

I walk back to the patrol car to call Emergency Control about Bentley High Street and Toll Bar – once again, I am told that everything is under control, that Bronze Command is based in both Toll Bar and Bentley and, as FLO, it is monitoring the situation and reacting accordingly.

I'm stunned – not only is it bordering on a riot out here but I'm getting conflicting information about the police and/or emergency services presence. Who is telling the truth? And where are they?

Sitting in the patrol 1 car, I just don't know what to do – although I can cope with almost any situation I've ever had to handle, here I could be responsible for two minsters being assaulted!

I just don't know what to do for the best – if I try to engage these people it may make things worse. There are a great many agitators already making a very difficult situation impossible – the police presence is negligible and the situation extremely volatile. Having said that, many of these people need our help and have completely valid grievances, yet Bronze Control is seemingly non-existent.

I sit in the car for a good ten minutes contemplating a way forward and trying to understand why I'm sitting here away from the affray; is it because I'm hiding? That I'm frightened of the public?

I have never been afraid before – but I decide I'm best getting Ed, Hilary and Mags away because, with the troublemakers, our presence is actually making matters worse.

I get out of the car, clearly shocked over the situation – and Trevor McDonald comes across to me.

"Are you alright Martin?"

"Yeah... I'm fine thanks Trev' Are you?"

"Me? I'm fine....But I'm not 'aving to deal with these like you are..." he gestures towards the 'man from Toll Bar'. *"Don't worry about that mouthpiece Martin, you're doing a good job in unbelievable circumstances... and he's deliberately stirring things up.*

ooo

I manage to extract Ed, Hilary and Mags and suggest we try to visit Bronze Command in Toll Bar, and then the 'Adwick Sports Centre [Rest Centre]'.

Hilary can see I'm struggling. *"Don't worry Martin"* he tells me *"You're doing a great job – their reaction is only to be expected."*

A considered silence falls on the car as we journey to the next location.

"Just thinking about that madness back there..." says Hilary, breaking the silence *"Where were the local councillors?"*

"Well Tony Sockett's on holiday in Portugal," I say, looking to Ed for acquiescence *"... and Di Williams was there... but I haven't seen or heard from Stuart Hardy all week."*

ooo

7.30 pm – A19 Bentley [New Village], South of Toll Bar

As we drive a further two miles up the A19, there is no traffic at all coming towards us – the road is deserted. We leave Bentley [New Village] and drive over the bridge into Toll Bar.

I brief the two ministers as we drive – explaining we are now approaching what I call the 'southern shoreline' of Toll Bar – but as we near the crest of the bridge, I am fearful of what we may find.

Starting down the other side, I can see immediately that the water's edge is further up the bridge and the many abandoned cars I saw yesterday are fully submerged. The water must be nearer to five feet deep now and, Emergency Control says, still rising.

However, this time it's not the silence but what I see that stuns – and enrages me. There, parked at the water's edge, is a white transit van with its sliding side door pulled open. And sat in the van are a dozen or so police officers, all laughing and joking whilst they eat a Chinese take-way together.

We've found Bronze Command.

Astonished that the mayor, deputy mayor and two ministers should suddenly be peering into their communal feast, the police officers' reactions are two-fold:
- one, who is clearly embarrassed that we should have stumbled upon their soirée, attempts to engage with us and report on how they are 'monitoring' an emerging situation;
- the remainder continue to consume their banquet – laughing and joking;

As the first officer steers us away from the mobile eatery towards the shoreline, our own police driver joins us.

So are you FLO? I ask the officer rhetorically, explaining to the ministers how Gold, Silver and Bronze Command [should] work; and we proceed to question him on the problems the community is experiencing.

I contain my frustration, as the officer paints a picture of Bronze Command's responsibilities – in true command and control fashion, they are keeping a watching brief.

When I ask them what are they monitoring? What are they watching for? He tells me any changes to the present situation". And when I ask him what the present situation is, he just nods at the submerged cars and the road in front of him.

"Well it's relatively quiet," he tells us *"It's evacuated [abandoned]."*

When I ask him for the picture on the 'northern shoreline' he is much less decisive and refers to "others" who are advising Emergency Control. They clearly don't know!

Obviously uncomfortable with their lack of knowledge, our police driver jumps in: *"They stoned the fire engine in Toll Bar today, didn't they?"* looking at me as if I'd witnessed it with him... *"So emergency services are keeping away."*

ooo

8.00 pm – Adwick Sports Centre [Rest Centre]

Adwick Rest Centre is heaving – this is the second time we have visited today and there must be a good three hundred people in the main sports hall.

Once again, our officers are doing a sterling job, welcoming residents, assessing their immediate needs and coordinating the arrival of beds, bedding, food, clothing, toiletries, medical equipment and all other manner of humanitarian support for the evacuees.

Generally speaking, the reception is good although individuals are frightened and tired. But there is a sense of a growing frustration with "the council" even though I believe we have fulfilled our duties admirably.

9.00 pm – A19 North of Toll Bar – the Toll Bar "Northern Shoreline"

Driving down Bentley Moor Lane the water is a lot deeper now – a good three feet – and it's coming over the bonnet of the Range Rover.

As we leave the low-point of the road behind us and it becomes dry again, we travel on to the A19 and then drive onto what is, for all intents and purposes, the island enclave of Toll Bar.

At the "northern shoreline" I notice that the caravan and brazier are now a lot further up the road than yesterday. In the distance, I can see inflatable boats being rowed up the high street.

As we pull up in the patrol car, we are met by the young men – the self-styled "protectors" of the community. *"Don't get out Martin!"* instructs the police driver as I undo my seatbelt, clearly experienced at avoiding conflict situations.

And he's right, the welcome party is more aggressive than before, vicious even, in its verbal condemnation of the politicians – and me in particular – telling us again how the community have been left to fend for themselves and seen no support or individuals from the council, Police or Fire Service.

We're struggling here and I think the fact we are in a police car is inflaming them. Not only are we in a really nasty, confrontational "us-and-them" situation, but we've got to get the ministers to the station for the 9.37 pm train!

After a good 20 minutes of arguing – over whether the residents of Toll Bar have been abandoned by the emergency services and left to drown, and with a mayor and two ministers all wanting to take charge of the discussion [!], we've made no progress at all. It's a complete stand-off.

ooo

9.25 pm

Finally, we manage to extract ourselves when the police driver interjects and offers a resolution He personally gives the "protectors" his word that he will report back and police officers will be sent to the northern shoreline of Toll Bar to see what help and assistance is required.

ooo

9.32 pm

We arrive at Doncaster train station, having made the journey from Toll Bar in seven minutes – courtesy of South Yorkshire Police's newest Range Rover's

"Blues" [emergency flashing lights]!

As the two ministers disembark, I congratulate the driver, telling him I didn't think we would make it in time. *"Oh I knew we would get you here on time,"* he answers matter-of-factly.

"I would've got you here quicker if I could've found the Twos [sirens] *to go with the Blues."*

ooo

9.45 pm

After being dropped off, Mags and I attend Emergency Control. Taking Paul Hart, Paul Reed and Silver Commander to one side, I express massive concern that Gold Command is not working correctly and that the community of Toll Bar has, in effect, been abandoned.

I ask why nobody thought to tell me about the stoning of the fire engine in Toll Bar and the resultant decision to keep emergency services away. However, all three officers deny any knowledge of the stoning incident and any decision to withdraw emergency services.

I tell Paul I have significant concerns for the Toll Bar community which is existing as an island enclave, cut off from the rest of Doncaster and that there are approximately two hundred residents living in the upstairs of their properties – with no electricity, access to fresh water or sewage treatment facilities. He tells me this is not Emergency Command's understanding of the situation.

I say I have no confidence whatsoever in Gold Command's ability to deal with our situation from Sheffield. As such, I tell him I want four council officers to meet me at 8.00 am tomorrow morning, on the northern shoreline. I also want one inflatable boat; four pairs of waders [in various sizes]; two hundred bottles of water; emergency food rations and two first aiders and/or medical officers. Additionally, I tell him I expect a Neighbourhood Management Team to be in attendance and any other resources they see fit to provide.

I explain to Paul that, having never been here before, I am making this up as I go along – and would value some technical and/or operational expertise from the Emergency Planning & Safety Manager and Officers…

I tell Paul I think we will very probably find people in poor health and, possibly dead bodies in the properties and that because of this, I want officers to be prepared to undertake an audit of every home, through a combination of door knocking and assessment of Rest Centre records to make sure nobody is trapped in their house.

11.30 pm – Our House, Kirk Sandall

As we drive back, I call Tony Socket in Portugal to brief him on the crisis. I also call Ed Miliband and brief him on the instructions I have given our officers for tomorrow morning.

ooo

Thursday June 28th 2007

6.30 am

Emergency Control informs me that we now have four large-bore pumps pumping water from the Bentley High Street area back onto the surrounding farmland and the Bentley Road [Tattersfield] area back into the Don at Marshgate.

However, we have a problem, they say, in that hydrology engineers from the Environment Agency have told them the water they are pumping from Bentley Road is simply being replaced by the water being pumped away from Bentley High Street, through the drains and culverts on the farmland to the rear of the properties.

We are, in effect, just moving water around – and the only solution is to pump it from Bentley High Street directly into the River Don at Marshgate, a distance of nearly 2 miles. We have an additional problem at Bentley Road [Tattersfield] where there is significant concern about water permeating through the base of the Don's flood banks.

Furthermore Paul Reed informs me that Thorpe Marsh electrical substation is now in danger of being inundated by the floods and that the army has been engaged to provide boats to facilitate movement around the site.

ooo

I like to think, and others have frequently commented that I cope very well in emergency situations; an almost subliminal level of capability seems to kick in as I deal with the situation at hand.

Having said that, my assessment here is that we are really beginning to struggle; not only are significant swathes of Doncaster disappearing under water – stretching our staffing capacity beyond expectations – but the information flow between Bronze and Silver; Silver and Gold and *vice versa* is struggling to keep up with the crisis.

To be quite honest, we appear to have been forgotten in Doncaster – my evidence is being treated as apocryphal by Gold Command. Here we are on

Thursday morning, three days after the crisis began, and the Gold-Silver-Bronze command and control structure is failing our communities; and more specifically, failing Doncaster's [atypical] political governance structure.

My understanding is that this should be a 'strategic', 'tactical', and 'operational' command structure and the chain of command should be the same as the order of rank.

However, Bronze does not appear to be dealing with operational issues but constantly "monitoring" or "awaiting direction". This may be how it was designed to work – but because of the scale of this crisis, both geographically and operationally, we are in need of something more in terms of direction and deployment.

The crises in Sheffield [Mon/Tues] and Rotherham/Ulley [Tues/Weds] have rightly been prioritised by Gold Command. However, both Gold and Silver have taken their collective eye off the ball. Wallowing in a job well done, they have become blind to the emerging disaster in Doncaster.

Although this will probably become the subject of more rigorous academic analysis in the future, the sheer scale and status of the differing "crisis" making up the overall "crises" has a lot to do with this oversight – with some already having moved to 'Recovery Phase', whilst others are in 'Consolidation Phase' or [as with Toll Bar and Bentley] still in 'Rescue Phase'.

This is particularly apposite when you consider the differing obligations of the statutory authorities and emergency services; even before you overlay the atypical political governance structure, and expectations, in Doncaster.

We [and I personally] have entered a very dangerous situation here, where the "command and control" structure appears to be failing one part of our community terribly – and I must somehow communicate the seriousness of the matter to them. But how?

ooo

7.30 am – Interview with BBC Radio [Sheffield]

I decide I'm getting nowhere and must go on the attack – so I express my concerns over Gold Command's response to the emerging crisis in Toll Bar and Bentley.

ooo

8.00 am – A19 North of Toll Bar – Toll Bar "Northern Shoreline"

We arrive at the northern shore to be met by several officers from the

Neighbourhood Management Team bearing sandbags, bottles of water and food supplies. However, there is no inflatable, no waders, no first aider and no medical supplies. I change into my jeans and a sweatshirt, while I consider my options.

So as not to lose my temper, I text Paul Hart, explaining the situation and he promises to have the resources sent immediately.

Fortunately, the residents have access to a tractor and trailer and we are able to drive onto the Toll Bar island enclave with the water and sandwiches. As we do so I am completely dumbfounded by what I see. There must be a good fifty to a hundred residents going about their lives – as if living in up to eight feet of floodwater were the norm.

ooo

When word gets around that we have food and water on the tractor, people open their upstairs windows and climb onto outhouse roofs, so we can pass the supplies to them. I could cry. We all witnessed the devastation of hurricane Katrina and how the people in New Orleans were left to die – yet here we are in the UK with a comparable situation!

On the plus side, as word gets round that we're here, more and more people come to the tractor, to tell us that there's somebody living upstairs in a house at the end of that lane; at the Post Office; near to the rugby ground or elsewhere.

As we near the southern shoreline – the scene of Bronze Command's communal feast last night – there is a photographer, a young Asian man called Faisal at the water's edge. He hitches a lift on-board the trailer.

ooo

9.30 am

There's still no boat, waders or medical supplies – but two Police Community Support Officers [PCSOs] have arrived, as has an ITV film crew who we leave on the northern shoreline with the promise that I'll give them an interview at lunchtime.

Our Neighbourhood Management Team is doing a fantastic job but we [I] have become absorbed by the immediate humanitarian need for us to provide food and water when we still don't know if there are fatalities. And I have to accept that I might have to deal with such 'worse case scenarios'.

Seventy two hours after the crisis began, the water is still rising in Toll Bar, and I'm being compromised by the conflicting demands of 'Rescue Phase' and 'Consolidation Phase' protocols.

The Neighbourhood Management team is now utilising the tractor and trailer working with the community to distribute sandbags. One of the 'protectors', a young man, whispers in my ear.

"Get on the trailer Martin and help with the sandbagging... it'll do you some good." Taken aback that he should suggest this I ask him:

"Who are you... my new political advisor?" and we both laugh.

"You can't win," he tells me *"... and some of these are after killing you, so you need as many supporters as you can get. So let them see you helping them rather than defending yourself and the council"* he advises.

I join the locals and the Neighbourhood Management Team loading and unloading the sandbags and attempting to protect the houses on the Manor Estate and also the Central Club, on the western side of Toll Bar.

Again I find myself shocked to see one of our care-workers continuing about her daily visits – as if it were routine.

When I ask who she's visiting, she tells me we still have elderly and infirm residents living without electricity, access to fresh water or sewage treatment facilities; and when I ask what advice and/or support she has had from Doncaster Council, she says none!

ooo

10.30 am

One of the Neighbourhood Management Team approaches me. *"Martin – we're struggling here can you help us?"* He has a worried look on his face.

"Sure – what is it?"

"It's just that we can save some of these houses," he tells me *"But this 'prize fighter' won't let us through"*

"I'm sorry?" I try to get my head around what he's just said.

"We're sandbagging these homes but we've reached an impasse with this 'prize fighter' who's not allowing us on – we think we can still save some of the properties but only if he lets us through..." he nods towards a group of the 'protectors'.

"Who? What 'prize fighter'? Where?" I ask in quick succession.

"Him over there," he nods again towards the group.

"How do you know he's a 'prize fighter'?"

"Because everyone knows he is... and he's threatening everyone." As I walk across to them, I can see one or two faces I recognise from the previous hostilities and last night's stand-off with the Minsters.

"What's the problem?" I ask the group.

"*You fucking are!*" replies one – the one who was particularly vocal during the stand-off with the ministers.

"*Don't fucking listen to this bastard!*" he orders the group "*He'll fucking sell you down the river, will this twat!*"

Now I've never been one to take incorrect criticism well, and I am certainly not going to stand for this level of abuse. "*Why do you say that?*" I ask him, not realising the stupidity of the question – I'm loading the gun for him.

"*Why? Fucking why!*" he shouts, clearly loving the situation he is creating and the crowd that is gathering. "*I'll tell you fucking why... you lying bastard!*"

"*You and that fucking Pig last night told us that the police would be coming!*" he tells his audience.

"*And you just fucking left us... Again – you bastards!*"

Oh bollocks, I think to myself – the only way we got away last night was because the police officer promised them the help they were demanding and now I find we've shafted them [and I've been shafted] again...

ooo

What follows this initial verbal assault is one of the most stressful situations I have ever been involved with. We [I] have to engage in a full-on public debate/row with the 'protectors' as to whether or not we have failed them and whether or not "we" should be allowed to continue to work in the community.

To all intents and purposes, they have taken control of their community – creating a scene reminiscent of a picket-line during the 'Miner's Strike' – with their caravan and brazier as their gateway into the village.

There's simply no way of avoiding this confrontation. It's been brewing for more than two days now – as I have tried to placate the residents with excuse after excuse for Gold and Silver Command's [my] failings.

Now I am not one to unnecessarily walk into a lion's den – but sometimes in life you can't avoid these situations and just have to accept that you're going to take a kicking; hopefully figuratively speaking but in this case, probably literally as well unless I can calm the situation down.

I always enjoy speaking to an audience that is against me – and it's only with respect from the group, that a silverback Gorilla can become a great leader! But if I get this wrong I shudder to think what the consequences might be.

To wit, I'm stood in the middle of a crowd of twenty or so Toll Bar residents, a couple of members of the Neighbourhood Management Team, two PCSOs, the photographer we'd picked up earlier and one or two others; but the main protagonist is a strong, athletic-looking man in his late thirties who, it transpires, is a full-on bare knuckle 'prize fighter' and both respected and feared, in the Toll Bar community.

He's a frighteningly aggressive individual who is used to getting things his way. Yet some of his reasoning is plausible and, I have to accept, there's a fairly strong case that we have failed his community.

Each time I think I'm getting the top side of the debate, he changes the subject to some other aspects of "the Council"; "the Mayor"; or "Gold Command's" failings and we're getting nowhere.

Finally, after nearly two hours one of the residents says: *"You've sacrificed us to save Donny and your new university."*

"What? How have I done that?" I say almost in disbelief.

"When you blew the flood banks up" comes the response.

"When I blew the flood banks up? Have you any idea how stupid a statement that is?" I ask him.

"I'm telling you," he addresses the crowd *"I heard the explosions... two of 'em at about half two in the morning."*

Oh, this is absolute bollocks, I think to myself. *"Look!"* I exclaim to what is developing into a mob.

"Don't you think that, if that was the case, all the TV coverage would be showing us where I'd blown up the flood banks?" I plead in exasperation. I detect a sense of acknowledgement from the mob. *"You show me where the banks have been blown!"* I demand... and I spot my way out. It's high risk way but if you want to win, you have to be prepared to lose...

"Okay... okay" I command their full attention. *"We're getting nowhere and simply wasting valuable time – we've been arguing for nearly two hours now"*

"What if you and me... right now... had a fight on that tarmac over there," I challenge the 'prize fighter' – pointing to a tarmac area – and mime rolling up my sleeves for effect.

"You and me can have a dust-up right now," I tell him *"... and it will end in one of two ways."*

He raises his eyebrows, as if to say does this guy know what he's saying? I'll tear him limb from limb...

"Either you, quite probably, will give me a good hiding," I continue, almost taunting him. *"And everyone will say that I got what I deserved..."*

And then I say in a quieter voice *"... or maybe I might put you on your arse..."* and I stare deep into his piercing blue eyes. *"In which case everyone will say... that they didn't expect that."*

And I look at everyone present. *"But what will it have done for this* community? Your community? You tell me how it will have helped this community in one positive way?"

I can see it's working… *"It won't have moved us forward one inch – it won't have helped one little bit!"* And I can see it's making the mob, and more importantly the 'prize fighter' really think…

"Instead of all this aggression… tell me what you want me to do – and I'll do it"

He's mellowing in front of me…

"You tell me what you want me to do – and I'll do it… Although I won't bare my arse on TV," I add – to a few laughs.

"You tell me, what you want me to do…" I reiterate *"… and I'll do it… or I'll try and make it happen for you."*

And I can see him trying to puzzle me out.

"Tell me what you want," I plead once again.

And before he really has time to think about it: *"I want you to apologise!"* he says – and looks around at the mob *"But you won't do that… will you?"* he's becoming aggressive again.

"I want you to go on TV and apologise to this community for letting them down," taunting me now.

To which I respond straight away *"Okay… I'll do it… I'll apologise for failing you… and can we then get on with saving this community?"*

And to be fair to him, he calmed down. *"Aye… when you've apologised,"* he smiles.

I turn to the photographer and say *"You've got some dynamite there Faisal – a right exclusive!"*

ooo

1.00 pm

We make our way to the northern shore, where the ITV camera crew is set up and I do a TV interview, during which I say:

"… I have to say that, as the Mayor, the buck stops with me… and that I believe I have failed this community… It's my job to work with Gold and Silver Command – and I have not been able to communicate effectively to them how bad the flooding is affecting this community in Toll Bar."

As usual, the media has a field day I would've thought the story was about a politician taking responsibility – but they'd just got someone to blame!
High risk strategy or not, it seems to have worked; the self-styled "community

leader" and his colleagues calm down and start to work with us to get the resources they need.

The 'prize fighter' is still very wary of me, however, and both he and the other 'protectors' remain aggravated about our failings. Each time I am introduced, he interjects:

"I still haven't decided whether he's legit'... and he wants to help us... or whether he's conning us... For the time being I think he wants to help us – but he might turn out to be a snake... just like all politicians [are snakes]".

What do they say about damming by faint praise?

ooo

2.00 pm

Still no boat, waders or medical supplies have arrived but things are moving now and the whole community is helping to sandbag the properties on the higher ground.

We have discovered an un-adopted road/track in extremely poor condition that works its way around the back of the houses and Toll Bar Club – which then services the Manor estate; despite outward appearances, the community is not physically cut-off.

ooo

2.30 pm

Emergency Control [Comm's] call me. Either the shit's hit the fan or my strategy has worked. Gold Commander at Sheffield is asking to speak to me about the misunderstanding that's taken place on BBC Radio this morning!

I agree to speak to him at 4.00 this afternoon – and ask Comm's to set this up.

ooo

3.30 pm

I am very conscious about how volatile the "peace" is in Toll Bar; so I check in with the locals explaining that I'm going to have to visit Emergency Control, Bentley Rd [Tattersfield] and Bentley High Street and giving my word that I'll be back in Toll Bar before 6.00 pm. All seem very amenable to my absence [!] on the basis that activity is now beginning to happen within their community.

4.00 pm – Council House, College Road

I have had to call into my office to sign some papers. As I sign them, Karen whispers to me that Gold Commander is on the line.

Gold Commander starts by briefing me as to where we are with Sheffield City Centre, Ulley Reservoir and the dam wall, and Sheffield Forgemasters; where there had been an immediate and direct danger of water entering the casting works and flooding a working forge, with potentially catastrophic consequences.

As the discussion moves around South Yorkshire, we have a rather staccato conversation and it is clear that, even now, he has very little understanding of the circumstances in Doncaster.

He starts to suggest I may have not understood how bad things were in Sheffield and Rotherham, hence my outburst this morning, which he puts down to poor communication between Gold and Silver. Outburst? The cheeky bastard!

Not really listening to my protestations that I completely understand how bad it was in Sheffield and Ulley, he tells me that, having dealt with the crisis:

"We are standing Gold Command down now – perhaps you would like to come through [to Sheffield] *tomorrow and have a pot of tea with us while we show you what we do, did and have been doing."*

The arrogant twat, I think to myself, he still has no understanding whatsoever of how bad it is and remains in Doncaster – or that it is still getting worse. As a minimum, he should have requested a brief on what the present situation is.

"With all respect, Gold Commander" I begin [always a bad sign] *"... the very fact that you are telling me that you are standing Gold Command down – and asking me to 'pop along' for a 'pot of tea and a chat' – shows me you have no grasp whatsoever of the situation here in Doncaster..."*

"We are twelve feet underwater in some areas [and still rising], with whole villages cut off; people having not been seen for three days [and potentially drowned in their homes]... and now you're asking me to come and have a pot of tea with you!"

"You may be entering Recovery Phase in Sheffield – but we're still in Rescue Phase here in Doncaster where we're still trying to save lives – and I would respectfully request that you convey this to your colleagues".

ooo

5.00 pm

I attend Emergency Command [Silver]...

There is significant water permeating through the base of the River Don flood banks at Bentley Road [Tattersfield], which is now threatening to flood the static caravan site there.

Call me paranoid, but I detect the senior police officers present at Silver are very distant; and when I suggest this to Paul Hart, he tells me staff have not taken my radio comments well. I tell Paul I'm livid – I understand that all the staff at Silver are exhausting themselves trying to deliver, but we can't be so precious about the crisis that the mayor isn't allowed to speak his mind.

I tell him he needs to get over to Toll Bar and see how bad it is – and then tell me that Gold/Silver got it right.

ooo

Notwithstanding the above, I have maintained my calm throughout the previous three and a half days of "command and control" systems... But it's not easy and I'm reminded of James Cameron's comments about his allegedly aggressive approach as a director:

> "You know, I think I was much more of a bastard in my earlier years as a director... and, frankly, the system rewarded it. I always said that the problem with the job of directing movies is that there is too much positive reinforcement for bad behaviour..."
>
> "And the positive reinforcement is... if you try to be completely calm and rationale all the time... everybody's under the gun and sometimes they're not listening and you'll get to the set and something that was discussed very rationally, maybe several times, is just simply not done..."
>
> "... and then you blow up and you pitch a big fit... and you storm around and then suddenly it just manifests itself – everybody scrambles around and solves the problem."

ooo

5.30 pm

I have had to pick up Joss and he is to accompany me for the rest of the day again.

ooo

6.00 pm – A19 North of Toll Bar – Toll Bar "Northern Shoreline"

The inflatable boat has arrived! But there are still no waders or medical supplies...

I speak to Paul and explain that we may have a boat now but until we have the waders we are unable to audit every flooded property to make sure there are no residents lying injured or dead inside.

He assures me once again that everything will be in place tomorrow morning – and that he personally will be attending on site to ensure this is the case. I tell him I'm relieved to know he's going to be here [to witness their arrival!].

ooo

7.00 pm – Visits to Rest Centres

Ed Miliband is up from London again and I brief him on the chaos. We attend the Don Valley and Adwick Rest Centres where the complaints are coming thick and fast – including one that I am dressed scruffily in jeans and wellingtons!

I have to concede this is a valid complaint – we have nearly three hundred people sleeping in the sports hall and such communal living, over time, will become unsanitary unless we are very strict on how we manage hygiene issues.

We agree, through Silver Command, that we need to brief the evacuees on hygiene, have antiseptic wipes for those entering and also provide disposable shoe covers to prevent the spread of germs.

ooo

9.00 pm – Toll Bar "Northern Shoreline"

We drive slowly and carefully down Bentley Moor Lane because the water is coming over the bonnet.

I have been briefing Ed on the disgraceful scenes we witnessed today and we arrive to be greeted by 'the protectors'. Adjacent to the caravan is the boat that has been left on the Northern Shore by the Neighbourhood Management Team; safe in the knowledge that it will not be removed!

Having introduced Ed to the 'prize fighter' and his colleagues, we agree that we will utilise the boat so Ed can see first-hand the "island enclave" that Toll Bar has become; it's a large inflatable, capable of carrying five or six adults comfortably and Joss immediately sits at the prow.

The 'prize fighter' passes the oars to me and Ed, and smugly announces that we can 'ferry' him around the village.

Whilst we are making ourselves comfortable, the remaining 'protectors' ready themselves to 'launch' us into the lake that Toll Bar has become.

We surge forward with the initial impetus from the 'launch party' and I press my oar tightly to the side of the boat to steer us in a more direct line – but we just glide around in a circle. As I struggle with a combination of forward, backward, sweep and pry strokes, the boat is still not steady – and I notice Ed is paddling as if he were in a race...

"Whoa... steady Ed," I tell him *"I'm trying to hold her steady..."*
But he's not listening.

"You need to paddle a lot less frantically," I tell him, but he's still not listening to me. And I realise the 'protectors' are laughing hysterically as we spin round and round in circles.

"Whoa... Ed... Ed... stop paddling so quickly," I tell him, trying to recover from the absolute scene of buffoonery we are [he is] creating. But it's having no effect whatsoever. For all his huge intellect [!], Ed is clearly unable to grasp the most basic tenet of rowing a boat...

I look at our 'passenger' and his face is a dual picture of amusement – and annoyance.

"Look at them bastards," he states nodding towards the protectors on the shore.

"They're pissing themselves at yer."

"Paddle slowly" he orders *"... and firmly – like you might massage a good woman"* – which amuses me more than ever.

"Fucking 'ell," he immediately dismisses... *"Give me the fucking paddle"* and he lunges towards Ed, pushing him to one side and grabbing his oar. The boat is rocking dangerously with all this activity; but soon calms once Ed is substituted.

Adjusting to our now functional rowing technique, nothing more is said; and like an end scene from the film 'Deliverance', we paddle south – down Askern Road – with the sun setting over the Manor estate to our right.

"I don't think you were ever a boy scout – were yer?" the fighter asks Ed rhetorically as we paddle into the distance.

ooo

10.00 pm

Dismayed at what he has witnessed at first hand on the island enclave, Ed is now desperate for us to be seen to be doing something.

"How can this happen?" he asks me. *"How were they left to fend for themselves? Why were they left to fend for themselves?"*

Ed has to return to London for a meeting with Gordon tomorrow morning but we agree he will be back up to Doncaster at lunchtime and that I will request a meeting with Silver Commander to discuss Toll Bar, Bentley and Arksey.

We drop Ed off at Doncaster station so he can get the 10.15 pm train to Kings Cross.

ooo

10.45 pm

As I arrive home, Emergency Control briefs me that serious flooding has now occurred in forty plus separate areas of Doncaster and we have more than 2,000 people presenting themselves at our Rest Centres.

ooo

Friday June 29th 2007

6.30 am – Our House, Kirk Sandall

Emergency Control briefs me that the Thorpe Marsh Electrical Substation was partially restored to operational service by six o'clock yesterday and fully restored by four this morning.

Hungerhill School is still closed and Marcey is with friends, so Joss has to spend the day with me again. Beth's school is open so she is functioning as "normal".

ooo

7.30 am – Toll Bar "Northern Shoreline"

At Toll Bar Paul Hart is beaming at me with a pair of waders on! Standing alongside Paul are several of the 'protectors', members of the Neighbourhood Management Team, two, fully-fledged, police officers and two PCSOs.

As I climb out of the Cab, Paul is clearly ecstatic that he has "delivered" and begins to issue orders to the team. I ask what we are doing and he tells me he has agreed they will undertake a full audit of every property, through a combination of door knocking and assessment of Rest Centre records.

ooo

fall out   In search of FLO [the calm before the storm]

8.26 am

I receive my twice-daily EPIC Summary from Emergency Control and make it available for the MPs:

From:	MJW
To:	'ennisj@▮▮▮.uk'; 'flintc@▮▮▮.uk'; 'milibande@▮▮▮.uk'; 'Rosie@▮▮▮.uk'; 'LindaMcAvanMEP@▮▮▮.uk'
Date:	29/06/2007 08:26:20
Subject:	EPIC Summary 28 June 2007 07.00 to 19.00

Please find below a summary of the key activity recorded on EPIC system for 28 June 2007.

I hope this information is useful in terms of providing a snapshot of yesterday's main activity.

Cheers – Martin

To be honest, I'm livid when I see the EPIC record for the previous day's activity:

"12.07 pm [yesterday] South Yorkshire Police Under Water Search Unit have requested the use of at least 1 possibly 2 of the rigid inflatables at Hatfield Water Park".

The inflatable only arrived at Toll-bar at 6.00 pm yesterday – despite me requesting [nay pleading] for its delivery some thirty-six hours previously... This means that we had them all along, and Gold/Silver and Emergency Control must have been aware of that!

ooo

9.00 am

Following concerns expressed by the community I need to look at the damage to Toll-bar Primary School. Having donned a pair of waders for a closer inspection, it is clear that the school is significantly underwater – to a depth of about four feet across the campus.

ooo

10.30 am

There are murmurings that Prince Charles is to visit the "floods" today – but I am a little irked that this apparently means he visits Catcliffe [Rotherham] and Sheffield.

Not that we're in a suffering competition, but it would seem our colleagues in Gold Command have deemed these two sites to be the priority for a royal support visit!

ooo

11.00 am

I take a pre-arranged call from the new Prime Minister, Gordon Brown. He is hugely supportive of me and the quality of advice and guidance I'm giving Ed.

"*Ed tells me you've made some courageous decisions in very difficult situations, Martin*".

"Well... I don't know about courageous... But I've been petrified when I consider the ramifications of some of them"

And then he says something I will always remember... "*Well courage is not the absence of fear, Martin – it is the triumph over fear.*"

And while I'm still taking in what he's said, he tells me I can safely rely on him and Ed, to support my every move, and that they – and the government will be there for me.

I tell him I have massive concerns about the costs of the floods. "*You don't need to worry about costs, Martin... that's the least you need to be worrying about...*" replies Gordon.

"*I'll make sure that they're covered for you.*"

Well that's good enough for me, I think. If you can't trust the word of the Prime Minister...

ooo

11.15 am

The Sheffield Civic Mayor has launched an appeal for the floods victims. Although I am informed that there has been an extraordinary reaction from the general public in the form of bedding and clothing, toiletries and food, I am concerned that any appeal needs to be a larger, South Yorkshire, national even, appeal.

I put in calls to the Leaders at Sheffield, Brantley and Rotherham and we agree there needs to be a bigger, more co-ordinated campaign.

ooo

fall out   In search of FLO [the calm before the storm]

11.30 am

Although Mags has been with me almost every step of the way during the last five days, she has also been holding forth with regard to cabinet and she tells me I have to attend a cabinet briefing meeting to discuss a variety of business issues and give them a steer.

Generally speaking, cabinet are pleased with the reporting they have received from Emergency Control; they are also very pleased that I have kept them all in the loop with regard to their wards and also Bentley and Toll Bar.

Despite "emerging grumblings" over my leadership, the Labour group is very satisfied with the manner in which we have politically dealt with the floods and how I have kept them up-to-date.

ooo

12.30 pm

Ed is back up from London and we have requested a private briefing with the [Silver] Emergency Commander. There is a growing sense of helplessness within Emergency Control – and more specifically the Environment Agency – as to the intransience of the floodwater in the Bentley and Toll Bar areas.

My briefings are now talking of the largest peacetime evacuation ever witnessed in the UK with statistics of 400 million tonnes of water a second falling across South Yorkshire, West Yorkshire and Humberside; the equivalent of 18 Olympic swimming pools every second, according to the Environment Agency.

We now have eight big bore pumps operating – pumping twenty-four hours each day – and it is having no impact whatsoever on the water levels. Silver Commander informs us that they have requested additional pumps and support from fire services nationally.

Ed is desperate to parade his capabilities to Silver Commander but he's really struggling. He is lacking in both experience and knowledge – factors which don't seem to impede his thought process!

Finally, in a desperate bid to be seen to find the solution, Ed proffers: *"What if we get oil tankers involved? What if we access oil tanker lorries to vacuum up the water and take it away?"*

I am mortified by the idiocy of the question – surely Ed must be able to see what a stupid suggestion he's making? I look at Silver Commander and his eyes roll, as if to say, "do I have to waste my time answering idiotic questions like these?"

"Let me explain further, Minister" I say in my best Sir Humphrey voice. *"I*

think we are talking in the manner of trillions of cubic litres of water – in Toll Bar alone..."
"Even if we could get access to an unlimited stock of tankers, it would take forty or fifty to empty one Olympic sized swimming pool... you do the maths."

Clearly not understanding the maths, Ed went on ... "But it would be possible?"

"Look," I interject in an exasperated tone *"We need to take advice on this one... and from somebody such as the Environment Agency – but let's be under no illusion... we are talking of hundreds and thousands of vehicle movements a day. Even if you could – hypothetically – get access to such a fleet of tankers..."* I begin almost apologetically to Silver Commander. *"Where are we going to park them? Where are they going to park 'off site' while they wait to fill up?"*

"And where do they then take the water to? Where's 'away'? We can't just take it to Whitby and run a pipe off the edge of the cliff."

"And that's before you have everyone up in arms about the number of heavy vehicle movements thundering through their communities each day..." I'm beginning to rant...

"... and before you've destroyed the roads – at a cost of millions!

"Let's not forget... Minister" I begin imitating Sir Humphrey once again. *"That the Stainforth Community were up in arms when 'RJB' wanted to reopen the pit – creating hundreds of jobs – and this was specifically because he projected fifty coal lorries running through the community each day..."*

"Fifty!" I say calmly – noting that Ed has realised the idiocy of his intervention.

ooo

1.15 pm

After Silver Commander leaves us, Ed and I continue the discussion – I tell him we need Gordon to come up because we're getting nowhere. We can't get rid of the water – and we can't get the resources we require.

Despite having now sat down with Silver Commander, Ed is completely flummoxed and keeps referring to the situation with Hurricane Katrina, where the world watched helplessly as the people in New Orleans were left to die.

"You can see how it happened... can't you?" he asks me *"You can see how the system failed them. There's no-one actually capable of making the decisions that need making on-the-ground – nobody has access to the information* [they require] *to make the decisions."*

"This is my argument entirely..." I agree with him *"... it's the case for*

mayoral subsidiarity – but within the context of Emergency Control. I can argue 'til I'm blue in the face that I'm elected to be 'accountable'... but Gold/Silver Command is in charge"

ooo

6.30 pm

I speak to David Moody, the South Yorkshire Lord Lieutenant with regard to Prince Charles' visit to Sheffield and Rotherham today – he tells me Prince Charles is extremely keen to visit Toll Bar and Hull and they are looking to arrange something during next week, but urges me to keep this completely confidential.

ooo

Saturday June 30th 2007...

8.00 am

Rather like a poor manager, believing something will only be done correctly if he [or she] does it themselves, I am reluctant to leave the Toll Bar community and allow history to repeat itself.

There is an emerging tension between Silver Command wanting to monitor the Rescue and Consolidation phases whilst the Local Authority staff, and our other partners, want to move into Recovery phase and physically support the communities.

Ed realises this and, even though he is unable to be here for the full weekend, I've assured him I will keep him fully briefed on events. Although he isn't saying as much, Paul has a similar view – and he's working with me in Toll Bar again to oversee the immediate Rescue and Consolidation work. Five days into the crisis, the water seems to have stabilised, although with further rain expected, the River Ea-Beck, the river that burst its banks contributing to the flooding at Toll Bar, remains the subject of a severe flood warning.

There is, of course, another way of looking at this situation – that Paul is so concerned about what I might do that he's chaperoning me! Nonetheless, during the day I get the opportunity to ask him if he has received any feedback on Ed and my meeting with Silver Commander the previous day.

"Nothing really... Although I'm told Ed had a novel proposal for dealing with the flood water..."

I laugh with him. *"Look... I know that in true 'brainstorming' style, we have to consider all options... but where on earth... how... and why on earth... would you ever think that taking it away in lorries [when there's oceans of the stuff] is a good strategy?"*

ooo

12.00 pm

As we enter Emergency Control, one of the Comm's staff passes us a copy of today's Yorkshire Post. *"Mayor claims town 'let down' in crisis"* reads the headline and the newspaper goes on to report:

"As hundreds of people faced up to their flood nightmares yesterday, Mayor of Doncaster Martin Winter said he felt that the emergency response system had "failed" people in the town."

"Sheffield, Rotherham and Barnsley were recovering from the effects of Monday's rain but some areas of Doncaster were still being pumped out, with about 300 people in refuge centres." [sic.]"

"Mr Winter spent several hours in Bentley and Toll Bar, the neighbourhoods hit hardest, travelling by boat to meet people who were trying to come to terms with what had happened to them."

"But he said he felt that communities in Doncaster, which is downstream of Sheffield and took longer to bear the brunt of the rain, had been "unable to access the resources they needed"."

As I digest the rest of what the newspaper is actually reporting, I exclaim: *"The set of tin-pot bastards!"* to anyone willing to listen. *"Those fucking twats at South Yorkshire Police are having a go at me".*

"Shh...Shh..." mimes Paul and quickly moves me into the Communications & Marketing syndicate room.

"I did warn you," he says. *"South Yorkshire Police don't take kindly to being criticised"*

"But South Yorkshire Police are briefing against me now," I cry *"Look at this load of bollocks... They are putting forward a counter narrative in an effort to discredit me because I had the gall to criticise them. But if you're going to put forward a counter narrative – you need to have the facts to back it up... And they can't get their figures right – even now – look, they're reporting that we've got 300 people in refuge centres – when we've got closer to 3,000 evacuees!"*

"They're 90% wrong..."

"90% – wrong – can – not – be – a – good – case – for – being – right!" I enunciate. But I'm on a roll now *"And I know... because I am 100% right!"*

"The stupid bastards. How can the Police give out figures [to a newspaper] *that are 90% wrong to support their case that they've got it right [and that I am wrong]? We've got nearly a thousand displaced in Toll Bar alone!"*

"Well you will 'tickle the tail of the tiger'... I think you would say Martin," says Paul.

"Yeah – but these stupid bastards are gonna create a war – with me – and I don't do losing."

"Well... I think we need to talk to ▮▮▮▮▮▮▮▮ *and Comm's..."* says Paul, slightly more nervously, and noticeably adopting a more corporate stance. *"Particularly if you're planning on going to war with them. I don't think we really want an on-going war [or sore] with South Yorkshire Police."*

"I don't give a toss! They are putting forward a counter narrative in an effort to discredit me – and they haven't got the facts to back it up. These phony bastards never even requested an interview – which I wouldn't have given anyway! So the only people they can have asked is Gold Command!

"And they're always keen to oppose Labour party politicians – so the Yorkshire Post is complicit with them... So we have no arbiter to challenge the 'facts' they're putting forward."

"Whatever happened to the impartiality of the press?" asks Paul rhetorically.

"It's the same every time with South Yorkshire Police," I rant *"They want to be judge and jury too – and woe betide anybody who criticises them, because they'll destroy them! Well they've picked on the wrong fucker here!"* And I move into classic pedant mode – dissecting the article line by line...

> He said "I feel that, as mayor, I should have been making a much stronger case to those directing the emergency services and that they should have been sending more resources into these communities.
>
> "I feel personally that we have let them down. I understand that Ulley dam was the priority, but these people have been left alone to manage the disasters in their own communities. We couldn't get pumps in here to take the water away."
>
> "But a spokesman for South Yorkshire Police said senior officers, who had chaired the response command, did not accept that the emergency services had treated the Doncaster area differently."
>
> "The spokesman said: "Our focus, as it has been throughout, is on looking after all the people affected by flooding across the county. No requests from Doncaster have been refused by any members of the Gold control centre, which includes fire, military and other services, as well as a representative of Doncaster Council."

I feel personally that we have let them down – *"I said I had let them down – me 'THE MAYOR' had let them down! ... the stupid bastards "They're just creating a story here to suit their editorial line against the Labour Party".*

I understand that Ulley Dam was the priority, but these people have been left alone to manage the disasters in their own communities – *"Well... that's true they were!"*

"For whatever reason, Bronze Command were just sat there having a Chinese – at 8.00 o'clock on Wednesday night! – and I would argue because Gold had said to them – 'rest at ease boys, you've done a good job and we're getting ready to stand down'.

We couldn't get pumps in here to take the water away – *"Well firstly, I accepted we couldn't get the pumps in because of Ulley – I was fairly relaxed about that – but we still can't get the fucking pumps in now!"*

I am in full rage by now – *"And why? Why? Because Gold didn't [and still doesn't] understand the scale of the fucking crisis we're dealing with in Doncaster!*

"As for taking the water away – well I simply would not say that – and I pointed this out [yesterday!] to Silver Command [and Ed Miliband] – THERE IS NO "AWAY"

"This is a classic case of the Yorkshire Post misreporting on the basis of an interview I gave on Thursday to a local Radio station."

"It is a matter of regret that despite an open invitation Mayor Winter has never attended Gold control, unlike the chief executives of the other boroughs affected. [sic.]"

"We understand that he has only visited the Silver control in Doncaster once and then only briefly, so it may be that he doesn't fully understand the situation."

It's a matter of regret... – *"It's a matter of regret... It's a matter of [fucking] regret... that South Yorkshire Police are briefing against me!"*

... despite an open invitation – *"They invited me on Thursday afternoon – for a pot of tea yesterday – on Friday!"*

... unlike the chief executives of the other boroughs – *"This is such a load of bollocks... I am not a fucking chief exec' – I am the mayor – I'm a fucking politician! We don't have a chief exec' – you are [our] Interim MD Paul – they can't even get my fucking status right."*

"I'm elected to be 'accountable'... but Gold/Silver Command is in charge and, at this point in time, they are physically hindering our recovery work."

... only visited Silver Command once and then only briefly, so it may be that he doesn't fully understand the situation – *"The fucking lying bastards! I visit Silver on a daily basis and or speak to either you Paul, Silver Commander or Paul Reed [as the 'EPO'] several times a day"*

"The cheeky fucking bastards," I sigh, almost in resignation... *"Right Paul... we need to be in charge of resource deployment – not Silver Command – how do we do that?"*

"Well you don't – or won't – whilst ever Silver Command is active. We can only take charge when we've formally moved to Recovery Phase."

[There is a long pause while we consider our options]

"That's what we need to do then Paul. We need to close Silver as soon as possible and wrest back control. We need to meet as a Strategic Management Group on a daily basis to consider local authority resource deployment and other issues," I say with glee. *"That'll teach the bastards"*

And I turn to look at Mags [and Joss] and laugh apologetically *"It's a good job we encourage you not to swear, isn't it Joss?"*

"You don't swear do you, Joss?" asks Margaret *"You're a nice lad aren't you?"*

"Well I didn't... until today!"

ooo

As if the cross-briefing from South Yorkshire Police isn't enough, the Yorkshire Post article [on Saturday June 30th] compounds matters further by going on to report how bad the situation is in Doncaster.

> "Yesterday South Yorkshire Fire and Rescue deployed most of its high volume pumps to the Bentley and Toll Bar areas and chief fire officer Mark Smitherman admitted the Ulley dam had been "a major pull on resources".
>
> "Meanwhile police, the Environment Agency [EA], and council and health workers continued to work around the clock to help evacuees."
>
> "With more wet weather expected, the Ea-Beck at Toll Bar last night remained the subject of a severe flood warning – the EA's most serious flood alert."
>
> "Severe flood warnings also remained in place at four points on the River Don – at Bentley, Bentley Moor, Willow Bridge caravan site and the areas of Thorpe in Balne, Kirk Bramwith, Braithwaite and Trumfleet."
>
> "As a precaution Kirk Bramwith and Braithwaite residents have been told to be prepared to evacuate their properties. Nearby Arksey and Almholme are also at risk..."

Still, I can have every confidence that Bronze Command are in place!

ooo

1.30 pm

Paul Hart calls to inform me we will be having a meeting on Monday with Prince Charles' Private Secretary and security to go through a programme for a visit next week.

ooo

Sunday July 1st 2007...

Work continues to protect and support both Toll Bar and the Bentley communities and, during a long day, Mags and I visit all eight Rest Centres, where we calculate we have a total of more than 500 evacuees.

Generally speaking they are happier and the Neighbourhood Management Model and our staff seem to be responding magnificently to the myriad demands being placed on them.

ooo

Monday July 2nd 2007...

9.30 am – Strategic Management Group [SMG] Meeting

As we sit down to the first meeting of this new group, Paul Hart introduces me to John Mallinson, Head of Scrutiny and Emergency Planning at Carlisle City Council, who has joined us this morning and will be advising Silver Command.

There is a general feeling of frustration – we now have access to eight High Volume Pumps [HVP] – and they are having no effect whatsoever. My briefing notes tell me that one Olympic size swimming pool could be emptied by a pair of High Volume Pumps in 3 hours... and a road tanker containing 28,000 litres [roughly 6,200 gallons] could be emptied by a single HVP in 4 minutes.

I point to this and whisper to Paul: "That makes a mockery of Miliband's strategy."

ooo

Following on from this morning's SMG, the discussion turns to housing demand and the fact that a great many residents are not going to be able to move back into their accommodation – whether public sector, private sector or privately owned – for many months.

As a result, we know we are going to be severely tested in terms of how we rise to the challenge of catering for their numerous demands. However, there is a lot of confusion over the numbers and status of the "evacuees":
- Those presently residing in Rest Centres.
- Those presently residing with "friends and families".
- Those presently residing in a flood damaged property.
- Those presently residing in accommodation provided by insurers, which might be:
  - Hotel accommodation.
  - Privately rented accommodation.
  - Caravan accommodation within their own curtilage.

With all the confusion, we simply don't know the exact requirements and our interim Director of Housing informs me that our staff are attempting to put together the most accurate figures available.

The issue of the future for Toll-Bar Primary School is becoming acute. Ordinarily, the massive damage the school has sustained would be a huge blow to the community but the current problem is compounded by the fact that the school has been identified for potential closure due to its surplus places.

Officers are suggesting we might take the opportunity to permanently close the school... which would go down terribly within the community and provide the media with a new spin on what is proving to be a rolling news story.

ooo

10.30 am

I call to thank Mike Mitchelson, the Leader of Carlisle City Council for his support, advice and assistance.

ooo

11.00 am

After a conference call with other South Yorkshire Leaders, we agree to the establishment of the South Yorkshire Flood Disaster Relief Fund and that the South Yorkshire Community Foundation should administer it.

ooo

12.00 pm

Government announces that John Healey – who was moved to the Department of Communities and Local Government in GB's first Cabinet – has been appointed 'Floods Recovery Minister', with special responsibility for assisting the recovery from flooding across the United Kingdom.

ooo

2.00 pm

Mags and I meet Prince Charles' Private Secretary and the Lord Lieutenant, David Moody, who is attending with two of Charles' security team, and we have been asked to physically run through a proposed programme and itinerary for the visit.

Charles' aides are incredibly impressive and have an uncanny ability to let us think we're in control, encouraging us to plan an exciting, dynamic visit, presumably in line with the direction from Prince Charles. In truth they are actually in charge and busy vetting every logistical aspect for timings, safety, security, resource and presentational implications. After approximately an hour and a half, we visit Adwick Rest Centre where the aides appear taken aback by the scale of the humanitarian aid being provided.

Prince Charles' Equerry is particularly well dressed, wearing a faultless, well-cut dark grey suit, a delightful pair of classic oxford shoes and sporting an umbrella over his arm. In short, he looks the perfectly tailored classic English gentleman and sticks out like a sore thumb!

I am concerned that we are having increasing difficulty discussing the royal visit in code, so I ask the Leisure Centre Manager – who has been briefed that I will be attending with some high profile guests – if he can organise refreshments for us and access to one of the sports centre's syndicate rooms so we can have a private chat.

Having taken this reconnaissance visit as far as we can, I suggest we retire upstairs and use one of the sports centre rooms to run through the visit and agree any action points or requirements.

As we reach the top of the stairs, the Centre Manager is stood attentively outside the room and shows the six of us in. Settling down in some comfy chairs, two female members of staff wearing blue 'Metro Catering' tabards enter, carrying a catering box containing cups, saucers, flasks and other accoutrements.

They put them on the floor near the door and start to empty the contents: *"I don't know who you are... or where you come from..."* says one of the women as she lifts the coffee and tea flasks out of the box and walks over to us.

Then, pausing for dramatic effect, she plonks them on the table with a fair degree of aggression and stares intently at me. *"... but if you think we've got nothing better to do... than to do this... then you want shooting!"*

She's quite right, of course. I could argue she's unprofessional, or that she has no right to speak to me and the guests in the manner she does, but I quite admire her boldness.

Now that doesn't mean I'm not annoyed and embarrassed, but it does mean I have to moderate the situation I now find myself in. *"I am terribly sorry,"* I begin *"It's entirely my fault – I merely wanted us to be able to have a discussion in privacy. And I certainly didn't expect anybody to be put out or diverted from other activities."* But neither of them cares what I have to say. They simply collect themselves together and leave the room.

I turn to our 'guests', struggling to make light of the situation...

"I trust she won't be serving His Royal Highness on Wednesday?" said Charles' Equerry, in marvellous understatement.

"Yes Sir..." I laugh, relieved he can see the funny side. *"I think we should just put it down as an example of what I call South Yorkshire chutzpah Sir!"*

ooo

Tuesday July 3rd 2007...

9.30 am – SMG Meeting

We are now seven or eight days into the crisis, with the problem in Toll Bar and, to a certain extent, Bentley showing no signs of abating. We have become the centre of the country's 'flood story' with the water still present and providing humanitarian, health, heroism and myriad other stories.

Our Officers have just briefed the SMG on an emerging problem identified through problems at one of the Rest Centres, and also through calls to the Council, where residents are seeking clarification with regard to their rent and Council Tax obligations.

We agree to suspend rent requirements for flood damaged properties and evacuees and I have requested a further report being brought to me which advises on the potential legal position if we suspend council tax obligations; with the subsequent revenue implications for future years and poor corporate performance assessment [CPA] scores through lower council tax collection levels.

ooo

fall out   In search of FLO [the calm before the storm]

Wednesday July 4th 2007...

9.30 am – SMG Meeting

During the meeting, we discuss an emerging problem at the Adwick Rest Centre with drunkenness! To a certain extent, it's understandable in that the majority of the people are there reluctantly and are killing time.
    Additionally the evacuees have been put in a position where they no longer have to pay their rent, council tax, electricity, gas and other utilities – while their food, clothing and toiletries are being provided for them. Suddenly they have a lot of disposable income and it's burning a hole in their pockets!
    We agree an alcohol and behaviour policy for the Rest Centres.

ooo

11.34 am

As we ready ourselves for Prince Charles' visit, it becomes apparent there's a rumour going round that the "Rest Centres" are closing; somebody's been saying things they shouldn't... As a result, the residents are unhappy and it's been leaked to the press, who are stirring the situation up. I send Paul Hart an email in response to a suggested line from Comm's:

From:	MJW
Sent:	04 July 2007 11:34
To:	ECC8; Hart, Paul
Subject:	Re: Statement re: rest centre move

Cheers

I'm fine with this but, as I said yesterday, shouldn't we be saying something about the strategy being... Firstly putting people into Emergency Accommodation, then into Interim Accommodation and then Temporary or more Permanent Accommodation.
    And should we not be pointing out that the communal living of "Emergency Accommodation" becomes ever more unhygienic and stressful with a complete lack of privacy etc.

Cheers

Martin

ooo

12.00 pm – Prince Charles' Visit to Toll Bar.

Following Monday's reconnaissance visit, the Prince of Wales is today making his second trip in less than a week, to the worst hit flood areas. Everybody's attendance is synchronised via the Lord Lieutenant, David Moody, and we are all awaiting Charles' arrival.

As we gather at Doncaster School for the Deaf, Ed is with us, of course. We are told that we will then follow Charles' vehicle and police outriders in convey to Toll Bar, where the visit will then commence.

Whilst he has been with us today, Ed has continued to display a worrying fascination, obsession even, with Kate Middleton, the girlfriend of Prince William. I'm worried that this appears to be all he is interested in discussing, when clearly he should be highlighting concern for his constituents' plight.

For a man who has been raised as part of the Westminster political elite and the glitterati, Ed appears almost 'star struck' with Charles and has a child-like excitement about the visit, constantly asking how it might look if he 'bummed' a ride back to London in the helicopter with him [!]

I have come to know Ed's unbridled arrogance well but this really does take the biscuit; *"Of course it'll be fine,"* I tell him – *just run it past the Lord Lieutenant and his equerry first"*.

Frighteningly, Ed saunters over to David Moody and does just that – completely oblivious to the fact that such a request will have put David in an invidious position.

I can't quite make out what they are saying but the Lord Lieutenant appears very cooperative and Ed returns to say David is fine about it, in principal, and will have a word with Charles' equerry; I am flabbergasted.

ooo

As a child, my father used to insist that I sat down for the national anthem at the Rugby League Cup Final each year, so I am frequently surprised how respectful I am of the Royal Family; but Charles is his usual extremely impressive self. His empathy and understanding for the evacuees is acute, as is his awareness of the operational and strategic demands of the crisis.

As we reach the southern shoreline, Charles considers the deserted high street, which is still under as much as 5ft of water. Suddenly, taking the residents and his security people by surprise, he climbs into an inflatable dinghy and is rowed by a fire fighter to inspect the flooded houses at close quarters.

ooo

2.00 pm

Having waived Prince Charles off – plus one hitch-hiker – we debrief on the visit.

ooo

Saturday July 7th 2007...

Most of the water has gone now, and we have very much moved into "recovery stage" as the huge clear up task begins.

The Prime Minister, Gordon Brown, visited Toll Bar today and was very good value, as usual. He has had a pretty torrid first couple of weeks since becoming PM – with fire and floods; the Glasgow Airport terror attack last week and the floods here and elsewhere across the country.

Note: In terms of pestilence, the foot & mouth crisis began in early August.

The Prime Minister assures the community and me, as the mayor, of the government's full support; and once again, he re-affirms that I mustn't worry about the money.

I am worried though – I don't believe the Bellwin Scheme will go anyway near satisfying our full expenditure...

ooo

11.52 pm – Our House, Kirk Sandall

I have just got home and decide I need to email Paul Hart:

From:	MJW
To:	Hart, Paul
Sent:	Sat Jul 07 23:52:44 2007
Subject:	Housing Demand

Paul

Forgive me for this but I am incredibly concerned that we are teetering on the edge of a logistical time bomb with regard to the flood victims.

This afternoon in Toll Bar was so unstructured, I have severe concerns that we will descend into anarchy. SITA staff were saying at 2.00 pm that this was the last "pick up" before the Civic Amenity sites shut at 3.00 pm – until I intervened and insisted we bring in another crew and open the sites until 10.00 pm !

The public meeting ▇▇▇▇▇ has organised for Thursday – unless very carefully choreographed – with a clearly managed message will descend into chaos. We have been talking of the housing logistics for two weeks now but I have seen very little information to

suggest we have a hold of the size and type of housing problem we have. As a result, for Monday evening, can I request the first estimates of the numbers of flood victims we have on the basis of the following criteria [or at least something approaching it]:
- Evacuation home status – eg Rest Centre, "Friends & Family", Insured Accommodation.
- Geographical home – eg Toll Bar, Bentley, Thorne, other.
- Family size and accommodation required.
- Special requirements: ages, disabilities, dependents, other needs.

Can we then map this against the provision we have identified so far and that we could provide through public and private housing, hotels and the use of the static mobile homes.

This way we may be able to usefully deliver a structured message of Thursday and request further information to enable timescales to be estimated and proffered.

Cheers

Martin

ooo

Monday July 9th 2007...

9.30 am – SMG Meeting

Following my midnight email to Paul Hart, I feel there is a greater sense of control; we are in charge of the full recovery programme now that "Silver Command has stood down. However, I am struggling to get some of our staff to grasp the notion that…"This is not a 9.00 'til 5.00 disaster – our residents are living with it 24-7!"

ooo

I am minded to find fifty caravans and set up a "trailer park" for the evacuees. All the advice I get tells me to avoid this strategy like the plague, but I feel it's right for this close-knit community, who want to stay together and fear the floods is a signal for the loss of their local school.

Ed plays a blinder, putting me in touch with contacts in the states who established them after hurricane Katrina. He has also linked me up with Peter Tallantire at the Cabinet Office [Director for Sustainable Development – later Deputy Director, Civil Contingencies Secretariat] – a fantastic contact, who has given me excellent advice and support.

Consequently, against specific officer advice, I make the decision to provide for a 50 pitch Caravan Park' which the government has pledged to fully fund.

I also make the decision to buy a "new school" – of temporary modular construction. I have chosen to purchase and not rent this because, once again, government has pledged to fully fund it's purchase; and we can then use the "school" elsewhere. We constantly struggle to find temporary and semi-permanent accommodation – a problem highlighted by the appalling temporary sixth form facilities at Ridgewood Comprehensive School. This disaster might prove to be an opportunity to acquire a permanent [temporary] school that we can use across the borough...

ooo

Footnote

A gold–silver–bronze command structure is used by emergency services of the United Kingdom to establish a hierarchical framework for the command and control of major incidents and disasters. The so-called "platinum control" is government level [COBRA].

ooo

Serious flooding occurred in 48 separate areas of Doncaster [any one of which would have warranted some type of emergency response by the Council]; it affected 3,286 homes, of which 2,275 suffered major damage.

ooo

Were the community of Toll Bar forsaken by the emergency services? People say perception *is* reality...

Toll Bar-on-Sea" was published in January 2008...

"Our Heroes. This book is dedicated to all who helped during the floods but especially to those who protected, cared for and rescued day and night, 26 to 29 June 2007, until the emergency services arrived".

ooo

There were no actual records of looting taking place but people were having to kick their doors in because the water had expanded them to.

Exit stage right – pursued by…

"Nothing in life is worst than been hated or punished for what is morally or spiritually right."

Bamigboye Olurotimi

Friday August 31st 2007…

I send an email to Martyn Vickers, President of Doncaster Central CLP…

From: MJW
To: martyn.vickers@▮▮▮▮▮.co.uk
Date: 31/08/2007 14:37:38
Subject: Mayor's Political Advisor

Martyn

Just to let you know that I have appointed John Curry as my new Political Advisor and following Ian Spowart's resignation to develop his wider career.

As you're aware, John is currently employed as a Regional Organiser for the Labour Party at Wakefield and will be joining us at the beginning of October and after the Labour Party's Annual Conference in Bournemouth.

I am really looking forward to working with John and building an ever stronger relationship with the Labour Party locally, regionally and nationally.

Thanks

Martin

ooo

Friday September 7th 2007…

The floods disaster has provided a hiatus from the internecine war being waged against me by several militant Labour Party members. I've been managing the problem for several years but it's been getting a lot worse of late; they have begun to take over some of the key positions in the group and exact vengeful and spiteful retribution against loyalist mayoral supporters like Margaret Ward.

I now refuse to attend group meetings. John Hardy collapsed after one recent "sortie"; and is unlikely to return... As a result, the Labour Party National Executive's Local Government Committee has commissioned a "Panel review" of relations within the Labour group in Doncaster and between the Labour group and mayor; although I won't hold my breath!

Perhaps what is more concerning is the complete lack of interest, involvement or action from any MPs. Jeff Ennis is outside of it all, with no Doncaster councillors in his CLP now; however, he does understand dysfunctional [local] Labour politics and tries to support me as much as possible at our regular MP's briefings. And to be fair to Caroline Flint, despite the fact that Aidan is frequently interfering, it's not any of her councillors either – and anyway, she always has tight control over any rebel tendencies they might exhibit!

The real problems lie with several of the councillors in Ed's constituency, the likes of Mounsey, Kitchen, Blackham, Jones, *et al* ; and Jameson and one or two bit-part players in Rosie's CLP. What makes this even more perturbing is that due to a boundary change, Carolyne and I are now in Rosie's "Doncaster Central" CLP and no longer part of Ed's "Doncaster North" constituency.

I'm pretty pissed off myself, I must confess, however, Carolyne is really disgusted with the Labour Party; particularly Miliband's disloyalty towards me – which is tantamount to betrayal – and Rosie's ambivalence to my plight.

She can see that the MPs and the Regional Labour Party seem to be backing the militant councillors [through their inaction], even though the party, the town and the borough are suffering because of it. Carolyne has never been keen on elected officials who go in for self-promotion and the councillors themselves are playing true to form, behaving less like politicians and more like bully boys and thugs.

We have discussed her disenchantment for a while now and, even though she knows it may not help me, she cannot let her name *"be associated with a private club that allows and promotes the actions of cheats, liars and thugs"*. She can no longer stand to be near such people and refuses to acknowledge them.

She is a lifelong socialist but this isn't the Labour Party she joined when she was eighteen. After being a long-serving, paid up member for many years, she decides to leave.

This is a massive move for her and serves to highlight our complete dismay at the situation we find ourselves in.

I communicate her decision to Rosie.

ooo

Monday September 10th 2007...

Carolyne has received a hand-written letter from Rosie, penned on House of Commons paper, asking her to reconsider her decision to leave the party *"because of personalities"*. In it she states:

> *"I do hope that you reconsider your decision on the Labour Party – we have too few people with real political conviction like yourself and it's a tragedy if you are driven out by personalities..."*

The letter just infuriates Carolyne. Her point was not about personalities, but about bullying, harassment and betrayal, and the need to behave with decency and loyalty. Furthermore, the person penning this "plea" is one of the politicians who, by her failure to intervene, is effectively condoning their behaviour.

Her decision stands.

ooo

Friday September 14th 2007...

We have a visit from our twin town Herten in Recklinghausen in Germany. I have become good friends with Herr Bürgermeister, Dr Uli Paetzel, in the four years since the death of Klaus Bechtel.

During his time in Doncaster, we visit Toll Bar to consider the effect of the floods and climate change; and I take the opportunity to introduce him to Ed Miliband.

ooo

Monday September 24th 2007...

12.30 pm – The Labour Party Conference, Bournemouth

The issue of who has the authority to appoint to outside bodies is becoming a massive sore in my side, with the Labour group now openly defying my wishes and forcing the council into stasis.

This is compounded by conflicting guidance in the 2000 and 1989 Local Government Acts. As a result of the stasis, the Monitoring Officer is having to prepare a "failure of statutory duty" report – with the resultant effect that this will have in terms of bringing the Labour party into disrepute and on our "Use of

Resources" score within the CPA/CAA process, as the Labour group tries to push us towards a "1 Star" rating!

This is another area where the government guidance and LGA2000 has not covered all the subtle nuances, or tribal ramifications [!] of the politics of the mayoral model. Because it is not covered in the 2000 Act, the default is the 1989 Act. As a result:

- If I appoint as per my wishes, and not the majority Labour group's wishes, I will be in breach of the 1989 Local Government Act and <u>the Council cannot action my appointments</u>.
- If I appoint as per the majority Labour group's wishes, then I will be adhering to the 1989 Local Government Act and the Council can action my appointments – but <u>I will be failing to follow the Labour Party Rule Book in doing so</u>.

My apologies for those not *au fait* with such byzantine systems and procedures but this is the life blood of UK Governance; and the straws that break camel's backs!

As a result, I am now driving down to the Labour Party Conference in Bournemouth for the day [!] specifically for a meeting with Patrick Heneghan, the party's Head of Local Government and Election Organisation – but also to listen to Gordon's speech.

ooo

The meeting with Patrick Heneghan proves an excellent use of my time, as he agrees with my stance; that the 2000 Act "missed" this issue and the legislation needs to catch up with the mayoral model.

Patrick has agreed he will clarify the matter for the Labour Group.

ooo

As I listen to Gordon's speech it becomes very apparent he's going to call a snap general election in October.

ooo

5.30 pm

Making my way back to Doncaster, I listen anxiously to the radio and widespread reports that Gordon's going to call a snap election.

ooo

Tuesday September 25th 2007...

9.30 am

I text Ed, asking him to call me because I'm really worried about Gordon's speech. He doesn't come back to me. I've clearly outlived my usefulness!

ooo

3.00 pm

The Newspapers are kicking up a fuss with the headline "Controversial Mayor's assistant to start". We really do need to move to a more mature level of political debate in Doncaster.

ooo

Monday October 1st 2007...

4.46 pm

I receive a copy of an email from Patrick Heneghan to Ros Jones, Secretary to the Labour Group.

From:	Patrick_Heneghan
To:	Jones, Ros
CC:	Jameson, Mick; Blackham, Joe; MJW:
Sent:	Mon Oct 01 16:46:35 2007
Subject:	Your letter - Doncaster Labour group

Ros,

Thanks you for your letter which arrived this morning. I do think over the long term we should tidy up the standing orders especially in relation to running of Labour Groups where there is also an elected Mayor as I think some of terms can be confusing.

It is my view that Labour is in control of Doncaster Council by virtue of the fact that your Mayor has full executive powers. It is also my view that the wording of this section can lead to confusion as the standing orders have been adapted from standing orders for the Leader/Cabinet model. My advice is that section 10.6 refers specifically to a situation where an executive mayor is not Labour – clearly in these circumstances the lack of a Labour Mayor requires that the group make Labour's nominations.

Section 10.5 refers to where Labour is in control and this is the method I suggest you use. *10.5 Where the Labour group is in control of the council and civic appointments, nominations to outside bodies and other council positions are made by the Mayor, or the Mayor and cabinet, the Labour group and the appropriate local government committee of the*

party shall have the right and opportunity to submit names to the Mayor for consideration, but formal nomination and selection shall rest with the Mayor, or the Mayor and cabinet. [13A.8].
I have copied this email to the group leader, group chair and the executive Mayor.

Patrick Heneghan
Head of Local Government and Election Organisation, The Labour Party

ooo

Saturday October 6th 2007...

After months of speculation, Gordon Brown has announced he will not be holding a snap general election next month – or even next year – unless there are exceptional circumstances.

In a pre-recorded interview with Andrew Marr he set out his reasons for not going to the country, claiming that he wants to be judged on his "vision" for changing Britain and not his "competence" at dealing with crises.

He says: *"I will not be calling an election, and let me say why. Over the summer months we have had to deal with crises – we have had to deal with foot and mouth, terrorism, floods, financial crises. And yes, we could have had an election based on competence, and I hope people would have understood that we acted competently.*

"But what I want to do is show people the vision that we have for the future of this country in housing and health and education and I want the chance, in the next phase of my premiership, to develop and show people the policies that are going to make a huge difference and show the change in the country itself."

Phew!

ooo

Two weeks later

Ed has surprised us by popping in unexpectedly. His old bedroom has now reverted back to the children's play room and Carolyne, Ed and I all sit on the large settee, with Ed in the middle, whilst we talk... I'm pleased to see him, and I tell him so; that I was beginning to feel forsaken. But I also acknowledge his ever increasing workload; particularly now he is the Chancellor of the Duchy of Lancaster, as Minister for the Cabinet Office [!].

I give him a gentle hard time [if that isn't an oxymoron]; pointing out that he should speak to me more often; that I can let him know what the feeling is "on the street" so to say, and not just in Doncaster, that I speak to real people up and down the country; and that it's not good out there – despite what Gordon's pollsters and 'focus group's' are telling him.

I ask him what on earth led them to believe it was a good idea to call a snap election.

"I know what you're saying Martin... But if the truth be known it was only Ed [Balls] really, who was wanting to call it. He was desperate for us to go now... because it was our best chance of winning.

"He kept arguing and arguing that we've got to go now..." Then Ed gets up from the settee and pulls a stool from against the wall, positioning it directly in front of me, so we are face to face. *"The simple fact is Martin... that economy is going to fall off a cliff and this was our best chance of winning."*

What do you mean?" I ask him and he explains.

"What I say – the economy is going to get a hell of a lot worse over the next two or three years and we'll get the blame for it; so it was either going now and risk losing, or wait and know that we're going to lose."

We don't realise [then] how significant this statement is, some ten months before the Lehman Brothers collapse.

ooo

Tuesday October 30th 2007...

2.00 pm

Paul Hart has just forwarded this email from the Leader of the Labour Group.

From:	Blackham, Joe
Sent:	30 October 2007 13:24
To:	Hart, Paul; Evans, Paul [Legal Services]; ▅▅▅▅▅▅ ;
Cc:	Labour Group
Subject:	Nominations to outside bodies

We have been instructed by Patrick Heneghan Head of Local Government in the Labour Party that we The Labour Group must nominate the individuals selected by the Mayor to be the Labour Party representatives on outside bodies. Please make the necessary arrangements to implement this decision.

Joe Blackham
Leader of the Labour Group

It must have been painful. It's taken 29 days to send it out!

fall out   Exit stage right – pursued by...

Nonetheless the damage is done; it was done last year, when our CPA rating went down to "2 Stars", but "they" have been inflicting damage on us [me] now for a good eighteen months.

ooo

Wednesday November 7th 2007...

Albert Halls, Nottingham

I am attending the "Core Cities Summit" in Nottingham.
Since Ed has been appointed to ministerial office he has become very difficult to pin down and seldom attends the regular "MPs Briefings" we hold in my office. Because of this, I have to journey down to London tonight to brief Ed on various issues; not least the £7 million shortfall on the floods compensation money from central government, which GB told me I hadn't to worry about [!]; the Labour party NEC investigation into the war that is raging between the militant members of the Labour group [all but one who are councillors in Ed's constituency] and "the mayor"; and also an emerging position with regard to the Audit Commission Public Interest Report, which it would appear is going to be damming of the Labour party in Doncaster and specifically his councillors' behaviour.
I again ask Ed to get his councillors on side but he tells me that he sees their behaviour as none of his responsibility.

ooo

8.49 pm – on the train returning from London

I email Ed.

From:	MJW
To:	'miliband▇▇▇▇▇.com'
Sent:	Wed Nov 07 20:49:14 2007
Subject:	MP's Briefing

Ed

Thanks for the meeting and nice to see you again. Just to confirm the salient points of our discussion;
     The £7m shortfall on the floods funding – we agreed that you would speak to John Healy about this issue and also to our other MPs so that we have a consistent line. I expressed the urgency of the situation *vis a vis* the extremely tight budget forecast we are working on and,

if support wasn't forthcoming, the need for us to consider making up the shortfall via the Council Tax adjustment process and the resultant failure to keep our Zero % rise above RPI election pledge.

Building Schools for the Future submission – we talked about the need for a clear line of support from the MPs, Mayor, Heads and Chairs of governors. You agreed to read the submission and that you would seek out a potential sponsor contact with the Cooperative Society and that I would brief you when I had briefed the Labour Group.

ECO Towns/Growth Pole – we discussed the exciting and radical nature of this submission and the need for it to factor in a radical transport model including several new QBCs with a borough wide orbital, several new park and rides, a sunken gyratory, a potential private sector FARRRS scheme and as the last aspect to be delivered – the potential for a linked congestion zone. You agreed to read the submission and agree a clear line of support from the MPs [pending the MPs brief next week] and also to speak to Yvette Cooper on this matter.

LEGI – we agreed for the need to coordinate our approach to MP briefings in order that we don't duplicate our officer's work and briefings. We agreed that, subsequent to the MP's briefing next week, that I would request a private briefing for you from Julie Wilson on LEGI activity in your constituency. This would support the brief that Julie will give the other MPs.

I hope that summarises our discussion.

Best wishes
Martin W

ooo

Thursday 8th November 2007...

Core Cities Summit

I receive a response from my political assistant with regard to the email I sent to Ed last night:

From:	Curry, John
To:	MJW
Sent:	Thu Nov 08 08:13:34 2007
Subject:	MP's Briefing

Did you talk about the Audit report?

John Curry
Mayors Political Assistant.

From:	MJW
To:	Curry, John
Date:	08/11/2007 08:14:50
Subject:	Re: MP's Briefing

fall out   Exit stage right – pursued by...

Yes but I didn't want to put it into an email.

ooo

I have just sat in on a speech delivered by Joan Ruddock, the Parliamentary Under-Secretary at Department for Environment, Food and Rural Affairs.

It's an excellent speech for me and I particularly note: *The Government will launch a zero waste places initiative with the aim of inviting a number of places to become exemplars of good environmental practice on all waste. Ensure that national and regional government agencies understand and reflect the important role of Core Cities in their climate change policies, programmes and where appropriate, funding allocations.*

I send an email to the [Acting] MD and members of our CMT

From:	MJW
Sent:	08 November 2007 14:58
To:	Curry, John; ▮▮▮▮▮▮▮▮▮; Hart, Paul;
Subject:	Joan Ruddock and Zero Waste

John

We need to write to Hilary Benn/Joan Ruddock with regard to her speech at Nottingham today - for the SoS - and where she announced a new move to promote "Zero Waste" around the country. We need to corner the Labour Party credits for this one.

Jane - can you prepare a first draft of a letter that espouses our ZW virtues and rapid recycling increases during the past 4 years – I will then top it and tail it.

Cheers

This is a massive turnaround from the government and makes a mockery of Elliot Morley and his advisors; who messed us about for nearly eighteen months with our bid to the Waste Implementation Programme [New Technologies] Demonstrator programme. Their procrastination and duplicity cost us approximately £400,000 and I have never forgiven him! Nonetheless, government has now moved and I would like some kind of acknowledgement that it is Doncaster that is driving this agenda.

ooo

My sense that Brown is going to let us down with the floods money is now acute – I send an email to Ed.

fall out   Exit stage right – pursued by...

From: MJW
To: 'miliband■■■■■.com'
Date: 08/11/2007 16:04:03
Subject: Floods Funding Shortfall

Ed

I've just spoken to Sir Bob Kerslake at the Core Cities Summit and he said that DfT has given Sheffield the "go ahead" to spend against the £30m capital repairs they need.

Which puts our paltry £3m revenue and £4m capital shortfall into perspective!

Martin

ooo

Saturday November 10th 2007...

"Rethink on buses" reports the Doncaster Star and explains how "Planned new bus laws would be a move towards giving Doncaster residents control of their public transport."
    The article explains how the new transport bill being introduced by Transport Minister, Rosie Winterton [appointed by Brown in July] will hasten this "new era".
    Although I am quoted as welcoming the news, its' simply another government obfuscation tactic – cop-out might be a better way of putting it.

ooo

Thursday November 15th 2007...

"Firm's £110m talks on waste" reads the Star headline, reporting on the sub-regional waste treatment facility we are negotiating with Rotherham and Barnsley councils.
    I have been battling with the other two local authorities for eighteen months now *vis a vis* more demanding recycling rates; a move towards zero-waste; and my refusal to sign up to a waste incinerator in Doncaster or elsewhere.

ooo

Tuesday November 27th 2007...

The whole issue of Ed being briefed is becoming a real problem. To protect myself, I send an email to him copied to the other three MPs.

From: Winter, Martin
Sent: 27 November 2008 15:22
To: ED MILIBAND; MILIBAND, Ed
Cc: WINTERTON, Rosie; FLINT, Caroline; ENNIS, Jeff

Subject: Serious Case Reviews

Dear Ed,

Attendance at our MP's briefing sessions has been poor and, as a result, I have not been able to brief you on the issue of child deaths in the Borough.
    You may know that there will be a sentencing session at Sheffield Crown Court next Monday relating to the father of child XY, who is a constituent of yours. I am not aware if the Police have briefed you but if you require any further information please contact my office.
    Ministers have been kept informed by ourselves via the Government Office.

Regards Mayor Martin Winter

ooo

Thursday November 29th 2007...

"Residents celebrate U-turn on homes – Victory as mayor announces demolition plan will not go ahead," cries the Doncaster Star. "You've got to credit the Mayor, the cabinet and council officers for listening," says a leading community representative. "The Mayor promised he would listen to the feelings of the community and he did – they've done right by us."
    I feel pretty battered at the moment and I need as many friends as I can get!

ooo

Wednesday December 5th 2007...

"Councillors still want poll on elected mayor" reports the Star in response to the government ruling which stipulates communities can only poll the electorate once every ten years.

ooo

The Chief Constable of South Yorkshire Police, Meredydd Hughes, was found guilty of speeding at Wrexham Magistrates Court today and banned from driving. He was caught driving at 90 mph where the speed limit was 60 mph. Wrexham Magistrates court disqualified Hughes from driving for 42 days and fined him £350.

ooo

Friday December 7th 2007...

"Council Children's Services praised" declares the Star focusing on a report by the Office for Standards in Education and the Commission for Social Care which says: "The council is making a good contribution to improving outcomes and is now better equipped to deliver a more efficient and effective service to children and young people thanks to some important developments, as well as having good capacity for further improvement..."

ooo

Monday December 24th 2007...

"Community Spirit shines through" is the paper's response to my Christmas message to the residents of Doncaster, which praised those who had suffered and helped communities as a result of the floods.

ooo

Monday January 7th 2008...

A nice start to the new year! The Star runs with the front page headline "Labour in prejudice wrangle – disabled councillor in legal row". It reports on the [now] public row over the Labour Group's discrimination and derogatory treatment of my cabinet member John Hardy.

Joe Blackham became the Leader of the Labour Group last year; since then there has been a noticeable increase in the aggression shown towards the mayor, my cabinet and any of the "loyalists" displaying support for the mayor.

It's pretty horrible and the Labour Group's attacks led to John collapsing at Full Council.

ooo

Wednesday January 16th 2008...

"Council tax at 7%" screams the front page of the Doncaster Star which would, of course, break my "zero percent above inflation" election pledge of 2005. However, I have introduced the "concept" as part of my budget-setting consultation process, aimed at stimulating the discussion that Brown has failed to cover our flood costs. "Council tax in Doncaster may soar by nearly seven percent this year to pay for damage caused by the summer's floods, Mayor Martin Winter has warned at a closed council meeting," the newspaper reports.

I am quoted, saying: "At this stage we are looking at budget proposals which assume an increase of council tax [0%] in line with inflation. However, given the on-going financial effects of the floods last year, it makes sense to introduce the options..."

I'm only asking the question...

ooo

As part of my ongoing battle with the Labour Group's more militant members, I have appointed Andrea Milner to the South Yorkshire Passenger Transport Executive, where she has been elected as Chair.

Andrea is a very capable politician and has worked at a high level with Unite – the former Transport & General Workers union – supporting issues on women, race, equality and diversity.

I know she will play a full and strong role leading the SYPTE.

ooo

Friday January 25th 2008...

3.00 pm – The Mayor's office, Council House

Some time ago, the Labour Party National Executive's Local Government Committee commissioned a "Panel review" of relations within the Labour group in Doncaster and between the Labour group and mayor.

I am not happy with the investigation, which is also wrapped up in the legal action John Hardy is now taking against the Labour party for disability discrimination. The "panel" has attempted to calm a completely unsalvageable situation without attaching any blame or accountability for actions...

In an effort to pre-empt the report, which will be presented next week, I instruct my political assistant to send an email about the group "providing me" with a replacement member for John Hardy, who is in a poor state of health and has been ill for several months now, following the Labour group's attack on him:

From:	Curry, John
Sent:	25 January 2008 15:45
To:	Jones, Ros; Blackham, Joe; Jameson, Mick
Subject:	Lead Member for Older People

Dear All

Following on from the Labour Group meeting on Monday, Martin has asked me to contact you to remind you of his request for assistance in finding a member of the Labour group to assist in the role of lead Member for Older People.

Martin would be very grateful if you could suggest one or two members for his consideration as it is becoming increasingly important that we identify someone as quickly as possible.

Thank you for your assistance.

John Curry
Mayor's Political Assistant

ooo

Tuesday January 29th 2008...

4.30 pm – Priory Suite, Mansion House

The Labour Party internal report into relations within the Labour group in Doncaster and between the Labour group and mayor is presented tonight.

An extremely pedestrian report is presented which basically tells us all to "kiss and make up" and all work together for the greater good of the people of Doncaster.

It reports that "The Labour group is seen as polarised. However, very little of the hostility relates to policy differences: the points of tension focus on personality."

Outrageously, the report stipulates that I have to make explicit to the group whether I will be standing for election next year…

It makes explicit the "unacceptable threats of political retribution against those supporting the mayor, including moves to deselect sitting councillors or not support their campaigns with group funds."

It stipulates a few specific actions, including that the mayor ask officers to review the council constitution and procedures for appointment to outside bodies, and to <u>clarify which are executive functions</u> – which has already been done, hence the previous argument.

There is also to be a separate investigation into breaches of Labour party rules including leaks to newspapers etc. but the main outcome is that the Labour Group is to have an external peer to advise them on their behaviour and *modus operandi* – as is the mayor.

ooo

Wednesday January 30th 2008...

Despite all agreeing to "kiss and make up" last night we receive the following email:

From:	Blackham, Joe
To:	Curry, John
Sent:	Wed Jan 30 10:31:01 2008
Subject:	RE: lead Member for Older People

Dear John,

The group officers have decided that in the current circumstances and having received legal advise [sic.] we feel it would be inappropriate to put forward any member of the Labour Group to fill the role of lead member for older people.

Regards Joe.

ooo

Thursday January 31st 2008...

Most officers are aware of the turmoil the Labour group is in; specifically the behaviours of the like of "Ted and John", who are both elected members for the Adwick ward. One of our officers makes mischief and sends me a text message:

Martin – I thought you should be aware, several bodies have been found in Adwick!

When I ring them back immediately, they take great delight in reporting that an ancient burial site has been unearthed in the grounds of North Doncaster Technological College, where John Mounsey is the Chair of Governors.

This thirty five body burial site, uncovered as part of the building works at the school, proves to be one of South Yorkshire's most significant archaeological finds.

Tuesday February 5th 2008...

The cat's out of the bag! The Labour party has a ruling which states that a Labour mayor cannot stand for more than two successive terms, which will rule me out of standing in May 2009, and the Labour group has "leaked" this story to the newspapers.

This "two terms" ruling is a classic case of the Labour Party's internal struggles between good and bad; in this case, the struggle between those driving a progressive agenda forward and its membership's resistance to change. The "two term" ruling was inserted to appease those against the model's propensity to create "too powerful" individuals.

The Party insists it is planning to change its rules in time for the 2010 elections when the three London Labour mayors in Hackney, Lewisham and Newham all wish to stand for third terms, having previously stated that they would be "two term mayors".

Despite the fact that I have previously told the Labour Group that rather than constantly opposing me, they would be better off identifying my successor – getting behind them and building them a platform for the election in 2009 – they're more concerned about the battle with me. For what it's worth, I tell them I will be getting behind Sandra Hollands as the Labour Party's preferred candidate... you could hear a pin drop!

Nonetheless, we are where we are and the Star devotes a front page headline to the story "Winter out in the cold – Mayor facing election KO after Labour Party ruling" and tries to infer this has been brought in to "get rid" of me.

ooo

Wednesday February 6th 2008...

What a surprise, the Labour Group has leaked the [internal] Labour Party report. "Mayor may get pair of 'minders' – Labour party plans to oversee Winter are slammed".
I give up!

ooo

Friday February 8th 2008...

Despite the Labour group bullying and harassing the man, and the NEC having to insist that the mayor should sit on the appointment's panel, Paul Hart is appointed as the new Managing Director.

ooo

Tuesday February 12th 2008...

10.00 am – Economy & Enterprise OSMC Panel

The malcontents are behaving very strangely at the moment. I am at the Economy & Enterprise OSMC [Overview & Scrutiny Management Committee] Panel's meeting to present my [Executive] proposals for the CCQ. I go because the members have been using the process to bully the officers within "3D" and the Development Directorate, and they have requested my support...
  As I sit down to present my proposals, one of the elected members actually moves an objection to my being there – in attendance to present my own proposals!
  Notwithstanding his "objection", which I quickly dismiss – ridiculing him for behaving "stupidly" – he then reacts aggressively to the fact my Political Assistant is there – on the basis that he is a "member of the public". Aren't we all?!

ooo

Wednesday February 13th 2008...

The Star reports on a "£100,000 project on Christ Church" – to illuminate Christ Church and also to provide some new railings and other security measures.

This "Lapwing Economics" strategy seems to work...

ooo

Sunday February 17th 2008...

12.15 pm – Our House, Kirk Sandall

This whole issue of the government's paltry support for the floods damage is getting out of hand; and particularly so, given that Ed is neither pushing for us to get the "promised" finance for Doncaster, nor is he delivering on his [Gordon's] obligations to me...

I decide to draft a letter to the Prime Minister...

From:	MJW
To:	███████; Hart, Paul
CC:	Curry, John
Sent:	Sun Feb 17 13:11:13 2008
Subject:	Final Draft Letter to PM

Can you prepare this letter to go out by post tomorrow please.

Paul - we will also need to prepare a very robust and hard-hitting press release to go out Thursday/Friday of next week re the budget and the huge impact of the floods – to Doncaster Taxpayers – despite the Government [PM's] promise to shoulder the costs.

Martin

Private and Confidential

Dear Prime Minister [hand written by MJW]

I write to thank you for orchestrating an exceptionally speedy and helpful response to the floods suffered within our community in Doncaster last year. Not least, I am most grateful that you found time to visit Toll Bar and publicly reassure our residents, as well as the Council's Managing Director and myself, of the Government's total financial support.

You will be aware that I delivered on my promise to keep the community together, building the temporary school, refurbishing the existing building and establishing a highly successful caravan park [from scratch] and all within 7 weeks of the disaster befalling us.

As a result, my Council and its officers have worked diligently on the recovery plan; and I firmly believe we are second to none in terms of our emergency planning and recovery work. We have spent some £14m in total, dealing with the floods and, whilst we are grateful for the Government's financial support, this amounts to less than 50% of the total cost to DMBC.

You will no doubt recall when you visited us that you publicly asked me for my commitment to re-build our communities and I gladly gave you my pledge that I would deliver for you. I fully accept that the Local Authority should pay a percentage of the costs, but I am sure that you did not foresee, or intend that, the taxpayers of Doncaster would have to cover such a high percentage of the costs. I should also point out that the Government Office for Yorkshire & the Humber has had nothing but praise for our efforts, our close co-operation, honesty and accuracy in the reporting of flood damage.

It is possible that I have been naïve or that this always was a chimera; but we are now in an extremely difficult financial position as a result of having to bare the majority of the flood costs ourselves – with our reserves now at their lowest point ever.

The above situation has also put me in a very difficult personal situation locally. I have tried to support both you and my government at every opportunity throughout this period. However, in the face of an apparent failure to deliver, I feel I cannot continue to hold the line with local people who know the truth of your original promise.

You will also recall, of course, my support for Ed Miliband's identification, selection and subsequent election as MP for Doncaster North; a stance which eventually led to the resignation of my Deputy Mayor and all that ensued. The rest is history and my family and I have suffered tremendously. Had Ed been able to deliver on commitments, then I am sure the personal problems would have eased. Unfortunately, I now have two broken promises to manage on top of all the suffering my family and I have had to endure over the last 2 years.

I am therefore respectfully asking for:

- the reimbursement of a much greater percentage of the Council's flood costs, for example, a further 20% of the costs would mean an extra £2.8m which would go some way towards replenishing our much depleted reserves;

and secondly:

- whilst I welcome the report by the Councillors' [sic.] Commission and the possibility of "parachute payments" to outgoing Mayors, I have no intention of standing down as Mayor of Doncaster. I am good at my job, I always deliver, and it is often the Doncaster Labour Party that seek to limit my power to deliver.

I would welcome a discussion on an exit strategy for me as Labour Mayor for Doncaster, including how this can be achieved in a logical, positive, and developmental manner for the sake of Doncaster, the Labour Party and myself. Such a discussion would be in keeping with the one between you and I at the Treasury in early 2005; when I stated that I would look forward to discussing my record of delivery for the Labour Party in Doncaster and my support for the establishment of our MP, Ed Miliband, for Doncaster North; when I had "delivered him" and at a date in the future.

Thanks

Martin

Surprise, surprise – we [I] never received a response!

ooo

Friday February 22nd 2008...

"Mayor's former ally asked to contend job – Labour members approach Rave as winter battles to keep his role" reports the Star, saying he has "unofficially been asked to stand".

What a lovely Mounsey inspired piece of non-reporting... You have to ask why newspapers insist on writing such non-stories.

ooo

Sunday February 24th 2008...

10.53 pm – Our House, Kirk Sandall

I have reliably been informed that Martyn Vickers is trying to get one of my cabinet members to stand for election as the mayoral candidate next year.

From:	MJW
To:	martyn.vickers@▇▇▇▇▇.co.uk
Date:	24/02/2008 10:53:12
Subject:	Mayor of Doncaster

Martyn

I was somewhat surprised to learn that you have been actively seeking support for a candidate for the mayoral elections.

I would have thought it better advised taking a more impartial view particularly given that you, as the Chair of the LGC, will be responsible for overseeing the decision on whether to sanction the Mayor standing for a third term, or not, in 2009.

I am furthermore surprised that neither you nor we, as a party, seem to have grasped the hard learnt lessons of our own Leader being forced into announcing his decision to stand down, more than two years before he actually did so as Prime Minister.

SY Police is now investigating allegations into the misuse of up to £3million of public money within Doncaster Council. These are issues I have been raising for the past three years and include the role of senior Doncaster Labour Party members; some [potential] mayoral candidates. This is a position I have personally briefed you on and, as a result, I am stunned that you have taken such a stance – particularly given your own position on the bench.

I would welcome your views on this very serious and sensitive matter, at the least by return of email and preferably through a meeting to discuss options and a way forward.

Martin Winter

ooo

Monday February 25th 2008...

I receive a response from Martyn Vickers

Dear Martin,

Thank you for your e-mail. You were not as surprised as I was that it had been reported to you that I was actively seeking support for a candidate at the mayoral election. Perhaps you would be good enough to tell me who this "candidate" is so I could find out more. Of course I would be pleased to meet you to talk this situation over and look forward to suggested times and dates. In the meantime I would like to make my position clear :

1. It has been made clear to us that the Labour Party has a rule that successful Mayoral candidates can only serve two terms. This position may be untenable, the situation may change and we may have to rethink in due course but that is how we stand at the moment. Again please let me know if you have a different or updated view on this position. I am certainly not aware that the LGC will be given the freedom to set aside or re-interpret party rules.

2. You have said publicly and privately, as at the meeting with the NEC lately, that you would not be seeking the Labour nomination in 2009. I would like to know if this remains your position.

3. I gave you my word at the meeting we had at Carlos back in 2003 that I would give you my full support through your first term and this I did willingly and unflinchingly. I also undertook to support you in 2005 and through the second term and this I have done. Indeed you will not find any occasion when I have been anything else but supportive and constructive. You may know [and I hope you will] that I have spoken up on your behalf and supported you on many occasions privately and publicly in the last year and have made it clear to those in the Party who have opposed you that I deplore and will not take part in any personal or political attacks against you and this I have resolutely done.

4. However we are now in a new position in which you cannot or will not stand for a third term. In this situation it is incumbent on those who want to see a Labour mayoral victory in 2009 that we encourage suitable people to consider a nomination particularly since some of those who have declared themselves to be possible candidates would seek to undermine the work you have done and destroy the real gains of your mayoralty which I could not support. However this is a far cry from actively seeking support for a new candidate.

I hope that we shall be able to meet soon to explore these points. At the moment you seem to be aware of more information [and misinformation?] than I am!

Kind regards, Martyn

Saturday March 1st 2008...

Somebody is making mischief again, leaking internal papers. "Stadium debts hit £2.5m – losses at the Keepmoat worry councillors". Papers have been leaked which show the "naming rights" purchased for the stadium as an on-going contingent [and theoretical] liability over the stadium's first fifteen years.

ooo

Tuesday March 4th 2008...

"Red-letter day for flood victims" cries the Star as the first council tenants return to their homes following the floods last June.

ooo

Friday March 7th 2008...

10.00 am – Full Council – Doncaster Council Chamber

Further to the malcontents' strange behaviour over the CCQ project, we have been informed they are going to kick off at today's Full Council because I described their
behaviour as "stupid".
   As we move to 'Questions to the Mayor', Councillor David Hughes tries to be clever, quizzing the Chair of OSMC, John Mounsey:

> In putting a question to Councillor. John Mounsey, the Chair of Overview and Scrutiny Management Committee, Councillor David Hughes JP stated that it had been reported in the Free Press that at the Cabinet meeting held on 20th February 2008, Mayor Winter had made a statement that it was not the place of Overview and Scrutiny to 'recommend' things and accused Councillors on the Overview and Scrutiny Panels of pulling apart his plans for selling off council assets and spending £300m on the Civic and Cultural Quarter for the Waterdale area of the town centre. The Mayor had also said they pulled the plans to pieces, not because the plans weren't any good, but because they were stupid. Councillor Hughes asked Councillor Mounsey what was the function of the Overview and Scrutiny Panels and did he think that Councillors on those panels were stupid?
>
> The Chair of Council indicated that, as there were still Members wishing to question the Mayor, this question would be put to Councillor Mounsey when questions to Mayor Winter had been concluded

As we move towards the end of my questions, Ken Knight asks a question of "the Mayor"... wondering what the mayor thought about Councillor David Hughes' earlier question to Councillor John Mounsey?

In response, I say it was an interesting question but that often what is said and what is reported are two different things. With no disrespect to the press, there is the saying "never let the truth get in the way of a good story".

As I answer, I explain what I had actually said... and that I consulted the Oxford English Dictionary to look up the definition of the word "stupid"...

Stupid: *1.* lacking in common sense, perception, or intelligence. *2.* dazed or stupefied: *stupid from lack of sleep.* *3.* slow-witted. *4.* trivial, silly, or frivolous...

... *and it was in this context that I said some ... [not all] but some.... of the members of scrutiny were "stupid" and had behaved "stupidly"; and I apologise if members of OSMC took it to mean anything else.*

So my apologies [Councillor Bissett] if this was the case – I certainly had no intention of insulting you...

Having said that, I thought members were behaving "stupidly"... when they objected to my attendance at the Economy & Enterprise OSMC Panel on the 12th February... to present my [Executive] proposals for the CCQ. As the [Executive] Mayor, I thought they were behaving in a trivial, silly, or frivolous [manner] when they objected to my attendance to present my own proposals.

Similarly, I thought that you personally, Councillor Bissett, were acting "stupidly" when you raised objections, in a hostile manner... to my Political Assistant [John Curry] [at that same 12th February meeting].

When you said your objection, Councillor Bissett, was that you considered my staff member to be "a member of the public" and therefore not in a position to attend. I thought you were behaving in a trivial, silly, or frivolous [manner], Councillor Bissett.

I thought that members of this panel were "stupid" when they, and you personally Councillor Bissett, tried to stop our Economic Strategy – probably the most important strategy proposed for some time – being agreed because it had made reference to the CCQ project. I thought you were behaving in a trivial, silly, or frivolous [manner], Councillor Bissett, and I thought that, as a member of this panel Councillor Bissett, you were behaving in a "stupid" manner when you personally alleged that a significant investor in Doncaster, had a "conflict of interest" because this businessman had written to the Free Press stating that he supported the Economic Strategy and the CCQ project. And that he thought they were fundamental to Doncaster, and his business's success [in Doncaster].

Let me be clear, Councillor Bissett, this is an investor – someone who runs a locally based creative and digital business [in Doncaster]. And a man who was encouraging the further development of this emerging business sector in Doncaster. I thought that you, and other members Councillor Bissett, were behaving in a trivial, silly, or frivolous [manner], in insulting a significant member of the business community in Doncaster. A man whose company employs many, many Doncaster people.

I'm proud to use the English Language correctly Councillor Bissett. We should all be proud to use words in their correct context – and not merely in their bastardised form.

So [once again] Councillor Bissett, it was in the trivial, silly, or frivolous [context] that I stated some of the members of scrutiny were "stupid" and had behaved "stupidly".

I consider this Council sacrosanct, Councillor Bissett. It is a place where one tempers one's language. It is not a place where one is trivial... nor silly... nor frivolous.

I apologise if you took it to mean anything else, I certainly had no intention of insulting you and I am glad you have allowed me to put that position on the record.

ooo

Friday March 21st 2008...

Some twelve months after Full Council attempted to set up another "Kangaroo Court", and I moved that we ask the Audit Commission to investigate what has been happening in Doncaster; I have received a second draft of the Public Interest Report [which the Audit Commission has insisted on preparing]. Quelle surprise!

I quote from my letter to the report's author: Paragraph 41 - you have changed your view here from your first draft report where you stated that "... the MD's support of the Deputy Mayor compromised her political neutrality". You now state that "The Managing Director was entirely within her rights to refer matters to the police in respect of the conduct of the Mayor"... could you please specify what evidence you have seen to support this change of sentiment?

Susan Law had to go into the archives to get these [previously and subsequently audited] files out. This was her attempt to get the Mayor off her back as an underperforming Head of Paid Service – by becoming a whistle blower – and was a completely calculated and political act! You know this to be the case, hence your first draft statement.

Paragraph 43 – Is the issue of Susan Law physically organising and choreographing a political press conference [on TV]. When considering this in the light of your statement in Paragraph 41 of your earlier draft "... but yet no one referred this matter [the compromising of the MD's political neutrality] to the Monitoring Officer... I am somewhat surprised by your change of view. For the avoidance of doubt, let me be quite clear, Cabinet witnessed Susan Law, Aidan Rave and John Mounsey attempt to overthrow the Mayor. This is fact – and the public need to know this. As part of this, they physically witnessed Susan Law orchestrating a political press conference for Aidan – whilst the attempted *Coup d'état* was taking place.

ooo

Monday April 14th 2008...

Dr Paul Gray is appointed as the Interim Director of Children's Services [DCS]. We have an emerging problem with children's' services and Dr Gray is the third interim DCS we have had in place during the last twelve months.

ooo

Thursday April 17th 2008...

"Council was 'distracted' by row between mayor and MD" reports the Star and comments: "It is among the findings of the Comprehensive Performance Assessment which gave Doncaster three stars"

ooo

Tuesday April 22nd 2008...

Despite me speaking to opposition members every year, the Star has decided to make mischief. "Mayor's secret bid for coalition cabinet – Winter talks to opposition leaders as he considers break with Labour" The newspaper reports that I am "... considering standing for a third mayoral term as an independent – because Labour Party guidance is against elected mayors standing for a third stint in office".

I have no intention of standing for another term – I want my life back! However, having witnessed Tony Blair lose his "power of authority" by announcing too early that he would not be seeking a fourth term, I have no intention of becoming a "lame duck" mayor.

It would appear "Lapwing Economic" strategies are transferable to other areas…

ooo

Wednesday April 23rd 2008…

The Institute for Public Policy Research [IPPR] has produced a report calling for more mayors – saying they have proved "highly capable" in the few places which already has them… the report says their introduction would "reinvigorate local politics" and persuade ministers to devolve more powers.
This must be what reinvigorated politics feels like then…

ooo

Tuesday April 29th 2008…

By their very nature, cabinet members have a higher profile and are arguably more capable as politicians, so they tended to be the councillors who secured the highest number of votes and "four year terms" at the all-out elections in 2004.
Thus, the majority of my cabinet are up for election on Thursday.

All politicians get jittery at this time but some are very worried with "threats of political retribution" being recorded in the "Labour Party inquiry"…

ooo

Friday May 2nd 2008…

Yesterday was a poor day for democracy; a poor day to be a member of the Labour group in Doncaster.
What played out was the militant Labour members' strategy to wipe out the mayor's cabinet. As a result my loyal deputy mayor, Margaret Ward, lost her seat, as did Pat Haith – the well-respected councillor brought in to a "portfolio" aimed at addressing the damage done by Susan – entitled "Supporting Front Line Councillors".
Perhaps the most unsettling aspect was the behaviour at the count, when Ted, John *et al* were seen cheering and applauding when it was declared that Mags had lost!

"Deputy shot down in poll – 'Good night for democracy' as Winter looks for new second in command" shouts the front page of the Doncaster Star. The paper adds: "Doncaster Mayor Mr Winter said Mrs Ward had been a fantastic councillor for nine years and a very loyal deputy".

ooo

We have received the final draft of the Audit Commission's Public Interest Report [PIR] – for publication on Monday May 11th.

During the last two or three years, we have witnessed some of the most appalling behaviour possible from several senior Doncaster Labour Group members. I have sought to "protect" the Labour Party's name throughout; attempting to deal with these issues in a private and confidential manner. However, the publishing of the PIR puts this behaviour right into the public domain.

It is very damming of [militant] Labour councillors; and makes clear that, in 2006, senior Labour Party politicians colluded with DMBC officers in a failed attempt to overthrow the mayor. A situation we know was "payback" for me delivering Miliband in Doncaster North.

Furthermore, the report describes how the cross party committee [established to investigate the subsequent allegations concerning the Managing Director's behaviour] was racked with political prejudice – driven by Labour Party members – and, as a result, ignored some of the most compelling evidence available rather than suspend the MD for gross misconduct.

ooo

Wednesday May 7th 2008...

Labour Group AGM [Part 1]

Rosie calls, tipping me off that the militant members of the Labour Group will be "taking over" completely at the AGM [in 40 minutes]. She also tells me that the party nationally is sending out new guidance to support the group's nomination to outside bodies; in effect, the Labour party is pulling the rug out from under me!

At the AGM [Part 1] the behaviour is pretty bad, with the militant member's language both appalling and threatening. I ask for nominations to various cabinet positions – as I do every year – but, in a co-ordinated "re-buff", receive only five nomination papers back.

ooo

After the meeting three different Labour councillors approach me to say they were frightened to put themselves, or other names, forward for fear of retribution from the militants.

ooo

This is getting really messy and we have to find some way to bring the militancy to the attention of the Party – its internal investigation having completely fudged the issue – even though individuals on the panel could see what was happening.

As a result, rather than sign up to the militant Labour group, Stuart Exelby, Eva Hughes and I try to get our retaliation in first by "signing up" with the council as "the Labour Group" before the Labour Group sign themselves up!

In essence, we have become a separatist "Labour Group".

ooo

Thursday May 8th 2008...

"Labour turned back on Mayor Winter" reports the Doncaster Star and comments on yesterday's [internal] Labour Group meeting.

In a thinly-veiled symbiotic relationship, the leader of the Alliance of Independent Members, Garth Oxby, says: "It would seem the majority of the Labour group has turned its back on the mayor".

I'm glad we've sorted this "leaking" issue out!

ooo

Saturday May 10th 2008...

Life goes on – and the Doncaster Star reports "Borough Treasures' pass success" hailing the massive success of this over 60's leisure scheme.

ooo

fall out   Exit stage right – pursued by…

Monday May 12th 2008…

2.00 pm

Stuart Exelby attends a Doncaster Council political groupings meeting [as a group leader] to discuss issues of proportionality. As he walks in, Councillor Joe Blackham, the leader of the [original] Labour Group walks out.

ooo

3.00 pm

The Labour Group is freely leaking stories to the media and the Doncaster Star has received a letter regarding Roy Kennedy, the Party's director of finance and compliance, giving Stuart, Eva and myself 14 days to sign up to the party or face action.
"Winter facing party ultimatum – Labour headquarters concerned about breakaway plan" reads page 2 of the newspaper.

ooo

5.00 pm

The whole issue of bullying and harassment within the Labour Group is in danger of destroying us all...
I email Stuart and Eva to see if we can agree a press release in which I paraphrase Kinnock's expulsion of Militant in the eighties, where he described Militant as "a maggot within the body of the Labour Party".

From:	MJW
Sent:	12 May 2008 17:16
To:	Hughes, Eva; Exelby, Stuart;
Subject:	Establishment of a [break away] Labour Group

Eva, Stuart

Please find attached – for release on Thursday – is this something that we can agree to?

Statement regarding the establishment of a [break away] Labour Group in Doncaster.

Collectively, the three of us have been members of the Labour Party for more than 80 years. We do not wish to leave the Labour Party – nor do we consider our actions lightly or hysterically. However, the publication of yesterday's Public Interest Report has now highlighted some of the most appalling behaviours of several Senior Doncaster Labour Party members.

These members are attempting to "rule" the Labour Group in Doncaster through intimidation, fear and victimisation and, as a result, we can no longer stand by and ignore what has been happening.

As a result, we are not willing to recognise this behaviour, nor this "group" as being reflective of the ethics and culture of our Labour Party – this type of behaviour is reflective of the militant activity seen in Liverpool in the 1980s.

Bullying behaviour of any kind should always be challenged, yet throughout history individuals have stood by and ignored those most in need of help.

We now call upon the Labour Party, nationally, to end the activities of this maggot in the body of the Labour Party in Doncaster.

ooo

Tuesday May 13th 2008...

3.00 pm

"Leader walks out as rebel 'leader' walks in – 'gang of three' incur wrath of Labour Party over mayor breakaway" reports the Doncaster Star – having had the story leaked to them.

ooo

Wednesday May 14th 2008...

10.00 am – Cabinet Meeting, Priory Suite, Mansion House.

Today is the day I believe I will be vindicated.

We are to receive a presentation from Sue Sunderland, the Audit Commission District Auditor, over her investigation into issues relating to the conduct and capability of the former Managing Director, Susan Law.

She states that "Section 8 of the 1998 Act requires me to consider whether, in the public interest, I should report on any matter coming to my notice in the course of the audit in order for it to be considered by the body concerned or brought to the attention of the public."

Consequently she takes us through the report and highlights the overall conclusions contained in the report's Summary:

My overall conclusions are as follows:

1] *The people of Doncaster expect, and are entitled to receive, the highest standards of governance but the Council has failed to achieve those standards in certain instances.* *Individual members and officers I interviewed expect these standards to be achieved* <u>*but the actions of a few members and officers, including the former Managing Director, fell short of those standards.*</u>

That's it. I knew it was coming and it's as explicit as the Audit Commission can make it. *Individual members and officers I interviewed expect these standards to be achieved* <u>*but the actions of a few members and officers, including the former Managing Director, fell short of those standards.*</u>

Not "the mayor". *"... the actions of a few members and officers, including the former Managing Director, fell short of those standards."*

Rave, Mounsey and others colluded with officers in a failed attempt to overthrow the mayor; and then, along with Ros Jones, conspired to "pay the MD off"; rather than risk a capability investigation, which would have uncovered what they'd done. It's there in black and white and they can't keep denying it now.

Sue Sunderland continues: *I noted a range of instances involving different people including breaching confidentiality, failing to show strict impartiality or not applying procedures fairly or most appropriately. Confidential information was also passed to the press during the investigatory process. Overall, these actions are very disappointing and, in my view, unacceptable particularly given the Council's well publicised governance problems highlighted in the 1990s.*

2] For the Council to move forward most effectively, I believe its new Managing Director must lead by example and ensure that the highest standards of governance are consistently practised at the Council.

3] In my view, the breakdown in relationships between the Mayor and the former Managing Director was partly caused by existing tensions between the Mayor and a key group of Doncaster MBC Labour councillors and the local Labour party. These tensions continue to hamper the effectiveness of the Council.

4] While the Mayoral system does give extensive power to the Mayor, its effectiveness in Doncaster is reduced by the current breakdown in relationships. To improve this situation, the Mayor and key groups need to recognise that movement and concessions will be required from all of them. Even if the groups concerned indicate a willingness to build bridges, mediation may be required to establish common ground for future improvements in working relationships.

5] As part of my review, I have considered whether to invite the Audit Commission to decide whether a separate corporate governance inspection of the Council should be carried out in view of the issues arising. Although several people encouraged me to make such an invitation, I believe it is better to allow the Council and its new Managing Director a year to demonstrate that they are moving rapidly forward on the governance agenda. I will reconsider this point in the light of the Council's progress.

Rosie can't avoid this issue now, nor can Ed – his councillors are bringing the council and the Labour Party into dis-repute and he must intervene.

ooo

Thursday May 15th 2008...

"Labour bullies made me leave" splashes the Doncaster Star and says the mayor "... described a maggot in the body of Doncaster Labour Party" in a statement issued along with fellow defectors Councillors Stuart Exelby and Eva Hughes.
"The statement was described by Labour Group chairman, Councillor Mick Jameson as outrageous and appalling."
Inside, the paper comments on the PIR, with the headline "Work together or the future is bleak – Auditor's hard-hitting report highlights divisions within council". The Star explains that the Audit Commission has said... "The key reason that you are not improving adequately is the weakness in the way you behave. You need to work together – if you do not the future is bleak." It also highlights the specific areas that the DA has said are in danger of failing. It cites children and young people and social care for vulnerable adults.
Are they reading a different report?! Can they not see that the first conclusion states.. *"but the actions of a few members and officers, including the former Managing Director, fell short of those standards"?*
I must be on a different planet – what are they looking at? Or perhaps they continue to want to deny the truth – "the mayor was right" isn't good copy...
My comments to the District Auditor are quoted: "Thank you for giving a very frank presentation. It highlights our consistent frustration at the internecine war that has been taking place. We spend a huge amount of time dealing with internal issues rather than concentrating on the wider issues – that has an impact on staff welfare and motivation."

ooo

Friday May 16th 2008...

11.00 am – Full Council AGM

I have to say I am ashamed of my behaviour today. The militants within the Labour Group have moved Ros Jones as the Chair of Council for next year in a clear move to de-stabilise my mayoralty. They will then seek to promote Ros as "mayor" in the months ahead.

I vote with the Lib-Dems, and all manner of malcontents, to see Paul Coddington [Lib-Dem], an odious man, elected to the position for the coming year.

000

3.00 pm

The Star reports that the Labour Group and the Conservatives have worked as a coalition to carve up all chair and vice-chair [paid] seats on all the panels between themselves just hours after Sue Sunderland warned them about their behaviour! The newspaper prophetically paraphrases the DA's report and places the sub-caption:

"You need to work together. If you don't the future is bleak – Audit Commissioner"

000

The paper also reports on the Lib-Dem call for a by-election for Eva Hughes' seat. Eva has come under massive pressure from all sides and finally "signs up" to the Labour group again. I understand and respect her decision. Eva's statement is: "After witnessing the behaviour of certain Labour party members at the count on May 2nd, and on numerous occasions in meetings, I joined two other Labour party members to form a separate Labour group."

"At no time did I intend to leave the Labour party, however, I am informed that according to National Labour Party rules I must join the Labour Group or I will be expelled from the Labour party."

"It is important for me to make it clear I have supported the mayor since his election. He has moved Doncaster forward in a way nobody could have imagined. You only have to look around the whole borough."

000

7.00 pm

For the first time ever, I do not attend tonight's Chair of Council's Ball. I don't particularly relish the thought of "celebrating" Coddington's appointment, but I do have an excuse… It's my first born's eighteenth birthday party – and I have always said that family must come first!

ooo

Monday May 19th2008…

I write to Roy Kennedy

> Can I say first of all that I have been a member of the Labour Party for more than 20 years. I am proud to be a Labour Mayor as I was proud to be the only Labour Mayor outside of London for several years.
> I am proud of my record of delivery, as a Labour Mayor – which stands comparison with the best and I do not wish to leave the Labour Party.
> Having said that, the depths that we have seen the Labour Group in Doncaster sink to during the last three years, with the constant rejection of my cries for help, from both the Regional and National Labour Party officials, left us with few options.
> In this period, we have witnessed some of the most appalling behaviour possible from several Senior Doncaster Labour Party members. I have sought to "protect" the Labour Party's name throughout; attempting to deal with these issues in a private and confidential manner. However, the publication of last week's Public Interest Report [PIR] has now placed this behaviour into the public domain.
> The PIR makes clear that, in 2006, Senior Labour Party politicians colluded with DMBC officers in a failed attempt to overthrow the Mayor. The report describes how the cross party committee [established to investigate the subsequent allegation's concerning the Managing Director's behaviour] was racked with political prejudice – driven by Labour Party members – and, as a result, ignored some of the most compelling evidence available rather than suspend the MD for gross misconduct.
> The corruption continues – with these members "ruling" the Labour Group in Doncaster through a culture of intimidation, fear and victimisation. 'If you support the Labour Executive – we will destroy you' appears to be their mission statement. Indeed, these members were seen to be threatening to, and actively campaigning against, my Labour Cabinet members at the last election; and were witnessed cheering when my Deputy Mayor lost her seat as a result of their activity. Consequently, I feel I can no longer stand by and ignore what has been happening.
> The registering of a separatist Labour Group, was not necessarily the most sensible "cry for help" but was the only option open to us, arguably, when we were notified via a phone call [40 minutes before the Labour Group AGM Part 1 was to begin] that the NEC had changed its ruling _vis a vis_ executive appointments to outside bodies in mayoral authorities. This placed me immediately in a position whereby the Labour Group leadership would take great delight in parading their "control" of the appointment process. A stance they took with relish – notifying good labour party members immediately "… now that we're in charge, we expect you to resign from your appointment".

Alongside these, there are many, many more examples of this despotic behaviour with the Labour Group in Doncaster. Some of them are recorded within our Labour Party minutes and were commented upon within the Audit Commission's PIR. Indeed, these auditable examples were available when the NEC/LGA undertook its "investigation" [sic.] in September last year – with the investigation deciding that "… we should ignore what's gone before and move forward", stating that "… there were faults on all sides".

As a result of the above, and many more, we have decided that we were not willing to recognise this dysfunctional behaviour, nor this "group" anymore as being reflective of the ethics and culture of our Labour Party. We took the view that bullying behaviour of any kind should always be challenged, yet throughout history individuals have stood by and ignored those most in need of help. We feel that we have been let down badly by the Labour Party that we have been proud to be members of, collectively, for more than 80 years – hence our stance.

This type of self-serving behaviour is reflective of activities of "Militant" in Liverpool in the 1980s. Indeed, the Labour Party records will show, ▇▇▇▇▇▇▇▇▇▇ was expelled from the Labour Party for being a member of "Militant" in the mid-1980s along, with others, and the suspension of the ▇▇▇▇▇▇▇▇▇▇ branch for several years.

To summarise, after seeking counsel from many quarters, Eva, Stuart and myself, withdrew our "registration" of a separatist Labour Group. Councillor Eva Hughes has signed up to the "official" group again. Both Councillor Stuart Exelby and myself are willing to sign up to the Group again but we are only willing to do so as part of an agreement that would see the Labour Party undertake an investigation into the behaviour of certain members of the Doncaster Labour Group.

I would welcome the opportunity to discuss the situation further with you – perhaps we could meet up as a matter of urgency?

ooo

Tuesday May 22nd 2008…

"Winter's job eyed up by pair" reports the Doncaster Star and comments that both Ted Kitchen and Joe Blackham are considering standing for mayor next year.

ooo

Friday May 25th 2008…

Things are hotting up – I attach a text conversation thread with Roy Kennedy

May 25th – 18:14:32

Roy – I've looked at both my diary and Stuart's and the best time for us is Wednesday afternoon - we can both do from 5.30 onwards. Having said that, at a push, we could both do 2.00 pm onwards on Thursday and 3.00 onwards on Friday. We are working on a letter to you - can you come back and let me know ASAP re the dates please?

Many thanks – Martin

May 25th – 18:22:57

2pm on Thursday best 4 me. I am happy 2 come 2 yr office. You both have 2 sign up 2 the group on Tuesday for me 2 come up on Thursday though.

Roy

May 25th – 18:31:58

Thanks Roy

We wish to sign up in your presence on Thursday Roy, with an agreed statement for the press. This is because we've had promises of action before and no follow up and we know the Labour Group will leak our signatures and make mischief...

Many thanks

Martin

ooo

Monday May 26th 2008...

I receive a response from Roy Kennedy

May 26th – 16:02:53

Thank u 4 yr text. U both need 2 rejoin gp 2morrow and then i will come up on Thursday. I will not agree 2 any press release. Far 2 much has been in press. Roy

ooo

6.00 pm

We are holding a "Mayoral Reception" for Doncaster Rovers, who have been promoted into the Championship.

ooo

Tuesday May 27th 2008...

I text Roy Kennedy again

May 27th – 10:24:06

Thanks for your response Roy

If we sign up before you come to Doncaster we feel some members of the Labour Group will leak a damaging story to the press.

I/we have never pro-actively issued any statements, we have always sought to adhere to the Party Rule Book but the LG has constantly gone to the press. There is massive media interest in our predicament - hence the need for an "agreed" strategy as part of any signing

Many thanks

Martin

May 27th – 10:24:06

I have made my position clear. Today is the deadline. Roy

Following Roy's text messages, Stuart and I decide to try another, last letter to him:

I write as a result of our on-going conversation…
I have to say I am somewhat disappointed by the inflexible stance you have taken on this issue. Stuart and I have said throughout that we do not wish to leave the Labour Party but that we are only willing to "sign up" again as part of an agreement that would see the Labour Party undertake an investigation into the behaviour of certain members of the Doncaster Labour Group.

In view of the seriousness of our allegations, the issues being made public in the Audit Commission's Public Interest Report and the fact that South Yorkshire Police has been investigating some of these allegations and the links to senior Labour Party Politicians in Doncaster for over six months, I would have thought the position merited more serious consideration from you on behalf of our Party.

I thought we had reached a positive position when you agreed to come up to see us on Thursday afternoon and we stated the need for an "agreed" press statement as part of any signing – this was to avoid the Labour Group leaking our "signing up" and making mischief.

Certainly, I find it quite ironic that you state "I have made my position clear. Today is the deadline." [for us to sign up again] when some of the issues we are raising are issues of bullying and harassment. It certainly feels like an overly draconian response when we offered to sign up in your presence 48 hours later.

Collectively, Stuart and I have been members of the Labour Party for more than 60 years. We do not wish to leave the Labour Party – nor do we consider our actions lightly or hysterically. However, the publication of the Public Interest Report has now made public some of the most appalling behaviours of several Senior Doncaster Labour Party members. These members are attempting to "rule" the Labour Group in Doncaster through intimidation, fear and victimisation.

We have been raising these issues for almost three years now and we cannot stand by and ignore what has been happening.

As a result of your statement today, we can only surmise that the Labour Party condones such behaviour and judges the protection of these perpetrators much higher than the support of two long standing members.

ooo

Wednesday May 28th 2008...

11.00 am – Full Council EGM, Council Chamber, Mansion House

The Public Interest report is to be debated at today's EGM. Noticeably though, for such an important meeting, only forty four of the sixty three councillors attended!

In a bad tempered meeting, the members behave true-to-type – which underlines the problem. Several of the malcontents refuse to accept the report shouting comments such as *"... its written as if the Mayor's just an afterthought"* and *"... the Mayor's the problem – not us!"* to which I simply smile at the Audit Commission's officers.

In a bizarre attempt at, I know not what, David Hughes actually moves that "Council Members should instruct the Managing Director to re-submit a more considered set of recommendations for consideration at a later date and withdraw the report before Council today."

The motion is lost by 16 votes to 29 – but it's another attempt at a Kangaroo Court!

When the subsequent vote is taken to accept the MD's recommendations, which have been developed and agreed with the Audit Commission [!], the vote is only 32 for – with 7 against and 6 abstentions – although only one actually votes as "abstained".

I feel ashamed by their behaviour – although somewhat vindicated that the Audit Commission officers have witnessed it.

ooo

5.00 pm

Martin Herron, a journalist from the Doncaster Star contacts me to ask if I would like to respond to the Labour Party's statement:

From:	Peter Morton
Sent:	28 May 2008 16:52
To:	Martin Herron
Subject:	Doncaster Mayor – Yorkshire and Humberside Labour Party quote

Here is the quote – please quote it as a spokesperson for Yorkshire and Humberside Labour Party:

Martin Winter and Stuart Exelby have failed to register as members of Doncaster Labour Group which is a clear breach of the Labour party rules. They were both informed by the Labour Party Head office on 9 May 2008 that they were required to re-join the Doncaster Labour Group within 14 days.

This has not happened and as a result the matter has now been referred to the Labour Party's Constitutional Officer, who will advise them that by leaving Doncaster Labour Group they are deemed to have auto-expelled themselves from the Labour Party.

Doncaster Labour Group is working hard for the town, and to build the mature leadership the council needs. Despite many offers of advice and support from the Labour Party, and the Audit Commission's concerns, the Mayor has walked away from our work to improve Doncaster in favour of political posturing. Doncaster deserves better and Doncaster Labour Group and its Labour MPs will focus on putting the people first

Cheers,

Peter Morton
Press Officer
Labour Party

I am appalled by the press release and forward a copy to Sir Jeremy Beecham commenting:

This is rather unfortunate, given that we are technically classed as "Whistle blowers".

Given the nature of the correspondence we have from the Labour Party, we'd like to give the LP the opportunity to withdraw the statement...

Many thanks

Martin

To which Jeremy responds:

From: Jeremy Beecham;
To: MJW
Sent: Wed May 28 20:50:10 2008
Subject: Re: Fw: A Labour Party Press Release?

Martin,

Thanks for the e-mails. I must say I think it's a pity things haven't been resolved, and I wasn't consulted about the press release!

Jeremy

ooo

Thursday May 29th 2008...

"You're out of Labour" reads the front page of the Doncaster Star "Mayor and colleague expel themselves from party".

The Yorkshire Post's headline states "New war of words as mayor insists audit report puts him in the clear" and then the journalist, Rob Waugh, goes on to report incredulously...

"DONCASTER'S elected mayor yesterday insisted a damning district audit report on the chaotic affairs of the town's council had absolved him of any blame".

"Martin Winter reiterated his belief that the public interest report, which focused on how the authority had controversially removed its former managing director, Susan Law, had vindicated his involvement in her departure."

Waugh then reports *inter alia* on the infamous Press Conference "Ms Law had been asked to arrange by then deputy mayor Aidan Rave..." So Waugh acknowledges Susan Law was guilty of misconduct [in that act].

He goes on to comment on Councillor Margaret Pinkney, who was herself criticised by the audit report for breaching confidentiality rules when she was a member of the sub-committee investigating Susan Law... but he doesn't say it was him who was receiving the confidential papers – and reporting on them!

ooo

Friday May 30th 2008...

"New cabinet will include Tories" reports the Doncaster Star.

ooo

Sunday June 1st 2008...

Stuart and I have been discussing the scenario with regard to our "auto-expulsion" from the Labour Party with Rodney Bickerstaffe, the former General Secretary of Unison. Rodney has been speaking to Chris Lennie, the [acting] General Secretary of the Labour Party.

"BIC" is a giant – and has a very loveable reputation. His hard advice is that we should do whatever we can not to leave the party but we have explained that we have nowhere else to go with this one.

We draft a final letter where we explain our predicament fully...

fall out   Exit stage right – pursued by...

Private & Confidential
Chris Lennie
Acting General Secretary
c/o The Labour Party
39 Victoria Street
London
SW1H 0HA   1st June 2008

Dear Chris

Mayor Martin Winter, Membership No: A238296
Councillor Stuart Exelby Membership No:A095306

"Auto-Expulsion" as members of the Labour Party

I write as a result of Rodney Bickerstaff's discussion with you on Friday 30th May which resulted from our ongoing conversation regarding the above.

I enclose a variety of information for you that describes the case we have been making to the national Labour Party, for it to intervene under Rule 13A [b] [iv] of the Party's rules. This is on the basis that the Labour Group's *"... political management has* [created] *a failure in public service and performance of the authority and where there is a lack of commitment displayed by leading members in the improvement agenda".*

Obviously you are an incredibly busy man and I have highlighted the salient areas, so as to assist you with your scanning of the material.

We have consistently repeated our misgivings and fully understand that the Party cannot investigate every complaint made by malcontents. However, this complaint has been verified by the detailed statements within the independent Audit Commission Public Interest Report [PIR] – published on 14th May 2008. It is our view that the Labour Group and Local Party, collectively, is in breach of rule 13A [b] [iv] if it does not carry out an appropriate investigation – and that any action and criticisms labelled against ourselves by Roy Kennedy, as the Director of Finance and Compliance, are completely unfounded and, in themselves, do not comply with our own rule book.

The basic thrust is that I and several Labour Party colleagues have been requesting support from MPs and the Party for several years now with respect to the most appalling of behaviours of several senior labour politicians in Doncaster. These issues have now been made public by an extremely damming Audit Commission PIR.

In view of the damaging effect this behaviour was/is having on the performance of the authority, we used this publication as the catalyst for our "final" request for support from the Party – under Rule 13A [b] [iv] of the Party's rules. We were naturally pleased that the Party agreed to Ann Black leading a panel to review "*... the relationship between Doncaster Labour Group and Doncaster Labour Mayor*" last September – but this never undertook to investigate the allegations, choosing to perform more of "mediation and cleansing" exercise.

We believe, and have always stated, that this PIR is "new evidence" and should constitute sufficient grounds for a full Labour Party enquiry under Rule 13A [b] [iv] of the Party's rules.It has certainly put us in an invidious position as two members of the Labour Executive – one where we are in danger of breaking any one, but not both, of two party rules:

    i]   the first states that we must sign up to the Labour Group – failure to do this will mean we are clearly in breach of 13A.1 [b] [iii] and we have been "Auto-expelled".

ii] the second states that we cannot act in a way where our management leads to a failure of the authority – to do this will mean we are clearly in breach of 13A [b] [iv].

The Audit Commission Public Interest Report clearly states that behaviour of leading members of the Labour Group continue to hamper the council [in contravention of rule 13A [b] [iv]]. Therefore, if we "sign up" to 13A.1 [b] [iii], we are opening ourselves to a collective responsibility for the "failure" of the Labour Group – a position that, in itself, would lead to expulsion.

To put it succinctly, we were/are obliged under rule 13A [b] [iv] not to sign up to a potentially corrupt Local Labour Group and Party. Similarly, rule 13A [b] [iv] compels the Party Nationally to take action; yet we have been "auto-expelled" for breaking the party rules.

Given this dilemma, we have always suggested a compromise to Roy Kennedy, whereby the two of us would register with the Labour Group, subject to an investigation into rule 13A [b] [iv] in order to clarify behaviours and statements within the PIR. The investigation should be independent but seemingly it has been refused at a national level by the Director of Finance and Compliance. If the outcome of the investigation is to absolve the Labour Group's members of wrong doing, then we will sign up to the Labour Group as rule 13A [b] [iv] no longer applies.

Our viewpoint regarding the breaking of rule 13A [b] [iv], is not a position we have taken based on our individual conclusions – and which any member would raise. But one made explicit and contained within the independent PIR from the Audit Commission – which the Mayor and Cabinet is bound to accept. Therefore the issue of our "Auto-expulsion", at this stage, is unconstitutional, and the Party is honour-bound to investigate the points made within the PIR; so that the Party can clarify the situation and thus enable us to comply with the rules.

We retained our membership throughout the "Donnygate" years and our Labour Party credentials cannot be faulted. We remain committed socialists and trust that you can inject a sense of objectivity, logic and fairness into this whole situation.

Mayor Martin Winter
Councillor Stuart Exelby

ooo

Monday June 2nd 2008...

"Lib-Dems expel former Leader" reports the Star, after Councillor Patrick Wilson is expelled from the party [locally?!] for accepting a position in my cross-party cabinet.

This will mark the dawn of a new era in political relationships in Doncaster. Doncaster is doing fantastically well but there are still many challenges to the delivery of top quality services. Now is the time for a new mature approach to opposition politics in Doncaster and I am delighted with the way that some elected members have risen to this challenge.

My Cabinet Consists of Stuart Exelby [Ind]; Eva Hughes [Lab]; Andrea Milner [Lab]; Martin Williams [Ind]; and Patrick Wilson [Ind]. I will not accept the Conservatives' nomination, which is done to antagonise me.

Wednesday June 4th 2008...

Having reflected on the media coverage the District Auditor's Report has received, particularly the coverage in the Yorkshire Post, I have had enough and email Paul Hart...

From: MJW
To: Hart, Paul
Sent: Wed Jun 04 08:56:12 2008
Subject: A Paradigm shift for the Media

Paul

I might have lost the plot here but I think we need to have a chat with ▇▇▇▇▇▇ in Comm's *et al* about shifting the media's thinking.
    As I understand it, I am not a Councillor, neither am I an elected member of this Council – although I am counted in as the 63 plus "1" for proportionality purposes. Neither our elected members, nor the media understand this simple concept.
    The argument that is "raging" is a self-fulfilling argument – it's an argument in the media, stoked and fed by the media who then wish to feature "stories" about the [unethical] elected members running to them with stories. The members are saying that *"The Mayor's a dictatorship!" and "The Mayor's in denial that he is the problem!"*. Therefore this is "newsworthy".
    The Audit Commission PIR has actually made the behaviour worse – not better – by not making a strong enough distinction about "whose behaviour" it is commenting on. We all saw the member's conduct and statements in Full Council "... it's written as if the Mayor's just an afterthought", "... the Mayor's the problem – not us!" etc. And, of course, the media duly report on this "news" – further stoking the [self-fulfilling] argument.
    Surely the "news" here is that of a "Council's" collective refusal to accept a legislative model. And, arguably, the media's failure [or refusal] to understand the relevant legislation – or to attempt to report on this to its customers.
    Given that the argument centres around a failure/refusal to understand the mayoral legislative model – can we not issue a joint statement/letter with the Audit Commission, to the media, to this effect?
    Similarly, given the ever increasing level of damage this is doing to Doncaster, can we not seek an injunction against the press for a failure to print the "news" but stoking a cyclical argument; and/or injunctions against the members for the damage they are wreaking on Doncaster – because of their immature "political" expediency [which would become the "news" of course!].

Can we discuss?

Many thanks

Martin

ooo

Tuesday June 10th 2008...

The government has announced plans for a new high speed rail system connecting the north to London. The "Atkins Report" has been commissioned to consider the project and I am slightly worried that they are talking up a "London – Birmingham – Manchester – Leeds" route, which will totally alienate the north eastern side of England, including Doncaster, York, Hull and Newcastle!

I speak to Ed and tell him he needs to start banging the drum for Doncaster or we risk being left behind. Ed's response is quite telling – or deliberately misleading...

He says the Atkins Report is a chimera – a purely political stalling tool to keep AGMA [Association of Greater Manchester Authorities] off the government's back- and will never be delivered! Furthermore, he tells me there is no way he would support £20 billion plus being spent on such a project.

Once again I have to explain to Ed that JP's legacy – the "Northern Way" – aims to do just that and identify the large-scale intervention/s required to address the trading gap between the north and the south; this is what the my "northern diamond" is all about...

He tells me that regardless of government spending £20 billion plus on "Crossrail" these high-speed rail links will never be built and I should stop worrying about the Atkins Report.

ooo

Friday June 13th 2008...

Pat Hagan has been awarded the MBE in the Queen's Birthday Honours.

This is absolutely fantastic news for Doncaster and nothing less than Pat deserves. It's also a tremendous honour for him, his family, his team and the community of Toll Bar.

ooo

Ray Collins has been appointed the new General Secretary of the Labour Party – he's an ex T&G [Unite] man and Stuart knows him quite well...

ooo

3.00 pm

I'm really battling against it now. "Cold wind blowing in the winter palace" reports a Star two page special featuring a whole host of criticisms from former Labour supporters – not least Aidan Rave and Caroline Flint!

"It's the final act of a desperate man" reads the sub-heading and Aidan is quoted, describing me as an enigma: "He can be brilliantly insightful one minute and appallingly pedantic the next. This mercurial nature is directly responsible for the carnage that we now see in Doncaster politics."

Sometimes they hurt – particularly when those commenting are the ones really responsible for the carnage!

ooo

Thursday June 19th 2008...

Labour searches for successor to Winter – reports the Star.

ooo

Monday June 23rd 2008...

"154 flood families still waiting". A year on from the floods and The Star reports that 42 of those families are council tenants and 34 are still living in caravans.

ooo

Tuesday June 24th 2008...

"Stadium scores a profit" says the Star – just three months after leaked internal papers prompted their tale of woe: "Stadium debts hit £2.5m – losses at the Keepmoat worry councillors". Strange that such a "bad news" story can be turned around so quickly...

ooo

Tuesday 1st July 2008...

Eva Hughes is coming under massive pressure from the Labour Party to leave my cabinet. The Doncaster Star reports on its front page "Ultimatum to quit cabinet –

Labour tells councillor to walk out on Mayor, or leave party" and reveals that Eva has received a letter telling her she must withdraw from the cabinet by tomorrow.

A Yorkshire and Humberside Labour Party spokesman said "Following discussions between Doncaster Labour Group and the Regional Labour Party, we have contacted Councillor Eva Hughes and requested she withdraws from Mayor Martin Winter's cabinet by Wednesday in order to remain a member of the Labour Party."

I am quoted as being disappointed with the Labour Party's position: "The Labour Party appears to be going against its own rules by refusing to co-operate, as rule 13 states that it has a duty to intervene where there is a lack of commitment displayed by leading members in the improvement agenda."

"All this flies in the face of the recent Audit Commission report where everyone on Doncaster Council has been charged with working together for the good of the borough."

But we are [I am] fighting a losing battle. We have been beaten by the Labour Party... that's the thanks I have received for all I have done for them...

For the avoidance of doubt, Rule 13A [b] [iv] states *"The Labour Party... will intervene where political management leads to a failure in public service and performance of the authority, and where there is a lack of commitment displayed by leading members in the improvement agenda".*

The Party is supporting the militants as they push the organisation towards complete stasis.

ooo

Wednesday July 2nd 2008...

Pat Hagan has been named Local Government Council Worker of the Year. "I am delighted that Pat has been named Council Worker of the Year. The floods were a disaster for many in Doncaster but Pat is a shining example of the countless employees who gave up so much of their time to help with the floods. It's thanks to them that many individuals and families across Doncaster, and specifically in the Toll Bar community, have been able to make such a positive recovery."

ooo

Friday July 4th 2008...

Andrea Milner has been performing fantastically as Chair of the SYPTE and has given me some excellent personal support when dealing with a significant health & safety issue at St Leger Homes.

She is a relatively new Labour councillor, having been elected to the Rossington Ward in May 2007, but has seen at first hand the bullying behaviour of the Labour group's leadership.

As a result, Andrea is in no mood for their shenanigans and has accepted my offer of a position in cabinet. Like most members of the Labour group, she is disgusted with their attempt to force the mayor out and the council into seizure but has decided she must make a stand and try to work for the best interests of the people of Doncaster.

ooo

Monday July 7th 2008...

I have received a letter from Chris Lennie. As a result I email Stuart

From:	MJW
To:	Exelby, Stuart
Date:	07/07/2008 20:44:19
Subject:	Response From Chris Lennie

Stuart

We've had a response from Chris Lennie. I haven't read it yet – it's at home but basically he's telling us we can do a running jump – I'll get Carolyne to fax it across when she gets back on Wednesday.

I think we need to do several things – firstly you need to speak to ▆▆▆▆▆ about Chris Lennie's response and what he intends to do ref you, me, Eva and [depending what the Party do] Andrea all being members of the T&G/UNITE;

Secondly – you should speak to Ray Collins – particularly after Andrea's position becomes clear, official and public on Tuesday;

Thirdly – can you speak to Cliff Williams – he rang me yesterday and left a message – we need to meet up with him as a matter of urgency to discuss the emerging situation.

Fourthly, you and Andrea need to speak to the likes of Eva, Barry Johnson, Bill Mordue and even Tony Sockett about the bullying and see if they'll break away.

Martin

ooo

Wednesday July 9th 2008...

"Cabinet row expel threat" reads the Star "Labour Party threaten to dismiss councillor after accepting role from Winter."

Andrea is a respected and considered councillor and is quoted as saying "I know full well the consequences of my decision. I've been thinking about it for some time and I believe it is an opportunity to help take Doncaster forward."

ooo

Monday July 14th 2008...

Full Council move a vote of "No Confidence" in me.

> "The Elected Members of this Council and the Electorate of Doncaster are growing more dissatisfied with the style of leadership and conduct of the Elected Mayor."

> "To protect the integrity of the Council and Elected Members and the communities they represent, this Council supports a vote of 'No confidence' in the Elected Mayor's style of leadership and conduct, which conflicts with the best interests of this Council."

Rather than debate the issue, I choose not to comment – but still have to sit through a humiliating tirade of abuse. It's pretty demoralising but I have become used to such "kangaroo courts".

In the voting, 8 support me, 7 abstain and 6 don't attend – so you could argue I have a third of the council's support! What's very interesting though is that of the seven members of the Chief Officer Investigatory Sub-committee [COISC], six remain as elected members. One votes for me and two abstain – they know that Susan Law should have been suspended and that this is all part of the subsequent "kangaroo court"!

Furthermore, six previous members of my cabinet either vote for me or abstain

ooo

The Doncaster Star reports: "Police probe into council contracts" and says South Yorkshire Police has launched an investigation into the awarding of contracts by Susan Law.

We approached South Yorkshire Police with this matter some five months ago, so why have they chosen now to inform the media?

The piece also seems to have been written pretty strongly in Susan's favour – saying in one breath that the investigation "coincided with a vote of no confidence in Mayor Winter" then contradicting itself by commenting that it has been going on for months...

Surely the newspaper chooses when to report issues – do they really think I knew four months ago that a vote of no confidence would be taking place?

Therefore, the newspaper made the decision to report on it to coincide with the vote of no confidence... which is interesting...

Susan's union rep claims the allegations made to police have already been dismissed by the council's own inquiry – and suggests the investigation has been prompted by the Mayor of Doncaster, "to deflect attention from his own political problems".

Now this is a really interesting statement to make – because <u>these allegations were never investigated</u>. This is exactly why I have stated all along that Susan "cut-and-ran" – to avoid the investigation and because the Audit Commission were now insisting that she must be suspended, pending an investigation...

ooo

Monday September 22nd 2008...

I host my "Achieving Success in Doncaster" conference at the racecourse, looking at the implications to schools and communities of my building schools for the future programme.

ooo

Fifteen months after the flooding in Toll Bar we have opened the primary school again.

After an absolutely wonderful day for the community, I ask the education officers where the temporary school we purchased is now. Following a suitably embarrassed silence, they tell me that despite my instruction otherwise, we didn't buy the school – we hired it for a twelve month period!

Sometimes you just can't get "best value"!

ooo

Friday 3rd October 2008...

Ed is appointed Secretary of State for Energy and Climate Change.

Our "relationship" has ended. I have served my purpose and there is no reason to continue the charade. I have become a burden to him...

I expect Ed to deal with the militants in his constituency but he is frightened of them; he sees no obligation to me [or Carolyne]; and does not accept that Aidan's behaviour has been coloured in any way as a result of my support for him, rather than Aidan, for the MP position.

ooo

Thursday October 9th 2008...

We are in the throes of the Icelandic bank crisis and appear to have lost £3 million that we had invested in Iceland. Interestingly, as a result of all this, we receive a high-level letter from government advising us to get all our money out of continental Europe and put it into Ireland and the Irish banks!

ooo

Monday October 27th 2008...

"Woman up for Mayor" screams the front page of the Doncaster Star, struggling to contain its misogynist predilections as it reveals that Sandra Holland has secured the Labour Party nomination for the mayoral election next year – defeating Joe Blackham and Glyn Jones.

ooo

Thursday October 30th 2008...

"Buses in council return? – Government U-turn opens way to local authority control" says The Star splash, reporting that the Local Transport Bill will end the 20-year "deregulation disaster" and stop the "free-for-all" at bus stops.

Although I welcome the developments, which will allow the SYPTE to impose quality contracts and strict franchise deals which will dictate routes, it's just another "half-way house" and a stalling tactic.

ooo

Tuesday November 11th 2008...

11.00 am – Mansion House Steps

As part of the malcontents' campaign to persistently rubbish "The Mayor", they have delighted in constantly blurring the lines between "The Mayor" and "Chair of Council" or "Civic mayor" for certain duties and functions; a strategy frequently abetted by the local newspapers.

To deal with the situation, and avoid arguments about the conflicting roles and responsibilities, I had a 'protocol and guidelines' prepared by the civic office in my inaugural year. These made explicit when the Chair of Council was "Chair of Council"; when he or she was functioning as "Civic Mayor"; and which dress codes were appropriate – Civic Badge; Chains; Chains and Suit; Full Chains and Robes etc.

Full Robes and Chains are worn for the Armistice Remembrance Sunday event, which the "Civic Mayor" leads and "Chain and Suit" are worn for the 2 minute "Armistice Day" silence on the Mansion House steps, which the Executive Mayor leads.

I lead a suitably humble and respectful silence, always conscious of the sacrifices of so many men, women and families over so many wars and conflicts.

ooo

Thursday November 13th 2008...

Children's Minister Ed Balls orders an inquiry into the role of the local authority, the health authority and the police, in the case of Baby P at Haringey.

ooo

Friday November 14th 2008...

3.00 pm

"ROBES BAN DISRESPECT" screams the front page of the Doncaster Star and continues with the sub-heading "War tribute downgraded as civic mayor told not to dress up".

Despite operating the protocol with few problems over the past six years, the Lib-Dem "Chair of Council" has decided he wants to change it and kicked up a fuss – ably supported by the militant Labour members, other malcontents and the newspaper, which sees fit to disregard the legislation, operating precedents or protocols – but why shouldn't they? They've got a good front page!

ooo

Wednesday November 26th 2008...

10.00 am – Cabinet

We are due a Cabinet update on the CCQ [Civic and Cultural Quarter] Project. This has proved a contentious project over the last two years and one which several of the more militant Labour members want to ditch.

Within reason, I have had to 'curb' my enthusiasm for the CCQ and, in some classic "Lapwing Economics" work I have played down my interest, linking it closely with the major improvements on the A6182 White Rose Way. As such, I have sat back and watched it trundle through relatively unopposed.

Today's meeting is an "Update on the Development Agreement and Preparatory Works Carried Out to Date and Approval of Costs for Further Preparatory Works".

ooo

Thursday November 27th 2008...

3.00 pm

Page 2 of The Doncaster Star is running with the headline "Mayor defends £350m scheme – Council clash over Waterdale transformation plan". It tells how Lib-Dem Councillor Paul Bissett "stormed out" of yesterday's meeting, claiming that to go ahead with the scheme would devastate the council's finances and bring Doncaster to financial ruin!

The "Lapwing Economics" have worked and I no longer need to keep my powder dry...

"Mayor Martin Winter said: 'I think it is very important that we move forward plans like this – it is a significant piece of the jigsaw to £300 million worth of investment, and if we don't we will be left with a huge hole in terms of Doncaster moving forward."

"We are being encouraged regionally and nationally to move forward and it is about showing that people can have confidence in making an investment in

Doncaster." "This is a time when we need strong leadership which I have always tried to exert as mayor."

ooo

Monday December 1st 2008...

10.00 am – Full Council – Doncaster Council Chamber

Interestingly enough there's a motion been put forward today by Councillor Edwin Simpson [Lib-Dem] and seconded by Councillor Garth Oxby [Alliance of Independent Members]:

> "This Council, will continue to uphold the long traditions of the civic mayoral functions. This Council, in order to support the above, calls for a protocol to be prepared by officers and agreed by the Elected Mayor and the Civic Mayor on their different functions."

I thought we already had such a protocol... they clearly want to further confuse the two roles. But, on the basis that I have to keep my "power of authority" until next June, I need to feign interest and "worry" about the ramifications on my "third term"!

ooo

Thursday December 18th 2008...

As part of the CPA/JAR process we have had a hugely damming report on our children's services. "Town's children services failing – inadequate rating in five out of seven areas" reports the page two article.

We know we have difficulties in children's services, including having had three interim Directors of Children's services in the past eighteen months; however, I am fairly confident that our present DCS, Dr Paul Gray, has a hold on the area and has put together a robust plan of action. He has identified three key issues needing attention:
- The structure of children's services.
- A shortage of qualified social workers, which is an issue in other parts of the county.
- The very high level of referrals into the system at 600 – 700 per month and frequently from partner organisations such as the police.

In addition to the above, I have now been made aware of a number of young people's suicides in Doncaster across a two-year period. I have expressed concern that we may have a similar situation to the one manifest in Bridgend, South Wales – being reported nationally as a "suicide sect" – where a considerable number of young people have hanged themselves during the previous eighteen months.

I ask Paul for a brief on the situation but say we need to be incredibly sensitive to the potential parallels with Bridgend…

I also ask him if he can draw some comparisons between the report we have just received and the report from December last year, where our children's services were assessed as "making a good contribution to improving outcomes" and "now better equipped to deliver a more efficient and effective service to children and young people thanks to some important developments, as well as having good capacity for further improvement…"

ooo

Friday December 19th 2008…

The Pilkington Glass factory finally closes its doors – after nearly ninety years of operation on the site. I am devastated.

We knew it was imminent but had been battling to support the company for at least a dozen years. Indeed, the "Glass Park" project, originally conceived in an attempt to assist the company's operational arm though the sale of land for residential development, became something of a saviour for it. If the "Glass Park Phase 4" had not faltered [after becoming embroiled in the smear campaign against the mayor], the land development revenue may have given the company another five years reprieve.

In the great scheme of things, I always expected to complete my second term as a successful Labour mayor and then move into the House of Lords as "Lord Winter of Sandall Parva" – the ancient name for the original village of Kirk Sandall, where I spent the majority of my childhood years.

ooo

Monday December 22nd 2009…

Despite the initial review of the child deaths suggesting we do not have a "suicide sect" issue, we do have a problem.

Children's Minister, Beverley Hughes has written to us to say they are sending in a "diagnostic team" to work with our children's services function, which has ordered "serious case reviews" into seven children's deaths over a period of five years; three of those have already been made public and involved toddlers aged under one, who were abused and neglected before they died.

Nonetheless, the shit has hit the fan with elected members kicking off that they only became aware of the children's deaths as a result of press reporting! With a media full of the story of "Baby P" at Haringey Council, the members are understandably furious.

ooo

Tuesday January 13th 2009...

10.00 am – Extraordinary Full Council – Doncaster Council Chamber

An EGM has been called into the issue of child deaths. To be honest, I have nowhere to go with this one.

Members may be concerned that they only found out about the cases from the media, but I wasn't that far ahead of them myself; only becoming aware of "an issue" after Carolyne listened in on a private discussion between Paul Hart and Paul Gray at my "Discover the Spirit" awards evening three months ago.

Having said that, there is the issue of "confidentiality", which councillors have continually failed to understand. Ethical governance has collapsed in Doncaster over the past two years – and was specifically reported on in the District Audit Public Information Report in May last year.

The Director of Children's Services [DCS] has a legal obligation to protect the safety of children in the council's care but is not legally obliged to inform the mayor or managing director. Indeed, even when we found out about the children's deaths and were in the middle of the storm, another child died and the DCS did not tell me or the MD!

So there are massive sensitivities about statutory responsibilities versus political responsibilities and our officers were often placed in an invidious situation; frequently not being "allowed" to perform their duties because of the internecine war that was taking place between the politicians.

Nonetheless, the following motion is put forward and I prepare to take a kicking:

"To debate and discuss as a matter of urgency the matter related to all the 5 serious child protection cases that have been highlighted to Councillors, not by officers but the local press. In view of the importance of the matters related to child protection in this Borough, to seek to put in place safeguards that fully ensure that this never happens again. The safeguarding of children is obviously of utmost concern for all Councillors and people of the Borough."

But the kicking doesn't come. Obviously members give me a pretty rough ride but the debate isn't as bad as I expect it to be. As expected there are a few calls for me to resign – but rather than just being passive, I go on the attack.

The Audit Commission warned of this failure in public services last May and it is the direct result of the militants' attempts to push the council into stasis. Yes, I have to take some responsibility – I'm the mayor and it's happened on 'my watch' – but so do all the councillors who are in denial about their part in this sorry tale.

This is exactly why I have been trying to get the MPs, but mainly Miliband, and the Labour Party, to deal with the militant extremism in Doncaster North [predominately].

ooo

Wednesday January 14th 2009...

3.00 pm

"Abysmal – Mayor Winter ignores resignation calls as 'ashamed' councillors condemn leadership".

The newspaper gives me a real kicking and I am really struggling to hold this thing together. Clearly the whole issue of "children's services" is a multi-agency affair and there are some faults with our partner organisations, most notably the police who are constantly referring cases into the system rather than using their own professional judgement.

But in the members' rush to hold the mayor responsible for everything they have chosen to forget this. I try to explain that we are all guilty of being misinformed, and I feel as let down as anyone; I commission a rapid and independent review to find out exactly how we arrived at this situation.

I ask members to stop playing politics with a difficult situation and not to be so quick to blame me before the outcome of the inquiry.

ooo

4.30 pm

Now there's a great danger that this "Lapwing Economics" strategy I have been using might backfire on me.

Since I chose to leave the party last year, I have been giving a standard reply to questions about whether I am standing as an independent candidate in June or not – always emphasising that "I am looking forward to a successful third term", although I've never said *whose* successful [third] term!

Even though I know I have no intention of standing for a third term, the Labour Party is becoming quite convinced that I *am* standing and seems desperate for me to announce that I'm not…

To this end, Rosie has sent Martyn Vickers to see me… Martyn is quite aware how the militants in the Doncaster Labour Party have destroyed my [political] career and is very supportive of my mayoralty. He is also fully aware of the "Labour Peer" exit strategy I pitched at Rosie in 2004, so he knows how "abused" I feel.

He tells me he thinks I will enter the House of Lords – but that I'll have to wait a couple of years for the fuss to die down.

"What do you really think?" I ask Martyn *"Do you think I really want another four years of this shit?"*. I tell him "they" should just let me disappear into the background and I'll quietly go away. If they continue to harangue me, they'll force me in to a corner and I'll probably stand just to spite the party – as a spoiler for the official Labour candidate, Sandra Holland.

He says he understands the message and will relay it back to Rosie.

ooo

Friday January 16th 2009…

I've always got on well with Ed Balls who is, I think, fully aware of how badly the party and the other Ed have treated me, and of the Labour Party's dysfunctionality in Doncaster.

In today's questions at parliament he says he is "encouraged" that Doncaster is "doing the right things" to address the problems in its child protection services. But he also says: *"The situation in Doncaster is a materially different situation to that of Haringey"*. In contrast to Haringey, he says, Doncaster Council *"understands the issue it faces and has been sorting it out"*.

ooo

Monday January 19th 2009…

A further EGM has been called into the issue of child deaths… This time the militant Labour Party members are really going for my throat!

Joe Blackham, the Group leader [and the man John Hardy is suing for disability discrimination], has put forward a motion, which has been seconded by Councillor Mick Jameson:

> "This Council calls upon Martin Winter the Elected Mayor to accept full responsibility regarding the failure of the Children & Young Peoples Service that has occurred within his period of office. We request he does the only honourable thing and resigns with immediate effect."

However, the malcontents have attempted to put the Labour Party under the hammer by moving an amendment to the motion:

> "This Council calls upon the Labour Party and Mayor Winter, the former Labour Elected Mayor, to accept full responsibility regarding the failure of the Children's and Young People's Service during his term of office."

Surprisingly, the amendment falls – I thought the majority opposition were desperate to pin the collapse of services on the Labour party – but it would appear they hate me more!
Suffice to say the meeting is awful – I have to accept the rough and tumble of politics but the manner in which the militant Labour Party members seek to destroy me is both frightening and heart-breaking...
This is a motion which relates to the deaths of children, yet Joe Blackham introduces it stating: *"It is with great delight and enormous satisfaction that I speak to this motion today"* and goes on: *"People should be under no illusions that this is a political motion and borne of vengeance against this man."*
With a completely biased Chair operating politically, I have no "right to reply" and am constantly shouted down and subjected to further disgraceful scenes and language, where members call me a liar, a cheat and a murderer; comparing me to Mugabe and more.

ooo

Tuesday January 20th 2009...

3.00 pm

"Go Now!" screams the front page of the Star and continues with "Fresh vote calls for mayor to resign as pressure mounts over child welfare row".
Adjacent to a photograph of those "campaigning for the mayor's resignation" is a picture of Ray Nortrop and the usual malcontents, as well as a comment from

Mick Jameson, Leader of the Labour group: "I think we made it clear to Martin Winter how we felt about his leadership".

"Winter is Doncaster's Robert Mugabe" says the inside pages, as the paper reports that I lost this vote of no confidence by 46 votes to 6.

ooo

Thursday January 22nd 2009...

"Stadium close to breaking even" declares the Star – which sounds like a political turn-around if nothing else!

ooo

I send a letter sent to Paul Coddington with regard to his Chairing of Monday's Full Council – quoting British trade unionist Walter Citrine:

> I write further to Monday's Full Council and also your letter requesting that I qualify my comments, which I received yesterday.
> It is my view that, during the meeting, you allowed members to conduct themselves in a manner completely unbecoming of Councillors, for example:
> Allowing one member to state that it was with "great delight" and "enormous satisfaction that [he] speaks to this motion today" [based on issues relating to the deaths of children and young people] and further stating that people should be under no illusions that "... this is a political motion..." [borne of] "... vengeance... against this man...".
> You allowed members of your own party – surely a neutral Chair should be particularly sensitive to this issue – to call me a liar and a cheat, and imply that I am a murderer, stating that I am "Doncaster's version of Robert Mugabe..." and, at no point were you inclined to challenge the choice of words, aggressive behaviour or choose to ask for a retraction.
> Your chairmanship of this meeting, and previously, has shown a complete disregard to the impartiality and political neutrality demanded by the position. To allow a comparison to Mugabe is totally out of order and, it is my contention, would not have been allowed in any other public arena in this country.
> Notwithstanding the above, I felt that your refusal to allow me to complete my response – with your interjection after 3.55 secs, further displayed a complete lack of understanding of the rules of impartiality and balance within debate and a total inability to offer any discretion to facilitate said debate. You clearly failed to recognise that the continual allowance of insults and totally unjustified claims and interruptions was eating up my allocated time and is seriously dragging the reputation of the whole council down.
> Consequently, it is my view that you have brought the position of Chair of Council into disrepute. As I have said to you before, you have failed completely to protect the neutrality of the position of Chair of Council through voting on such motions.
> Even the most basic grasp of Citrine would have enabled you to direct and conduct Full Council with the most rudimentary level of capability and I would strongly urge you familiarise yourself with his writings. Certainly I would advise you to read a copy of Citrine's "The ABC of Chairmanship". In the vernacular of Chairmanship, Citrine is known as "The

Chairs' Bible" – and what does Citrine say about the chairman seeking to impose his or her views on a council?

"Impartiality: Above all, the chairman must be impartial. Where there are differences of opinion, the chairman should give both sides an equal chance to express their views. There is a difficult balance to strike between being too firm and becoming almost dictatorial; and being too weak, which can lead to rulings from the chair being questioned..."

I have expressed to you before the requirement that the Chair protects his position of neutrality and impartiality; compromising this position in extremis, but you constantly feel the need to parade your bias.

Your behaviour on Monday, and previously, has clearly transgressed the rules of impartiality and political neutrality. In saying this, I wish to point out three counts:

Firstly, on Monday you allowed 20 occasions for people to speak for the motion and against me, giving a total of well over an hour of colluded attack. Subsequently, I and my two Cabinet colleagues were allowed a total of less than 14 minutes to respond; hardly a balanced equal opportunity to express our views as per Lord Citrine. In essence, you denied me my right of reply to some of the most heinous of allegations possible.

Secondly, that during last week's [13th January] Extraordinary Full Council, a similar pattern of debate ensued. I would argue that the one member of council who should have been afforded a certain level of discretion in his response, the portfolio holder for Children's Services was similarly denied the opportunity by your over-zealous attitude.

Thirdly, at a previous meeting through registering your vote on a similar issue, you failed to protect the Chair's historic position of neutrality.

ooo

Dear Martin

Thank you for your letter of 22nd January 2009. I have noted the views you express in your letter and have considered them very carefully.

I do not intend to trade written insults and disagreements over individual issues. Suffice to say that I disagree with a great deal of your views, but that I do see some merit in one or two of your arguments regarding impartiality and political neutrality which I have taken into account, especially in the way I will chair Council meetings in the future.

Whilst I do not agree that I have brought the office of the Chair of Council into disrepute, nor to my certain knowledge do the vast majority of councillors, I will be reviewing practices and approaches with officers in the light of your remarks.

There is of course a fine line between political banter, which does sometimes contain personal remarks, and offensive language which I will strive to banish from the Chamber.

We have four busy months to carry out our respective duties, where our protocols and ways of working will continue to be tested to the full. I ask that we work together from now on to deliver our best for Doncaster.

Yours sincerely
Paul Coddington

ooo

Saturday January 24th 2009...

Surprise surprise, the members are playing politics with the children's services crisis and we are having difficulty getting the message out there, despite me being quoted:

"The real issue we should be debating is how, and why, this council was not made aware of a developing crisis in our children's services. And because we are not debating the real issues, this council is in danger of putting politics before service delivery."

As a result, I have written to all mayoral candidates and leaders of political parties inviting them to take part in the briefings I receive with regard to children's services.

ooo

Thursday February 12th 2009...

Mick Maye announces he's standing [again], focusing on essential services from rubbish collection and recycling to housing issues [!]

ooo

Friday February 13th 2009...

6.30 pm – Mount Pleasant Hotel

Life goes on and I am speaking at "The Met Club" – a Yorkshire-wide business club for senior decision makers and entrepreneurs.

Christine Armstrong, The Met Club managing director, introduces me: "Martin continues our theme of high-profile speakers able to engage diners with important local issues. Martin has had such an incredibly varied life, and we are all looking forward to hearing his views on Doncaster and the credit crunch."

ooo

Friday February 27th 2009...

Since the Audit Commission report last year the elected members' behaviour has deteriorated to the point of total collapse. As a result, we have been undertaking an

"Ethical Governance Health Check" with support from the Improvement & Development Agency [IDeA]. The team consists of:

Paul Rogerson – Chief Executive Peer, Chief Executive, Leeds City Council
Kirsty Cole – Monitoring Officer Peer, Newark & Sherwood District Council
Malcolm Grimston – Member Peer, Cabinet Member, Wandsworth Borough
Vanessa Walker – Improvement Manager, IDeA

I am ambivalent about this project and its work, having witnessed countless attempts to deal with the members' behaviour during the previous two or three years. However, one of the team's key initial statements bears some resemblance to what I have been saying for the past while:

"Often ethical problems do not relate to probity, but to relationships and behaviour. They can serve to divert effort away from serving the community."

After requesting copies of their interim feedback for some time now, I respond as follows:

    From: MJW
    To: Hart, Paul; Evans, Paul [Legal Services]
    Date: 27/02/2009 15:10:06
    Subject: IDeA Feedback 12th Feb09.ppt

Thanks for this

I would've thought I would be copied in to this [last week] rather than having to request it.
    My immediate thoughts are that, obviously this presentation was just the headline messages but it appears fairly dry and very biased towards the officers, which is only to be expected; the IDeA do not appear to have grasped that it was I who was constantly challenging member behaviour and, when I gave up, this exacerbated the situation.
    I would have expected to have seen "a complete failure to understand or respect the mayoral system of governance and legislation" in there somewhere. As would "officers petrified of members"... I have several examples of where officers have lodged, with me, their fears and records of threats from councillors.
    I also think people never understand the power of stating "problems between the mayor and members" when "problems between the members and the mayor..." would be more accurate [and less inflammatory or value laden against an individual].
    Also, during the interview with me, they majored on my "stupid" comment and also the media and member reports that I called the members "maggots" which I did not – as examples of me leading on the poor ethical governance...
    They appear to dismiss the raison d'etre of politicians, which it could be argued, is to avoid stating or covertly stating what a person means. The "stupid" argument was, in my view, a classic piece of political oratory – did they ask to see my script? The "maggot" comment was a deliberate quotation from the Labour Party's Militant history used for

effect in a press release – and taken out of context by the media and members – did they ask to see the press release or context in which it was said?

Thank you

Martin

ooo

Thursday March 5th 2009…

"Council 'warned' lives were at risk – Child protection problems raised four years ago – claim" reports the Star and quotes an officer who left the authority in 2006.
It's getting to the point where if I don't do something to try to take the political sting out of the situation it will never get better…

ooo

Thursday March 12th 2009…

I decide to make a statement to the press and media…

"I have been saying for several weeks now that we should not rush to judge and that we should await the findings of the Government's diagnostic process.
I have never been in denial about the need for fast and immediate improvement in the safeguarding of our children in Doncaster.
The simple fact is that as soon as these issues were brought to my attention I took action, and I took decisive action. I made the finances available immediately [a total of over £6m extra investment].
But the reality is that this situation has arisen on my watch, as mayor, and because of this it has become something of a political football before the election in June, which I deplore.
I therefore feel it is important to take the politics out of this situation so that we are able to concentrate on the job in hand.
I have decided to announce today that I will not be seeking re-election as Mayor of Doncaster in June.
I have made this decision to stop another bout of political infighting which interferes with the crucial task of improving the safeguarding of children in Doncaster.

I have given the Government my assurance that for the remaining 12 weeks of my term of office, I will ensure that co-operation is maintained and everything possible is done to achieve the improvements needed.

It saddens me beyond belief that some factions have attempted to use this issue politically and as a way of undermining the mayoral system of local government. No doubt, if I had not made this decision there would have been a continuation of the political game-playing.

I sincerely trust my announcement will bring people back to what should now be the main focus of attention – the safety of the children of Doncaster.

I would like at this stage to pay tribute to my fellow cabinet members and to the staff of the council – many of whom do extremely important and difficult jobs, day in day out and wholly for the people of Doncaster. I thank you all for your support.

I have already held the first of regular briefing sessions with declared Mayoral candidates and Group Leaders on Doncaster Council to ensure the new Mayor, whoever it is, hits the ground running on the crucial issue of safeguarding. I will continue to do this until June."

Martin Winter
Mayor of Doncaster

ooo

Friday March 13th 2009...

3.00 pm

"You can't blame me – mayor Winter to quit but he won't be saying sorry" screams the front page of the Star.

ooo

Inside, it reports: "Legacy of grandiose schemes and declining services"– which hurts, given that we were nudging at an "excellent" CPA rating in 2006/7.

ooo

fall out   Exit stage right – pursued by...

Monday March 16th 2009...

"Ditched mayor title set to be brought back" reports the Star, commenting on councillor's moves to change the "Chair of Council" title back to that of "Mayor".

ooo

Wednesday April 1st 2009...

"Warning signs in children's services – two reports detailed serious problems before children died" says the Doncaster Star and refers to internal officer reports from 2006 and 2008, which painted a picture of poor mental health with overworked social workers.

To be fair, Susan had referred to a "report" given to her by an officer around the time of the restructuring in 2006 – but then dismissed it as scaremongering by a staff member opposed to her restructuring!

ooo

Monday April 27th 2009...

Not satisfied with the mayor having tended his resignation and the feedback from an extremely poor "Ethical Governance Heath Check", the members are after even more blood...

They are kicking off about the "appearance" of these two [internal] operational officers' reports and, as such, have decided to have another go:

> "This Council deplores the total absence of any meaningful Political and Managerial Leadership within Doncaster's Children's Services following the [internal] reports from Mark Eales in January, 2005 and Bron Sanders in March, 2007. The result of which was the direct intervention of Government into Children's Services within Doncaster. The principle reasons given for this intervention are as followings:
> - The lack of a strong and settled management team.
> - Ineffective political leadership.
> - Weak local partnerships.
> The Council requires the Elected Mayor to account for this situation."

I have expressed to both the MD and the Acting Director of Legal and Democratic Services that the organisation [collectively] is "hanging me out to dry" on this one and that I am minded not to attend yet another "kangaroo court".

As such, the Acting Director of Legal and Democratic Services wrote to all members over the weekend for legal advice in relation to the debate of the motion and asked members to have regard to that advice during the course of the debate.

The Chair also reminded members to consider the impact of inappropriate conduct and comments in the Council Chamber and asked members to refrain from personal attacks and the use of offensive expressions in reference to other members, officers or anyone else.

Nonetheless, I refuse to attend and ask Stuart Exelby to read a prepared statement to Full Council.

ooo

The motion is proposed by the Labour group leader, Joe Blackham, Ros Jones [Lab], Garth Oxby [AIM], John McHale [Lab] and Edwin Simpson [Lib-Dem]; and in a marvellous piece of double bluffing, Edwin then rounds on the Labour group, with an amendment:

> "This Council deplores the total absence of any meaningful Managerial leadership and Political leadership from Labour Cabinet Members and the then Labour Mayor within Children's Services, this following the reports from Mark Eales in January, 2005 and Bron Sanders in March, 2007. The result of which has been the direct intervention of Government into Children's Services within Doncaster. The principle reasons given for this intervention are as follows:
> - The lack of a strong and settled management team.
> - Ineffective political leadership from Labour Cabinet Members and Labour Mayor.
> - Weak local partnerships.
>
> The Council requires the Cabinet at that time and the Elected Mayor to account for this situation."

The amendment is carried. How stupid can the Labour group be?! In essence they are now moving and voting on a motion that criticises themselves – as the Labour Party!

Technically correct, in terms of the Audit Commission Public Interest Report and my argument with regard to 13A [b] [iv]] of the Labour Party Rule Book – *"The Labour Party... will intervene where political management leads to a failure in public service and performance of the authority, and where there is a lack of commitment displayed by leading members in the improvement agenda".*

But then what do you expect from a group of militant extremists pushing the organisation towards complete stasis.

ooo

Tuesday April 28th 2009...

The Doncaster Star reports that Council refused to hear my prepared statement yesterday but reports extracts from it. For completeness here it is:

Statement to Full Council. Officers, Members of the Public and Press

I shall not be attending today's Special Full Council Meeting. The reasons why I will not be attending are as follows:

    Firstly, I have received legal advice from Susan Law's Lawyers and I have also taken advice from the Acting Head of Legal Services, the Interim Monitoring Officer, Robin Hooper and the Managing Director; all have stated, to a lesser and greater extent, that I shall be restricted in what I am able to state with regard to the previous Managing Director with reference to this motion.

    This Council knows that the Compromise Agreement with Susan Law binds the Council, and therefore me, in respect to many of the issues you wish me to answer for. Anything I say about past structures, protocols and behaviours, risks costing this council a fortune in legal fees; you know this from the letter that has been circulated to you all prior to this meeting.

    Secondly, I have requested advice from the Chair of Council as to my freedom of speech and his use of discretion in allowing my response – the Chair will only commit to "...considering using [his] discretion... in allowing [me] additional time [should it be required] and fair and proper to do so".

    Thirdly, I have previously reported that I have assured the Minister that I will do all that is within my powers to make sure the authority is best placed to move forward with the Child Safety agenda. What I do not understand is what the councillors seeking this debate think is to be gained by demanding answers which they know I cannot give for legal reasons and which will not help us to address, as the urgency dictates, the improvements which are needed now and in the future.

Doncaster's Councillors have become famous throughout the country for their immoderate and insulting behaviour towards me, towards each other and towards our officers. Support for this motion will once again be immensely damaging to Doncaster's reputation and will not move us forward one iota – and how will this help the children of Doncaster?

    But finally, I will not be attending today's Special Full Council Meeting because the motion to be debated does not itself require my attendance. It is my view that today's Full Council Meeting is designed purely to provide members with one last opportunity to attempt to create political mayhem hours before the commencement of purdah.

As such, if members, fully cognisant of the irreparable damage it may do Doncaster, support this motion today, then I shall be more than happy to respond to it and account for this situation, through the correct and proper fora.

ooo

Friday June 5th 2009...

Now the shit has really hit the fan!

In yesterday's mayoral election, English Democrat, Peter Davis was elected as Mayor of Doncaster – the Labour candidate, Sandra Holland came third, just ahead of the Tories.

Be careful what you wish for...

ooo

fall out – an afterword...

> *"When the burdens of the presidency seem unusually heavy,*
> *I always remind myself it could be worse...*
> *I could be a mayor.*
>
> Lyndon B. Johnson

Throughout my life, I have always believed in the abiding principle that truth is stranger than fiction; when it comes to my time as mayor of Doncaster, it's certainly the case.

The story I have attempted to map out here can be viewed in two ways; as a complex series of inter-linked stories like some byzantine plot worthy of a John Le Carré novel, or as an example of the above maxim.

The simple fact is that this is a true story – the true story – and the one I have always said I would write. It's my version of what really happened and it's supported by countless reports, testimonies, investigative transcripts, emails, text messages and other forms of evidence.

Having said that, the vast majority of what I say here has already been said, published previously, or is already in the public domain, should the reader wish to look for it.

ooo

I have always tried to do what is best, and to do *my* best, whether in business, sport, recreation, relationships or parenthood. I wrote the "Loved and Trusted" years to convey this adage and principles.

The "Hated & Abused" years highlight how I was harangued, berated, criticised and persecuted for serving the people of Doncaster – particularly so during the three years from 2006 to 2009.

The main reason I chose to write this book was to put my side of the story "out there"; so that in the future my children, and my children's children, can know the truth and won't have to rely on media coverage or any urban myths about my mayoralty.

This is the view from where I am standing or where I stood; so this is "my truth" and frankly, I'm sick of hearing other versions!

My objective, therefore, has always been the delineation between right and wrong; between truth and innuendo; fact and fiction; reality and insinuation –

issues the Stuart Dobson Report and the Audit Commission's Public Interest Report both struggled to convey. I was up against an increasingly vocal opposition and an immature press that became ritually antagonistic towards me, obsessed with reporting matters of opinion rather that the facts.

To this end, I quote one last time, the introduction to the Stuart Dobson Report: *"If nothing else, I hope that the report will now enable judgements to be made on the basis of the facts, rather than on the basis of anecdote or rumour"*. Something that a short-term, inward looking media was sadly, and shamefully, incapable of achieving...

I have found the whole process to be therapeutic, cleansing even, as I have unpacked this eight year period and described the activities and behaviours I witnessed during that time – my two terms as mayor of Doncaster. In preparing this manuscript I have read some of the media's coverage for the first time and I genuinely don't know how Carolyne and my wonderful children coped with such an unremitting torrent of abuse and intrusion into our [their] lives. For this I will be forever humbled. I just thank God that it pre-dated the social media tsunami that is today's zeitgeist.

When times were good they were fantastic – and my earlier years as leader and mayor were like pushing at an open door. Our many partners and investors were desperate to break from the past and, alongside the phenomenally capable David Marlow, we made rapid progress in moving the borough forward, away from the disgraces of the preceding years...

Fourteen years on, people forget what we had to deal with – how far we moved over a short period of time in securing the "closure" of Donnygate. They forget, principally because of the new smokescreen that was created – by the Labour group ironically – in an attempt to destroy any legacy I may have had – "Donnygate 2 – the sequel"!

ooo

Doncaster had been known as the byword for council corruption and having been asked, mandated even, by Blair to deal with this mess once and for all, I became the saviour of the town and its Labour party.

With everyone working towards re-invention, progress was relatively easy and all partners were desperate to buy-in to a new "shared vision" – not just the mayor's vision. It was an opportunity and a period where we had everything to achieve and nothing to lose.

We swiftly rose to prominence in UK local government through our unstinting anti-corruption stance and the campaign to rebrand Doncaster as a major economic driver in the north of England.

A Labour Mayor working with a Labour Government, four Labour MPs and with a majority Labour Council, was a recipe for success, or so we thought.

What we eventually witnessed was a Labour administration, bitter at the "loss" of executive control, trying to hang onto power by opposing its own Labour mayor and mayoralty. That political weakness was accentuated by a legislative framework which was not fit-for-purpose in terms of mayoral governance – being merely a "bolt-on" to existing legislation.

Nonetheless, this was very much a slow-burning fuse and I enjoyed a euphoric first term. Doncaster witnessed a massive economic resurgence and fantastic improvements in service delivery; huge economic regeneration; cleaner streets and safer neighbourhoods; a greater focus on recycling and waste collection; and vastly improved housing services. The mayoral approach was certainly working. Delivering a more responsive mayor [and council], particularly though the "cutting edge" green and white paper approach to establishing policy and holding the mayor and council to account.

Doncaster was booming and it didn't happen by accident. These first four years reached a crescendo when Gordon Brown asked me to "deliver" Ed Miliband's selection and election as the next MP for Doncaster North.

Oblivious to the fact that I had reached the peak of my political prowess, and with Ed ensconced in his new seat, the exhilaration at being part of a new Labour "leadership" agenda was short-lived...

Despite year-on-year improvements in services, achieving a "good local authority" Comprehensive Performance Assessment [CPA] in the first mayoral term, and coming desperately close to being classed as an "excellent local authority" in the 2005 CPA process, the natives were indeed becoming restless.

As the malcontents and majority opposition developed a more "joined up" insurgency campaign, and the efficacy of the mayoral model and specifics of Local Government Act 2000 became more apparent, they were joined by some less than supportive Labour Party members.

A recently appointed and struggling managing director united with a [now] severely disenfranchised deputy mayor and defeated parliamentary candidate, to create a situation where the planets aligned. As a result, a manipulative MD colluded with senior Labour Party politicians in a failed attempt to overthrow the mayor.

The consequences of the above were threefold: firstly, the MD was forever protected through her "whistle-blower" status; secondly, a self-serving, egotistical former "colleague" paraded his duplicity and disloyalty for all to see; and lastly, and perhaps most significantly, Doncaster suffered a recurrence of the damage inflicted by previous' self-serving politicians. The town's undoubted recovery was sacrificed – as was the mayor – as "payback" for delivering Miliband as the MP for Doncaster North.

During the next two to three years, it became apparent that Miliband and Brown could not be trusted, welching on their obligations to the town and to the mayor, who was becoming embroiled in simultaneous, and coordinated, insurgency strategies leading to myriad investigations.

During this time, we witnessed appalling behaviour from several senior Doncaster Labour group members. Meanwhile my political protection *from* the Labour Party transformed into political assassination *by* the Labour Party...

The publication of the "Dobson Report" in November 2006, alongside the successful conclusions to all investigations, should have prompted the media to adopt a more mature, evidence-based reporting style – focusing on the facts rather than [opposition] anecdote, rumour and opinion. It should have spurred them on to report on the real story of mayoral delivery in Doncaster and the birth of a new city. Sadly they chose to let that opportunity slip by.

Shamefully, the floods disaster that befell so many of our communities in June 2007 actually provided a respite from the day-to-day guerrilla warfare I was facing. What we witnessed was a community forsaken and senior, well-paid professionals struggling with the decision-making and leadership requirements of the crisis – a hiatus that provided me with a stage from which to lead the emergency response and later the recovery for many of our communities.

I always acted in a statesmanlike manner as I sought to "protect" the Labour Party's name – trying to deal with issues in a private and confidential manner and requesting support from MPs and the Party throughout this period. It was the publication of the Audit Commission Public Interest Report in 2008 that put the political infighting right into the public domain.

The report made explicit that the MD had colluded with Aidan Rave and other Labour politicians, and failed the people of Doncaster. Furthermore Ros Jones then led the subsequent "investigatory" sub-panel, which conspired to "pay off" the MD rather than risk a capability investigation, which would have uncovered what they had done; Ros Jones – who would herself become a future mayor of Doncaster!

Yet leopards can't change their spots, particularly journalistic leopards, and the newspapers collectively chose not to report on this, preferring to underline the urban myth that the entire fault lay with me. The media also chose to ignore the prophetic warnings from the Audit Commission that councillors were so obsessed with destroying "the mayor", that it was affecting council services. Despite such warnings, I wish I could say we saw the problem in children's services coming, but we didn't.

The whole area of the statutory responsibilities of the Director of Children's Services [DCS] needs to be considered in more detail. The DCS was [is] under no legal obligation to share information with the mayor or any other politician' whether local or national. Indeed, in 2008, whilst we were right in the middle of the storm, the DCS chose not to make me aware of another child's death; a point not lost in the early days of the new mayor, in June 2009, when political leaders were again not told about a baby dying.

Certainly this underlined that the fault was never with "Mayor Winter" singularly; and was exacerbated when Peter Davis became mayor in 2009. Not because of any shortcomings of his, but because the Labour Party then waged a full-on war on *his* mayoralty – pushing the local authority into complete seizure.

ooo

Recorded history will show that, following a wretched second term, I stood down as the first elected Mayor of Doncaster in June 2009 – ending a quite spectacular fall from grace.

All I ask is that you, the reader, consider the facts of these matters – there is a multitude of evidence to support my claims – rather than disregarding the evidence and giving credence to issues that were a matter of opinion or based on the politics of innuendo and rumour…

This was my experience.

This is my truth.

Acknowledgements

Political books are notoriously bad sellers, only really appealing to those in the immediacy and one or two other interested bystanders. Because of this, I have not attempted to find a "publisher". I did not want to be editorially constrained by their objectives, preferring to spend my energies writing, researching, triangulating and verifying this manuscript.

However, I would like to show my appreciation to the countless individuals who have supported me and offered advice and guidance as the book developed.

I would like to thank those who assisted in the editing, proofreading and design of the book – and to apologise, in advance, for any grammatical mistakes herein, I accept they are mine. I hope you will see them as some of the smaller scars of life, rather than hurdles to obstruct your enjoyment.

More than anything I would like to thank the countless staff working for DMBC and its partner organisations. To you, I am truly sorry that I could not prevent the politics from breaking our organisation once more... The vision we aspired to was [is] the right one, hampered only by self-serving politicians and the media.

I must say thank you to "John and Gary" for their comments – predominantly on the background story before I became Leader/Mayor – and for drafting Chapter 2 for me.

I also want to thank my loyal supporters; those who have always defended my character and known some of the truth... I would particularly like to thank one of my most stalwart supporters, without whose help this book would not have been published. You know who you are and I will be forever grateful to you and respectful of your own objectives and motivations.

Above all, I want to thank my partner, Carolyne, and the rest of my family, who supported and encouraged me tirelessly whilst I was mayor - in spite of all the times it took me away from them, then, and more recently as I wrote this book. Both have been long and arduous journeys and I will be forever in their debt.

Last and not least, I will apologise in advance to all those who have been with me over the years and whose names I have failed to mention; it does not reflect any ingratitude on my part – and in some cases is done to protect you!

Photographs

Front cover [Shaun Flannery]; Rugby Player [Page 4 – Phill Callaghan]; with Rudy Giuliani [Page 354 – YIBC]; with Ed Miliband [Page 510 – the author's own library]; with Tony Blair [Page 633 – NLGN]; Floods Images [Page 672 – Ben Gurr]; [Page 674 – Graham Stott]; [Page 681 – Reuters];